All the Cardinal's Men and a Few Good Nuns

THE SYMPTOMS

TED DRUHOT

Brilliant Books Literary
137 Forest Park Lane Thomasville
North Carolina 27360 USA

INTRODUCTION

For over two centuries nearly ninety five percent of hospitals in the United States were owned and operated by Religious organizations, i.e. Baptist, Lutheran, Jewish, Presbyterian, Catholic, to name a few. Caring for the sick and injured was considered a ministry. The hospitals operated as charities dependent upon donations and some reimbursement from the patients. A gradual change began in the 1930's as pre-paid hospital and physician insurance gained popularity. By the 1950's Insurance plans became a popular source of reimbursement for medical services. By the 1960's most patients had some form of medical coverage. In 1965 Medicare and Medicade were initiated and the United States Government became the primary payor for health Services. Hospitals became profitable. The trend began to reverse as the National Affordable Health Care program was initiated 2008.

As hospitals became solvent, they used their capital gains to expand their capacity and services to additional tertiary levels. The quality of care was on a rapid increase. The growing fiscal prominence of hospitals caught the interest of entrepreneurs who either bought the Church hospitals or developed their own proprietary hospitals. The conversion of the healing ministry to an industry caused many Religious Organizations to reduce their involvement or withdraw from the hospital ministry.

This is a fictitious story about a hospital, Religious sponsors, proprietors, and people caught in the confusion of change from hospital ministry to medical industry as it began to peak in the late 1990's.

The story also includes characters who participate in a society punctuated by a drug culture suggesting the advent of a revised healing ministry.

ALL THE CARDINAL'S MEN AND A FEW GOOD NUNS

CHAPTER ONE

The little man in the expensive suit parked the midnight blue Mercedes in the small parking lot at the end of the circle drive marking the entrance to the Cardinal's Residence. The Chancery, Seminary, and Library buildings spread around the wooded rolling campus opposite the Residence all looked deserted. The Seminary was only partially used when classes were in session because of the steady declining enrollment. The rest of the central campus of the Boston Catholic Archdiocese seemed to be standing at ease waiting for orders. It would be at least a week before the busy offices and agencies of the Archdiocese would be in full swing. The new Cardinal had been installed in office last week and the many celebrations marking the event were only completed a few days ago. It was at the Installation Ceremony in the great Cathedral of the Immaculate Conception in downtown Boston that Kevin Hardly, First Leading Knight of the Equestrian Order of the Knights of the Holy Cross, had been advised by Bishop Hanks, Auxiliary Bishop and Vicar General of the Archdiocese, that Francis Cardinal McMahon requested a meeting at their earliest convenience to discuss serious fiscal matters regarding the Church's healing ministry. Kevin Hardly was proud to be of service to his Church and the Cardinal. He had served the recently deceased Cardinal Riley as the First Knight for several years. Hardly was sworn to be a Knight of the Church—sworn on his Mother's grave.

The Beacon Street Campus of the St. James Seminary that also served as the main administrative complex for the large Catholic Archdiocese of Boston was in full bloom with manicured lawns and large oaks casting refreshing shade from the penetrating brightness of the sun. Kevin breathed the cool air as he walked to the entrance of the Cardinal's Residence. Once there he paused to straighten his tie before ringing the ornate bell. The door opened suddenly and Bishop Hanks beckoned him to enter. Hanks was also anxious to make a good impression on his new boss by making sure that Hardly was in place and waiting at the appointed time. He was quick to point that out to Kevin in his first statement. "Ah, Mr. Hardly we are right on time. I expect His Eminence will join us shortly. Did you bring the information?"

Kevin nodded as he patted the brief case under his arm. "Yes, Bishop, I have all the data regarding St. Anslem's. I'm sorry that I had not brought this here before but Cardinal Riley, bless his departed soul, never asked for a report. We will certainly miss him. May he rest in peace? Cardinal McMahon seems very nice but very different don't you think?"

Bishop Hanks was not about to discuss the relative merits or demerits of Cardinals past or present. He simply gave Kevin a bland look and gestured for him to sit on the old English wooden bench next to the conference room door. Kevin took the hint and tried to change the subject, "Bishop, I hope you don't mind if I take some time today to brief His Eminence on the work of the Knights of the Holy Cross. The Knights were highly regarded by Cardinal Riley."

Bishop Hanks was quick to respond, "Kevin, His Eminence has a complete file on the Knights and their good work. He is well aware that you are the First Leading Knight and I'm sure he will ask you for a briefing in time. Today he is interested in the institutional healing ministry and particularly the fiscal status of St. Anslem's Hospital. I explained to him that you and your Bank have served the Archdiocese well. He expects you to give us your suggestions and assistance on reversing the potentially scandalous bankrupt condition of the hospital. Are you prepared for that?"

Hardly began to open his briefcase when the conference room door popped open. A tall well-built man in his mid-fifties dressed in black slacks and short sleeved collared white shirt stood briefly in the doorway and then without saying a word, waved Hanks and Hardly into the room. Cardinal McMahon was in excellent physical condition. His six foot two inch frame was tanned and muscular. Only the gray hair betrayed his age. Otherwise he could easily be mistaken for an athlete. His appointment as Cardinal Archbishop of Boston was well received by the faithful. McMahon was almost a native son. He was born and raised in Falmouth on Cape Cod by middle class parents who managed to send him to Harvard where he studied the performing arts. After graduation he discovered his vocation and entered St. James Seminary. Following ordination, he volunteered to be a Chaplain in the Marine Corps. Twenty-five years later he retired as a Brigadier General and head of the Chaplain Services for the entire United States Armed Forces. Following his military retirement, he served as Director of the National Shrine in Washington where he learned the fine art of Church politics. From there he was appointed Bishop of the Diocese of Scranton, Pa. where he perfected the art of Church administration. It was a foregone conclusion that he was destined to lead a principal Diocese and be a Cardinal Prince of the Church. He waited in Scranton for the opportunity. Boston was the first opening and McMahon moved up in the ranks.

Graciously he greeted Kevin Hardly and invited him to sit down at the long hand-carved wooden conference table. Bishop Hanks in true servant fashion moved to serve coffee from the tray behind the Cardinal. The Cardinal acknowledge the cup of coffee that Bishop Hanks put before him. After Kevin had been served, the Cardinal motioned for the Bishop to take a chair. Hanks moved promptly and the Cardinal began the conversation. He got right to the point.

"Mr. Hardly, I am aware that The Hardly Security and Trust Bank has served the Archdiocese for many years. You, your parents, and your grand-parents, have generously contributed to the support of the Church. It is on this basis that I have asked you here to help me as I begin my assignment in this Archdiocese. From all the information that has been provided me so far by Bishop Hanks and the Chancellor it seems that we are in deep trouble."

The thought of admitting to the Cardinal that the Archdiocese had fiscal trouble was very discomforting to Kevin Hardly. He felt that it was his personal responsibility to maintain fiscal stability since all the

Archdiocesan funds including St. Anslem's treasury had been entrusted to his bank. In truth, the problem had been the result of the deceased Cardinal Riley. John Cardinal Riley, a Prince of the old Church, who led the Boston Catholic Archdiocese for nearly thirty years. During that time he expanded the teaching, charity, and healing ministries of the Church to serve the entire Diocese especially the poor and disadvantaged. In Robin Hood style, he extracted funds from wealthy parishes and services to create and support ministerial programs that had not a prayer of fiscal success. Deeply religious, he led his flock with great affection for the members of the Mystical Body of Christ. His charity was evidenced by his determination to preserve the teaching and healing ministries in the very poor neighborhoods of his Archdiocese. At the time of his death the financial condition of the Archdiocese of Boston was deplorable. His successor, Francis Cardinal McMahon, had been appointed with specific instructions from the Holy See to solve the fiscal problems of the Archdiocese and avoid the scandal of bankruptcy. Prominent in that regard was the prospect of financial failure of St. Anslem's Hospital.

The Hardly Security and Trust Bank with Kevin Hardly as Chairman of the Board and Chief Executive Officer, was the primary bank for the Archdiocese and the Hospital. Acting upon the advice of Bishop Hanks, the Cardinal invited Kevin Hardly to meet with him to plan for the return of fiscal security to the Archdiocese. St. Anslem's Hospital was the most prominent of the Archdiocesan services and as such became the focus of public scrutiny. The Hospital sat on the highest ground in Brighton Center overlooking the semi blighted commercial area of taverns, beauty parlors, ethnic food stores, and video stores. An antiquated precinct station of the Boston Police Department sat a block away on the opposite side of the street. Next to the Police Station was the Knights of Columbus Hall directly across from the Masonic Lodge. The Elks Lodge was on the corner. Churches of various denominations dotted the landscape a block west of Cambridge Avenue, the main street of the community. Trolley tracks still ran down the middle of Cambridge although the wires had long been removed. Originally, the trolley served to link Brighton with the North End and South Boston where the population originated. In modern times the famous Boston MTA replaced the trolley although the nearest station was several blocks from the hospital and Brighton Center. Those who ventured out of the original ghettos and migrated west to Brighton built the churches and supported the hospital. Their offspring eventually moved to the affluent suburbs and were replaced in Brighton within the past twenty years by an influx of Vietnamese and Russian Jews. Absentee landlords bought many of the original triple-deckers and converted them into apartment houses for student housing and low-income rentals. Hospitals and Churches exempt from taxes were then viewed by the property owners as elements of cost because of their tax-exempt status. The landlords opposed expansion of the institution's services. The hospital fought back, arguing that it was a valuable institution in the provision of health services, now recognized as the leading industry in Boston. Alienation between the hospital and its neighbors was typical of the age. Not only was the Cardinal interested in fiscal security for this Catholic institution, he was interested in restoring it as a friend of the Community as well.

Aside from the community attitude, St. Anslem's held fast to its original Church affiliation. It was the only remaining hospital in Boston to be operated under direct Church control. Others made reference to their religious origination within their name but had moved to a corporate mode apart from Church sponsorship. It was difficult for St. Anslem's to make such a departure since the Code of Canon Law within the Catholic Church prohibited alienation of Church property and therefore prevented a separation of the ministries to lay control. Consequently, St. Anslem's faced the difficult task of functioning in a secular medical environment that presented countless ethical challenges, Regardless, the Cardinal Archbishop of the Boston Catholic Archdiocese was resolute that the healing ministry would be conducted by and through St. Anslem's Hospital.

Kevin Hardly thought briefly about how his warnings to Cardinal Riley had been brushed aside with the admonition that, "God will provide." Kevin had faith and did believe a miracle would bring the money necessary for the Church to continue its mission. Now a new Cardinal dispelled that myth and asked him to bring forth the miracle from his knowledge of business and finance. Kevin opened his brief case and spread several of St. Anslem's recent operating reports on the long table as he spoke.

"Your Eminence, as you will note from these financial reports of the current year, St. Anslem's is losing money each month at an increasing rate. Revenue is experiencing a slight decline while expenses are rapidly increasing. Mr. O'Shea, my executive vice-president and controller, is very confident that with the right management the hospital could reverse the situation. It is his suggestion, and I agree, that the Hospital should have new leadership and governance. We propose that a lay businessman be installed as the chief executive of the hospital and that a Board of Trustees comprised of Catholic businessmen be established."

St. A's, as it was affectionately called by the Residents and Interns, was a teaching hospital far removed from the geographic center of the medical academic centers on Longwood Ave. The hospital began in South Boston over a century ago through the initiative of three poor Irish spinsters who walked the streets caring for the poor and bringing them to their home for care. When the Bishop of the time learned of the work of these fine ladies, he arranged to buy them a more appropriate place on the outskirts of the City in the Brighton neighborhood. The ladies fit well into the desire of the Bishop to form a healing ministry. A year later the house was formally dedicated as St. Anslem's Hospital and the three ladies were organized into an order of Nuns known as the Poor Sisters of Charity of Boston following the rule of Elizabeth Ann Seton and the dictate of the Bishop, A century later the small house on the top of the hill grew into a very large tan brick and glass institution resembling a space ship overlooking Brighton from the heights. Its many buildings of modem design dominated the landscape and cast the small neighborhood into comparative blight.

Under the direction of the Sisters, St. Anslem's became the heart of the Community. Its compassion and charity were revered by patients, employees, nurses and physicians. Many young ladies were trained as nurses by the Sisters and from that experience several accepted the vows of Religious life. The St. Anslem's School of Nursing was a special quality of the hospital and eventually became the foundation for the neighboring Boston College School of Nursing. Additionally, the physicians who sought the opportunity to serve the Brighton community were well trained practitioners who in time created a teaching service affiliated with Tuffs University School of Medicine. A Research Center for Cardiac

Disease was established in the 1960's that brought St. Anslem's into the big time with the downtown hospitals. Full time faculty crowded the halls and cafeteria. Residents pushed into the required conferences. Administrators pondered the plight of sophisticated data processing. New buildings replaced old. Bonds were issued. Fund campaigns were conducted. The Sisters watched, wondered, and worried about their advancing age and declining numbers, but continued to look for ways to serve the poor.

The physicians, on the other hand, continually looked for ways to better serve the patient. They pressed for advanced state of the art technology. Specialists were recruited to administer the new discovered miraculous cures. Special Nursing Units were created within new and remodeled buildings that housed the equipment and gave office to the specialists. Nurses and technicians also became specialized in intensive care of medical, surgical, and other critically ill patients. Intensive care units (ICU's) of several varieties absorbed a significant part of the hospital and provided the greater part of the revenue as well as momentum for the institution's spiraling costs.

Bishop Hank's mouth popped wide open when he heard Kevin's suggestion for lay control of the Hospital. He knew that the dear departed, Cardinal Riley was spinning in his fresh grave. He was about to express his opposition to the idea when he saw Cardinal McMahon give a slight positive nod. Then the Bishop opted for a different tact, "Kevin, your suggestion is unexpected but well intended, I'm sure. It seems that His Eminence will want to give it time as he reviews the total integration of the laity into the various ministries of the Archdiocese. Is money available that we could use in the meantime to shore up the Hospital?"

Cardinal McMahon was a man of action. He was not interested in a detailed study of lay ministries. He was anxious to plug the leaks and stop the ship from sinking. He gave Bishop Hanks a quick disapproving glance and then turned his view to Hardly. "Mr. Hardly, what you suggest is that good business management will repair the situation. I believe that to be so. Do you have suggestions on who we could get to volunteer to serve on the Hospital's Board?"

Hardly pulled another sheet of paper from his briefcase. It was on the Bank's best bond and carried the name of Thomas O'Shea under the banner on the letterhead. O'Shea had told Hardly to expect this question when they discussed the meeting. O'Shea had also prepped Hardly that St. Anslem's Hospital was overdrawn in its operating account and several months delinquent on its mortgage payments. O'Shea further explained to his boss that St. Anslem's Hospital generated over two hundred million dollars in revenue each year. The accelerator effect of that amount of business through Boston Security was delicious.

Hardly handed the paper to the Cardinal and explained, "Your Eminence, in order to support our suggestion, Mr. O'Shea prepared this list for me to give to you if you were interested. It contains three names with their background in addition to my own who are Knights of the Holy Cross and proven loyal to the Church. The four of us could be on the Board with you as the Chairman and Bishop Hanks as Vice Chair. That would give us five people. I have a few other names that have been suggested if you would like to increase the Board."

Cardinal McMahon took the list from Kevin. He reached in his shirt pocket and pulled out his tri-focal glasses that with some embarrassment he pushed on his head. After focusing the glasses and moving the paper in view of the proper lens he began to study the list. Bishop Hanks glared at Hardly. He resented the layman, regardless of his prominence, pushing the laity into a position of control without at least informing the Bishop's office in advance. Bishop Hanks felt he had been betrayed. As the Cardinal scanned the paper, Bishop Hanks decided to pout.

The first name on the list was Kevin Hardly. The Cardinal was already acquainted with some of Kevin's background. The recommended appointees to St. Anslem's Board were wealthy Catholics that had penetrated the Protestant-controlled commerce of the greater Boston community. Catholic wealth had registered its strength over the past thirty years and was demonstrated by the vast amount of Archdiocese real estate in Boston. Certainly, the most prominent on the list was the very wealthy Kevin Hardly. Mr. Hardly, benefited from his grandfather's seafaring interest that evolved into one of the world's largest shipping fleets in the 19th century, coupled with his father's combined import and export business. The Hardly family of which Kevin was now the patriarch, was repudiated to be one of the wealthiest families in New England. He was very prominent as well in political affairs especially the Democratic Party. President Kennedy had appointed him to a special commission to investigate the trade imbalance and President Carter had appointed Hardly chairman of a special Presidential commission to investigate waste in purchasing practices of the Department of Defense. The resulting Hardly Commission Report had given Mr. Kevin Hardly international acclaim that he flaunted on every occasion. Kevin Hardly was perpetually inebriated with his own exuberance. A power broker well-positioned, he was convinced that he would command the wealth of the Church to benefit God with a return better than the Dow. His immortality was assured by his staunch support of the Church which he also reasoned gave him a license to modify specific moral practices in the interest of profit.

Remarkably, Kevin Hardly was not an offspring of Catholic tradition. The Hardly clan, staunch Protestants from Scotland, was one of Boston's first families arriving on the legendary ship, Mary and John, from England in 1632. This gallant ship managed to traverse the tricky currents of Massachusetts Bay and landed on the shore of a hospitable area that the settlers named Dorchester. The Puritan tradition of hard work and thrift carried the family through the next two centuries with compounding wealth and prominence.

However, Kevin Hardly's grandfather in his youth committed an unpardonable sin that seriously offended their Protestant heritage. He fell in love and married an Irish Catholic lass from South Boston. Kevin's grandfather was disowned by the family so he took his portion of the family's wealth and started the Catholic branch of the Hardly clan. Kevin's grandmother became determined that her descendants would be strong in their Catholic faith and defenders of the Church. The two factions of the Hardly clan from the time of the unforgivable marriage shared only the hate of religious differences. Both sides continued to prosper and eventually became major competitors in business, finance, politics, and religion. Although they shared the same ancestors there was absolutely no love lost between their Protestant and Catholic descendants.

The second name on the list was that of the author of the recommendations, Mr. Thomas O'Shea. Cardinal McMahon was not previously aware of Mr. O'Shea although the O'Shea name was well known through-out the Archdiocese. He was the son of poor Irish immigrants who gained respectability by serving on the Boston Police Department, attending Catholic schools, and joining the Knights of Columbus. Thomas extended the ambition of the O'Shea clan by becoming the first of the family to earn a college degree and then a master's degree in finance both from Boston College. He began working in the mail room of The Hardly Security and Trust Bank when he was a senior in high school. Eventually he became a clerk in the trust department, passed the CPA exam, promoted to Internal Auditor, then to Vice President, and ultimately Treasurer—the first Irish Catholic to be admitted to the executive structure of Boston's leading financial institution. Needless to say, his friendship with Kevin Hardly established during their undergraduate days at Boston College also contributed to his ascension at the Bank.

Richard Folley, MD, was next on the list. In addition to being the Chairman of medicine and medical staff power broker, he was also O'Shea's son-in-law. Cardinal McMahon was very much aware of the great Doctor. Dr. Folley had been Cardinal Riley's personal physician. Before his death, Riley had the opportunity to discuss the transition of the Archdiocese with then Bishop McMahon of Scranton, Pa. Riley had sworn Folley to secrecy when his unannounced successor, Bishop McMahon, came to Boston for an orientation visit. McMahon met with Folley and discussed Riley's care. McMahon began administering the Archdiocese several months before Riley's death. Folley knew who was in charge and he managed to keep it secret.

The last name on the list was that of Charles Patello. Mr. Patello was an investment banker, broker, and member of the Board of Hardly Security and Trust Bank. Little was known about Mr. Patello in Church circles. Charlie did not court the clergy as Hardly did. Yet, Patello was known as a generous man who made sizable contributions to activities and charities of the Archdiocese. Bishop Hanks knew the name but he didn't know the man. Just the same he was a proven supporter of the Church and friend of Kevin Hardly.

Charles Patello was always a man destined for success. Raised on Boston's North End, he learned the fine art of integrating business ventures to his personal benefit from the knee of his favorite uncle, Big Frank Patello, who eventually became head of the largest juice operation in the Northeast known in the legitimate world as National Associated Investors of New York City. Through Uncle Frank's support, Patello became the owner of a successful investment firm in Boston that specialized in financing small businesses. He also became a prominent partner in Uncle's operations in New England although that part of his business was never publicly disclosed. In addition, and as a result of his careful cultivation of his college association with Hardly and O'Shea, he became a board member of the Hardly Security and Trust. What was not known was that the relationship between Hardly, O'Shea and Patello began at Boston College during exam week of their junior year. The poor O'Shea sought out the very rich Hardly because it was known to O'Shea that both of them were destined to flunk their Ethics course. O'Shea explained to Hardly that he knew Charlie Patello had acquired an advance copy of the examination that Patello was willing to share for negotiated consideration. Hardly bought himself and O'Shea into the proposition and as a consequence each earned a passing grade in Ethics. From that point on Hardly saw to it that O'Shea and Patello were always positioned to support his goals and ambitions.

Cardinal McMahon turned to the second page of Hardly's list of recommended hospital board members. This page was actually a letter written to Hardly by Patello that thanked him for being recommended to the Cardinal. In addition, the letter contained two names that Charlie asked Kevin to bring to the Cardinal's attention. The first was Mr. Mark Meehan, CEO of Advance Waste Management Company. The second name was Mr. Phil Mondi, Manager of Patriot Courier Service. The letter was written in haste by Patello. He was taken off guard when Kevin Hardly informed him that the Cardinal would be contacting him to be a member of the St. Anslem's Board. Patello agreed to serve and then called his Uncle, Big Frank Patello to discuss the prospects of such a venture.

Big Frank Patello was quick to recognize the potential of getting into the hospital treasury. He was uncertain how to develop the opportunity, but advised his nephew to gain as much influence as possible while the matter was researched. Big Frank also suggested that Philip Mondi, owner of Patriot Transport and Courier Service, the front organization for Patello' drug dealing business in Boston and Mark Meheen, a young graduate from Notre Dame and Harvard Business School who was making it big as the CEO of Action Waste Management, another of Patello's public service skimming ventures, be added to the St. Anslem's Board. Meehan and Mondi were to serve as additional eyes and ears for an opportunity for National Associated Investors.

Charlie Patello had called Hardly and convinced him to add both Meheen and Mondi, good Catholic businessmen, to the list. O'Shea refused to add them to his recommendations, so Patello sent his own list that Hardly included in his report to the Cardinal.

After completing his review of the letters, Cardinal McMahon passed them to Bishop Hanks. While Hanks scanned the names, Cardinal McMahon responded to Hardly, "Mr. Hardly, assuming that these men are all good Catholics and active in their parishes, I will accept them on the St. Anslem's lay Board. Now there are some others that need to be included. Bishop Hanks, of course, will be on the Board but as my personal representative since I will have honorary chairman status. You, Sir, will serve as Chairman of the Board. May I suggest that your Mr. O'Shea be vice-chairman? Perhaps Mr. Patello could be Secretary. In addition to Dr. Folley, Mr. Meehan, and Mr. Mondi, I believe it proper that the Religious Leader of the Poor Sisters of Charity also serve on the Board. I know you want to remove them from the operation but I believe their one hundred years of sponsoring and administering the hospital mandates their continued participation. Don't you agree?"

Hardly was not prepared for the question. He made a quick glance at Bishop Hanks who chose to look at the ceiling. Hardly was on his own. Carefully, he began a shaky reply, "Of course, Your Eminence, we want the Sisters to continue to serve the patients with the love and kindness that they have given for so long. Having a Sister on the Board will be good for us and good for her I'm sure."

The Cardinal smiled at the response. Bishop Hanks glanced back at the letters.

Kevin fidgeted. Sweat was very visible on his forehead. Somewhere a clock chimed and the Cardinal looked at his watch. "Well gentlemen, unfortunately we have to cut this short. I have a few other details to contend with this afternoon. Can we say that we agree on the Hospital's board? Tell me, Bishop, do the recommended members seem to be in good standing with the Church?"

Hanks knew that he had to agree. A Church politician at his best, he managed a political response, "Your Eminence, I have no information that any of the candidates are less than active Catholics. Mr. Hardly has recommended them so they must be acceptable."

Hardly saw an opportunity to make a pitch for the Knights, "Your Eminence, you will be pleased to know that all of the gentlemen are members with advanced rank in the Knights of the Holy Cross. Since Bishop Hanks is also a Knight it seems that the Board is made up completely of the Equestrian Order. I guess the Sister would be an exception since she doesn't qualify to be a knight and since she isn't married to a Knight she doesn't qualify to be a Lady. We really don't need a Lady—just a Nun. That shouldn't make a difference. We have yet to discuss the hospital's CEO. I believe that a Knight should do that as well. Your Eminence, all the Knights are reviewed by the Chancery before they are installed in the Order. Our files are current and complete. You can be certain that a Knight is a practicing Catholic in good standing."

The Cardinal looked at Kevin as if to say that enough had been said. Bishop Hanks thought too much had been said and was having a difficult time controlling his contempt. Cardinal McMahon recognized the Bishop's body language. It was time to bring the Bishop into the game and make him own the decision. "Bishop Hanks, I thank you and Mr. Hardly for these recommendations. In time, we will see the benefit of new leadership at the Hospital. For the immediate future, we will inform the members of their appointment to the Hospital Board. Please send them the appointment letter. But before any of the letters are sent please meet with Sister Elizabeth, I believe that she is the Religious Leader of the Poor Sisters, and inform her of this reorganization. She will need to explain it to the Sisters at the Hospital"

Suddenly Bishop Hanks came back to life. He had just been given the proverbial dirty end of the stick. He needed to counter. "Your Eminence, what about the reserve powers, Canon Law requires us to control the Board."

The Cardinal had gotten out of his chair and was at the door when the Bishop brought up the Reserved Powers. He turned slowly and glared at the Bishop. "Bishop, I expect that you will see to it that the Code of Canon Law is properly applied. Nothing that we have done here this afternoon was intended to absent that. Do you understand?" I expect you to represent me and the Church in the conduct of the Board so you are the authority of the Church in by behalf"

"I understand Your Eminence, but the Chief Executive Officer has always been appointed by the Cardinal. Will you appoint the layman as well?"

The Cardinal's response was brief, "Yes, Bishop, I will." Then he walked out of the conference room without saying another word.

Kevin Hardly was uncertain about what had happened. He had been called to the Cardinal's Residence by Bishop Hanks at the Cardinal's request to discuss the financial status of St. Anslem's Hospital. The conversation centered on the appointment of a lay Board that the Cardinal accepted. Now his friend, Bishop Hanks was apparently upset over the outcome. Kevin wanted to know why. "Bishop, I think we had a good meeting although I'm not sure. Are you disturbed with the appointment of the Board?"

The Bishop was pensive," Kevin, you are a married man of many years. I've not had the pleasure of marital bliss. I opted for Holy Orders because I felt the calling of Christ's Church. My new boss accepted your recommendation and left me with the task of telling the Sisters that they are out and you are in. Kevin, my good man, I may be celibate but I fully understand that hell hath no fury like a woman scorned. You can be sure that His Eminence knows that even better than me. That's why I have the task. The Holy Spirit will need to guide me through this. I wonder if I'm up to it. Pray for me, Kevin"

oOo

The Motherhouse of the Poor Sisters of Charity sat on twenty acres of valuable land on the top of the same hill that St. Anslem' Hospital was located. The Sisters' Motherhouse was very controversial in the Community because it was rumored at one time that the Hospital was going to tear down the ancient buildings and develop the area into low rent condos. The Community, to counter such a possibility, attempted to have the Buildings registered as a National Historic Site. The Poor Sisters of Charity supported the proposal but the Archdiocese, as owners, strongly opposed the Historic Registry claiming that is was confiscation of Church property and a violation of the principle of separation of Church and State. In the end the Church lost and the Motherhouse was entered on the list of National Historic Sites in the Boston area. Prominent in the decision was a letter to the Historical Commission from Sister Elizabeth, Religious Leader of the Poor Sisters of Charity, stating that the Sisters would be proud to have their building and their history established permanently in the history of Boston and the United States. Other letters and testimony from the lawyers of the Archdiocese had no impact. After the decision had been made, Bishop Hanks gave Sister Elizabeth a non-spiritual talking to that evolved into a shouting match about who was boss. Now the good Bishop was again given the task of talking to the tough little Nun who didn't take any of his guff

In addition to the subtle conflict of running a hospital to serve the patient and creating a good payer mix, the good Sisters experienced the not-so-subtle conflict of serving God in a male dominated Church that saw them as hand maidens to the tasks of the ministries. The many changes within the conduct of the Church that resulted from Vatican II seemed to enhance their frustration as the Sisters adjusted to the modern world and struggled for position in the modem Church. St. Anslem's Hospital, even after the Reform by Vatican II and the subsequent revisions to the Code of Canon Law, remained the property of the Cardinal Archbishop of Boston and his Holy Roman Catholic Church. Sister Elizabeth resented the subordination of her Religious Community and herself as the Religious Leader within the spiritual and temporal affairs of the Church. She had made this very clear to the Bishop.

It seemed reasonable to Bishop Hanks that the Sisters would welcome the opportunity to reduce their governing responsibility and yield to the lay Board. The Sisters were declining in number. They had less than one hundred and twenty-five members and their average age was seventy-five. The only Sister still functioning in a full-time position was the hospital's CEO, Sister Celest. Otherwise the elderly Sisters volunteered in the Hospital's Pastoral Care Department and served as hostesses and greeters in Admitting and Reception. Kevin Hardly and the Bishop felt they performed a valuable service in those functions. Bolstered by this logic the Bishop arrived at the Convent door two weeks after being dispatched by the Cardinal, somewhat confident that his mission might not be as traumatic as he originally expected

Sister Elizabeth received the Bishop with great courtesy. The obligatory coffee and cookies were in place on the coffee table in the Convent reception room. Sister preferred to meet in the comfortable room with its padded chairs and couch rather than her convent office that only had a desk and a few ancient wooden chairs. The Bishop had been in the conference room before and knew what to expect. The two exchanged pleasantries, sipped coffee, talked about the weather, and munched cookies.

After a half hour, Sister Elizabeth prompted the purpose of the meeting, "Bishop, I'm sure that you were sent here on a mission. Let's get on with it. What, pray tell, is His Eminence up to?"

The good Bishop was somewhat blindsided by Sister's sudden thrust to the point. He emptied his coffee cup and reached for the last cookie. "Sister, His Eminence asked me to convey to you his deep appreciation for your dedication to the healing ministry. You have carried the burden of caring for the ill for over a hundred years. He wishes to offer you some relief and assistance."

Sister Elizabeth felt the chill. Relief and Assistance meant that the Sisters were being ousted from the hospital and put on the retirement shelf. She had expected it but was determined that the Poor Sisters would not be canned while she was their Religious Leader. "Bishop, we appreciate the Cardinal's concern. Please inform him that we are able to continue serving the poor, ill, and injured. There is no need to give us relief and assistance when so much is needed in his parishes. We can continue as we are."

Hanks had to get the message delivered. The coffee had fired him up, his temper was hot, and his bladder was about to burst. "Sister, let me be direct. His Eminence has decided that the Sisters will be replaced in the Governance of the Hospital by a group of lay Catholic businessmen. You and I will represent the Church. Sister Celest will be replaced by a person with a business background who will be charged with straightening out the hospital. We don't have to discuss this. The Cardinal expects the change to happen immediately."

The response from Sister Elizabeth was just as direct, "Hanks, you can tell the Cardinal that if he wants to kick the Sisters out then he should do it himself rather than send his boy. We aren't going to give anything up and Sister Celest will stay as the hospital administrator. That's it. Don't let the door hit you on the way out."

She had done it again. The tough Nun had bounced the Bishop out the Convent door with a strong message for his boss. He delivered the message in the same words that Sr. Elizabeth had used. The Cardinal listened to the report and without hesitation picked up the phone and dialed the Convent. He was put through to Sr. Elizabeth who was expecting the call. However instead of being summoned to the throne for a dose of discipline, the Cardinal announced to Sister that he was coming to see her to discuss the St. Anslem's changes. When they met, the Cardinal carefully explained that the use of businessmen in governance was an attempt to secure the hospital as an instrument for the continuation of the ministry in the future. He allowed that as long as the Sisters were able they could continue to be a part of hospital's governance and administration providing that the Sister appointed to the post was qualified.

Cardinal McMahon left the Convent with Sister Elizabeth's support for the reorganization of the Hospital's Board. In return for her support, Cardinal McMahon agreed to allow Sister Celest to continue as the hospital administrator as long as a lay businessman could be employed as an Executive Vice President and chief operating officer. Executive Officers as second in command were common in military organization.

Sister Elizabeth didn't think this change was significant enough to merit an in-depth explanation to Sister Celest. She would let the new Chairman of the Board handle that. The Sister and the Cardinal had a deal.

Sister Celest was a qualified hospital executive. Her twenty years of experience in hospital administration was backed by a Master's degree from the Harvard School of Public Health, a Master's degree in nursing from Regis College, and a bachelor degree in nursing from Boston College. She had inspired St. Anslem's to fulfill its mission by opening several store front clinics in Dorchester, Roxbury, and Chelsea that used considerable resources thus contributing to the expanding deficit of the hospital.

The medical staff, particularly the Department of Medicine, complained bitterly about the apparent waste of money when priorities demanded that teaching and research personnel be increased and better compensated. Doctor Richard Folley produced an extensive slide presentation at the meeting of the entire medical staff documenting the many benefits and profits available to the hospital by adding two cardiac catheterization laboratories, expanding the cardiac care intensive care unit, and employing three additional cardiologists and one more cardiac surgeon.

Folley made his presentation again at the first meeting of the newly reconstituted St. Anslem's Board meeting that met in executive session without Sister Celest. The Board voted to close the clinics with Sister Elizabeth casting the only descending ballot. Cardinal McMahon was recorded as absent and excused. They also voted to build the cath. labs, raise faculty salaries, and hire the recommended physicians. In executive session the Board appointed Hardly, O'Shea, and Patello as an executive committee authorized to recruit, select, and employ an executive vice president for St. Anslem's Hospital. The Terrific Trinity consisting of Hardly, O'Shea, and Patello felt they were in substantial control. They were determined that the Catholic nature of the hospital would be conducted always as a credit to the healing ministry of the Cardinal who they fully recognized as the boss of the Archdiocese.

oOo

It seemed reasonable to Kevin Hardly that the Executive Committee of St. Anslem's Board of trustees consisting of himself, O'Shea and Patello would seek first of all a Catholic gentleman dedicated to the propagation of the faith to assume the Executive Vice President position at their Hospital. Finding a person with qualification was no problem. Within the Order of the Knights of the Holy Cross that Kevin Hardly commanded as the Leading Knight, there was unquestionably a defender of the faith who would ride forward to the challenge given by the Cardinal.

However, that loyal Knight must be a trustworthy person who would attain the goal of fiscal stability and avoid public scandal. The trinity discussed the matter at lunch and concluded that Knight Joseph Bauman was the man for the job. Bauman was a democrat and recently retired as an Inspector in charge of Vice for the Boston Police Department. He had been installed in the Knights by Hardly with expectation that he would be Boston's top cop.

However, the unpredictability of the Boston voters had placed a non-believer in the mayor's office thus putting Bauman's ascension on permanent hold. The portly appearance of Bauman coupled with his red nose and ever-present grin seemed appropriate nonetheless for the hospital position. The good officer had graduated from the Boston Police Academy with honors thirty-five years ago. Otherwise, his education was supplemented by occasional night classes in law enforcement and continuing education at the school of hard knocks on Boston's South Side. A natural ability to compromise law, politics, and personal financial need into an accommodating personality led him through the ranks of Boston's Finest to a top job in the Department. Since his retirement, he had been waiting for the call to again serve humanity.

Bauman was elated when Hardly informed him of his new charge. The compensation was double his former salary as a Police Inspector. His experience in hospitals was limited to a three day stay riding the sheets while the, "pagan clowns in white at a downtown medical center," pondered his suspected ulcer. By virtue of this experience, he made critical observations from a horizontal perspective that he was certain would complement his proven leadership skills.

Bishop Hanks pushed the appointment letter into the Cardinal's hands as the Cardinal was about to board a plane for Rome. The Cardinal, grateful that the executive committee had found a qualified person, immediately signed the letter. Banks asked Hardly to inform Sister Elizabeth of Bauman's appointment so she could inform Sister Celest. Sister Elizabeth told Hardly that it was his duty to inform Sister Celest since he was Chairman of the Board. Hardly agreed. A few days later he took Bauman by the hand as they entered Sister Celest's office. He gently placed that hand in Sister Celest's hand and explained that this was a joining of their efforts to forward the healing and spiritual mission of St. Anslem's. They sat in Sister's comfortable but sparsely furnished office while Hardly explained that the role of the Sister was to represent compassion and caring while the role of administration was to deal with the hard realities of business.

Sister Celest, as President, Hardly explained, "Would have the assignment of seeing that the Sisters would continue to be present and that the patient was comfortable." Bauman would "run the hospital" and report to Hardly and the board of directors. "Of course, Sister will keep her office." Hardly added with emphasis. He then asked Sister Celest if she could, "arrange for a suitable office for Mr. Bauman and see that he was well received by the members of the staff" Having given Sister her charge he released their hands and looked at Sister for a reply.

Sister Celest, for the first time in her many years as a Religious, was overcome with uncontrollable anger. The decision of the lay Board to close the clinics was about all she could take. Now she was presented with the crowing blow to her dignity as a nurse, administrator, and a Religious. She could hardly speak and managed to avoid shedding tears. Instead she seemed to be pondering the matter as she looked at the ceiling of her office. After a long pause, Sister smiled at Mr. Bauman and slowly turned her head to gaze into Hardly's eyes. The sunlight from the window in back of Sister Celest was directly in Hardly's face causing him to squint deceptively and blink frequently. Celest recognized his sincerity and his innocence cloaked in ignorance. Hardly actually thought he was doing a service to her and the hospital. In true charity, the good Sister thanked them for their good intentions. She carefully avoided accepting or even implying that Hardly and his man of wisdom were reasonable assistance to the Hospital. With great tact she managed to escort them out the door realizing that she could not get them out of her life.

When Sister Celest was sure that Hardly and Bauman had cleared the front door, she called Sister Elizabeth and in words uncommon to a Religious explained to Elizabeth where she could "park this damn job." Sister Elizabeth, after a long and heated conversation, eventually convinced Sister Celest that punching out Hardly and "his damn fat faced friend" was not a proper course. Celest wouldn't let go. She pushed Sister Elizabeth to fight the Bauman appointment by organizing a protest march by the Sisters to the Cardinal's Residence.

Sister Elizabeth had her hands full when Sister Celest was mad. Celest had been an outspoken rebel throughout her Religious life. Elizabeth thought it time to remind her of that, "Celest, a march on the Cardinal's mansion would not work. First of all we don't have that many Sisters that can walk that far. Second, the Cardinal is in Rome and won't be back for a month. I don't think we could stay out in his yard that long. More importantly, the people of Brighton are not sympathetic to your long walks. That trip you made to Selma in the sixties was one thing but marching with the Gay and Lesbian Coalition in the St. Patrick's Day Parade in South Boston was something else. No, my dear, we are not going to protest this thing with one of your favorite walks for freedom!

Sister Celest went from red hot to white heat when Sr. Elizabeth mentioned the Gay and Lesbian March. Now she began to shout, "Elizabeth, damn it, you gave me permission to be in that march. We agreed that it was a case of public discrimination that required our involvement as a matter of social justice. You can't hold that against me."

"Permission might be somewhat of an overstatement, Cecile. You told me you were going to march in the parade. I had no idea that you would be carrying a sign espousing Gay Rights. I'm sure that little escapade is well instilled in the memory of the fine Irish clergy that dominate our Diocese. My suggestion is that we find another way to deal with Mr. Bauman other than public protest. Do you understand?"

Sister Celest remembered the many hate letters that she had received after her participation in the St. Patrick's Day Parade had made the evening television news. She knew that Sr. Elizabeth was right. A public demonstration would possibly make things worse. Together the two agreed to conspire for the eventual crash of Joe Bauman and the restoration of the healing ministries' preferred option of caring for the poor.

Bauman began his career in hospital administration one week after his introduction to Sister Celest. She complied with Mr. Hardly's request and converted a reception room opposite the chapel into an attractive office. Several get acquainted sessions were held in the hospital's cafeteria so the employees could meet and greet the new executive. Bauman was received with courtesy for the most part. An exception was the environmental service department employees who expressed resentment over the hiring of another executive instead of adding service workers. Bauman promised the housekeepers a complete review of the matter and charged the director of human resources to satisfy the, "Troops," within the week. "This administration stuff was a breeze for a seasoned street fighter," he thought. Otherwise, what Bauman didn't understand about the hospital was covered up by his friend and ally Dr. Folley who became the power behind the throne. Gradually, Folley's power became evident and an informal structure formed around the Chairman of Medicine. Bauman walked the halls as he once walked the streets as a policeman greeting the public, shaking hands, and admonishing staff for improper dress or conduct.

Sister Celest fully anticipated that Dr. Folley would be in control. She knew that she could not stop his power play. Alternatively, she set her sights on Mr. Bauman with the objective in mind to, "stick it in the ear of a male chauvinist Cardinal and his male dominated Church." One good shot was all she wanted and then it was off to the Sisters' Retirement House of Prayer on Cape Cod. Sister Elizabeth had already given her permission. The Sisters at the hospital had agreed as well.

The Reception Room opposite the Chapel entrance that served as Bauman's office was originally a store room and actually part of the Sisters Convent. It was windowless and very small. Heating pipes running along the ceiling made a constant hissing sound. They also made the room unbearably hot unless the door was constantly left open.

The Convent was contained within the hospital on the east wing of the first floor adjacent to the main entrance lobby. Most of the Sisters had opted to live in small homes in the community or had moved to the spacious Motherhouse on the hill. Consequently, the hospital's convent was nearly empty except for a few Sisters who had chosen to remain and take care of the Sisters admitted to the infirmary.

Bauman's office/reception room was always seen as a part of the Chapel. On that same floor was the Sisters' infirmary where the Order's sick Sisters were treated. When a Sister passed away her funeral was held in the east wing Chapel. The Reception room that Bauman occupied had always had been used for the wake. A special team of Sisters from the Motherhouse was permanently assigned to make arrangements and conduct the Sisters' funerals. All of the protocols and procedures had been preapproved by the Master of Ceremonies for the Cardinal who frequently attended the wake and funeral Mass. No person or power on earth could change a pre-approved protocol or procedure.

So it was on a Wednesday afternoon two weeks after Bauman began his distinguished career that he was in his office having a chat with a very attractive young lady who had applied to be the hospital's food and nutrition director. Suddenly three Sisters pushed a casket containing a deceased member of the Order through the open door. They positioned the casket on the wall opposite Bauman's desk, placed two kneelers beside the casket and left, followed in short order by the attractive young lady who decided to withdraw her application.

Bauman knew that this was nothing Folley could handle so he placed a call to Hardly. Hardly remembered that he had charged Sr. Celest with finding an office for Bauman. A call to Sister Celest revealed that the Convent Reception Room was the only available space since the new cardiologists and surgeons had occupied the only remaining offices in the hospital. Hardly next placed a call to Bishop Hanks to see about changing the reception room. Bishop Hanks was sympathetic but explained that he had no control over these kinds of things. The Cardinal's Master of Ceremonies was the sole source of authority, other than the Cardinal himself, in these matters. Furthermore, Bishop Hanks explained that the Master of Ceremonies was, "an independent little cuss" that only listened to the Cardinal. Banks ended the conversation by informing Hardly that, "The Cardinal was out of the country for at least another month and the matter will have to wait his return."

While waiting for the Cardinal's return three more Sisters gained their eternal reward. Bauman became a basket case not knowing when the deceased would appear before him. He began having nightmares. His lack of sleep caused him to doze while sitting in the lobby waiting for the funerals to begin. One afternoon the hospital's director of maintenance told him about a plan that Sister Celest had designed several years ago to remodel the spacious chapel and build a new reception room in the Chapel proper. Bauman was over-joyed. At his request the maintenance director called the hospital's architect who still had the remodeling plans on file. Without even looking at the plans or asking the price Bauman authorized the job. Three days later Bauman put a chain and padlock on the Chapel door in order to prepare it for remodeling. That night a construction crew cut a hole in the Lobby wall for the new entrance to the Chapel. However, the new entrance was boarded up waiting for door frames and the old entrance was still locked when the Sisters assembled for Mass the next morning.

A lock on the Chapel door was beyond Sister Celest's most extreme expectations of Bauman's stupidity. At most, she had expected him to lock the Sisters out of his office and that way force a confrontation between the Cardinal's fair haired boys and his gofer master of ceremonies. She had the early cooperation of the Sisters and benefited from the loyalty of her maintenance director in setting him up. But locking the Chapel was an invasion of the Sanctuary unequaled since the Turks' heathen acts caused the Crusades.

The war started within minutes after Father Curley, Pastor of St. Gabriel's Parish across the street from St. Anslem's, arrived to say the Seven O'clock Mass for the Sisters and the staunch Catholic members of the hospital's night shift. They were gathered in the corridor confused and bewildered when Curley came on the scene. Sister Celest was among the assembled faithful. Carefully, she explained to the angry Father Curley that she was omitted from the decision loop but with his support she would ask the maintenance man to pry open the Chapel door. Curley gave her the necessary support and after Mass placed a heated angry call to the Cardinal's secretary reporting that the lay administration of St. Anslems, for whatever reason, had decided to deny the Sacraments to the Sisters, staff and patients of the largest and most prominent Catholic hospital in the archdiocese. While the secretary was frantically attempting to locate the Cardinal, Father Curley was contacting every cleric in God's kingdom to report that St. Anslem's Hospital under lay control was no longer Catholic.

It took five hours for the Cardinal to receive the message to call his office. He delayed responding until there was a break in the Council of Bishops meeting that he was attending in Dallas. By that time his entire flock of ordained men were ranting at the Chancery. There was no room for mediation—only reparation. The Cardinal took the first flight back to Boston and within an hour after landing at Logan airport had convened an executive session of St. Anslem's' Board of Trustees, of which he was the honorary chairman, and keeper of the reserved powers. The most significant reserved power was the appointment of the hospital's executive and the Cardinal felt he also had the power of disappointment. Sr. Elizabeth reminded him that the hospital's chief executive was Sr. Celest and that he had permitted the terrific trinity to select the executive vice president His Eminence caught the drift and knew that he had been had. With careful terms he requested that Sr. Celest be remembered for her many years of dedicated service to St. Anslem's and to the healing ministry. Sister Elizabeth mentioned that Sr. Celest was looking forward to her retirement at the Sisters House of Prayer.

The Cardinal then emphatically suggested to Mr. Hardly that Mr. Bauman be provided a warm handshake as he left the hospital with the reminder that he would always be remembered in the prayers of the faithful. As a concluding point His Eminence decreed that St. Anslem's Hospital would be administered by an experienced, professional Catholic health care Executive of the kind that he had heard about at the Council of Bishops meeting in a session conducted by the Catholic Health Association.

The Cardinal realized that the good Nuns were determined to make his life miserable. He also recognized that the terrific trinity was his Achilles heel but he desperately needed their financial strength. The solution, he reasoned, would be to insert a buffer between them and his office that they could both love and hate. This would require an innocent well intentioned, good natured, loving, strong, intelligent, educated, person who understood Church politics and teaching. If such a person could be found and if such a person, once found, became corrupted by faction on or off the Board, then His Eminence would simply apply his reserved powers and look for another boy. In his mind, he stressed the word "boy". He calculated that the new boy would have to be from a distant land and therefore, viewed as an expert divorced of hospital politics.

Hardly left the Chancery and went to Bauman's office to give him his warm handshake. He didn't intend to mention the prayers of the faithful. When he arrived, a wake was in process. In response to Kevin's inquiry the Sister in attendance suggested that, "Himself', usually drank lunch at the Emerald Tap. As he entered the comforting surroundings of the Emerald, Kevin spotted the former Police Inspector of Vice turned Hospital Executive Vice President seated at the long ornate bar in the dark recesses of the large room taking another taste. Kevin slid onto the next barstool and ordered Irish double and neat.

Bauman felt the presence of the Leading Knight but offered no sign of recognition. He simply gazed into his small glass of whiskey that reflected a distorted image of Hardly. Without a greeting, Hardly began to speak to him. "Joseph, my friend, when you were but a mere lad at St. Patrick's don't you remember the good Sisters telling you that you never were to fuck with the Chapel."

Bauman didn't look up. He took a short sip of his whiskey before he replied, "I do Kevin. I do indeed. But I don't think they'd be saying it in just that way which is why I forgot, I suppose. Are you to tell me that I'm to pick up my time?"

Hardly gave an affirmative nod into the mirror visible to Bauman, "That I am, Joseph, and as one good Knight to another, hear me when I say that it will be a short time until we find a more suitable place for a man with your talent."

Bauman was a man of faith who trusted friendship. He was confident that Kevin would soon have him reinstated in a prominent position. Kevin was not as confident but was loyal to his brother Knight. He would try. With a pat on the back he wished Joseph the best of the day and signaled the bartender to put his drink on Joe's tab. Then he slipped off the barstool and left for his plush corporate office with the satisfaction of knowing that he had completed another task for his Church.

CHAPTER TWO

The entire Bauman affair extended over six months. There were an additional few months of healing while the Cardinal pondered a way to recruit a new hospital chief executive officer. In the interim Sister Celest remained in office under the careful eye of Sister Elizabeth. The Terrific Trinity of Hardly, O'Shea, and Patello, walked in the shadows using Doctor Folley as their agent. Folley became an adept medical politician using his power base wisely to build an empire that would prevail regardless of the chief executive be he or she religious or lay. All of the employed faculty physicians regardless of department or specialty were in some manner beholding to Dr. Folley's informal control of the budget. The community based private practice physicians used Folley to reserve special rooms and surgery times and Folley in turn used the private practitioners to expand his political base. Through his connection with Patello, he became a regular at political dinners, cocktail parties, and even wedding receptions. He eventually became the personal and confidential physician to leading State representatives and senators whose medical record contents bought Folley their unlisted telephone numbers and a first name relationship. There wasn't a door that Doctor Folley couldn't open or an arm he couldn't twist. He reached the summit when Francis Cardinal McMahon asked Doctor Richard Folley to advise him about his chronic hypertension, weight gain, and nutrition problems.

Cardinal McMahon recognized the need to expedite the selection of the hospital's chief executive officer. He sought the counsel of the Washington office of the Council of Bishops who in turn sought counsel from the Catholic Health Association who recommended their immediate past chairman of the board, Mr. Joseph Durant. Joseph Durant was well known in Catholic Health Care. He was a professional administrator who for some unknown reason had only been employed in Catholic hospitals. His career extended over four decades and three different positions in three large mid-western cities. The Archbishop Cardinal of Chicago knew Durant well as an Executive at the Daughters of Charity Hospital. He advised Cardinal McMahon that Mr. Durant would be a fine Catholic to administer St. Anslem's Hospital. Acting on the good advice, Cardinal McMahon directed Bishop Hanks to retain an executive search firm to contact Mr. Durant and recruit his services. The Cardinal also appointed Bishop Hanks to chair a search committee that would recommend Mr. Durant to him as the new hospital CEO. Other members of the search committee included Sister Elizabeth, Dr. Richard Folley and Mr. Thomas O'Shea.

The search firm selected by Bishop Hanks was deliriously happy to charge a big fee to recruit a single candidate pre-selected by the client. Durant had no idea that he had been pre-selected. The head hunters promoted the job with the idea that many qualified applicants were fighting for the position. Durant put on a pretty face, shined his shoes, and went for it. His background check was squeaky clean. His interviews with the search committee were flawless except for the time spent with Mr. O'Shea. O'Shea regarded Durant as a carpet bagger. He resented Durant's statement that mission was the first consideration over margin. He later informed Hardly that Durant was a male nun and therefore no different than Sr. Celest. At the second and final meeting of the search committee O'Shea protested Durant's selection and refused to allow a unanimous recommendation to the Cardinal. Folley provided some consolation to O'Shea by reminding him that Dr. Folley was the real authority at Sr. Anslem's and would, "control the clod from the mid-west."

The search firm represented the Archdiocese and the trustees in negotiating the employment agreement with Durant. O'Shea contemptuously noted that the $250,000 salary was more than twice the amount paid to Bauman. The termination clause provided eighteen-months continuation of salary and benefits, except for cause, which most certainly would include putting a lock on the chapel door. All expenses of moving the Durant family from their comfortable three-bedroom ranch in Waukegan to a four-bedroom colonial in Hingham was paid by St. Anslems. Again, O'Shea protested by pointing out that selection of a local candidate would have avoided this outrageous expense. The Cardinal confided to Bishop Hanks that the salary and benefits were far more than he had expected. He wondered if the amount would be the cause of scandal if the public media exposed it in view of the hospital's fiscal plight. Bishop Hanks offered no consolation. The employment agreement was signed and Joseph Durant became the chief executive officer of St. Anslem's Hospital.

Kevin Hardly was on a world tour as a guest of the State Department during the month that the St. Anslem's search committee was doing its work. Consequently, Joseph Durant was installed as the CEO by O'Shea in his capacity as vice-chairman. The fanfare was reserved for Durant and more directed to Sr. Celest's retirement. The Boston Globe, in an editorial, took delight in bashing the Cardinal and the Catholic Church as a male dominated bastion while praising Sr. Celest as a heroine of modem time. Durant was completely overlooked by the media as was typical of St. Anslems in a City over- crowded with major and numerous world famous medical centers. It was five weeks later before Hardly met Durant. That first meeting left Durant wondering if he had made a fatal mistake.

Joe Durant knelt in a slouched way as he reflected on his first months as St. Anslem's CEO. Somehow in the back of his mind he heard the words "Lord Jesus Christ, you said to your apostles; I leave you peace, my peace I give you. Look not on our sins but on the faith of your Church, and grant us the peace and unity of your kingdom where you live for ever and ever." The familiar words spoken by the Priest and the responding, "Amen", by the assembled worshipers brought Durant back to paying attention to the Mass. He heard the Priest say, "The peace of the Lord be with you always." He responded with the congregation, "and also with you."

Durant was mentally engrossed in the circumstances that had pressurized the hospital's Board as he and his wife sat in a side aisle pew at St. Francis by the Sea Catholic Church in Hingham, a quiet suburban New England town where he settled after being recruited to St. Anslem's from Illinois. The small Church was less than half occupied on this warm Sunday morning as the elderly Priest noticeably struggled through the liturgy. The most solemn part of the Mass brought Joseph Durant out of his contemplations of temporal matters to the realization that, according to the teachings of the Church, the Body and Blood of Jesus Christ was about to become present, transformed from bread and wine. Joseph was baptized a Catholic a few weeks after his birth and had been educated in the teachings of the Church by the Sisters of the Holy Cross through elementary and high school followed by a Jesuit undergraduate and graduate education at Xavier University; He was comfortable in his religion and practiced it faithfully but not scrupulously. The Jesuits had convinced him that faith and morality were matters of personal moral convictions supported by the teachings of the Church. He concluded early in his Jesuit years that religious regimentation and dictate was for the benefit of the uneducated who required procedure to establish belief. Attention to his personal spiritual well-being was conducted without intellectual conflict as he ignored the confusion of the faithful brought about by modifications in Church practice. He sometimes pondered the inconsistency of the Church Hierarchy in moral dictates from diocese to diocese but as a Catholic hospital administrator of nearly thirty five years he had come to realize that the Church was, above all else, human. Those human qualities were the focus of the healing ministry.

Durant had been deep in thought about the many problems of St. Anslem's Hospital when the words of the Eucharist recalled his spiritual attention. In less than forty-eight hours the Board of Trustees was scheduled to meet and hear, among other things, a report by the finance committee that St. Anslem's operating result for the past month was in severe deficit, as it had been for the past ten months. Gallant attempts by Rod Weaver, St. A's Vice President for Finance, to explain the deficit as a consequence of market reorganization had failed to convince, much less satisfy, the Finance Committee consisting of Thomas O'Shea and Dr. Folley. Their reaction was to shoot the messenger. After the last finance committee meeting O'Shea told Durant that Weaver had to go. Durant attempted to explain the injustice of that to Mr. O'Shea only to be advised that if Weaver stayed, the CEO would go. He then appealed to the O'Shea's sympathy pointing out that Weaver was forty-seven years old with two children in grammar school, one in high school and one in her second year at Boston College. To relocate at this time in his life would be extremely traumatic for his family. O'Shea was unmoved.

As the Priest gave the final blessing Joe was again pondering St. Anslem's. He had learned about the hospital's corporate history from Sister Celest during the two months that she stayed on after his appointment to help with the transition. She respected Joseph as a professional and he appreciated her dedication to the religious community and the ministry. In contrast to Bauman, Sister recognized that Durant was a sincere professional administrator who understood charity and compassion for the poor and under served as primary to the healing ministry. Durant realized that Sister Celest had attempted to equate modem technical medical expertise with the hospital's mission. He respected her for the attempt and became determined to expand the mission as she had done. When time came for Sister to formally retire she did so with the assurance that Joe Durant would direct St. Anslem's as the Poor Sisters of Charity had intended. Sister Celest and Joe Durant were good friends.

The Hospital continued to experience hard times in spite of the pseudo expertise of the reconstituted Board of Trustees. Within the halls and units of the Hospital there was continuous bickering over the demands by administrators to reduce spending. Folley acted as the consummate politician in soothing the ruffled feathers of the many prima donnas who paraded into his office seeking special exemption and favors at the expense of their colleagues. Doctor Ronald Anderson, MD, Ph.D., Director of St. Anslem's Hospital's Chemical Addiction Program, referred to as SACAP, was specialists of a different breed. He was a primary care physician boarded in Internal Medicine who had great compassion for the addicted and chronically ill. Anderson was a passionate Catholic who had deep appreciation and loyalty to the Church, the Cardinal, and the Sisters. The slightly built somewhat lanky man remained focused on his patients and tried to be oblivious to the changing patterns of health delivery. However, the fiscal pressures put upon him by administration frequently spirited his temper causing an outburst of profanity directed at the source of agitation. He began his day at 7 AM with the usual review of the administrative junk scattered on his cluttered desk. Pressure to reduce staffing in the face of increasing census in the program seemed ludicrous. Cutbacks in reimbursement by the State Department of Public Aid had almost destroyed the program last year and now the encroachment of managed care practices by the insurance companies were threatening to finish the job. Administration had put increasing pressure on his boss, Doctor Richard Folley, Chairman of St. Anslem's Department of Medicine to either dump the program or find a way to make it profitable. To make matters worse the Budget Director was scheduled to meet with him to question him about over spending in last month's supply expenses.

Anderson had built the substance abuse program from the ground up in times when money was plentiful thanks to the generosity of cost based reimbursement structured in the original Medicare and Medicaid programs. In his mind so called health care reform was detrimental to the Nation's health. He was about to launch into one of his early morning tirades about the Fascist plot to destroy the practice of good medicine when his secretary mercifully informed him that his lead patient counselor, Bob Markley, was holding on line one. Anderson immediately changed his mood as he answered the phone. "Bob-- What's happening? Don't ask for more because administration won't give us anything but grief. What's on your mind?"

Markley was the most respected member of Anderson's staff. He was a recovering alcoholic and one of Anderson's success stories who didn't fear the old man's bark or bite. He held his mentor in high regard. After a brief pause and an audible deep breath, he managed to reply, "And a cheery good morning to you, Dr. Anderson. I take it from your warm greeting that all goes well. Perhaps you could digress from your routine aggressive behavior for a while to consider a clinical matter. You do remember patientcare—if not I could take this matter to Doctor Folley who I'm sure would give me the immediate assistance of the senior resident."

Mentioning Dr. Folley was a quick jab to Anderson's ego. Folley was the Hospital's Chief of Medicine and leading medical politician.

Anderson was Folley's senior but had declined the opportunity to lead the Department of Medicine in deference to Folley. Anderson respected Folley as an administrator, teacher and physician but despised his political techniques that he thought were unbecoming to the physician's image. Somewhat irritated, he fired back, "Markley, you have made my day. The VP for finance is looking to roll some heads out of the salary lines and you just volunteered. Maybe I should take that bit of news to Folley with whatever else you have banging on that pickled brain of yours."

Markley sensed that Anderson was running a bit hot so he switched to a more tactful approach. "Sorry, Doctor. I need your advice and professional help with a client. His name is Jay Marquart who has been in the program for only a week. He managed to clear the first hurdle and now some things are entering into the mix that are explosive and I mean with a big bang. The chart is on its way to your office. I'd appreciate it if you would review it, especially the social history, and then set a time when we can discuss it. Please take very careful note of the incident report clipped to the back of the record. It has not been sent to Risk Management yet so you can judge how far this thing needs to travel. I'll fill you in on all the gory details after you review the chart."

Anderson was delighted to be inserted into clinical matters. He was personally convinced that was where a physician was supposed to be instead of wasting clinical skills arguing about the need to justify every penny lost or found. He couldn't understand the young residents who openly announced their intent to be public health administrators or worse yet, hospital administrators. "Why go to medical school and study science to be custodian of the farm," was his constant lament. He was about to work himself into another emotional fit when his faithful secretary politely placed Jay Marquart's medical record on the desk. Anderson sat back in his comfortable desk chair. He pushed aside the administrative clutter and placed the medical record in its metal cover on the desk in front of him. He switched on the desk lamp and began a close inspection of the record as if he was the attending physician. The record was complete up to the time of the patient's last encounter with his counselor. The many blood and urine lab tests recorded a steady decline in the adverse chemical substance levels of an abuser. Anderson noted with disgust that the test results were not available when the patient came for his counseling sessions. This forced the attending physician to fly blind in assisting the counselor in prescribing the course of treatment. Anderson damned the pathologist for her inefficiency and the hospital CEO for his continual cutback of lab technicians. He made a mental note to make this an issue at the next meeting of the medical staff Quality Assurance Committee.

The admitting notes recorded that Jay Marquart checked into the SACAP unit of St. Anslem's Hospital in response to and at the direction of the Employee Assistance Program of Action Waste Management Company. In fact the EAP Director drove Jay to the hospital after Jay had gone into a severe depression at a staff meeting. Anderson's curiosity began to peak as he scanned the clinical data. His professional research in the field of substance abuse supported his contention that inherited physiological qualities of a potential addict required an environmental trigger usually related to emotional stress coupled with depression. The cure often required medication to supplant an absent chemical in the patient's blood that erased the addictive urge for the so called recreational drugs. As a young Ph.D. pharmacologist and researcher at Tuft's University School of Medicine he wanted to expand his theories to the test. His professional curiosity heightened and he eventually enrolled in the School of Medicine to earn his MD and board certification in internal medicine. He joined the St. Anslem's Medical Staff following his residency and gradually over the years promoted his theories about the treatment of substance abuse. The Sisters were captivated by his dedication and with the support of the physicians gave him some unused space, formally the Sisters' Infirmary, to be developed into the St. Anslem's Substance Abuse Program.

Jay Marquart's medical record contained social history notes entered by various counselors doing the admitting evaluation. They all concluded that Jay's quasi voluntary admission into the program was the beginning of a long overdue turn around in his thirty six years. Typically, Marquart denied his problem but after several sessions took the first step and admitted his dependency. His motivation was based on his resolve not to lose shared custody of his five year old daughter, Kirstie. She was the focus of his adult life and the only reason he held for living. Anderson was becoming increasingly disturbed that the notes seemed to avoid pinpointing the trigger of the patient's emotional collapse. He remembered Bob Markley'S request that he take careful note of the social history to be followed by an in depth discussion of the case. He also remembered Bob informing him about an incident report attached to the chart. The incident report was clipped to the back of the metal chart cover. Anderson pulled it off and placed it aside. He intended to review it after he completed reviewing all the clinical data.

Unfortunately the social history in the medical record was only a sketch of Jay's current life. It detailed his family, job, income, and interests but failed to reveal the evolution of his addiction that began as an adolescent determined to lead his life as a free spirit. His natural intelligence and average athletic ability were set aside for the good times with his buddies who invented ways to bypass the rules at Brighton High School. Marquart set a record at the High School for breaking more rules than anyone else in history. The revised student handbook published after his graduation was referred to by the exhausted faculty as the Marquart Manual of Mischief

Jay loved life and he was extremely loyal to his family and friends. He always came home for birthdays and holidays and then would disappear after dinner. He would hug his mother with true affection before leaving the house. Anyone who offended his brothers or sisters or the family dog would find Jay in their face ready to do combat. Anyone who Jay considered a friend had his full loyalty and access to his last joint. He would defend his shiftless friends to his parents who constantly pleaded with him to hang out with a better class. As Jay was quick to love, he was also quick to hate. His temper tantrums as a baby seemed to carry forward through his teens and into his young adult years. When he became angry he became violent as well. Scars from his street encounters were apparent on his face and arms. On two occasions his parents were called to the hospital where Jay was treated for a concussion and then released. Aside from being happy go lucky, free-wheeling, and occasionally violent he somehow managed to avoid being charged of any form of crime.

Jay's high school academic record would not have qualified him for admission to Harvard. This was not a matter of great concern. In fact, Jay, was not interested in advanced studies of any kind except what he might learn partying and hanging out. Funds for his various adventures were scarce since Dad announced that Jay had reached a point of finding a means of supporting himself. Jay's first job out of high school was driving a Senior Citizen Van for a nursing home. He loved the job and he loved helping the old folks. The men would tell Jay stories about fishing, hunting, and drinking that convinced Jay that the life in the wild was the true course of happiness. Unfortunately, the money that he earned from Senior Citizens was not adequate for him to support his increasing habits so he followed his compassionate instincts to St. Anslem's Hospital where he was first employed as a janitor and eventually became trained as a cardiac technician by a Nun who adopted Jay as a project.

Jay Marquart married Cecile Kelly when they were both twenty and ironically employees at St. Anslem's. Jay was a technician in the Cardiac Catheterization Laboratory and Cecile a licensed practical nurse in the Medical Intensive Care Unit. Their marriage lasted twelve painful years during which time they drank booze, smoked pot, and sniffed cocaine for recreation and socialization. Jay's efficiency eventually became hampered by a perpetual hangover that, combined with a companion state of depression, led him away from gainful employment and for lack of a better option into taking classes at the University of Massachusetts in Boston. His parents, pleased at his apparent effort to improve himself, picked up most of the tab.

Cecile contributed to the effort by continuing to work at St. Anslems and, in addition, entered the associate degree program for registered nursing at Bunker Hill College. After three years of questionable social existence they both graduated. Jay, with a degree in political science, became a slave of the political bosses in Boston. This eventually led to his employment at Action Waste Management. Cecile passed her Massachusetts State Nursing Boards and was elevated to registered nurse in St. Anslems Medical Intensive Care Unit.

Cecile's life had been a constant struggle since her father abandoned her and her Mother when she was ten. The petite, feisty, five-foot Irish lass accepted her fate and companion poverty with the resolve to control her adult life free of domination from any direction. Her marriage to Jay was more for convenience and economy than affection and companionship. Jay was acquainted with the people on the street and supplied her with the good times and obligatory high of their youth. Now she held the respected status of a professional nurse and resolved to be excellent. As she became established in her nursing profession she became less dependent on the particulars of her relationship with Jay. Within a year after her graduation from Bunker Hill she knew that her marriage was no longer of benefit.

Kristie was an accident of fate following the usual weekend binge. Sex was never enjoyable for Cecile. She responded without emotion to Jay's passionate begging and ignored him most of the time. It was a tremendous shock when she discovered her pregnancy. They had been married eight years and over that time had gradually moved into different worlds. Now the threat seemed real that a child could merge their relationship into a traditional family. Furthermore, Cecile feared that as a Mother she could possibly be subordinated to the role of a domestic. In her mind this meant the loss of all that she had accomplished in her quest for professional status. Her Catholic upbringing never offered her the thought of terminating the pregnancy. Instead she became determined to dominate her child and eliminate the involvement of the father.

Jay was elated over the prospect of becoming a father. He had the benefit of a stable family background that included three brothers and two sisters. The warmth of family gatherings at Thanksgiving and Christmas would become more appealing as their baby entered the extended family with new cousins, brothers and sisters in law. Jay remembered these same good times as a boy and recalled as well how he had rejected the family circle for the attraction of a joint, cheap wine, and hanging out with his buddies. He was the one who had the use of Mom's car to roam the streets looking for the connection and then using a motel for a rousing party. While still in high school he also tried his hand as a delivery boy for local drug dealers but found it not to his benefit when his dad found the unpaid for stash in the garage and threw it in the garbage can. Somehow Jay convinced his supplier that the loss of the stash, while tragic, was not of great consequence since he had talked his father out of reporting the matter to the police and, worse yet, the school authorities. The supplier had accepted Jay's foggy reasoning without breaking either of his legs but as punishment the delivery concession was transferred to Jay's best friend, Brian, who was well recognized as the main mule for both the senior and junior high schools in Brighton.

Actually, Jay had been sleeping off a jag when Dad decided to clean the garage and found the stash. Dad was pondering his find when the garbage truck pulled into the driveway. As the garbage man was wrestling with the family trash Dad handed him the stash and asked him to dispose of it. The environmental attendant was immediately responsive. Subsequently the Marquart household had the benefit of extraordinary attention by an array of City Sanitation Employees who made frequent and unscheduled checks on the trash accumulation in the Marquart garage

Cecile's pregnancy was uneventful but very uncomfortable. As she approached term it was apparent that a cesarean delivery was required. Kristie was born without complications but Cecile became determined that Kristie would be her one and only child. She would have the best education and formation for her child which certainty required divorce from a father who lacked social foundation, direction, and ambition. It would take time to reorganize her life to maintain her career advancement, accommodate the seemingly limitless requirements of her baby, and maneuver herself to the desired status of a single parent. In the interim she would see that Jay became disciplined in his conduct and correct in taking care of the child. She began by volunteering for as much overtime and extra duty as the hospital could offer in order to maximize her income.

She also made sure that she and Jay had separate bank accounts so their respective contributions to the family income was well recorded. Jay's various endeavors such as fishing, hunting, smoking, drinking and gambling were financed by his own earnings except for the times that she went along.

Jay's life was one of constant instability but that was the way he liked it. Following graduation from UMass he attempted to find a position that would provide him with a moderate sense of dignity that he reasoned a college graduate should have. He purposefully steered away from anything to do with healthcare especially St. Anslems Hospital. His degree in political science and persuasive personality led him to the Democratic Party Headquarters where he offered to assist office seekers in campaigns.

At first, he was strictly a volunteer, but eventually he gained the confidence of a few people on the first level who recommended him to a few of people on the middle level who asked permission of a few people on the top level who authorized a few patronized bucks to provide Jay a small salary, provided he kicked back a piece to the Party's Widows and Orphans' Fund. Jay accepted the draw as part of the cost of doing business. He also accepted the rigors of long hours, endless meetings, standing on comers holding campaign signs, and brown nosing as the price he had to pay for the good times at campaign parties with lots of good booze. His daughter, Kristie, put a new perspective to his life, however, and Jay found himself wheeling and dealing within the Party's power base for a real job. Eventually he was able to convince a power broker from the North End to sponsor him on the patronage role for an entry job with the Massachusetts Department of Environmental Services.

Jay, at first, enjoyed his life as a low-level bureaucrat. The flexible hours allowed by the State accommodated his night time sorties for the party bosses. He found that he was in great demand to attend to seemingly endless details of real or imagined office seekers. Occasionally his sponsor would ask Jay to do a few minor tasks apparently not related to the work of the Democratic Party. Jay presumed the tasks were benefits of being a party boss so he delivered the packages, picked up the envelopes, washed the car, and mowed the lawn. Eventually the good times began to wear thin and he began looking for improved status. His sponsor, Mr. Charles Patello, was reluctant to consider promoting him up the patronage ladder and instead advised Jay to seek an opportunity in the private sector.

Mr. Patello was an investment banker of sorts who was well acquainted with expanding companies. Jay was appreciative of Mr. Patello's assistance but sought to find his own opportunities. He responded to a notice on the public bulletin board in the cafeteria that announced several openings with a State grant supported private company called Action Waste Management. Jay had reviewed several parts of their grant request and had the honor of presenting the Action proposal to the Grant Committee. While it was a minor role in the process of obtaining State favor, Jay was certain that the Action executives who were at his presentation would remember his efforts and be attracted to bringing him on board.

As he had hoped he was well received by Action's personnel clerk who, after an hour and a half- moved Jay on to meet Ken Ryan, Supervisor of the Quality Control Section of Action's waste recycling program. Jay's knowledge of waste recycling was nearly perfect. Ryan offered him the position on the spot. Following the required two-week notice Jay left the world of politics and patronage for a career in private enterprise- -or so he thought.

Ryan was only five years older than Jay, in his second marriage, had a great sense of humor, and seemed tolerant if not understanding of Jay's difficulties in adjusting from the loose working requirements of the State to the precise time clock practice of good business. In fact Ryan had started as a State employee, like Jay, in the Department of Environmental Services. He stayed less than a year until the opportunity in industry came through. An executive of Action approached him after a legislative hearing on recycling where Mr. Ryan had been a key witness for the Representatives proposing mandatory recycling for all municipalities by the year 2000. He accepted the offer to head the Quality control section of Action on the spot. That was five years ago and while he was still in the same position his salary had doubled. On two occasions he had received a generous bonus for assisting the implementation of the Action Recycling System in Foxboro and Braintree—a fact he was quick to point out to Jay. Otherwise Ryan had not been subjected to the political scutt work of ward healing and patronage.

Jay enjoyed the status of a real job. He responded to his duties with genuine effort and sincerity. Cecile, while favorably impressed with his demeanor, remained critical of his slothful attitude at household duties. She prepared a list of tasks for him to accomplish each day after work with the understanding that they would be completed before she left the hospital at the end of her twelve-hour shift. Little Kristie was to be picked up each day by Jay on his way home from work at Cecil's parents. As Kristie grew older Jay would take her to the zoo or for a late afternoon walk in the park. Their bonding grew in spite of Cecile's objective to remove Jay from the family.

Kristie was four years old when her mother's nagging finally broke Jay down. He was at the point of violence on several occasions but backed away due to the good advice of his boss and friend, Ryan. However, Ryan also advised Jay that he was bringing his troubles to work too often. Jay knew that a solution had to be found. He thought of moving out of their small house but again Ryan suggested that he should avoid any action that would appear as an act of abandonment. Jay compensated for his misery by playing softball and bowling with his old high school buddies that included Brian. Brian shared his pot with Jay as they compared tales of misery about women, jobs, and get rich quick schemes.

Cecile refused to let Brian in their house and threatened to have him arrested if he came into the neighborhood. Jay, always loyal to his friends, countered with the announcement that the house was his as much as it was hers and that Brian could visit any time he wanted. Cecile explained to Jay that she had made the down payment, qualified for the mortgage, made the monthly payments and paid the taxes out of her bank account. It was all documented and available for review by lawyers, judges, or J. Christ if necessary. She was ready for the contest of a divorce. Jay knew that divorce was the only possible answer and was opting for a no contest settlement until the question of child custody came up. Cecile was determined that she would have exclusive custody of Kristie and Jay would be forever removed from both her and Kristie's life. She was certain that the divorce settlement would uphold her position that Jay was unsuitable as a father.

Cecile's confidence in winning her way in the divorce was well founded. Jay's support of the family was indeed minimal. He contributed little to the necessary where with all of the economic household unit. He could offer little evidence to the contrary.

Aside from his all too frequent consumption of booze and pot he had somehow been able to keep his reputation intact. He did have a job and above all else he demonstrated true love and affection for Kristie that could be proven. Jay was determined that the one person in his life for whom he cared the most would not be taken from him. There was one weakness that he was certain Cecile would exploit in forcing a settlement to her liking. Jay was broke and could not afford a complicated and costly legal battle. He knew that Cecile had the upper hand when it came to the money. His attempts to offset Cecil's determined child custody with total concession on all matters of property were accepted by her without compromise. Cecile sensed total victory and filed for divorce.

Throughout his adult life, Jay had wanted to be independent. He, nevertheless, was sensitive about his parents, brothers and sisters. They in turn always stood by him in time of crises. The Marquarts were a strong family anchored in love. Over the four years since Kristie's birth she had become a true member of the Marquart clan and held status equal to any other member. It was inconceivable that she would be separated from the family and her father by the cunning aspirations of her mother who had never gained the complete acceptance of Jay's sisters. Jay entered the initial steps of the divorce process with his usual air of independence and was blindsided by Cecile's lawyer who made a forceful demand for custody of Kristie.

Jay entered into a deep state of depression and, as he had done on many occasions in his developing years, called his sister, Martha, who in addition to being Kristie's aunt, was a lawyer. Martha recognized Jay's call to arms. The family circle was convened with Dad and Mom fronting the necessary cash to carry the day. Martha amassed her professional chits that brought the firm's leading divorce attorney forward to represent Jay in all proceedings. She backed the legal team with her own pro-bono efforts. What followed was an ugly brawl that ended with the Court granting joint custody of Kristie. Her time with each parent was to be mutually determined.—was obligated to pay the usual amount of child support to Cecile with whom Kristie would reside. Cecile contended throughout the proceedings that Jay's conduct was unfitting as a parent. The Court took careful notice of her contentions and warned Jay that any inappropriate conduct including failure to pay child support could result in loss of joint custody. It was also noted that Jay would be responsible to provide Kristie with an appropriate safe environment during the times that she was in his care.

Jay came out of the divorce as he had gone into it-flat broke. He was grateful for the help that Martha had provided even though he thought the efforts of the firm's super divorce attorney should have, "slammed dunked Cecile into the shitter." He let Martha know that her Law Firm could use better help which resulted into a brother and sister shouting match not unlike their teen age years. He was free of Cecile's nagging and had the occasional opportunity to be a real loving father. He was also free of a place to live. He had a monthly check to write for child support. His ten-year old Jeep needed a valve job and his fishing license had expired. Other than these few minor problems he was a new man. He picked up the phone and gave his old buddy, Brian, a call.

Finding a place to live was a real problem for a man of very limited means. A house or an apartment was prohibitive until Jay could recover from the divorce. As a temporary measure, he arranged to sleep on the sofa in Brian's dingy studio pad in Chelsea. In addition to his many other remarkable qualities Brian was also a slob. The apartment was decorated with an assortment of trash that would have required an all-out effort by Action Waste Management to correct. Jay knew that he could not bring Kristie to Brian's pad. He also suspected that if Ken Ryan knew an employee of Action was living in such squalor he would see his job on the line. On the positive side, he was Brian's guest at no charge. He reunited with some of his old contacts in the Party and started earning a few bucks on the side doing the routine delivery jobs. He also had the eerie feeling that Cecile was watching his every move. To keep her off the trail he would take Kirstie to visit Aunt Marie or Uncle Mike or Grandma on her weekends with Dad. Aunt Martha would usually appear at the family homestead during Kristie's visit and take the opportunity to remind Jay of the terms of the divorce. She told him about a livable shack in Waltham that she had recently repossessed for a client. It was available and affordable on Jay's meager income provided he would attend to a disciplined budget. Mom came across with the security deposit and the first month's rent. Martha prepared the lease. Jay told Martha to mind her own business and moved to the shack in Waltham.

The town of Waltham was a few miles west of Boston. It sprang to life after World War Two when the need for housing the returning servicemen resulted in the town tripling its size with acres of two-bedroom prefab houses. Waltham became the first blue collar bedroom community in New England. Jay's drive to work was around a half hour depending on traffic. His living conditions were definitely Spartan, however. He had no furniture except for a bed that was used by Kristie on weekends and Jay on week nights. He stood in the small kitchen to cook and eat except when Kristie visited. Then they had a picnic in the empty living room sitting Indian fashion on the floor. The plumbing was a sometimes thing and the old oil furnace just managed to keep the pipes from freezing in the winter. If there was any redeeming qualities about the place it was his neighbor who taught Jay how to maintain his old Jeep and do a lot of the home repairs that the landlord ignored. Again the family pitched in and gradually Jay collected modest furnishings including a used color TV that Kristie adored.

Jay realized that he was heading for trouble when Cecile arrived on a cold February evening to collect Kristie and found her sitting in the middle of the living room in her snowsuit playing fish with her Daddy. The temperature in the shack was slightly above fifty degrees and Kristie had a cold. Cecile, on the other hand, was definitely hot under the collar and proceeded to put Jay's feet to the fire. Jay called Martha who put him in touch with an out of firm attorney who successfully carried Jay through the resulting court appearances. It was apparent that Jay would have to find suitable housing if he was to counter future challenges to joint custody.

By the end of the first year following the divorce Jay had managed to pocket the down stroke on a small three-bedroom ranch in good condition just a few blocks away from his shack. Martha maneuvered him out of his lease and used her connections to get him a mortgage that He felt was a rip-off. He was now a homeowner in a respectable neighborhood that had working sewers, inside plumbing, and electric lights. His career as a quality control technician at Action Waste Management was apparently secure evidenced by a satisfactory evaluation and a six percent raise. His life was improving in spite of all the "crap" he had to crawl through to keep that "bitch off his back." Now he began to plan a counter-attack. By next year he intended to turn the tables and take full custody of Kristie. Ken Ryan said it was possible. Ken didn't have any kids when he went through his divorce but his attorney said it was possible. The attorney offered to represent Jay when the time was right. Jay also had overcome his total acquired distrust of the female persuasion and began to have an occasional date.

Jay enjoyed his freedom, his times with Kristie, his frequent hunting and fishing trips, his job at Action, and partying. Brian had become his constant companion. They would meet every night after work for a few pops that frequently extended into "all-nighters." Brian's career in the parcel delivery business had expanded to include a whole new line. He offered to introduce Jay to the business. Jay declined the offer but did agree to sample the products from time to time. Brian also introduced Jay to a young lady whose husband had been in the business until an unfortunate sale to an undercover agent put the man on extended leave. Alice had a daughter that she dearly loved and in her best interest gave testimony under protection about her husband's business affairs. This led to his conviction and eventually his parole. It also led to their divorce coupled with a bout with the Internal Revenue Service and Bankruptcy Court. Needless to say, Alice was flat broke when she met Jay and it was love at first sight. She moved in—lasted three months and abruptly moved out contending that Jay had more affection for his fishing pole than her. Jay did not contest the issue except to offer the excuse that the similar appearance of Alice and his fishing pole caused the problem. He once again vowed that women were no damn good.

A few weeks after the Alice Fishing Pole incident, Jay and Brian were positioned in the Waltham Tap and Keg when Jay spotted a familiar face among the five o'clock boozers. Her name was Susan Testa. Susan had been a regular participant at the high school pot parties that seemed to have been in another century. Jay had never gotten to know Susan in those days and he now had the urge to make up for lost time. After a rather clumsy approach he took the direct route and asked if she remembered him as the one and only good looking guy in the class. Susan remembered him but not so much for his good looks as his constant burnt out expression which seemed to her to be a lasting quality.

It was obvious that the two understood one another and had a lot in common. After a prolonged courtship of three months they were married by a justice of the peace on the Boston Commons at three in the afternoon. The hour was perfect for passersby to view the proceedings and extend best wishes. Jay's buddy Brian and his boss Ken Ryan were also present along with his Sister, Martha. After the ceremony, the entire party went to dinner at Mama Roses in the North End. Once again Jay was a married man.

Susan was small like Cecile but her Italian ancestry was accented with coal black hair and fiery eyes that were occasionally clear. She moved into Jay's house and brought with her several rooms of furniture, cooking utensils, linens, a washer and dryer, and two sons, ages eight and four, from a previous marriage. Jay now had a real house with a real family that included three kids and a good cook, His life seemed complete. Susan was no nag. She shared Jay's love for children, family, fishing, hunting and partying. They knew a lot of the same people and enjoyed the same culture.

Susan's former husband, an employee of Patriot Transport and Courier Service, was Brian's boss. Eddie the Enforcer, as he was known, had the task of collecting accounts receivable from delinquent customers. It was common knowledge that his habit of practicing his technique on Susan a couple times a week led to their break-up. Contrary to Jay, Susan's first husband apparently had no love or interest in his kids. He had gladly adhered to the restraining order served on him after he gave her the last bashing. Susan also shared Jay's attitude that the Mother should attend to the proper raising of the children in the home and not be employed full-time away from the children. Jay was determined to be the sole support of his family.

Contrary to Jay's hopes, Cecile had not abandoned her quest for sole custody of Kristie. Over the years since their divorce she had also learned that a single parent offered little confidence to a judge in matters of custody when the other parent presented the prospect of a stable family environment. This created a matter of great concern. Cecile detested the thought of marriage. She especially hated the idea of a sexual relationship of a permanent nature. A one night stand now and then was more than adequate to solve occasional biological urges. Her social life had presented several such opportunities that were satisfying but marginally enjoyable. However, one Friday evening at a nursing staff TGIF party she was introduced by a nursing buddy to a good looking cop from the Brighton precinct. He not only was good looking but was a true gentleman who didn't try to score on the first try. Cecile decided to pursue the relationship and since the officers from the Brighton precinct ate lunch in St. Anslem's cafeteria it was easy to meet at lunch and get better acquainted. After three weeks of a steady diet of salad and yogurt, Cecile popped the question and asked if he wanted to modify their lunch breaks into a more extended relationship. The good policeman took the hint and offered to have dinner at Cecile's house that very evening.

Their first nocturnal affair was a shocking but satisfying experience for Cecile and Officer Michael O'Sullivan. Contrary to Cecil's expectations of a rocking night in the sack, she was exposed to a person of sincere good nature with honorable intentions who explained that he occasionally enjoyed the alternate life style. He confessed that his association with Cecile was to cover his opposite life while his superiors considered his application for undercover assignment to Narcotics Division of the Boston PD. Cecile also let it be known that she was looking for a front to recover her kid. After extensive analysis by both parties they mutually agreed to a working relationship within a formal marriage. The event took place a month later when the former Mrs. John Marquart RN became Mrs. Cecile O'Sullivan RN, wife of Officer Michael O'Sullivan—Boston Police Department—recently assigned to Narcotics.

Dr. Anderson learned little of Jay's history from reading the medical record. It simply mentioned that Jay had admitted to habitual heavy use of intoxicating substances and that he had been on a week end binge prior to his collapse at his workplace, Action Waste Management. Markley's notes described Jay's violent behavior. The course of treatment was routine. The patient's background was typical of a user who was capable of being helped. Anderson liked what he saw. Markley had found another prospect.

The Chief Executive Office of St. Anslem's Hospital had no idea that there had been an incident in the SACAP involving Patient, Jay Marquart. Such matters rarely, if ever, required the attention of the hospital's chief executive. More appropriately, Joe Durant, St. Anslem's chief executive, consistently thought about the institution's occupancy, staffing, quality and fiscal well-being. Operational problems were handled by the extensive chain of command that blended physicians directing departments of medical specialists with vice presidents administering nursing, business affairs, hotel services such as food, housekeeping, engineering, and the like. Frequently the various medical disciplines conflicted with each other or more often with the lay administrative activities. Durant felt that he served more as a referee in these struggles. He tried to administer the institution to the benefit of the patient and the goals of the hospital established by the Board of Trustees. The inconsistency of patient care and corporate goals that had occurred in recent times seemed to put him in an impossible position but as a seasoned professional he was confident that he could better any challenge.

CHAPTER THREE

Charlie Patello at first gave little thought to St. Anslem's Hospital. He placated Hardly at the board meetings by appearing to be interested in the loose discussion. Otherwise he thought that Folley's wining about the hospital's administration was pure crap. He, Meehan and Mondi had plenty of other things to worry about in addition to finding a way to bring St. Anslems into their web. Mondi's distribution and sale of cocaine to Boston's rich and famous under the cover of National Assocated Investors, was rapidly expanding and needed more outlets. Meehan's Action Waste Management Company was not as established. It was riding the crest of a new wave industry that required a great amount of political lubrication to be supplied by Patello if the right people could be bought. Patello was totally absorbed in doing the undercover work for the benefit of the firm. If successful, National Associated Investors through Action Waste Management would add another major revenue source to its grand list of money laundering and skimming operations. At a casual dinner one evening Patello and Meehan hit on an idea to combine Action's future with the hospital. The combination of the two could be the entree that Big Frank Patello had asked them to develop.

Waste management in the Boston area and in most towns and cities in the State was provided by the municipal administration. By convincing the politicians that it was to their personal benefit to privatize the service, Action Waste Management could get the market base it was seeking. Typically, hospitals created large waste disposal problems for the municipalities because of the infectious nature on their waste material. This gave Action an angle. Promote hospital waste as a municipal problem and then ride to the rescue on a white horse of a private company dedicated to save the day.

Initially, tax increases were tolerated by the voters but soon became a burden for political incumbents trying to stay in office. Party bosses on both sides of the aisle warned the administration that other forms of revenue for water reclamation and waste control had to be found. The next alternative was an increase in utility rates particularly water and sewer services. Eventually the naive users became sensitive to the highest water rates in the United States and strongly challenged, once again, the concept of taxation without representation. Massachusetts Governor Dukar's handlers sensed that the cost of the Water Reclamation Project could not only sink their man's chances of re-election but forever end his political career. Dukar was the property of the Republican Party and the Party was the supported in no small part by big money from big business. It was essential to maintain control of the State administration in the heavily populated Northeastern United States. However the reaction of the public to taxes and water rates provided an opportunity for the NAI syndicate to initiate the project called Privatization. Patello and Meehan knew that NAI's experiences in other States proved that the public, given the right motivation, would demand that waste management be placed in the hands of competent private companies that would guarantee a cleaner, safer environment. Dukar they reasoned would want to be the named author and hero of the privatization program. Big Frank had schooled his nephew, Charlie Patello, early in life that the first step in any good business venture is to create the demand.

That demand was initiated by an angry mother, compensated by Patello, who summoned the Boston Globe Investigation Team to Squatum beach in North Quincy. The beach had been closed to swimmers for several years because of the water pollution but it still was a popular place for sunbathing, jogging and family recreation. The caller's voice went beyond angry to violent as she described how her three-year old had found and began playing with a syringe with needle that apparently washed onto the beach. She claimed the place was littered with trash that contained bloody bandages, toilet paper, and other items that she couldn't identify. Within minutes Boston's number one newspaper had its crack Investigative Team with photographer on the scene. The next edition carried the story on page one with a four-column photo of the trash. The banner story detailed the incompetent procedures that area hospitals used in collecting and bagging trash. It concentrated on the disposal of the trash by City Sanitation Service that indiscriminately threw the trash bags on open trucks and carted the debris to barges that supposedly dumped the material miles off shore. Other area Newspapers, not to be out done by their Big City competitor, ran front page stories with focus on the infectious waste that contributed to the rapid spread of AIDS. Television and radio stations throughout New England picked up on the story with syringe and needles spotted on every beach from Maine to New Jersey. In less than a week an irate public was demanding that the Governor mobilize the State's resources to eliminate the threat to public safety.

Mayor Cowan of Boston represented the demands of the citizens to the Governor's office. He pointed out to the governor and the assembled media that the City Sanitation workers were overwhelmed by the enormous task of segregating infectious hospital waste from ordinary trash. To place such a burden on the municipality would require extensive subsidization from the State. He emphasized that significant increase in taxes was not only required but well worth the investment. The Boston Taxpayers Association countered the Mayor's contention that additional taxes were necessary to solve the problem. They pointed out that private companies could be invited to collect and dispose of infectious waste and other debris on a fee for service basis that would place the burden on the producer of the waste thus relieving the taxpayer. The Governor acknowledged the wisdom of the Tax Payers Association and appointed a blue-ribbon commission to formulate a plan for the privatization of waste collection and disposal for Massachusetts' municipalities. The resulting report of the commission titled Infectious Waste Control for Towns and Cities in Massachusetts served as the basis for enabling legislation that established an Office of Waste Management within the State Department of Public Health that, among other things, applied to the Federal Government for block grants to be used to support Towns and Cities in the development of recycling and waste control. The Office of Waste Management reviewed all local grant applications and passed them on for final review and recommendation to the former blue ribbon commission now named The Governor's Special Taskforce for Waste Management. Once the Taskforce gave its positive recommendation on a specific grant application it was forwarded to Governor Dukar for final approval. Once a grant was approved by the Governor it was placed in the capable hands of the Secretary of Public Health who delegated it to the Director of the Office of Waste Management who assigned the project to a Regional Coordinator of Waste Management Services who assigned the project to a grant manager who regulated the local implementation through the municipal public health official and the recognized private contractor named in the grant award.

The legislation was initially opposed by the Massachusetts Hospital Association that contended the whole program was politically motivated. The Association attempted unsuccessfully to demonstrate that private companies would charge outrageous fees to hospital thus dramatically increasing the cost of health services. The media destroyed the Hospital Association's arguments with a series of programs and articles about the Boston teaching hospitals' enormous wealth and extreme profits. Faced with the embarrassing truth the Hospital Association retreated to safer grounds and fortified itself against the Governor's promised assault on hospitals' tax exempt status.

Organized Labor took up the fight and denounced the entire privatization program of the Governor as a scam certain to lead to a criminal conviction. The Boston Workers' Guild organized a strong campaign to counter the privatization of waste management that was diminished by editorial sentiment pointing to the advantage of private cost effective companies that would create jobs and contribute to the tax base of the local community and State. The fact that none of the companies named in the grant applications approved by the Governor had union contracts was somehow overlooked by the media in spite of Union commentary and editorial reply.

Somewhat as the last resort, the Boston Workers' Guild organized a massive rally to be held on the Capitol steps to protest the signing of the legislation by Governor Dukar. They had convinced the Massachusetts Hospital Association to cosponsor the rally. The gathering was large by usual protest standards and equally unruly. The steps of the Golden Domed State Capitol Building were packed with demonstrators. The crowd overflowed into the street and onto Boston Commons where tourists mingled with the protesters. The bright, warm sunny afternoon gave the affair a festive mood. Many openly drank beer and sang. The local media had a field day filming staged fist fights between hecklers and angels of mercy in white uniforms. Hospital CEOs stood side by side Union leadership and angrily denounced the private control of waste management. Statements issued by hospital administrators were cheered by hospital employees and union members. The excitement grew to a fever pitch and came to an explosive climax when Bob Muldoon, President of the Boston Workers' Guild came to the podium. He waxed eloquent about the solidarity of the Guild and the unyielding opposition to the privatization of waste management. Then to the sudden dismay and surprise of the hospital officials he announced a City wide strike of organized hospitals in the Boston area if the Hospital Association endorsed the signing of contracts with private waste management companies. He also pledged that any union hospital that signed a waste management agreement on its own would be faced with a strike vote post haste.

Dukar took special note of the furor in the local Boston media and silently prayed that it would blow over. He had been well advised that the union might try a grandstand play with a strike threat. He had also been advised by the attorney general that a strike of this kind was illegal and could be dissolved by injunction. Muldoon was also well aware of the legal status of the threat. He knew and fully expected any strike that occurred not to be sanctioned by the union. Muldoon also knew a big threat made big news that would draw national attention. As he had hoped all the wire services and networks filled their nightly news with scenes from the latest edition of the Boston Tea Party. Muldoon had bigger fish to fry and now the skillet was hot and ready.

oOo

Number One Park Ave in New York City is a very tall prestigious building located a block south of Grand Central Station. The name has no relationship to the building's location on Park Avenue. It simply represents the wealth and influence of the developers and the way of doing business in New York. A significant amount of money found its way into the hands of the NYC zoning and planning commission that, in turn, rewarded the developer for improving the image of the City with its grand edifice. The true address of One Park Ave is classified information held by the United States Post Office that delivers mail routinely throughout Manhattan by building name and area code.

The occupants of the thirty fifth floor at One Park Ave, National Associated Investors, had little concern about the building's name. NAI's purpose was to build new and highly profitable business ventures for its wealthy stockholders. Mario Capizzi, President of NAI, had initiated the formation of Park Environmental Inc., a subsidiary of NAI, two years earlier following the passage of the Federal Environmental Protection Act. Cappizi had convinced the Board of NIA that public demand for waste management and the motivation for States to use available Federal funds to establish waste management standards by and through the use of private enterprise offered excellent profit potential, respectability, possible tax advantages, and opportunities for cash investors to launder income from other sources. Big Frank Patello, NAI's chairman and head of the Patello family formerly of Brooklyn and recently Providence, Rhode Island, accepted Cappizi's recommendation and, with unanimous consent of NAI's board of trustees, funded the formation and operation of Park Environmental Inc.

Cappizi as Chairman of Park Environmental Inc. and President of National Associated Investors, selected Anthony Marone as President of Park. Marone built Park into a prominent national consulting firm on environmental and waste management practices that offered quality, inexpensive advice to State legislators and governors on acquisition and use of Federal grants for waste management in addition to making the obligatory contributions to election campaigns. Park also became recognized as the foremost consulting firm to private investors and entrepreneurs interested in the formation and operation of Waste Management Companies. Using the resources of NAI, Park invested in each of the Companies that it helped to initiate. NAI found working capital loans from local banks and investment companies for their various waste management ventures. Park, because of its particular method of financing, was able to guarantee cost/price advantage to its companies. Park also provided an exclusive franchise. As a consequence, there was little competition that favorably compared to Park's services.

Marone, following Cappizi's direction, used the national organizational structure established by NAI to access local markets. This well-established organization, staffed with well-connected prominent individuals, provided Park instant success. The New England Region was based in Boston and therefore would best be initiated in Massachusetts. Rhode Island was an alternate consideration because of Patello's banking influence but was dismissed due to a sudden and unexpected defection that caused a prominent publicized disruption in the savings and loan business. NAI's man in Boston was Charles Patello. Uncle Frank had enjoyed bouncing little Charlie on his knee when he was a toddler and now enjoyed contributing to his success as a member of the family. Little Charlie responded to his Uncle's kindness by ushering NAI into many profitable ventures in the New England region.

A particular benefit that Patello brought into the NAI ventures in Boston was his close connection with the Irish gang that controlled an estimated one third of the area's wealth including the City of Boston's municipal spending and the spending of the Boston Catholic Archdiocese. Charlie had convinced Uncle Frank many years ago that two Irish kids he had met at Boston College could be compromised for future use, One, Kevin Hardly, came equipped with lots of money, family influence, and little brains—the other, Tom O'Shea, had lots of ambition, no money, and few morals. It seemed to be a perfect combination that only required two hundred dollars to bribe an ethics professor for an advance copy of the final exam. Uncle Frank gave Charlie the money to swing the deal. Charlie pulled it off and returned the two hundred with fifty bucks splitting a hundred-dollar profit down the middle. Big Frank Patello knew at that time that his Sister's youngest son was destined to be his successor and head of the largest operation east of Chicago.

The remaining two thirds of Boston's wealth seemed problematic to Charles Patello and the interest of National Associated Investors.

The Puritan Ethic of avoiding association with Papists and non-Christians created a block that Patello tried vainly to overcome. He also recognized that the WASP strength was based on the unfortunate split in the Hardly family. He decided that a frontal attempt to penetrate the WASP fortification against Catholics and non-Christians was destined to failure. On the other hand, the WASPs were nearly desperate to stop the Irish from controlling key elected posts at Federal and State level. He suspected that a covert action supporting a political WASP candidate might give the NAI a foot in the door. The Governor was a true WASP that offered the NAI the opportunity it was looking for by making him the hero of the Massachusetts' Waste Management Program.

The Governor was also a true politician that recognized the power of organization. He knew that the Mayor of Boston was the strongest opposition to his re-election. The Waste Management issue could give the Governor a powerful base to overcome any threat to re-election.

Patello found his way into the WASP fortress through the backdoor of the Boston Tax-Payers Association that was essentially controlled by WASP business interest, the Boston Chamber of Commerce, and the Republican Party. His offer to the TP A was to use his lobbing strength to support the Governor's Waste Management legislation, to provide campaign contributions anonymously in support of the Republican Governor and the election of a Republican candidate to the US Senate, to mount a media campaign in Boston that would hang the Mayor out to dry for misuse of campaign funds and to use the combined influence of National Associated Investors to promote Boston as the site for the Olympic Games in the year 2008. In return for his generous support the TPA agreed that the Governor would name Richard Folley MD as a member of the Governor's Special Taskforce on Waste Management, Park Environmental Inc. would be retained by the State as consultants to the Office of Waste Management, and Action Waste Management of Boston would be given a grant to initiate privatized waste management programs for the Boston Metropolitan area.

Patello, delighted at his success, reported to Marone at Park's New York office that it was time for Action Waste Management to set up shop. A day later the Capitol steps experienced the rally turned into a brawl by the Boston Workers' Guild causing Patello to remember that a third of

Boston's wealth and influence was held by organized labor and virtually uncontrolled.

Patello telephoned Marone and reported the problem with Muldoon. Marone in turn called his contacts with the National Federation who called Muldoon. The Federation subsequently advised Marone to schedule an off the record never happened type meeting with himself, Patello, and Muldoon at an inconspicuous place as soon as possible. Marone called Patello who called Muldoon who arranged the meeting in the back room of Stinger's tavern in Dorchester two blocks from the offices of the Boston Workers' Guild.

Stinger's appeared to be a typical neighborhood tap on a frontage road to Interstate Ninety Three. Its small neon sign was barely visible. On top of the two-story frame building was a large lighted billboard that pointed to the Workers Guild Building. The electronic billboard flashed Union slogans and pronounced the strength of organized labor for all traveling the Interstate to see. Inside the tavern was dingy but reasonably clean. Wooden tables and chairs were haphazardly spread around the bar room that also contained an old-fashioned bar with a foot rail and no stools.

Stingers was primarily a standing man's drinking establishment. In back was a fairly large room that seemed to be for the private use of the Workers Guild. Four square tables with padded chairs comprised the furnishings. The bland decor of the dirty painted walls featured the latest advertisements of local breweries. Green shade lights hanging from the ceiling were centered over each table making the atmosphere perfect for poker games. A slide window to the bar commanded the attention of the bartender in service of the room's occupants.

Twenty-four hours after the Capitol Steps Rally, three men gathered in the back room of Stinger's. Muldoon, first to arrive, came alone. When Patello and Marone arrived they correctly recognized that this was not a meeting of record with the Workers' Guild. Muldoon had apparently been waiting at Stingers for a few hours and his speech offered a slight expression of a man who had enjoyed a liquid lunch. Patello introduced Marone and ordered a round of Sam Adams beer.

Muldoon remained seated, nodded an acknowledgment to Marone, and motioned the two visitors to sit. He was cordial and asked Marone about his flight from New York, commented about the weather, damned the government, and got to the point. "Patello, you son of a bitch, you put your stinking deal together without asking me in. You know you can't ignore labor. You also know now that I can bring this whole mess down on your head like a rock. I used that two by four on your skull yesterday just to get your attention. You got this thing with waste hauling bagged as far as the City goes but you don't move one truck or get one hospital under contract without me saying so. You need my help and that's worth something. I need a piece for labor and I need a piece for me."

Marone became flushed and it was apparent to Patello that good old Mouldy had just bought himself a long ride on a dark night. He felt that there might be an opportunity to gain more than he gave by bringing Muldoon into the program but only at the operational level. To negotiate to that end he needed to penetrate Muldoon's mind and discover how much information he had about the total operation. He also had to be careful to prevent Marone from reverting to his previous life and dusting Muldoon on the spot.

Patello looked at the aging, small Muldoon and recognized that the Union Leader had seen better days. Muldoon hands seemed to shake slightly, his hair was very thin on top, and he needed a shave. Best to try a soft sell he thought, "Bob, you are right about my oversight. For that I apologize. You know that I'm kind of inexperienced at these things. I have never been involved with unions and union contracts."

Muldoon leaned forward to get into Patello's face, "That's an understatement. Why did you let New York call the Federation? It took me over an hour to convince them that this was a local fire fight that didn't need their attention. Now they think they can muscle in on your national organization, Park whatever. If they get into this it gets the attention of the US Attorney General and we all lose."

"Score one for our side," thought Patello. Muldoon apparently was unaware that the Workers' Federation through its various pension funds was a heavy investor with National Associated Investors. Marone had contacted the head of the Federation through NAI President Cappizi who made the contact through the Secretary of the Federation who held a seat on the NAI Board. The Federation had all the information about Park but, for reasons that were becoming more obvious, decided not to let their information available to Muldoon and the Boston Workers' Guild. It occurred to Patello that the Federation had advised Muldoon that the mess he created was all his to handle.

Patello glanced at Marone who was pouring the balance of his Sam Adams into his glass with a slight smile on his face. This indeed was a local matter. "Look, Bob, the last thing we want is trouble with the Feds. Sure we use influence to get what we want but it is all legal."

This time Muldoon rocked back on the legs of his chair and displayed an air of confidence in place of arrogance, "Legal my ass. Your deal with the TPA to fry Cowan's butt is about as legal as murder one."

"Score one for the goons," thought Patello, "He knows about the deal with the TPA because the Workers' Guild has a seat on the Chamber of Commerce that ties in with the TPA. Okay so now what does he want?"

Muldoon shook his empty bottle at the window to the bar and with expert precision the hefty bartender, who seemed disinterested in the trio, produced another round of Boston's finest. Muldoon poured slowly and seemed to be pondering his next comments, "Charlie my boy, I'm sure it's no surprise for you to hear that the Workers' Guild was a big contributor to the Mayor's election fund. In addition, most of the Locals in the City kicked in as well. Now you and your egg sucking Ivy coated swells are going to arrange for the Mayor to be exposed for using campaign funds for personal use. It's also no surprise for you to know that all of the Mayor's big dollar contributors not only knew but encouraged his honor to pocket the cash in return for certain concessions. Of course, that means that you and your people got yours the same way that I and my people got ours. It also means that the Mayor is not going to take the fall without dragging his loyal contributors into the mud. Some might even go to the slam with him. Maybe someone else should take the dive."

The point was getting sharper to Patello. The Workers' Guild was fronting for the Mayor. Actually the Guild was protecting its interest and investment in control of municipal services that included garbage collection and sanitation. Patello guessed that Muldoon would back off if he could somehow maintain control of the same services in the private sector without losing the money invested in City Hall, "Look Bob, I explained to the TPA that I had no knowledge about the Mayor's use of his campaign funds. Consequently, I am not in a position to make any accusations. I am only in a position to suggest to certain media representatives that looking under certain rocks might produce some interesting results. Are you concerned that I might finger the Workers' Guild?"

Muldon shot forward in his chair and again leaned into Patello who was sitting with his arms resting on the edge of the table, "You should be careful how you use your finger, Charlie, because you wouldn't wanna get it stuck where it didn't belong. What I'm suggesting is that some other guy like the Commissioner of Public Health who before he got appointed commissioner of Public Health was the Mayor's campaign manager, might be responsible for money being directed to diverse use. This is the same campaign manager who as Commissioner of Public Health has advised the media that the Union local is featherbedding at Boston Hospital. Now it seems to me that if the Commissioner of Public Health resigns because of misuse of funds and if the new Commissioner of Public Health not only happens to be a friend of labor but a strong proponent of waste management, recycling, and whatever else Action Waste Management sells, then we are all better served. You get my drift."

Patello caught the drift. In effect, he was being told to renege on his agreement to fry the Mayor. This would preserve the Mayor as the most likely candidate to unseat the Governor at the next election which was the foundation of the deal cut with the governor. Patello was in a vice. They had finished their third beer and Marone made a swayed but hasty trip to the john. The expedient bartender brought a fourth round. Bob and Charlie sat silently waiting for Marone's return. He was back in a few minutes but Muldoon had a sudden urge to urinate and wandered off. Patello felt the urge but he did not want to be anywhere with Muldoon without Marone. He decided to be patient if his bladder would cooperate. Muldoon returned looking refreshed.

When Muldoon was seated, Patello made another try, "Look Bob, you and the Guild are the ones with the information about the Commissioner. If someone other than me got to the media with the facts about campaign funds first, then whatever I came up with would be yesterday's news. The Mayor could direct fire as he wants. If he gets a little dirty in the trenches it's the cost of doing business so to speak."

"No good, Charlie, my boy, but it's a nice try." Muldoon seemed to regain control, "You have to understand that if hizzoner gets just a little dirty in this roust then he won't be credible in naming our man to succeed the commissioner. The Mayor stays clean and your organization provides the soap. You understand?"

For the moment Patello was speechless as he thought about Muldoon's last pitch. He wasn't sure he understood the crafty Union leader but he decided to act like he did, "Robert my man, it seems to me that what your organization needs is grease not soap. We have plenty of grease to slip your man in regardless of the stuff hanging on the Mayor. Trust me. Look at it this way. We convince the Governor's taskforce on waste management to allow Boston to start its conversion to privatized waste management on a voluntary basis. Then we get the hospitals to switch from City trash pick up to a private company with union employees and that little dance you did at the Capitol yesterday gets forgotten"

Muldoon heard the offer to gain a sweetheart deal with Action Waste Management. None of Patello's ventures had union shops so this was a major concession. The temptation to deal was strong but he remembered the call from the Mayor who told him in specific terms that Hizzoner would see him in hell if he failed to get Patello off his back. The Mayor was the common man well respected by the working class. He had used the Unions to advance his political career and eventually became their champion. His continued election success and established acceptance among the poor and lower middle class gave him power that tended to make his creators, such as the Workers' Guild, his eventual subjects. Muldoon was uncertain if Patello knew that the Mayor had the Guild by the throat. He pondered the question and fixed his eyes on his beer.

Marone noticed the change in Muldoon's body language. The lowered eyes was a definite sign that Patello had scored. Patello saw the change as well but was uncertain if he had closed the deal or simply concluded article one of a longer agreement yet to be determined.

Muldoon's reputation as an expert negotiator was well deserved. His emotional control or lack of same was part of his language in doing business. He moved his hands, eyes, and his butt in the chair as a calculated signal to the other side that he had applied a period to a sentence or started another paragraph in the discussion. Muldoon raised his eyes and fixed them squarely on Patello. Discussion was about to begin on article two. "You son of a bitch. Where do come off offering me a contract with Action. I can organize that sweatshop in a minute. You got to come up with an idea that gives me something other than the sleeves off your vest. Suppose you use your power base to give our squeaky-clean Mayor a real job like running the Catholic Church. Yeah, that's it—let's see you make him Pope. I hear you got connections all the way up with the Democrats by that lard ass Hardly so get Cowan a plush job like ambassador to Pago Pago. You do that and he don't buck the WASP for Governor. You can push one of your flunkies against Dukar that will guarantee Dukar wins and you look good all way round."

Now it was Patello's turn to blink, "Let me make sure I'm reading you, Robert. You think the Mayor will resign and accept a job in the Federal administration if we, you and me, can come up with the right appointment. How do we know that he will stand hitched? As for making him Pope we first have to make him Catholic."

"It's better than jail, Charlie." Muldoon was about to go on a roll, "He stays clean which gives him the chance to come back and kick your ass in the future but we can bury a lot of stuff in the meantime. Besides you get a piece of him in the process. Also, you realize that the President of the City Council will step in as the interim Mayor. Siro is one of your boys, a good Catholic kid from Roslindale that holds a union card, He didn't go to BC but nobody is perfect. He's democrat—steps in as Mayor, fires Logan, and appoints Mike Megan Commissioner of Health. Logan sees it as part of the transition and disappears. Everybody wins. Logan is a young kid that you can take care of with a job in one of these companies that you juice up. Maybe he can work in Hardly's bank and get a night job teaching at Harvard."

Patello glanced at Morone who had his eyes fixed on Muldoon, "Well we have several problems with your "everybody wins plan," Bob. First of all, we have to wait for the right opening at the Federal level. That could take some time. Second, the Massachusetts Hospital Association will take this on in the media as another excuse for the high cost of health care. The public will buy in giving the Attorney General an opening to push for an investigation which puts us back in the soup. Maybe while we are waiting for a place to plant the Mayor you could convince him to sign a City contract with Action to handle the waste from Boston Hospital. That would break the MHA hold on the cost thing when the Mayor points to the savings the hospital will experience by using a private contractor. The Tax Payers Association will want to endorse the Mayor's good wisdom which means they won't pressure me to start dragging him in the mud."

Muldoon adopted a conciliatory position as he moved sideways and sat on one hip, "Charlie, it seems to me that we aren't too far apart. I am in a position to know that the Secretary of Labor will be looking for a prominent elected Democrat to step in as the Undersecretary of Labor. Of course, the person to be selected has to be a friend of Labor and a known supporter of the President. The National Workers' Federation wants the recommendations of its affiliates on possible nominees. Once the Federation decides on the best possible nominee that person has a lock on the appointment. But just to be sure that the right person gets the job it might pay for a big outfit that has a lot of influence to join up with the Federation, say like National Associated Investors, and work out a deal like we're doing here. When I was talking with the Federation earlier they suggested I mention it. That way the confirmation would sail through, you know."

"So much for the local fire fight bullshit," thought Patello. Marone remained impassive. His expression didn't change. This was top floor stuff that he would carry to Big Frank Patello in a few hours followed in short order by a NAI Board meeting and negotiation that set national policy on such matters. The Federation knew the process. They had been through it on other occasions. There was apparently something else on the national agenda that could be advanced by the relatively insignificant Boston item. Muldoon was obviously the messenger boy. He had accomplished his mission by giving a subtle message to the NAI that a pow-wow was requested with the big chief. That being done he could move back to the details of the local issue. The ball was squarely in Patello's court who decided to go to the men's room. Marone went along.

The usually neat appearance of the NAI and Park executive seemed ruffled, "Charlie, I think you got what you need from that mick. Let's blow this cookie farm. I can't stand this goddamn tasteless Boston beer.

It runs right through me. I'll see Big Frank in the morning after he meets with the Board. If there's anything that we need from here we'll let you know. Old Muldoon is good, damn good. Your Uncle might want you to visit with him about this Cowan stiff I doubt that Cowan means that much to the Federation. Me thinks the goons got a big deal in the offing that merits our combined interest. We'll see. Meanwhile you keep Cowan's ass out of the mud. I'll take care of the WASP side but you got to make sure that Hardly doesn't piss off his cousins and get the locals all stirred up. This Commissioner Logan should find a nice job in the private sector. Next month maybe he starts as a vice president with Patriot. I'll arrange it with Mondi. He'll contact this kid and cut him a deal he can't refuse. You check out this Mike Megan guy and see if he can be loyal."

Patello nodded his assent to Marone's comments and the duo returned to the table.

Muldoon had a fresh beer in hand with two more set waiting for his party. The expedient bartender was behind the bar tending to other orders. Marone grimaced at the sight of another Sam Adam's but followed Patello's lead in rendering a gratuitous sign to Muldoon.

Patello picked up the conversation, "OK Mouldy, we got your message and Mr. Marone will see that the proper people are advised. A representative from Action Waste Management will be appointed to work out the terms of a labor agreement with the appropriate Local. I'm sure that you can make those arrangements. It's my understanding that Commissioner Logan will accept a position in the private sector within the month. There is no basis to think that the Mayor or anyone in his administration has misused campaign funds. You can be sure that I have no intention at this time to imply anything of the kind to the media. We need assurance from the Mayor that Mr. Megan will be appointed to succeed Commissioner Loan. We also need to meet with Mr. Megan in the next couple of days to discuss the details of the Privatized Voluntary Waste Management Program for Boston. The Mayor will want to announce the new arrangement at Boston Hospital next week. I also believe that our mutual interest can be benefited with a private contractor waste management agreement with a private hospital in the City. Since organized labor and the Catholic Church are so supportive of each other it seems reasonable that St. Anslem's should start at the same time as Boston Hospital. Two Boston hospitals going to private waste management will pull the MHA's string. We may need the help of the City health department to convince the CEO of St. Anslem's that he needs privatized waste management. You take care of your end and keep in touch with me. Is there, anything that I left out? Oh yeah, no strikes or slowdowns at the hospitals. You keep the locals cool. Anything else?"

"Just one thing," Muldoon stood and turned toward the door; "when you pay the bar tab make sure that my friend Harry, the bartender, gets a good tip."

oOo

Phil Mondi was pleased to receive a phone call from an old friend. He and Tony Marone had been friends and teammates at St. Michael's High in the Bronx. They both attended Fordham but Phil later transferred to Pace. Marone graduated a year ahead of Mondi and began his career in the small business investment racket as an account analyst and collector. He was an immediate success and rewarded with a supervisory position and then his own branch of the business in lower Manhattan. Mondi, after graduation, went to work for Marone. He showed equal promise and with Marone's support in a few years was given the opportunity to manage one of NAI's courier ventures, The Patriot Transport and Courier Service of Boston. With the consent of NAI, Marone and Mondi diversified Patriot into other services and products beyond the basic transport activities.

Mondi enjoy talking to his friend, "Tony, my main man, how are you doing and how's that beautiful wife and kid?"

"Just fine, Phil. Things well with you?" Marone seemed to register a rhetorical tone, "I know you're making money because I see the reports. You know money isn't everything. You got to relax. Play more golf. Enjoy life you know what I mean?"

"Tony when you start with that relax stuff it means you got some bum that I got to put on the payroll for my own good and yours too. Who is the guy and when does he start?"

Marone seemed genuinely hurt that his friend suspected ulterior motives in the call, "I got to explain, Phil. You know about the waste management thing that Patello's handling? Well we cut a deal with this Muldoon guy at the Union that we take and stash the Boston Commissioner of Health in a private slot so the goons can put a guy they own in the Commissioner's job. So, I figure that we put the guy in with you so if we need to come back later and hit the goons we got this guy Logan to use as a club. You sort of keep him happy but don't let him get too involved if you know what I mean. Anyway, the goons put in a guy named Megan and he opens the door for us with the hospitals as a starter. We give the Union a contract at Action and let them load up on us a little."

The drift was obvious to Mondi, "Your talking about Michael Logan, Tony. He's a clean-cut kid that the Mayor appointed to the commissioner's job after the last election. We know him because he was active with the Young Democrats. I think his thing is public health work. Got a master's degree from Harvard or BU or something. He probably doesn't know squat about the transport business. He takes a job in this outfit and the press is going to smell a deal somewhere. It makes more sense for him to go into health in the private sector. That way the switch is less obvious and keeps him from being offended by a forced career change. Also, the public sees it as reasonable since the kid really isn't a politician. How about this? We get him a job with the Catholics, say at St. Anslem's Hospital. Patello and I convince Hardly that the hospital's CEO needs a guy to help with quality control or something that a master's degree in public health would want to do. Hell, he could be an assistant to our good friend and fellow hospital trustee, Dr. Richard Folley."

"Phil, I knew there was a reason why I put up with your bullshit all these years. That's a good idea. How do we know the boss at St. Anslem's will buy the idea? You got him wrapped?"

"The top job at St. Anslem's is a wild card, Tony. Hardly tried too early to move in and pissed off the Cardinal and the Nuns. They got a guy in there that is a common pro that tries to do a job. He's got some moxie but I don't think he'd take a wrapper. I think I have a better idea. We get Hardly and Folley to convince the Cardinal that he needs an office in the Chancery for health affairs. This guy Logan, obviously, a good Catholic, gets anointed to the post by the Cardinal and everybody cheers. He can still be an assistant to Folley that way we got a wrapper on him but it's transparent. I like it."

Marone jumped at the suggestion, "OK, Phil, makes sense except for a few management problems and a few bruised egos. Let's give it a try. You call Patello about our talk and work it out. Get back to me. In the mean-time I got to talk to Cappizi about what to do with Mayor Cowan and to make sure we got a tight wrapper on Siro. Speaking about wrappers you ought to see if you can get one on the top guy at the hospital. We might need it."

"Whatever. You stay cool my friend." Mondi closed the conversation.

CHAPTER FOUR

The idea of creating a central office for health within the Archdiocese directed by Mike Logan that could be controlled by National Associated Investors required careful cultivation. Phil Mondi gave the idea to Charlie Patello following the conversation with Marone. Patello knew that he could not advance the idea without opposition from O'Shea and his son in law, Dr. Folley. Folley had the clout to kill the plan by simply suggesting to the Cardinal that it was not a good idea. On the other hand, Patello reasoned, Folley could also convince the Cardinal to do it. The only way to get Folley to do that was to somehow make it his idea. Since Folley was best influenced by his father in law, Patello decided to plant the seed of wisdom with Hardly who was certain to mention it to O'Shea. O'Shea would probably slip the idea as his own to Folley who would run with it. The scheme worked like a charm.

Three days after Partello had a chat with Hardly about a central Office, Hardly, Pattello, O'Shea, and Folley met in Hardly's plush conference room to discuss the sad state of affairs surrounding the Church's healing ministry. Hardly was moved by Folley's representation of the lack of coordination among the Catholic hospitals throughout the Archdiocese. O'Shea was readily convinced that a coordinated administrative structure among the hospitals could produce significant cost reductions. O'Shea envisioned a centralized management structure that, among other things, used a central banking concept. Hardly assigned a member of his planning staff to write a complete proposal for the Office of Health Affairs for the Boston Catholic Archdiocese. He also called the Cardinal's office and asked to have a briefing session with Cardinal McMahon and Bishop Hanks at the earliest possible date. With their consent, the proposal would be given to St. Anslem's Board of Trustees at their next regular meeting.

O'Shea, at Patello's suggestion, was given the assignment of diverting CEO Durant from any anticipation of the proposal. Durant they reasoned, could convince Sr. Elizabeth that the Office of Health Affairs would be strong enough to force the Sisters completely out. The Sisters, if they opposed the idea, could convince the Cardinal to back down. The tactic was to have the Cardinal announce the plan as a fait accompli'. O'Shea decided that the best defense against any interference from Durant was to take the offense and charge the administration of the hospital with fiscal deterioration and managerial incompetence—a charge easy to make since the hospital had experienced increasing deficits with the advent of managed care plans in the Boston area. Hardly's call to the Chancery was promptly returned by Bishop Hanks who reported that the briefing with the Cardinal was set for the next Tuesday and was to follow his cabinet meeting. That meant the briefing would at best begin around three in the afternoon when the Cardinal's mood would be very unpredictable. Otherwise the next available date was in three months, much too far in the future for Patello to hold Action in waiting and the Governor, the Mayor, the Workers' Guild, the media, and the public under control. The terrific trinity plus one had to take a chance.

O'Shea began his campaign immediately after the meeting. He placed a heated call to Rod Weaver, CFO at St. Anslem's, demanding that the monthly financial statements be in his hands within a week following the end of the month. He half listened to Weaver's patient explanation why a minimum of ten days was required for accuracy in the reports and then blasted Weaver for not detailing the reports. His next target was cash. The accounts receivable had increased one percent in the last quarter since Durant had taken over. O'Shea asked Weaver what the CEO had done to cause this. Weaver was at a loss to respond. Then O'Shea wanted to know why the doctors weren't contributing to the building fund. He finished his one sided discussion with the announcement that all of the issues under discussion would be items on the agenda and the Board of Trustees meeting a week from next Tuesday.

Durant was in conference with Weaver when he received a call from a screaming O'Shea. Weaver was attempting to explain to his boss that O'Shea was on a tear. O'Shea confirmed Weaver's warning. Durant could only listen to O'Shea's incoherent screaming. The one-sided conversation lasted fifteen minutes during which time O'Shea called Weaver everything but rational and human. He demanded that Durant can Weaver on the spot. If he refused to dump Weaver, O'Shea promised he would have Durant's, "ass out of St. Anslem's in a New York minute." Durant offered to discuss Weaver's competence with the board but asked that O'Shea be patient and allow for time to make corrections. O'Shea would have none of it. Durant was definitely on the defensive and was tactically removed from control at the forthcoming Board meeting. Mission accomplished.

O'Shea met Hardly and Patello for lunch following his conversation with Durant. He was animated as he explained how he had that devoured Durant. His obsession with the kill concerned Patello. Patello suggested that Durant had to be held in office if for no other reason than to maintain order while the plan to justify the Office for Health Affairs fell into place. He asked Hardly to calm O'Shea down. O'Shea was offended and a bit angry at Patello's attitude and offered that Durant was an outsider that didn't matter. Patello remembered that Marone for some reason he had not discussed told Mondi to get a wrapper on Durant. Bouncing him wasn't what Marone had in mind. "This goddamn O'Shea had to calm down," he thought. Nevertheless, the mind game he worked on Durant was right for now. The more immediate objective was to convince the Cardinal to create the Office of Health Affairs. The proposal had to be protected from Durant and the Sisters for a week until the St. Anslem's Board meeting, In the meantime Patello decided he would have a preliminary meeting with Commissioner Logan.

Commissioner Logan grew up in South Boston and held a strong affection for his native Boston. He had no desire for public office but committed himself to public service with a strong passion. He respected the working man and felt that municipal services should be first devoted to the health and safety of the population, especially the poor. While attending Harvard's School of Public Health he made headlines by constantly hassling the City Department of Health about conditions in the disadvantaged neighborhoods of Boston. When Cowan announced his candidacy for Mayor based on a strong public health and safety platform, Logan became a member of his campaign cabinet and was promised early in the campaign that he would be Cowan's commissioner of Public Health. As Commissioner, he also became the nominal head of Boston Hospital that provided care for the majority of the poor from Roxbury, South Boston, and Dorchester. He noticed that the cost of providing sub-standard care was higher than the cost of high quality care provided by private teaching hospitals in Boston which he blamed on union feather bedding among other things. His passion to do the right thing coupled with a certain political insensitivity caused him to grow in disfavor with the Mayor's political supporters—especially The Boston Workers' Guild. Contrary to statements made by the Mayor and others on the City Council, Logan had not any access to campaign funds or the accounting of the funds. He had a growing uneasiness that he was being set up to take a big fall.

Patello had the Human Resource Director from Hardly Security and Trust give Logan a call at home to inquire about his interest in a position in the private sector. The Human Resource Director told Logan that while he was calling for the bank, the position was with a major client of the Bank and one of the largest private providers of health services in Massachusetts. If Logan was at all interested he should get his resume to the caller immediately since the client expected to fill the position within the month and there were many possible candidates. Logan hand carried his resume to the Bank the next morning. The HR Director called Patello who told him to tell Logan to expect an interview sometime after Tuesday but within the week.

Patello checked in with Muldoon to let him know that the skids were being greased for Logan's departure from public life. It was time, he suggested, to meet Megan and discuss the voluntary privatization of waste management for Boston. He also arranged for Muldoon to meet with Mark Meehan, the President of Action, so that management and labor could begin negotiations on their collective bargaining agreement, Muldoon and Meehan agreed to meet at the Marriott in Framingham, about fifteen miles west of Boston, for an early breakfast out of sight of the Boston Business Journal reporter who had been shadowing Muldoon since his Capitol steps routine. Muldoon, ever cautious, promised Patello that he would arrange a session with Megan when he was sure Meehan was rightly on the come. Patello had to admire the old labor warrior's guts. The guy was tough and careful.

Muldoon came to the Marriott equipped with a contract that was loaded for bear. The two men met in the spacious lobby and moved quickly to the comfortable restaurant with floor to ceiling windows overlooking the rolling fairways of the hotel's golf course. Meehan had arranged for a table away from the center of the dining room. He has also paid to have the surrounding tables kept vacant so the two could talk without being overheard. Muldoon immediately realized that the stage had been well set. To counter the effect, he decided to intimidate Meehan with an opening volley and force a quick conclusion. He was counting on Meehan being afraid of having to report to Patello, and especially Marone, that the deal was not done.

As the two sat down, Muldoon fired the first shot, "Let's cut this short. I haven't got time for any of your bullshit. Here's the contract. Just sign it and we can get back to town."

Meehan took Muldoon's opening blast with the unexpected calm of an experienced negotiator. He carefully avoided picking up or even glancing at the document that Muldoon pushed at him, "Mr. Muldoon, before we get to far involved in details, I suggest we have some breakfast. They have an excellent buffet. Otherwise, you might want to look at the menu. Personally, I'll have the buffet."

Muldoon had experienced this tactic many times before in his long career with the Workers' Guild but he was nearly blown away by Meehan's completely unexpected professionalism. Slightly flushed he followed Meehan to the buffet. He picked at his fruit and bagel while Meehan demonstrated total emotional control as he devoured a heaping plate of scrambled eggs, sausage, bacon, two pancakes, and toast. When the waitress poured the third cup of coffee Meehan went back to the buffet and returned with two sweet rolls and a bran muffin. Muldoon was both amazed and disgusted. He had lost his concentration and the initiative.

Between bites, Meehan began the conversation, "You know, Bob, in addition to having one hell of a buffet this place has the cutest waitresses in New England. I do my best work in these conditions. We seem to have the unique opportunity to come to a mutual understanding without the usual time consuming preliminary activities associated with the collective bargaining process. Let's not screw it up with a lot of irritating demands and counter-demands. We also have to be sure that what we agree on has the Department of Labor's good housekeeping seal of approval. I suggest that we have a standard but fast track election at Action that follows the course of collective bargaining. That way the contract will properly represent the employees' interest and maintain the integrity of process. What I'm prepared to offer you is the opportunity to name an individual of your choice to accept a management position in the sales force at Action. This person will be salaried and on commission based on gross sales on all Action contracts signed after, say, the date of our labor agreement. The offset to this is that I want to name the shop steward that the local appoints. That way everything remains in balance. Now if you think that we can agree on this, I'll have my HR director and lawyer meet with your people tomorrow and start the process. As you told Patello, you can organize our sweatshop in a minute."

Muldoon realized immediately that in his first conversation with Patello he had mentioned a piece of the action. He thought Patello had overlooked it so he was intending to bring it up again when the contract was in place. Now he was being offered a piece up front plain and simple. Commission based on gross sales was open ended. He could take the commission and let the stiff he named to the phony sales job take the salary or whatever piece he thought he should have and pocket the rest Muldoon was caught up in the offer. His mind identified several organizers employed by the Union that could be trusted and happy to take the job. All things considered he had what he wanted.

"Did you say twenty percent commission on the gross, Mark?"

Meehan took another bite, swallowed, and gently touched his lips with his napkin, "I didn't say. I usually pay five percent on the gross."

The counter was exactly what Muldoon had expected. Carefully, he held his emotion, "Fifteen percent is the least I could accept"

Meehan put down his fork and leaned forward on the table. He looked squarely into Muldoon's eyes. The final offer was about to happen, "Cut the shit, Muldoon. We both know that ten percent is the number."

Muldoon didn't say a word. He looked into Meehan's eyes and gave a slight nod.

Meehan extended his hand over the table and Muldoon extended his. They shook hands and the deal was done. They started to leave together but Meehan stopped to pay the check and give a tip with an affectionate pat on the shoulder to the waitress. Muldoon gave a slight wave and left. Meehan walked to the lobby gift shop and bought a roll of Tums that he desperately needed. By the time he got to his BMW he had popped four of the white tablets and was having stomach pains. He laboriously moved under the wheel, started the engine and pushed the speed dial on his telephone for Patello's office. Patello answered the direct line to his desk.

Meehan seemed to belch his greeting when Patello answered, "Charlie, this is Mark. The deal is done. You were right. He jumped at the commission. He'll get me a sales manager and I'll get him a shop steward. We can wrap this up in the week. I'll have the employees notified about the union this afternoon. My supervisors will keep it in line."

Patello was pleased, "OK, Charlie. Good work. Look, on this shop steward thing I recommended a young guy from the State Office of Waste Management to Action some time back. I think he told me that he works in your Quality Control section for Ken Ryan another one of our State alumnus. He might be a good man for shop steward. Name is ah—let me think- ah- yeah Jay Marquart. Anyway he's a good kid that did a lot of mule work for the party. Still helps out now and then. I think you can trust him to do as asked or told, whatever. Check it out."

Meehan felt miserable. He was sure he had ulcers. Quickly he accepted Patello's suggestion, "I know Ken Ryan, Charlie. He's clean and innocent. Best we keep it that way. This Marquart guy I guess is like Ryan. We could make him steward without getting him or Ryan dirty. As long as we have Muldoon on the take the steward only has to tell Ryan and Ryan tells us or vice versa. I'll check it out but I'm inclined to go with Marquart. I'll make sure Ryan keeps Marquart available for the appointment."

Within minutes after completing his call from Meehan, Patello's phone rang again. This time it was Hardly calling to report that the proposal for the Cardinal's Office for Health Affairs was ready for a pre-briefing by the terrific trinity plus one. The Bank's planning staff had practically worked around the clock to create logical text, definite recommendations, slides, and graphs that all supported the concept. Hardly suggested that they get a room at the Alleton Club that evening, review the proposal, and have dinner. Patello stated his availability and left it to Hardly to make the arrangements.

More pressing in Patello's mind was the deal with the Workers' Guild and the need to get the Guild in line with the Waste Management program. Anxiously, Patello telephoned Muldoon. When the Union Leader answered, Charlie pressed the point, "Bob this is Charlie. I understand that you and Mark worked things out. Now I believe that Mr. Logan will be well placed in short order. We should have a conversation with Mr. Megan sometime today or tomorrow".

Muldoon had expected Patello's call. He was prepared for the questions and gave immediate answers, "Right, Charlie. We still have a couple of loose ends. The big piece is the Mayor. I have to get him comfortable about the WASP before we can get Megan into the Commissioner's job. We need to hear from NAI or the Federation or both if the Mayor has a shot for the Federal post. Let's go with the WASP issue first. Can you get a signal that they're going to back him"

Patello had been put on the defensive. He needed time to make sure that the pieces would stick together, "I'll get back to you, Bob"

Patello hung up and immediately placed a call to Marone in New York. The secretary explained that Mr. Marone and Mr Capizzi had left early to drive to Providence for a conference with Mr. Frank Patello. She suggested that he could reach Mr. Marone on his car phone or at Mr. Frank Patello's residence. She offered both telephone numbers to Mr. Patello since his name appeared on the approved list now flashing on her CRT. Patello knew Uncle Frank's unlisted number and had Marone's car phone on his index so he graciously declined the secretary's offer. He knew that the questions he had to ask could not be answered until after Marone and Capizzi had met with Big Frank.

Big Frank had been briefed by Capizzi about the Boston issue. He immediately called the Federation's representative on the NAI Board to ask why the Union had not been direct about whatever was on their mind. The Federation rep was Jim Ebber, a former U S Senator from New Jersey who was the choice of Iabor only to be unseated after four terms by a professional basketball player. Ebber explained to Big Frank that his knowledge of the Federation's interest in Boston was limited but he could have a special advisor from the Washington Headquarters' come with him to explain the matter. Big Frank suggested that they come to Providence and attend the briefing the next morning with Capizzi and Marone. The meeting was scheduled at Big Frank's estate on millionaires' row in Newport.

By ten o'clock the next morning everyone had arrived, introductions were complete, and coffee with Danish was available. At Big Frank's request Ebber opened the meeting with an explanation about the Federation's unusual method of bringing their interest to the NAI table. The underlying reason was that the Federation was uncertain about its interest in an expanding industry that had exploded on the West Coast and seemed about to impact in Boston. Ebber asked Big Frank if the staff man from Washington could be allowed to explain the matter in more detail. Big Frank nodded his approval.

The consultant began by pointing out that over the past ten years Union negotiators, especially on the West Coast, had been making major concessions in health benefits for their members in contract renewals. Cost conscious employers had abandoned the traditional indemnity plans offered by Blue Cross/Blue Shield for a less expensive form of coverage provided by health maintenance organizations. As the plans became more popular they became more profitable. New companies came into the market, generated profits and were bought out and consolidated into major conglomerates. The key to their fiscal success was enrolling a healthy population, limiting and controlling use of services, and putting the providers at financial risk. Now that the conglomerates were expanding into the national market with their managed care plans it occurred to the Unions that the only way to protect their members in contract negotiations was to have an interest in Health Maintenance Organizations. A direct attempt to form a Union Health Maintenance

Organization would face a limited market and limited profits. It was reasoned by the Federation that they should partner with an organization that did not have a direct identity with Labor in the formation of this venture. The consultants also pointed out that a national HMO did not sell as well on the local level as an HMO that looked and smelled like it was home grown.

Patello seemed to be tracking on the presentation but Capizzi and Marone were helplessly lost. Ebber continuously glanced at Big Frank to measure his attitude. When he sensed that Big Frank was becoming frustrated he jumped in, "Mr. Patello, the third highest topic in the minds of the people these days is healthcare. They rate crime and the economy as one and two. Fourth is the environment. The Federation joined with AARP, the national hospital associations, and many other organizations to bring about a national health reform bill. It got clobbered by the republicans because it was too damn expensive. Many members in the house and the senate were defeated because of their support of the President's health reform proposal. The mood of the nation is to control health cost by local determination. It seems to us that there is an opportunity to form a national syndicate on the same order as Park Environmental that will meet the interest of the people and, I hasten to add, be extremely profitable. You ask why we targeted the Boston area to stake our claim. Please let our consultant explain."

The young consultant put down his cup of coffee, adjusted his glasses, and glanced at his notes. He straightened his tie and made eye contact with Big Frank, "Actually, we hadn't considered Boston as a player in this thing until our conversation with Mr. Marone last week regarding Mr. Muldoon's demonstration at the rally on the Capitol steps. During our conversation, it occurred to us that Boston was well saturated even over saturated with health services that controlled the economy or at least a major piece of the economy. We also had in place through Action, a cover for our investment in health services. What we needed to establish was an arrangement with the Workers' Guild and your local operation that gave us the opportunity to create this new venture.

We didn't want Muldoon to be fully informed about the program because of his, shall we say, tendency to seek personal gain at the risk of the major objective. Nevertheless, a man of his ambition and limited intellect can be helpful in arranging the preliminary details and doing spade work. I expect that by now you have managed to compromise Mr. Muldoon to your own interest. Following our conversation with Mr. Marone, we contacted Mr. Muldoon who explained that the deal cut by your Mr. Patello with the tax payers association was a threat to labor's interest. Actually, we saw it as rather helpful but we did not want to disillusion Mr. Muldoon. We simply directed him to cut the best deal he could, and in the process, get your attention by bringing up the need to get Mayor Cowan a Federal appointment. The good Mayor has been well supported by us over the years and deserves a place in history where we can keep him in line. You can help by using your influence to protect the Mayor from suffering any public embarrassment while we maneuver his appointment."

Marone quickly glanced at Capizzi and then at Big Frank. He caught a nod from the boss that indicated that he had the floor, "I think it's safe to say that Mr. Muldoon will represent our mutual interest from this point forward. We respect his ability. He was very helpful in bringing your message to our attention. We are in process of establishing a labor contract between Action Waste Management and a Guild local. To further advance our interest we must be assured that the Mayor will be happy with a Federal appointment and not seek an elected post in State government."

Senator Ebber leaned forward on the table and glanced at the three gentlemen opposite him, "We quite frankly are unable to control all of the Mayor's ambitions. He has stated to our political action committee that he would be content with a Federal appointment at a high level. However, our people on the President's staff are reluctant to have the slob too close to the top. He could bolt from the Under-Secretary post and run back to the State. We think that the campaign fund issue needs to be held by us as a trump card. If we have to play it, Muldoon and some of his cronies could take a heavy dive. We would appreciate your help in convincing the Democratic leadership that the Mayor can scrub up to look and act respectable."

Big Frank pushed back his chair and stood up. He walked slowly around the table and glanced out the window at the rolling waves breaking against the rocks. The temperature in the room had been elevated by the sun so he took off his jacket and hung it over his chair. The others in the room followed. It was time for a break.

When the meeting resumed, Big Frank took the floor, "This healthcare business is confusing. Everybody says it's expensive and you say it's profitable. Yet I hear the hospitals hollering for more money. The insurance companies want more money from the employers. Doctors are all rich. The States are closing the nut houses because they can't afford them. This new business, HMO, how's it different so it makes money? I don't understand how we get ours. If we go in then we got to have some vigor to stay in. I didn't hear anything that sounded like a good deal. Or did I miss it?"

The young consultant became energized at Frank's commentary, "Let's begin at the top. Healthcare spending is expected to absorb a third of the nation's gross national product in the next ten years. Where is all that money going to be spent? Almost entirely in the private sector. Who spends the money depends on how the Nation's health policy is formed but it's a good bet that the mood of the Country continues to favor the private sector as both buyer and seller of health services. We expect the interest to center on private providers of health care for a minimum often years—maybe forever. You form a company that sells health care and you form another company that buys health care. You take the profits off the top on both sides and let the medical providers worry about the bottom line. You have to be careful that you don't get suckered into giving to much away and losing your service base in the process. That's why we supported a tax based program for the poor. The government would prepay for the poor just like the employer would prepay for the employee. We still skim off the top. To get established you need a service base like a big group of doctors and a hospital in a large population area. You also want to begin in an affluent community so that you don't get overrun with the problem of caring for poor people or old folks."

Big Frank looked to be partially convinced but still carried a confused look, "I don't understand this buyer and seller business. Hospitals and doctors sell and the insurance company buys. How am I going to make out selling doctors services when I ain't a doctor? Those bastards are all independent. So are the hospitals."

The consultant smiled at the question and stood to respond, "That's the point, Mr. Patello. As the buyer you determine how you want to buy the product. Setting specifications on health services for your subscriber clients requires the provider groups to provide care according to your specifications. You control the market by controlling volume and cost. The providers are forced to form an organization or join one that you own. It's called a medical services network. Boston is well positioned to accept the reformed model of health services delivery, In fact the Boston medical community has been converting to managed care for the past ten years without being aware of the transition. The Boston based medical schools, Harvard, Boston University and Tufts, have extensive medical practice plans for their teaching faculty who are mostly employed and salaried by the hospitals. Almost all of the employed physicians are specialists that control referrals from the primary care physician in private practice. In order to maintain the revenue to the practice plans the medical schools and their affiliated hospitals created their own HMO's several years ago that have successfully competed with Blue Cross and other indemnity programs. The attraction of the patients to the medical centers away from the community hospitals and community based specialists caused the community docs to form group practices that compete with the university practice plans. Right now, the community doctors and the hospital guys are at each other. It's called a town and gown battle."

Big Frank was looking directly at Capizzi who was totally confused. He changed his glance to Marone who slowly shook his head in confusion. Frank breathed deeply and returned eye contact to the consultant who was now seated, "OK, I can see that there is big money in healthcare and more is going to be in the pot. I understand that the way we get ours is by taking it off the top. I understand that to do that we got to control both ends. That's all very simple. I don't understand this HMO business and I don't understand this doctor to doctor stuff. That is a big mystery. What is even more confusing is how do we get into the act and how do you figure in?"

The consultant nodded an acknowledgment to Frank. He reached into his pocket and distributed business cards to the three men. He then went to his briefcase and extracted brochures that he placed on the table, "I apologize for not beginning with introductory statements. I thought that perhaps Mr. Ebber might have provided this in advance of our meeting but I now realize that he had no time to send any preliminary information. As you can see on the business card, my name is Tom Callahan and I'm a senior partner with Debur and Tandy. We are a public accounting firm and management consultants specializing in public service industries. Our practice has focused over the past five years on consultation to major users and purchasers of health care services. We have been advisors to the Federation for nearly ten years. We hope to become the consultants to the joint venture that results within the Federation in the formation of a national health services network. We are confident that the venture could begin with a strong push in the Boston area and spread rapidly across the country. Through our other clients in several industries we could influence the progress. Debur and Tandy is well positioned."

Young, Mr. Callahan had their attention, "Allow me to further explain the Boston opportunity. Boston is saturated with health services that are extremely expensive for employers. The high expense is the direct result of over utilization. The over utilization is caused by the control of the payers by the big providers, teaching hospitals. The payers are on the edge because the providers take all the money that the payers exhort from the employers. Our approach is to force an HMO over the edge and pick it up under Chapter Eleven, Bankruptcy. We appear to be riding to the rescue of the subscribing employers and the unfortunate providers wanting for their accounts receivable as well as anyone bonds or mortgages. Wearing our white hats, we convince the employers that our brand of managed care is the suitable answer to control the surging costs of healthcare benefits. From the other direction, and with another identity, we convince the community doctors and the community hospitals that by joining our network of providers they can control patient volume and thereby maintain income. Now Here's what we have going for us. Boston experiences one thousand hospital patient days per one thousand population per year. In California the number is three hundred fifty days per thousand. That difference gives us a lot of room to make some impressive change. The average cost per hospital stay in Boston is the highest in the country. This tells us that there is a lot of room to skim and still reduce the cost. Obviously, the teaching hospitals have been skimming all along. We just take their piece or a part of it and give the rest back. Meanwhile we take the referring community physician and put him on incentive to reduce the referrals to the high price specialists. In the interest of their own pocketbook they treat the patient at low cost. The specialists eventually come around and accept a negotiated arrangement on our terms."

Big Frank began to get the drift, "What about the hospitals? They got a ton of money stashed from years of skimming. Why can't they do the same as us since, as you said before, they already control both ends?"

Callahan gave a positive response, "They can do it. And they are in the process of moving into managed care arrangements. But they have to get organized. Right now, the hospitals are scrambling to form their own networks. They are concentrating on merging with community hospitals and overlooking the doctors. We move in by buying up the doctors who make the referrals, the so called primary care doctor. The hospital utilization rate drops like a rock. They can't cut costs fast enough because of the teaching and research load. Big deficits result and we pick'em off."

Big Frank nodded his gratitude to Mr. Callahan. He then directed his comments to Ebber, "Senator, my colleagues and I are grateful and pleased with your candid statements and honesty in making known your intentions. I will ask Mr. Cappizi to work with Mr. Callahan in formulating a detailed proposal for the consideration of the NAI board of trustees. I'm confident that the due diligence on the matter will give us good reason to initiate our so called joint venture. I have not forgotten the matter regarding the Mayor. We will use whatever influence we might have to cause his appointment as the Under Secretary of Labor. You can appreciate I'm sure that in so doing we will be discreet."

After the meeting adjourned, Big Frank advised Cappizi to check out Debur and Tandy, especially Tom Callahan, although he held a sudden attraction to the man's style. He also directed Marone to signal Patello that NAI was with the Federation on the deal with Mayor Cowan. He expected the Union to shoulder the matter with NAI in a supporting role. That's why he stressed the discreet aspect to Senator Ebber. In response to Marone's question regarding filling Patello in on the prospect of getting into the Healthcare business, Big Frank opted to have Patello informed in general but not burden him with scant details until after the NAI board had heard the full proposal from Debur and Tandy. Frank knew well that his nephew would call him direct if he wanted the full scope.

On the drive back to New York, Marone placed a call to Patello. Patello expected the call and was pleased to hear Marone's voice, "Charlie, this is Tony, we are on our way back to New York from a meeting with Big Frank and the Union guys. Thought I'd fill you in."

Patello for some reason got out of his chair and stood glancing out the window, "Good to hear from you, Tony. What's this big deal with the Federation?"

The signal faded on the cellular phone as a truck passed. Tony waited a second before continuing the conversation. "Healthcare, Charlie. They want us in the healthcare business. Anyway, we're going to look at it at NAI next week. Big Frank seems like he wants to go along. Not much I can tell you about it because I'm not too sure I understand it. You want to know more maybe you should call Frank."

Patello understood and respected Marone's requirement to limit details about the meeting. He also appreciated Tony's hint that Uncle Frank wanted to explain the details to him personally. With slight hesitation he asked, "Look, Tony, did anything get resolved about the Mayor?"

"Yeah. Big Frank said we would support the Federation's push to get the Mayor out of Boston. You know I don't think they like the son of a bitch."

Patello thought the comment was an understatement, "Thanks Tony. That's all I need for now. I have to call Muldoon and tell him to relax. Then I need to see that the labor deal between Action and the Local gets done. We also have to see that Meehan and the hospitals sign a trash deal, not to mention getting this guy Logan onto the Cardinal's staff and this Megan into Logan's former job as Commissioner. And, of course, let's not forget to have the Mayor announce the voluntary privatization of waste management project. So, look, if you want to be in the healthcare racket and want my help maybe you should wait until I get a few irons out of the fire."

Marone gave a slight laugh as part of his good bye, "We'll be in touch, Charlie. When and if this health thing gets approved you know Big Frank will want you to move it along. Don't work too hard."

Patello moved back to his desk and hung up the phone. Then he sat in his comfortable chair and pondered the conversation just ended. It was very reasonable for NAI to go into the health business especially in Boston. The problem is that one Charles Patello was over extended and not in a very good position to give the matter all the attention it would need. He thought about calling Uncle Frank and suggesting that health be given a stand by status until the waste management thing, the union, the Mayor, and God knows what else got resolved. Such a call to Uncle Frank would also disclose that Charlie was bending under pressure and maybe not the boy wonder that Frank thought he was. This would be very disappointing to Frank. Charlie would never disappoint Uncle Frank. On second thought it was best to let things happen.

Patello never had a chance to finish his second thought. The private line to his office began to buzz and the light began to flash. An important call was in the offing and it no doubt was Uncle Frank. Charlie pulled up the receiver and rendered a friendly greeting, "Hello, Frank. I knew you would be calling. How are you? I was just about to give you a call."

Frank was not surprised that Charlie had guessed that he was calling. Nothing that Charlie did surprised Frank. Frank simply passed on the greeting and went to his agenda, "Yeah, Charlie. I guess maybe Mario and Tony got to you already about this thing the Federation wants to do with the health business. See, I think it's a good thing but it's not the big thing. We need to shoot for something higher. Don't you think?"

Charlie was perplexed. He had no idea what Frank might be thinking, "Uncle Frank, if you think the health business is where we belong then that's where we'll go. I'm sure that I can bag Hardly, O'Shea, and his idiot son in law. Beyond that, you have to tell me what to shoot for. I have no idea what you mean by something bigger."

The big picture was only in Big Frank's mind. Suddenly he realized that his favorite nephew was not on the same wave length, "Sorry, Charlie, I'm running way ahead of you. Here's what I'm thinking. We capture waste management but what we really got is City Hall. That's cool. Now we take over health services through waste management. What we got? We got City Hall and the biggest piece of business in town. What's left? Banks! Boston has no industry. All there is in that town is State Government, City Government, a bunch of hospitals and medical schools, and a lot of Colleges and stuff with the Banks sucking up the revenue. We get control of City Hall, the Hospitals, and the Banks, and we own the town. It's a lot better deal than we got in New York because here we got to share the pie with a lot of other interests. Besides, it ain't safe to walk the streets here at night anymore. My thing is to move our show to Boston where we could run everything. Then I retire and you take over. I can hang out in Newport and help when you need me. How's it sound?"

Patello was standing again and looking out his window. He was almost in shock as he tried to contemplate the scope of Uncle Frank's idea. "Uncle Frank, that's a pretty tall order. It could take years to pull it off"

Before Charlie could finish, Frank interrupted, "No Charlie, it's not such a big deal. You got waste management greased with the Mayor and Union guys. The Hospital thing with the Catholics is a hanger. What you got to do is push over this nitwit Hardly and grab his Bank. Then we pull in a few more Banks and the deal is set. I got faith in you. You can do it. For now it's just you and me who got the idea. I'll spring it on Mario and Tony when you got an angle on the Banks. Then we bring NAI along. You got it?"

There was a lot of truth in what the old man said. Patello had thought for some time that Hardly was losing it. He would eventually have to be replaced as the Bank's new chief executive. Before the Bank's Board of Directors focused on that prospect it might be well to have the Board focus on the prospect of being bigger and richer. Greed was the best tactic.

"Uncle Frank, just off the top of my head, I think what we could do is subtly promote a bank merger between Boston Security and Cambridge Bank. That would undermine Hardly and his goofey cousins at the same time. While the investors whip it about we could move in and buy up the controlling interests. I'll check it out."

That was the attitude Big Frank was hoping for. His nephew was on the move. "You got it, Charlie. Keep me posted on your progress so I know when to spring it here. You also got to remember that the waste management deal and the hospital thing have to come through so we have a solid base of control. Get the Catholics in line. Nice talking to ya. I gotta go."

That was it. Frank hung up before Charlie had a chance to say good bye. Charlie now had the big picture. Next to Frank, he was the only one who did.

oOo

The Terrific Trinity plus One arrived at the Alleton Club at five in the afternoon. Hardly had reserved a room on the third floor of the stately club that was almost as old as the Hardly family tradition. The Hardly clan had been charter members of the exclusive gentlemen's sanctuary reserved then and now for the ancestors of Boston's Brahmans.

Kevin Hardly had membership by default since Catholics were not easily admitted into membership. For sure had he been subjected to a standard application process his Protestant cousins would have had him black balled. For that reason he kept a low profile in club activities and always paid his bill on time. Inviting his Irish and Italian friends to dine was risky. Using a third floor club room was not only appropriate but guaranteed that the Club provided quality service without engendering the wrath of the other members with proper heritage. The room was spacious for at least twenty diners. A small table set for·six was squarely set in the middle of the room with the unused tables moved to the inner wall. The extra chairs had been removed and a serve yourself bar had been inconspicuously placed in the corner. At the end of the room opposite the door were two easels with poster boards reversed and waiting. A flip chart was positioned between the easels.

Two staff planners from The Hardly Security and Trust Bank had arrived about an hour before the Terrific Trinity plus one and arranged the room for their presentation. Now satisfied that all was in readiness they initiated proceedings at the self-serve bar. Hardly arrived promptly at five and was served his first martini-extra dry, rocks and a twist by his subjects who had done their homework. Patello and O'Shea arrived at the same time and rode the elevator to the third floor. O'Shea was cool to Patello and still nursed his anger from their last meeting when Charlie admonished him about his attitude toward Durant. Patello tended not to notice the typical Irish grudge and extended a cordial greeting. When they entered the room Patello mistakenly thought that one of the young planners was the bartender and ordered a Duers and water. The young man seemed pleased to be of service. Patello later apologized for the mistake with his usual charm. O'Shea made a cutting comment about how some people were always in need of help. Patello felt a surge of anger that nearly erupted in a Roman response learned years back in the neighborhood. In his mind he knew that, "this Irish son of a bitch was going to get his—but not now." O'Shea appeared oblivious to Patello's concealed anger and nosily gargled a beer.

The Terrific Trinity and the two planners were on their third round when the magnificent Richard Folley MD was escorted into the room by the club manager. Folley thanked the manager for his courtesy and made a grand gesture to his compatriots ignoring the hired help from the Bank. In response to Hardly's invitation, he declined his usual martini opting for an ice tea explaining that he was on call for the department and indeed lives were to depend on his clear thinking. With all on board, thirst amply quenched, Hardly beckoned to a waiter standing just outside the door. It was time to eat.

The extensive menu of the Alleton Club allowed each participant to exercise their knowledge of fine dining. Hardly encouraged exploration of all facets of the menu. He enjoyed playing host and making suggestions to his guests about the quality of his favorite entrees. When the orders were complete, he accepted the wine list and made a prominent French selection. He also directed the waiter to continue to pour the wine throughout the meal—no need to ask if another bottle was required—just make sure that his guests were amply refreshed. An hour and a half later the diners were finishing their desert. Hardly suggested that brandy and a good cigar would be a fitting end to their dining experience. Everyone except Hardly declined the cigar but they all enjoyed the brandy. Hardly allowed the bottle to be left on the bar. The waiter brought coffee and asked if could be of additional service. Hardly signed the chit and thanked the man for his excellent attention to his guests. It was time for the staff planners to give their briefing. Both had poured themselves another double shot of brandy.

Hardly explained to Patello, O'Shea and Folley that the Planning Department at Hardly Security and Trust was staffed with Harvard Business School graduates. Their capability was the envy of the banking industry. It was the Planning Department that first recognized the potential of automated teller machines and gave BSTB a big lead in the retail banking market. It was the BSTB planners that engineered the acquisition of rural banks thus forming a network that was the beginning of the BSTB becoming the largest retailer of banking services in the State and the nation. Following the build-up, he invited Stephen and George, BSTB's crack planning team, to begin the briefing that would justify the formation of the Office of Health Affairs for the Boston Catholic Archdiocese.

The evening had lasted beyond the endurance and sobriety of the BSTB crack planning team. Stephen sat at the end of the table with a silly grin on his face. George was laboriously trying to stand. Having accomplished that feat, he proceeded to knock down the first easel. This was too much for Stephen who broke out into uncontrollable laughter. George brought the easel back to an upright position and acknowledged his partner with a wave of his tie signaling the start of their best Laurel and Hardly imitation.

George spoke the opening line, "Well, this is another fine mess you got us into."

Stephen's facial expression turned to remorse and he began to fidget with his fingers. He seemed to be on the verge of crying, "I'm sorry, George. It's just that I'm not used to speaking in public."

George looked at the executives waiting for the report and then cast a disapproving glance at Stephen, "Well all right, Stephen, I'll do the talking and you handle the cue cards. Can you do that?"

Stephen hung his head in mock remorse, "I'll try, George. What do you want me to do?"

Now in full command, George spoke with authority, "You just stand next to the easel, Stephen, and when I point with my fingers you take one off. Do you think you can do that?"

Stephen appeared confused with the assignment but moved next to the easel with cue cards in place. George strolled to the center of the room above the dining table and introduced the presentation, "Gentlemen, our assignment was to study the possibility and benefit of establishing an office of Health Affairs for the Archdiocese. I'm pleased to report to you that an office for this purpose could be of valuable service in assisting the Archdiocese meet the expanding demand for health care in the Boston metropolitan area. As I will demonstrate on the charts, the health care market in Boston has been on a growth curve for the past ten years"

With a flourish, George gestured to the first easel and looked at Stephen. Stephen grabbed George's hand and proceeded to twist his fingers. George began clubbing Stephen who promptly dropped George's hand. Both convulsed with laughter. The humor was lost on Hardly who looked confused. Folley and O'Shea were angry. Patello concealed a smile, not as a result of these expert planner buffoons, but more at the build-up let down posture of Hardly. George took quick note of Hardly and signaled Stephen that fun time was over. Do the job and hope to be still employed in the morning seemed to register with the crack presenters?

George pointed to the first chart that Stephen had placed into view. "Gentlemen, as you see on this graph, hospital admissions in Boston have increased at ten percent per year for the past ten years. This next chart shows that the admissions at St. Anslem's has increased on average of eight percent over the same period. We can conclude that St. Anslem's is losing market share but closer inspection will reveal that St. Anslem's is benefiting from higher intensity than any other major teaching hospital in the area. This high intensity provides a higher revenue per admission than any other hospital and of course contributes to the bottom line. We are confident that St. Anslem's will continue to expand its tertiary market if it becomes the tertiary referral hospital for the three other Catholic hospitals in the Archdiocese. The coordination of this referral base becomes the major function for the Office of Health Affairs."

The time seemed right for Patello to make his pitch. Carefully, he interrupted the presentation by the crack planning staff by offering support for their conclusions. Then he suggested that the Office would require a special type of leadership that was adept at coordinating diverse interests. Finally, he very tactfully mentioned that Michael Logan, the current Commissioner of Health for the City of Boston, was an excellent candidate for the position. Hardly agreed. O'Shea was silent, while Folley seemed to applaud the prospect.

Folley was thinking that the presentation was right on. He needed to find a way to take credit for the thinking. Perhaps he could make a call to Bishop Hanks or the Cardinal and suggest that he was best prepared to direct the office. On the other hand, he didn't want to bump off Logan and in the process, bring Patello down on his back. The matter required some thought.

George resumed his commentary, "In addition to the coordination of in patient tertiary care the Office could be a central agency for insurance, personnel administration, benefit coordination, purchasing, and any number of administrative tasks. This centralization would noticeably reduce overhead and, therefore, increase profits. We think in time that the Office would become the administrative structure for health care and the hospitals in the Archdiocese under a single corporate structure. What we have on the remaining charts are organization diagrams and we have also asked our legal staff to prepare a sample set of articles of incorporation and bylaws that can be used when the hospitals are merged. All of this information is contained in the packets that we have prepared for each of you."

The buzz was beginning to wear off. Stephen was in pain and could feel the prospect of vomiting. George noticed that pale look on his partner's face and said a quick prayer for Stephen's life and recovery. George felt fatigue. He had been at the presentation for only about fifteen minutes including the stand-up comedy routine, but had been under pressure from these "stiffs" for nearly four hours. He had a pounding headache. What he needed was a quick ending that gave these "clowns" what they wanted to hear. He chose to distribute the information packets and abandon any further use of the easels and cue cards. Stephen helped distribute the packets and disappeared to the men's room.

George sat at the table and began to explain the information. "Gentlemen the information contained in these packets is the result of extensive research of the hospital markets in the Boston area. You will note that page one and two are the same charts previously displayed. On page three we begin with the statistical data that shows the growing prospects of the area hospitals. The continuing increase in revenues measured against expenses showing less increases obviously is represented in growing profits. While the last three years have shown what appears to be a slowing of the occupancy rate we note on page four and five that enrollment in the emerging manage care companies is steadily increasing. This leads us to conclude that the increased enrollment will tend to restart the utilization of the hospitals. The growth period will continue as long as the managed care companies continue to expand. The insurance companies are very supportive of the hospital base. Contracts between the providers and the HMOs are in good order."

Patello noticed that the information contained in the packets was nearly two years old. The poor copies still exposed the Massachusetts Hospital Association logo. Apparently, this crack research team had spent all of a half hour collating material faxed to them by the MHA. O'Shea seemed uncomfortable as well but could not afford to embarrass BSTB by exposing the shabby material. Instead he decided to explore the depth of Frank's analysis. He glanced at Patello and at George, "George, your positive report about the prospects of the hospitals is encouraging. However, St. Anslem's is experiencing increasing deficits over the past ten months. Is this in any way indicative of a trend or are we just experiencing poor management?" George wasn't sure what answer the man from the big office wanted. He opted for the middle road, "I don't have the detail of St. Anslem's operations, Mr. O'Shea, but I would have to guess that the St. Anslem circumstance is unique. My suggestion is that you press management for detailed comparative data. You could just well have a management problem."

"Right answer," thought Patello. The kid just saved his ass by accidentally giving O'Shea more ammunition to blow Durant out of office."

It was late and Patello decided to end the session. He directed his attention to Kevin Hardly who appeared to be dozing. "Kevin, your staff has made an excellent presentation. I personally believe we have what we need to adequately advise His Eminence about the status of his health care ministry. Let's bring this to a close and get ready for the presentation at the Chancery."

Kevin's eyes opened when Patello addressed him. Not sure of what was asked he nodded his concurrence. With that the participants began to leave the room. Stephen had just re-entered the room and began to pack the easels and other material. When the executives had left the room he lit a joint and sat down. George sat next to him and shared. Stephen complained bitterly about the senior executives' lack of humor. The "Laurel and Hardy" routine had wowed 'em in graduate school.

The smell of pot saturated the room when the Club Manager came in to check the room and turn off the lights. He noticed the glass eyed stare of the young bankers and the particular aroma. This was a serious violation of club rules and seemed to be what Kevin Hardly's cousins were expecting and hoping for. Stephen and George sheepishly picked up their junk and headed for the elevator.

CHAPTER FIVE

The events that brought Jay Marquart under the care of St. Anslem's Chemical Abuse Program began weeks before the incident that now sat in report on Dr. Anderson's desk. Marquart's habitual use of substances that started when he was in high school seemed to him to be occasional use especially on weekends when he "let it all hang out." During the week he would drink a few after work with his buddy Brian and have a few more before and after dinner with his wife, Susan. The weekends, however, were non- stop affairs that included plenty of booze, pot, and if he could afford it, cocaine.

Friday afternoon was Jay's second favorite time of his second favorite day. His first favorite time was after Friday afternoon and before Monday morning. Action Waste Management was not a pressure packed company. By Friday morning things started to relax. By Friday afternoon the staff was busy making arrangements for the week end. Jay Marquart was an expert in arranging the week end. His routine was to first make sure that his loving wife was in a party mood and that the kids' activities were covered. Susan's oldest son, Benny, was in his first year of Little League. Jay enjoyed watching and coaching Benny. He remembered with pride that as a little leaguer he swung a mean bat. Passing a few tips to young Benny was a real blast. He also had to be sure that he picked up Kristie on time from Cecile's when it was his turn to have her. The

"Bitch" gave him no end of grief if he was late. Then it was a call to "Ol'" buddy Brian to arrange for a party with appropriate sustenance. The partying frequently began with late night fishing followed by sleeping in on Saturday morning. The effects of Friday night were dispatched by three or four hours of doing yard work or house repairs in the hot sun. By late Saturday afternoon John was ready for the next blast. He stoked up the Webber grill around four and waited for Brian and, his "main squeeze," Louise to appear. Then Jay, Susan, Brian, Louise and the kids would have a fish fry with soda, cold beer, loud music and, after the kids hit the sack, a few sniffs to complete the high that kept going until well after midnight. Sunday was recovery time. A little quality time with the kids sparked by gin and grapefruit usually brought the week end to a close by midnight. B ack to work on Monday gave time to rest up for next Friday.

Step one in the process was to check in with Brian. Brian was running his delivery route for Patriot Courier Service on Friday afternoon, but Jay knew he was available by beeper. He called the operator at Patriot and asked her to page his buddy and have him call Action Waste Management.

Within the hour Brian responded with a call back to Jay's desk. As usual, Brian was upbeat and eager to, "get it on." He almost shouted over the phone when Jay answered, "Jay, my main man, how's it look from your end? I'm in good shape if you know what I mean. I got to carry the beeper this week end but that's no thing. We goin' fishing?"

Jay smiled at Brian's youthful attitude. He leaned back in his desk chair and braced his foot on the edge on the open bottom desk drawer. "Yeah, Brian. Benny's got a game at five so I'll be hung up till about seven by the time we get through the Dairy Queen. You want to meet me at the park. Susan can take the kids. I got Kristie this week end and I gotta pick her up at four thirty or else her mother, the Bitch, will have a hemorrhage. Then it's over to the ball park. I'll hook up with the family there. Then after, we can cut out for Hingham. You got a boat?"

Brian took the question as a compliment. He loved to boast about his friend and the boat that he borrowed. "Sure. I always got a boat. My customer says I can use it whenever I want. If he wasn't stoned out of his mind on Fridays he would be a good man to have along. He really knows the spots around the Boston light. We just got to be sure we fill it with gas and clean it out when we bring it back in."

Jay closed his conversation with Brian and checked the clock. Two more hours and he was on the move. He had to call Susan and tell her about the arrangement with Brian. He also had to touch base with buddy and boss Ken Ryan to see if he could get a head start on quitting time. With Ken's support, he could sneak out a half hour early in order to pick up Kristie. Ken had disappeared after lunch. Jay suddenly feared that Ken had taken the afternoon off which meant he was stuck on the job until four thirty. This was definitely bad news. He was not interested in starting the week end with a shouting match with "dear old Cecile."

Ken Ryan had been called into a staff meeting right after the noon hour. This was unusual for a Friday. Action Waste Management routinely held supervisor meetings on Tuesdays. As it turned out this was a special meeting for the big boss, Mark Meehan, to spark the troops about the big opportunity for the company that would result with the advent of privatized waste management in Boston. He pointed out that while growth of the company had been slow, the boom was near. He stressed the need for longer hours as new contracts were obtained. The topper for the meeting was the introduction of an incentive program that could increase earnings by about twenty five percent if all projects were on time and under budget. Ryan came back to his desk highly motivated. Jay was waiting for him.

Before Ryan had a chance to take a seat, Jay was posing his question, "Ken, I got to get away at four to pick up my kid at her mother's. OK?"

Jay's lack of tact irritated Ryan. He looked at Jay with disgust and then gave an abrupt answer, "Jay, you have to make some other arrangements for Kristie. Today is OK, but Mr. Meegan says that we are going to get very busy. No more short shifts. This Boston thing means big bucks for the company and they are going to cut us in. We all need the money, especially you. Start figuring on late hours on Friday's and every day."

"Christ," thought Jay, "this is a real bummer." He lived for the week ends. Freedom and time with Kristie meant more to him than money. He only needed the job to earn money for his child support payments. One missed payment and "that Bitch" would have him in court in a second. He suddenly remembered that Susan and her kids also figured into the deal and his life. He felt trapped. Frustration turned into anger. He felt the urge to pop off to Ken with a blast of profanity but retreated from his anger back to frustration. All he could do was glare at his friend and boss signaling everything he had in mind.

Ken Ryan read Jay like a book. He knew what Jay was thinking, "Jay, don't look at me that way. Keep it cool buddy. You screw this up and you are back to running junk for the syndicate. That can only lead to big trouble and doing time. You think I'm a pain in the ass? What do you think the mob is when they get their hooks into you?"

Jay's glare suddenly turned into a look of amazement. He had no idea that Ken was aware of his work as a party mule. Especially the times when he was doing special trips. Jay had no direct knowledge what was contained in the packages. He only guessed and now was wondering if Ken was guessing too. His anger returned and he popped off.

"You son of a bitch. Where do you come off with that shit about running junk? You don't know shit, man. I'll carry my load around here and you can stick that syndicate up your ass. You want me on the job, man, I'll stay on the job till hell freezes over. Fuck you."

Abruptly, Jay turned and stormed away from Ken's desk. Ken felt bad about the exchange. He also knew that Jay would leave at four anyway so the sentiments were mostly academic. Jay, on the other hand, was depressed and angry that the week end had begun with a fight with his boss. He saw this as an omen of bad things to come. At four o'clock he was on his way to Cecile's

After Cecile had married Officer Michael O'Sullivan of the Boston Police Department, she sold the small house that she and Jay had owned and, with Michael, purchased a larger home in Roslindale. It was located in a middle-class neighborhood on a quiet and peaceful street, a perfect setting for the double income parents of a charming little girl. They were accepted by the neighbors who were proud to have an angel of mercy and one of Boston's finest on the block. Some wondered about the beat-up jeep that routinely pulled up in front of the house and collected Kristie, Cecile usually walked her to the jeep so she could bomb Jay with a ritual of do's and don'ts concerning Kristie. Mostly she reminded Jay that the matter of joint custody was subject for review at the slightest indication of his misconduct. Furthermore, as the mother of the child she was the parent expected to protect the child from any inappropriate influences. She told Jay she suspected that he was doing drugs in Kristie's presence and she intended to make that an issue before the judge, given the opportunity.

Jay drank a lot of booze in front of the kids and usually had a buzz, but to the best of his foggy memory he could not remember ever smoking pot or sniffing coke in front of the kids. He was convinced that Cecile was on a fishing expedition. To counter her wrath, he persistently threatened to take her to court to have the support money eliminated based on the fact that Kristie spent more time with him and received most of her life's necessities from his meager income. Somehow, they managed to avoid coming to blows or even shouting so the neighbors could hear. Unfortunately, their sharp exchanges and threats were not out of sight or hearing of a little girl who always looked very sad.

Jay arrived in front of the O'Sullivan household promptly at four thirty. Kristie waved at him from the front window but did not move toward the door. Obviously, she was waiting for her Mother's escort. It took about fifteen minutes for the "Bitch" to open the front door. As Jay was waiting his anger was mounting. He could feel another fight on the way. Good. He was in the mood to tell the "Bitch" off. This whole day had turned sour after his bout with Ken. He opened the car door and stepped out to give Kristie a big hug and in the process, antagonize her mother.

To Jay's surprise the first person out of the door was not Kristie or Cecile, but a guy that looked like Rock Hudson wearing a tight pair of jeans and polo shirt. Jay quickly estimated that he went six three and about two hundred pounds of real man stuff. The giant glared at Jay, gave Cecile a peck on the cheek, and hugged Kristie. After that he sauntered to the Toyota in the driveway, backed into the street, and rode off into the sunset never giving Jay a second look.

Jay held a slight smile on his face as Cecile approached. "That's the new Stud? You got a lot to handle. Think you are up to it?"

Cecile tried not to let Jay's comment upset her. In turn she tried to counter his remark, "And that is the kind of comment that makes you such an endearing person, Jay. Yes that is my husband. He loves me and he loves Kristie. You need to keep that in mind."

The look in Cecile's eyes signaled to Jay that maybe this marriage wasn't all that it appeared to be. He was envious of the house and the apparent material comfort of their dual income life. But something was strange about the way that dude brushed by him and the way he registered a peck on Cecile. He didn't look too serious about any of it. Rumor had it that Cecile had married a cop. It seemed like a good time to verify the fact.

"What's it like sleeping with a cop? He is a cop, right?"

Cecile was uncomfortable with the conversation and noticed that Kristie was very interested in both the tone and content of the discussion. Kristie had crawled into the back of the jeep and was leaning on the front seat perched on her elbows. Her blue eyes sparkled at what she thought was a rare peaceful exchange between her parents. Cecile reached into the car and hugged her daughter, brushed back Kristie's golden locks, and returned to the conversation.

"Yes, Jay. Michael is a policeman and well regarded. It's sufficient for you to know that we love one another. Other than that, our lives are none of your business."

What's with all this love shit," thought Jay. She seemed to give a lot of emphasis to the marriage thing. He made a mental note to keep pushing the point and see if over time he could find a crack in her solid front. Just one angle and he would drag her into court and even the score. "Well it's always a pleasure, Cecile. You pick up Kristie about seven Sunday?"

Cecile shook her head and answered with an authoritative tone, "Jay, I'll pick her up at four on Sunday. We are going to a family get together with some of Michael's friends."

Jay was not about to let Cecile call the shots. "No way. This week end is with me. You and Muscles can go to the policeman's brawl. Susan can bring Kristie to you on Monday."

"Jay, be reasonable. We are invited to a picnic where children will be present. Why shouldn't my child be with me? She deserves to be with other children." Cecile was now pleading with Jay for some concession.

Jay sensed the opportunity to strike a blow, "She will be with other children. Benny and James are two of the best kids on earth. How do I know who these other brats are? No way. I'll bring her back to you late Sunday night if you are too drunk to pick her up or Susan can bring her to you Monday morning. You make the call. Remember she is my kid too and we have joint custody—that's joint custody"

Little Kristie took immediate notice of the change in tenor of her parents' conversation. She released her grip and slipped into back seat. Her usual sullen expression returned. Both Cecile and Jay recognized the change. It was time to go. Cecile gave in. "Jay, we expect to be home by ten Sunday night. You bring Kristie here by ten thirty."

Jay decided to press his advantage, "That's awful late for a child of her age. What kind of a mother are you? Don't bother to answer. I think I know. Kristie will be here before ten thirty Sunday night. Just make sure you're here."

That was the departing shot. Jay walked around the jeep, got behind the wheel and started the engine. As he was pulling away Kristie leaned out the back and gave her Mother a cheery wave. Cecile returned the gesture. Jay slammed through the gears leaving Cecile in a cloud of dust. The neighbors noticed and wondered.

Jay had called Susan from work and arranged for her to get Benny and Brother James to the ballpark in time. He expected to be at the game with Kristie well before the first inning. Kristie and James enjoyed playing around the park while Benny played baseball. Susan and Jay took turns keeping an eye on them and pulling them out of mud puddles or sand piles or from under the bleachers or whatever else a four and five-year-old could get into. In spite of his debate with Cecile, Jay sensed he was on schedule to make the first inning. His mood moderated slightly from the downer at work. He thought he had bested the "Bitch" in their last exchange, but he remained irritated at her attempt to pry Kristie away from him on Sunday afternoon. His stomach turned and his mad returned.

The drive from Roslindale back to the Waltham Little League Park was obstructed by the usual Friday afternoon traffic jams. Jay's mood deteriorated at every stop light. He shouted at slow drivers and gave the finger to a few thousand more. His anger was nearly uncontrollable when he blasted through a yellow light and just missed creaming a baby Benz. The driver looked at Jay through his tinted window from an automatically controlled environment with contempt. Jay looked back and rendered the expected middle finger salute. Kristie followed her Father's example and gave the Benz a final tribute with the same sign. Jay saw Kristie render the salute out of the corner of his eye and at the same time caught the open mouth expression of the Benz driver. The combined emotions of anger, shock and humor twisted Jay into control with a resulting smile that he concealed from Kristie. She was most certainly her father's daughter.

The game was in process when they arrived. Jay's anger climbed another octave but simmered when Susan told him that Benny was scheduled to play the last half of the game. He hadn't missed a thing. He was also pleased to see Sister Martha with Susan. Martha had her camera and was taking a picture of Benny in the dugout. James ran to Kristie as she jumped from the jeep that Jay parked in a towing zone. The two kids immediately emerged themselves in a dirt mound in back of the bleachers. Jay and Susan climbed to the third row and sat down. Martha joined them. Suddenly Jay felt relaxed. The week end was officially here. Let the good times begin. He unbuttoned his shirt and leaned back.

Martha needed the relaxation as much as Jay. She was the only woman attorney in a firm of forty. She had made partner in nearly record time but she suspected her advancement, while deserved, was salted by a degree of tokenism. Since becoming a partner, the pressure to better her male counterparts was immense. Competition for clients and billings within the firm was cut throat. Her colleagues were determined not to be outclassed by a woman. She, in turn, found it necessary to double her efforts in order to prevent the male animal from burying her professional presence. Her usual practice on Friday night was to frequent the bar a block from the office and exchange war stories with attorneys from the neighboring firms. This often led to referrals and sometimes a date. In either event, it was an extension of business and not complete relaxation. This Friday she left the office earlier than usual in order to pick up her sister in law Susan, Ben and James, and take them to The Waltham Little League Park where she would watch her step nephew, Benny, play ball and in the process, expand her bonding with her niece Kristie and step nephew James. Martha loved family and she especially loved children. Later she had a date with a young attorney who worked as an investigator for the State Attorney General's Office.

Benny's turn to play came at the end of the third inning. He was positioned at second base. Jay had played the same position from little league through junior high and still played an occasional second base as a substitute on Actions' slow pitch softball team. He shouted position instructions to young Benny while a patient and tolerant coach nodded to Benny to accept the instruction. Jay was in the game as much as Benny. He relaxed when the third out was made and Benny returned to the bench to wait his turn at bat. Jay made a quick check with the coach and learned that Benny was the number six hitter. He had time to check on Kristie and James.

The fun loving little cherubs had moved from the dirt in back of the bleachers to the gravel and dirt parking lot. Jay noticed the change and signaled Susan to get them back in the corral. Susan was on her way when Jay heard her shout at James. He turned in time to see James pitch a rock in perfect form at Kristie who adeptly stepped aside. The rock with high velocity slammed loudly into the door of an Oldsmobile leaving a prominent impression in the door and the door's owner who happened to be leaning against the opposite fender. The owner immediately moved between Susan and the car. James was hot footing it in the other direction and Kristie hid behind Susan. Jay jumped off the bleachers and headed for the scene of the crime. By the time he got to the Oldsmobile the owner was inspecting the damage to his four-year old rust marked, pitted, and now newly dented sedan.

Jay approached the victim with conciliation in mind. "I'm sorry about the damage. The kids somehow got out of our sight. I'll pay for the repair."

The gentleman stood tall and folded his strong arms across his chest. He looked at Jay as if to size his ability to pay. Perhaps he sensed an opportunity. It was certainly worth the effort to see if this sucker was good for a load. "Well I know that kids will be kids and all that, but you see this door is dented and they got to replace it. When they do that they got to paint to match and that means the panels have to be primed and coated so we're talking considerable costs I imagine."

Jay's boiling point was near. "Another fight—goddamn it another fight. First Ken, then the Bitch, that idiot in the Benz, and now this jerk. "Jay knew that combat was out of the question. First of all, it wouldn't play well with Susan and the kids. Second, they were in a public park that was patrolled by the local constabulary. Third, and most important of all the considerations, was that this guy was more than big enough to eat Jay's lunch.

Susan sensed Jay's anger. She had the urge to begin proceedings by kicking the gentleman in the groin but realized that his counter attack could render Jay useless. As an alternative she took Kristie by the hand and left to pull James from under the bleachers where he had established sanctuary.

Jay recognized her departure as permission for him to work this thing out as best he could. "Look, friend, I am willing to pay to fix the door but the rest of the car is not my responsibility. I've got a friend who does body work who could do a quick estimate. You get an estimate on the door from whoever you want and then we can reach an understanding."

The man starred down at Jay, "First of all I'm not your friend. You are going to pay for the damage in full. None of the compromise crap. Your kid rocked my car and you pay. It's pretty simple. I'll tell you how much. You don't tell me!"

Susan had returned to the bleachers and captured James. He began to sob and leaned against his Aunt Martha. Kristie held on to Susan and looked back at her Daddy. Both men were animated and pointing, but not shouting. Martha carefully moved James to his Mother's side and then walked over to where Jay and his new-found friend were getting acquainted. She heard the last exchange and began to make her own observations as an attorney schooled in artful negotiations. She noticed that the subject automobile had a sizable crack in the windshield and that the inspection sticker on the same windshield had expired six months ago. The taillight cover was missing and the absence of the rear wheel cover revealed a missing lug nut. This gentleman was not prone to investing funds in automobile maintenance or safety requirements. Best bet is that he is a cash hound.

Jay had reverted to his classical angry stare that usually preceded a gigantic screw up. He was unaware of Martha's presence. She caught the signal and moved in. "Sir, I'm Martha Marquart, Mr. Marquart's sister and attorney. We recognize your interest in seeing that this matter is properly concluded. I suggest that we ask the Waltham Police to come to the scene and make an official report of the damage as well as a record of the incident in case of insurance claims or litigation. Of course, I'll represent Mr. Marquart and if you have counsel you may want to suggest that he or she contact me after the police report is on file."

Martha offered her business card to the gentleman who looked at it but with a wave refused to take it. Jay was stunned at his Sister's assertion. Both men were totally disarmed. Martha took to the offensive. "Two hundred bucks. Cash. You take it and get that piece of junk out of here. We'll forget this unfortunate incident ever happened."

She held out ten twenty dollar bills. The gentleman looked first at the money, then at Jay, then Martha, and back to the money. Martha raised her arm as if to let the gentleman smell the cash. He paused for a brief moment and took the money. Martha nodded to the man, took Jay by the arm, and escorted him back to the bleachers.

Jay was speechless. He looked out at the field only to notice the final out of the game. He learned later that he had missed Benny's clutch single that drove in the winning run. James cuddled next to Jay in gesture of seeking forgiveness. Jay, still stunned, placed his arm around James and gave him a hug. Susan counseled Benny not to bug Jay about his outstanding play. There would be time for that later. For the time being it was best to let Daddy alone. Kristie held onto Martha because she knew that Aunt Martha did something to cause peace. Suddenly Brian appeared in their midst.

Jay, Susan and the kids piled into the jeep and headed for the post game team meeting at the Dairy Queen. Martha said her good byes at the ballpark and headed for the nearest Automated teller machine to replenish her cash supply before her date. Brian drove his beat up pick-up truck behind Jay to the Dairy Queen. He enjoyed a Buster Bar while he waited for Jay to complete his father bit. Somehow Brian remained a kid in spite of his occupation. He was Uncle Brian to the kids and a good time buddy for their parents. He enjoyed being a surrogate uncle and at work often told their natural father, Eddie the Enforcer, about his kids. Eddie seemed disinterested.

The Dairy Queen was over-run with kids from age six to sixty getting a sugar fix after a victory or defeat. It didn't seem to matter if they won or lost. Jay sat amidst the confusion and for the time being forgot about the incident at the Park. It was amazing to Jay how Dairy Queens around the world over remained indestructible to the continuous onslaught of Little League baseball teams. He pondered which came first, "Did Little League find Dairy Queen or did Dairy Queen find Little League? What was probably more important was who was going to survive the longest. If Dairy Queen disappeared who would be next—Dairy Delight—Dairy World—Dairy whatever until the whole soft ice cream universe disappeared? On the other hand, if Little League baseball was discontinued or went on strike like the majors, the Dairy Queens of the Universe would go without notice and eventually disappear anyway. The whole thing was much too horrible to contemplate. He looked at Brian and realized that there was one saving factor. Brian was hopelessly hooked on Buster Bars. Brian's uncontrolled consumption could be the salvation of Dairy Queen. The thought brought a smile to Jay's face. The first one since Kristie gave the finger to the nerd in the Benz. Brian noticed Jay's smile and raised his dripping Buster Bar in a toast. He also rocked his head toward the door as a signal that it was time to go fishing.

Jay caught Brian's signal and, looked for Susan. He spotted her corning out of the ladies' room with Kristie and James at hand. As he waved, she gathered the three kids and joined him. Uncle Brian also joined the group and they spent a few more minutes together. Brian complimented Benny on his game winning single. This was the first that Jay heard of Benny's heroics. Benny beamed at his step-father and accepted his great hug with pride. Jay explained to the kids that he and Uncle Brian were going fishing and he would see them in the morning. They were also going to have a party tomorrow afternoon after the lawn was cut and the house was cleaned. They were to help Susan tonight by taking a bath and going to bed when she said. He would see them in the morning. Benny wanted to know if he could go along. Jay promised him a fishing trip, kissed the three kids, added another for Susan and headed for the door with Brian.

Brian's old Dodge Ram pick-up truck was filthy and cluttered. The ash tray was overflowing with cigarette butts, candy wrappers and miscellaneous pieces of paper. The floor held last winter's mud, a tire tool, and parts from the non-functional radio. Jay kicked the derbies aside and carefully cranked open the door window. It was off track forcing him to guide the window to its lowered position. Brian pumped the gas pedal and turned the key. On the third try the tired old truck came to life. He steered free of the crowded Dairy Queen parking lot and headed for the Mass. Pike. Traffic had cleared so the time to the Hingham Town Boat Dock was less than an hour.

Jay slumped in the seat. "Shit, Brian. I say shit."

Brian gave a quick glance at the sulking Jay, "Now what's buggin' you, man?"

Jay straightened up when he heard Brian's question. He pounded his fist on the dashboard and made a quick left jab motion. "Martha gave that robbin' son of a bitch two hundred bucks. How am I gonna' come up with that kind of money? Shit. I say shit."

Brian casually flipped his cigarette out the window and followed it with a quick spit. Then he gave Jay another glance. "Well, I only saw the tail end of the action and it looked to me that she saved your ass. You got that man mad and he was fixin' to kick your butt, maybe. She say you had to pay her back?"

Jay lit a cigarette, fished a beer out of the cooler between them and pondered Brian's question. He took a long swallow and belched. "She's my sister. I'll pay her back. No way am I gonna stiff my sister. She can be a real pain in the ass—a real pain in the ass."

Brian seemed philosophical. "Yeah, well everybody should have a pain in the ass like that. Wish I did. How come she ain't married? Why you bitching? Everything's cool."

Jay was slightly offended at Brian's personal question about Martha. He looked at Brian and decided that he meant no harm. It was a reasonable question for Brian to ask, but it didn't deserve an answer. He finished his beer, dug in the cooler for another, popped the top, and handed it to Brian. Then he pulled another out for himself. "You know' Brian, I figure Martha will get married when she has me straight. Then she can concentrate on her own life. Right now I'm about all she can handle. Man, that son of a bitch had me hassled. I think I could have beaten him out completely if Martha hadn't bought the bastard off. He would have blinked. I was givin him the evil eye and I could see his lip quiver. The dude had no stomach for a fight. He was a con—a goddamn con job. Yeah, I was ready to rumble. He wouldda made the first move then I roll him out. Shit."

Brian laughed at Jay's comments. He had heard Jay talk this way before. Jay talked a good fight but was slow to actually engage. "I know you ain't had nothin to smoke, man but you talkin like you on the clouds. No way you gonna punch that dude. You got Susan and the kids standin there. A lawyer by your side. That low-grade hassle could keep you in the slam all week end. Then you got to explain at work why you got to go to court. Man, if I got into a fuss over something like that Patriot would fry me good."

Now it was Jay's turn to smile, "Yeah, well Patriot can't afford to have its employees looked at too closely by the fuzz. Action doesn't have quite the same situation. You see that dude wasn't gonna go with the hassle I was givin him about estimates and all that, and he wasn't about to duke it out. So, when I give him the stare down he says let's forget it happened. He was about to cave when Martha comes up and pays him off. You see how fast he grabs the cash?"

Brian didn't answer. He was occupied with trying to merge left in heavy traffic on to State Route Three. The exit to Hingham was just two miles beyond the intersection of Interstate 93 and State Route 3 which was the main route for Boston weekenders to take to Cape Cod. Traffic was bumper to bumper and barely moving. The flashing blue lights of a State trooper vehicle were visible ahead near the exit to Hingham. Brian became tense. He handed Jay his half-consumed beer and gestured for him to stash the empty cans in the cooler. Brian maneuvered the truck onto State Route 3 and carefully merged to the right lane. He was holding the wheel with his left hand and attempting to open a box of Tic Tacs with his right hand and thumb. Having succeeded he poured the contents into his mouth.

The truck swayed as Brian turned to talk to Jay. "Jay, can you see what we got up there? Is it an accident or are they doing sobriety tests? Man, I don't want them looking close at this truck. They find my stash and its iron bar city. Drink the rest of my beer. We get stopped I'll tell them you been doing the drinking and I been driving. You OK with that?"

Jay strained to look ahead. He could see two cars in the break down lane ahead of the State Trooper. Suddenly he caught the flash of a yellow light in front of the vehicles. It was either a towing vehicle or CVS Good Samaritan van. "Christ, Brian, relax. Looks like it's a breakdown or accident. No sweat. Just act normal. I realize that may be difficult for a man of your status."

Brian was not amused. In spite of the cool sea breeze he was sweating and perspiration was evident on his brow. He feared arrest. The strain was becoming very apparent as the truck began a slow weave from the right lane onto the breakdown lane and back. Jay glanced at Brian as the truck began to move to the right. His grip on the wheel was overly tight and he appeared to be fighting the steering. Fortunately, traffic was moving about fifteen miles per hour so the irregular movement was not noticed by the busy troopers directing traffic. As the truck came close to the scene Brian moved to the left and cleared the trooper's car with little room to spare. He somehow managed to exit Route 3 without incident. Jay glanced out the rear window to be sure they were not being followed.

Brian stared straight ahead and as they came to the stoplight, he released a deep sigh. "Jay, my man, I live in fear that I' m gonna take a dive. You know I'm only carrying a little for us. Not like it's a big thing. But it seems that I freak out more than I used to when the cops are around. Wonder why?"

Jay leaned out the window and looked back at the traffic jam before he answered. "I don't know what's eating you, man. You might be getting old in this business. You ever been hassled?"

"Nope, never have."

Little more was said. The Hingham Boat Dock was busy as pleasure boaters and fishermen launched and retrieved their boats. Brian's customer had tied the boat to the dock a few hours earlier and had managed to frustrate the launching process by occupying precious pier space. The Hingham Harbor Master was standing next to the boat when Brien and Jay arrived at the dock. Brian noticed him and went to the rescue. Jay began removing the fishing gear, radio tape player, and cooler from the truck.

Brian tried his best brand of soft-soap, "Sorry about the delay, Officer. We'll be loaded and out of here in a few minutes. We were delayed in traffic. There's an accident up on three."

The Harbor Master was not convinced. He nodded at Brian and handed him a ticket for inappropriate use of Public Launching Facilities. Brian glanced at the ticket that contained a twenty-five dollar fine. The Harbor Master walked away without saying a word. Brian shoved the ticket in his pocket and went to help Jay with the gear. In a few minutes, they were ready to go.

The boat, a twenty-foot blue Sea Sprite with a closed bow and padded seats, had seen better days. It was a pleasure boat of the run about class and definitely not built for fishing. The old Inboard/outboard power drive system displayed leaking seals, low compression, noisy water pump, and a tendency to overheat when pushed over 3000 rpm. Its most significant quality was its tendency to float. The outdated Massachusetts' registration tags were properly displayed on the bow. The Windshield held a Coast Guard Safety Inspection decal from 1988. It was typical of the boats cruising Boston Harbor on a summer Friday night. Brian nursed the engine to life while Jay tended to the lines. They were free of the dock, free of the harbor master's stare, and free of life's pressures. The tranquility of the open water with the glide of the boat through the relative calm brought both men to full relaxation.

Brian made headway for the first fishing spot just outside the Boston Lighthouse that sat on the end of a reef marking the entrance to Boston Harbor. Jay attended to his fishing tackle as Brian moved toward the outer harbor. Susan had brought the gear to the park and transferred it to Brian's truck before Jay had checked it. He kept his fishing box and rods at the ready in the basement and Susan only had to bring it along. His preparedness brought rewards as he found everything available. His next act was to pull a couple of beers from the cooler for Brian and himself. The hassle with Ken, the beef with the jerk at the ballpark, Brian's freak out, the fine from the harbor master didn't mean a thing. Lean back and relax, man, relax. The week end was just beginning.

The plan was to fish the structures outside the harbor around the Graves Reef, as it was called, then as the tide continued its ebb, move in to the inner reef and fish close to the edge. Mackerel, flounder, cod and possibly a sea bass were if the offing with a little luck. These areas were heavily fished by the locals so a number of boats were already in position as Brian came onto the spot. He maneuvered the boat close to the reef and signaled Jay to set the anchor. When he was confident that the anchor was holding he shut off the motor. It was dusk with the final glow of the sun behind the horizon—the time when most small fishing boats began to return to port.

Two hours later Brian and Jay had the spot all to themselves. Boats that had not returned to port had moved to the inner harbor. The fish were not cooperating. Not even a nibble had been registered since the anchor had been set. "Time to move," thought Brian. "Jay, I guess we better move inside. They ain't hittin out here anyway. I didn't see any body pulling anything in. What do you say?"

Jay started to reel in, "Yeah, I'll clean the hook and pull the anchor. Crank it up and let's get outta here."

The old engine kicked in on the first try. Jay had the anchor on board. Brian carefully steered the craft past the rocks now visible and into Nantasket Roads. He followed the buoys past Boston Light and then began a gradual approach toward the reef just becoming visible above the tide.

"Brian, bring her in close to the rocks" Jay urged, "They'll be feeding on the structure. We can use drop lines if you can get next to the reef. Get right on top if you can."

The current from the ebb was particularly strong. Brian powered the boat forward until the bow hit the rocks. He kept the power forward while Jay pitched the anchor onto the reef. The night prevented Jay from seeing the anchor grasp the rocks but a pull on the line convinced him that they were secure. He signaled Brian to cut the engine. Once again, they baited their hooks and waited for results. An hour later they experienced the result of their efforts. Instead of a fish they felt an unusual rock of the boat followed by the sound of the outdrive bouncing on the rocks. Brian instinctively pushed the raise button on the outdrive control and brought it to its highest position. Now the thump was heard from the bottom of the boat. Within what seemed like a few short minutes they were firmly grounded on the reef. Brian leaned back in the seat and relaxed. "Jay, or buddy, guessed we're screwed here for about four hours if my estimation of the tide is near correct. We ought to be able to get off 'bout three hours into the flood if we ain't too high. We could be stuck for four maybe five hours max. This thing probably draws a foot and a half with outdrive up—three feet with it down. We just got to wait it out."

Jay had the benefit of several beers working on his attitude. "Yeah, we sure as hell ain't goin' to do much fishing in the process. Break out the stash. I could use a smoke."

Brian dug into the depths of his tackle box and produced a nickel bag. He handed it to Jay and helped himself to another beer. "Jay, you know that we sittin' here like this, there is only one boat that gonna pass us that gives us a close look. That's gonna be the Harbor Patrol. Water Cops. They come over and check us out all the way. They check for booze, pot, and everything else. They find any and we go to the slam, they impound the boat, and the whole world comes down on us. We gotta pray that they don't come around."

The thought of being hassled again irritated Jay. He felt his anger rise as he fired back at Brian, "Man, you starting that paranoid shit again? We're fishing that's all. We fucked up and ran aground. Hell, they see that all the time. Ain't no reason for them to do a body search. They don't mind us having a few beers as long as we don't hurt nobody. Stay cool. I'll finish the joint and if you want I'll throw the stash overboard. How we fixed for beer?"

Brian simply shrugged an answer to John's questions. He slowly sipped his beer. After a while he looked up at Jay, "Jay, I gotta know, would you rat on me?"

"Would I what?"

"Rat on me. You know. If a guy, say a cop, started asking you questions about me, what I do, who I work for, and all that would you tell him?"

Jay was completely distracted by the conversation. He wondered what Brian was trying to say, "No, Brian. I wouldn't rat on you. Who's going to be asking questions about you anyway? You don't own the business. You're a truck driver that delivers packages. I don't know nothing about your business."

"But what if you got caught with some stash they want to know where you got it. You gotta think of the kids and don't wanna take a dive then you tell em you got the stash from me. Would you do that?"

Irritation and anger started to ebb into Jay's emotions. He tried to remain calm, "Brian, if it's a choice between you and the kids, I take the kids. Yeah, under those conditions I'll tell them where I got the stash if that is what it takes. You gotta expect that. Anybody would. You wanna take me off your list?"

"You gotta know I got insurance." Brian's expression seemed secure.

Whatever Brian had in mind was not clear to Jay, "Insurance? What the hell you talking about? Insurance. You got insurance from taking a dive? Brian, they don't sell that kind of insurance."

Brian was more confident as he fired back, "Its company insurance. The company insures me. They got insurance."

"What company insurance—hospital, life, disability, workman's compensation, unemployment, and dive. Gimmie a break, Brian." Frustration mixed with anger mounted in Jay's clouded mind.

Brian assumed the role of an instructor, "No shit, man. It's self-insurance. They provide it. You see, when we get a new customer and I go to make the first delivery Eddie goes along to make sure everything is OK and the customer is satisfied and everything. You know Eddie, Susan's ex? Well he explains to the customer how everything works. You know about payments and delivery and order and all that. He also explains that we got to be sure that the customer stays satisfied and don't have no beef that they take to the fuzz cause if they do Eddie breaks both their legs. That's my insurance. The customer knows that if he rats, Eddie gonna break both his legs or blow up his car or something. That's my insurance, man. You gotta know that."

Suddenly the small boat got very small. Jay felt the sting of an outright threat from his best friend. The surge of anger that he had felt several times earlier in the day was overpowering. This time he could be violent and succeed. He grabbed the grappling hook and took straight aim at Brian who now stood in the boat with his back turned. Jay began his swing but checked it as they became illuminated in a spotlight from a Harbor Patrol Boat closing on their position.

The patrol boat moved in cautiously. A man in the distinctive gray uniform was on the bow, "You boys OK? Anyone hurt? The boat OK? How hard did you hit the rocks?" The patrol boat moved to within twenty feet of the Sea Sprite before it touched bottom. Close but not close enough to do a full inspection without getting very wet.

Brian waved at the officer and replied, "We're OK. We were at anchor when the tide went out. Just grounded. No damage. Guess we'll just have to wait for the flood. Thanks for checking."

The Officer moved the spotlight back and forth as it to do his own check on the condition of the boat, "Yeah, we gotta check it out. We'll stop by every hour to make sure you're still OK. You got a VHF?"

Brian's response was quick, "No radio. It's on the blink so we took it in for repair. Guess we should have asked for a loaner."

The Officer turned off the light and sat down. "Shouldn't be out here at night or anytime without a VHF. You got flares? Anything happens use a flare. We'll see it and be here fast. Take care."

The Patrol Boat reversed its engine and backed away from the reef. Brian waved to the Officer and sat down facing Jay. He began to sob. Jay's anger dissipated when Brian unemotionally and skillfully dealt with the harbor patrol. Now he felt deep sympathy for his friend who was experiencing what Jay thought to be a nervous breakdown. Brian's sobbing increased to an uncontrollable rate and he began to hyper- ventilate.

"My God," Jay thought, "will I need those flares. Where in the hell are they?" Brian began to take deep breaths. His sobbing stopped. He eventually looked up at his friend. Jay's eyes filled with tears as he looked back at Brian's exhausted expression.

Brian slowly gained control. He was no longer the instructor on matters of insurance. Now he was a lonely man and scared, "Jay, I gotta get outta this racket. I can't take it anymore. Man, it was fun when we were in high school but now it's getting to me. Man, I don't want to do no time. I'm scared shitless that somebody's gonna cop on me. Eddie gives me this insurance shit. He says don't worry cause nobody's gonna wanna mess with him. Shit. I say I wanna quit and Eddie says I ain't gonna. He says I gotta keep on muling. He says I just got to cover my ass. Says that I gotta tell you about my insurance. He won't bust Susan or his kids but that asshole might bounce Kristie if he figures you gonna rat. I try to make a move and that son of a bitch will break me in two. What we gonna do, Jay?"

Jay couldn't believe the turn in events. He now understood the bizarre conduct of his buddy. Eddie the Enforcer, AKA the Insurance Man, was leaning on Brian to make Jay's life miserable. It was unclear if Eddie was knocking Jay because of Susan and his kids. He might be trying to hurt Susan by putting the pressure on Jay. On the other hand, this might really be a business matter. Eddie and the firm might be simply pressuring Brian to tidy up his security measurers since he obviously told them he wants to quit.

The uncertainty denied Jay an answer to Brian's question. He slowly shook his head as a negative response. Brian folded his arms across his chest and cuddled into the seat. In a few minutes, he was asleep. Jay starred into the sky, had another smoke and waited for the tide.

It was almost two AM when Jay felt the boat begin a slow rock accompanied by the sound of water slapping the side. The tide had advanced on the reef and the boat was beginning to float. Jay tapped Brian on the shoulder, "Brian, I think we're about free. I'll try to get the anchor loose. Damned if I know where that son of a bitch landed. It won't pull so I gotta go over the side and fish it out. We got a flashlight?"

Brian handed Jay the flashlight. Jay had a good jag on from the smoke and beer. He dropped off the side of the boat into a foot of water. The reef was ragged and the footing uncertain. He held the anchor line and followed it to the anchor securely wedged between the rocks. He pulled the anchor free but fell backwards as he lost his footing. The cold-water shock was accompanied by a nauseating pain in his lower back.

Brian saw him fall but was unable to assist since the boat had become free. Jay, realizing his predicament, struggled to his feet, cradled the anchor in his arms, and painfully returned to the boat. He was standing in water up to his thigh. Brian tried to steady the boat against the rapid current and help him back into the boat. Jay tossed the anchor into the boat and made one major effort to come over the side. Brian gave him a boost by pulling his arms. He landed in the bottom of the boat with a loud thud joined by a blast of profanity that would embarrass a sailor's parrot.

The spotlight from the Harbor Patrol boat caught them as Jay was struggling to get up. "You boys free? Everything all right? We'll stand by till you are under way."

Brian gave an affirmative wave to the Patrol boat and attempted to start the engine. After a few turns the motor kicked in. Brian hit the switch for the navigation lights that thankfully worked. He maneuvered off the reef and steered for Hingham. The Patrol Boat followed in their wake for a while then veered to starboard toward Boston. Jay was in pain but the jag made it tolerable. He noticed the turn by the Patrol Boat and nudged Brian. Brian gave Jay a big smile and the two exchanged a high five followed by uncontrolled laughter. Their fishing trip had lasted over six hours with not one catch or even a bite. Brian had experienced a nervous breakdown. Jay had attempted murder, fell on his butt in two feet of water, injured his back, and was wet and cold. They had barely escaped arrest. This was truly a fun filled adventure that they would talk about forever.

The Hingham Town Boat Dock was quiet as Brian made his approach to the pier. The Harbor Master was probably in town at Dunkin Donuts. Brian purposely landed the boat in the same spot where it had been tied in the afternoon. He secured the boat as Jay removed the gear. When he was satisfied that the Sea Sprite was properly birthed he took the twenty-five dollar ticket wrapped it around the keys and put them in the glove box. The customer would grease out of it.

It was four in the morning by the time Brian dropped Jay at his Waltham estate. Jay showered and managed to crawl into bed by five. In two hours Susan and the kids would start the Saturday rituals. Jay would have none of it. He slept past noon and awoke with severe pain in his back. He could barely move. Susan responded to his pleas for help and held him upright as he dressed. There was no way that he was going to be able to mow the lawn in his condition. It didn't look too bad and could wait his recovery.

The first priority was pain control. Doctor Marquart's remedy for back pain was a generous quantify of gin in grapefruit juice taken constantly until the pain disappeared or the patient passed out. The therapy began as Susan was feeding lunch to the children. The kids accepted Susan's explanation that daddy was a bit under the weather so the usual Saturday afternoon games would be delayed. Daddy was opting for total postponement.

By three in the afternoon Daddy was literally feeling no pain. He had supplemented his therapy by taking a few sniffs of coke out of sight of the kids. Although a little stiff in the back he managed to referee the kids through a backyard run through the hose, a game of darts in which Kristie decided that James was the target, and a game of horse with Benny on the garage hoop. He was aglow and on a good high. Time to get out the old Webber. Brian and Louise were about due.

Fortunately, the fish fry was not dependent on last night's catch. The Marquart freezer was heavily stocked with the results of more productive trips. Susan had removed a generous quantity of flounder and blue fish that was in the process of defrosting. Jay pulled the Webber out of the garage, loaded it with charcoal, and placed the lighter fluid on the small folding table with his cooking utensils. He then joined Susan in the kitchen and helped prepare a special dish of vegetables in oil that they would bake on the Webber with the fish. Susan accepted Jay's offer of a tall, powerful gin and grapefruit. It was time for her to start to gain altitude. Jay was in full orbit. He stretched out a couple of lines that they inhaled.

Brian and Louise arrived at five-thirty, a little later than usual. Louise explained that Brian had to answer his page and make a few unscheduled deliveries. Jay looked at Brian who dropped his eyes. The insurance conversation of the prior evening was not forgotten by either man. A sudden anxiety caused Jay to begin to shake. He sat down. After a few minutes, he recovered and made a drink for Brian and Louise. The kids had pulled Uncle Brian into the backyard for a game of tag. Louise joined Susan in the kitchen. Jay lit the Webber. The pain returned only not in the back. It was in the abdomen, high, just below the chest and in the middle. He became dizzy. The pain grew in intensity and seemed to radiate to his arms. He was sweating. His breathing was difficult and painful. Susan came out of the kitchen with the fish as Jay fell to his knees. She ran to him and shouted for Brian to help. The pain dissipated as they placed him in a chair.

Jay had worked in the Cardiac Catheterization Laboratory at St. Anslem's for a few years after high school. He was classified as a technician but was no more than a gofer in a high-tech environment. Nevertheless, he learned about the symptoms of cardiac arrest and saw patients experience the pain associated with failure. He was certain that he was on the verge of a heart attack but he also felt that he had time to get to the hospital unassisted.

Jay took Susan's hand, "Susan, look, I think I need to get checked out. If Louise and Brian can feed the kids and look after them, you can drive me to Waltham hospital emergency. We ought to leave now. They can check me out and we can be home in a couple hours."

Louise, standing next to Jay, heard the conversation, "Susan, you take off. Me and 'Brian can take care of the kids. They'll be all right. Jay has gotta get to the hospital. You want Brian to take you? I can feed the kids and see they get to bed."

Susan nodded. Brian handed his truck keys to Louise. Jay gave Brian the keys to the jeep. Susan and Brian helped Jay into the Jeep. Fifteen minutes later they arrived at the Waltham Hospital Emergency Room. Jay walked into the Emergency Room with Susan at his side. He explained to the clerk that he had experienced radiating pains in his chest and abdomen accompanied by dizziness and sweating. The clerk immediately put him in a wheelchair and pushed him into an emergency room. A nurse followed them in and asked Jay the same questions as the clerk while she took his blood pressure and pulse. She asked Jay to lay on the emergency room gurney and to take off his shirt. Jay was feeling better but remained worried about the sudden unexplainable pain. In a few minutes, a physician came into the room.

The doctor was younger than Jay and Susan. He had a boyish face and seemed a little unsure of himself. Great," John thought. He was on his death bed and they throw in a rookie. Obviously, a moonlighter from one of the teaching hospitals. Suddenly Jay had an anxiety attack of a different nature, "Holy Christ! Not St. Anslems. If this guy knows the Bitch"—relax Jay—"he don't know me so he won't be able to put it together even if he knows Cecile." The physician greeted Jay and Susan and asked the same questions over again. He then began to examine Jay closely with his stethoscope. He looked at Jay's eyes very closely, his fingernails, and tapped his body in various places. As he was completing his exam the nurse reappeared to extract some blood for the lab. She also asked Jay to urinate in a small bottle. No small task for a guy lying flat on his back. The nurse suggested that he use the lavatory across the hall if he felt up to it. Jay's pains had gone and his anxiety level was back to normal. He felt weird but said he could make it to the lavatory unassisted. Susan helped him off the table. He had to pea in the worst way so the trip was welcomed. Hitting the bottle was the most difficult part of the whole experience. He returned to the room with the specimen and handed it to the nurse. She accepted it and placed the bottle on the counter then assisted Jay back on the table. The EGK machine had been placed next to the table. The nurse explained the process as she placed the leads on his body.

Jay knew the process very well. He had taken many EKGs in his day as a cardiac tech at St. Anslems—no few of them in the emergency ward. At St. Anslem's any patient that presented symptoms like Jay's would be treated by a team of cardiologists, fellows, residents, medical students, nurse specialists, and technicians from the lab, cardiac care unit, and x-ray—not to mention a cardiac surgeon lurking about just in case. This cast of thousands was now being represented by a sleazy looking nurse and a kid playing doctor. She completed the EKG, made a few notes on the record and took Jay's pulse again.

The doctor came back into the room a few minutes later and casually looked at the nurse's notes before he commented, "Mr. Marquart, my name is Doctor Barker. I'm the emergency physician on duty. We've reviewed your symptoms and given you a preliminary examination. At this time I believe that you do not have cardiac failure but we need to wait for the blood and urine tests before we can come to any definite conclusions. The EKG looks normal but, again, we will have it read by a cardiologist later tonight or in the morning. We are going to admit you to the observation area for monitoring overnight. That way we can rule out cardiac distress. If everything goes as I expect you should be able to go home in the morning sometime before noon I think. Tell me, have you been taking medication of any kind or using the so called recreational drugs? How about alcohol? My guess is that you had quite a lot to drink today. That so?"

Susan wanted to crawl under the table. "Had he used recreational drugs? Does a bear shit in the woods?" Jay had sniffed up his week's supply of coke as he knocked down a fifth of gin. She had her share too. Hopefully this guy would not test her blood. He obviously knew the answers to the questions. Jay had over dosed, plain and simple and now the jig was up. That overnight bit for observation was a polite way of saying detox. They were going to detox her Jay and then throw him into rehab or some "do- gooder" program. Maybe he would go from the hospital direct to the tank downtown. For a moment she thought that a heart attack would have been a better deal.

Jay's response to the doctor was classical. "Yeah, I started popping pain killers early this morning. I hurt my back last night fishing and the pain was killing me. They didn't seem to help so I used some dope. When that didn't help I went to booze. Sort of screwed myself up I guess. You want to look at my back—still hurts like hell." Jay turned on his side and put his hand on his lower back. A large bruise was present.

The doctor looked at the area and gave it a slight touch, "Well we need to get a few x-rays. You would have been better off to come in this morning and have this looked at instead of punishing your body with over medication. You could have bruised ribs—maybe broken. Any sharp pains when you breathe? We'll know by morning."

The nurse listened to the conversation and made notes. She nodded when the doctor mentioned x-rays. The order forms were quickly obtained for his signature. Jay looked at Susan and winked. He had, at least for the moment, diverted further discussion about drugs.

The doctor directed his attention to Susan. "Mrs. Marquart, there's no reason for you to stay. Mr. Marquart will be closely monitored overnight. If anything happens we will call you. Do you have transportation? We can give you a ride home if you need one?"

Susan explained to the doctor that a friend had brought them to the hospital. He was in the waiting room and would take her home. If necessary she could drive herself back to the hospital. Otherwise she would bring the kids with her in the morning to collect their hero. The doctor nodded and left the room in response to an audible page. The nurse put down the chart and followed. Jay sat up on the table and asked Susan to have Brian come in. He needed a few minutes with him to assure him that nothing was wrong. Susan caught the drift that Jay wanted to speak to Brian alone. She gave Jay a kiss and left to find Brian.

A few minutes later Brian came into the room looking like the one who needed treatment. He was smiling and tried to be reassuring, "Jay' man you scared the shit out of me. Susan says you gonna be OK. Man, what hit you? You looked like hell. Susan's calling Louise and telling her everything is OK. Why they keeping you, man? Oh yeah, Susan needs your insurance card for the desk. You got it? I'll take it out when I leave. You scared me, man."

Jay dug in his wallet and began to look for his Bay Area HMO membership card provided by Action. He found the card and handed it to Brian. "Yeah, well Brian, I was scared myself. I never been hit like that before. They got me figured out I think which is what I want to tell you about. They got my blood and pea in the lab right now. What they gonna find is a lot of coke and maryjo. They gonna know that I OD'ed. That's gonna be in my medical record at this hospital. No way anybody else is gonna know so don't worry about your insurance or anything like that. You know what I mean?"

Suddenly Brian became noticeably upset. "Why you tellin me this, man? If this thing is air tight then we got nothing to worry about, unless they got to tell the fuzz. They got to do that?"

Jay gave his friend a negative wave off, "No way. I'm a private admit. Came in under my own steam so to speak. If I would have been in a car wreck or fell down on the street or got caught doing drugs then my record would be in the public domain. As it is I'm a private patient and these people got to preserve my confidentiality. Wanted you to know that and not worry about your insurance man. No way is he gonna know. You OK with that?"

Brian tried to look comfortable, "Yeah, man. I'm OK with that. You been in this hospital racket so you outta know. I'll take this card to Susan. She says she will get you tomorrow so I'll check in with you then. Don't get frisky with that nurse. Looks like she could eat your lunch."

Susan carne to the door of the room looking for Brian and the HMO card. Brian handed her the card. She blew John a kiss and left with Brian. A few minutes later an x- ray tech moved John onto a gurney and pushed him to the x-ray room for a series of pictures. Moving around the x-ray table was painful for John but gave him assurance that the effect of his excess drugs was wearing off. After the X-rays he was pushed to the observation area and placed in a bed with heart monitoring equipment.

The night attending nurse took his temperature, pulse, and respiration rate every hour. They kept him awake most of the night. In the morning, he was served a bland breakfast of cereal, skim milk, dry toast, and hot tea. Except for a lack of sleep, he felt fine.

Around eight thirty a man dressed in a blue suit approached his bed. "Mr. Marquart, I'm Dr. Hendricks, internist and cardiologist. How are you feeling this morning?"

Jay sat up and tried to look as if he was in fine form. "Fine, Doctor. A little tired. No problems. How do I look from your point of view?"

Hendricks rapidly turned the pages in the chart and talked at the same time. "Well you had a good night. All signs are back to normal. I looked at the EKG and it is normal. I guess you are a lucky man. You just missed a big problem. The lab tests revealed an extremely high presence of cocaine, alcohol and other drugs. You experienced a mild overdose. Had you not had the reaction when you did and continued to consume you could be in bad shape. If you are prone to habitual use I would like to recommend a treatment program. St. Anslem's Hospital has an excellent program that is discreet and personal. The Director of the program, Dr. Ron Anderson, is a friend of mine who would be glad to give you his personal attention."

That was the last thing Jay wanted to hear but he didn't want to offend the Doctor. He tried to give a reasoned response. "Doctor, I know that you have my best interest in mind. Right now I don't consider my habit as being out of control. I got caught up in a lot of things this week end and sort of lost control. I can handle it. This won't happen again, I'm sure. You think from what you saw in the blood and urine that I'm hooked. Well so is half the world. Illicit drug use is big business and so is drug treatment. Hell, you can't have one without the other. For now I'll continue to use and eventually get the treatment. It's sort of like Little League Baseball and Dairy Queens."

The metaphor was lost on Dr. Hendricks. He looked at Jay with pity in his eyes.

Jay wondered what caused him to say something that stupid and far removed. Hendricks wondered about the comment briefly and then attempted to counter Jay's reluctance to accept counseling, "Jay, you know I hear that from a lot of patients. You're right it seems that the whole world is addicted to something. That doesn't change biology. Eventually your resistance to the drug breaks down and you begin to experience physical breakdown. Your system collapses and you experience cardiac failure or stroke. If you are not dead you are a vegetable. That's a guaranteed outcome my friend. You can count on it unless you get help. Drug rehabilitation and counseling works. The sooner you start the better. You are thirty-six. Well if you continue to treat yourself as you did yesterday you won't see forty. If you have people that depend on you, that should mean something."

Jay remained determined to best the physician. "Come on, Doc. They say the same things about cigarettes. We been puffing away for hundreds of years and all of a sudden, we're killing ourselves. I admit we're all going to die from something. Cigarettes, drugs, sugar, pork or old age—when you're dead you're dead. I hear you and I'll be careful. Right now, I need some slack."

Hendricks knew he was not about to convince this patient. Unfortunately, the man would have to learn the hard way. "I'll write the discharge order, Mr. Marquart. The record will contain a note that I recommended continuing treatment and counseling. You need to know that especially if you decide later to take my advice. Your insurance will cover the treatments as they have been prescribed by a treating physician. When you check in remember to refer your treatment facility to your medical record here. I'll give you my card. Call anytime."

Doctor Hendricks extended his hand and Jay shook it. He gave a short wave and walked over to the nurses' station. Jay waited a few minutes after the doctor had left the observation area. He carefully got out of bed and walked toward the counter. The nurse looked up as he approached. She asked if he was all right and gestured for him to sit down at the chair next to the desk.

Jay stood next to the desk instead of accepting her invitation to rest. He tried to act nonchalant, "Did he write the discharge order?"

The cute but slightly portly nurse smiled and gave a positive nod, "Sure did. You can go home anytime you're ready. Is there someone who can pick you up or do you have your car here? You need to stop at Out-Patient on the way out and make sure that they have all the billing info.

While you're waiting for someone to pick you up you can get dressed and take care of the paper work. Let me know if I can help."

"Why out-patient? I thought admitting took care of the discharges. "Jay tried to impress her with his knowledge of hospital procedure.

The nurse was not impressed. She maintained her smile as she attempted to explain, "You were admitted to the observation area that is part of the Ambulatory Services Department. You were never an in-patient. Your stay was less than twenty four hours so it's not an admission. The face sheet on your record is out-patient/emergency service. Less cost and a better bang for the buck"

Jay, the hospital expert, was the one who became impressed. "Man, this hospital business has changed in the few years since I left St. A's, he thought. No wonder the emergency room wasn't packed with white coats. This was a bare-bones cost effective operation. Jay asked permission to use the desk phone to call Susan. She answered promptly. It would be an hour or so before she could get to the hospital since she was in the middle of feeding the kids. Jay got dressed and ambled to the out-patient desk. The clerk was efficient. His billing record was complete. Having completed the discharge process, he wandered into the cafeteria for donuts and coffee. He desperately needed the caffeine.

Susan and the kids arrived about fifteen minutes after Jay had returned to the out- patient waiting area from the cafeteria. The kids were happy to see that Daddy was healthy and happy. Kristie seemed especially pleased. Benny wanted to know about Daddy's heart attack pointing out that some of his buddies on the team had daddies with heart attacks. This caused Jay to suddenly recall his statement to Doctor Hendricks that half the world was addicted. He was tempted to ask Benny if the daddies were also junkies. Otherwise the ride home in the overcrowded jeep was uneventful.

Once home the excitement about Daddy subsided and the kids found other things to occupy Sunday afternoon. Susan was extremely curious about his diagnosis. Jay attempted to explain. "Susan, the doc said I had a mild overdose reaction to cocaine. He said I was lucky that I didn't get the big one. Seems I stopped at the right time. Anyway, he figures I'm an addict that needs treatment, rehab, and all that. I told him no soap."

Susan shook her head as a sign of opposition to the Doctor's advice as if it had been directed to her. "Jay, we don't do that much coke. A lot of people do more than us. Ask Brian he knows. Louise tells me about the stuff he delivers to some people. We don't do near that much. I can't see that we're addicts. We do a lot of booze and smoke but not much coke. We don't need that goodie two shoes stuff, do we?"

Jay wondered about Susan's constant me of first person plural. To the best of his recollection he was the one with the reaction. Susan must have felt it as much as he. Again he had the thought that half the world was addicted. "No, Susan, we don't need that goodie two shoes shit. I'll be more careful about overloading. We're OK. You feeling all right? Louise get along all right with the kids?"

Susan was pleased to get off the discussion about addiction. "Louise and Brian are great. She had the kids bathed and in bed when I got home. Brian cleaned up outside then we talked past midnight. He sure seemed worried about you. What are you going to do now?"

"Sleep, Susan, Sleep. I feel like a brew but I'll pass that up for now. If Brian calls tell him what I told you. I'll give him a call tomorrow night. Right now I need some sack."

Jay was in bed at two in the afternoon. He fell sound asleep in a matter of minutes. Susan entertained the kids for the rest of Sunday. The boys were pleased that they could stay up late and ride with their mother to take Kristie to her other house. At ten thirty Sunday night Susan escorted Kristie to the front door of her mother's house in Roslindale.

Cecile answered the door surprised to see her instead of Jay. Before she could speak Kristie opened the conversation. "Mommy, Daddy got sick and had to go the hospital. He came home but is sleeping. He was very sick. I guess he is good now."

Susan attempted to explain. "Cecile, Jay had a mild attack of something. I think it was related to the heart. They kept him overnight to check him out. He carne home this afternoon and went to bed. The doctor says that he's all right. He asked me to bring Kristie to you".

Cecile's nursing instincts caused her to realize that this was not a runny nose type incident. She immediately suspected that good old John had stepped over the line and hit the wall. This might be the incident she was waiting for. She hugged Kristie and pushed her inside. Then she gave Susan a friendly and cordial good bye. "Thank you for being so considerate, Susan. I hope Jay is feeling better. Tell him of my concern. I'll call him later this week. Thanks, again."

Kristie ran into the house. Officer O'Sullivan picked her up and tousled her hair.

Susan said her good-by, returned to the Jeep, and drove home. She was uncomfortable with the conversation with Cecile. She wondered what Cecile was going to contact John about next week.

Jay was up earlier than usual on Monday. He had slept for nearly sixteen hours. The effects of his weekend experience was not apparent. He bounced around the kitchen making coffee and slamming the refrigerator door. Susan finally appeared. She had juice and coffee with him while explaining the events of Kristie's return to Cecile. Jay actually seemed amused at the prospect of Kristie telling Cecile that Daddy was in the hospital. He really didn't give a damn about the prospect of a call from Cecile. He could handle that "bitch." No sweat. At seven thirty he kissed Susan and left for Action Waste Management-- a half hour ahead of schedule.

By seven thirty Cecile had been at work for a half hour in St. Anslem's Medical Intensive Care Unit. She had taken report from the night shift, and had made rounds with the chief resident in order to decide on the AM transfers to general units. The attending physicians were beginning to come to review their patients' progress and teach the residents and medical students rotating through the service. Nursing students were scheduled to arrive at nine o'clock. Patient acuity was exceptionally high. The pressure was on.

As Cecile was breezing by the desk the unit secretary signaled her that she had a telephone call. Cecile made a quick turn behind the desk, grabbed the phone, and answered with professional style, "Good morning, this is Nurse O'Sullivan. Can I help you?"

The caller was obviously not under the same pressure as Cecile. Her greeting was evident of the fact, "Cecile! Kathy Berry. Do you know what they call a nurse with two assholes? Married! How do like that one, my old Bunker Hill buddy?"

Cecile had great affection for her former classmate. They talked often and shared the events of their lives. It was a surprise that her friend would call at this busy time. Cecile suspected that behind the relaxed greeting was an important message. "Kathy, it's always a pleasure to have these deep intellectual discussions with my favorite classmate, but I'm up to your favorite part of the anatomy in alligators right now. Do you have something else on your mind?"

Kathy caught the cue. "Yes, my dear I do. Knowing that you have a great interest in researching nursing functions in cardiac care I thought you might be interested in doing a case study on an interesting patient. I was doing a temp job at Waltham's observation unit Saturday night and encountered an interesting case that seemed to fit your research protocols. You get the drift?"

The drift was that Kathy had confidential information about a patient that she knew Cecile could use. However, it was necessary to give the message in a way that did not violate the law or nursing ethics regarding patient confidentiality. It was up to Cecile to give the good opening for Kathy to respond, "Look, my research centers on Caucasian males, middle age, who experience cardiac symptoms from excessive use of recreational drugs. Did this patient present that way."

The reply was right on. Kathy let it happen, "That he did, my dear. The man had a good course with discharge in twenty hours. You might want to make note that the patient came in through the Emergency Service Saturday PM complaining of abdominal and chest pains. Blood and urine was in orbit. Good case for your review. Anyway, you know where it's at. Know you're busy this time of the morning but wanted to get you the information. Keep in touch."

"Thanks, Kathy. See ya." Cecile hung up and waved her fist in the air. That was it. Jay had spaced out on Saturday afternoon. Probably in front of the kids. He went to Waltham Hospital. Was discharged on Sunday. Kristie knew Daddy was sick so she probably saw what made him sick. Now the challenge was to get Jay's medical record before a judge. That would prove her point. He would lose custody. She made a mental note to call her lawyer at lunch.

Jay arrived at Action Waste Management early enough to accidentally meet his boss, Ken Ryan, in the parking lot. That had never happened before. Ken was blown away. Usually Jay arrived fifteen minutes late looking like he hadn't slept for a week. Ken greeted his charge with

Monday morning warmth, "Good morning, Jay. Looks like you're ready for another week. Have a good week end with plenty of rest?"

Jay acted as if the world was well within his grasp. "Same 0, same 0, Ken. Got a good night's sleep last night. Bring it on."

A large notice in bold print hung on a pedestal sign at the employee entrance announcing a meeting for all non-management employees in the cafeteria at nine o'clock. A notice for a management meeting was on Ken's desk. That meeting was to start promptly at eight-thirty and conclude no later than nine. This was most unusual. Jay and Ken both realized that something big was about to happen. Both thought that the Boston project was about to begin

Ken went immediately to the management conference room. He was one of the last to arrive. The other ten supervisors were already present guessing about the purpose of the meeting. Promptly at eight thirty, Mark Meehan entered the room accompanied by three men, two of whom looked like interior linemen for the Patriots. He invited everyone to have coffee. When everyone appeared comfortable he called the meeting to order.

"Gentlemen, let me introduce our guests. The man on my right is Robert Muldoon, President of the Boston Workers' Guild. To his right is Mr. Martin Hart, President of The Service Workers Local Number 936, and on the end is Mr. Veto Celli who has joined our staff as sales manager for the Boston area project. You will all get to know Mr. Celli better as he becomes involved in the Boston project. The primary reason for this meeting is to advise you that at the employees' meeting to begin in less than a half hour they will be advised of their opportunity to join Local 936. We have decided not to contest an election. The union has agreed not to obstruct proceedings in the Boston project. A contract with 936 will be worked out this week as soon as the employees have completed their enrollment. Action Waste Management will be a Union Shop. Any questions?"

The room was silent. Finally, a supervisor asked if the contract would change work hours and production schedules. Mr. Hart explained that the current working conditions were to be included in the contract without change. Of most importance would be the economic issues that would be subject of a reopened clause next year. For now, everything would remain the same. Ken asked if the contract would require management to deal with a business agent on work rules and hours. Again, Mr. Hart explained that no change in practice was intended. There would be a Shop Steward appointed who would represent Union member concerns to the local. The Business Agent would be the agent for the Shop Steward to the Local and would not generally be involved in day to day matters. When no more questions were presented Mr. Meehan thanked the Union officials for their assistance. It was nine o'clock and time for them to attend the employees' meeting.

He asked the supervisors to remain, have another cup of coffee and meet Mr. Celli. As Celli circulated among the supervisors, Meehan pulled Ken to the side for a private conversation. "Ken, I want you to know that the Union wants Jay Marquart as the shop steward. It's OK with me. How do feel about it?"

Ryan seemed puzzled. "It's OK with me, Mark. I wonder what Jay will say. He's an independent cuss that doesn't seem to me to be inclined to join a union. He might tell them to shove it."

Meehan was insistent. He held Ken by the shirt as he pressed the point, "Well they won't bring it up at this meeting. You can help Jay decide. If all goes well at the employees' meeting and the cards get signed they'll ask Jay to be the Steward this afternoon. I'll let you know later this morning where it stands. Then maybe you can prep Jay to go with it. You two get along?"

"Yeah. We get along." Ryan wondered about the question as Meehan walked away.

The small company cafeteria had several tables in line with Service Workers Local 936 signs. A few clerks from the Union sat behind the tables but said nothing to the employees as they mingled about waiting for the meeting to begin. The purpose of the meeting was very evident. In spite of it the employees were careful not to express an opinion. At a time like this it was best to keep your opinions to yourself. Action's Human Resource Director was chatting with one of the clerks who seemed to be in charge. Jay noticed an absence of stress in the environment. He remembered when the Union tried to organize St. Anslem's an all-out war erupted until the Cardinal declared peace by recognizing the Union. Jay carried a union card until he decided to go to school. He thought

Unions sucked. He too kept his opinion to himself as he enjoyed the free coffee and donuts. At least the Union had provided that and he hadn't even joined.

At a few minutes after nine three men entered the room greeted by the HR Director. They proceeded to the head table while the HRD asked everyone to take a seat. He then introduced Mr. Muldoon of the Boston Workers' Guild. Mr. Muldoon, dressed in a shirt with an open collar, moved to the podium and began the pitch.

"Ladies and gentlemen, I am Bob Muldoon of the Boston Workers' Guild. I am pleased to inform you that Action Waste Management has agreed to allow The Service Workers of America Local 936 to represent you and your interest in collective bargaining. This of course will only happen with your consent. We want to inform you of the advantages of collective bargaining and to inform you about Local 936. Marty Hart, here at the table, is the president of the Local. He'll tell you all about it in a minute. With him is Dave Donovan who is the business agent for 936. He'll be working with your Shop Steward once we get organized."

Muldoon explained at great length about the history of the Union movement in the United States. He eventually narrowed his focus to the Boston Workers' Guild pointing out that The Service Workers of America Local 936 was a charter member of the Guild. The local had a long and distinguished history in rightfully representing its members. On cue, the clerks at the tables would prompt applause from the assembly. Eventually Muldoon had the assembly applauding and cheering. The time was right to introduce Marty Hart. When Hart took the floor, he was met with a standing ovation again prompted by the clerks now positioned around the room. He continued firing up the emotions. Jay stayed calm taking note that nothing of substance was being said. The meeting reminded him of the high school pep rallies that he attended to get out of study hall. No sooner had the thought crossed his mind when Hart began leading cheers. Jay couldn't believe it. He was considering walking out when Hart completed his speech by inviting everyone to sign the enrollment card. Jay got in line with everyone else. As each person signed the card they were ushered into a receiving line where they shook hands with Muldoon, Hart and Donovan in that order. As Jay was shaking hands Donovan took special notice of his name and commented that he was looking forward to working with him. Jay was surprised at the comment but made no response except an affirmative nod of the head.

It was all over by ten-thirty. Jay was in the Union. He didn't feel any different. He wondered if Ken would be upset when he found out. Certainly, the management meeting earlier was about the Union thing. Muldoon said it had already been worked out with management. "So, everything's cool," he said out loud as he strolled past Ken's desk and gave him a wave.

Ken looked up and motioned Jay to have a seat at his desk. When Jay seemed comfortable, Ken passed him a piece of paper and explained.

"Jay, there's a note here for you from HR. They want you to meet with the Union at one o'clock. Guess I'm not going to get much work out of you today. What's up?"

Jay threw his hands in the air in mock confusion, "Hell, I don't know, Ken. This whole thing came out of the blue. You know this was up? I never had much use for the Union. It was a war at St. Anslem's. My old man said the only way to join a union was if you could run it. Maybe they are going to ask me to run this thing. How about that?

This was the right answer and gave Ryan the lead that he needed to carry out Meehan's order. "Well now, Jay, you could just be right. This place will need a Shop Steward who has some brains, can respect the business, and represent the employees. You might be the right man for the job. Would you take it if they asked?"

"Yeah, if they ask. I'm not about to run for office. Anybody else is interested they can have it. I'll get along fine as I am. What makes you think they might ask? "Jay looked at Ryan with a degree of suspicion.

Ken winked at Jay and smiled, "I heard the Union guy mention it. Mr. Meehan said it was OK with him if you accepted. He thinks you're all right."

"Cut the bullshit, Ken. "Jay straightened up in the chair and then stood up, "If Meehan goes along then it's because you suggested me. He don't know I exist. What's in it for you if I take the Steward job? Oh hell, what's important is what's in it for me. Don't bother to answer I'll figure my end."

Jay walked back to his desk and began to review grant applications. Ken waited until he was sure Jay was occupied, then called Meehan's office. He reported his conversation with Jay to Meehan. Meehan thanked him for the information. Jay's interest in finding something in it for him could be accommodated with trips and time off for meetings. All this would be explained by Donovan. Things were coming together just fine.

Promptly at one o'clock Jay reported to the HR department. The receptionist ushered him into an interview room where Dave Donovan was waiting. Donovan stayed seated as Jay came into the room. He extended his hand and pulled Jay into the chair next to him at the small round table. Donovan was friendly and had a fatherly like appearance. He leaned back in his chair and tried to put Jay as ease as he spoke.

"Jay, Mr. Marquart, how are you doing? Things went well this morning. The troops selected us to represent them. Everybody signed up. No contest. How about that? So now we have to get to work. Check off of dues start the first of the month and the troops are going want to see something for it. Somebody has to be here to see that what they want is registered, put into writing and sent to the Local. Also, if anybody has a beef with management it has to be dealt with on the spot. So, we need a guy that's tough and has the guts to put it on the line. The troops think you can do the job. You up to it."

Jay tried to look tough. He tilted himself back of the rear legs of the chair and put his thumbs in the waist of his pants. Then he glared at the Union official. "Yeah. Donovan, I'm up to it. Somehow, I don't think the troops have the slightest idea that I'm being selected for the job. You guys got your reason for picking me. That's OK with me but you got to explain to me why I should go along."

Donovan didn't need this attitude. He was not happy with the way that Muldoon and whoever had selected this person for a key and important post. Now he had to deal with his arrogance, "Well life's full of little surprises. Maybe a little fairy popped Muldoon on the head and told him to pick you, I really don't know. I was told that you were the Shop Steward and that's the way it is. Now, if you don't want the job I can mention it to the muscle and they will find someone else. You got a problem?"

Jay didn't pick up on Donovan's irritation. Instead he pushed further, "No problem, Donovan, except I figure there's gotta be some vigorish. This is a tough job the way you describe it. It seems I'm at personal risk. You got any insurance that keeps me from getting canned or worse yet wasted?"

The George Raft imitation amused Donovan. He saw through the phony exterior and recognized a person that could be formed to be of service to the Local. He rocked back on the legs of his chair and gave Jay a fatherly answer, "You watch too much TV. There is no vigorish. You have the protection of the US government. The law requires the company to give you time to do your duties as Shop Steward. That includes time off to attend meetings. You can spend a lot of time traveling. The Union pays the expenses. What else you do want to know? Make up your mind. Are you in or out?"

Jay gave an affirmative nod, "I'm in Donovan. Definitely in."

CHAPTER SIX

The Honorable Robert Cowan, Mayor of the City of Boston, returned from his trip to Washington over the weekend and was in no mood for a press conference. The media broke the news on Friday that the Mayor was going to DC to chat with the Secretary of Labor and the President about the position of Under Secretary in the Labor Department. The Mayor's office at first denied the reported purpose of the trip but later confirmed that some meetings with the Secretary were scheduled. There was no confirmation that the President was involved. Cowan had advised his staff before the trip about its purpose but also advised that the tentative nature of proceedings required caution if not deception in dealing with the media. When he returned, the local media had the benefit of the national press in Washington that shadowed the Mayor for the entire time. There were no secrets. There were also no definitive answers. Pressure for a news conference came from the Mayor's staff.

There were things that Mayor Cowan could not tell the press. For example, he did not want to disclose that the appointment as Under Secretary was a dead end in his quest for national prominence. Even if the President was re-elected it was doubtful that Cowan would be advanced in his administration. The President as much as said so. Furthermore, the pay as Under Secretary was slightly less than Mayor of Boston and living expenses in Washington, considering the Mayor's living allowance from the City, were higher. The economics of the opportunity did not recommend the position. Why would he bailout of his native Boston for the cut throat Washington scene?

The answer to the question was another fact that the Mayor did not want to discuss with the media. The political scene in Massachusetts, while always cut throat, was becoming hazardous to the Mayor's political health and personal freedom. If a scandal broke over the misuse of campaign funds he would be dead as a candidate for Governor. There was reasonable assurance that his contributors would rally in his defense should any accusations be made. He had strengthened that position by bringing Bob Muldoon and the Labor Bosses to his aid in the Party. However, the Republicans were determined to re-elect Dukar and position the Governor as a potential presidential candidate. To do this they needed to re-elect Dukar for another term as Governor by a wide margin. Since Cowan could carry Boston and most of eastern Massachusetts, he stood as an upset candidate and threat to the Republican plan. Cowan suspected that a deal had been cut by his friends and the opposition to mow him out of the way. Things went too well in Washington. Apparently, the skids were greased for his appointment. Who paid for the deal? Who would he really be working for? Where did Muldoon and the Labor Guild fit in? And of most importance, who was going to take the fall when the campaign fund issue finally carne to the surface as it eventually would? He needed answers. So did the media. Hopefully not to the same questions.

As a first item, the Mayor requested that Alfonse Siro, President of the City Council, meet with him to discuss the change in City Government in the event that the Mayor resigned to accept the Federal appointment. Siro had routinely supported Cowan in City Council. He held the Mayor's trust but not his confidence. Cowan wisely kept his campaign and personal business restricted to a few close associates and friends. Siro didn't belong to the inner circle but was a confidant for the Mayor in dealing with the politics in the Council. Siro was also a seasoned politician who realized that it was necessary to hold certain matters close to one's vest. One of Siro's closest associates in politics and personal friend was Michael Francis Megan, Deputy Commissioner for

Parks and Recreation——City of Boston. Siro had been advised by his political supporters that the Mayor would support Megan's appointment to the Commissioner of Health job should Commissioner Logan resign. Logan would resign as a result of an advantageous opportunity in the private sector. This transition would follow the initiation of the waste management voluntary privatization project.

It was necessary for Cowan and Siro to have a detailed discussion about the complex agenda of change. Once they had a meeting of the mind on dates, times, places, and people, they could begin a calculated campaign of conditioning the media that of course included the usual informal leaks for the benefit of the inquiring minds.

Siro was the first person the Mayor contacted after his return from Washington. The two met at the Mayor's office at seven o'clock Monday morning. The time and place for the meeting was well selected since Siro routinely met with the Mayor on Monday to go over agenda items for the City Council meeting held on Thursday morning. City Hall beat reporters waited outside of the Mayor's office for Siro's exit then would badger the Mayor for an advance look at the agenda. The Mayor routinely passed the reporters to his secretary who provided them a draft copy immediately after sending a fax copy of the rest of the Council members. If the agenda was not agreed upon at the time of the meeting the Mayor would truthfully inform the reporters that the agenda was not ready for distribution. This was already decided to be the case as Siro walked into Cowan's office.

Cowan had arrived at the office at six AM. He had gone over the telephone calls, reviewed the messages on his desk and listened to voice mail. Sharon, his secretary, arrived at six forty five. She usually arrived at seven but the Mayor called her Sunday to ask her to be a few minutes early in case the reporters needed to be diverted with coffee and Danish. She had the usual office pot ready with a full tray of donuts. Inside the Mayor's office coffee and Danish waited Siro's arrival. Siro walked past her with a good morning nod and entered the Mayor's office without benefit of being announced. The reporter sitting on the couch in the reception area did not have time to move from under his cup of coffee and donut to ask preliminary questions. He would remain on stake out.

Siro, as President of the City Council, considered himself an equal to the Mayor and always addressed him with informality and friendliness, "Good morning, Bob. How'd things go in DC?"

The Mayor looked up from the messages spread on his desk and extended his hand to his political colleague, "Well its progressing, Al. We need to talk about some things in case it all comes together soon."

Al Siro liked the comfort of the Mayor's roomy office. He thought often about being mayor and occupying the corner room. When he became Mayor he intended to keep all the furniture as is. He patted the arm of the chair as he sat down and when comfortable responded to Cowan, "I think so. You have a bird dog outside. Probably be a covey of them in a few minutes. They're going to have a million questions. What's our approach?"

Cowan plopped into his double padded desk chair and leaned back to the limits. He stared at the large ornate chandelier in the center of the ceiling, "AI, I'm not certain if this thing in Washington is the best bet for me. My people say it's the way to go. I'm inclined to take their advice but to make it work I understand that a few things need to be completed here. You have any idea what I'm talking about?"

"Yeah, Bob. I guess that the waste management thing is the key to getting things straightened out. That's probably the first priority. "Siro mentally went over the facts given to him an hour earlier.

The Mayor came forward in his chair and looked at Siro with a questioning expression, "Well I'm willing to authorize the voluntary thing for the City but it will require the support of the City Council. You guys willing to go along?"

The response from Siro was quick and direct, "Bob, you know that I can deliver the Council. I'll need a few things to keep things in line regardless if I become acting Mayor. You know that Commissioner Logan could be a problem on the political end. The kid is sincere but acts like a loose cannon. He ought to have another job. If you don't move him then I have to do it. It would be best if Logan resigns and you appoint Megan to the acting job as Commissioner of Health. Then when and if I step in I give him the permanent appointment. He's my man. I'll take responsibility. If I don't step in, you put up with him long enough for the waste project to get settled then make a decision about Megan. We can talk about Megan's permanent appointment as we go along."

Cowan turned in his chair and gazed out the window at the snarled early morning traffic moving slowly around City Hall. "Al, you know that labor will back Megan's appointment because Logan stuck his finger in their eye at Boston Hospital. They have been pressuring me to bounce the kid ever since. Do your sponsors have any opinions on Megan or Logan?"

"Labor has contacted me about Logan," Siro began as an understatement. "They want something done. I also have some word that the Boston Taxpayers Association likes the private waste management idea. They will support Megan if he's in office. I guess that means that they would back you and me if we put him there. Labor and the BTA is a tough combination to beat. That's both sides of the aisle. Don't think we could do better. Anyway, that's the way it was explained to me."

That was what Cowan was waiting to hear. Siro was in the tank. Big money had made a move on him. Good. He had it explained to him by somebody other than Labor. The contact had been made. Siro would stick to the script as long as it was the script that Big Money had written. He also now knew that the reason things went well in Washington was due to an alliance made high up in the power politics game. That gave him some assurance in accepting the Federal appointment. He had just been promoted from the rank of pawn to castle.

Siro noticed the appearance of a slight smile on Cowan's face. Obviously, the message had been received just as Patello suggested it would. Cowan was a seasoned, smart politician who heard the unspoken word clear as a bell. When Patello met with Siro he had carefully explained the approach to Cowan. Siro had rehearsed the script over and over while waiting for Cowan to return from DC. He knew the call for a meeting was inevitable. Patello had said so.

In his mind, Siro turned the script to page two. "Bob, we need to avoid any talk about improper use of funds and things like that. Some people believe that Logan pocketed funds for you when he was in your campaign. If you drop him will he implicate you in any way? If that hits the fan the whole thing would be diverted. To me Logan seems too innocent to be guilty of stealing."

The Mayor was standing now. He calmly made his way to the coffee pot and poured a cup for himself and offered to refresh Siro's, "Not to worry, Al. Mr. Logan had nothing to do with my campaign funds. The kid never saw a nickel. If fact he not only donated his time to the campaign he donated his own money as well. The man is a one hundred percenter. They might want to nail him but they can't. I always thought that the TPA was targeting the kid to get me to do something in his defense so that I would automatically incriminate myself. Labor picked up on the rumor as a way of forcing the kid out. I let it happen as a diversion. The more they chased Logan the further they were from the facts. It's nice to have a guy like him around. Could he take a fall? Well you know that anything is possible in the courts but it would be a real travesty of justice."

Siro was pleased with the exchange. He had the answer to Mr. Patello's second question. Logan was an innocent man and possibly an innocent victim. Cowan kept the kid in the dark about campaign funds but allowed the shadow of suspicion to fall over him as a diversion. Siro recognized the tactic. He knew that if things got hot for Cowan he could set Logan up for a fall by a simple adjustment to the books. Cowan's greatest crime at that point is being hoodwinked by an honest man. It happens all the time. You just can't trust honest people.

"I understand, Bob. Let's do it. Are you going to talk to Commissioner Logan about his future? It seems to me that he has to make the move in order for the rest to happen. He gets a new job. You appoint Megan to take Health as an Interim appointment. Megan announces the waste management deal. You make your decision. Then I make mine. That puts it in order. Sound good to you?"

Cowan now realized that he had to take a risk. If he appointed Megan to the Health slot it would be a signal to the boys upstairs that he could be trusted. On the other hand, if he fired Logan he would be without any insurance that the Big Boys were going to deliver the Federal job. He needed a sign from above. Logan was the sign. If Logan resigned then the game was on. If Logan had to be fired, the deal was screwed.

"Al, I think the best thing to do is wait for Logan. If he finds a job on his own in the next couple of weeks then we can proceed. If I force him to move it seems to me that he will become defensive and create a lot of media interest on his plight. You know, a young married man with a couple of kids put on the bricks by an unfeeling Mayor who puts politics in front of the family. If my Federal job comes up first then when I resign you can advise Logan that he ought to go with me or move to the private sector. You have a right to put your own people in the job. The press will understand. So will Logan. Tell you what I'll do. I'll have a staff meeting with all the Commissioners and confirm that I have looked at a Federal appointment. They know it anyway. I'll remind them that according to the Articles the President of the City Council steps is as the acting Mayor until the Council sets a date for an election. These people are politically savvy and capable of doing their own thing. Could be that I have all their resignations. You want to come to the meeting?"

Siro was shocked at the Mayor's suggestion, "Bob, the press would have a field day with that action. I don't want any part of it. Your first suggestion is right. If Logan can find a job on his own in the next week or so that would be best. I'll pass the word along and see if something comes up. That way the power base has to do its part. Let's do it that way. Speaking of the press how are you going to respond to those vultures when I leave?"

Cowan had what he needed. Siro was his messenger to the inner sanctum. In less than an hour he was certain that somebody way up would recognize that for the deal to move a sign of security was required. The sign was a job for Logan

With a show of conciliation Cowan appeared to agree with Siro. "Al, for the time being, I think we should stick to the routine of City business. No comment about the Washington thing. I know that the President and the Secretary of Labor are only going to acknowledge that I'm being considered for the post. I'll acknowledge the same thing. No decisions have been made and none are expected soon. As for the Council agenda, we can say that we have not completed it. Frankly, I would like to move the Waste Management on Thursday but that depends on what happens relative to our discussion. Let the press hang out for a while."

Council President Alfonse Siro nodded his agreement, shook the Mayor's hand and opened the office door. A wild gang of reporters stormed the door nearly pushing Siro back into the office. He used his bulk to push forward and through the crowd. When asked if he had a statement, he paused long enough to be courteous. His report to the media was that the Mayor had acknowledged the prospect of a Federal appointment. No, they had not discussed succession. Several items of City business were proposed for the Council that were to have some staff analysis. The agenda was not complete. He was sure that the Mayor's secretary would furnish them a copy of the agenda when it was ready. He rendered a salute to the cameras and walked into the corridor. The Mayor had taken the opportunity to close his door and stayed sheltered from the media at least for the time being.

Siro moved quickly to his office in City Hall and waited for the procession of reporters to dissipate. When his secretary signaled that the hall had cleared he asked her to hold all calls. Siro picked up his phone and dialed Charles Patello's direct line. Al Siro and Chuck Patello had met years ago at the Roman Cultural Society. Although they came from different neighborhoods they had maintained contact as each had progressed in their respective careers. Their occupations were different so there was no basis for a business relationship. Social occasions of the Society offered the continuing contact. As Siro moved forward in politics his friends at the Society became major supporters. They met late that night following Kevin Hardly's dinner meeting about the development of an Office for Health Affairs for the Archdiocese. Patello explained his interest in Commissioner Logan as a possible candidate for the job as well as the political advantages to Siro if Megan became the new Commissioner. He also explained that the Voluntary Waste Management Program was the underlying issue. For everyone to benefit it was essential for Mayor Cowan to accept a Federal appointment that was being arranged.

Siro was a quick study. He well understood the issues. He agreed to all facets of the transition including keeping Mr. Megan in line. His report to Patello was positive and he was pleased to give it when Charlie came on the line, "Charlie, this is Al Siro. Just met with the Mayor. He's in good form. As you thought Logan is clean. Bob is using the kid as a decoy. Now here's the way J think he wants things to happen. First thing is that the deal in Washington has got to be right financially. He thinks the Labor Secretary will call him today with good news. Then before he makes any announcement about his leaving, the Logan kid gets another job. I guess he would see Logan getting a new job as a sign of good faith—from whom I don't know. Then he appoints Megan as interim-commissioner before he announces that he is going to DC. Oh yeah, he pushes the button on the waste management thing as soon as Logan resigns. I guess that's about it."

Charles Patello was not usually a religious man, but in his mind he thanked God for the apparent break before responding to Siro. "Thanks, Al. The job at the Archdiocese has to be cleared by the Cardinal. We meet with him tomorrow afternoon. If all goes well, and I think it will, we can make an offer to Logan Tuesday or Wednesday. If the Mayor waves notice Logan can start next week. The Mayor can appoint Megan as soon as Logan resigns. The Waste Management Project could pass the Council on Thursday. Is all this possible? How about Megan? Is he on board?

Again, Siro had good news. "Megan is fine, Charlie. I've been keeping him informed. He knows the Project and is poised to contact Action Waste Management as step one. The soft spots are the Archdiocese and the US Department of Labor. Sounds to me like we are violating the principle of separation of Church and State. Maybe we need a constitutional lawyer."

Patello appreciated the humor. "I hear you, Al. My guess is that the Federal thing will happen as the Mayor believes. I have no idea how the Cardinal will respond. The man is unpredictable. No way that I can get a handle on him."

"Have you tried money, Charlie? I understand he is a sucker for a buck. Let me know if I can help."

Patello hung up the phone. He thought about how much money had been invested in the Church by his various companies since he had hooked up with Hardly and his glorious Knights. It was good business to support the Church even if you couldn't own one. At least he owned Hardly and that meatball, O'Shea. The thought brought him a sudden chill. "Can those clowns put on a convincing act for his Eminence at tomorrow's briefing? My God all this work and influence clear to the Office of the President of the United States could be for naught if Laurel and Hardly did their routine at the Chancery." Somehow, he had to direct that presentation. He called Kevin Hardly and offered to buy him lunch. Hardly accepted. Next, he placed a call to Marone to give him a status report and check on the Federal scene.

Tony Marone was in conference with Mario Capizzi when the secretary forwarded Charlie Patello's call. Patello was on the top priority list in Marone's office. That meant his calls were always put through. Tony's greeting was energized, "Charlie, my man. How you doin? I'm in with Mario now. We're getting ready for a meeting tomorrow on getting into the health business. It looks like Boston is the place to be. You got any action?"

Action was just the word that Patello wanted to hear. He pushed the point back to Marone, "Things are shaping up, Tony, and coming to a head rapidly. The deal with the Union went down without a hitch. Action is being organized as we speak. Muldoon is in the wrapper. Al Siro, President of the City Council and next Mayor is on board. Megan checks out. He belongs to Siro. The Waste Management Project could go by Thursday. But ~ we have two big If's. The first is getting the Cardinal to go along with our scheme for an Office of Health Affairs where we stash Logan and the second is getting the Federal job for the Mayor. I have to deal with the Cardinal but you and your friends have to deliver to the Mayor. You heard anything from Washington?"

Marone turned away from the phone to ask Capizzi if he had a report from Washington. Mario gave an affirmative nod and offered to talk to Patello. Marone handed him the phone. "Yeah Charlie, this is Mario. I had a call Sunday from the Federation. It seems that your good Mayor pissed off the Feds by asking for a deal better than the President. After a little reality check his Honor caught on that he was begging, not choosing so he narrowed his focus. What he really wanted was some dough to get his kids in private schools, a living allowance, and a little slush for moving around. The Feds got the slush in the budget for his office. The other stuff is being taken care of on the QT. He is going to get a call around noon that fills him like he wants. That should do it. He could resign anytime that makes sense. Now Tony and I been talking about what might be needed if we go into the health business. We think that you need a good wrapper on this guy Logan and that top guy at that Catholic hospital, St. Whatever. I'll let Tony explain. You need anything else from me?"

Capizzi's rapid commentary always confused Patello as he tried to follow the point. He wanted to make sure he had a good understanding of what was required, "You've answered my question, Mario. I've got what I need for now. Put Tony on. I need to understand this wrapper for Logan."

There was a pause before Marone answered, "Charlie, Tony. Listen we been thinking that this guy Logan being clean ain't in our best interest. See, your Mayor Cowan is asking for a shelter and Labor wants to give it to him. OK. So that gives the Mayor no collar. He can bolt from the Federal job, go back home and raise hell. That makes you look bad but also puts us at odds with the Federation who we don't want no hassle till we get our end of the health thing. What we think we ought to do is slip a collar on Logan that he doesn't know about but the Mayor does. That way if the Mayor bolts he has to drag Logan. Logan's collar serves evidence that the Mayor played with money. This keeps the Mayor in line. The Federation stays out of it."

Patello's head began to ache as he tried to follow the scheme. "I understand what you want and why you want it, Tony. You need to explain to me how we are going to get it done."

Marone seemed exasperated at Patello's comment. "OK. Try this. We convince the Mayor to free up ten grand to reimburse Logan for campaign expenses. The ten-grand will be donated by us on a special check made out to the Mayor but after the Mayor endorses it we deposit it to a special personal account that you set up for Logan in that bank you control. You tell Logan that the money is a signing bonus from the Catholic guys supporting the Church. He can draw on the account or transfer it to his own. Our accountants can cover it. We end up with a canceled check made out to the Mayor that he endorsed over to Logan's special account. That bit of evidence keeps him in line."

"How do you get Hizzoner to go along with this?" Patello's question was actually an audible thought.

Marone accepted it as if he expected the question. He hardly paused as he rapidly explained, "Logan ain't the only one getting a signing bonus. The Mayor thinks he gets an under the table twenty-thousand-dollar bonus. We show him two checks made out to him for ten-grand each. He endorsees one check and gives it back to us so we can deposit it in a special account that is released to him when he properly completes his term as Under Secretary of Labor. The account will have joint signatures, his and a trustee that we appoint. When he gets to Washington the cards will be there for his signature. We take the endorsed check, altar the endorsement and deposit it in Logan's account. Then we cover the ten-grand from another source. Costs us thirty-grand over all, but that's cheap for a collar. What do you say?"

"Sounds crazy enough to work. How do I figure in?"

Marone was convinced that he had given Patello a good explanation. He slowed his speech to a relaxed tempo. "We'll have a guy deliver the Mayor's endorsed check to you. You see that it gets deposited into Logan's special account. Logan won't need to sign the check for a deposit only but if the Bank looks for it maybe you can have an officer initial it, that way it will go through. You got the bank guys under control?"

Patello was uncomfortable with the plan but decided to let the New York staff worry about it. For now he would do what was being asked of him, "Sure, Tony. We can get it done. The tough part is putting a wrapper on Durant at the hospital. He's innocent but not as much as Logan. Been around a little longer and is more independent. It might take a while to bring him in. I'll work on it."

"Yeah, do that. Keep us posted on the deal with the Cardinal. You doing OK?"

Patello didn't answer Marone's question. He said his good bye and wished them well. The conversation came to a close with Charlie's promise to report on his Tuesday meeting. A glance at his Rolex signaled time to grab a cab for his lunch with Kevin Hardly in the Chairman's Suite at The Hardly Security and Trust Bank. When he arrived, Mr. Hardly's executive assistant ushered him into the private dining room. The dining room was a part of the extensive executive suite that Hardly had built for himself over the years that he directed Hardly Security and Trust Bank. The Chairman's Suite occupied the entire twenty eighth floor of the BSTB Building. The dining room was positioned on the east side with ceiling to floor windows looking out over Logan Airport, Boston Harbor and Massachusetts Bay. Occupants of the room became instantly mesmerized by the view. Hardly had used their loss of concentration on business matters to his and the Bank's benefit on many occasions.

A waitress from the Bank's catering staff was in attendance. She took Mr. Patello's order for ice tea and returned shortly with the beverage. Kevin was on the phone in his private office that adjoined the dining room. The connecting door to his office was wide open giving him a view of the occupants as they arrived. He waved to Charlie indicating that he would join him soon. Charlie acknowledged the wave and turned to enjoy the view of the Boston Harbor. As he turned away from the panoramic view Thomas O'Shea walked into the dining room. He asked the waitress for a glass of white wine, looked coolly at Charlie, and starred out the window.

Patello looked at O'Shea to give a greeting but O'Shea stared out the window seemingly ignoring Charlie. After a few cold minutes, O'Shea spoke but without making eye contact with Patello.

"Charles, Kevin had the decency and courtesy to invite me to this meeting. I cannot understand why you would attempt to exclude me from a briefing about the Archdiocese. I am an officer of the Hospital. Anything you have to say to Kevin you need to say to me as well. Why wasn't I asked to this meeting?"

Charlie was about to unload on Thomas when the waitress returned with the glass of white wine. Another glass was on her tray that Kevin Hardly picked off as he followed her into the dining room. Kevin noticed that the chill in his colleagues' expression matched that of the wine. He decided to take charge. "Gentlemen, good afternoon. A beautiful day. I truly enjoy this view. We ought to be on the water taking a cruise toward the Cape. Better yet—doing eighteen—I've got a three o'clock tee time so we'll have to make this short. Charlie, you suggested that we have this session. Let's order lunch then we can eat and meet. Tom agreed to join us at my request."

The three men sat at the dining table large enough for ten. Kevin instinctively sat at the head of the table. O'Shea moved quickly to his right. Patello waited until the others were seated then sat on Kevin's left. The waitress distributed menus and explained the very special preparations of the day. Hardly made a brief speech about the diet he had started that morning and ordered a cup of clam chowder, to be followed by a chef's salad. O'Shea and Patello both ordered a turkey club sandwich. The waitress took the orders with dispatch to the kitchen.

Kevin's expression turned troubled, "Gentlemen, I received this disturbing letter from the Alleton Club requesting that I appear before the discipline committee to explain my improper conduct on the night we had our dinner meeting. For the life of me I can't figure out what they mean by improper conduct. I thought we were well behaved. This could mean my dismissal or suspension from the Club. I wonder if I should refer this to my attorney. It could be a plot by my lovely cousin to disgrace me. Did either of you get unruly?"

Patello recognized the set up. He guessed that the two experts from the Bank's crack planning department got buzzed and littered up the place after the terrific trinity of Hardly, O'Shea and Patello left. No need to target the young men at this point. They might be needed tomorrow although they would be the last people he would put before the Cardinal.

O'Shea carne to the same conclusion as Patello. He was less tactful in response. "Kevin, my guess is that those nitwits from planning lit up the place after we left. They were both looped to the gills. Thank God we got the report before they passed out. My suggestion is that you plead guilty and throw yourself on the mercy of the court."

Kevin looked as if he was going to cry. The humiliation of appearing before his dreaded cousin on a discipline rap was more than he could tolerate. He starred at O'Shea in disbelief. Patello gave him a reassuring pat on the shoulder. "Well Kevin, we have to admit that we all had quite a bit to drink. The gentlemen from planning were our guests or more properly the guest of Mr. Hardly. Whatever they did as your guest is seen by the Club, I imagine, as an act of the member. I also suspect that the club manager earned a few points from your cousin for turning you in. Let me see if I can be of some help before you go to court so to speak. Can you give me a list of the members who serve on the discipline committee? A list of the board of trustees might also be helpful. I'll have a friend of mine go over the list and see if we can find a friend in court. We can probably put this matter to rest in no time. Our major concern, I suggest, is convincing the Cardinal that the Office of Health Affairs is the way to go."

Kevin Hardly was relieved. He had the same look on his face that he had when he received his passing mark in Ethics back at good old Boston College many years ago, "Charlie I'll have the list in your hands by the time we leave this meeting. I'll appreciate anything you can do. I didn't know who were connected with the Alleton Club. It

"I'm not, Kevin. "Patello did not want to pursue the matter, "But I am connected—that's usually good enough. As for the meeting tomorrow, we need to be explicit, I imagine, about the mission and fiscal benefits of the Office. We have the information that we can provide but my observation is that the Cardinal appreciates a concise to the point recommendation. He is decisive."

The waitress arrived with the food so time was taken to begin its consumption. O'Shea was animated while trying to eat and talk at the same time. "The key to the Cardinal is Dr. Folley. His Eminence will take his advice before any of us. He respects the Doc. Let's give him the ball and let him sell it. He knows health care in Boston. If any of us do the talking the Cardinal will only get confused. I say we let Richard be our spokesman."

Patello felt the sting of O'Shea's whip. O'Shea had maneuvered Folley as the spokesman in order to gain control of the operation. Folley was O'Shea's son in law and blood runs thick in the Irish clan. On the other hand, to oppose the suggestion could be counter-productive to the main objective. If necessary, Patello felt he could force the O'Shea clan out in the future. He wondered how much he should inform his associates about the circumstances surrounding Mr. Logan. Some preliminary information seemed appropriate. While he had mentioned the potential availability of the Commissioner of Health for the City of Boston as the first Director of the Office of Health Affairs for the Archdiocese to Hardly and O'Shea he had not finalized their support for the recommendation. This was the time to get their support.

Artfully, Patello moved the question to O'Shea as a way of gaining acceptance by letting the opposition game the idea, "Gentlemen, an essential part of our recommendation to the Cardinal is the inclusion of competent leadership of the health services within the healing mission. The corporate structure suggested by the Bank's crack planning staff is essential as well as the person who is to head the organization. We must recommend both to the Cardinal. Tom, I recall that Dr. Folley was impressed with the corporate structure. He also supported the idea of a Director for the Office when we had our meeting at the Club. Can you check with him to see that he is comfortable in recommending that same concept tomorrow?"

O'Shea was excited to be put in control by Patello. He jumped at the opportunity, "I can and I will, Charlie. It's too damn bad that Richard wasn't included in this meeting. Why are you trying to be so secretive?"

Patello felt the burn of anger. He was certain that his face was flushed giving away his otherwise controlled emotions. He held back the profanity forcing its way through his mind. There remained more important matters to be resolved. "I apologize for the oversight, Tom. Time is so short that I felt a need to get together with Kevin and review things for tomorrow. It would be presumptive of me to call a meeting of our executive committee. Kevin is the chairman and I very much appreciate his wisdom in asking you to attend. The item that now concerns me the most is the Director's job. As you remember, I agreed to make initial contact with Commissioner Logan to see if he is interested in working for the Archdiocese. 1 am pleased to report to you that he is interested in changing from public life to the private sector. I have not informed him that the opportunity is with the Church but from everything we know about him he would fit well into our organization. He is a very active Catholic. You are also aware that the Mayor is considering a post in Washington. This makes Logan very available. We should make him an offer this week if the Cardinal buys into the Office idea."

Kevin Hardly listened to the exchange between his two friends. The subtle animosity between them was lost on Kevin who believed that he never had an enemy other than his cousin. Conflict was something that a gentleman of means delegated to staff. He was still somewhat preoccupied with the letter from the Alleton Club but forced some concentration on the discussion. He especially heard Patello's comment that Logan was an active Catholic. That gave cause for his reply. "Gentlemen, we definitely need a good Catholic in the job. Mr. Logan should also be a Knight. I'll recommend him. We can have him installed at the next Knights of the Holy Cross Installation in October. It's on the Cardinal's calendar. We'll need to have him complete the application and get the recommendation of his Pastor. Do you know if he belongs to Malta or the KC's. I'll check on it. I'm sure the Cardinal will go along."

O'Shea was amazed. He sat with his mouth wide open staring at his boss. There was no room for discussion. Hardly, in his usual fog, had accepted Logan as a part of the Archdiocesan team. There was no need to look at Patello. O'Shea could feel the joyful vibration of the big wop. Well, bring in Logan and see if Folley can drop him out.

O'Shea maneuvered for some room, "Kevin, we agreed earlier that Dr. Folley was our spokesman. We have now apparently agreed that Mr. Logan will direct the Office for the Archdiocese. All of this is contingent on the Cardinal's decision. I will call Richard immediately after this meeting and inform him of our discussion. Is there anything else he should be told?"

Patello reached into his coat pocket and produced an envelope addressed to Hardly. He opened it pulled out two copies of a resume. "Tom, I have copies of Michael Logan's resume for each of you. You might want to fax a copy to Dr. Folley. I think you will be favorably impressed with his background. He will work well with Mr. Durant, Dr. Folley, and the other Catholic hospital administrators in the Archdiocese. When and if the Cardinal accepts our recommendation, we need to make immediate contact with Logan. Salary, fringes, and perks should be decided now or no later than tomorrow."

The rush to conclude on Logan's selection was not to O'Shea's liking. He again attempted to stall. "Kevin, Charlie, I feel that we are going too far at this time. We don't know how the Cardinal is going to react. I want time to review this resume. I'm sure Richard will feel the same way. We have time after tomorrow's session to conclude the details of Mr. Logan's employment"

Kevin Hardly was leaning toward the position of his Executive Vice President because he wanted to conclude the meeting and take a pea before dealing with the more important matter of the problem at the Alleton Club. By agreeing with O'Shea, he thought the meeting would end quicker, "Charlie, I think Tom is right. Let's wait until tomorrow to deal with Mr. Logan. I'm sure Tom has to get back to work. I need to get you the list of people from the Alleton Club so you can deal with my little problem. Let's call it quits for now."

The session adjourned with little more being said. Patello was led by Hardly to the desk of his executive assistant who handed Patello a copy of the Alleton Club Year book containing a list of the Board of Directors and the various committee members. Hardly made a quick run to the Men's Room. All the members in good standing were listed alphabetically on following pages. Charlie counted twenty-three Hardly names and wondered if there would be one less when the book was reprinted. When he returned to his office he telephoned Philip Mondi at Patriot Transportation and Courier Service. He explained to his good friend that he wanted to cross check the Alleton elite with the special service customer list of Patriot Transport. He also explained the purpose of the analysis. Mondi was very cooperative. He sent a Courier to pick up the membership lists and return it immediately to his attention.

Hardly and O'Shea's refusal to consider salary and benefits for Logan worried Patello. Time was short to demonstrate to the Mayor that the Washington appointment was secure. If the Cardinal didn't go along with the deal or if he even delayed a decision the whole basket of fruit could spoil which included the prize plum—waste management. He desperately needed a fallback position. The more he pondered the situation the more he became convinced that he was locked in. The deal with Logan was a must. If that "goddamn O'Shea" screwed around with Logan's appointment he would put in a hit order. No. That would only make things worse by drawing a big investigation perhaps closing all Uncle Frank's business ventures in New England. He needed to be patient. Maybe work for time on the other end. He thought about convincing the people in Washington through NAI that they should stall the Mayor for another week or so. That probably wouldn't fly. The NAI and the Federation were working out the health deal this week. A delay didn't figure in. He remembered Bishop Hanks advising the Terrific Trinity that the Church saw time in centuries while business measured time in minutes. The decision-making processes of the Church and of business were basically incompatible. Yet, the Church seemed to be holding all the marbles. Maybe he was in the wrong racket. His mother wanted him to go to the seminary. Instead he took Uncle Frank's advice and went to Boston College. The Jesuits taught him that time was the essence of imperfection. At the moment, their wisdom seemed to be the essence of perfection. What logic could be applied for solution?

Patello sat at his desk with his hands holding his head as if more in pain than in thought. The ring on his private line brought him out of his meditation. Phil Mondi was calling to report on the Alleton Club analysis. As Patello had thought, six board members were special service customers of Patriot. Of the six, two served on the Discipline Committee. Another committee member's spouse had used Patriot for special parties at their Cape Cod estate. The spouse was a particular client who had become well acquainted with a gentleman named Eddie in the Accounts section of Special Services. At Mondi's request Eddie had placed a call to the lady asking that the matter regarding Mr. Hardly be resolved without further consideration. The spouse in turn had a conversation with her husband. She reported back to Eddie that apparently, the whole matter was a misunderstanding. Mr. Hardly would be receiving a letter by Patriot courier this afternoon apologizing for the unfortunate mistake. Case closed. Now if the Church could be just as expedient.

Patello was about to return to his deep concentration when his secretary announced that a Mr. Muldoon was holding on line one. Great. Muldoon was hardly what was needed at the moment. Obviously, the goon wanted answers that Patello didn't have. He advised his secretary that he was on another call and would return Mr. Muldoon's call later. That didn't work. The secretary came back on the intercom and reported that Mr. Muldoon insisted on being put through. His call was urgent. He insisted that Mr. Patello take his call. If necessary he would hold until Patello completed his other call.

Patello conceded and answered the phone. "Robert, my cheery little man, what pray tell is of such urgency that you demand my attention. You know I'm a very busy executive."

Muldoon chuckled at Patello's frustration. "Ah Charlie you need to be busy with all you've got to do. We have it goin' now my friend but we need to get hizzoner to Washington soon. Do you know what might be slowing things down? We have Action Waste organized as I'm sure you know. Mr. Meehan and I would like to begin selling waste management agreements to the hospitals. Time is money—perhaps you didn't know. I have it on good authority that the big boys are in New York resolving the little matters while we tend to the world's problems. What can you tell me?"

Patello really needed to hear that time is money crap. Good or Muldoon was having a ball rubbing his nose in it. He obviously figured out that the Church was the delay. He just wanted to hear Patello admit that there was a force in the world that he couldn't control.

"Bob, we have to wait for the Cardinal to open up the job for Logan. Then the Mayor moves Megan in. When that's done Mr. Cowan goes to Washington and we go to work. It should all fall in place before the weekend. You see things any differently?"

"No different, Charlie," replied an apparently relaxed Muldoon, "I'm scheduled to meet Dave Donovan with 936 this afternoon. He is going to introduce me to the Shop Steward at Action. I wanted to make sure that things were progressing according to plan so I wouldn't have to tell the new guy to pull Action's troops out on the bricks. Keep me posted."

Patello placed the phone on the hook and nursed his anger. After a few deep breaths, he transitioned to frustration. He wondered if Muldoon knew that the Marquart kid was well wrapped by the syndicate. Certainty he knew that he was wrapped by Action. That was the deal. He guessed that Muldoon suspected that Marquart was a syndicate plant and was making initial reconnaissance to determine the depth of Marquart's connection. He would learn little or nothing from his meeting with Marquart. The kid had no idea that he was a lynch pin in the operation.

oOo

Jay Marquart was elated with his new status as Shop Steward for the Action Waste Management Bargaining Unit of Local 936. Donovan had promised to teach him all he needed to know about his duties. He had even offered to buy him a few beers after work. Some big wig from the Workers' Guild was going to join them and press the flesh. He thought about pushing his luck and asking buddy/boss Ryan for an early out so he could meet Donovan. Then again Jay didn't need a repeat of last Friday. On second thought, he would work the full shift. He would hold back on pulling rank for the time being.

Donovan had invited Jay to meet him at Stinger's Tavern in Dorchester between five and five thirty. Jay knew he wouldn't get there until after five thirty since he had to cross the entire City in rush hour traffic. Donovan could wait. From the looks of him he had spent a few hours in a bar before so he wouldn't feel out of place. The other stiff would probably knock down a few extras as well. Jay called Susan and reported his new status. He also advised her that his new duties required him to attend a special training session with the Union leadership this evening so don't hold dinner.

Susan recognized the ploy and reminded him of his delicate condition resulting from the weekend binge just ended. She also told him that Brian had called and desperately needed to make contact. Cecile had also called and left a message on the answering machine. She asked that Jay call her at home this evening to discuss a very important matter. Jay completed his conversation with Susan. He immediately dialed the page operator at Patriot requesting that Brian contact him at Action Waste Management.

It took a half hour for Brian to answer Jay's page. He apologized to Jay for the delay in response. Brian was excited over his new assignment as a special assistant to Eddie. He wanted Jay to know that Eddie had chosen Brian to do special courier jobs to elite clients. This meant that he was no longer a truck driver. He was expected to wear a shirt and tie since he was going to be delivering to lawyers, bankers, doctors and all kinds of important people =He had made his first run this afternoon to some rich broad who took the delivery and gave him a letter that he took to the chairman of Hardly Security and Trust. Eddie wasn't the monster that Brian thought he was. The topper was that he was driving a four-door sedan instead of a van. He felt like celebrating and wanted Jay to join him for a few after work.

Jay tried to invade Brian's excitement with his own exuberance but to no avail. He agreed to join Brian after work if Brian would agree to meet him at Stinger's in Dorchester. Brian offered the opinion that thirty at the Waltham Tap and Keg where they had held court for years. No sense changing a good thing. As Jay hung up the phone he made a mental note to return Cecile's call between the evening's sessions. Hopefully the "bitch" wouldn't screw up the celebrating. The clock on the wall registered four forty-five which meant that boss buddy was out the door. Jay straightened out his cluttered desk containing grant applications pending review and headed for the door. He was now on a mission for God's own union.

Jay found Stinger's Tavern at about five forty-five across the street from the Boston Workers' Guild building. He parked his jeep in the Guild parking lot figuring that it had to be the safest place in the neighborhood. His buddy Donovan was standing at the bar when Jay arrived. Donovan saw Jay as he came in. He moved away to meet Jay in the middle of the bar and escorted him to a table in the rear. He then introduced Jay to a grumpy old fart named Muldoon. Muldoon remained seated and simply nodded to Jay. Jay recalled that Muldoon had opened proceedings at the Union meeting that morning. He obviously was a member of the Union hierarchy. As a gesture of respect Jay slid into the chair next to Donovan.

Muldoon ordered a round of his favorite Sam Adams beer for the three of them and began the conversation. "I hope you like Sam Adams, son. If you don't you better learn to like it because it's Boston beer and it's Union beer. Union is solidarity. We support those who support us. You know what I mean? All union members are your brothers and sisters, not just your buddies at Action, I mean every working son of a bitch who holds a card. You been chosen to represent the members at Action in 936 but also to become a member of the team that carries the ball for every Local in this area. Donovan and I expect big things from you. You up to it?"

If it was confidence that Muldoon was looking for, Jay had plenty of it. He put a fist on the table as emphasis for his reply, "Sure, I'm up to it. I told Mr. Donovan that when we met this afternoon. But this thing came on all of a sudden. You are going to have to explain a hell of a lot to me if I'm going to do what is expected. I don't know diddly squat about this Union stuff. How in the hell did I get this Job? Was I really selected by the troops or did someone finger me? You gotta know, I been drinking Sam Adams since I was sixteen. Drinking beer is something I know a lot about."

Muldoon put his hand over Jay's clenched fist as if to imply that Jay was subordinate to the Guild. "For now, all you got to know is that you are the Shop Steward. Donovan will see that you get the right information and experience. You just check with him every time you get a question. Eventually you will be able to figure things out for yourself.

We have training sessions on Saturdays and some evenings for the Shop Stewards. You'll attend those and learn more. Donovan will get you the right invitations."

Jay felt his familiar serge of anger. "Christ! Saturdays and evenings—what a lot of bullshit," he thought. Nothing was going to screw up his weekends, not Donovan, not Muldoon or any other mother's son in or out of the union. Weekends are sacred. He'll explain that to them later. For this meeting, the less said from him the better. Jay decided to let Muldoon have the floor.

Muldoon had already decided to take it. "Jay, what we want to do here now is begin to get to know one another. You from around here? Your Dad carry a card? Gimme a little life history. Maybe we got something in common. Let's have another beer."

Muldoon waved his empty bottle at the window to the bar. The bartender immediately responded with three brews. Jay thanked Muldoon and proceeded with his life history beginning with his first job out of high school at St. Anslem's, his marriage, college, Kristie, divorce, remarried to Susan, her family, State work and then to Action. He tactfully omitted mentioning his spare time activities with the Democratic Party and muling for party bosses.

Muldoon listened carefully and then carefully interrupted Jay, "You know, Jay, I kinda feel that you are holding something back. Were you ever active in politics say as a party worker or something like that? People who have a natural political side are usually the type that rise to the top in the Union. You seem to me to be the political type. You like politics? Ever hear of a guy named Patello?"

Jay felt the hook. He suddenly recalled Ken's comment about running junk for the mob. Now this Union chief starts with the "who do you know" games. He wondered if he should lie. Better not. This guy probably knows the answer or maybe he knows a little and wants to know a lot more. Best tact is to try to circle around the question. Lie just enough to get off the hook was his thought as he answered. "Well there was a time right after I graduated from UMass that I thought I would try to use what they taught me in political science. I was a poli-sci major. Anyway, I did some volunteer work for the Democrats. Couldn't eat it so I quit."

The answer wasn't enough for Muldoon. He pressed for more, "How'd you get with the State? Charlie Patello arrange it?'

Jay was uncertain if he was being set up, "Who? Charlie Patello. I guess I might have met him but I don't know if he helped me get with the State. I asked the Party for a recommendation that they gave but I don't think Mr. Patello was involved. At least I'm not aware that he was."

Again, Muldoon pushed for information, "How'd you get the job with Action? You friendly with Meehan"

Jay felt certain that Muldoon knew everything but Jay remained determined to force Muldoon to tell what he knew before Jay spilled his guts. "That's the second time I heard that in the last four days. I don't think Mr. Meehan knows who I am. I got the job at Action on my own. Applied from a notice on the State bulletin board. They liked my background and that was it. Why you want to know all this?"

It seemed as if Muldoon was beginning to back down at least for the moment. "Just trying to get acquainted, Jay. We like to know if we are working with a working stiff or a wimp from the back office. Which one are you? Take it from me, Meehan knows who you are. He might try to compromise you with goodies and special favors. You tough enough to resist?"

"Hell, Mr. Muldoon, just let him try to buy me. He'll get the surprise of his rich life." Jay swung his other fist as an emphasis of his tough hide.

Muldoon now seemed satisfied. He explained that he had another meeting across town, excused himself, shook Jay's hand and left. As he passed the bar he ordered another round for Jay and Donovan. The bartender delivered the beer and explained to Donovan that Mr. Muldoon had paid the tab. Donovan exchanged small talk with Jay as they drank the final round. Little was said about the conversation with Muldoon except the opinion offered by Donovan that he thought Muldoon liked Jay. Donovan finished his beer in a gulp and said good-bye to Jay, offering that he had to get with the family. He promised to call Jay in the next day or so to fill him in on the contract negotiations with Action.

Jay sat by himself and relaxed. He nursed the remainder of his Sam Adams while pondering the exchange with Muldoon. The guy was about as subtle as an atomic missile. He might just as well have said that he thought Jay was a management shill. In his mind, Jay reasoned,

"Well, what the hell, if that's what he thinks then there's no reason to disappoint him."

Jay left Stinger's in plenty of time to make his appointment with friend Brian. The trip across the City was miserable. Traffic was backed up on Interstate 93 inbound and jammed on the Mass Pike outbound. Somehow Jay didn't seem to care. He wore a nice glow from the three beers. The world still appeared to be his oyster. Gradually he steered to the Waltham Tap and Keg. Brian was perched on his favorite stool holding a few beer-leads on his buddy.

As Jay pulled alongside, Brian already had one perched for him. This was Brian's night to howl. The moon was full and Brian was half the same. Jay slapped his buddy on the back and gulped down the offered beer. He quickly ordered up another for Brian and himself. The code of celebrant drinkers required a reciprocal round before conversing. This time they touched bottles in mutual salute before guzzling the brine.

Their consumption rate slowed as they began the next round. Eventually conversation about the day entered the agenda. Jay fired the first volley, "Brian, you son of a bitch, what is this about you sticking your head up Eddie's ass? You tuning in on the big time?"

Brian had to swallow fast to respond. He almost choked, "No, man. It came out of the blue. I didn't know anything and he comes up and says they taking me off the route. I figure I'm canned. What the hell I wanted to quit anyway. So, Eddie sits me down and says how he needs an experienced field hand to run special orders for high rollers. The swells don't like to have a truck deliver their nose candy. Guess it makes the neighbors think they got a hefty stash. They gimme a Chevy with a tape player and everything. I'm on call around the clock though. Got this damn pager hanging on me all the time. Can you believe this shit."

Jay just smiled, "You get to keep the tips, Brian?"

"No way. I'm not supposed to accept any money." Brian seemed to assume an almost religious sincerity, "I only deliver. The collection is made by a bag man some other way. I never see the guy. That way if I get busted they can only nail me for possession not for dealing. It's an easier rap. Hell, I don't know what I'm delivering. I can only guess. None of the packages look alike and they sure as hell don't have labels. The dudes sign for it like anything else. Special courier that's me. Got a raise too. You ready for another?"

Another beer was produced by the hefty bartender. J on found the barstool difficult to his seating. They moved to a remaining open booth that proved more comfortable and conducive to conversation. The Waltham Tap and Keg was beginning to get crowded. Most of the booths were filled, people standing at the bar were two deep, the pool tables in the rear were occupied and the blaring music from the corner jukebox saturated the place with Country and Western music. Conversation was difficult and required a shout to be heard. Jay played with the napkin dispenser while Brian continued to ramble in a very loud voice about his new career opportunity. No matter how hard Jay tried he could not insert his own news about his appointment as a shop steward. He was becoming bored with the celebration. It seemed time to quit. He had a nice buzz. Brian was repeating himself for the fourth or fifth time. "Maybe one more round and we split." thought Jay.

He was about to suggest this to Brian when Brian's pager let out a shrill high pitch beep that gained the attention of the assembled faithful. Brian struggled to find the device clipped on his belt. When he finally located it, he could not find the page button. Eventually, he overcame the miracle of technology and noted the paging phone number on the small LED. With no small amount of pride Brian excused himself to answer the summons.

"Hell," Jay thought, "they ought to give him a cellular phone to go with the job. That would make things easier and really boost Brian's ego." He decided to mention it to Brian on his return.

It seemed like only a minute or two when Brian came back to the booth looking excited. "Jay, I got to make a run. You wanna go along? I could use your help."

Jay was now more than a little drunk. He thought the request from Brian was ridiculous. "You need my help? Shit, you delivering a ton of stash or something? How heavy can that stuff be? I never had any trouble lifting mine. Why you want me along?"

The sarcasm went over Bian's head, "Well, I gotta admit to being a little scared about this new deal. I mean it happened too sudden. One day Eddie was going to fry my ass and the next thing I'm his man. He could be setting me up. I gotta be careful for a while till I get used to this action. You know, man."

"What I know is that you're still a paranoid." Jay remembered the crying jag that Brian had on the last fishing trip. "Eddie try to sell you any more insurance for the new job? Shit, Brian you can't run scared all the time. Where we goin' and what do you want me to do?"

Brian assumed an important air and sat back in the booth to detail a reply, "Well I got to go over to the dispatcher at Patriot and pick up the load. Then I carry it to the fruit bowl down town. You take your car home and I'll pick you up on my way to town. It's eight thirty now. We can be back at your place by midnight."

Jay was amused at Brian, the executive. He leaned across the table and poked Brian in the chest to give emphasis, "You bet your ass I'll be home by midnight. I got a big day tomorrow. We got a Union at Action and I'm the Shop Steward. We're into contract talks. How about that? What's the fruit bowl? Never heard of it."

Now it was Brain's turn to lean back, "Jay, I been holding a union card since I joined Patriot. It don't hurt a thing, man. Don't worry about it. The fruit bowl is that queer bar down on Harrison. I think the name of the joint is the Troubadour or something like that. Anyway, what I want you to do is cover my ass so to speak."

"Sick, Brian. That is really sick. Man, you need a vacation."

If Brian realized Jay's implication, he gave it little credence, "No, man. I don't mean that. What I mean is that I want you to go in first and just look around. Order a beer and case the joint. You see something that you don't think is natural give me the high sign and we split. I tell the dispatcher that I think I had a hot LZ. It's SOP. We don't always deliver on the first try. The customer got to secure the zone or we don't come in. Eddie explains all that when the order is made."

Jay was still amused at the nature of the task. He continued to bait his friend, "Brian, when I go into that fruit bowl, I ain't gonna see anything that I think is natural. What the hell am I supposed to see that tells me we got to split? You're puttin' the wrong man on point, buddy."

Brian finally got the point but decided to ignore it. Instead he tried to flatter his friend into cooperating. "Jay, if there's one man on earth that's an expert on saloons and stash it's you. You done more pick-ups in this town than anybody. You been buying stash since junior high. You know what to look for. Just go in there like you was the deal and I'm the dealer. You think it's right give me the nod. Then I go to my contact. The dispatcher will tell me who to look for. They know I'm coming but they don't expect me to have a point man. You stay clear. If the deal gets busted you stand aside and walk away. Don't get involved. If there's a bust Eddie will get me clear. Patriot only runs a delivery service and they don't deal is the way that they explain it to the law. That's somebody else that I never see or know anything about. You know I could be delivering' a box of candy to some guy's sweetheart."

"Sick, Brian, really sick." Jay's response was again lost on Brian.

Jay and Brian divided the tab, waved goodnight to their friendly bartender, and processed to the dingy parking lot behind the bar. Brian insisted on giving Jay a tour of his assigned Caprice Classic with tape player and a Patriot Courier Service sign on the front doors. Jay complemented Brian on his new found status.

In his semi-inebriated condition, Jay drove home carefully. The boys were in process of preparing for bed. He supervised the baths while Susan warmed his dinner. Jay explained to her that he was going to help Brian with a job that would have him home by midnight. Susan didn't ask about the job but knew well that her hero was sticking his neck out for a friend. This was a prominent feature of Jay's personality that she both admired and feared.

Jay fixed a couple of gin and grapefruits that they consumed while waiting for Brian to arrive. A horn from the driveway announced the beginning of the mission. Jay hugged the kids, kissed Susan and left. On his way out the door Susan reminded him to call Cecile.

Jay's stomach ached from the hastily consumed meal, two gin and grapefruits, and the anxiety of having to call the "bitch." "Damn. What was her problem?" He suspected that she wanted to hassle him about the hospital thing on Saturday. "That's none of her business." he thought. "If she suspected an overdose so what. The record was secure." He wondered if she found a judge who could make him tell the cause of his hospitalization. The pain in his stomach and chest seemed to be progressing. He tried to ignore the pain and concentrate on Cecile, "Got to call Martha in the morning and ask her about this medical record thing. She is going to he really pissed when she learns about the hospital trip."

Brian took notice of Jay's pained expression. "What's the matter, man? You look like you got a fart caught sideways. See that package on the back seat. That's it. Looks like it might be a box of candy. What's inside is none of my business, man. I'm just the special courier delivering' a late-night order. How you feeling?"

Jay was doubled over in the front seat but tried to answer, "Like shit. My guts are killing me. Maybe we ought to open the box and help ourselves to some of that candy. You game for that?"

Messing with a delivery package was against the code and Brian was not about to violate the code. "Yeah, sure. We just tell the customer that it was our favorite kind so we helped ourselves to a small bite. Oh man, Eddie would chomp us up."

It took about fifteen minutes in late night traffic to drive from Waltham to the center of Boston. Brian took another fifteen minutes to locate the Troubadour Night Club. He pulled into a loading zone in front of the building next to the Club. They could see in the front door that the place was crowded.

Brian took charge of the operation. "Jay, it looks like there's an open spot at the end of the bar. I can see it from here. You go in, sit there, and order a drink. If things look OK then turn around on the barstool and look out the door. When you turn around that's my signal to come in. You just sit there and finish your drink. Wait until I leave then follow me out after a while. They might spot you coming out but then it don't mean nothing. Main thing is that you got to act natural like you belong there."

"Shit, Brian. Acting natural and looking like I belong there is a contradiction" Jay had his pain under control for the moment and was back at jabbing Brian, "I gotta tell ya if one of those freaks puts his hand on my knee we are going to have combat. Who you looking for?"

Brian reached into the back seat and brought the package into his hands. "Best you don't know. Otherwise you might look right at them and blow the cover. You do a general check and give me the sign. Oh yeah, if the place looks hot you keep looking forward, finish your drink and leave. I turn back to Patriot with a customer not found report. Eddie knows that means a hot LZ. Sometimes when that happens I make a second run."

"You make a second pass on this deal, you making it alone. I signed on for a single trip." Jay gave an emphatic point with his finger as he started to leave. He opened the car door and strolled to the Club. A bouncer stood outside smoking a cigarette. He gave Jay a quick once over as Jay opened the door and stepped in. Otherwise, Jay felt that he was generally unnoticed. He took the seat at the end of the bar as planned. From his vantage point he could see most of the customers. Surprisingly a number of women were present. Conversation was animated. People were having a good time. Whatever bizarre behavior Jay expected was not evident. The place seemed like a lively singles bar. He became comfortable. Eventually the busy bartender managed to ask him for an order. Jay asked for his usual gin and grapefruit. The bartender nodded. Jay noticed effeminate characteristics but without offense. He felt that he was in a nice place.

As the bartender was making his drink Jay, on impulse, spun around on his barstool. Just as he completed his one hundred eighty degree turn he realized with horror that he had accidentally given the all clear signal to Brian who was already out of the car and walking to the Club entrance with package in hand. It was in God's hands now.

Jay turned to his left and spun his stool back to the bar just as the bartender placed a drink in front of him. He tried to sip the drink but his hand was shaking uncontrollably. He then turned to his right to place his elbows on the bar. Brian had approached two men sitting in a booth. They apparently invited Brian to sit down. As he slid into the booth he placed the package in front of the larger man.

After a few deep breaths, Jay raised his eyes to give the crowd the visual check that he had failed to do before giving Brian the all clear. He suddenly had strong eye contact with a giant of a man that looked like Rock Hudson. The man was staring at Jay with a very serious look. As Jay returned the stare the man slowly turned his head in the direction of the booth where Brian was sitting with his new customers. Rock glanced back at Jay and walked over to the booth. With a start, Jay recognized the Rock Hudson look alike. It was Officer Michael O'Sullivan of the Boston PD presently married to one Cecile O'Sullivan RN. Jay was amazed at the realization, "Cecile's old man was hanging out in a queer bar. Holy shit! The guys a cop!" He made Jay with Brian. "It's a bust—a fuckin bust." The pain in Jay's stomach made him double over. He spilled his drink. The bartender came to Jay's aid and asked if he could be of some assistance. Jay thanked the man, paid for the drink, and tried to leave but he could barely manage to walk.

The pain brought tears to Jay's eyes. He was beginning to pray for an arrest so he could ask for medical care. He even thought about surrendering to O'Sullivan on the spot when the image of Krisitie came to mind. This is what the "bitch" needed to knock him out of custody. The combination of love for Kristie and hate for Cecile overcame the pain for the moment. He regained his composure. A glance at the booth where Brian was seated revealed the two customers, Brian, and O'Sullivan engaged in friendly humorous conversation. There was no bust. "What the hell was going on?" surged in his mind. He didn't wait to find out. Carefully he maneuvered out the door to the Chevy. Brian in his usual careless manner had failed to lock the doors. Jay slumped into the front seat. The pain had returned.

Brian came out to the car a few minutes after Jay. He got behind the wheel and started the engine. Brian happily chirped at his buddy. "Hey, thanks for your help, Jay. Those were a couple nice guys. That other guy must have been a user. They invited me to party with 'em. Told him I had a few other runs to make. Can you imagine that? They want me to take a few sniffs. They acted like I know what's in there. I act like I maybe know. Anyway, they gonna' ask for me special from now on. How you doin?"

Jay didn't want to talk but he managed to answer, "Hurtin bad, Brian. I got to get home. Man, I never want to see another drop of booze. Can you hurry up?"

In addition to the pain Jay was very anxious about being identified by Officer O'Sullivan as part of the delivery. Legally it didn't mean much. He could testily in Cecile's behalf at a custody hearing. Maybe he was under cover. Jay had reasoned an explanation. "Yeah that's it. He was under cover. He's going for something else. Maybe he's on to Patriot and the whole ring. Maybe he's trying to bust his queer buddies for possession. Hell, they might already be in the slammer. No good. He busts the users and they finger Brian who fingers him. Cecile wins. So how do I tip off Brian? Do I tip off Brian and he goes to Eddie for insurance? Eddie figures how I'm linked in and comes after me. I lose. Hell, there has to be a way out of this mess. Right now, I'm cornered. Maybe I'll die. Case closed. Yeah that's it. Maybe I'll die. Brian? How does Brian work in? Those guys got his name. They going to ask for him special. Why? Oh yeah! They are setting him up. I bet all three of those dudes were cops. Brian is their way into the Patriot racket. They get Brian on the hook and use him as a backward mule. That's not too bad if nobody gets killed in the process. Patriot goes down but Brian cops out. Man, got to get clear from the whole mess before it falls on me. Jesus how do I get clear?"

Brian pulled into Jay's driveway just after midnight. Jay managed to get inside and sat in the living room. Susan was sound asleep. She was unaware of Jay's misery or anxiety. She found him asleep in the chair at seven the next morning. The pain was still with him but he decided to go to work. His new status demanded the extra sacrifice of attendance.

At eight fifteen he shuffled past Ken Ryan's desk and slumped in his chair. Roughly, Jay figured he had three hours of restless sleep. The rest of the night had been constant sharp pains followed by anxiety attacks and visions of Cecile gloating over a court victory. Ken approached Jay's desk with a new work schedule for the Boston project. Jay was convulsing. He was incoherent. The company nurse responded to Ken's call. She took Jay's vital signs, asked him a few questions that he was now able to answer. She concluded that Jay was suffering from the DT's.

Ken realized that a 911 call would put Jay in the public record. He instead took the chance that Jay was not in a life-threatening condition. A few months prior Action had signed a corporate health contract with St. Anslem's that contained among many things an Employee Assistance Program for individuals suspected or known to be substance abusers. With the assistance of Action's EAP director, the health nurse, Ken, and a cast of thousands Jay was placed in the Company van and driven to St. Anslem's where he was introduced to SACAP or in the complete text, St. Anslem's Chemical Addiction Program.

Jay was placed in a regular hospital room and bed. Doctors and nurses hovered around him taking vital signs, asking him questions, and taking the mandatory blood and urine samples. He signed a treatment consent form that Ken suggested was appropriate if he was to be treated for his convulsions and pain. The form specified emergency treatment for detoxification and overdose. Jay noted the words but was in no condition to object. After a time, a nurse brought Jay some liquid medication that he took without question. Within a half hour he stopped shaking and the pain was less intense. He felt weak. The rebound that he experienced on Sunday at Waltham Hospital was not happening this time. He knew he was a sick cookie. Nailed. Tears came to his eyes as he drifted into a peaceful sleep.

Several hours later he woke soaked in sweat. The bed linen was more off the bed than on, displaying the significant restlessness of which he had been completely unaware. He felt totally fatigued and very weak. His throat was dry. An attempt to speak resulted in a burning sensation in his chest that seemed to consume what little breath he had in his lungs. As his eyes gained focus he became aware that no one else was in the room. Panic overcame fatigue as he attempted to get out of bed. His legs collapsed under him as he touched the floor. He fell on the terrazzo floor, unconscious.

An eternity later he opened his eyes. He was back in the same bed but with clean linens. The room was dark except for a small night light that seemed to be in the distance. The window offered no light causing Jay to realize that the day had passed. An intravenous pole and stand was adjacent to the bed. Jay looked up at the bottle and visually traced the line to his left arm. This time he did not panic. He recalled that somewhere within reach was a nurse call button. Find the button and a human being would appear. Unless—unless he was dead and experiencing the transfer to the life hereafter. Again panic. "Horseshit. No angel is going to hook up an IV. Where's that damn button?" He found it clipped to the linen just below his shoulder on the left side, somewhat out of range, causing him to reach across his body with his right hand. He made a mental note to explain to the nurse about the proper position of the call button as he gave it a push.

After a few minutes, a nursing assistant came into the room. She was very pleasant and seemed quite pleased with Jay's return to a rational state. It was a few minutes after ten. She explained that Jay had been in the detox mode for nearly fourteen hours. Susan had been with him most of the time but had gone home to care for the kids. They would continue to take his vital signs throughout the night. In the morning, a physician would explain his physical condition and a counselor assigned to him would explain the course of rehabilitation. He had fought most of the afternoon but eventually came to rest. The IV was to deal with dehydration. It probably would be discontinued in the morning. The doctor wanted it to continue through the night. If he was hungry or thirsty she could get him something. The nurse was busy with a new admit but would drop in to check on him when she was free. "Any questions?"

Jay listened to the nursing assistant with amazement. He didn't remember anything about the day. He recalled going to work and the night before at the Troubadour. He had no recollection how he got to St. Anslem's. To be sure, he asked the nursing assistant if he was in fact at St. Anslem's. She explained that he was in the SACAP Unit. He vaguely recalled that the Unit began about the time that he left St. A's. He also recalled that the doctor at Waltham had recommended the St. Anslem's program. Well, he certainly took his advice. He asked if he could call Susan. There were no telephones in SACAP rooms but phones for patient use were available at the nursing station. Jay was asked to wait until morning to place his call unless it was an emergency. He agreed to be patient and give Susan a call in the morning.

CHAPTER SEVEN

As Tuesday began with pain for John Marquart, it began with anxiety for Charles Patello. After a restless night, Charlie got out of bed at five AM. By the time he had showered and dressed it was five forty five. He decided against his usual juice and coffee opting instead to drive to his office arriving an hour and a half ahead of his routine schedule. He had not heard from his so- called buddy, Thomas O'Shea, since their meeting the day before so he had no idea if the good Doctor Folley was on board and willing to promote Logan to the Cardinal as the Director of the Archdiocesan Office for Health Affairs. The meeting with the Cardinal was scheduled to begin sometime after three thirty that afternoon. Patello wondered if he would develop a bleeding ulcer between now and then. He wandered aimlessly around the empty office until his stomach directed him to the all-night coffee shop across the street where he devoured two cream filled doughnuts, a large orange juice, and black coffee. Slowly his anxiety transitioned to the indigestion that was more his style. The chatter in the coffee shop diverted him from the thoughts of the pending meeting with the Cardinal. He allowed himself the pleasure of pondering the favor of the young waitress as a further diversion while he consumed three more cups of black coffee. Finally, at half past eight he paid the check and walked to his office. The caffeine had him wired for action.

Things were already happening at One Park Avenue in Manhattan. Mario Capizzi, President of National Associated Investors arrived at his office at six to prepare for the Board of Directors meeting scheduled for eight AM. His number one assistant, Anthony Marone, arrived a half hour later. The two executives carefully examined the Board members' information packets that had been place on the board room table the day before. Everything seemed to be in good order for the critical presentation on the prospect of NAI entering the business of health care. Slide projector, screen, podium, amplifier, tape recorder, television with VCR, and note pads were strategically placed to capture the details of presentation and discussion. At seven AM the executive assistant to Mr. Capizzi arrived and began to double check the arrangements. A few minutes later Mr. Marone's executive assistant arrived and began a test of the technical recording devices. The Caterer arrived at seven thirty to prepare the continental breakfast consisting of fruit, Danish, yogurt, nut bread, sweet rolls, bagels, jams, jellies, a variety of juices, tea, soft drinks, and caffeinated and decaffeinated coffee. The mammoth board room was immaculate. The plush chairs were positioned at the table. The executives, satisfied that all was in readiness, relaxed with a cup of coffee. The executive assistants moved to the outer reception area in order to greet the in-coming members.

As the caterer was arranging the nourishment, Mr. Tom Callahan, Health Consultant for Debur and Tandy, retained by the Federation, arrived and began to prepare for his presentation. He and his assistant placed special notebooks that contained statistics supporting his presentation at each chair. Copies of slides to be used in the presentation were also in the packets. His assistant carefully loaded the slide projector and tested the focus. He then placed a video tape in the VCR, cueing it to the start position. Callahan placed his presentation notes next to the podium after giving them a final review. At twenty minutes before the hour Mr. Frank Patello, Chairman of the Board of NAI, walked into the board room.

Patello huddled with Cappizi, Marone and Callahan to review the agenda and get a feel for the details of the presentation. The meeting plan was simple and directed to the single issue of health. After call to order and roll call the minutes of the last meeting would be brought forward for approval. They had been previously mailed to the members. No contest or amendment was expected. Since this was a special meeting of the Board, Big Frank Patello intended to ask the members to wave the routine reports and old business of the NAI in order to move promptly to the subject of Health as a new business venture. With the concurrence of the members, he would introduce Mr. Callahan who would explain the nature of the venture. The presentation would be followed by a period of questions and comments. The nature of the questions and comments from the members would give Patello a general sense of the attitude of the Board concerning the venture. After they had exhausted their inquiries, Big Frank would call for a break. During the forty-five-minute break Capizzi and Marone would lobby any apparent opposition. Callahan would be available for a one on one with any board member seeking more information or clarification.

Following the break, Big Frank intended to ask Mr. Capizzi to present a sketch of the NAI Health business plan. This would give the board better insight of the processes and methods to be employed by NAI in developing the health services programs and, of most importance, the expected profits. Again, questions and comments would be entertained after the presentation. If all went well Frank would ask for a motion to approve the venture with the capital allocation recommended in the business plan that was included in detail in their information packets. The representative of the Federation was already disposed to make the motion. If necessary, Patello would give the second but it was expected that the Federation had arranged for a second from the floor. After the vote was taken with a positive result, Big Frank would ask if there was any other business. Not expecting any other items to be brought forward he would then ask for a motion to adjourn. Following adjournment cocktails would be served in the reception area while the board room was prepared by the caterer for a very delicious gourmet style lunch. The executive assistants would be available to assist any board member in arranging travel, tours, or entertainment following lunch.

The four men felt that the meeting was well planned. Preparations were in order. At ten minutes to eight the first members arrived. By eight o'clock Frank Patello noticed that a solid quorum was present. Additional representatives were scheduled to arrive soon. The attitude among those present was jovial. Jim Ebber, representing the Federation, was circulating and apparently spreading the gospel. It all looked good. Big Frank decided to delay the start of the meeting in order to allow for more good will to develop and to allow late arrivals to sample the buffet. No need to press the issue since it seemed to be carrying itself

The members of the NAI Board of Directors had all been carefully selected by Frank Patello. They came from all parts of the United States but the majority were wealthy people from the Northeast. Each person's wealth was gained by hard work, albeit somewhat less than honorable. Nevertheless, they held a great amount of personal respect in society because of their wealth which they shared generously with special charities. The twenty-one members were also heavily invested in the NAI ventures. All in all, the NAI Board of Trustees comprised a solid mutual aid and admiration society that lived the motto of one for all and all for one. At exactly eight thirty, Big Frank asked everyone to be seated so the meeting could begin.

As planned, Big Frank moved through the preliminaries with ease and then introduced Mr. Tom Callahan. Tom expressed his gratitude for the opportunity to address the members of the Board. He introduced his able assistant then moved immediately to the subject, healthcare for fun and profit. "In the next year, over one trillion dollars will be spent on health services," he explained, "Nearly forty percent of that amount is expected to be spent on services traditionally provided by hospitals and another twenty percent for physician services. Si xty percent to be spent on hospitals and physicians while the remaining forty percent will be distributed over a wide range of services including nursing homes, durable medical equipment, drugs, and other health related programs."

As Mr. Callahan spoke his assistant presented slides demonstrating the statistics.

Callahan continued, "From a business perspective it is important to note that the money to be spent for hospital and physician services is ninety percent prepaid and held by insurance companies, health maintenance organizations, and government agencies to be eventually distributed to the point of service. The dominate method of conducting health insurance over the past decades was by use of an indemnity form of insurance that reserved the premiums and paid to the agencies on a schedule of fees usually negotiated and discounted. The insurance companies attempted to earn a profit on investment income. This method was not successful from a proprietary perspective because there was no control on the utilization of the services. Consequently, the providers were prone to over treat the patient in order to maximize their revenue and profits. Under the indemnity program the insurance companies made little profit, physicians and hospitals made big profits, and the purchaser of the health insurance, usually employers, paid ever increasing premiums."

At this point, Mr. Callahan's assistant displayed a chart showing the growth in employer spending on health insurance compared to salaries and wages over the past thirty years. The chart displayed that over the past three decades for every dollar on increased wages another two dollars was spent for health care benefits.

Callahan dramatized the Chart and continued, "The increasing premiums caused the rapid escalation of the health services component in gross national product. Automobile manufacturers complained bitterly to the government that the cost of health benefits in the cost of their products made them non-competitive with foreign companies. Federal initiative to reform the provision and payment methods for healthcare failed in Congress but did result in industrial attempts to modify the nature of pre-paid health services. The underlying concept in reform is the modified health maintenance organization as the payer networks / regulator coupled with the recently introduced concept of healthcare.

The networks are vertically organized hospitals and doctors who bid for the contracts to provide care for the health maintenance organizations. Fiscal control is maintained by a capitation agreement that only allows a given amount per person in the plan to be spent in a given year. The health network agrees to provide services as needed but stands at risk on total spending. If money is left over at the end of the year the network is given a bonus."

At this point Callahan paused. His assistant lowered the lights and immediately played a video tape of various congressional hearings on health care reform. Congressmen from California and Illinois spoke in depth about the cost of health care. Each offered a solution that differed in form but substantially admonished physicians and hospitals as culprits.

After the fifteen-minute tape was completed the assistant raised the light level as Callahan returned to the platform. He glanced at his watch and noticed that the presentation had passed the forty-five-minute mark. "Time," he thought, "to get to the point."

"Gentlemen, for the past hour I have attempted to give you a fairly comprehensive review of the status of health services from a fiscal point of view. I'm sure you noticed that the complex state of affairs that currently exists in health provides at best a very risky opportunity. What I want to point out, however, is that the opportunity for profit is not in health per se but in the transition of health services. Keep in mind that currently a trillion dollars in cash is floating around out there looking for a place to land. That trillion dollars is earmarked for health service. My recommendation is that you take advantage of the confusion that may exist in select markets, move in, and acquire the health payer and provider base, extract the short run profits while they last, and then divest as the markets move toward stabilization. You have effectively done this in the waste management venture. The strategy used in that venture is basically the same that you may want to employ in health. I imagine the tactics will vary however. You have what the industry needs to make its transition. What health needs is transitional dollars. I mean capital to acquire the franchise for service that includes the provider base. This acquisition gives you the cash drawer to collect the pre-paid dollars. As the cash flows into the drawer you extract your return up front, then pay for the services to the at-risk providers and at the end share in the profits. Basically, you have the opportunity to make out on both ends."

Callahan had their attention, "The time frame between confusion and stabilization is uncertain. Once you move in you will be better able to determine the time that you will want to remain in that particular market. In other words, if you have control of the market you pretty much can hold the window open for however long that you like. The dominate factor however is regulation brought by legislation. Right now, the Country in 1995, favors private enterprise and a conservative point of view toward health services. However, that could shift. For instance, a move toward any willing payer type legislation could dramatically affect your franchise and control over the provider. Once you get in, you need to keep a sharp eye on the political winds. Gentlemen, I've exhausted my material and I thank you for your kind attention. At this time, I conclude my remarks. Thank you."

Mr. Callahan stepped away from the podium and Big Frank took his place. As Callahan stepped down a hearty round of applause erupted form the board. Frank shook Callahan's hand and pulled him next to the podium in a position to respond to questions.

Big Frank politely asked for order. "Gentlemen, as I'm sure you have observed we have one of the leading authorities in health reform with us this morning. I thank Mr. Callahan for his excellent presentation. I also want to thank our friends at the Federation for bringing the discussion on the health market to our attention through Mr. Callahan. Now Mr. Callahan has agreed to entertain your questions and comments. The floor is open."

The question and answer period went on for another forty-five minutes. Patello noted with pleasure that the questions were of a genuine nature. There was no sarcasm or arguments. All of the Board members were attentive to the subject and seemed attracted to the proposition. Most of the questions centered on the temporary or time limited nature of the venture. It was generally agreed that this element posed the basis for risk as it did for profit.

The meeting schedule was now running a half hour late but otherwise in good form. Patello recessed the meeting for thirty minutes. During the break Callahan's assistant removed the charts, slides and video tape used earlier. As he completed his work, Mario Capizzzi's executive assistant distributed an outline of the next presentation to the respective chairs. She also placed several charts on the easel next to the podium.

Capizzi and Marone circulated among the board members and listened to their exchange. Again, all seemed well. Callahan was cornered by a small group who were actively exploring his mind about health transition in various parts of the country. There was no question that the NAI Board was focused on the topic.

Chairman Patello called the meeting back to order exactly thirty minutes into the break. As the members took their seats, he began the second session. "Gentlemen, we were advised in our first session this morning about the short run opportunity in the field of health services. The opportunity as I understand it requires that we select a market and move swiftly to gain control. Then as the market matures, we divest for capital gain in addition to extracting significant operating profits. We might also choose to enter several markets at the sometime depending on the opportunities. If you recall we recognized the same opportunities when we entered the waste management field. You are well aware, I'm sure, of the success of that venture. While we are not experienced in health we are well experienced in the waste management program. On that basis, I asked Mr. Mario Cappizi, our chief executive officer and Mr. Anthony Marone, President of Park Consulting, to develop a proposed strategy for our entry into the health venture. Mr. Cappizi and Mr. Marone have worked with Mr. Callahan in developing the business plan that Mr. Cappizi is about to present. The full details of the plan are before you in the blue notebook under section two. Mr. Cappizi."

Mario Cappizi stepped to the podium looking refreshed and energized. His appearance suggested confidence. The slight smile on his face and the glint in his eyes conveyed a winning attitude. He was ready to get started.

"Once again, good morning gentlemen. You know me well enough to realize that I wasn't going to let Frank do all the talking. Now it's my turn and I'm going to take full advantage of it. Seriously, your positive reception to Tom Callahan's presentation was most encouraging. Mario and I have been studying the prospect of a health venture in depth and we are convinced that it is a profitable, very profitable, venture. The details of what I am about to present are in your notebook and an outline of my presentation is also at your place. You may want to follow it and make notes for questions later. I will be asking for motions to support the venture at the conclusion. This will include a request for a significant capital authorization. The name of this project is TARGET BOSTON MEDICAL. We propose to penetrate the Boston medical market with the acquisition of a health maintenance organization currently serving that area. As we gain control of the HMO we will begin the process of selling coverage to employers at under market prices. As we market to employers we will through another entity, form an integrated delivery network that will appear to bid for and acquire an exclusive contract with our HMO for the provision of services to our insured. We intend to use the capitation model as the means of putting our providers in the network at risk. We will extract twenty per cent of the premium dollars from the HMO up front and will also extract another twenty percent of the capitation allowance from the network up front as part of our corporate fee. We also reserve the right to a major share of any profits at the end of each operating year. In view of the fact that we are underselling the market you may wonder about the prospect of profits. Believe me the potential for profit is great. I will ask Mr. Marone to explain."

Tony Marone took the podium looking less confident than his boss. He was unsure if he really understood the health racket. Cappizzi and Callahan had it cold and had convinced Marone that it was a boomer. Now Marone had to explain it to some hard business types that knew their way around a buck. Before speaking he carefully wiped his brow.

"Gentlemen, I am an expert in converting trash to cash. I suppose I appear less than confident about my ability to convert an ill to a bill. Well, that's only because I am new to the idea and have yet to master the lingo. However I do know a rip-off when I see it. The people of Boston have been getting the medical shaft for a long time. Regardless of our proprietary intent, what we propose is needed in Boston and will be viewed by the people as something welcome and well overdue. To demonstrate my point there are more physicians per capita in Boston than any other city in the United States. Furthermore, Boston has the highest percentage of medical specialists in the Country. The case cost per hospital admission is the highest in the country and the hospital length of stay again is number one. The number of hospital days per one thousand population is currently at eight hundred down from a thousand a year ago. This is compared to three hundred fifty days per thousand in Los Angles. With the right administration of our HMO and the network we can lower the use and cost of healthcare in Boston by forty percent in two years max, and at the same time extract our ROI off the top of the premium and get another big piece at the bottom line. Eventually the competition will catch up to our methods and true price/ quality competition will create equilibrium. As that begins to occur we will begin our withdrawal."

As Tony was talking, Mario was demonstrating the points with the charts and graphs on the easel. Tony would occasionally defer to Mario who would explain in some detail how the data was created and go more into its meaning. After fifteen minutes of explanation and discourse Tony returned the podium to Mario.

Mario continued his relaxed approach. "Tony has mentioned the impact of competition as an ally in our efforts. Boston has not experienced the effect of competition in health services. The community has never questioned the extravagant over served care because the health industry appeared to be the backbone of the local economy. We will cause that to change. In fact, the change is taking place without us.

At the present time, the major teaching hospitals are attempting to gobble up the competition at the community hospital level in order to preserve their referral base to their high-priced specialists. This has caused major disruption in the harmony of the medical community which gives us the opportunity to move in and get established virtually without notice. The existing HMO's are locally owned. The physicians and the hospitals have sucked them dry. I hasten to point out that the hospitals have the highest profit history in the country. Our first acquisition opportunity we believe is Bay Area Health Maintenance, an HMO that is in desperate need of capital. We could bail them out and gain a majority equity position. The remaining equity belongs to about a hundred physicians that we could buyout in groups or one at a time. We give them some vigorish to use in the partnership they take in the health network that we form. That same network should have an institutional partner that would eventually couple with the physicians in buying us out at the right time. Our contacts in the Boston area are well situated to deliver St. Anslem's Hospital to the network assuming that they can overcome the Church bureaucracy. Gentlemen that in a nutshell is "Target Boston Medical"

Several questions were asked by a variety of Board Members about the estimated time to be spent in the Boston market. Most felt that the NAI venture should start in several areas in order to maximize the prospect of success in the brief window of opportunity that Callahan had described. Eventually the motion was made and passed that initial studies be prepared for Dayton, Grand Rapids, and Raleigh. The capital allocation for each project was estimated and approved by the board. It was also recommended that Park Consulting change its focus from waste management to healthcare. The Board of Directors concluded that NAI should begin to divest from waste management enterprises. There being no further business to be brought before the Board of Directors, Mr. Frank Patello, Chairman, accepted a motion to adjourn.

oOo

Charlie Patello managed to control his emotions throughout the morning. He tried several times to contact O'Shea to learn if Dr. Folley had sufficiently prepped for the presentation to the Cardinal. O'Shea's office repeatedly reported that he was in a meeting and unavailable. A brief conversation with Hardly lacked substantive information but was reassuring enough to allow Charlie Patello to concentrate on other matters.

He left his office at noon for lunch at the coffee shop. In spite of his anxiety he sported a solid appetite. Refreshed, he returned to his desk at one fifteen in time for a call from Tony Marone. Tony was excited about the conclusion of the NAI Board meeting and wanted to give Charlie an update. Charlie listened to the report with great interest. The prospect of moving out of the waste management business in favor of the health venture seemed problematic in view of the state of affairs in Boston. The Mayor was in waiting for a Federal job. The Logan kid was being greased for the Archdiocese. A new Commissioner of Health for the City was positioned to approve the voluntary waste management program. The Union had been cut in at Action. Boston City and St. Anslem's were targeted for waste contracts. It was reasoned to suddenly back off would cause a real mess that would take years to repair.

Patello knew he had to persuade Marone to delay the retreat from waste management. Carefully he tried to counter, "Look Tony, we can't back off this waste project and move on health. There's too much at stake. Maybe instead of Target Boston you should Target Grand Rapids."

Marone, nevertheless, got the point. He offered a compromise, "I see it different, Charlie. The waste thing is tied to hospitals. It's a natural progression. We continue to move the waste project while doing the preliminaries on health. The two overlap, but don't conflict. We'll get you the help you need. Once the Mayor is taken care of Mark Mehan becomes point on the waste project and you can steer the health thing.

No sweat. We like the setup. You got control of the Catholic hospital and ought to be able to bring it in to the network when the time is right. That BayArea HMO is ripe for a takeover. It's got a load of Docs that we can con into the deal. Our consultant is pure genius and our guiding light. In the end, maybe we give him a piece of the action. We'll have a meeting of the Boston crowd to layout a work plan next week. You see what you can do to wrap up the waste project this week. By the way, the Mayor's deal is all set. It's critical that the Logan kid goes into the wrapper. You having any problem with that?"

Feeling some relief, Patello got back on track, "I'm not aware of any problem, Tony, other than the absence of a job to put him into. It all depends on that quack, Folley, convincing the Cardinal that he needs Logan to run his health business—excuse me—ministry. We meet in a couple hours. By five or six this afternoon I'll know if we have a problem."

Everything seemed in good order from Marone's point of view. He said as much to Charlie, "OK. You remember the signing bonus. When you have Logan let me know. I'll get the checks prepared for Cowan's endorsement. You see that an account is opened at the bank. We'll have Patriot hand carry the Logan check to the bank for deposit. To move this along Logan should resign his City job by Thursday. The Mayor will announce that Megan is the acting commissioner that same day. He also lets it leak that he is going to resign. On Monday, the Mayor meets with the President and the Secretary of Labor at a press conference in Washington to announce Cowan as the new Under Secretary. The Federation is taking care of all the details. Anything else?"

"Nothing at the moment, Tony" Patello knew it would be useless to complain about the work load, "I'll get back to you this evening or tomorrow morning. It's time for me to head for the Chancery. Say a prayer for our success."

"Yeah, right. You can count on my prayers. "Marone had not said a prayer since the third grade.

Patello hung up the phone and closed the files on his desk. He moved to the outer office and announced to his executive assistant that he would be at the Chancery for the rest of the day. He expected to be in the rest of the week but asked that his schedule be cleared for a number of priority meetings that he expected to develop. It was only two thirty.

The meeting with the Cardinal was expected to begin sometime after three thirty. Charlie knew that it would only take a half hour to drive from his downtown office to the Chancery in Brighton. Getting there a little early would give him time to check with Hardly, O'Shea and the distinguished Dr. Folley about their state of readiness. As he entered his car, he suddenly wished that he had eaten a light lunch.

The meeting with the Cardinal was to be held in the Cardinal's Residence, a stately edifice located a few hundred yards from the Chancery office building on the same campus. While the Residence resembled a mansion, it was used in the main for administration and as a conference center. The Cardinal used only a small portion of the building for his living quarters. Patello was unaware of the location of the meeting and had to be directed to the Residence by the receptionist at the Chancery. He was the first to arrive. A receptionist at the Residence answered the door. She directed Mr. Patello to a comfortable waiting area in a large corridor, gave him a cup of coffee, and immediately disappeared. Charlie sat alone in the corridor with his thoughts, surrounded by the life size portraits of Bishops, Archbishops, and Cardinals who over the past centuries had given spiritual guidance to the faithful of Boston and Eastern Massachusetts. He noticed that each portrait seemed to stare right at him. Was that planned or was he somehow being subjected to the spirit of these spiritual ancestors who knew that evil intent was more the agenda than advancing the ministry? He put his coffee cup on the small table next to his chair and walked to the nearest window where the magnificent landscape offered less imposing thoughts.

Kevin Hardly was next to arrive. Again, the receptionist answered the door. As she escorted Mr. Hardly to the waiting area she noticed that Mr. Patello had strayed to a nearby window. This was apparently some form of misconduct. As Kevin was provided the obligatory cup of coffee the receptionist summoned Mr. Patello back to his chair. He sensed a slight reprimand as she asked if he would like another cup of coffee. The message was plain and simple. Stay in your seat. Suddenly Charlie had a flashback to his days at St. Mary's grammar school. Kevin seemed relaxed in the sullen environment. As soon as the receptionist disappeared down the endless corridor, Kevin was on his feet inspecting the various portraits. He gave Charlie a historical review of each one noting his family's relationship with the Church during the particular reign of the Ordinary. In a way, it seemed that Hardly was right at home in the Cardinal's Residence. He, in his capacity as the First Leading Knight of the Equestrian Order of Knights of the Holy Cross, had frequently visited the Residence.

Kevin and Charlie exchanged small talk as the wait extended past the three thirty start time. It was curious to Charlie that O'Shea had yet to arrive. Kevin could offer no explanation for the absence of O'Shea or, of greater significance, the illusive Dr. Folley. Charlie's anxiety was mounting to anger and frustration. He was considering finding a telephone and searching out the missing persons when Bishop Hanks suddenly appeared from out of the darkness. Bishop Hanks apologized for the wait explaining that the Cardinal's cabinet meeting had extended well beyond its intended time allocation. The Cardinal required the extra time to resolve a number of matters before rushing for a plane to Rome. The Cardinal had asked Bishop Hanks to apologize to the distinguished gentlemen for not being able to meet with them but he was sure they would understand that the important matters waiting his attention at the Vatican required his immediate departure. Bishop Hanks asked Kevin and Charlie to follow him to the Cardinal's conference room where they could continue their discussion.

Patello was speechless. He could hardly breathe. The absolute need to settle the issue now was lost to everyone but him. He began to sweat. His stomach turned and he suppressed a belch. He was beyond anger. This was panic. No recourse. Just plain panic. As they walked to the conference room he barely was conscious of the conversation between Bishop Hanks and Hardly. Vaguely he heard something about the Cardinal's general consent to experiment with the concept but it seemed distant to the issue. He was concentrating on regaining his composure. What was the rule—never let them see you sweat. Under his coat, he was dripping wet.

As they entered the conference room, Patello got his second major shock of the day. Seated at the table was the distinguished Dr. Richard Folley with his favorite father in law, Mr. Thomas O'Shea. Bishop Hanks asked Hardly and Patello to be comfortable. The ever-present receptionist appeared from behind a paneled wall and offered coffee. She complemented the offer with a plate of large chocolate chip cookies that Bishop Hanks identified as the Cardinal's favorite. No one could resist taking a bite from the Cardinal's private stash. It was evident from the used coffee cups in front of Folley and O'Shea that there had been a pre-conference. Patello wondered if the Cardinal had been present. He made a quick glance around the room for evidence of another person but the efficient secretary had removed the used cups and saucers before disappearing behind the panel. He was left with the question.

As they began to sip their coffee and nibble at the Cardinal's favorite cookies, Bishop Hanks once again apologized for the Cardinal's absence. He then got immediately to the purpose of the meeting. "Gentlemen, when Dr. Folley called me to explain the purpose of the meeting this afternoon I advised the Cardinal. His Eminence requested that Dr. Folley give him a preview of the discussion and then detailed the matter to his Cabinet this morning. Dr. Folley was given permission to have Mr. O'Shea, the Cardinal's financial advisor, assist in the briefing. The bottom line is that the Cabinet agreed with the Cardinal's decision to establish an Office of Health Affairs for the Archdiocese. As an additional point, the Cardinal has asked Dr. Folley to be the Secretary of Health for the Archdiocese. In that capacity, he will direct the affairs of the Health Office. He will also be a member of the Cardinal's Cabinet. There is only two other laymen on the Cabinet so this is quite an honor."

Now Patello was in a slow bum. He knew that the Cardinal would not have made up his mind in that short of time. This was a well thought out decision that could only have been reached after many discussions. Apparently, the good Dr. Folley had wisely used his clinical time with the Cardinal to foster the concept and feather his own nest at the same time. Best guess was that Folley began his campaign right after the Alleton Club briefing. That would be about the right amount of time needed to cut the deal.

Bishop Hanks finished his introductory comments and then asked Dr. Folley to detail the nature of his conversation with the Cardinal. Folley appeared eager to explain, "Thanks, Bishop. Kevin and Charlie you know that I was completely sold on the idea of an Office for Health Affairs. I decided right after our review of the idea at the Alleton Club that it was an idea I would promote to the Cardinal. His Eminence has always confided in me his great concern that the healing ministry was losing prominence in Boston. Special emphasis on the ministry was needed. The Office was perfect for that to happen. Now the Cardinal is convinced that the best way to expand the ministry is to expand our influence over the physician. That's why he wants me to place emphasis on the teaching and physician training programs at St. Anslems. It's his idea that St. A's be identified as the teaching and tertiary care hospital for the Archdiocese. The community based Catholic hospitals will be expected to refer tertiary patients to the Catholic tertiary base, St. A's. We have the quality to match the big centers downtown. Once the word is passed that we have a Catholic system, the physicians will fight to be a part of it. The only downside to the prospect of success is our physical plant limitations. We will need to expand our capacity to accommodate the referrals. We will also have to recruit more specialists in medicine, surgery, and obstetrics. A quick fix might be to eliminate those programs at St. A's that are not tertiary such as the SACAP. I would like to add that the research done by the Bank's planning staff was very much appreciated by the Cardinal. He reviewed the material very closely. He is convinced that St. A's and the Office for Health Affairs can be very profitable for years to come. These profits will be the basis for the future expansion of the ministry. Tom gave the Cardinal a good review of the finances. Dad, would you like to comment?"

O'Shea sat back in his chair and looked directly at Patello as he responded, "Yeah. Dick. My involvement in this process was minor compared to the outstanding work that Dick did in convincing the Cardinal to accept our proposal. I hasten to add that Bishop Hanks was a champion in getting us onto the Cardinal's busy schedule. I explained to the Cardinal that St. A's was losing a ton of money because it was being mismanaged. The big money was in the more exotic procedures. To make it big you had to invest in super stars that would draw referrals from all over New England if not the Country. This kid, Durant, has no imagination or understanding of the business. He wouldn't last a week at the Bank. Having Dick as his boss will overcome the administration's stupidity. I expect that Dick will want to can him in a few months anyway. We need some good marketing. Development is also a key. People will want to give to the idea of a Catholic medical center.

Bishop Hanks became visibly anxious at O'Shea's comments about Durant. He raised his hand to silence O'Shea and then began his own commentary, "Gentlemen, you need to recall that Mr. Durant was selected by the Cardinal based on the recommendation of his fellow Bishops. He is an experienced administrator with a proven track record. The Cardinal is not to be easily convinced that Mr. Durant is incompetent. You also need to recall that your first recommendation, Mr. Bauman, was a serious embarrassment to the Cardinal. I believe it important that you concentrate on establishing the effectiveness of the Office for Health Affairs first before you concentrate on compromising Mr. Durant."

O'Shea suddenly had the look of a whipped puppy. He lowered his eyes and remained silent. The pause in the conversation was pregnant. Patello sensed the opening and proceeded to jump into the fray, "Bishop Hanks, I'm certain the Cardinal recognizes the need for competent management. Our intent is not to discredit Mr. Durant. More importantly, our intent is to ensure that the ministry remains credible to the public it serves. We indeed intend to place our emphasis on the Office for Health Affairs. Selecting Dr. Folley to be the Secretary and Director of the Office is genius. However, the selection could require Dr. Folley to resign his position as Chairman of St. Anslem's Department of Medicine. It will be extremely difficult for him to manage both positions without help. Ordinarily we would expect the Chief Executive Officer of the hospital to fill the gap. But as Mr. O'Shea has pointed out, the state of affairs at the hospital will require his full attention. We believe that the Secretary for Health should have an administrator to work the fields in behalf of the ministry. Our intent was to propose that Mr. Michael Logan be employed to staff the Office. He is an outstanding Catholic gentleman that is well recognized in the community for his dedication to the poor. His presence and identification with the Catholic ministry will only help our efforts. I have it on good authority that Mr. Logan will resign from the City when the Mayor accepts a Federal appointment. Apparently, Mr. Siro intends to appoint a new Commissioner of Health. I know Mr. Logan and am confident that he would accept a position with the Archdiocese."

Bishop Hanks nodded in agreement. Folley recognized that Patello had scored. He decided to parlay his own gains, "Bishop, I agree with

Mr. Patello. I will definitely need some help. As you know I am very active in State and City programs that include our ministry. My presence is necessary in many places with frequent conflicts in schedule. Mr. Logan could well represent me on such occasions. I hope we can move on Charlie's recommendation with dispatch."

It was now Kevin Hardly's turn to get into the action. He had sat quietly while Bishop Hanks, Charlie and Dick were discussing Logan's appointment. When Bishop nodded his head in apparent agreement Hardly saw that as his cue. "Bishop, I have listened with great interest to the discussion regarding Mr. Durant and Mr. Logan. There is no doubt that these are two fine Catholic gentlemen valuable to our ministry. It is my intent to see that these men are made Knights of the Holy Cross at the next installation. We will need their pastor's recommendation and a complete file on them as soon as possible. With your permission, I'll contact them immediately for the necessary information."

Bishop Hanks looked at Kevin in a questionable manner but supported his comments, "You have my permission, Kevin. I wonder if we should be a little more discreet and wait until we know that Mr. Logan wants to join us. We also have a Board meeting at St. Anslems next Tuesday. I assume the details of the Office will be discussed there. Mr. Durant has a lot of things to think about in that regard. He or rather St. Anslem's will have to foot the bill for the Office which will include Dr. Folley and Mr. Logan. That might not make Durant very happy. What do you think, Tom?"

O'Shea waved his hand as if to dispel Durant's anticipated opposition, "Bishop, it makes no difference if the administrators are Knights or not. They still have to produce a positive operating result. I believe Durant is incapable of coming up with a positive margin. OK, let's make him a Knight and see if that helps. As far as supporting the Office, St. Anslem's has no other choice. We have decided that's the way it is. Durant has to get off his butt and produce. One other thing I'm certain about is that Durant is not a leader. If we bring him into the Order of the Knights of the Holy Cross then he should be held as a member without opportunity for advancement. We don't want him to become an officer and destroy our work. We have to keep him silent."

Patello struggled to suppress his laughter. The words of the famous Christmas carol jumped to his head, "Silent Knight—Holy Knight all is calm. All is bright." The irony was diverting him from the intensity of the discussion. That stupid fool O'Shea completely missed the humor of his comment. Bishop Hanks either missed it or chose to ignore it. Probably the latter. Hardly was in his usual fog and Folley was busy, as usual, counting his trump.

Bishop Hanks lowered his head then raised it slowly as a signal to reorder the meeting. "Gentlemen, we seem to have come to an agreement. As the Cardinal expects, we will establish an Office for the Healthcare Ministry. Dr. Folley will serve the Cardinal as his Secretary for Health Affairs. Mr. Logan will be employed as the Director of Health Affairs reporting to Dr. Folley. St. Anslem's Hospital will provide the fiscal support for the Office assisted, as appropriate, by the other Catholic hospitals in the Archdiocese. Dr. Folley I trust you will take care of the details of locating the Office. Mr. Patello, I take it you will assist Dr. Folley in obtaining the services of Mr. Logan. We will announce all of this at the St. Anslem's Board meeting next Tuesday. Is that about it?"

"Excuse me, Bishop. You forgot to mention the Knights." Hardly fired his last salvo.

"Oh yes, thank you Kevin." The look on the Bishop's face was not one of gratitude. With the meeting concluded, Bishop Hanks escorted the participants to the door.

Patello and Folley lingered in the parking lot to discuss the employment of Logan. Folley agreed to offer Logan a salary of one hundred twenty-five thousand dollars plus an automobile and the usual benefits enjoyed by executives at St. Anslem's. Patello agreed to contact Logan and make the offer. If Logan was agreeable, Patello would arrange for a meeting between Folley and Logan to close the deal. Patello was satisfied with the outcome of the meeting but was uncomfortable with the amount of control held by Folley and O'Shea. "This deal could still go south," he thought.

oOo

Early Wednesday morning Patello placed a call to Commissioner Logan's office. He asked for an immediate appointment on a very urgent matter. The Secretary put the call directly into Michael Logan's office. Logan agreed to meet Patello at the Coffee Shoppe in South Station at ten o'clock.

Logan had no sooner completed the call from Patello when he received a call on his private line from the Mayor. Cowan was excited and breathless as he spoke, "Michael, I have it from a confidential source that you are considering a job with the Archdiocese. Look, I want you to know that this is an excellent opportunity. I'll be resigning within the next week so it would be to your advantage to take the offer. I can arrange for you to resign immediately in good standing. It will look natural since I intend to leak my resignation today or tomorrow. How does it sound to you?"

The call was very perplexing to Logan, "Your Honor, I'm grateful for the call and your support. Honestly, this is the first that I knew that the position was with the Archdiocese. I haven't any idea what the job is all about. Of course, an association with the Cardinal would be viewed as an honorable position so on that basis I'm prone to give it positive consideration. I expect to hear more about it in a few hours. Things seem to be moving at a fast pace."

Cowan began to push. "Michael, this is an excellent opportunity. I've been very involved in its development. The Cardinal is a close friend. I mentioned you to him on a number of occasions and he has been waiting for an opportunity to bring you on his staff. You go along with this. It will be a big advancement to your career. The Catholics collectively are the largest provider of healthcare in the State. That might be changing because of the new mergers and such but they will always be on top. I'm sure the money and benefits will be better than the City. Let me know how you decide. If possible I would like to announce your change at the Council meeting tomorrow. What do you think?"

Logan caught the drift. Essentially the Mayor was telling him in a nice way to resign or be fired. The sequence was simple. Scenario one, Logan finds a new job this morning and resigns this afternoon or, scenario two, the Mayor resigns to go to Washington and Logan gets fired by Siro. Better to resign with a bird in hand than get fired.

As Mayor Cowan hung up the phone he winked at Council President Siro. The deal was certain in the Mayor's opinion. He and Siro then began to work out the various tactics ordinarily employed in the transition of political power. At the City Council meeting on Thursday the Mayor would announce the resignation of Commissioner Logan coupled with the announcement that Commissioner Megan would be transferred from his post in Parks and Recreation to be acting Commissioner of Health. With that business completed the Mayor would announce the plan to immediately implement the voluntary privatization of waste management for the City. The Acting Commissioner of Health would detail the plan to the Council. Mr. Siro, as President of the City Council would move support for the plan. Other routine business of the Council would follow. However, by this afternoon the agenda for the Council meeting would be in the hands of the media as well as the members of the City Council. Obviously, the agenda would raise speculation that the Mayor's resignation was in the immediate offing. This speculation would be prompted by a leak from Washington. The Mayor would have no comment but Siro would confirm to the media that he expected the Mayor to resign within the week. The Mayor would announce his resignation the following Monday to be effective after the Council meeting the following Thursday. Siro would take office as acting Mayor at the close of the Council meeting.

Siro called Patello from the Mayor's office to let him know that Logan had been prepped for the ten o'clock meeting. The Mayor called Muldoon to let him know that the transition plan was being implemented. Patello called Marone to let him know that the waste management project was taking off. Marone called Meehan at Action to advise him to be ready for the implementation of the Boston project. Meehan called his management team including Ken Ryan in Quality Control and Veto Celli, Boston Project Sales Manager, to prepare them for the all-out effort. Muldoon called Celli as well to discuss personal business following which he called Donovan to press Action on the bargaining agreement. Donovan tried to call Marquart but he was not at work.

The meeting between Logan and Patello took place at South Station as planned. Patello arrived first and managed a small table away from the general milieu of patrons. As Logan entered the Coffee Shop, Patello waved him over to the table.

Logan was uptight and a bit irritated. "Mr. Patello, in our first meeting you gave me no indication that the opportunity you had in mind was with the Archdiocese. It was a shock to learn that the Mayor had actually arranged this with the Cardinal. What I don't understand is why you are involved?"

Patello, on the other hand, was amused to learn that the Mayor had told Logan that he had arranged the deal with the Cardinal. Quickly, Charlie easily concluded that Hizzoner was feathering his nest as usual. Nevertheless, the Kid's attitude was disarming. Setting aside the Mayor, Patello decided that a direct and almost truthful approach was best.

"Michael, the Cardinal, like all good executives in big organizations uses staff and delegates to carry out the details of direction. In the case of the health ministry the Cardinal has recently established an Office for Health Affairs under the direction of Dr. Richard Folley, Chairman of Medicine at St. Anslems. Dr. Folley has the title of Secretary for Health Affairs for the Archdiocese. Several of us who also serve on the Board of Trustees for St. Anslem's also serve to advise Dr. Folley. My assignment is to lead a recruiting effort to select and employ a Director for the Office of Health Affairs. We have counseled with the Mayor, the Cardinal, and several additional influential people in Boston. They have been unanimous in recommending you for the Directorship. As a public figure, we found it easy to gain perspective on your attitudes, manner, and so forth. Interviews were not necessary from our point of view. We are prepared to offer you the position. Hopefully, you are in a position to want to take it."

Reflecting on his recent conversation with Mayor Cowan, Logan seemed positive, "Mr. Patello, as a leading citizen in Boston I suspect you are well aware that events to take place in the next twenty-four hours will put me in a position where I cannot refuse your kind offer. However, I have no idea what your kind offer consists of. Furthermore, I have never met Dr. Folley much less the Cardinal. You are asking me to go into this deal blind. I'm willing to take a chance but I need some protection. I'll require a salary of one hundred twenty-five thousand plus two times salary in life insurance, full health insurance for myself and my family, guaranteed pension, and an automobile. I will also require the option to leave the position at any time in the first year of employment with one year salary and benefits extended from the date of my resignation. After the first year of employment the extension is only applicable if the Archdiocese requires or requests my resignation."

True to his negotiating instincts, Patello tried to shave the request. "Michael, your salary request is higher than we expected to pay. However. I can understand your request. The other items are also understandable. I would like to suggest another item that may help. The general employment agreements with the Archdiocese requires a thirty day probation period. Usually no benefits or perks are provided during this period. I feel that I can get a wavier to the thirty-day elimination period with the exception of the salary extension. To offset this, since I am going out on a limb on the salary, I will see that you are paid a signing bonus of ten thousand dollars. This amount is yours today with absolutely no recourse. We also will provide you with private banking services at Hardly Security and Trust without charge. We can have the account opened and the money deposited this afternoon. You can go home tonight ten thousand dollars richer. Tomorrow you meet with Dr. Folley. If you decide after the meeting that you don't want the job you can still keep the ten-grand. How's it sound?"

This was an unexpected twist. Logan had never heard of a signing bonus paid without signing. He decided to look the horse in the mouth, "It sounds like something out of the Godfather. If I wasn't dealing with the Church I would swear that you were working for the mob."

"That hurts, Michael." Patello appeared to be greatly offended, "I am trying to meet your requests. If you want to turn me down just say so. We have other candidates but none with your civic background."

Logan feared that the offer would be withdrawn leaving him unprotected. He made a quick grab, "OK, Patello. It's a deal. You have the employment agreement to me this afternoon. Keep it confidential. Deliver it to me for my eyes only. I'll review it and sign it after I have the ten thousand dollars in the bank. Let me know where and when I meet Dr. Folley."

"Done, Michael. We'll be in contact this afternoon. Are you going to be in the office?"

Logan nodded in the affirmative and shook Patello's extended hand as he departed.

A waitress appeared as he was walking away. She noticed that Patello was also standing to leave so she turned away. It was a free rent day at the Coffee Shop.

Patello returned immediately to his office and placed a call to Cappizi regarding the ten thousand dollar signing bonus. Capizzi informed Patello that the Mayor had endorsed the check for the ten thousand dollars that morning. The check had been taken by courier to Patriot dispatch where it was being held for further delivery instructions. Capizzi reasoned that Patello should direct the check into the bank account for Logan.

To that end Patello called Kevin Hardly and told him that he had offered private banking services at no charge to Mr. Logan. He asked Hardly to make the necessary arrangements. If Hardly could have the necessary account cards prepared, Patello would have a courier pick them up and take them to Mr. Logan for signature. The courier would bring the signed account cards and an initial deposit of ten thousand dollars back to the bank before close of business today.

Patello knew that Hardly would want to be as helpful as he could be. He also reasoned that an account opened through the office of the Chairman of the Board would not be subject to scrutiny. This way the initial deposit with the Mayor's endorsement would have little if any notice. Also, the lack of endorsement by Logan would not be an issue since the total amount was for deposit. He thought about having Hardly initial the check for good measure but dismissed the idea after realizing that it would set a trail back to the Terrific Trinity.

Hardly, as Patello expected, was very pleased to hear that Logan had accepted the Archdiocese's offer. Of course, he would see that Mr. Logan was given the benefit of private banking. He would see to the account personally. After he finished talking to Patello, Kevin Hardly immediately set about arranging the private banking service for Mr. Logan. Hardly had no way of knowing how to arrange such service. He immediately sought council of his efficient executive assistant. She advised Mr. Hardly that opening an account in the private banking service was not at all complicated. She would take care of the arrangements. Hardly was relieved to have her in charge of the assignment. He then left for an afternoon of friendly poker at the Alleton Club.

The executive assistant checked the Bank's procedure manual for private banking and discovered that all private bank accounts required the approval of the Treasurer. No problem. She would direct the courier to Mr. O'Shea's office. She than called the executive assistant in Mr. O'Shea's office and advised her that a VIP private banking account would be coming from Mr. Hardly's office this afternoon that required special attention and prompt dispatch. Mr. O'Shea's executive assistant assured her that he would be available to handle the matter.

Patello also called the Bank's Human Resource Department. The HR Director had been of great help in the initial phase of the Logan recruitment. Patello outlined the terms of employment except the signing bonus and asked the HR guy to prepare a legal type employment agreement. He then called Folley to advise that the deal was cut. The employment agreement would be in his hands this afternoon and, hopefully with Dr. Folley's signature, in Logan's hands an hour later, Folley listened to the employment terms short of the signing bonus but including private banking services. He agreed to the terms and said he would sign the agreement. A courier would transport the document.

Next Patello called Phil Mondi at Patriot Transport and Courier Service. He explained to his buddy, Phil, that he had a rather complex courier assignment that required a man used to details, who could follow orders, and get the job done no matter what. Mondi asked for time to review his staff and give him a call back. Patello explained that this was business for Marone and that the item was already at his dispatch center. Mondi knew immediately what the item was and promised to call Patello back in less than ten minutes. During that time, Phil met with Eddie who advised that the best man to handle this special assignment was Brian. Mondi returned the call to Patello and advised him that they had a man standing by. Patello said he would fax the courier instructions to Patriot dispatch in fifteen minutes.

Brian was in process of spending some quality time with Louise when his beeper let out its annoying screech. He first had to find his pants then the damned beeper. He dutifully returned the call to Dispatch and was told that Eddie wanted him on the spot now. He was to, "drop whoever he was doing and double time it back." Eddie seemed to have a sixth sense about Brian's whereabouts. Without delay Brian quit his conversation with Louise and powered the Chevy Caprice with tape deck back to station. As he arrived Eddie, waved him into the office and presented him with a list of assignments:

<u>Item 1</u>: Pick up item envelope at Patriot dispatch center.

<u>Item 2</u>: Pick up item envelope at Chairman's office Hardly Security and Trust See executive assistant.

<u>Item 3</u>: Pick up Items envelopes at Human Resource Office (Director) Boston Security and Trust.178

<u>Item:4</u> Take Item 2 to Commissioner Public Health—City Hall—Wait for his response in envelope (Commissioner's Eyes Only).

<u>Item 5</u>: Take Item 3 to Commissioner Public Health· City Hall- Wait for his response in envelope (Commissioner's eyes only)

<u>Item 6</u>: Take Item 1 and item 4 back to Chairman's Office Boston Security and Trust—Wait for response in envelope.

<u>Item 7</u>: Take Item 3 to Dr. Richard Folley—St. Anslem's Hospital- Wait for response in envelope.

<u>Item 8</u>: Take Item 6 and Item 7 back to Commissioner Public Health -City Hall Commissioner's eyes only)

<u>Out time EST 1400" Assign comp: EST 1630</u>

Brian was used to the complex type assignment. He also recognized the tight time frame for completion. Two and a half hours to move around heavy City traffic was tough enough but waiting for response was always dependent on the secretaries' breaks and other delays as the subjects quizzed each other about the documents. This was obviously some hot stuff that some big wigs wanted done in quick order. Well, he would do his end. The rest was up to the subject items. As he departed, Eddie requested that he phone in at every stop.

Brian checked out of Patriot dispatch with the envelope containing the ten-thousand dollar check in his courier pouch. He aimed the blue Chevy toward the financial district and Hardly Security and Trust. The trip took about twenty minutes in midafternoon. He parked the car in the loading zone and headed for the twenty eighth floor executive suite. The executive assistant in Mr. Hardly's office presented Brian with a very large promotional type folder that was to be delivered to Commissioner Logan's office. In addition, he was given a smaller envelope containing the private banking account signature cards. He was instructed to wait for Mr. Logan to sign the cards and then bring them back to Mr. Hardly's office. This was generally in accord with Eddie's orders. On his return trip, he would also deliver the envelope listed as Item one. Brian couldn't figure out why he couldn't deliver Item One now but his was not to reason why and orders were orders. He left the Executive Suite and dropped down to the tenth floor per instructions to pick up Item three from the Human Resource Office. The envelope was waiting for him at the reception desk. First phase completed he telephoned Eddie that he was on his way to City Hall.

When Brian arrived at Commissioner Loan's office he was escorted into the Commissioner's office. Mr. Loan asked Brian to sit in a comfortable chair while he examined the documents. It took about twenty minutes for the Commissioner to review the material. Mr. Logan made a phone call to someone who seemed to answer his question about a bank account. Item two was signed and placed back in the envelope. Item three took another twenty minutes of scrutiny before it was signed. Both items were given to Brian after Mr. Logan made copies. Brian called Eddie to report that the stop at the Commissioner's office had consumed an hour of the precious schedule. He departed City Hall and made his way back to Boston Security. He was actually doubling back over his original track. Brian would cover the same route three times. Again, he realized that his job was to follow Eddie's orders. He made a mental note to critique the process with Eddie at his first opportunity. To Brian the process seemed like, "pure bullshit."

Again, Brian managed to avoid the usual downtown traffic snarls. Fortunately, the unloading zone in front of the Bank was vacant. He ran for the elevator destined for the twenty fifth floor just managing to squeeze past the closing door. As he entered the executive suite the assistant waved to him to move ahead of others waiting her attention. At last he sensed some expediency toward restoration of the vital schedule. Then things began to unravel. She explained that the material for Mr. Hardly had to be taken to Mr. O'Shea's office on the twenty second floor. Mr. O'Shea was waiting for the material. He would complete the transaction and authorize the transfer of information back to Mr. Logan. Brian dutifully retreated from the executive suite and caught the elevator for twenty-two. The executive assistant in Mr. O'Shea's office took the envelope containing the check and the envelope containing the signature cards into Mr. O'Shea's office.

The door to O'Shea's office was left open. Brian saw that O'Shea seemed irritated with the material. He made a few telephone calls. Yelled at the ceiling and sent the executive assistant packing the material to an unknown location. Before she departed she made copies of the material and asked Brian for his log sheet that she also copied. She then disappeared and returned in less than fifteen minutes with a few slips of paper in her hand that she gave to O'Shea. O'Shea gave out with a blast of profanity that shocked Brian. Then he came out of his sanctuary with a sealed envelope in his hand. He pushed the envelope into Brian's hand and ordered him to tell Mr. Logan that the money, "where ever it came from," was now in his new account. Brian sensed that the messenger had just been shot. He didn't respond to O'Shea. Verbal messages by courier went out of vogue when Bell invented the telephone. Instead, he quietly retreated to the elevator, got into his car, and headed for his next destination, St. Anslem's Hospital.

Brian's attitude deteriorated completely when he attempted to park at St. Anslem's.

The traffic at the hospital was usually complex but today it was compounded by an unusual number of ambulances delivering nursing home patients for therapies. When he attempted to park in the fire zone next to the main entrance a burley security guard chased him out. He offered little consolation to Brian's plea for temporary parking. Eventually he found an unoccupied handicap slot. Once inside, he found the information clerk busy assisting visitors. She finally found time to direct Brian to Dr. Folley's office located a floor below the main entrance.

Brian was feeling his way toward Dr. Folley's office when he met Cecile. She glared at Brian in her usual manner. Brian had actually never seen Cecile that he could remember, without her hateful stare. He gave her a weak wave and attempted to pass.

Cecile blocked his way. She pushed him against the wall and put a clench fist in his face, "Brian, you worm, where is Jay? I've been trying to contact him for two days. He better return my call. You see to it, dimwit."

The fist was less alarming than her attitude. Brian untypically became somewhat sarcastic, "Cecile, I'm so happy that we had this pleasant chat. As soon as I leave here I'll let Jay out of my trunk so he can give you a call. Now if you'll go back to your cage, I'll get back to work."

The comment accelerated Cecile's anger, "You don't know the meaning of work, you crawling epidemic. Get out of here before you contaminate the place."

Having fired the last volley, Cecile popped back into the Medical Intensive Care Unit. Brian stood in the corridor totally disarmed. His mind was blown. He leaned against the wall pondering the exchange with Cecile. Gradually he remembered the task at hand and proceeded to locate the office of Dr. Richard Folley. The receptionist took the package from Brian and invited him to be seated. Dr. Folley was in conference but had left instructions to be interrupted when the courier arrived. The receptionist reappeared and told Brian that Dr. Folley would be with him in a few minutes. Then she went on break. Thirty minutes later Brian took the initiative and knocked on Dr. Folley's door. Dr. Folley responded with an invitation to come in. When Brian inquired about the package Dr. Folley nodded to the out box on his desk. He stated that it had been ready for the last twenty minutes and waiting for someone to pick it up.

Brian thanked the good Doctor and headed for his handicapped parking place. He headed for City Hall, the final destination. Eddie said he would call the Commissioner's office to let him know that the package was on its way.

It was nearly four thirty and traffic was becoming impossible. Brian arrived at the Commissioner's office at five fifteen. The Commissioner was alone in the office. He was packing files and personal affects in boxes that were stacked in the outer office. Brian handed him the envelope from the bank and the envelope from the hospital. He waited patiently as the commissioner looked them over. Finally, the Commissioner looked up as if to ask Brian if "there was anything else."

Brian caught the signal, "Ah Sir, the gentleman at the Bank asked that I tell you that the money, where ever it came from, was in your new account."

Logan nodded as if relieved, "Thank you. Do you remember who at the Bank gave you that message?"

"Yes sir. It was the gentleman on the twenty second floor, a Mr. O'Shea. He signed for the material I just delivered. Anything else, Sir?"

Michael Logan said nothing in response. He simply gave Brian a wave as a sign of dismissal and continued to pack.

Brian left the Commissioner's office after he had used the secretary's desk phone to notify Eddie that the run was complete. Eddie immediately informed Mr. Meehan who called Patello. Patello was already aware of the matter having, first, been informed by Logan who wanted to know why Mr. O'Shea was so caustic. Patello covered the matter by informing Logan that the signing bonus was provided by anonymous benefactors of the Archdiocese who did not want to reveal their identity. He offered that Mr. O'Shea was irritated that he did not know the source of the donations. He offered to calm Mr. O'Shea by giving him some insight to the signing bonus.

Logan accepted the offer. He also advised Patello that he had signed his letter of resignation and sent it by special courier a half hour ago. He had called the Mayor earlier. The Mayor was going to inform the media tonight and present the resignation as a matter of business at the City Council meeting in the morning.

Patello was furious. Everything had gone fine except that idiot Hardly had to involve O'Shea. O'Shea obviously took careful note of the deposit check. He most certainly realized that the Mayor's endorsement on the check signaled foul play. Nevertheless, he let the deposit go through. Why? Regardless, O'Shea was in the know. This made him a big problem in the conduct of the Waste project and possibly a bigger problem in the future health initiative. The guy had to be reported to the boys in New York. Since it was now a matter concerning the Waste project, Patello thought it best to advise Meehan as well as Mondi. He first called Meehan and told him about the conversation with Logan. Meehan was not aware of the way that Capizzi had arranged the wrapper so could offer little comment. He, nevertheless, did recognize the potential for a massive screw up. His recommendation was that Patello check with Phil Mondi at Patriot to see if the courier experienced anything unusual. Patello took the advice and called Mondi. Mondi promised to interview the courier and get back to him.

As Brian was about to take up where he had left off with Louise earlier in the day, his pager once again let out its annoying tone. This time Brian was being summoned by Mr. Mondi who wanted to meet him in the office immediately. Brian bid a quick farewell to his main squeeze and pointed his trusted Chevy back to the coral. Big Boss Mondi was very kind and grateful to Brian for returning to the office at the late hour. He asked Brian several questions about his afternoon run. Brian gave detailed answers about every stop. He left out the exchange with Cecile but was very explicit about the hassle in Mr. O'Shea's office including the verbal message that he relayed to Mr. Logan. He noticed that Mr. Mondi took careful notes on the part involving O'Shea. Mondi also was interested in the fact that O'Shea's secretary made a copy of Brian's log. He asked Brian for his log and then made a copy for himself. Brian became increasingly nervous during the interview. He wasn't sure if he had screwed up or not. If Eddie suddenly came through the door, Brian would know that he had messed up and Eddie was going to rearrange his anatomy. That never happened. To the opposite, Mr. Mondi shook Brian's hand, gave him five twenty dollars bills, and told him to take his best girl out to dinner. This was definitely a day and night to remember.

Mondi called Patello at his home around nine thirty that evening. He gave him the courier's report. Patello was now very certain that O'Shea was holding some very incriminating evidence. As he pondered the matter the local television stations were reporting the resignation of Commissioner Logan combined with information from a Washington source that Mayor Cowan was to be named as the Under Secretary of Labor. The Mayor acknowledged that Commissioner Logan had resigned to accept a post with the Archdiocese of Boston. However, at this time the Mayor would neither confirm nor deny the Washington report.

In an on-camera interview, Commissioner Logan stated he was very pleased to be joining the Archdiocese as the Director of the Office of Health Affairs. Cardinal McMahon was in Rome and unavailable for comment but a spokesman for the Archdiocese confirmed that Mr. Logan had been employed. No additional information was available at this time from the Archdiocese.

Sister Elizabeth was glued to her television set. The creation of an Office for Health Affairs was a recommendation that she and Sister Celest had made to Cardinal McMahon when he was first installed as the Archbishop of Boston. He rejected the proposal out of hand stating that it represented too much bureaucracy. At the time Sr. Elizabeth had recommended that Sr. Celest could run the office as a part of St. Anslem's Hospital thus avoiding additional expense and bureaucracy. Again, the Cardinal rejected the idea because of more pressing matters. She now recognized that politics of some nature created the moment for the Office. However, the fact that she and the other members of the Board of St. Anslem's were not consulted gave her a stomach ache. Her pain and discomfort was compounded with the realization that the Director of the Office was selected without any input from the Board. Indeed, she would again have recommended Sr. Celest for the job. She suspected that the Terrific Trinity had a hand in this and vowed to raise no small amount of hell at the Board meeting on Tuesday.

CHAPTER EIGHT

Jay woke early Wednesday. The light of the new day was beginning to filter through the dusty venetian blinds on his shabby hospital window. The previous two days were still a blur. He did recall several conversations with the hospital staff on Tuesday. Nothing of great substance. A few residents checked the progress of his treatment that consisted in the main of medication and bed rest. The lab jockey stuck him a few times and there was the persistent demand that he pea in a bottle. He recalled that Susan was with him for a few hours last night. Boss and buddy, Ken Ryan, also dropped in, said little and left. Susan mentioned that Brian inquired about his health and wished him well. The kids, Benny and James, wanted Dad home for the weekend. Kristie hadn't been told about Dad yet. He and Susan reasoned that Cecile would push Kristie for answers that she didn't have. Besides Jay wasn't sure what his diagnosis was. Nobody had given him the word. Today was supposed to be the day that Jay learned all. The real doctor was supposed to show up early in the morning to explain to him why he had been in captivity for the past two days. Jay had made up his mind that this was his last day in internment. He was going to bust out at noon, doctor or no doctor. He felt fine.

He was just beginning to dig into his breakfast tray when a distinguished gentleman with stethoscope in hand came into his room.

He was the first physician that appeared to be over thirty that Jay had encountered since he was admitted. The doctor introduced himself as Doctor Kenneth, an internist in private practice and part time attending with the St. Anslem's Chemical Addiction Program. He explained to Jay that he had been assigned to his case on the rotation schedule. If Jay preferred another Physician, Dr. Kenneth would make all the necessary arrangements. Otherwise, he would continue to direct Jay's care as he had been doing since Jay had been admitted to the Unit. Jay did not have a primary care physician although the HMO required him to name one. He knew that Susan and the kids had docs but Jay couldn't remember their names.

Jay reasoned that accommodating the doctor would be the best tact so he offered a proper reply, "Look, Doctor, I'm sure that you'll do fine. In fact, I think you have done wonders. I feel fine and think I can go home and back to work. I thank you for all that you have done. The staff has been wonderful. About all I need is a discharge order and I'll cease being your problem."

Doctor Kenneth shook his head from side to side as Jay talked. Then he answered, "Jay, you are not well. I'm here to advise you about your illness and work out a treatment plan. You have a long way to go for recovery. We might be able to discharge you from this bed but we cannot in good conscience discharge you from treatment. You have an illness that needs treatment. On the other hand, we cannot force you to follow our direction. This has to be a voluntary decision on your part."

The doctor's comments frustrated Jay. He wanted out of the hospital. He did not want to hear about an illness that he did not believe he had. This time he answered with sarcasm, "What, pray tell, is this terrible disease. Am I going to die? I don't feel like I'm what sick. If you are referring to my boozing, I've heard that song before. Some guy at Waltham Hospital handed me that line on Sunday. Said his name was Hendricks. Know him?"

Kenneth sat on the edge of the bed and looked out the window, "Mr. Marquart, you told the resident about your admission to Waltham's ER on Saturday. You also signed a consent release for us to access your records. We brought your records forward and have consulted with Dr. Hendricks. If you would like him to continue your treatment that can be arranged. Dr. Hendricks and I trained here at St. Anslems. We share a private office practice. In summary, you have a chemical dependency based on a deficiency in your blood. This deficiency causes you to use drugs to offset the imbalance in your system. The problem is that the chemicals that you are using while giving you emotional satisfaction are causing an increasing deficit in the quality of your metabolism. We intend to treat your deficiency with the right chemicals and restore your chemical balance. You also need to know that we suspect that you are developing ulcers. That is very consistent with addicted people. Without treatment, you will continue to experience physical as well as mental breakdowns."

Jay got out of the bed and began to pace around the room. His irritation was now very obvious, "Let me get this straight. You want me to start taking drugs in order to stop taking drugs. That's interesting. You guys have a neat thing going for you. Hendricks scoops 'em up in Waltham's ER and you take a chunk out of 'em at St. A's. Between the two of you every junkie in town gets fixed. Not."

Dr. Kenneth stood up and followed Jay. Eventually he got in front of him and looked Jay in the eye, "Mr. Marquart, I don't intend to argue with you about this. I also don't intend to take any of your crap. Your disease is the most difficult to cure. The main reason is because you and many like you do not believe that they are as sick as they are. A person who experiences cardiac arrest doesn't have to be convinced. They get religion real fast. An addict, in spite of the pain, wants to keep right on punishing himself because he thinks it feels so good. The cost isn't money. The real cost is the loss of dignity, family, and the love and respect of those close to you. You think you can handle it. Well, friend, look around you at your wife and kids and ask if they can handle it. They have to carry the burden."

"Doctor I'm sorry if I offended you." Jay realized that he had angered the physician and probably lost his chance to be discharged, "You've got a tough and thankless job. Yeah, I know that I have a problem. I like to party. Who doesn't? But I pull up short of saying I'm a junkie. I also realize that over doing it can screw me up big time. So, I'll slow down. No reason to quit. Just a little self-control and I can go on living. You take care of the poor bastard that's zonked out in the gutter. I'll take care of good or Jay and stay out of here. Tell me again how you got my record out of Waltham."

Dr. Kenneth backed away and seemed to regain his composure, "Mr. Marquart, I want to treat you now so you avoid being zonked out in the gutter. Your denial of the problem is very typical. I won't bother you anymore today but I will ask our counselor, Bob Markley, to have a chat with you. Will you see him?"

Jay sensed that things were about to go his way, "Sure, if it will make you feel better. Send him around. How about that discharge order? I don't want to walk out of here today against medical advice or AMA as you guys put it. That could screw up the insurance. We can both appreciate that."

Dr. Kenneth closed Jay's chart folder, put his pen in his pocket, and with a sigh followed by a slight wave to Jay walked out of the room. Jay watched the Doctor walk out. In a way he felt sorry for the guy. He had tried his very best to sell Jay a continuing treatment program. The effort and passion that the doctor displayed suggested to Jay that there had to be big money involved. Why else would the doctor try so hard to convince him that he needed the cure. Jay also recognized that the doctor's compassion was genuine. Several of Jay's verbal blasts almost brought the man to tears. "Why couldn't the guy just back off?" he wondered. "No need to make such a big deal out of the problem." Suddenly, he remembered that he had to make some telephone calls. The first one to Susan would be to arrange for her to pick him up this afternoon. He also had to call Ryan and, "oh yeah, the bitch." Must not forget the "bitch."

Jay dressed and packed what few items he had in a hospital container that he found in the closet. Satisfied that he was ready to go, he ambled to the front desk to get permission to use the patient telephone. The desk was unattended except for a gentleman in whites that, because of his somewhat unkempt appearance and relaxed poster, gave Jay the impression that he was a male nursing assistant. The man also looked a little shop worn and long of tooth. His ID badge was clipped on backwards so the name was not visible. His hair was overdue for a trim, the mustache drooping slightly to starboard, and his belly pulled the shirt buttons to maximum tension. The uniform was clean and the white shoes were spotless yet old. When Jay asked for permission to use a phone, the man flashed Jay an infectious grin and passed him the desk phone. Jay punched nine for an outside line and received a weird screech.

The man gently reached over and depressed the button causing disconnect. "Sorry, buddy, No need to punch nine. We now have the most marvelous advanced state of the art telephone system in the world. Administration bought this miracle of modem technology with the money usually paid to us slaves. Now we can call anywhere in the world without punching nine. Try again. Just dial your number. All the comforts of home right here in St. A's. Would you ever have guessed? Just look at the excellent device before you. We still have to train it to say only what we want to hear. I guess that will be part of next year's expensive upgrade. We can hardly wait."

Jay returned the man's smile. He loved the guy's sarcasm. This was the kind of person Jay was attracted to, a real cynic. This time he dialed correctly. Susan answered on the second ring. Jay explained to her that he was, "busting out of this funny farm by four thirty at the latest." The man heard the comment, smiled, and leaned back in his chair as if he was a party to the conversation. Jay noticed his interest and gave him a wink in acknowledgment that also served as an invitation to monitor Jay's particular style and humor. Jay appreciated an audience. He performed well using the best street terms in describing to Susan the quality of care at St. Anslems. He talked about how he humbled Dr. Kenneth and now was waiting for his next victim, "some dweeb named Markley" After he polished off this guy, he was leaving.

Susan was very pleased that Jay was being discharged. Trying to handle Benny and James, make visits to the hospital to see Jay, and run the household was no small challenge. She was looking forward to Jay's homecoming and the coming weekend party. She desperately needed a few belts and a couple of good laughs with Brian and Louise.

Her excitement was evident. "Jay, I'll be there to pick you up at four thirty. I'll bring the kids. They have been concerned about you. Cecile called several times but I told her you were on the road for Action. I think she smells something. Brian met her at the hospital today when he was delivering something. Anyway, she chewed him out about you not returning her call. He called about a half hour ago. He doesn't know where you are either. He thinks you are out of town. Maybe you ought to call him tonight after you get home."

Jay acknowledged the need to call Cecile. He also said he would call Brian that evening. His intent was to call Ryan after he finished his conversation with Susan but the fact that Cecile was making such a fuss motivated him to retaliate. He cut short his conversation with Susan. As he hung up the receiver he asked his new-found buddy if he could place an in-house call. The man nodded in the affirmative and instructed Jay how to locate the number in the house directory. It was a simple matter of dialing the four-digit number.

The unit secretary in the Medical Intensive Care Unit Answered the phone immediately and in response to Jay's inquiry, informed him that Mrs. O'Sullivan was on duty. He was asked if he wanted to hold for a minute until she was available or she could return the call. Jay opted to hold. He reasoned that a return call to the SACAP unit could complicate the conversation.

In less than a minute Cecile answered the phone with her usual professional greeting. "This is Nurse O'Sullivan. How may I help you?"

"Nurse O'Sullivan, this is Mr. Jay Marquart. The question is how can I help you, as if I really cared?"

Cecile was not in the mood for Jay's smart mouth. She fired back with a blast of her own, "Well, Mr. Marquart, your antics of the past week are of sufficient note that my lawyer is preparing the necessary papers to return you to court. You have placed Kristie in harm's way with your habitual and excessive alcohol and drug use. I am advised that I have an obligation to bring your conduct and Mrs. Marquart's conduct as well to the attention of the court that way protecting Kirstie from harm and undue negative influence. You will lose your custody. My call was to advise you that papers would be served to you in the next few days. I will add the information that for the past few days you have obviously been in treatment at St. A's drug unit. We will subpoena your medical record. You know, Jay, I don't care if you and Susan dope yourselves to hell. But there is no way that my daughter is going to be subjected to the influence of her drunken, spaced out father and his junkie wife. You can try to ignore me but that won't matter once we get to court. This time you have really screwed up."

Jay was speechless. He feared that Cecile was on his trail after Kristie spilled the beans about his trip to Waltham Hospital on Saturday. How did the Bitch know that he was at St. Anslem's? Everything was supposed to be so confidential. He thought he was in a protected unit. Suddenly he realized that he had accidentally violated his own confidentiality. As he stared at the marvelous marvel of modem technologic telephone he noticed the small screen LED on the top of the instrument flashing the number of the station he had called and the name of the unit secretary that had answered. Apparently, Cecile was now looking at the LED on her telephone that was flashing the number and name of the Unit from which the call had been placed. He was nailed. He was at the moment too shocked to get angry. Tears filled his eyes and he sobbed. His tough cocky attitude dissipated. Gone was the humor that he had exchanged earlier with the man at the desk.

The man at the desk took note of the change. He got out of his chair, walked around the desk and stood at Jay's side. Gently he placed his hand on Jay's shoulder. The touch of compassion was welcomed by Jay. God, how he was in need of a friend.

Jay struggled to regain his composure and best Cecile, "Cecile you and your lawyer can cram it. You have no right to my medical records and you have no knowledge that would give cause of improper influence on Kristie. I'll have you out of her life for good if you try to disrupt my relationship with Kristie. Kiss off"

Jay slammed the telephone on the desk. Now he was enraged. Inadvertently he swung his fist at the man whom he had befriended a few minutes before.

The man with the skill of a prizefighter gracefully dodged the blow. Jay threw a chair across the room that crashed against the wall then bounced into a lamp that it destroyed. His anger accelerated. Three more pieces of furniture were pitched across the room. The office, reception desk, and adjacent area were systematically reduced into piles of debris. Jay raged, shouted, cursed and beat his fist into the wall.

A Code 777 SACAP was called by the unit head nurse to the hospital communication center and relayed through the entire institution via the audible paging system. Three massive security guards responded, well trained in handling violent patients. As they appeared Jay's new friend waved then out of sight. He allowed Jay to wear out his anger. Eventually, Jay tired. He sat down in the middle of the room, exhausted, and began to cry. His friend sat down next to him among the broken furniture, glass, torn paper, and various personal items from staff lockers. Gently, he placed his arm around Jay. Jay reached up and took the man's hand as a gesture of relief. He was asleep within a few minutes.

Jay's new friend sat in the chair next to the bed and waited. It was well past time for his lunch break but he had missed that many times before. He waited, as he had also done many times before.

After a few hours, Jay opened his eyes. He was still very tired and emotionally drained. He was also bathed in sweat. His clothes were damp and he felt a chill. The very dry condition of his throat was stark contrast. He was in desperate need of water. The shame of his outrage clouded his mind. Above the discomfort and shame was the overriding issue of the pending court fight with Cecile. Martha was his only counsel. He desperately needed to talk to her. Carefully he raised himself up and sat on the edge of the bed. It was then that he noticed the man in the chair next to the bed. It was the same guy that was with him when he lost it at the nurses' station.

The good dude with the quick smile and wicked sense of humor that Jay had tried to cold crock with his famous right hook sat peacefully watching Jay struggle to the edge of the bed. "How you doing, partner? Thirsty I bet. I'm usually thirsty when I come off a tear like that. Man, you messed up the place. Administration's going to flip. Well, they have to have something to do to earn the big bucks. What set you off, anyway? Here, I got you a glass of water."

Jay accepted the glass of water with noticeable gratitude. He raised the glass in salute before he gulped it down. He handed the glass back to the man who poured him another from the pitcher at his side. Again, Jay drained the glass without taking a breath.

On the third glass Jay sipped the contents slowly. He was beginning to regain composure. "You know, buddy, you seem to have been my constant companion for the past several hours and we haven't even been introduced. I'm Jay Marquart, patient extraordinare and self-appointed interior decorator of St. A's drunk tank. Who might you be?"

The man's quaint smile returned, "My name's Bob Markley. I used to have your job and, I might add, did a much better job on a regular basis. Now I'm confined to the payroll as a counselor. I think before the action started that you referred to me as a dweeb. Doctor Kenneth wanted me to chat with you this afternoon. I have to admit, it was an interesting interview."

The comment surprised Jay. He leaned forward and supported himself by spreading his arms to his side and placing his hands on the side of the bed as he sat. "Yeah. You ain't what I expected either. I don't know what to do now. This fucking hospital has messed me up big time. I came in here thinking that I was protected by the usual code of confidentiality. Now that goofy telephone has told the world including my ex-wife that I'm a junkie. Man, I'm gonna sue their ass. She's taking me to court knowing that I'm in here. The goddamn records are open for public scrutiny, she thinks. Where does she come off as a nurse in this hospital exposing the records of a patient? My sister's a lawyer. Man, she is going to sue your ass."

Markley was shaken by Jay's comment about litigation but he remained calm. "Jay, I can't comment on the status of the hospital in your dispute with your ex-wife. I can say that under Federal law if a patient seeks or receives treatment at a general hospital that operates a certified substance abuse program recognized by the Federal Government then the patient's treatment and the patient's records in the program remain confidential. No one, including the courts, can access that information. Any member of the hospital staff in any capacity that uses that information outside of the treatment program is subject to criminal action. St. A's program is fully accredited and certified by the Federal government. You are protected as a recipient of our care. The only way that your records would transfer out of here is if you were never admitted to the program. While you have been in the Unit for the past two days you have been classified as a general hospital patient. What Dr. Kenneth tried so ineffectively to explain to you this morning is that we want to admit you to the program. You rejected the idea but you might want to reconsider in view of recent events."

Jay wasn't sure he had heard what Markley said. "OK, let's see if I got this straight. I join your little dance party and my records get locked up. Nobody gets to them. But if I don't join, then my records are treated like general hospital records. Hell, what's the difference? General medical records are supposed to be confidential."

Markley got out of his chair and placed his hand on Jay's shoulder to emphasize the point, "General medical records are easily subpoenaed by the courts. Lawyers force disclosure through discovery all the time. It's not as easy in substance abuse programs. You can have your lawyer check it out. Anyway, it gives you better protection than you have now. My suggestion is that you voluntarily admit yourself to the program as of your date of admission on Tuesday. You can do that since you have not been discharged. We simply transfer you and your records out of general hospital into the program. Everything is locked up including your trip to Waltham hospital because Dr. Hendricks made a referral in your record to St. A's program. It's a nice neat package."

"What's the catch?" Jay was suspicious.

Markley sensed that he had Jay's attention, "Well you have to be serious about your treatment. If you admit to the program and then withdraw or refuse to accept treatment, which is the same as withdrawal, then you lose the Federal protection. Your records flow back to general hospital for whatever consequence."

The thought of protection was appealing but the thought of continuing treatment was discouraging. "Man, what am I getting into? I thought Dr. Kenneth wrote the discharge order. How we going to get around that?"

Markley waved his hand in the air as if to brush away a fly, "No sweat. I asked him not to make any entry on your chart until we had our little chat. I really didn't have any idea things would shape up this way. I thought maybe I would just beat the hell out of you and leave it at that. So, what do you say? Try it. You'll like it."

Jay was caught by Markley's comfortable manner. "OK sign me up. Did you ever sell used cars or do recruiting for the Marines?"

Bob Markley invited Jay back to the nursing station. Housekeeping had cleaned the place up. Some of the broken furniture had been replaced and there was an odor of fresh paint. Jay attempted a weak apology that Markley discounted. Apparently, the nurses' station and lobby were frequently rearranged by irate clients

The two men entered a very small office in back of the nurse station. Markley produced an admitting form to the Program that Jay signed after giving the small print a quick glance. He also signed another series of consent and release forms. Markley back dated the forms to last Tuesday. He handed Jay several pamphlets about the program that he instructed Jay to keep and use if he ran into questions from family and friends about his disease and treatment. Otherwise there was no need to advertise his condition.

One pamphlet was strictly for the employer. Markley noticed that Jay seemed to be staring at this one, "Jay, you worried about your job?"

"Yeah. My boss and the company nurse brought me in here. They know about me. How they gonna keep this out of my employee file?" Jay's eyes were closed as if experiencing some pain as he mouthed the question.

Markley made a quick check of Jay's medical record, "It says on the record that Action Waste Management referred you to us through their Employee Assistance Program. The only thing that should ever appear in your work record is the time that you are off the job for illness, vacation, and things like that. If you had a medical problem at work that the company nurse assisted with then that would be a part of her daily log. There should be no indication in your work file regarding your dependency problem. If it concerns you, I'll have our staff check your file or you can do it yourself when you get back to work."

The response brought Jay out of his temporary depression, "When can I go back to work? I got things stacked up. I was counting on being there tomorrow."

"Monday at the earliest. That wild spree that you went on a few hours ago is apt to hit you again. We need to get better acquainted over the next few days. You can go home this afternoon but I want you to spend your days here for a while. When you get over the hit that detox gives you then we can let you take a little more mental pressure. It's hard to tell at the beginning what might light your fuse. Apparently, your ex-wife lights you up real easy." Markley knew he had made an understatement.

Anger flared in Jay's eyes. He stood and pounded his fist on the counter, "Yeah, well she's gonna drag my ass into court over custody of my daughter. This goddam place gave her the information she needed to fry my ass. You gotta know that I'm going after her big time. This hospital is in deep shit, I'll own this goddam place before it's over. That fucking telephone system is gonna cost you big bucks. I thought hospital employees were supposed to keep patient information confidential. Seems to me that I could have her nursing license revoked."

Markley tried to appease his patient, "Jay, you are getting agitated and in a few minutes your anger will erupt into violence. I'll see that it doesn't happen. You and I can talk about something else, or if you want, we can talk more about your concern. The key here is that we talk out your anxiety and anger. That's why I want you to spend a lot of time with me over the next few days. You'll meet some other people who understand your problem and the disease that causes it. In time, you will realize how beneficial it is to have someone to turn to when the pressure moves you to a breaking point. You will get to know a lot of people in the many support groups that are available."

The thought of a full-blown counseling program was not what Jay had in mind. "Look, Bob, you know that I'm not really big into this stuff. I'm hiding my record so my Ex can't take my daughter away from me. You gave me the idea. All the rest of this stuff is a little far out. Sounds like you figure me for a head case."

"In a way, you are." Markley came back at him. "What makes you different from a psycho is that the cause of your anger is very evident. You are going through a form of withdrawal. The change taking place in your body chemistry causes a psychic reaction that manifests in violent behavior. Dr. Kenneth will monitor your chemistry and give you supplements that moderate your emotions while your body adjusts to what we expect to be a permanent change in your life style. However, the type of disease that you have cannot be cured medically. It can only be controlled by a combination of medicine and a strong dose of individual will power. Dr. Kenneth will evaluate your physical needs and prescribe the appropriate therapy. I'll be your buddy during this process and together we can work on the will power bit. Take it from me, it's not going to be easy."

It was apparent to Jay that the price of protection from Cecile was cooperation with Markley. With some degree of courtesy, he tried to explain his position, "So you think that between now and Monday I'll get religion. Man, that's far out. I can't wait to get out of here. The only thing that will bring me back is Kristie, that's my daughter. No way am I going to swallow Kenneth's medicine. I told him this morning that taking drugs to stop taking drugs was bullshit. I'll listen to you but I'm not going to start taking those weird pills. You know I used to work in the cath. lab here. I saw those docs pump up the charges on those patients with a lot of stuff that didn't mean shit. What did the patient know? Nothing, man. They just wanted to live. Well, I just want to keep my daughter."

"OK, Jay, we'll take it one step at a time." Markley was satisfied that he had a taker.

One of the first procedures in the first step involved a telephone call to Ken Ryan at Action Waste Management. Jay's call was warmly received by Ken who emoted about the prospect of the Boston project. It was expected to start as early as tomorrow. Ken was in hope that Jay would be back on board. Jay reported that he had to continue treatment through the weekend and would possibly be back to work on Monday. His new buddy, Bob Markley, got on the phone at Jay's request and explained in careful terms that Jay's condition required careful monitoring for the next few days. The call concluded with Ken reporting to Jay that a Mr. Donovan desperately needed to talk to him. He gave Donovan's phone number to Jay.

Jay called Donovan and explained that he had been sick and in the hospital for the past couple of days. He had to stay home for another few days and would be back to work on Monday. Donovan asked Jay to call him tomorrow since it was noised about that the Boston project at Action was going to kick off. The Union contract had to be worked out so that the workers got a piece of the rewards. A good health plan was definitely a part of the discussion. Jay agreed to give Donovan another call in the morning.

At four thirty Susan came into the Unit. Benny and James were left in the main lobby with coloring books being carefully watched by the volunteers on duty. Susan was anxious to get back to her charges and became noticeably irritated when Jay asked her to take a few minutes to meet Bob Markley. She became increasingly agitated as Bob explained that

Jay was not being discharged but allowed to go home in the evenings. His days were to be spent in the Unit through the weekend. Susan realized that somehow Markley had got his clutches on Jay. She feared the goody two shoes life style that often accompanied the reformed. This could mean a damper on the weekend party that she desperately needed.

On the way home, she noticeably pouted about the days ahead. Jay didn't appreciate her attitude. He was concentrating on the legalities ahead of him while trying to form the details in mind so he could give Martha the material to hang Cecile and St. Anslem's in the bargain.

The happy Marquart family arrived home and proceeded to enjoy a welcome home dinner that Susan prepared for their hero. Jay was in very good spirits. In similar circumstances, he would have had two or three gin and grapefruits. Now he was sober and intent on staying that way. Susan missed the usual jag that accompanied the family's good times. Somehow things just didn't seem the same. After dinner Jay moved in front of the TV to take in the sports report on the evening news. His timing was perfect to see and hear the headline story about the pending resignation of the Mayor and the resignation of the Commissioner of Health who was to become a part of the Archdiocesan staff. Jay caught the comment that the former Commissioner was to be the Director of Health so he made a mental note to sue the Church as well as St. Anslem's although he wasn't too sure what he would do with a Church if he won. The kids hung around Jay until they were certain that he was home for the night. Then they disappeared to other haunts.

As the sports reports began, the Marquart telephone broke Jay's attention on the latest Red Sox win. When he answered the phone his concentration remained focused on the interview with the relief pitcher who managed to get the final out on three straight strikes. His attention shifted immediately, however, to Martha's greeting following his bland hello.

Martha was insistent on penetrating the events of the past few days. "Well, my dear brother, what have you been up to the past five days? My guess is that you have teased your former wife to a state of frenzy."

"Martha, thanks for calling." Jay was excited and began to ramble. "We got to talk. Man, that bitch really messed up this time. I want you to sue her ass and St. Anslem's Hospital. We goin' to nail them big time."

The strength of Jay's reply caused Martha to try a counter measure. "She apparently thinks you are the one who messed up. I don't know what to think. Your lawyer that handled the divorce was advised by her lawyer that you are going to be served with papers tomorrow claiming that you are an unfit parent, an alcoholic, drug abuser, and a few other things all of which is intended to return you to court for a custody hearing. He called me and asked me to tip you off. I wanted you to know that you will be served and advise you not to beat the shit out of the process server. Remember that he is a court official. Please be a good boy and accept the papers without contest or comment. Bring them to your divorce lawyer and we can take it from there. What have you been up to anyway?"

Jay detailed the events of the weekend beginning with his trip to Waltham Hospital. He proudly added his new status as Shop Steward with Local 936 and the Action union as prelude to the event Tuesday morning that caused his trip to St. Anslems. He omitted telling Martha anything about his experience at the Troubadour with Cecile's husband but he did explain that his illness of Tuesday was prompted by a drinking and smoking spree with Brian the night before. The big event, from Jay's point of view, was the telephone call with Cecile and the telephone system at St. Anslems. Jay was confident that he had complete immunity from Cecile's charges because of his enrollment in the St. Anslem's Chemical Addiction Program. Martha remarked that she was not familiar with the Federal law regarding substance abuse program immunity. She would check it out in the morning. She also advised Jay to stay cloistered in the SACAP during the day but to expect that the process server would find him at home or at work when he returned.

After some more thought, Martha conceded that Cecile may have compromised herself. Guardedly, she explained, "Jay, off the top of my head, I think that you may have a point about Cecile. She could be in big trouble. The hospital is another story. I'll talk to some plaintiff attorneys about the malpractice issue. If you have a case they'll grab it on contingency. We need to talk about it some more. Let's plan on getting together as soon as you can without messing up your participation in the program at the hospital. You need to maintain your status in that effort. Let me know when you are going to get sprung."

Martha was relieved that Jay was participating in the SACAP program. She and the rest of the Marquart clan knew that Jay needed help for years. Any mention of this to Jay was always ignored or met with angry response. In her own way, Martha prayed that Jay would stick with it this time. She was certain that without the benefit of the program he was without a defense to Cecile's custody challenge. Jay, on the other hand, concluded the call with Martha, encouraged over the prospect of gaining full custody of Kristie, receiving a generous settlement from the Hospital, and forcing Cecile on to welfare as a consequence of losing her nursing license. Things were definitely looking up. He felt good enough to give buddy Brian a call.

Brian answered the phone on the first ring and Jay fired a greeting, "Brian, my main man, I hear tell that the Bitch worked you over yesterday at St. A's. Man, you don't have to take nothing from her. I got her good this time. I been spending some time at St. A's myself, following up on Sunday. How you doing?"

"Hey, Jay. I'm fine, man. How about you? Why they hang on to you so long? You can't pay or something? I got a few bucks and maybe Louise can chip in. Say we get the crowd down at the Waltham to have a charity drink me down for your benefit. What do you say, man?"

The idea of a charity drink fest to help a drunk struck Jay as very funny. He decided to humor his friend in reply, "Well, Brian, the hospital says that I got to cut down on the partying. They got me coming back during the day for a while until I get straighten out. I'll be fine in a week or so. I just been hitting. It's nothing.

"Hey, we goin fishing Friday night? I got the boat out at Hingham. I hear from the Customer that the Blues are running. It's time we get out there, man. We got skunked last time. Time to get even."

"Not this time, Brian. Benny's got a game again and I got to rest after. The hospital wants me to come in on Saturday. They do a test and I got to be clean. I'm gonna be very dry for a while. Let's get together on Saturday evening as usual. Susan and the kids are looking forward to it."

Brian still didn't quite get the message, "Yeah, man. Louise and I enjoy it to. You want me to come packing? There's some quality joy in town."

"Oh, Brian, my man you are the party mule. I just told you I got to stay clean. You bring what you think you and the girls will want. I'm not having any, thank you."

oOo

Thursday morning was warm, bright and clear. The Mayor enjoyed his stroll to City Hall greeting well-wishers along the way. He was in very good spirits. The night before he had received final notice that he was the Nominee for the position as Under Secretary of Labor for the United States Department of Labor. Washington would release the information from the President's office before noon. The matter had been leaked to the wire services late last night and, therefore, would be the topic of interest by the media at the City Council meeting. His official resignation would take place next week at the Council meeting but would be a matter of routine for him. Siro would gain the spotlight next week. Between now and then it would be Mayor Cowan's time to celebrate and be celebrated by the Boston media. It was a real story about a local boy making it big on the national scene. Just what the Mayor needed to pave the way for his eventual return as the Democratic candidate for Governor. His plan was working well.

As Mayor Cowan entered City Hall a Boston Globe beat reporter came by his side and began asking questions about the transition. The questions were more for the reporter's information than as a matter of report. The Mayor invited the reporter to walk with him to the office where they chatted about several items in the process of resignation. The Mayor appeared successful in cultivating the young reporter. Sharon, the faithful secretary, filled their coffee cups and maintained the process of cleaning the files, packing personal items, and answering the phone that was now constantly ringing. At eight thirty she invited the reporter to step outside while reminding the Mayor that he had to prepare for the Council meeting scheduled for ten o'clock. As the reporter was leaving the office, Council President Alphonse Siro and Commissioner Michael Francis Megan, currently of Parks and Recreation and soon to be of Health and Hospitals, walked in. The reporter decided to wait around in the outer office.

Al Siro had in hand several press releases regarding the appointment of Megan to the Commissioner of health position. Of even greater importance, was the resolution supporting the initiation of a voluntary waste management program for the City of Boston. The resolution made the program effective immediately upon acceptance. The Mayor was quick to approve the resolution and press release. He was also delighted to begin to pass the routine of the Mayor's office to Council President Siro. The two men had conspired to have Siro actually run his office and the Mayor's for the past week and now going forward until after the special election that the City Council had to arrange. The tact was obviously to establish Siro in the minds of the voters so that he would be the choice for Mayor elect.

The three men conferred for about an hour. At nine thirty they left the Mayor's office for the City Council Chambers. The Globe reporter strolled with them as if one of the party much to the chagrin of the reporters from the electronic media crammed in the Council Chambers. The other members of the Council were already present. They surrounded Cowan and Siro as they entered the room. The Mayor accepted the individual acknowledgments with excellent poise. Everyone was very well behaved. Even the media seemed to respect the collegial order that prevailed this important meeting. At exactly ten AM, President Siro called the meeting to order. Several matters of routine business were handled with dispatch. Next on the agenda was the resignation of Commissioner Michael Logan.

Council President Siro asked Mayor Cowan to report the resignation of the Commissioner and to announce his interim successor. Mayor Cowan reported that Commissioner Logan had long sought an opportunity to enter the private sector and become involved in the direct provision of health services.

"It is to his credit and to the credit of the Boston Catholic Archdiocese that their mutual interest can be served by integrating the Church's healing mission with the dedication of a health professional committed to the public's interest" was the opening theme of the Mayor's report. He concluded by praising the work of the Church in carrying for the Boston community saying in conclusion that. "Michael Logan is truly an honorable public servant that deserves credit for his attention to the health needs of the community."

When the Mayor concluded his report, President Siro introduced a resolution of gratitude to Michael Logan. The resolution was passed unanimously.

The Mayor requested the floor again and announced Megan as his choice to replace Logan as Commissioner of Health. Megan needed no introduction to the Council, the media, or to the residents of Boston. His very active manner and enthusiasm for his job had endeared him to the public. He was a budding politician who was cutting his teeth in public service. Someday he intended to be mayor. As for now he was content to share in the bright lights of the Office transition. He was at this time becoming a prominent matter of record. At the Mayor's beckoning, Megan stepped to his side. The Mayor embraced the new appointee as the media cameras recorded the event.

President Siro called the meeting back to order at which time he accepted a resolution to endorse and support Mayor Cowan's appointment of Commissioner Megan as the interim Commissioner of Public Health. Again, the motion was passed unanimously.

The Mayor thanked President Siro and the Council for their supporting resolutions. He then baited the media by stating that the replacement for Commissioner of Parks and Recreation would be announced in the future. Perhaps next week. He however, had no one in mind at his time. The media became drawn to the reality that the Mayor's own resignation would be the topic of the next City Council meeting. The media seemed to surge at the inference. Siro noted the interest and immediately called a twenty-minute recess. The media swarmed to the Mayor and began asking questions about his Federal appointment, his resignation, and plans for transition.

Things were going exactly as planned by Siro and Cowan. They had decided at their morning conference to create a media diversion before the introduction of the voluntary waste management program to the Council. They reasoned that by creating interest in the Mayor before the recess, the media would have filled their notebooks and cameras with sufficient material. As expected, the majority of the electronic media were folding their equipment at the end of the recess time. When President Siro called the meeting back to order only the assigned beat reporters from the local newspapers remained.

Council President Siro introduced the subject of waste management as a matter of concern for the City Council. He explained the history of the project going back at least ten years when the City found it necessary to begin an expensive process of harbor clean up and water reclamation. He pointed out that the project although funded in the main by the Federal government had nevertheless required the City and surrounding Communities to experience the highest water rates in the nation. Now it was time, if not past time, to continue the cleanup of the area through a process of waste control and management of waste disposal. This included a recycling program for the City but more important it had to include a recycling and waste management program for private industry and private residences.

Siro concluded his remarks by pointing out that improper control of waste material and toxic agents was the fifth ranking cause of death in the United States last year. "These agents," according to Mr. Siro, "could be traced to environmental pollutants, food and water contaminants, ingredients in commercial products and many more related health problems." He proposed that the City had a large responsibility dealing with asbestos, childhood exposure to lead, as well as the new large-scale changes that the City needed to contemplate. "Therefore," he concluded after twenty minutes of information that he read from an Action brochure, "the City requires the assistance immediately of a qualified private company to assist in the protection and maintenance of a high standard of health for the citizens of Boston."

Following the presentation by the President of the Council, the Mayor explained that the City was particularly blessed to have the Nation's leading private waste management company located in Boston. This company, at the invitation of the Mayor, had submitted a bid to cover the Boston Hospital's waste management process at a saving of thirty percent under present costs. The City Budget Office had confirmed these savings. With the concurrence of the City Council the Mayor would sign the contract with Action Waste Management to implement a waste management program at City Hospital immediately. President Siro then called for a motion to approve the Action Waste Management/Boston Hospital agreement. Again, the motion passed without opposition.

After the vote on the City Hospital contract, and on cue, a member of the Council called for a vote supporting the voluntary privatization of waste management for the City. "This vote," he explained, "would open the door for private waste management companies such as Action to promote a healthy environment without imposing higher taxes on a community already overtaxed."

This time there was some dissension as several Council members argued that the citizens were not over taxed but perhaps under-served. The debate made for good theater and also served to tire the remaining reporters who were faced with deadlines. Siro allowed the debate to continue until it was obvious that the reporters had enough. He then called for the vote which passed by a sound majority exactly as planned. As the Council meeting came to a close, Siro noted with pleasure that the meeting had extended well beyond the two hour schedule. It was nearly one thirty. The Council had worked through the lunch hour. No one could say that the people were not getting their money's worth from the City Council.

Mark Meehan sat in the back of the City Council Chambers for the entire meeting. He had supplied Council President Siro with pages of material on environmental control. Most of the information had been published by Park in a sales handbook for their respective agencies. With Meehan was the company attorney who noted the time and date of the Council's votes regarding waste management. After the meeting the attorney went immediately to the office of the City Clerk to obtain copies of the resolutions. Meehan went straight to his office filled with the excitement of the Boston Project. It was now official. The project was underway. At his direction, his secretary called another management meeting on the Boston Project. These meetings were turning into daily affairs.

Bob Muldoon was also at the Council meeting. He sat with Meehan and commented from time to time about the actors on the stage. He seemed pleased with their performance. After the final curtain call Muldoon moved to the front of the Council. He sought out his friend, Megan, and congratulated him on his new assignment. Siro noticed Muldoon from across the room and made special effort to come to his side. Siro was very obvious about securing Labor's support in the mayoral special election. Muldoon did not hesitate to offer that support. Their relationship extended over Siro's entire political career. Marty Hart, President of Local 936, the only local in Boston having a contract or near contract with a waste management firm, was also at the meeting. With him was Dave Donovan, Business Manager of 936. They sat apart from Muldoon but moved to his side as he began to talk to Siro. Otherwise the two 936 officials chatted about the situation at Action Waste Management concerning their new shop steward. Donovan was concerned that Marquart was sick at a very critical time. Hart advised him to give it another week. Muldoon introduced his associates to Al Siro who seemed genuinely pleased to have their acquaintance.

Charles Patello was also in the back of the Council Chambers. He and Meehan intended to meet there but Patello steered away when Muldoon moved into the chair next to Meehan. Muldoon was Meehan's problem now. Patello had other matters at hand now that the Waste Management project was under way. There remained the mystery of O'Shea's interest in the check deposited in Logan's account. He left the Council Chambers as the meeting concluded and walked back to his office where he immediately placed a call to Mario Capizzi. Mr. Capizzi was very pleased that all the details for implementing the Action project were now complete save the minor issue of the Mayor's resignation. That was simply a matter of timing since the Mayor had publicly announced that he had accepted the Federal appointment. Capizzi gave Patello a well done and concluded with the question of what was next on Patello's agenda.

Patello saw the question as an opportunity to discuss the O'Shea matter, "Mario, we have one glitch that could be trouble. Boston Security's Executive Vice President, a guy named O'Shea, looked over the bonus check. He apparently noticed the Mayor's endorsement. He sent a verbal message to Logan via the courier that the money where ever it came from is in Logan's account. He essentially told Logan that he thinks the money is dirty. Logan called me to ask what's going on. I told Logan that O'Shea's nose is out of joint because he isn't in the know about the donors. Logan seemed to buy this. Then I told Mondi who checked the courier who tells him that O'Shea made copies of the check, the courier's log and I don't know what all. You know that O'Shea is a member of the

St. Anslem's Board. Hardly, O'Shea and I control the place along with a Dr. Folley, who happens to be O'Shea's son in law. Anyway, O'Shea and Folley pull a fast one on me and convince the Cardinal to make Folley the head of the Office of Health Affairs."

Capizzi was very confused at Patello's rambling explanation, "Charlie, you need to take a little time off. I can't follow you. About all I understand is that some big wig at the Bank is aware that the money in Logan's account came from the Mayor. Now the son of a bitch may have some ulterior motive in pimping Logan about the account. That motive is not clear. He knew that you were involved in cutting the employment deal with Logan but he didn't bother calling you about the check. In fact, he didn't bother calling Logan about the check. He chose, instead, to send a cynical message to Logan that essentially said that he was in the know. You think he might want a piece of Logan? He probably figures that Logan and the Mayor are in a deal. He knows that you arranged for the private bank account but he doesn't know, at least not yet, that you or we paid him a signing bonus. It seems to me that the best thing to do at this stage is nothing. You play it straight like you know nothing about a signing bonus. I doubt that Logan will bring it up to anybody but you. If he does, then we'll come up with a cover story. Right now, the trail is to the Mayor just like we wanted it. This O'Shea guy I bet is on that trail for his own good."

"That's probably true, Mario." Patello began to relax and realized that he had pushed the panic button, "I've been a buddy of O'Shea's since our days at Boston College. I'll tell you this, the guy is just smart enough to make him dangerous. Right now, he has the information about Logan's account that is just like a loaded gun. The fool could pull the trigger without thinking and screw everything up. Remember you put the wrapper on Logan as a trigger to nail the mayor. Now O'Shea has the same gun but doesn't know who or how to fire it."

Capizzi was pleased that Patello had regained control of his emotions, "That's right. If he was straight he would have made an issue about the check and never have processed it into Logan's account. My thought is that he might be smarter than you think and have a target in mind or he might realize that the information has great potential for future return. That's what you would expect from a banker. The bastards are all crooked at heart. Let's wait him out. Keep a close eye on him. Say nothing to anybody about this. Anything else?"

Patello answered, "We have a Board meeting at St. Anslem's on Tuesday. That's when we put Logan into the lineup. We'll see then if O'Shea has anything immediate in mind or is playing for the long run. I'll keep you posted."

In Capizzi's mind he thought it time to end the conversation, "OK. I'll brief Marone and Big Frank. Big Frank doesn't like surprises. You best tell Meehan and Mondi its business as usual. We play out the string as planned. Anything comes of this O'Shea issue we'll deal with it from New York. You keep me posted. You also got to play it cool with O'Shea. He may be looking at you just like you are looking at him. Don't tip your hand."

Patello felt relieved after his telephone conversation with Capizzi. He cleaned up his office, dictated a few letters, and placed a call to Siro for a round of golf later in the afternoon. The courting had begun.

oOo

Joseph Durant sat at his desk studying the Boston newspapers. Both the Globe and Herald devoted the entire front page to the pending resignation of Mayor Cowan. Cowan was glorified by both papers as a visionary Mayor that brought the City to new heights with his programs in environmental control, health and safety, and public recreation. Both papers featured pictures of the Mayor during his campaign talking to the man on the street or riding a fire truck The Globe also carried a side bar story about Commissioner Michael Logan's resignation and his new appointment as Director of the Office for Health Affairs for the Archdiocese. This was the main point of interest for Durant. He was both angry and offended that the Archdiocese hadn't informed him of the new Office. He also wondered if the Office would absorb any of the functions of the Hospital President. The newspaper accounts centered on the accomplishments of the Commissioner with little information about his new assignment.

The Herald carried the same stories about the Mayor but differed in its inside report about Commissioner Logan. It implied that the

Commissioner was over his head in dealing with the complex problems of the City. It pointed out that his extreme dedication to the inner-city health problems was admirable but he left healthcare in general get out of hand. The provision of health services was the City's third largest industry next to State government and Private education. That industry, according to the Herald report, was shameful due to the outrageous profiteering and gouging of the public trust by private hospitals. The report called for the new Commissioner and the Interim Mayor to appoint a special Blue-Ribbon Task Force to investigate the deteriorating status of health services in the Boston Metropolitan area.

The Boston Business Journal was published twice a week. It had been focusing stories about healthcare in Boston for over a year. For the most part, they watched the action of the major downtown teaching hospitals as the barometer of the industry. Hospital profits and executive salaries were a common focus. Their editorials were sharply critical of the major hospital Boards and Presidents. Reporters followed executives on weekends taking special note of their extravagant homes, yachts, and golf club memberships. In recent editions, the Journal had begun a series of reports about the excess utilization of Boston Hospitals. It predicted that Boston's over capacity of hospital beds would be eliminated by the new reimbursement methods currently being implemented by the Health Maintenance Organizations. One writer described it as a gigantic melt down of the healthcare industry that would eliminate over a third of the hospitals in the area and displace over six thousand employees. While not stated, the implication was that the smaller hospitals in the City would succumb to the change. It appeared that the rule of the jungle was being applied to healthcare reform in Boston.

Durant knew that the Journal articles, while colored in rhetoric, were based on fact. The future of St. Anslem's was a matter of great concern to him. He felt a desperate urge to express his anxiety and emphasize the need for survival planning at the Board meeting next Tuesday. Unfortunately, the great Thomas O'Shea had pre-emoted the agenda with his microscopic attention to the details of finance.

Durant nursed his frustration. He told himself over and over again that he could regain control by cooperating with the ridiculous demands of O'Shea. He also resolved in his mind to welcome Logan and the Office of Health Affairs. His intent was to capture the focus of the Office on the survival issue and in that way hopefully redirect the Board to the big picture. He decided not to make an issue about not being informed or included in the formation of the Office. It was best to make sure that his trusted vice president for finance was well prepared with every detail in response to Mr. O'Shea's criticisms of the hospital's fiscal status and operational deficiencies. After about three hours of contemplation he regained his composure and asked his Executive Assistant to arrange a time for him to have a pre-board briefing with Rod Weaver, Senior VP for finance. He also asked the executive assistant to invite Mitch Daly, the hospital's Senior Vice President for strategic planning to attend the briefing.

It was Durant's intent to have Daly well informed on the Board's focus on the fiscal item while Daly prepared the appropriate analysis on strategic issues. Durant intended to redirect the Board's attention to strategy for survival over the next three months as the new fiscal year approached. Strategic planning was an excellent complement to budgeting. The fiscal year for St. Anslem's began on October first. Between now and then Durant intended to combine the talents of Weaver and Daly into the most reliable authority on health services in the area. That team combined with his leadership would be the means by which Durant would lead the Board of Trustees and St. Anslem's into its future as the premier Catholic Hospital in New England.

oOo

While Durant pondered the future of St. Anslem's Hospital, Bob Markley pondered the life and times of Jay Marquart. It was nearly nine o'clock and Mr. Marquart had not appeared in the Unit. Markley was questioning his judgment in letting Jay go home last night. He was still very brittle. If his ex-wife hassled him or if his current wife began to mope, Jay could easily revert. He had not yet taken the first step toward recovery. That precious first step required the addict to admit that he or she was hooked. Markley knew that it would take Jay a while to come to that important conclusion. Durant also recognized in Jay an inner strength to meet the challenge of recovery. He was a fighter and a man with passion. He easily displayed compassion and love for others. On the other hand he required love from others. These were the qualities that Markley recognized as prospects toward recovery. He sat at the desk staring at Jay's chart and said his daily prayer for his friends, the recovering patients.

The telephone in front of Markley reminded him of a more immediate concern. From his point of view, "that damn thing," had indeed violated the rule of confidentiality when it signaled to Jay's ex-wife that he was in the unit. Certainly, the lawyers if they got involved would come up with a thousand mitigating circumstances that obliterated the hospital's liability. In the argument the patient would be lost from recovery. Markley was certain of that. However, Jay's determination to litigate the matter forced Markley to prepare an official hospital incident report that had to be submitted to the Risk Management Director who would notify the hospital's malpractice-practice carrier who would notify a defense attorney who would assign a claim manager who would do whatever it took to blame Jay for the whole thing.

Markley knew he had no choice but to prepare and submit the incident report. But he decided to send the matter through the Director of the SACAP Unit, Dr. Ron Anderson, for review before it was channeled to Risk Management. Dr. Anderson was Bob Markley's hero. He, in Markley's eyes was a miracle worker with addicted persons. A kind and compassionate man who was adept at moving around rules that obstructed patient care, Anderson would recognize the problem and find a solution to the administrative dilemma. Markley inserted the required form in the typewriter and began to peck out the answers to the numbered questions. He was pondering the wording and description of the incident when a shadow moved across the desk. He looked up into the smiling face of Jay Marquart. He extended a hand to him and commented, "Jay, you're late. Good to see you. Have a good night?"

Jay appeared in good spirits, "Yes I did, Bob. Nice of you to ask. I don't recall that you mentioned a starting time. We on a time clock?"

"Not exactly. You do remember that hospitals operate on a certain routine. It's rather convenient to have the patient around when the lab tech shows up to draw blood. Little things like that are seen by some as important. I'll call the lab and tell them that you have arrived. They'll be so pleased. Dr. Kenneth will be in shortly. Glad you arrived before him. Otherwise he would have to make a house call."

Jay was not impressed, "Yeah, right. Look I talked to my Sister last night about this flap with my Ex. Seems that I'm going to be served some papers. Can they do that to me in here?"

Markley was not about to let Jay worry about the presence of a court order, "Jay, no one knows you're here but us chickens. The front desk has you as discharged from general hospital. They don't know where you are. If, by chance, the process server gets by the front desk he won't get into this unit. We have a security force that loves to throw people into the street. You will probably be served at home or at work next week. And, by the way, could you manage to check in here by eight o'clock? We would appreciate it. Here, go pea in this bottle."

Jay complied with the request and returned the specimen to the desk. A Lab tech in a white coat two sizes too small met Jay at the desk and took the urine specimen. He then escorted Jay to a small room where he extracted a small vile of Jay's blood. Jay's attempt to make small talk fell on deaf ears. The tech was not a friendly sort. Jay was prone to suggest that the tech needed a stiff belt but thought differently as he saw Dr. Kenneth enter the Unit. The Doctor began reviewing several charts that Markley had selected for his review. The two men were conferring when Jay walked back to the desk. Markley nodded to Jay and then asked a nursing assistant to take Mr. Marquart to the patient library to view the video presentation. Jay obediently followed the attractive young lady to a former patient room now equipped with a couch and a few recliners facing a television and a VCR All of the furniture had seen better days. On each side of the room were battered bookshelves containing a few books and a lot of pamphlets.

The nursing assistant invited Jay to have a seat and be comfortable. She offered him a cup of juice or water that he declined. She then pulled down the tattered window blinds, turned on the television and started the VCR. As the video began she left the room. Jay realized that they only way he could escape the approaching propaganda was to leave the room or turn off the set. Either option would be seen as discourteous, rude, and obstinate, he thought. There was no need to be that offensive to kind people who seemed eager to be of service. Jay decided to go along with the game. He settled back in his recliner to enjoy the video. The flick began with an assortment of down and out bums aimlessly through littered streets and then panned to a well-dressed, up and coming, Harvard type sitting in a BMW smoking a joint. The scene shifted to a group of business types having lunch with several drinks. As the group departed one member walked to the bar instead of out the door. He ordered a drink and began a casual narrative about his decision to enjoy life by his standards. The key to the good life, according to the drinking narrator was maintaining control of your own destiny. He hastily drank his drink and ordered another. Following the consumption of the second drink and more narrative about his staunch independence he dropped the money on the bar and left, apparently in full control of his destiny. Following scenes depicted his failure to make appointments, loss of customers, arguments with his spouse, divorce, unemployment, fiscal disaster and eventual transition to the street aimlessly walking and looking for his lost destiny. He appeared in poor health. As he collapsed a friend picked him up and escorted him into a shelter where he was given nourishment, clothes, and assistance in his recovery.

The concluding scene showed the recovering alcoholic regaining his dignity and control of his destiny. He explained that controlling his destiny required control of his addiction. That type of control required the understanding of his disease and the benefit of support from others who understood the many difficulties faced by an addicted and dependent person. The final scenes pictured various support groups in the conduct of their meetings and providing individual support. The now recovering narrator praised the work of the groups and offered to be of assistance to the viewer as the telephone numbers of the groups rolled over the screen.

Jay, for lack of anything else to do, watched the video with mild interest He recalled the same type presentations in high school. Then he thought the corny acting was funny. He and his buddies would mock the flicks as they partied after school. Now he began of wonder if the film had some message for him. His life carried some of the tragedy depicted in the story but he had reasonable comfort and happiness. The struggle he had with Cecile over Kristie was rooted, he admitted, in his determination to party above all else. He also realized that his family and his life with Susan was centered on the good times associated with the high that he and Susan so often sought. They were always financially distressed. They were compatible. Were they addicted? He was holding the question in his mind when Dr. Kenneth greeted him from the hall.

Dr. Kenneth's inquiry about Jay's current state of body and mind brought a courteous response from Jay. The good Doctor noticed Jay's change of attitude from their first meeting. This was a definite sign of progress. He invited Jay to walk down the hall to his office. Once there he gave him a standard physical exam. A nurse appeared and stuck a thermometer in Jay's mouth. As Jay's temperature was being recorded, Dr. Kenneth flipped through the chart making various notes.

Kenneth eventually closed the chart, removed the thermometer, looked at it, and put it aside as he addressed his patient, "Jay, your body is responding well to treatment. Your lab and urine tests show that the presence of alcohol and cocaine use are substantially gone. This is normal. But you are in a fragile state. If you consume any substance of that sort over the weekend you could have another incident like the one that brought you in here. Your blood still carries very evident traces of marijuana. That shows little or no decline over the time that you have been with us. This does not necessarily mean that you have used marijuana in the last few days. The chemical trace of that substance in a habitual user will remain for a long time even if the person completely refrains. We should begin to see a decline after a week. It could be a month or maybe two before you test completely clean. That should be your goal. Test clean and then stay that way. In the interim we will provide you with the support that your body needs to adjust to the new you. I would like you to take some medication that will help you overcome your craving for these substances. We also have something that will help you control your anger. Mr. Markley told me about your incident yesterday."

Dr. Kenneth offered Jay three pills and a paper cup filled with water. Jay looked at the pills and reluctantly put them in his mouth, drank the water, swallowed, and attempted to talk. "Doctor, I'll give this medication thing a try. I don't know why but as long as I'm here I might as well play your game. If these things mess me up then you got to know that I won't take another one. I've heard about guys being hooked on methadone. They are as spaced out as dope heads on opium. I'll go cold turkey before I get hooked on that treatment."

Dr. Kenneth explained, "Jay, you are going through withdrawal from three substances, cocaine, alcohol and marijuana. You have used these substances in increasing quantities over the past several. Your dependency obviously was increasing so now we are reversing that biological trend. We are uncertain how you will react to this transition mentally and emotionally. Our attempt with the medication is to fortify you against a convulsive reaction like you experienced Monday and an emotional breakdown like you experienced yesterday. We know from experience that every patient experiencing withdrawal has physical and mental side effects. We can't predict the severity of those side effects. Your situation is better than most because we are treating you before you totally overdosed and experienced a severe major physical and mental breakdown. That's the up side. The down side is that we are faced with greater uncertainty about withdrawal side effects than we would be in treating what you describe as dope heads on opium. We do know that you are experiencing side effects. Markley watched you do it. We are confident that you will have more."

Jay tried to act sincere, "So how long am I gonna be a head case?"

Dr. Kenneth continued, "Well cocaine withdrawal which is the substance having the greatest impact is generally not predictable. We have recognized that cocaine abstinence syndrome has three stages. Phase one could last only a few hours. In some cases, we have seen it last up to nine days. Phase one is the most serious. This is when a patient becomes violent and does physical harm to himself or someone else. In phase two the patient becomes less violent but may experience severe depression. The depression eliminates harm to others but may cause the patient to harm himself. Phase one and two may overlap. There is no clear cut line between them. The second phase may take from one to ten weeks. Phase three is that time when the patient recognizes the problem and struggles to be free of the addiction. A failure in the attempt triggers the effects of one and two. Phase three has an indefinite time phase. It just goes on and on. What is important to the patient's recovery, just as it is to people addicted to alcohol, is the recognition of their addiction and the ability to seek the support from others in helping them avoid the crash. What I'm telling you is that there is no known cure from addiction. The disease can be controlled."

Jay seemed to modify his doubts, "Man this is weird. I been hanging around this place for the past four days and all of a sudden I got an incurable disease."

"Correction. You've been hanging around this place for four days and now know that you have an incurable disease. You were sick when you came in here, remember. You just didn't believe it." Dr. Kenneth tried to regain Jay's attention to the point

Jay remained skeptical, "Yeah, I'm still not completely convinced that I'm sick as you put it. Another way of looking at it could be that I was on a weekend drunk and took a bad trip. You know—like a bad hangover. Otherwise I feel fine."

"I recognize your disbelief" Kenneth attempted to be tactful but direct, "You weren't hit hard enough to be a believer. The guys that get hit the hardest are the first to admit the problem but are usually too far gone to do anything about it. You, at the moment, don't fully admit the problem but have the strength to do something about it. Hopefully you won't wait to get the big hit. This is the time to start your recovery."

"I'm here aren't I? What's the drill?" Jay's anger started to flare, "I give you my blood, pea in a bottle, watch a class B video—that's it? Where's the beef, man?"

"Good questions, Jay. The drill is rather loose except for the medication and observation. We will see that you get plenty of rest over the weekend. Mr. Markley will explain the support methods in place to assist with your recovery and I'll keep tabs on you medically. If you seem to be in control by Monday we will recommend that you go back to work. We'll know for sure by Sunday evening. Depends how you behave over the weekend. That medication that you took will make you drowsy. The nurse will show you a room where you can sleep if you like. Otherwise, feel free to go back to the lounge, have a cup of coffee or whatever. Read or watch television for a while. Bob Markley will catch up with you in an hour or so. He'll start you on the reinforcement. By the way lunch will be served in the lounge. You'll meet some other people there. I'll check in with you tomorrow."

Jay left the doctor's office in a quandary. He still didn't accept the idea that he had a disease. He was beginning to accept the thought that he raised a little too much hell. He began to feel sleepy. A little sack time seemed like a good idea. The nurse at the desk was very responsive to his request to lay down and rest his eyes. She escorted him back to the same room he was in the day before. Jay popped off his shoes, laid down, and fell asleep

The next thing he experienced was someone gently shaking him awake. He opened his eyes to the friendly smile of Bob Markley who extended a friendly greeting. "Wake up, Sunshine. You have been pounding your ear for nearly two hours. Another half hour and you would have missed lunch. Let's go. Got some people I want you to meet."

Jay gave Markley a light jab on the shoulder as he rolled out of bed. It took him awhile to find his shoes since he couldn't remember taking them off. Then he went to the powder room where he discovered that he forgot his comb. After straightening his hair with his fingers, he joined Markley for the walk to the dining room lounge. As they entered the room Jay noticed that the buffet lunch had been well consumed. Markley's estimate that Jay would have missed lunch in a half hour was off by a half hour. Jay picked up some bread, a slice of cheese, and the crumbs of a few potato chips that the swarm had mysteriously overlooked. Some sliced vegetables were all that remained in abundance. Jay filled his paper plate with the residue and took the remaining empty seat. Markley walked around the room greeting each person. Then he walked to the podium placed at the back opposite the food table.

"Good afternoon folks", Markley began, "My name is Bob and I'm a recovering alcoholic. How's everybody today?" Everybody applauded Bob's greeting and seemed to be in good spirits. Bob raised his hands asking for silence. Gradually the group came to order. Markley then continued his greeting, "Ladies and Gentlemen. It's always nice to have you here for our weekly meeting. It's especially nice to see so many of you attending on a regular basis. Now there are a few things, however, that the administration has asked that I point out. First is that you are using too many napkins. If this keeps up the vice president in charge of napkins is going to cut us off and we'll have to go back to using the drapes—that is if they ever get around to replacing the drapes that they took away from us last winter. Also, they have reminded me that we have used up our allotment of used and broken furniture for the remainder of the fiscal year. We will have to wait until next year before we will be given any more broken furniture. Until then we will have to make out with the good stuff. That means we will have to be on our worse behavior. Can you handle it?"

Again, the remarks were answered with laughter, applause, and cheers. The remarks about the furniture caused Jay to blush. He felt as though everyone in the room was looking at him but when he raised his head he saw that he was not being noticed.

As Bob paused in his remarks he looked directly at Jay. "My friends, we have a guest today. I hope my comments made in jest have not given him the wrong impression. You are a wonderful group dedicated to your own recovery and the recovery of those around you. You have done a marvelous if not miraculous service for one another. Some of you will want to talk about that today but before we do I want you to introduce yourself."

Following his comments each person in turn rose and faced Jay. They introduced themselves giving their first name only followed by the comment that he or she was a recovering addict. At the end of the introductions Bob asked Jay to introduce himself

Jay carefully stood before the group uncertain what he was going to say, "Ladies and Gentlemen, ah, I'm Jay. Bob, ah, I mean when Bob said he was going to buy me lunch I didn't know that, ah, he had this in mind. You see I'm, ah, I mean I been getting some treatment here and he said he wanted me to meet some wonderful people. Well, ah, I know what he meant. You are great folks. Thanks for having me."

The people responded with a loud round of applause. A few waved a sign of acceptance to Jay. Another person reached out and shook his hand. Jay was somewhat embarrassed at the friendliness of their reaction. When the group came back to order Bob asked if anyone had anything that they wanted to report or discuss. One by one individuals stood to report on the success or failure of their efforts to stay sober. One man reported in detail about his fall from the wagon and how a friend rescued him. He was back on the road to recovery. Others commented on the days, weeks, or months that they had been clean. They all thanked each other for the support to continue.

After the reports were completed Bob congratulated the group for their continuing success in recovery. He mentioned that the meeting would be held again next week at same time and place. He encouraged them to return and bring a friend in need. As the meeting concluded several of the attendees approached Jay and shook his hand. They stated that they hoped to see him again.

Jay accepted their expressions of friendship with courtesy. He noticed that the group consisted of people several years his senior. They were clean, poorly dressed, but well groomed. Their age was more in line with his parents. He realized that these were not his kind of people. Bob was beginning to pick up the paper plates and cups from the tables so Jay broke off his thoughts and began to help.

Markley, at first, seemed to take Jay's help for granted. Then he casually asked, "So Jay, what did you think of our little gathering?"

Jay was waiting for the question, "Nice people, but I felt really out of place. I mean these people were old enough to be my parents. That really threw me off. I was surprised to hear you admit to being a drunk. You gave me enough hints over the past few days that I should have realized it. Anyway, it was an eye-opener. I couldn't believe how many of these people fell off the wagon. Man, I guess when you been sopping it up as long as they have there ain't no way that you're gonna quit. Right?"

"Wrong!" Markley fired back, "Many of those people have been dry longer than you have been alive. They come here to give help and be an inspiration to the rest of us. We need all the help we can get. The key to recovery is to admit that you are sick and be willing to get help when you need it. Age makes no difference. An addicted person experiences the same difficulties. Help is the answer. That's what I wanted you to see and hear. I want you to have confidence in the ability of others to help you when you are under pressure."

"Man, you guys have been pushing this sick shit at me since I came in." Jay reverted to his defensive style, "I'm not ready to buy it. Sure, I overloaded and had a bust. You guys can dry me out and everything is jake. I go back out on the street and take care of myself No way I want to go through this again. I got that religion, man. Don't need this gang bang routine, no way."

The response caused Markley to put down the paper plates and directly confront Jay, "Jay we know what we know about you. You can't take the street. Eventually you'll find that out. Here's a card with the Unit's call number. Keep this in your wallet.

Right now, I'm your friend as well as your counselor. When the pressure builds call this number. If I'm not in, somebody else just as qualified, if not more qualified than me, win come to your aid. We can even pick you up and bring you in if necessary. Things might get rough for you in your free time this weekend. Remember, Dr. Kenneth explained that you were in Phase One of your recovery. You could experience a serious reaction to your detox. You need to be on guard. You mentioned that you had religion, well say a few prayers that you get by without taking a big hit. I'll say a few for you myself."

"Screw that religion stuff, partner. I'm supposed to be Catholic. Went to a Catholic grade school and had that God stuff crammed down my throat. Never bought it either. This is a Catholic hospital, right? How come they screw me over with their goddamn telephone letting my Ex know that I'm in "Dope-Ville." It's nothing but a freaking racket, man. All they want is money. Bring in my insurance. Too bad you ain't on the cash side of this deal, partner. They got you suckered. Looks like the Pope trained a drunk to dance to his tune and bring in the trade. Shit, I ain't buying."

Jay's anger accelerated. He suddenly grabbed a chair and threw it across the room into the food table. He kicked violently at another chair, missed and slammed his foot into the wall mounted air conditioner. The resulting pain brought his emotions to overload. He screamed and sat down in chair. As he rubbed his aching foot he shouted continuing profanities at the top of his lungs. The head nurse and a nursing assistant heard the commotion and rushed to the aid of Bob Markley. As they entered the room Markley was calmly leaning against the wall waiting for Jay's temper to cool. They opted to stand across the room at the door out or Jay's sight. Eventually Jay began to run out of steam. He placed his face in his hands and his elbows on his knees. He sat that way in silence taking deep breaths.

As his breathing began to slow Markley sat in the chair next to Jay and gently put his hand on Jay's shoulder, "Jay, you've had a long day. It's time for a rest. Let's go back to your room. It's time for another pill. Then you can sleep for a few hours before you go home. I'll be with you and check on you before you go leave. We can pick up on all this conversation in the morning. What do you say?"

"Yeah, OK. I'm sorry about messing the place up. OK?"

"Sure, it's OK, man. It's nothing. Let's go."

Jay got out of the chair unassisted. Markley waved the nurse and her assistant out of the room before Jay noticed their presence. As Bob reached to assist, Jay indicated to him that he could, actually preferred, to walk unassisted. Markley wondered if Jay was signaling that he still denied that he need for help in his recovery. However, Jay did not seem to object to Bob walking beside him to his room. As they neared Jay's room Markley noticed that Jay's energy and good nature had returned.

Jay picked up the pace and gave Bob a smile as they entered the room, "That was a short trip. Hope I didn't break anything expensive."

"Not likely, Jay. The administration gives us the hand me downs that are usually shot to hell by the time we get them. If that stuff wasn't in SACAP in would be in the junk. Feeling Better?"

"Yeah, sure. I don't think I need that pill."

"Take it anyway. That way the Pope won't get upset when the cash is low. I'll check you out about four. If you feel all right then you can go home for the night. OK?"

"Sure." After Jay took the medication Markley busied around the room until he was confident that Jay was relaxed and under control. Then he returned to the nursing station and completed his work on the incident report concerning Patient John Marquart and the St. Anslem's telephone system. He read his description of the incident over several times, uncertain on the emphasis given to the apparent misconduct-conduct of a certain staff nurse. Finally, he put the report in his confidential file for safe keeping. He intended to think it over some more before sending it to Dr. Anderson.

oOo

Joseph Durant, President of St. Anslem's Hospital, habitually arrived at his office every day at seven AM. This Friday was no exception. His diligent executive assistant somehow always managed to arrive at least fifteen minutes before the boss and routinely had the lights on, voice mail recorded, and coffee perking when he came in. Durant's routine was to go through the messages, read correspondence, dictate replies, review the appointments for the day and then begin shouting usually about, "that son of a bitch, Folley," followed by whoever else came to mind. He could never quite handle the fact that while he arrived at seven most of the other executives began filing in after eight. The executive assistant could only shrug when he demanded a stat meeting of his executive staff at seven thirty. The only one available was Dr. Folley who was the last person Durant wanted to see.

Durant's frustration centered on the lack of information for the Board of Trustees meeting agenda next Tuesday. O'Shea, Folley and, "the rest of those bastards that had screwed things up royally with that crap about the expense reports and now the prospect of this Logan character getting into the act," made for more uncertainty. He had tried to call Hardly, Chairman of the Board, on Thursday but he was out playing golf. Hardly eventually returned the call through his secretary who advised Durant to consult with Mr. O'Shea about the board agenda. Durant had that experience last week. No further contact was necessary.

He sat at his desk with his head in his hands wondering who on the Board might have some interest in an agenda and be available for a telephone conversation before eight AM. Suddenly he remembered Sister Mary Elizabeth. Nuns always got up early, went to Mass, and then to work. She would know about Logan and the Office of Health Affairs. After all she was part of the Official Church. He hastily dialed her number. Sr. Mary Elizabeth answered with a cheery good morning. After that it was all downhill.

Sister Mary Elizabeth became emotional when Durant asked her if she could give him any information about the change at the Archdiocese. She pulled up an inch short of using gutter terms in describing the basic intellect of the male dominated Board and the Chancery. She had tried to discuss the matter with Bishop Hanks who said that he would report in full at the St. Anslems Board meeting. Until that time, he in effect told her to cool her jets. He did explain that Dr. Folley had been anointed by the Cardinal as the guru of Health and would be the king of kings as far as the health ministry was concerned. End of report.

As a closing comment Sister mentioned that she had talked recently to Sister Celest who would be calling Mr. Durant in the next week. She concluded by telling Joe that he was constantly in her prayers.

Durant's next move was a call to Bishop Hanks at the Archdiocese. He felt certain that he would get a better reception than Sister Mary Elizabeth. In fact, he got no reception at all. The switchboard operator at the Chancery reported that the Bishop was not available. She took the name and number for an eventual return call. She had no idea when the Bishop would be available.

Charles Patello was a mystery to Durant, He was, on the surface, a very friendly type who always had a useful opinion when asked. At Board meetings, he seemed content to let Hardly get pushed around by O'Shea and Folley. Durant felt that Patello was not a part of the inner circle that ran things for the Archdiocese and the Universe. He observed that Mr. Patello preferred to be removed from the politics of business and government. He was a successful self-made man, content in his own right. It, therefore, seemed inappropriate to call him for an opinion on the agenda and the Office for health Affairs. On the other hand, Mr. Patello was a member of the executive committee. Durant had already called O'Shea, Hardly, Sr. Elizabeth, and Bishop Hanks. To omit calling Patello would appear improper and look like a selective omission if the matter became a topic of discussion. He realized then that he needed to call Mr. Patello and the remaining board members as well. He would first call Mr. Patello. After that he intended to call Mr. Mondi and Mr. Meehan. With luck, he would have made contact or at least attempted to make contact with the entire Board before noon with the exception of that jerk, Folley.

The medical staff was scheduled to have its monthly meeting in the auditorium at noon. Durant usually gave a brief report at the meeting. Folley always showed up for that part. Durant decided to collar him after the medical staff meeting and after he had talked to the other members of the Board.

Durant had seldom called Patello in the past since Patello always seemed as though he preferred to remain distant from the administrative chores of the hospital. However, on this occasion Patello seemed pleased that Durant had called. He answered the phone with a cheery greeting followed by an immediate offer of assistance. Durant first apologized for having to call then explained that the purpose of the call was to determine Mr. Patello's preference in dealing with the formal and informal items that were becoming apparent for the St. Anslem's Board meeting. Charlie Patello replied in a gentlemanly manner with complete courtesy. He stated that he felt the most immediate concern of the hospital and of the Board was the deteriorating fiscal position. He was aware that Mr. OShea was very intent on that point. He also mentioned that he had met Logan and felt that he could be of great help to St. Anslem's especially in getting the hospital into a better competitive position with the leading Teaching Hospitals of the world.

As Patello talked his mind was searching for an opportunity to link Durant's apparent anxiety to Capizzi's suggestion that Durant, "be put in a wrapper." It seemed to Patello that Durant needed a friend in court. There was the opportunity to compromise him. Durant had suddenly walked into his arms. The question was how best to embrace him.

Patello needed time to consult with New York. For the moment he would compromise Durant, "Joe, my friends Mr. Hardly and Mr. O'Shea have been very active with the Archdiocese in bringing about these changes. They have given me some insight to the duties of Mr. Logan but I really don't know enough about it to comment. Dr. Folley has also been involved I believe and as you know he has the ear of the Cardinal. I suspect your best source of information is Dr. Folley. If you haven't talked to him about it I suggest that you do before the Board meeting. Personally, I'm confused how your position and Logan's interact. I consider the CEO of the Hospital as the key person in the health structure. We need to make sure that is the way things are structured."

Durant was relieved to gain a friend on the Board, "Thanks Charlie. Obviously, you realize that I'm concerned about this new structure. Of course, the Cardinal has every right to make whatever changes he wants in the conduct and direction of his health ministry. I'll go along no matter what but in this very competitive environment we cannot afford expensive duplication of executive talent and complicated levels in decision making. The Mass General and Brigham merger has eliminated a big hunk of bureaucracy. They are streamlined. Our decision making must be very accurate and timely."

"Joe, I know far less than you do about health reform and what's going on in Boston," confessed Patello. "The newspapers carry a story everyday about the changes taking place. St. Anslem's is never mentioned in the new networks that the downtown hospitals are forming. It seems to me that we need to move rapidly before we are left out completely. With all the pressures, you have in just trying to make ends meet it must be nearly impossible to keep up the pace. Mr. Logan will be able to help I'm sure. However, we need to develop a plan that fits the future. We need a true strategic plan. I have used national consultants in my business and have been amazed and pleased at the amount of insight that a large national firm can give you. I would like to recommend to the Board that we form a strategic planning committee and hire a national consulting firm to help us. I'll fix it so you direct the effort. What do you say?"

"Yeah, that's great." Durant was elated. "Mitch Daly our Planning VP, as you know has been bugging me to hire a consultant to help us do a strategic plan. The problem is money. We are struggling to meet payroll. O'Shea is constantly raising hell about the deficit. I understand that a major consulting job could go over a hundred grand. In all good conscience, I couldn't spend that kind of money when I'm laying people off. How are we going to justify it?"

Patello saw the opening but decided to play it slow and easy, "At the moment I don't have an answer. Let me explore some options. I have some contacts with national organizations that have provided grants and planning assistance to charitable agencies in various parts of the Country. I'll make a few phone calls and see if I can come up with something. I'll get back to you on Monday. In the meantime, just enjoy the weekend. You're a boater, aren't you? I understand that it's supposed to be a great weekend for sailing."

"Actually, I'm a power boater. We don't always appreciate high winds like the rag flappers but I expect to get out for a few hours on Sunday. How do you intend to bring this planning effort up to the Board?" Joe asked.

"Tactically, I think it best that the agenda remain as loose as possible," commented Patello, "That way I can slip it in when the opportunity presents itself. My guess is that Kevin will let things just happen as he usually does. Tom will want to beat you on the head about money. Bishop Hanks will want to tell us about Folley and Folley will tell us about Logan. The combination of all of this will create enough confusion for me to suggest that we bring about order through a strategic plan. The other Board members will welcome the comic relief."

Durant was relieved, "OK. I'll stop worrying about an organized meeting and agenda and let things just happen. I was going to call Mr. Mondi, and Mr. Meehan for their input. Should I still do that? What does the Bishop have to tell about Dr. Folley?"

The question about the Bishop brought Patello up short. Suddenly he realized that by pressing his interest to compromise Durant he had inadvertently tipped his hand that he was in the know more than he wanted Durant to realize. At this point Folley's appointment as Secretary of Health for the Archdiocese was only known to a few insiders. Patello did not want Druant to see him as a member of the Cardinal's gang. On the other hand, to deny having any knowledge about the appointment and have Durant learn later that he was one of the first informed would destroy the trust with Durant that he was now trying to firmly establish. Patello opted to give an honest reply.

"I'm sorry, Joe. I thought that Dr. Folley might have informed you. The word I got from Bishop Hanks is that the Cardinal has named Dr. Folley to be his Secretary of Health. Logan will be reporting to Folley as I understand it. I expect that the Bishop will report that to the Board on Tuesday."

The news was a real downer for Durant, "Christ! That really sucks, Charlie. How in the hell can I run this hospital to the satisfaction of the Cardinal, the Board, that jerk Folley, and Logan, who I've never met? That really sucks!"

Patello recovered, "Well it only serves to justify the need for an organized plan of action. Let's get the planning committee organized. Maybe Mondi and Meehan could serve on the Committee with you and me. That would create some balance while Logan, Folley, O'Shea and Bishop Hanks handle the fiscal crisis. Hardly can be the mediator. Why don't you let me talk to the others? That way you won't be seen by O'Shea and his associates as an insurgent."

Suddenly Durant remembered, "How about Sister Mary Elizabeth? Where does she fit in? Her nose seemed well out of joint when I talked to her about an hour ago. Think she would fit into the planning committee?"

"Good question, Joe. I'm not really sure. Let's give it some more thought and talk on Monday."

As the conversation ended Patello felt certain that he had gained the trust of Durant. Even more important he felt that Durant had allowed himself to become dependent on Patello for leverage against the apparent power play that Folley had engineered by his appointment as Secretary of Health. A side bar advantage is that the counter move the planning committee could cause O'Shea to expose his motive for holding the evidence about Logan's bank account. This was a long shot worth taking. Now Patello needed the assistance of Park consulting. Tony Marone wasn't in to answer his call but got back to him within the hour. Charlie detailed the conversation with Durant to Marone who immediately opted to consult with Cappizi and get back to Patello. Three hours later a meeting had been arranged for Monday morning in Patello's office. Capizzi and Marone would be there. Tom Callahan, world class health consultant of De bur and Tandy, would also be with them.

Durant was fuming mad. Twice he picked up the telephone to call Folley. Each time he thought better of it and returned the phone to the receiver. He pounded the desk in anger, shouted at the ceiling, and yelled for his executive assistant. She walked into his office and calmly sat in the chair in front of his desk. Her matronly deportment and professional style caused the near mad executive to reign in his own emotions. They sat looking at each other for a few minutes before he spoke.

"Dam it, that jerk Folley has got me by the shorts. I need to have a stat conference with Weaver and Daly. Get 'em here in the next fifteen minutes. Tell 'em whatever they are doing can wait. Have you mailed out anything for the Board meeting?"

The executive assistant was very curious about the Folley remark. Some rumors about the good Doctor becoming Durant's boss had been circulating among the secretaries. Obviously, this was not the time to engage the boss in small talk about a trivial thing like his job. She thought it best just to answer his question. "The only thing that has been sent to the Trustees is the meeting notice, Mr. Durant. I expected to fax an agenda to everyone today. Do you have it ready?"

"Negative. We'll surprise them with some of Hardly's mystic commentary. Folley can do the dance of the Seven Veils and I'll do some slight-of hand tricks with the cash balance. For my big finish, I'll make Weaver disappear. That ought to make 'em go bananas"

This was the opening the Executive Assistant had been waiting for. Now was the time to pop the question, "You are obviously upset about the meeting. What has Dr. Folley done this time?"

Durant's anger brought him out of his chair. He paced back and forth as he began to explain to the faithful executive assistant, "God's gift to the medical profession, one Dr. Folley, has apparently used his clinical relationship with the Cardinal as a means to achieve prominence and glory in the Chancery. He got himself appointed Secretary of Health for the Archdiocese. I think the son of a bitch is running for Pope. The Cardinal had to be drunk when he made that decision, Jesus!"

Having extracted the information of interest, the executive assistant redirected Durant back to the business at hand, "Mr. Weaver called earlier for an appointment. I gave him one o'clock. Usually Mr. Daly prefers to meet with you on Monday morning. Should I cancel his Monday meeting and bring him in at one with Mr. Daly?"

The relationship between Weaver and Daly had always been strained. Weaver by nature and profession was cautious. Every detail needed to be accounted for in an exact fashion. Accounting was an art that Weaver mastered and bookkeeping was an exact science that he commanded. Daly was an artist of a different sort. Since his days as a student activist during the Viet Nam War, Daly had used estimates and trends as a gauge of measurement. Details were always contained but hidden in the packaged conclusion. Durant had discovered that Weaver's exact nature in budgeting and Daly's wide lens approach to planning often led to the same conclusions. When that happened the hospital could set a course with accuracy. When the two perspectives differed, Durant took the time to analyze the differences in depth before proceeding. During the analysis of the difference Durant would attempt to get the two executives to collaborate and come to a uniform compromised conclusion. Collaboration was difficult and often forced. The two men were not only professionally different but were on the opposite extremes politically. Weaver epitomized the arch conservative while Daly was an outspoken liberal who still wore a Castro style beard. Bringing the two together in a small conference or in a general executive staff meeting was always potentially explosive. Apart each man was extremely competent and possibly the best in their respective positions in all of the Boston area hospitals, a fact not fully known therefore not appreciated by the Board.

Durant intended to inform Weaver and Daly about the conversation with Patello at the same time. He wanted to measure their individual reactions and see if they could come to an immediate common perspective on the conduct of a strategic planning process.

It was important that the executive staff have a united effort in order to keep planning under management control. He would emphasize that point by telling the executives about Folley's latest claim to glory. The political strategy within the Board would be obvious. No need to explain all of this to the executive assistant.

Instead Durant gave a simple answer to her question, "No. Let Daly's Monday meeting stand. Tell him to be here at one for a discussion with Rod on strategic planning. We can detail today's meeting on Monday. Schedule Rod to come back on Monday. That Way they'll both be upset.

Actually, one PM was the best time for Durant to meet with Weaver and Daly. The General Medical Staff meeting was less than an hour away by the time he had finished his morning routine, called the board members, ranted and raved, then had a discussion with his executive assistant. For the next thirty minutes Durant would busy himself making notes for the President's report to the Medical Staff. The meeting would begin at noon and usually conclude by one. He could then move immediately to the meeting with his two senior vice presidents.

At eleven forty-five Durant entered the hospital's main auditorium. Several physicians had arrived and were enjoying the buffet lunch. Physicians are customarily attracted to a free lunch. It is an integral part of their residency training that lasts through out their entire career. Hospital Presidents are taught to always cater to the physicians. Gradually the room became crowded as the teaching faculty, hospital based specialists, and community based physicians assembled for their obligatory meeting. Some signed the attendance forms, ate lunch and left. Most stayed obediently through the reports and presentations. The agenda for the general staff meetings is purposely short since the physicians attend a number of departmental quality review sessions on a routine basis. In addition, the medical staff has a major scientific session each month called grand rounds that is always very well attended. Actually, the general staff meeting was more of a social gathering where the elected leadership of the medical staff would report on medical administrative matters and the members of the medical staff could register a complaint about parking, medical record transcription, or anything else that came to mind. The president of the medical staff moved quickly through the agenda to the concluding item, The Hospital President's Report.

Durant's style in dealing with the general medical Staff was to be concise, factual, and always upbeat. His years of experience had taught him that placing a burden on the physicians with a lot of crape hanging always generated a negative reaction. This was especially true in the current environment where the specialists were losing income because of the increasing denial rate by Health Maintenance Organizations. The primary care physicians were becoming busier but they were also being held far more responsible and accountable under the capitation payment method.

Durant cautiously steered around conflict between members of the staff. He began his report by thanking the physicians for their continuing support during these difficult times. He noted that the occupancy of the hospital was nearing a record low but the diagnostic and therapeutic procedures were running ahead of last year. From a fiscal perspective, the hospital's cash flow was excellent. Days in the accounts receivable were slightly under this same period last year. The employee to patient ratio was on the decline. Spending was being modified to become consistent with revenue. He concluded his remarks, as he began, by thanking the physicians for their loyalty and support.

As Durant was giving his report, most of the physicians were finding another cup of coffee, talking to a colleague, or lining up a consultation. No one seemed to realize that the President's report was packed with bad news. The Hospital was losing money. Admissions were at a record low. Intensity was declining. Expenses were being cut. Employees were being laid off. Revenue was declining. As always Durant asked if anyone had any questions or comments. Hearing none he returned the podium to the President of the Medical Staff who adjourned the meeting.

Durant lingered in the auditorium as the physicians filed out. Some of the doctors remained in little groups chatting about matters of practice and referrals. Others socialized and talked about the Red Sox, golf, or vacations. Often individual physicians would take the time to whisper the latest gossip in Durant's ear. He wondered if anyone would bring Folley's latest escapade to his attention. None did. He also noticed that Dr. Folley, Chairman of the Department of Medicine at St. Anslem's Hospital, Member of the Board of Trustees, Professor of Medicine Tuft's University School of Medicine, Distinguished servant of the Commonwealth and City, gentleman, scholar, man of letters, and soon to be announced Secretary of Health for the Boston Catholic Archdiocese was not present. "Good" thought Durant, "this is not the time or place for a confrontation."

While Durant was hanging around the auditorium, Weaver and Daly had arrived at his office. Daly was the first. He properly announced himself to the executive assistant and took a chair in the office reception area. Weaver arrived within minutes of Daly. He walked past Daly without comment, waved to the executive assistant, entered the President's office and sat down. Both executives remained in their own solitude until Durant arrived. As the boss entered his office Daly walked in and took a chair opposite Weaver at the small conference table. Durant joined them and sat at the end of the table so that he was flanked on both sides by his capable assistants. The boss tried to warm the meeting by commenting about the weather, the week end relaxation, and some trivial gossip about who was doing what to who. As the execs took to the discussion with their own commentary Durant carefully measured the compatibility scale.

When he determined the time was right, he brought their attention to the purpose of the meeting, "Boys we have another interesting challenge given to us by the great Dr. Richard Folley. This time he has managed to get himself appointed Secretary for Health on the Cardinal's Cabinet. He has also been appointed boss of the new Office for Health for the Archdiocese. I'm sure that you have heard that former City Commissioner Logan is going to direct that office. What we don't know at this time is how all of this impacts on our work in administering St.

Anslem's. I expect to be enlightened at the Board meeting on Tuesday. There are some Board members who feel that the CEO of St. Anslems should be the principal agent for the Board of St. Anslem's. They are going to recommend that St. A's establish its destiny through a strategic planning effort led by the administration of the hospital. We need to be prepared to take charge of the planning effort. I wanted to have an initial discussion about this with the two of you today so you begin to prepare your thoughts over the week end. We will meet again on Monday morning to begin to flesh out our approach."

Daly sat up straight and began to be energized by Durant's comments. His black eyes flashed from Durant to Weaver and back. As Durant finished his comments Daly jumped in, "This could be the opportunity that we have been looking for to focus the Board on the changing pattern of health delivery going on in Boston and away from the micro perspective of money. The only reports they ever see are financial. Has anyone thought about a planning committee?"

Weaver slumped in his chair and began rubbing his temples. He seemed irritated by Daly's eagerness. With a quick flick of the wrist he popped open his ever-present Briefcase, laid copies the draft financial operating statement for the recent month on the table, and began his commentary. "What we need to plan is how we are going to get out of the toilet. We went down a million two hundred and change the past month. If this keeps up the only viable plan is bankruptcy. Folley and that goddamn Department of Medicine is way under budget in revenue and way over on expenses. That jerk needs to start cutting losses. Why don't we start with him and bounce his ass full time to the Archdiocese? Another cut could be in administration by chopping back on wild hair planners who only know how to plan to spend. We need more tertiary admits to cover the overhead load. O'Shea will jump all over this planning shit."

Durant took quick notice of Weaver's slam at Daly. Daly hadn't missed it either. He was leaning forward in his chair as if he was about to lunge at Weaver. Durant came forward in his chair in an attempt to separate the two. "Look guys what I need is your collective wisdom not your antagonism. We know that this place has got warts. We also know that O'Shea is screaming about the losses. If our only answer is to gut this place with layoffs and cutbacks then we are in a death glide. I'm not ready to admit that, although it might be the fact. We owe it to the Board to do a very careful review of our situation and look for viable alternatives. Maybe the Office for Health can help generate more referrals to St. A's. We ought to at least get the Catholic market."

With a wave of his hand Weaver dismissed Durant's comment. "Boss you are kidding yourself if you think the Catholics are going to let the Archdiocese tell them where they are going to get health care. Have you been to Church lately? The place is nearly empty on Sunday. People listen to the HMO's. Our docs have to sell their excellence to the HMO's. That's where the action is. The only thing you are going to get from that stupid Health Office at the Archdiocese is a bill to pay for Folley and Logan. That's the only kind of plan they care about."

Daly remained focused on Weaver but directed his remarks to Durant. "I believe the only way out of the fiscal crisis is to reposition the hospital into new markets. Our emphasis on cardiac disease has brought us into the most competitive market. We might have the best product but who knows it. If we are going to stay with that emphasis then we have to put big bucks into the marketing end. We could be a small player with high quality in cardiac and create another high- profile service that draws the referrals. A planning effort would help determine where the new markets are. Again, my learned fiscal wizard, you better be prepared to open the purse strings because a real planning effort costs money."

As Daly concluded his comment, Weaver leaned forward and put his fist in the middle of the table. He glared at Daly. "If I'm a wizard you're a mystic. What in the hell do we need to spend money on? We need to stop spending, not start, for Christ's sake. Your goddamn planners and consultants are not going to tell us anything that we don't know. What we need to do is kick some ass. Let's start with Folley."

Daly sat back in his chair and seemed to relax. He looked at Weaver with a slight smile before commenting, "Rodger, my dear friend, you are a real asshole."

Before Durant could call for order, Weaver jumped from his chair and made a move for Daly. Daly, the smaller of the two but far quicker, was on his feet in time to duck Weaver's blind punch. Weaver's second punch landed harmlessly on Daly's upraised arms. The two combatants then went into a clinch and proceeded to waltz around Durant's office knocking pictures off the wall and rearranging the top of the boss's desk.

Durant was at first speechless and then began to repeatedly shout, "knock it off!" to little avail except to draw the executive assistant into the office. She watched the dance for a few seconds before announcing that, "You two jerks couldn't get noticed at a walrus convention." That comment ended the fray.

Weaver and Daly picked up their material and left together. Durant wondered if they were headed for the parking lot to finish the battle. As the door closed he joined his faithful executive assistant in putting the office back in order. "Another executive conference brought to a productive conclusion," he thought. It was now three thirty on Friday afternoon. Time to start the week end. Durant turned out the lights in the office and went home.

As he drove home, Durant worked over in his mind the exchange between his two capable Vice Presidents. He dismissed the physical combat as something of no consequence. Instead he searched for a common point to base a planning review. Points of agreement were the fiscal crisis and low occupancy. There seemed to be mixed attitudes about the hospital's emphasis on cardio vascular disease. Yet, putting the insults aside, the two executives seemed to acknowledge that as the hospital's strong suit. Neither seemed to suggest that the hospital had any other area of prominence. Daly would not acknowledge that cost reduction methods were required. Weaver, on the other hand, felt that immediate cutbacks were necessary. On the last point, Durant completely agreed with Weaver. Monthly losses of over a million dollars could not be sustained. The hospital was required to drastically scale back its spending. The challenge was to reduce spending without impacting the revenue base. On the other hand, revenue enhancement would be served if the doctors would become salesmen to the HMO's, as Weaver had suggested, and if the hospital would find new profitable markets as Dally had suggested.

In summary Durance focused on three combined efforts. The first would be a detailed fiscal analysis of all hospital functions. Those that were not essential would be eliminated. The second analysis would be a review of all hospital services from a revenue to cost perspective. Those services that were not profitable would be eliminated unless they materially contributed to enhancing revenue for another service such as the cardiac catheterization laboratory in medicine contributing to the volume of cardiac surgery. The third analysis would be the strategic planning effort. The intent of that effort would be determining new markets that offered opportunity for growth and prominence.

This last analysis is where Durant intended to focus the planning committee. He prayed that Patello would find a funding source for the planning program. Such a find would eliminate the objection that Weaver raised about the cost of consultants. In his heart, Durant felt that Weaver was being the Devil's advocate as a conditioner for O'Shea. "Yes, all things considered it was a productive meeting," was his last thought on the subject as he turned into his driveway.

w enjoyed contributing to his success as a member of the family. Little Charlie responded to his Uncle's kindness by ushering NAI into many profitable ventures in the New England region.

A particular benefit that Patello brought into the NAI ventures in Boston was his close connection with the Irish gang that controlled an estimated one third of the area's wealth including the City of Boston's municipal spending and the spending of the Boston Catholic Archdiocese. Charlie had convinced Uncle Frank many years ago that two Irish kids he had met at Boston College could be compromised for future use, One, Kevin Hardly, came equipped with lots of money, family influence, and little brains—the other, Tom O'Shea, had lots of ambition, no money, and few morals. It seemed to be a perfect combination that only required two hundred dollars to bribe an ethics professor for an advance copy of the final exam. Uncle Frank gave Charlie the money to swing the deal. Charlie pulled it off and returned the two hundred with fifty bucks splitting a hundred-dollar profit down the middle. Big Frank Patello knew at that time that his Sister's youngest son was destined to be his successor and head of the largest operation east of Chicago.

The remaining two thirds of Boston's wealth seemed problematic to Charles Patello and the interest of National Associated Investors. The Puritan Ethic of avoiding association with Papists and non-Christians created a block that Patello tried vainly to overcome. He also recognized that the WASP strength was based on the unfortunate split in the Hardly family. He decided that a frontal attempt to penetrate the

WASP fortification against Catholics and non-Christians was destined to failure. On the other hand, the WASPs were nearly desperate to stop the Irish from controlling key elected posts at Federal and State level. He suspected that a covert action supporting a political WASP candidate might give the NAI a foot in the door. The Governor was a true WASP that offered the NAI the opportunity it was looking for by making him the hero of the Massachusetts' Waste Management Program.

The Governor was also a true politician that recognized the power of organization. He knew that the Mayor of Boston was the strongest opposition to his re-election. The Waste Management issue could give the Governor a powerful base to overcome any threat to re-election.

Patello found his way into the WASP fortress through the backdoor of the Boston Tax-Payers Association that was essentially controlled by WASP business interest, the Boston Chamber of Commerce, and the Republican Party. His offer to the TP A was to use his lobbing strength to support the Governor's Waste Management legislation, to provide campaign contributions anonymously in support of the Republican Governor and the election of a Republican candidate to the US Senate, to mount a media campaign in Boston that would hang the Mayor out to dry for misuse of campaign funds and to use the combined influence of National Associated Investors to promote Boston as the site for the Olympic Games in the year 2008. In return for his generous support the TPA agreed that the Governor would name Richard Folley MD as a member of the Governor's Special Taskforce on Waste Management, Park Environmental Inc. would be retained by the State as consultants to the Office of Waste Management, and Action Waste Management of Boston would be given a grant to initiate privatized waste management programs for the Boston Metropolitan area.

Patello, delighted at his success, reported to Marone at Park's New York office that it was time for Action Waste Management to set up shop. A day later the Capitol steps experienced the rally turned into a brawl by the Boston Workers' Guild causing Patello to remember that a third of Boston's wealth and influence was held by organized labor and virtually uncontrolled.

Patello telephoned Marone and reported the problem with Muldoon. Marone in turn called his contacts with the National Federation who called Muldoon. The Federation subsequently advised Marone to schedule an off the record never happened type meeting with himself, Patello, and Muldoon at an inconspicuous place as soon as possible. Marone called Patello who called Muldoon who arranged the meeting in the back room of Stinger's tavern in Dorchester two blocks from the offices of the Boston Workers' Guild.

Stinger's appeared to be a typical neighborhood tap on a frontage road to Interstate Ninety Three. Its small neon sign was barely visible. On top of the two-story frame building was a large lighted billboard that pointed to the Workers Guild Building. The electronic billboard flashed Union slogans and pronounced the strength of organized labor for all traveling the Interstate to see. Inside the tavern was dingy but reasonably clean. Wooden tables and chairs were haphazardly spread around the bar room that also contained an old-fashioned bar with a foot rail and no stools.

Stingers was primarily a standing man's drinking establishment. In back was a fairly large room that seemed to be for the private use of the Workers Guild. Four square tables with padded chairs comprised the furnishings. The bland decor of the dirty painted walls featured the latest advertisements of local breweries. Green shade lights hanging from the ceiling were centered over each table making the atmosphere perfect for poker games. A slide window to the bar commanded the attention of the bartender in service of the room's occupants.

Twenty-four hours after the Capitol Steps Rally, three men gathered in the back room of Stinger's. Muldoon, first to arrive, came alone. When Patello and Marone arrived they correctly recognized that this was not a meeting of record with the Workers' Guild. Muldoon had apparently been waiting at Stingers for a few hours and his speech offered a slight expression of a man who had enjoyed a liquid lunch. Patello introduced Marone and ordered a round of Sam Adams beer.

Muldoon remained seated, nodded an acknowledgment to Marone, and motioned the two visitors to sit. He was cordial and asked Marone about his flight from New York, commented about the weather, damned the government, and got to the point. "Patello, you son of a bitch, you put your stinking deal together without asking me in. You know you can't ignore labor. You also know now that I can bring this whole mess down on your head like a rock I used that two by four on your skull yesterday just to get your attention. You got this thing with waste hauling bagged as far as the City goes but you don't move one truck or get one hospital under contract without me saying so. You need my help and that's worth something. I need a piece for labor and I need a piece for me."

Marone became flushed and it was apparent to Patello that good old Mouldy had just bought himself a long ride on a dark night. He felt that there might be an opportunity to gain more than he gave by bringing Muldoon into the program but only at the operational level. To negotiate to that end he needed to penetrate Muldoon's mind and discover how much information he had about the total operation. He also had to be careful to prevent Marone from reverting to his previous life and dusting Muldoon on the spot.

Patello looked at the aging, small Muldoon and recognized that the Union Leader had seen better days. Muldoon hands seemed to shake slightly, his hair was very thin on top, and he needed a shave. Best to try a soft sell he thought, "Bob, you are right about my oversight. For that I apologize. You know that I'm kind of inexperienced at these things. I have never been involved with unions and union contracts."

Muldoon leaned forward to get into Patello's face, "That's an understatement. Why did you let New York call the Federation? It took me over an hour to convince them that this was a local fire fight that didn't need their attention. Now they think they can muscle in on your national organization, Park whatever. If they get into this it gets the attention of the US Attorney General and we all lose."

"Score one for our side," thought Patello. Muldoon apparently was unaware that the Workers' Federation through its various pension funds was a heavy investor with National Associated Investors. Marone had contacted the head of the Federation through NAI President Cappizi who made the contact through the Secretary of the Federation who held a seat on the NAI Board. The Federation had all the information about Park but, for reasons that were becoming more obvious, decided not to let their information available to Muldoon and the Boston Workers' Guild. It occurred to Patello that the Federation had advised Muldoon that the mess he created was all his to handle.

Patello glanced at Marone who was pouring the balance of his Sam Adams into his glass with a slight smile on his face. This indeed was a local matter. "Look, Bob, the last thing we want is trouble with the Feds. Sure we use influence to get what we want but it is all legal."

This time Muldoon rocked back on the legs of his chair and displayed an air of confidence in place of arrogance, "Legal my ass. Your deal with the TPA to fry Cowan's butt is about as legal as murder one."

"Score one for the goons," thought Patello, "He knows about the deal with the TPA because the Workers' Guild has a seat on the Chamber of Commerce that ties in with the TPA. Okay so now what does he want?"

Muldoon shook his empty bottle at the window to the bar and with expert precision the hefty bartender, who seemed disinterested in the trio, produced another round of Boston's finest. Muldoon poured slowly and seemed to be pondering his next comments, "Charlie my boy, I'm sure it's no surprise for you to hear that the Workers' Guild was a big contributor to the Mayor's election fund. In addition, most of the Locals in the City kicked in as well. Now you and your egg sucking Ivy coated swells are going to arrange for the Mayor to be exposed for using campaign funds for personal use. It's also no surprise for you to know that all of the Mayor's big dollar contributors not only knew but encouraged his honor to pocket the cash in return for certain concessions. Of course, that means that you and your people got yours the same way that I and my people got ours. It also means that the Mayor is not going to take the fall without dragging his loyal contributors into the mud. Some might even go to the slam with him. Maybe someone else should take the dive."

The point was getting sharper to Patello. The Workers' Guild was fronting for the Mayor. Actually the Guild was protecting its interest and investment in control of municipal services that included garbage collection and sanitation. Patello guessed that Muldoon would back off if he could somehow maintain control of the same services in the private sector without losing the money invested in City Hall, "Look Bob, I explained to the TPA that I had no knowledge about the Mayor's use of his campaign funds. Consequently, I am not in a position to make any accusations. I am only in a position to suggest to certain media representatives that looking under certain rocks might produce some interesting results. Are you concerned that I might finger the Workers' Guild?"

Muldon shot forward in his chair and again leaned into Patello who was sitting with his arms resting on the edge of the table, "You should be careful how you use your finger, Charlie, because you wouldn't wanna get it stuck where it didn't belong. What I'm suggesting is that some other guy like the Commissioner of Public Health who before he got appointed commissioner of Public Health was the Mayor's campaign manager, might be responsible for money being directed to diverse use. This is the same campaign manager who as Commissioner of Public Health has advised the media that the Union local is featherbedding at Boston Hospital. Now it seems to me that if the Commissioner of Public Health resigns because of misuse of funds and if the new Commissioner of Public Health not only happens to be a friend of labor but a strong proponent of waste management, recycling, and whatever else Action Waste Management sells, then we are all better served. You get my drift."

Patello caught the drift. In effect, he was being told to renege on his agreement to fry the Mayor. This would preserve the Mayor as the most likely candidate to unseat the Governor at the next election which was the foundation of the deal cut with the governor. Patello was in a vice. They had finished their third beer and Marone made a swayed but hasty trip to the john. The expedient bartender brought a fourth round. Bob and Charlie sat silently waiting for Marone's return. He was back in a few minutes but Muldoon had a sudden urge to urinate and wandered off. Patello felt the urge but he did not want to be anywhere with Muldoon without Marone. He decided to be patient if his bladder would cooperate. Muldoon returned looking refreshed.

When Muldoon was seated, Patello made another try, "Look Bob, you and the Guild are the ones with the information about the Commissioner. If someone other than me got to the media with the facts about campaign funds first, then whatever I came up with would be yesterday's news. The Mayor could direct fire as he wants. If he gets a little dirty in the trenches it's the cost of doing business so to speak."

"No good, Charlie, my boy, but it's a nice try. Muldoon seemed to regain control, "You have to understand that if hizzoner gets just a little dirty in this roust then he won't be credible in naming our man to succeed the commissioner. The Mayor stays clean and your organization provides the soap. You understand?"

For the moment Patello was speechless as he thought about Muldoon's last pitch. He wasn't sure he understood the crafty Union leader but he decided to act like he did, "Robert my man, it seems to me that what your organization needs is grease not soap. We have plenty of grease to slip your man in regardless of the stuff hanging on the Mayor. Trust me. Look at it this way. We convince the Governor's taskforce on waste management to allow Boston to start its conversion to privatized waste management on a voluntary basis. Then we get the hospitals to switch from City trash pick up to a private company with union employees and that little dance you did at the Capitol yesterday gets forgotten"

Muldoon heard the offer to gain a sweetheart deal with Action Waste Management. None of Patello's ventures had union shops so this was a major concession. The temptation to deal was strong but he remembered the call from the Mayor who told him in specific terms that Hizzoner would see him in hell if he failed to get Patello off his back. The Mayor was the common man well respected by the working class. He had used the Unions to advance his political career and eventually became their champion. His continued election success and established acceptance among the poor and lower middle class gave him power that tended to make his creators, such as the Workers' Guild, his eventual subjects. Muldoon was uncertain if Patello knew that the Mayor had the Guild by the throat. He pondered the question and fixed his eyes on his beer.

Marone noticed the change in Muldoon's body language. The lowered eyes was a definite sign that Patello had scored. Patello saw the change as well but was uncertain if he had closed the deal or simply concluded article one of a longer agreement yet to be determined.

Muldoon's reputation as an expert negotiator was well deserved. His emotional control or lack of same was part of his language in doing business. He moved his hands, eyes, and his butt in the chair as a calculated signal to the other side that he had applied a period to a sentence or started another paragraph in the discussion. Muldoon raised his eyes and fixed them squarely on Patello. Discussion was about to begin on article two. "You son of a bitch. Where do come off offering me a contract with

Action. I can organize that sweatshop in a minute. You got to come up with an idea that gives me something other than the sleeves off your vest. Suppose you use your power base to give our squeaky-clean Mayor a real job like running the Catholic Church. Yeah, that's it—let's see you make him Pope. I hear you got connections all the way up with the Democrats by that lard ass Hardly so get Cowan a plush job like ambassador to Pago Pago. You do that and he don't buck the WASP for Governor. You can push one of your flunkies against Dukar that will guarantee Dukar wins and you look good all way round."

Now it was Patello's turn to blink, "Let me make sure I'm reading you, Robert. You think the Mayor will resign and accept a job in the Federal administration if we, you and me, can come up with the right appointment. How do we know that he will stand hitched? As for making him Pope we first have to make him Catholic."

"It's better than jail, Charlie." Muldoon was about to go on a roll, "He stays clean which gives him the chance to come back and kick your ass in the future but we can bury a lot of stuff in the meantime. Besides you get a piece of him in the process. Also, you realize that the President of the City Council will step in as the interim Mayor. Siro is one of your boys, a good Catholic kid from Roslindale that holds a union card, He didn't go to BC but nobody is perfect. He's democrat—steps in as Mayor, fires Logan, and appoints Mike Megan Commissioner of Health. Logan sees it as part of the transition and disappears. Everybody wins. Logan is a young kid that you can take care of with a job in one of these companies that you juice up. Maybe he can work in Hardly's bank and get a night job teaching at Harvard."

Patello glanced at Morone who had his eyes fixed on Muldoon, "Well we have several problems with your "everybody wins plan," Bob. First of all, we have to wait for the right opening at the Federal level. That could take some time. Second, the Massachusetts Hospital Association will take this on in the media as another excuse for the high cost of health care. The public will buy in giving the Attorney General an opening to push for an investigation which puts us back in the soup. Maybe while we are waiting for a place to plant the Mayor you could convince him to sign a City contract with Action to handle the waste from Boston Hospital. That would break the MHA hold on the cost thing when the

Mayor points to the savings the hospital will experience by using a private contractor. The Tax Payers Association will want to endorse the Mayor's good wisdom which means they won't pressure me to start dragging him in the mud."

Muldoon adopted a conciliatory position as he moved sideways and sat on one hip, "Charlie, it seems to me that we aren't too far apart. I am in a position to know that the Secretary of Labor will be looking for a prominent elected Democrat to step in as the Undersecretary of Labor. Of course, the person to be selected has to be a friend of Labor and a known supporter of the President. The National Workers' Federation wants the recommendations of its affiliates on possible nominees. Once the Federation decides on the best possible nominee that person has a lock on the appointment. But just to be sure that the right person gets the job it might pay for a big outfit that has a lot of influence to join up with the Federation, say like National Associated Investors, and work out a deal like we're doing here. When I was talking with the Federation earlier they suggested I mention it. That way the confirmation would sail through, you know."

"So much for the local fire fight bullshit," thought Patello. Marone remained impassive. His expression didn't change. This was top floor stuff that he would carry to Big Frank Patello in a few hours followed in short order by a NAI Board meeting and negotiation that set national policy on such matters. The Federation knew the process. They had been through it on other occasions. There was apparently something else on the national agenda that could be advanced by the relatively insignificant Boston item. Muldoon was obviously the messenger boy. He had accomplished his mission by giving a subtle message to the NAI that a pow-wow was requested with the big chief. That being done he could move back to the details of the local issue. The ball was squarely in Patello's court who decided to go to the men's room. Marone went along.

The usually neat appearance of the NAI and Park executive seemed ruffled, "Charlie, I think you got what you need from that mick. Let's blow this cookie farm. I can't stand this goddamn tasteless Boston beer. It runs right through me. I'll see Big Frank in the morning after he meets with the Board. If there's anything that we need from here we'll let you know. Old Muldoon is good, damn good. Your Uncle might want you to visit with him about this Cowan stiff I doubt that Cowan means that much to the Federation. Me thinks the goons got a big deal in the offing that merits our combined interest. We'll see. Meanwhile you keep Cowan's ass out of the mud. I'll take care of the WASP side but you got to make sure that Hardly doesn't piss off his cousins and get the locals all stirred up. This Commissioner Logan should find a nice job in the private sector. Next month maybe he starts as a vice president with Patriot. I'll arrange it with Mondi. He'll contact this kid and cut him a deal he can't refuse. You check out this Mike Megan guy and see if he can be loyal."

Patello nodded his assent to Marone's comments and the duo returned to the table.

Muldoon had a fresh beer in hand with two more set waiting for his party. The expedient bartender was behind the bar tending to other orders. Marone grimaced at the sight of another Sam Adam's but followed Patello's lead in rendering a gratuitous sign to Muldoon.

Patello picked up the conversation, "OK Mouldy, we got your message and Mr. Marone will see that the proper people are advised. A representative from Action Waste Management will be appointed to work out the terms of a labor agreement with the appropriate Local. I'm sure that you can make those arrangements. It's my understanding that Commissioner Logan will accept a position in the private sector within the month. There is no basis to think that the Mayor or anyone in his administration has misused campaign funds. You can be sure that I have no intention at this time to imply anything of the kind to the media. We need assurance from the Mayor that Mr. Megan will be appointed to succeed Commissioner Loan. We also need to meet with Mr. Megan in the next couple of days to discuss the details of the Privatized Voluntary Waste Management Program for Boston. The Mayor will want to announce the new arrangement at Boston Hospital next week. I also believe that our mutual interest can be benefited with a private contractor waste management agreement with a private hospital in the City. Since organized labor and the Catholic Church are so supportive of each other it seems reasonable that St. Anslem's should start at the same time as Boston Hospital. Two Boston hospitals going to private waste management will pull the MHA's string. We may need the help of the City health department to convince the CEO of St. Anslem's that he needs privatized waste management. You take care of your end and keep in touch with me. Is there, anything that I left out? Oh yeah, no strikes or slowdowns at the hospitals. You keep the locals cool. Anything else?"

"Just one thing," Muldoon stood and turned toward the door; "when you pay the bar tab make sure that my friend Harry, the bartender, gets a good tip."

o O o

Phil Mondi was pleased to receive a phone call from an old friend. He and Tony Marone had been friends and teammates at St. Michael's High in the Bronx. They both attended Fordham but Phil later transferred to Pace. Marone graduated a year ahead of Mondi and began his career in the small business investment racket as an account analyst and collector. He was an immediate success and rewarded with a supervisory position and then his own branch of the business in lower Manhattan. Mondi, after graduation, went to work for Marone. He showed equal promise and with Marone's support in a few years was given the opportunity to manage one of NAI's courier ventures, The Patriot Transport and Courier Service of Boston. With the consent of NAI, Marone and Mondi diversified Patriot into other services and products beyond the basic transport activities.

Mondi enjoy talking to his friend, "Tony, my main man, how are you doing and how's that beautiful wife and kid?"

"Just fine, Phil. Things well with you?" Marone seemed to register a rhetorical tone, "I know you're making money because I see the reports. You know money isn't everything. You got to relax. Play more golf. Enjoy life you know what I mean?"

"Tony when you start with that relax stuff it means you got some bum that I got to put on the payroll for my own good and yours too. Who is the guy and when does he start?"

Marone seemed genuinely hurt that his friend suspected ulterior motives in the call, "I got to explain, Phil. You know about the waste management thing that Patello's handling? Well we cut a deal with this Muldoon guy at the Union that we take and stash the Boston

Commissioner of Health in a private slot so the goons can put a guy they own in the Commissioner's job. So, I figure that we put the guy in with you so if we need to come back later and hit the goons we got this guy Logan to use as a club. You sort of keep him happy but don't let him get too involved if you know what I mean. Anyway, the goons put in a guy named Megan and he opens the door for us with the hospitals as a starter. We give the Union a contract at Action and let them load up on us a little."

The drift was obvious to Mondi, "Your talking about Michael Logan, Tony. He's a clean-cut kid that the Mayor appointed to the commissioner's job after the last election. We know him because he was active with the Young Democrats. I think his thing is public health work. Got a master's degree from Harvard or BU or something. He probably doesn't know squat about the transport business. He takes a job in this outfit and the press is going to smell a deal somewhere. It makes more sense for him to go into health in the private sector. That way the switch is less obvious and keeps him from being offended by a forced career change. Also, the public sees it as reasonable since the kid really isn't a politician. How about this? We get him a job with the Catholics, say at St. Anslem's Hospital. Patello and I convince Hardly that the hospital's CEO needs a guy to help with quality control or something that a master's degree in public health would want to do. Hell, he could be an assistant to our good friend and fellow hospital trustee, Dr. Richard Folley."

"Phil, I knew there was a reason why I put up with your bullshit all these years. That's a good idea. How do we know the boss at St. Anslem's will buy the idea? You got him wrapped?"

"The top job at St. Anslem's is a wild card, Tony. Hardly tried too early to move in and pissed off the Cardinal and the Nuns. They got a guy in there that is a common pro that tries to do a job. He's got some moxie but I don't think he'd take a wrapper. I think I have a better idea. We get Hardly and Folley to convince the Cardinal that he needs an office in the Chancery for health affairs. This guy Logan, obviously, a good Catholic, gets anointed to the post by the Cardinal and everybody cheers. He can still be an assistant to Folley that way we got a wrapper on him but it's transparent. I like it."

Marone jumped at the suggestion, "OK, Phil, makes sense except for a few management problems and a few bruised egos. Let's give it a try. You call Patello about our talk and work it out. Get back to me. In the mean-time I got to talk to Cappizi about what to do with Mayor Cowan and to make sure we got a tight wrapper on Siro. Speaking about wrappers you ought to see if you can get one on the top guy at the hospital. We might need it."

"Whatever. You stay cool my friend." Mondi closed the conversation., excused himself, shook Jay's hand and left. As he passed the bar he ordered another round for Jay and Donovan. The bartender delivered the beer and explained to Donovan that Mr. Muldoon had paid the tab. Donovan exchanged small talk with Jay as they drank the final round. Little was said about the conversation with Muldoon except the opinion offered by Donovan that he thought Muldoon liked Jay. Donovan finished his beer in a gulp and said good-bye to Jay, offering that he had to get with the family. He promised to call Jay in the next day or so to fill him in on the contract negotiations with Action.

Jay sat by himself and relaxed. He nursed the remainder of his Sam Adams while pondering the exchange with Muldoon. The guy was about as subtle as an atomic missile. He might just as well have said that he thought Jay was a management shill. In his mind, Jay reasoned, "Well, what the hell, if that's what he thinks then there's no reason to disappoint him."

Jay left Stinger's in plenty of time to make his appointment with friend Brian. The trip across the City was miserable. Traffic was backed up on Interstate 93 inbound and jammed on the Mass Pike outbound. Somehow Jay didn't seem to care. He wore a nice glow from the three beers. The world still appeared to be his oyster. Gradually he steered to the Waltham Tap and Keg. Brian was perched on his favorite stool holding a few beer-leads on his buddy.

As Jay pulled alongside, Brian already had one perched for him. This was Brian's night to howl. The moon was full and Brian was half the same. Jay slapped his buddy on the back and gulped down the offered beer. He quickly ordered up another for Brian and himself. The code of celebrant drinkers required a reciprocal round before conversing. This time they touched bottles in mutual salute before guzzling the brine.

Their consumption rate slowed as they began the next round. Eventually conversation about the day entered the agenda. Jay fired the first volley, "Brian, you son of a bitch, what is this about you sticking your head up Eddie's ass? You tuning in on the big time?"

Brian had to swallow fast to respond. He almost choked, "No, man. It came out of the blue. I didn't know anything and he comes up and says they taking me off the route. I figure I'm canned. What the hell I wanted to quit anyway. So, Eddie sits me down and says how he needs an experienced field hand to run special orders for high rollers. The swells don't like to have a truck deliver their nose candy. Guess it makes the neighbors think they got a hefty stash. They gimme a Chevy with a tape player and everything. I'm on call around the clock though. Got this damn pager hanging on me all the time. Can you believe this shit."

Jay just smiled, "You get to keep the tips, Brian?"

"No way. I'm not supposed to accept any money." Brian seemed to assume an almost religious sincerity, "I only deliver. The collection is made by a bag man some other way. I never see the guy. That way if I get busted they can only nail me for possession not for dealing. It's an easier rap. Hell, I don't know what I'm delivering. I can only guess. None of the packages look alike and they sure as hell don't have labels. The dudes sign for it like anything else. Special courier that's me. Got a raise too. You ready for another?"

Another beer was produced by the hefty bartender. J on found the barstool difficult to his seating. They moved to a remaining open booth that proved more comfortable and conducive to conversation. The Waltham Tap and Keg was beginning to get crowded. Most of the booths were filled, people standing at the bar were two deep, the pool tables in the rear were occupied and the blaring music from the corner jukebox saturated the place with Country and Western music. Conversation was difficult and required a shout to be heard. Jay played with the napkin dispenser while Brian continued to ramble in a very loud voice about his new career opportunity. No matter how hard Jay tried he could not insert his own news about his appointment as a shop steward. He was becoming bored with the celebration. It seemed time to quit. He had a nice buzz. Brian was repeating himself for the fourth or fifth time. "Maybe one more round and we split." thought Jay.

He was about to suggest this to Brian when Brian's pager let out a shrill high pitch beep that gained the attention of the assembled faithful. Brian struggled to find the device clipped on his belt. When he finally located it, he could not find the page button. Eventually, he overcame the miracle of technology and noted the paging phone number on the small LED. With no small amount of pride Brian excused himself to answer the summons.

"Hell," Jay thought, "they ought to give him a cellular phone to go with the job. That would make things easier and really boost Brian's ego." He decided to mention it to Brian on his return.

It seemed like only a minute or two when Brian came back to the booth looking excited. "Jay, I got to make a run. You wanna go along? I could use your help."

Jay was now more than a little drunk. He thought the request from Brian was ridiculous. "You need my help? Shit, you delivering a ton of stash or something? How heavy can that stuff be? I never had any trouble lifting mine. Why you want me along?"

The sarcasm went over Bian's head, "Well, I gotta admit to being a little scared about this new deal. I mean it happened too sudden. One day Eddie was going to fry my ass and the next thing I'm his man. He could be setting me up. I gotta be careful for a while till I get used to this action. You know, man."

"What I know is that you're still a paranoid." Jay remembered the crying jag that Brian had on the last fishing trip. "Eddie try to sell you any more insurance for the new job? Shit, Brian you can't run scared all the time. Where we goin' and what do you want me to do?"

Brian assumed an important air and sat back in the booth to detail a reply, "Well I got to go over to the dispatcher at Patriot and pick up the load. Then I carry it to the fruit bowl down town. You take your car home and I'll pick you up on my way to town. It's eight thirty now. We can be back at your place by midnight."

Jay was amused at Brian, the executive. He leaned across the table and poked Brian in the chest to give emphasis, "You bet your ass I'll be home by midnight. I got a big day tomorrow. We got a Union at Action and I'm the Shop Steward. We're into contract talks. How about that? What's the fruit bowl? Never heard of it."

Now it was Brain's turn to lean back, "Jay, I been holding a union card since I joined Patriot. It don't hurt a thing, man. Don't worry about it. The fruit bowl is that queer bar down on Harrison. I think the name of the joint is the Troubadour or something like that. Anyway, what I want you to do is cover my ass so to speak."

"Sick, Brian. That is really sick. Man, you need a vacation."

If Brian realized Jay's implication, he gave it little credence, "No, man. I don't mean that. What I mean is that I want you to go in first and just look around. Order a beer and case the joint. You see something that you don't think is natural give me the high sign and we split. I tell the dispatcher that I think I had a hot LZ. It's SOP. We don't always deliver on the first try. The customer got to secure the zone or we don't come in. Eddie explains all that when the order is made."

Jay was still amused at the nature of the task. He continued to bait his friend, "Brian, when I go into that fruit bowl, I ain't gonna see anything that I think is natural. What the hell am I supposed to see that tells me we got to split? You're puttin' the wrong man on point, buddy."

Brian finally got the point but decided to ignore it. Instead he tried to flatter his friend into cooperating. "Jay, if there's one man on earth that's an expert on saloons and stash it's you. You done more pick-ups in this town than anybody. You been buying stash since junior high. You know what to look for. Just go in there like you was the deal and I'm the dealer. You think it's right give me the nod. Then I go to my contact. The dispatcher will tell me who to look for. They know I'm coming but they don't expect me to have a point man. You stay clear. If the deal gets busted you stand aside and walk away. Don't get involved. If there's a bust Eddie will get me clear. Patriot only runs a delivery service and they don't deal is the way that they explain it to the law. That's somebody else that I never see or know anything about. You know I could be delivering' a box of candy to some guy's sweetheart."

"Sick, Brian, really sick." Jay's response was again lost on Brian.

Jay and Brian divided the tab, waved goodnight to their friendly bartender, and processed to the dingy parking lot behind the bar. Brian insisted on giving Jay a tour of his assigned Caprice Classic with tape player and a Patriot Courier Service sign on the front doors. Jay complemented Brian on his new found status.

In his semi-inebriated condition, Jay drove home carefully. The boys were in process of preparing for bed. He supervised the baths while Susan warmed his dinner. Jay explained to her that he was going to help Brian with a job that would have him home by midnight. Susan didn't ask about the job but knew well that her hero was sticking his neck out for a friend. This was a prominent feature of Jay's personality that she both admired and feared.

Jay fixed a couple of gin and grapefruits that they consumed while waiting for Brian to arrive. A horn from the driveway announced the beginning of the mission. Jay hugged the kids, kissed Susan and left. On his way out the door Susan reminded him to call Cecile.

Jay's stomach ached from the hastily consumed meal, two gin and grapefruits, and the anxiety of having to call the "bitch." "Damn. What was her problem?" He suspected that she wanted to hassle him about the hospital thing on Saturday. "That's none of her business." he thought. "If she suspected an overdose so what. The record was secure." He wondered if she found a judge who could make him tell the cause of his hospitalization. The pain in his stomach and chest seemed to be progressing. He tried to ignore the pain and concentrate on Cecile, "Got to call Martha in the morning and ask her about this medical record thing. She is going to he really pissed when she learns about the hospital trip."

Brian took notice of Jay's pained expression. "What's the matter, man? You look like you got a fart caught sideways. See that package on the back seat. That's it. Looks like it might be a box of candy. What's inside is none of my business, man. I'm just the special courier delivering' a late-night order. How you feeling?"

Jay was doubled over in the front seat but tried to answer, "Like shit. My guts are killing me. Maybe we ought to open the box and help ourselves to some of that candy. You game for that?"

Messing with a delivery package was against the code and Brian was not about to violate the code. "Yeah, sure. We just tell the customer that it was our favorite kind so we helped ourselves to a small bite. Oh man, Eddie would chomp us up."

It took about fifteen minutes in late night traffic to drive from Waltham to the center of Boston. Brian took another fifteen minutes to locate the Troubadour Night Club. He pulled into a loading zone in front of the building next to the Club. They could see in the front door that the place was crowded.

Brian took charge of the operation. "Jay, it looks like there's an open spot at the end of the bar. I can see it from here. You go in, sit there, and order a drink. If things look OK then turn around on the barstool and look out the door. When you turn around that's my signal to come in. You just sit there and finish your drink. Wait until I leave then follow me out after a while. They might spot you coming out but then it don't mean nothing. Main thing is that you got to act natural like you belong there."

"Shit, Brian. Acting natural and looking like I belong there is a contradiction" Jay had his pain under control for the moment and was back at jabbing Brian, "I gotta tell ya if one of those freaks puts his hand on my knee we are going to have combat. Who you looking for?"

Brian reached into the back seat and brought the package into his hands. "Best you don't know. Otherwise you might look right at them and blow the cover. You do a general check and give me the sign. Oh yeah, if the place looks hot you keep looking forward, finish your drink and leave. I turn back to Patriot with a customer not found report. Eddie knows that means a hot LZ. Sometimes when that happens I make a second run."

"You make a second pass on this deal, you making it alone. I signed on for a single trip." Jay gave an emphatic point with his finger as he started to leave. He opened the car door and strolled to the Club. A bouncer stood outside smoking a cigarette. He gave Jay a quick once over as Jay opened the door and stepped in. Otherwise, Jay felt that he was generally unnoticed. He took the seat at the end of the bar as planned. From his vantage point he could see most of the customers. Surprisingly a number of women were present. Conversation was animated. People were having a good time. Whatever bizarre behavior Jay expected was not evident. The place seemed like a lively singles bar. He became comfortable. Eventually the busy bartender managed to ask him for an order. Jay asked for his usual gin and grapefruit. The bartender nodded. Jay noticed effeminate characteristics but without offense. He felt that he was in a nice place.

As the bartender was making his drink Jay, on impulse, spun around on his barstool. Just as he completed his one hundred eighty degree turn he realized with horror that he had accidentally given the all clear signal to Brian who was already out of the car and walking to the Club entrance with package in hand. It was in God's hands now.

Jay turned to his left and spun his stool back to the bar just as the bartender placed a drink in front of him. He tried to sip the drink but his hand was shaking uncontrollably. He then turned to his right to place his elbows on the bar. Brian had approached two men sitting in a booth. They apparently invited Brian to sit down. As he slid into the booth he placed the package in front of the larger man.

After a few deep breaths, Jay raised his eyes to give the crowd the visual check that he had failed to do before giving Brian the all clear. He suddenly had strong eye contact with a giant of a man that looked like Rock Hudson. The man was staring at Jay with a very serious look. As Jay returned the stare the man slowly turned his head in the direction of the booth where Brian was sitting with his new customers. Rock glanced back at Jay and walked over to the booth. With a start, Jay recognized the Rock Hudson look alike. It was Officer Michael O'Sullivan of the Boston PD presently married to one Cecile O'Sullivan RN. Jay was amazed at the realization, "Cecile's old man was hanging out in a queer bar. Holy shit! The guys a cop!" He made Jay with Brian. "It's a bust—a fuckin bust." The pain in Jay's stomach made him double over. He spilled his drink. The bartender came to Jay's aid and asked if he could be of some assistance. Jay thanked the man, paid for the drink, and tried to leave but he could barely manage to walk.

The pain brought tears to Jay's eyes. He was beginning to pray for an arrest so he could ask for medical care. He even thought about surrendering to O'Sullivan on the spot when the image of Krisitie came to mind. This is what the "bitch" needed to knock him out of custody. The combination of love for Kristie and hate for Cecile overcame the pain for the moment. He regained his composure. A glance at the booth where Brian was seated revealed the two customers, Brian, and O'Sullivan engaged in friendly humorous conversation. There was no bust. "What the hell was going on?" surged in his mind. He didn't wait to find out. Carefully he maneuvered out the door to the Chevy. Brian in his usual careless manner had failed to lock the doors. Jay slumped into the front seat. The pain had returned.

Brian came out to the car a few minutes after Jay. He got behind the wheel and started the engine. Brian happily chirped at his buddy. "Hey, thanks for your help, Jay. Those were a couple nice guys. That other guy must have been a user. They invited me to party with 'em. Told him I had a few other runs to make. Can you imagine that? They want me to take a few sniffs. They acted like I know what's in there. I act like I maybe know. Anyway, they gonna' ask for me special from now on. How you doin?"

Jay didn't want to talk but he managed to answer, "Hurtin bad, Brian. I got to get home. Man, I never want to see another drop of booze. Can you hurry up?"

In addition to the pain Jay was very anxious about being identified by Officer O'Sullivan as part of the delivery. Legally it didn't mean much. He could testily in Cecile's behalf at a custody hearing. Maybe he was under cover. Jay had reasoned an explanation. "Yeah that's it. He was under cover. He's going for something else. Maybe he's on to Patriot and the whole ring. Maybe he's trying to bust his queer buddies for possession. Hell, they might already be in the slammer. No good. He busts the users and they finger Brian who fingers him. Cecile wins. So how do I tip off Brian? Do I tip off Brian and he goes to Eddie for insurance? Eddie figures how I'm linked in and comes after me. I lose. Hell, there has to be a way out of this mess. Right now, I'm cornered. Maybe I'll die. Case closed. Yeah that's it. Maybe I'll die. Brian? How does Brian work in? Those guys got his name. They going to ask for him special. Why? Oh yeah! They are setting him up. I bet all three of those dudes were cops. Brian is their way into the Patriot racket. They get Brian on the hook and use him as a backward mule. That's not too bad if nobody gets killed in the process. Patriot goes down but Brian cops out. Man, got to get clear from the whole mess before it falls on me. Jesus how do I get clear?"

Brian pulled into Jay's driveway just after midnight. Jay managed to get inside and sat in the living room. Susan was sound asleep. She was unaware of Jay's misery or anxiety. She found him asleep in the chair at seven the next morning. The pain was still with him but he decided to go to work. His new status demanded the extra sacrifice of attendance.

At eight fifteen he shuffled past Ken Ryan's desk and slumped in his chair. Roughly, Jay figured he had three hours of restless sleep. The rest of the night had been constant sharp pains followed by anxiety attacks and visions of Cecile gloating over a court victory. Ken approached Jay's desk with a new work schedule for the Boston project. Jay was convulsing. He was incoherent. The company nurse responded to Ken's call. She took Jay's vital signs, asked him a few questions that he was now able to answer. She concluded that Jay was suffering from the DT's.

Ken realized that a 911 call would put Jay in the public record. He instead took the chance that Jay was not in a life-threatening condition. A few months prior Action had signed a corporate health contract with St. Anslem's that contained among many things an Employee Assistance Program for individuals suspected or known to be substance abusers. With the assistance of Action's EAP director, the health nurse, Ken, and a cast of thousands Jay was placed in the Company van and driven to St. Anslem's where he was introduced to SACAP or in the complete text, St. Anslem's Chemical Addiction Program.

Jay was placed in a regular hospital room and bed. Doctors and nurses hovered around him taking vital signs, asking him questions, and taking the mandatory blood and urine samples. He signed a treatment consent form that Ken suggested was appropriate if he was to be treated for his convulsions and pain. The form specified emergency treatment for detoxification and overdose. Jay noted the words but was in no condition to object. After a time, a nurse brought Jay some liquid medication that he took without question. Within a half hour he stopped shaking and the pain was less intense. He felt weak. The rebound that he experienced on Sunday at Waltham Hospital was not happening this time. He knew he was a sick cookie. Nailed. Tears came to his eyes as he drifted into a peaceful sleep.

Several hours later he woke soaked in sweat. The bed linen was more off the bed than on, displaying the significant restlessness of which he had been completely unaware. He felt totally fatigued and very weak. His throat was dry. An attempt to speak resulted in a burning sensation in his chest that seemed to consume what little breath he had in his lungs. As his eyes gained focus he became aware that no one else was in the room. Panic overcame fatigue as he attempted to get out of bed. His legs collapsed under him as he touched the floor. He fell on the terrazzo floor, unconscious.

An eternity later he opened his eyes. He was back in the same bed but with clean linens. The room was dark except for a small night light that seemed to be in the distance. The window offered no light causing Jay to realize that the day had passed. An intravenous pole and stand was adjacent to the bed. Jay looked up at the bottle and visually traced the line to his left arm. This time he did not panic. He recalled that somewhere within reach was a nurse call button. Find the button and a human being would appear. Unless—unless he was dead and experiencing the transfer to the life hereafter. Again panic. "Horseshit. No angel is going to hook up an IV. Where's that damn button?" He found it clipped to the linen just below his shoulder on the left side, somewhat out of range, causing him to reach across his body with his right hand. He made a mental note to explain to the nurse about the proper position of the call button as he gave it a push.

After a few minutes, a nursing assistant came into the room. She was very pleasant and seemed quite pleased with Jay's return to a rational state. It was a few minutes after ten. She explained that Jay had been in the detox mode for nearly fourteen hours. Susan had been with him most of the time but had gone home to care for the kids. They would continue to take his vital signs throughout the night. In the morning, a physician would explain his physical condition and a counselor assigned to him would explain the course of rehabilitation. He had fought most of the afternoon but eventually came to rest. The IV was to deal with dehydration. It probably would be discontinued in the morning. The doctor wanted it to continue through the night. If he was hungry or thirsty she could get him something. The nurse was busy with a new admit but would drop in to check on him when she was free. "Any questions?"

Jay listened to the nursing assistant with amazement. He didn't remember anything about the day. He recalled going to work and the night before at the Troubadour. He had no recollection how he got to St. Anslem's. To be sure, he asked the nursing assistant if he was in fact at St. Anslem's. She explained that he was in the SACAP Unit. He vaguely recalled that the Unit began about the time that he left St. A's. He also recalled that the doctor at Waltham had recommended the St. Anslem's program. Well, he certainly took his advice. He asked if he could call Susan. There were no telephones in SACAP rooms but phones for patient use were available at the nursing station. Jay was asked to wait until morning to place his call unless it was an emergency. He agreed to be patient and give Susan a call in the morning.

CHAPTER NINE

As Tuesday began with pain for John Marquart, it began with anxiety for Charles Patello. After a restless night, Charlie got out of bed at five AM. By the time he had showered and dressed it was five forty five. He decided against his usual juice and coffee opting instead to drive to his office arriving an hour and a half ahead of his routine schedule. He had not heard from his so- called buddy, Thomas O'Shea, since their meeting the day before so he had no idea if the good Doctor Folley was on board and willing to promote Logan to the Cardinal as the Director of the Archdiocesan Office for Health Affairs. The meeting with the Cardinal was scheduled to begin sometime after three thirty that afternoon. Patello wondered if he would develop a bleeding ulcer between now and then. He wandered aimlessly around the empty office until his stomach directed him to the all-night coffee shop across the street where he devoured two cream filled doughnuts, a large orange juice, and black coffee. Slowly his anxiety transitioned to the indigestion that was more his style. The chatter in the coffee shop diverted him from the thoughts of the pending meeting with the Cardinal. He allowed himself the pleasure of pondering the favor of the young waitress as a further diversion while he consumed three more cups of black coffee. Finally, at half past eight he paid the check and walked to his office. The caffeine had him wired for action.

Things were already happening at One Park Avenue in Manhattan. Mario Capizzi, President of National Associated Investors arrived at his office at six to prepare for the Board of Directors meeting scheduled for eight AM. His number one assistant, Anthony Marone, arrived a half hour later. The two executives carefully examined the Board members' information packets that had been place on the board room table the day before. Everything seemed to be in good order for the critical presentation on the prospect of NAI entering the business of health care. Slide projector, screen, podium, amplifier, tape recorder, television with VCR, and note pads were strategically placed to capture the details of presentation and discussion. At seven AM the executive assistant to Mr. Capizzi arrived and began to double check the arrangements. A few minutes later Mr. Marone's executive assistant arrived and began a test of the technical recording devices. The Caterer arrived at seven thirty to prepare the continental breakfast consisting of fruit, Danish, yogurt, nut bread, sweet rolls, bagels, jams, jellies, a variety of juices, tea, soft drinks, and caffeinated and decaffeinated coffee. The mammoth board room was immaculate. The plush chairs were positioned at the table. The executives, satisfied that all was in readiness, relaxed with a cup of coffee. The executive assistants moved to the outer reception area in order to greet the in-coming members.

As the caterer was arranging the nourishment, Mr. Tom Callahan, Health Consultant for Debur and Tandy, retained by the Federation, arrived and began to prepare for his presentation. He and his assistant placed special notebooks that contained statistics supporting his presentation at each chair. Copies of slides to be used in the presentation were also in the packets. His assistant carefully loaded the slide projector and tested the focus. He then placed a video tape in the VCR, cueing it to the start position. Callahan placed his presentation notes next to the podium after giving them a final review. At twenty minutes before the hour Mr. Frank Patello, Chairman of the Board of NAI, walked into the board room.

Patello huddled with Cappizi, Marone and Callahan to review the agenda and get a feel for the details of the presentation. The meeting plan was simple and directed to the single issue of health. After call to order and roll call the minutes of the last meeting would be brought forward for approval. They had been previously mailed to the members. No contest or amendment was expected. Since this was a special meeting of the Board, Big Frank Patello intended to ask the members to wave the routine reports and old business of the NAI in order to move promptly to the subject of Health as a new business venture. With the concurrence of the members, he would introduce Mr. Callahan who would explain the nature of the venture. The presentation would be followed by a period of questions and comments. The nature of the questions and comments from the members would give Patello a general sense of the attitude of the Board concerning the venture. After they had exhausted their inquiries, Big Frank would call for a break. During the forty-five-minute break Capizzi and Marone would lobby any apparent opposition. Callahan would be available for a one on one with any board member seeking more information or clarification.

Following the break, Big Frank intended to ask Mr. Capizzi to present a sketch of the NAI Health business plan. This would give the board better insight of the processes and methods to be employed by NAI in developing the health services programs and, of most importance, the expected profits. Again, questions and comments would be entertained after the presentation. If all went well Frank would ask for a motion to approve the venture with the capital allocation recommended in the business plan that was included in detail in their information packets. The representative of the Federation was already disposed to make the motion. If necessary, Patello would give the second but it was expected that the Federation had arranged for a second from the floor. After the vote was taken with a positive result, Big Frank would ask if there was any other business. Not expecting any other items to be brought forward he would then ask for a motion to adjourn. Following adjournment cocktails would be served in the reception area while the board room was prepared by the caterer for a very delicious gourmet style lunch. The executive assistants would be available to assist any board member in arranging travel, tours, or entertainment following lunch.

The four men felt that the meeting was well planned. Preparations were in order. At ten minutes to eight the first members arrived. By eight o'clock Frank Patello noticed that a solid quorum was present. Additional representatives were scheduled to arrive soon. The attitude among those present was jovial. Jim Ebber, representing the Federation, was circulating and apparently spreading the gospel. It all looked good. Big Frank decided to delay the start of the meeting in order to allow for more good will to develop and to allow late arrivals to sample the buffet. No need to press the issue since it seemed to be carrying itself

The members of the NAI Board of Directors had all been carefully selected by Frank Patello. They came from all parts of the United States but the majority were wealthy people from the Northeast. Each person's wealth was gained by hard work, albeit somewhat less than honorable. Nevertheless, they held a great amount of personal respect in society because of their wealth which they shared generously with special charities. The twenty-one members were also heavily invested in the NAI ventures. All in all, the NAI Board of Trustees comprised a solid mutual aid and admiration society that lived the motto of one for all and all for one. At exactly eight thirty, Big Frank asked everyone to be seated so the meeting could begin.

As planned, Big Frank moved through the preliminaries with ease and then introduced Mr. Tom Callahan. Tom expressed his gratitude for the opportunity to address the members of the Board. He introduced his able assistant then moved immediately to the subject, healthcare for fun and profit. "In the next year, over one trillion dollars will be spent on health services," he explained, "Nearly forty percent of that amount is expected to be spent on services traditionally provided by hospitals and another twenty percent for physician services. Si xty percent to be spent on hospitals and physicians while the remaining forty percent will be distributed over a wide range of services including nursing homes, durable medical equipment, drugs, and other health related programs."

As Mr. Callahan spoke his assistant presented slides demonstrating the statistics.

Callahan continued, "From a business perspective it is important to note that the money to be spent for hospital and physician services is ninety percent prepaid and held by insurance companies, health maintenance organizations, and government agencies to be eventually distributed to the point of service. The dominate method of conducting health insurance over the past decades was by use of an indemnity form of insurance that reserved the premiums and paid to the agencies on a schedule of fees usually negotiated and discounted. The insurance companies attempted to earn a profit on investment income. This method was not successful from a proprietary perspective because there was no control on the utilization of the services. Consequently, the providers were prone to over treat the patient in order to maximize their revenue and profits. Under the indemnity program the insurance companies made little profit, physicians and hospitals made big profits, and the purchaser of the health insurance, usually employers, paid ever increasing premiums."

At this point, Mr. Callahan's assistant displayed a chart showing the growth in employer spending on health insurance compared to salaries and wages over the past thirty years. The chart displayed that over the past three decades for every dollar on increased wages another two dollars was spent for health care benefits.

Callahan dramatized the Chart and continued, "The increasing premiums caused the rapid escalation of the health services component in gross national product. Automobile manufacturers complained bitterly to the government that the cost of health benefits in the cost of their products made them non-competitive with foreign companies. Federal initiative to reform the provision and payment methods for healthcare failed in Congress but did result in industrial attempts to modify the nature of pre-paid health services. The underlying concept in reform is the modified health maintenance organization as the payer networks / regulator coupled with the recently introduced concept of healthcare.

The networks are vertically organized hospitals and doctors who bid for the contracts to provide care for the health maintenance organizations. Fiscal control is maintained by a capitation agreement that only allows a given amount per person in the plan to be spent in a given year. The health network agrees to provide services as needed but stands at risk on total spending. If money is left over at the end of the year the network is given a bonus."

At this point Callahan paused. His assistant lowered the lights and immediately played a video tape of various congressional hearings on health care reform. Congressmen from California and Illinois spoke in depth about the cost of health care. Each offered a solution that differed in form but substantially admonished physicians and hospitals as culprits.

After the fifteen-minute tape was completed the assistant raised the light level as Callahan returned to the platform. He glanced at his watch and noticed that the presentation had passed the forty-five-minute mark. "Time," he thought, "to get to the point."

"Gentlemen, for the past hour I have attempted to give you a fairly comprehensive review of the status of health services from a fiscal point of view. I'm sure you noticed that the complex state of affairs that currently exists in health provides at best a very risky opportunity. What I want to point out, however, is that the opportunity for profit is not in health per se but in the transition of health services. Keep in mind that currently a trillion dollars in cash is floating around out there looking for a place to land. That trillion dollars is earmarked for health service. My recommendation is that you take advantage of the confusion that may exist in select markets, move in, and acquire the health payer and provider base, extract the short run profits while they last, and then divest as the markets move toward stabilization. You have effectively done this in the waste management venture. The strategy used in that venture is basically the same that you may want to employ in health. I imagine the tactics will vary however. You have what the industry needs to make its transition. What health needs is transitional dollars. I mean capital to acquire the franchise for service that includes the provider base. This acquisition gives you the cash drawer to collect the pre-paid dollars. As the cash flows into the drawer you extract your return up front, then pay for the services to the at-risk providers and at the end share in the profits. Basically, you have the opportunity to make out on both ends."

Callahan had their attention, "The time frame between confusion and stabilization is uncertain. Once you move in you will be better able to determine the time that you will want to remain in that particular market. In other words, if you have control of the market you pretty much can hold the window open for however long that you like. The dominate factor however is regulation brought by legislation. Right now, the Country in 1995, favors private enterprise and a conservative point of view toward health services. However, that could shift. For instance, a move toward any willing payer type legislation could dramatically affect your franchise and control over the provider. Once you get in, you need to keep a sharp eye on the political winds. Gentlemen, I've exhausted my material and I thank you for your kind attention. At this time, I conclude my remarks. Thank you."

Mr. Callahan stepped away from the podium and Big Frank took his place. As Callahan stepped down a hearty round of applause erupted form the board. Frank shook Callahan's hand and pulled him next to the podium in a position to respond to questions.

Big Frank politely asked for order. "Gentlemen, as I'm sure you have observed we have one of the leading authorities in health reform with us this morning. I thank Mr. Callahan for his excellent presentation. I also want to thank our friends at the Federation for bringing the discussion on the health market to our attention through Mr. Callahan. Now Mr. Callahan has agreed to entertain your questions and comments. The floor is open."

The question and answer period went on for another forty-five minutes. Patello noted with pleasure that the questions were of a genuine nature. There was no sarcasm or arguments. All of the Board members were attentive to the subject and seemed attracted to the proposition. Most of the questions centered on the temporary or time limited nature of the venture. It was generally agreed that this element posed the basis for risk as it did for profit.

The meeting schedule was now running a half hour late but otherwise in good form. Patello recessed the meeting for thirty minutes. During the break Callahan's assistant removed the charts, slides and video tape used earlier. As he completed his work, Mario Capizzzi's executive assistant distributed an outline of the next presentation to the respective chairs. She also placed several charts on the easel next to the podium.

Capizzi and Marone circulated among the board members and listened to their exchange. Again, all seemed well. Callahan was cornered by a small group who were actively exploring his mind about health transition in various parts of the country. There was no question that the NAI Board was focused on the topic.

Chairman Patello called the meeting back to order exactly thirty minutes into the break. As the members took their seats, he began the second session. "Gentlemen, we were advised in our first session this morning about the short run opportunity in the field of health services. The opportunity as I understand it requires that we select a market and move swiftly to gain control. Then as the market matures, we divest for capital gain in addition to extracting significant operating profits. We might also choose to enter several markets at the sometime depending on the opportunities. If you recall we recognized the same opportunities when we entered the waste management field. You are well aware, I'm sure, of the success of that venture. While we are not experienced in health we are well experienced in the waste management program. On that basis, I asked Mr. Mario Cappizi, our chief executive officer and Mr. Anthony Marone, President of Park Consulting, to develop a proposed strategy for our entry into the health venture. Mr. Cappizi and Mr. Marone have worked with Mr. Callahan in developing the business plan that Mr. Cappizi is about to present. The full details of the plan are before you in the blue notebook under section two. Mr. Cappizi."

Mario Cappizi stepped to the podium looking refreshed and energized. His appearance suggested confidence. The slight smile on his face and the glint in his eyes conveyed a winning attitude. He was ready to get started.

"Once again, good morning gentlemen. You know me well enough to realize that I wasn't going to let Frank do all the talking. Now it's my turn and I'm going to take full advantage of it. Seriously, your positive reception to Tom Callahan's presentation was most encouraging. Mario and I have been studying the prospect of a health venture in depth and we are convinced that it is a profitable, very profitable, venture. The details of what I am about to present are in your notebook and an outline of my presentation is also at your place. You may want to follow it and make notes for questions later. I will be asking for motions to support the venture at the conclusion. This will include a request for a significant capital authorization. The name of this project is TARGET BOSTON MEDICAL. We propose to penetrate the Boston medical market with the acquisition of a health maintenance organization currently serving that area. As we gain control of the HMO we will begin the process of selling coverage to employers at under market prices. As we market to employers we will through another entity, form an integrated delivery network that will appear to bid for and acquire an exclusive contract with our HMO for the provision of services to our insured. We intend to use the capitation model as the means of putting our providers in the network at risk. We will extract twenty per cent of the premium dollars from the HMO up front and will also extract another twenty percent of the capitation allowance from the network up front as part of our corporate fee. We also reserve the right to a major share of any profits at the end of each operating year. In view of the fact that we are underselling the market you may wonder about the prospect of profits. Believe me the potential for profit is great. I will ask Mr. Marone to explain."

Tony Marone took the podium looking less confident than his boss. He was unsure if he really understood the health racket. Cappizzi and Callahan had it cold and had convinced Marone that it was a boomer. Now Marone had to explain it to some hard business types that knew their way around a buck. Before speaking he carefully wiped his brow.

"Gentlemen, I am an expert in converting trash to cash. I suppose I appear less than confident about my ability to convert an ill to a bill. Well, that's only because I am new to the idea and have yet to master the lingo. However I do know a rip-off when I see it. The people of Boston have been getting the medical shaft for a long time. Regardless of our proprietary intent, what we propose is needed in Boston and will be viewed by the people as something welcome and well overdue. To demonstrate my point there are more physicians per capita in Boston than any other city in the United States. Furthermore, Boston has the highest percentage of medical specialists in the Country. The case cost per hospital admission is the highest in the country and the hospital length of stay again is number one. The number of hospital days per one thousand population is currently at eight hundred down from a thousand a year ago. This is compared to three hundred fifty days per thousand in Los Angles. With the right administration of our HMO and the network we can lower the use and cost of healthcare in Boston by forty percent in two years max, and at the same time extract our ROI off the top of the premium and get another big piece at the bottom line. Eventually the competition will catch up to our methods and true price/quality competition will create equilibrium. As that begins to occur we will begin our withdrawal."

As Tony was talking, Mario was demonstrating the points with the charts and graphs on the easel. Tony would occasionally defer to Mario who would explain in some detail how the data was created and go more into its meaning. After fifteen minutes of explanation and discourse Tony returned the podium to Mario.

Mario continued his relaxed approach. "Tony has mentioned the impact of competition as an ally in our efforts. Boston has not experienced the effect of competition in health services. The community has never questioned the extravagant over served care because the health industry appeared to be the backbone of the local economy. We will cause that to change. In fact, the change is taking place without us.

At the present time, the major teaching hospitals are attempting to gobble up the competition at the community hospital level in order to preserve their referral base to their high-priced specialists. This has caused major disruption in the harmony of the medical community which gives us the opportunity to move in and get established virtually without notice. The existing HMO's are locally owned. The physicians and the hospitals have sucked them dry. I hasten to point out that the hospitals have the highest profit history in the country. Our first acquisition opportunity we believe is Bay Area Health Maintenance, an HMO that is in desperate need of capital. We could bail them out and gain a majority equity position. The remaining equity belongs to about a hundred physicians that we could buyout in groups or one at a time. We give them some vigorish to use in the partnership they take in the health network that we form. That same network should have an institutional partner that would eventually couple with the physicians in buying us out at the right time. Our contacts in the Boston area are well situated to deliver St. Anslem's Hospital to the network assuming that they can overcome the Church bureaucracy. Gentlemen that in a nutshell is "Target Boston Medical"

Several questions were asked by a variety of Board Members about the estimated time to be spent in the Boston market. Most felt that the NAI venture should start in several areas in order to maximize the prospect of success in the brief window of opportunity that Callahan had described. Eventually the motion was made and passed that initial studies be prepared for Dayton, Grand Rapids, and Raleigh. The capital allocation for each project was estimated and approved by the board. It was also recommended that Park Consulting change its focus from waste management to healthcare. The Board of Directors concluded that NAI should begin to divest from waste management enterprises. There being no further business to be brought before the Board of Directors, Mr. Frank Patello, Chairman, accepted a motion to adjourn.

oOo

Charlie Patello managed to control his emotions throughout the morning. He tried several times to contact O'Shea to learn if Dr. Folley had sufficiently prepped for the presentation to the Cardinal. O'Shea's office repeatedly reported that he was in a meeting and unavailable. A brief conversation with Hardly lacked substantive information but was reassuring enough to allow Charlie Patello to concentrate on other matters.

He left his office at noon for lunch at the coffee shop. In spite of his anxiety he sported a solid appetite. Refreshed, he returned to his desk at one fifteen in time for a call from Tony Marone. Tony was excited about the conclusion of the NAI Board meeting and wanted to give Charlie an update. Charlie listened to the report with great interest. The prospect of moving out of the waste management business in favor of the health venture seemed problematic in view of the state of affairs in Boston. The Mayor was in waiting for a Federal job. The Logan kid was being greased for the Archdiocese. A new Commissioner of Health for the City was positioned to approve the voluntary waste management program. The Union had been cut in at Action. Boston City and St. Anslem's were targeted for waste contracts. It was reasoned to suddenly back off would cause a real mess that would take years to repair.

Patello knew he had to persuade Marone to delay the retreat from waste management. Carefully he tried to counter, "Look Tony, we can't back off this waste project and move on health. There's too much at stake. Maybe instead of Target Boston you should Target Grand Rapids."

Marone, nevertheless, got the point. He offered a compromise, "I see it different, Charlie. The waste thing is tied to hospitals. It's a natural progression. We continue to move the waste project while doing the preliminaries on health. The two overlap, but don't conflict. We'll get you the help you need. Once the Mayor is taken care of Mark Mehan becomes point on the waste project and you can steer the health thing.

No sweat. We like the setup. You got control of the Catholic hospital and ought to be able to bring it in to the network when the time is right. That BayArea HMO is ripe for a takeover. It's got a load of Docs that we can con into the deal. Our consultant is pure genius and our guiding light. In the end, maybe we give him a piece of the action. We'll have a meeting of the Boston crowd to layout a work plan next week. You see what you can do to wrap up the waste project this week. By the way, the Mayor's deal is all set. It's critical that the Logan kid goes into the wrapper. You having any problem with that?"

Feeling some relief, Patello got back on track, "I'm not aware of any problem, Tony, other than the absence of a job to put him into. It all depends on that quack, Folley, convincing the Cardinal that he needs Logan to run his health business—excuse me—ministry. We meet in a couple hours. By five or six this afternoon I'll know if we have a problem."

Everything seemed in good order from Marone's point of view. He said as much to Charlie, "OK. You remember the signing bonus. When you have Logan let me know. I'll get the checks prepared for Cowan's endorsement. You see that an account is opened at the bank. We'll have Patriot hand carry the Logan check to the bank for deposit. To move this along Logan should resign his City job by Thursday. The Mayor will announce that Megan is the acting commissioner that same day. He also lets it leak that he is going to resign. On Monday, the Mayor meets with the President and the Secretary of Labor at a press conference in Washington to announce Cowan as the new Under Secretary. The Federation is taking care of all the details. Anything else?"

"Nothing at the moment, Tony" Patello knew it would be useless to complain about the work load, "I'll get back to you this evening or tomorrow morning. It's time for me to head for the Chancery. Say a prayer for our success."

"Yeah, right. You can count on my prayers. "Marone had not said a prayer since the third grade.

Patello hung up the phone and closed the files on his desk. He moved to the outer office and announced to his executive assistant that he would be at the Chancery for the rest of the day. He expected to be in the rest of the week but asked that his schedule be cleared for a number of priority meetings that he expected to develop. It was only two thirty.

The meeting with the Cardinal was expected to begin sometime after three thirty. Charlie knew that it would only take a half hour to drive from his downtown office to the Chancery in Brighton. Getting there a little early would give him time to check with Hardly, O'Shea and the distinguished Dr. Folley about their state of readiness. As he entered his car, he suddenly wished that he had eaten a light lunch.

The meeting with the Cardinal was to be held in the Cardinal's Residence, a stately edifice located a few hundred yards from the Chancery office building on the same campus. While the Residence resembled a mansion, it was used in the main for administration and as a conference center. The Cardinal used only a small portion of the building for his living quarters. Patello was unaware of the location of the meeting and had to be directed to the Residence by the receptionist at the Chancery. He was the first to arrive. A receptionist at the Residence answered the door. She directed Mr. Patello to a comfortable waiting area in a large corridor, gave him a cup of coffee, and immediately disappeared. Charlie sat alone in the corridor with his thoughts, surrounded by the life size portraits of Bishops, Archbishops, and Cardinals who over the past centuries had given spiritual guidance to the faithful of Boston and Eastern Massachusetts. He noticed that each portrait seemed to stare right at him. Was that planned or was he somehow being subjected to the spirit of these spiritual ancestors who knew that evil intent was more the agenda than advancing the ministry? He put his coffee cup on the small table next to his chair and walked to the nearest window where the magnificent landscape offered less imposing thoughts.

Kevin Hardly was next to arrive. Again, the receptionist answered the door. As she escorted Mr. Hardly to the waiting area she noticed that Mr. Patello had strayed to a nearby window. This was apparently some form of misconduct. As Kevin was provided the obligatory cup of coffee the receptionist summoned Mr. Patello back to his chair. He sensed a slight reprimand as she asked if he would like another cup of coffee. The message was plain and simple. Stay in your seat. Suddenly Charlie had a flashback to his days at St. Mary's grammar school. Kevin seemed relaxed in the sullen environment. As soon as the receptionist disappeared down the endless corridor, Kevin was on his feet inspecting the various portraits. He gave Charlie a historical review of each one noting his family's relationship with the Church during the particular reign of the Ordinary. In a way, it seemed that Hardly was right at home in the Cardinal's Residence. He, in his capacity as the First Leading Knight of the Equestrian Order of Knights of the Holy Cross, had frequently visited the Residence.

Kevin and Charlie exchanged small talk as the wait extended past the three thirty start time. It was curious to Charlie that O'Shea had yet to arrive. Kevin could offer no explanation for the absence of O'Shea or, of greater significance, the illusive Dr. Folley. Charlie's anxiety was mounting to anger and frustration. He was considering finding a telephone and searching out the missing persons when Bishop Hanks suddenly appeared from out of the darkness. Bishop Hanks apologized for the wait explaining that the Cardinal's cabinet meeting had extended well beyond its intended time allocation. The Cardinal required the extra time to resolve a number of matters before rushing for a plane to Rome. The Cardinal had asked Bishop Hanks to apologize to the distinguished gentlemen for not being able to meet with them but he was sure they would understand that the important matters waiting his attention at the Vatican required his immediate departure. Bishop Hanks asked Kevin and Charlie to follow him to the Cardinal's conference room where they could continue their discussion.

Patello was speechless. He could hardly breathe. The absolute need to settle the issue now was lost to everyone but him. He began to sweat. His stomach turned and he suppressed a belch. He was beyond anger. This was panic. No recourse. Just plain panic. As they walked to the conference room he barely was conscious of the conversation between Bishop Hanks and Hardly. Vaguely he heard something about the Cardinal's general consent to experiment with the concept but it seemed distant to the issue. He was concentrating on regaining his composure. What was the rule—never let them see you sweat. Under his coat, he was dripping wet.

As they entered the conference room, Patello got his second major shock of the day. Seated at the table was the distinguished Dr. Richard Folley with his favorite father in law, Mr. Thomas O'Shea. Bishop Hanks asked Hardly and Patello to be comfortable. The ever-present receptionist appeared from behind a paneled wall and offered coffee. She complemented the offer with a plate of large chocolate chip cookies that Bishop Hanks identified as the Cardinal's favorite. No one could resist taking a bite from the Cardinal's private stash. It was evident from the used coffee cups in front of Folley and O'Shea that there had been a pre-conference. Patello wondered if the Cardinal had been present. He made a quick glance around the room for evidence of another person but the efficient secretary had removed the used cups and saucers before disappearing behind the panel. He was left with the question.

As they began to sip their coffee and nibble at the Cardinal's favorite cookies, Bishop Hanks once again apologized for the Cardinal's absence. He then got immediately to the purpose of the meeting. "Gentlemen, when Dr. Folley called me to explain the purpose of the meeting this afternoon I advised the Cardinal. His Eminence requested that Dr. Folley give him a preview of the discussion and then detailed the matter to his Cabinet this morning. Dr. Folley was given permission to have Mr. O'Shea, the Cardinal's financial advisor, assist in the briefing. The bottom line is that the Cabinet agreed with the Cardinal's decision to establish an Office of Health Affairs for the Archdiocese. As an additional point, the Cardinal has asked Dr. Folley to be the Secretary of Health for the Archdiocese. In that capacity, he will direct the affairs of the Health Office. He will also be a member of the Cardinal's Cabinet. There is only two other laymen on the Cabinet so this is quite an honor."

Now Patello was in a slow bum. He knew that the Cardinal would not have made up his mind in that short of time. This was a well thought out decision that could only have been reached after many discussions. Apparently, the good Dr. Folley had wisely used his clinical time with the Cardinal to foster the concept and feather his own nest at the same time. Best guess was that Folley began his campaign right after the Alleton Club briefing. That would be about the right amount of time needed to cut the deal.

Bishop Hanks finished his introductory comments and then asked Dr. Folley to detail the nature of his conversation with the Cardinal. Folley appeared eager to explain, "Thanks, Bishop. Kevin and Charlie you know that I was completely sold on the idea of an Office for Health Affairs. I decided right after our review of the idea at the Alleton Club that it was an idea I would promote to the Cardinal. His Eminence has always confided in me his great concern that the healing ministry was losing prominence in Boston. Special emphasis on the ministry was needed. The Office was perfect for that to happen. Now the Cardinal is convinced that the best way to expand the ministry is to expand our influence over the physician. That's why he wants me to place emphasis on the teaching and physician training programs at St. Anslems. It's his idea that St. A's be identified as the teaching and tertiary care hospital for the Archdiocese. The community based Catholic hospitals will be expected to refer tertiary patients to the Catholic tertiary base, St. A's. We have the quality to match the big centers downtown. Once the word is passed that we have a Catholic system, the physicians will fight to be a part of it. The only downside to the prospect of success is our physical plant limitations. We will need to expand our capacity to accommodate the referrals. We will also have to recruit more specialists in medicine, surgery, and obstetrics. A quick fix might be to eliminate those programs at St. A's that are not tertiary such as the SACAP. I would like to add that the research done by the Bank's planning staff was very much appreciated by the Cardinal. He reviewed the material very closely. He is convinced that St. A's and the Office for Health Affairs can be very profitable for years to come. These profits will be the basis for the future expansion of the ministry. Tom gave the Cardinal a good review of the finances. Dad, would you like to comment?"

O'Shea sat back in his chair and looked directly at Patello as he responded, "Yeah. Dick. My involvement in this process was minor compared to the outstanding work that Dick did in convincing the Cardinal to accept our proposal. I hasten to add that Bishop Hanks was a champion in getting us onto the Cardinal's busy schedule. I explained to the Cardinal that St. A's was losing a ton of money because it was being mismanaged. The big money was in the more exotic procedures. To make it big you had to invest in super stars that would draw referrals from all over New England if not the Country. This kid, Durant, has no imagination or understanding of the business. He wouldn't last a week at the Bank. Having Dick as his boss will overcome the administration's stupidity. I expect that Dick will want to can him in a few months anyway. We need some good marketing. Development is also a key. People will want to give to the idea of a Catholic medical center.

Bishop Hanks became visibly anxious at O'Shea's comments about Durant. He raised his hand to silence O'Shea and then began his own commentary, "Gentlemen, you need to recall that Mr. Durant was selected by the Cardinal based on the recommendation of his fellow Bishops. He is an experienced administrator with a proven track record. The Cardinal is not to be easily convinced that Mr. Durant is incompetent. You also need to recall that your first recommendation, Mr. Bauman, was a serious embarrassment to the Cardinal. I believe it important that you concentrate on establishing the effectiveness of the Office for Health Affairs first before you concentrate on compromising Mr. Durant."

O'Shea suddenly had the look of a whipped puppy. He lowered his eyes and remained silent. The pause in the conversation was pregnant. Patello sensed the opening and proceeded to jump into the fray, "Bishop Hanks, I'm certain the Cardinal recognizes the need for competent management. Our intent is not to discredit Mr. Durant. More importantly, our intent is to ensure that the ministry remains credible to the public it serves. We indeed intend to place our emphasis on the Office for Health Affairs. Selecting Dr. Folley to be the Secretary and Director of the Office is genius. However, the selection could require Dr. Folley to resign his position as Chairman of St. Anslem's Department of Medicine. It will be extremely difficult for him to manage both positions without help. Ordinarily we would expect the Chief Executive Officer of the hospital to fill the gap. But as Mr. O'Shea has pointed out, the state of affairs at the hospital will require his full attention. We believe that the Secretary for Health should have an administrator to work the fields in behalf of the ministry. Our intent was to propose that Mr. Michael Logan be employed to staff the Office. He is an outstanding Catholic gentleman that is well recognized in the community for his dedication to the poor. His presence and identification with the Catholic ministry will only help our efforts. I have it on good authority that Mr. Logan will resign from the City when the Mayor accepts a Federal appointment. Apparently, Mr. Siro intends to appoint a new Commissioner of Health. I know Mr. Logan and am confident that he would accept a position with the Archdiocese."

Bishop Hanks nodded in agreement. Folley recognized that Patello had scored. He decided to parlay his own gains, "Bishop, I agree with

Mr. Patello. I will definitely need some help. As you know I am very active in State and City programs that include our ministry. My presence is necessary in many places with frequent conflicts in schedule. Mr. Logan could well represent me on such occasions. I hope we can move on Charlie's recommendation with dispatch."

It was now Kevin Hardly's turn to get into the action. He had sat quietly while Bishop Hanks, Charlie and Dick were discussing Logan's appointment. When Bishop nodded his head in apparent agreement Hardly saw that as his cue. "Bishop, I have listened with great interest to the discussion regarding Mr. Durant and Mr. Logan. There is no doubt that these are two fine Catholic gentlemen valuable to our ministry. It is my intent to see that these men are made Knights of the Holy Cross at the next installation. We will need their pastor's recommendation and a complete file on them as soon as possible. With your permission, I'll contact them immediately for the necessary information."

Bishop Hanks looked at Kevin in a questionable manner but supported his comments, "You have my permission, Kevin. I wonder if we should be a little more discreet and wait until we know that Mr. Logan wants to join us. We also have a Board meeting at St. Anslems next Tuesday. I assume the details of the Office will be discussed there. Mr. Durant has a lot of things to think about in that regard. He or rather St. Anslem's will have to foot the bill for the Office which will include Dr. Folley and Mr. Logan. That might not make Durant very happy. What do you think, Tom?"

O'Shea waved his hand as if to dispel Durant's anticipated opposition, "Bishop, it makes no difference if the administrators are Knights or not. They still have to produce a positive operating result. I believe Durant is incapable of coming up with a positive margin. OK, let's make him a Knight and see if that helps. As far as supporting the Office, St. Anslem's has no other choice. We have decided that's the way it is. Durant has to get off his butt and produce. One other thing I'm certain about is that Durant is not a leader. If we bring him into the Order of the Knights of the Holy Cross then he should be held as a member without opportunity for advancement. We don't want him to become an officer and destroy our work. We have to keep him silent."

Patello struggled to suppress his laughter. The words of the famous Christmas carol jumped to his head, "Silent Knight—Holy Knight all is calm. All is bright." The irony was diverting him from the intensity of the discussion. That stupid fool O'Shea completely missed the humor of his comment. Bishop Hanks either missed it or chose to ignore it. Probably the latter. Hardly was in his usual fog and Folley was busy, as usual, counting his trump.

Bishop Hanks lowered his head then raised it slowly as a signal to reorder the meeting. "Gentlemen, we seem to have come to an agreement. As the Cardinal expects, we will establish an Office for the Healthcare Ministry. Dr. Folley will serve the Cardinal as his Secretary for Health Affairs. Mr. Logan will be employed as the Director of Health Affairs reporting to Dr. Folley. St. Anslem's Hospital will provide the fiscal support for the Office assisted, as appropriate, by the other Catholic hospitals in the Archdiocese. Dr. Folley I trust you will take care of the details of locating the Office. Mr. Patello, I take it you will assist Dr. Folley in obtaining the services of Mr. Logan. We will announce all of this at the St. Anslem's Board meeting next Tuesday. Is that about it?"

"Excuse me, Bishop. You forgot to mention the Knights." Hardly fired his last salvo.

"Oh yes, thank you Kevin." The look on the Bishop's face was not one of gratitude. With the meeting concluded, Bishop Hanks escorted the participants to the door.

Patello and Folley lingered in the parking lot to discuss the employment of Logan. Folley agreed to offer Logan a salary of one hundred twenty-five thousand dollars plus an automobile and the usual benefits enjoyed by executives at St. Anslem's. Patello agreed to contact Logan and make the offer. If Logan was agreeable, Patello would arrange for a meeting between Folley and Logan to close the deal. Patello was satisfied with the outcome of the meeting but was uncomfortable with the amount of control held by Folley and O'Shea. "This deal could still go south," he thought.

oOo

Early Wednesday morning Patello placed a call to Commissioner Logan's office. He asked for an immediate appointment on a very urgent matter. The Secretary put the call directly into Michael Logan's office. Logan agreed to meet Patello at the Coffee Shoppe in South Station at ten o'clock.

Logan had no sooner completed the call from Patello when he received a call on his private line from the Mayor. Cowan was excited and breathless as he spoke, "Michael, I have it from a confidential source that you are considering a job with the Archdiocese. Look, I want you to know that this is an excellent opportunity. I'll be resigning within the next week so it would be to your advantage to take the offer. I can arrange for you to resign immediately in good standing. It will look natural since I intend to leak my resignation today or tomorrow. How does it sound to you?"

The call was very perplexing to Logan, "Your Honor, I'm grateful for the call and your support. Honestly, this is the first that I knew that the position was with the Archdiocese. I haven't any idea what the job is all about. Of course, an association with the Cardinal would be viewed as an honorable position so on that basis I'm prone to give it positive consideration. I expect to hear more about it in a few hours. Things seem to be moving at a fast pace."

Cowan began to push. "Michael, this is an excellent opportunity. I've been very involved in its development. The Cardinal is a close friend. I mentioned you to him on a number of occasions and he has been waiting for an opportunity to bring you on his staff. You go along with this. It will be a big advancement to your career. The Catholics collectively are the largest provider of healthcare in the State. That might be changing because of the new mergers and such but they will always be on top. I'm sure the money and benefits will be better than the City. Let me know how you decide. If possible I would like to announce your change at the Council meeting tomorrow. What do you think?"

Logan caught the drift. Essentially the Mayor was telling him in a nice way to resign or be fired. The sequence was simple. Scenario one, Logan finds a new job this morning and resigns this afternoon or, scenario two, the Mayor resigns to go to Washington and Logan gets fired by Siro. Better to resign with a bird in hand than get fired.

As Mayor Cowan hung up the phone he winked at Council President Siro. The deal was certain in the Mayor's opinion. He and Siro then began to work out the various tactics ordinarily employed in the transition of political power. At the City Council meeting on Thursday the Mayor would announce the resignation of Commissioner Logan coupled with the announcement that Commissioner Megan would be transferred from his post in Parks and Recreation to be acting Commissioner of Health. With that business completed the Mayor would announce the plan to immediately implement the voluntary privatization of waste management for the City. The Acting Commissioner of Health would detail the plan to the Council. Mr. Siro, as President of the City Council would move support for the plan. Other routine business of the Council would follow. However, by this afternoon the agenda for the Council meeting would be in the hands of the media as well as the members of the City Council. Obviously, the agenda would raise speculation that the Mayor's resignation was in the immediate offing. This speculation would be prompted by a leak from Washington. The Mayor would have no comment but Siro would confirm to the media that he expected the Mayor to resign within the week. The Mayor would announce his resignation the following Monday to be effective after the Council meeting the following Thursday. Siro would take office as acting Mayor at the close of the Council meeting.

Siro called Patello from the Mayor's office to let him know that Logan had been prepped for the ten o'clock meeting. The Mayor called Muldoon to let him know that the transition plan was being implemented. Patello called Marone to let him know that the waste management project was taking off. Marone called Meehan at Action to advise him to be ready for the implementation of the Boston project. Meehan called his management team including Ken Ryan in Quality Control and Veto Celli, Boston Project Sales Manager, to prepare them for the all-out effort. Muldoon called Celli as well to discuss personal business following which he called Donovan to press Action on the bargaining agreement. Donovan tried to call Marquart but he was not at work.

The meeting between Logan and Patello took place at South Station as planned. Patello arrived first and managed a small table away from the general milieu of patrons. As Logan entered the Coffee Shop, Patello waved him over to the table.

Logan was uptight and a bit irritated. "Mr. Patello, in our first meeting you gave me no indication that the opportunity you had in mind was with the Archdiocese. It was a shock to learn that the Mayor had actually arranged this with the Cardinal. What I don't understand is why you are involved?"

Patello, on the other hand, was amused to learn that the Mayor had told Logan that he had arranged the deal with the Cardinal. Quickly, Charlie easily concluded that Hizzoner was feathering his nest as usual. Nevertheless, the Kid's attitude was disarming. Setting aside the Mayor, Patello decided that a direct and almost truthful approach was best.

"Michael, the Cardinal, like all good executives in big organizations uses staff and delegates to carry out the details of direction. In the case of the health ministry the Cardinal has recently established an Office for Health Affairs under the direction of Dr. Richard Folley, Chairman of Medicine at St. Anslems. Dr. Folley has the title of Secretary for Health Affairs for the Archdiocese. Several of us who also serve on the Board of Trustees for St. Anslem's also serve to advise Dr. Folley. My assignment is to lead a recruiting effort to select and employ a Director for the Office of Health Affairs. We have counseled with the Mayor, the Cardinal, and several additional influential people in Boston. They have been unanimous in recommending you for the Directorship. As a public figure, we found it easy to gain perspective on your attitudes, manner, and so forth. Interviews were not necessary from our point of view. We are prepared to offer you the position. Hopefully, you are in a position to want to take it."

Reflecting on his recent conversation with Mayor Cowan, Logan seemed positive, "Mr. Patello, as a leading citizen in Boston I suspect you are well aware that events to take place in the next twenty-four hours will put me in a position where I cannot refuse your kind offer. However, I have no idea what your kind offer consists of. Furthermore, I have never met Dr. Folley much less the Cardinal. You are asking me to go into this deal blind. I'm willing to take a chance but I need some protection. I'll require a salary of one hundred twenty-five thousand plus two times salary in life insurance, full health insurance for myself and my family, guaranteed pension, and an automobile. I will also require the option to leave the position at any time in the first year of employment with one year salary and benefits extended from the date of my resignation. After the first year of employment the extension is only applicable if the Archdiocese requires or requests my resignation."

True to his negotiating instincts, Patello tried to shave the request. "Michael, your salary request is higher than we expected to pay. However. I can understand your request. The other items are also understandable. I would like to suggest another item that may help. The general employment agreements with the Archdiocese requires a thirty day probation period. Usually no benefits or perks are provided during this period. I feel that I can get a wavier to the thirty-day elimination period with the exception of the salary extension. To offset this, since I am going out on a limb on the salary, I will see that you are paid a signing bonus of ten thousand dollars. This amount is yours today with absolutely no recourse. We also will provide you with private banking services at Hardly Security and Trust without charge. We can have the account opened and the money deposited this afternoon. You can go home tonight ten thousand dollars richer. Tomorrow you meet with Dr. Folley. If you decide after the meeting that you don't want the job you can still keep the ten-grand. How's it sound?"

This was an unexpected twist. Logan had never heard of a signing bonus paid without signing. He decided to look the horse in the mouth, "It sounds like something out of the Godfather. If I wasn't dealing with the Church I would swear that you were working for the mob."

"That hurts, Michael." Patello appeared to be greatly offended, "I am trying to meet your requests. If you want to turn me down just say so. We have other candidates but none with your civic background."

Logan feared that the offer would be withdrawn leaving him unprotected. He made a quick grab, "OK, Patello. It's a deal. You have the employment agreement to me this afternoon. Keep it confidential. Deliver it to me for my eyes only. I'll review it and sign it after I have the ten thousand dollars in the bank. Let me know where and when I meet Dr. Folley."

"Done, Michael. We'll be in contact this afternoon. Are you going to be in the office?"

Logan nodded in the affirmative and shook Patello's extended hand as he departed.

A waitress appeared as he was walking away. She noticed that Patello was also standing to leave so she turned away. It was a free rent day at the Coffee Shop.

Patello returned immediately to his office and placed a call to Cappizi regarding the ten thousand dollar signing bonus. Capizzi informed Patello that the Mayor had endorsed the check for the ten thousand dollars that morning. The check had been taken by courier to Patriot dispatch where it was being held for further delivery instructions. Capizzi reasoned that Patello should direct the check into the bank account for Logan.

To that end Patello called Kevin Hardly and told him that he had offered private banking services at no charge to Mr. Logan. He asked Hardly to make the necessary arrangements. If Hardly could have the necessary account cards prepared, Patello would have a courier pick them up and take them to Mr. Logan for signature. The courier would bring the signed account cards and an initial deposit of ten thousand dollars back to the bank before close of business today.

Patello knew that Hardly would want to be as helpful as he could be. He also reasoned that an account opened through the office of the Chairman of the Board would not be subject to scrutiny. This way the initial deposit with the Mayor's endorsement would have little if any notice. Also, the lack of endorsement by Logan would not be an issue since the total amount was for deposit. He thought about having Hardly initial the check for good measure but dismissed the idea after realizing that it would set a trail back to the Terrific Trinity.

Hardly, as Patello expected, was very pleased to hear that Logan had accepted the Archdiocese's offer. Of course, he would see that Mr. Logan was given the benefit of private banking. He would see to the account personally. After he finished talking to Patello, Kevin Hardly immediately set about arranging the private banking service for Mr. Logan. Hardly had no way of knowing how to arrange such service. He immediately sought council of his efficient executive assistant. She advised Mr. Hardly that opening an account in the private banking service was not at all complicated. She would take care of the arrangements. Hardly was relieved to have her in charge of the assignment. He then left for an afternoon of friendly poker at the Alleton Club.

The executive assistant checked the Bank's procedure manual for private banking and discovered that all private bank accounts required the approval of the Treasurer. No problem. She would direct the courier to Mr. O'Shea's office. She than called the executive assistant in Mr. O'Shea's office and advised her that a VIP private banking account would be coming from Mr. Hardly's office this afternoon that required special attention and prompt dispatch. Mr. O'Shea's executive assistant assured her that he would be available to handle the matter.

Patello also called the Bank's Human Resource Department. The HR Director had been of great help in the initial phase of the Logan recruitment. Patello outlined the terms of employment except the signing bonus and asked the HR guy to prepare a legal type employment agreement. He then called Folley to advise that the deal was cut. The employment agreement would be in his hands this afternoon and, hopefully with Dr. Folley's signature, in Logan's hands an hour later, Folley listened to the employment terms short of the signing bonus but including private banking services. He agreed to the terms and said he would sign the agreement. A courier would transport the document.

Next Patello called Phil Mondi at Patriot Transport and Courier Service. He explained to his buddy, Phil, that he had a rather complex courier assignment that required a man used to details, who could follow orders, and get the job done no matter what. Mondi asked for time to review his staff and give him a call back. Patello explained that this was business for Marone and that the item was already at his dispatch center. Mondi knew immediately what the item was and promised to call Patello back in less than ten minutes. During that time, Phil met with Eddie who advised that the best man to handle this special assignment was Brian. Mondi returned the call to Patello and advised him that they had a man standing by. Patello said he would fax the courier instructions to Patriot dispatch in fifteen minutes.

Brian was in process of spending some quality time with Louise when his beeper let out its annoying screech. He first had to find his pants then the damned beeper. He dutifully returned the call to Dispatch and was told that Eddie wanted him on the spot now. He was to, "drop whoever he was doing and double time it back." Eddie seemed to have a sixth sense about Brian's whereabouts. Without delay Brian quit his conversation with Louise and powered the Chevy Caprice with tape deck back to station. As he arrived Eddie, waved him into the office and presented him with a list of assignments:

<u>Item 1:</u> Pick up item envelope at Patriot dispatch center.

<u>Item 2:</u> Pick up item envelope at Chairman's office Hardly Security and Trust See executive assistant.

<u>Item 3:</u> Pick up Items envelopes at Human Resource Office (Director) Boston Security and Trust.178

<u>Item:4</u> Take Item 2 to Commissioner Public Health—City Hall—Wait for his response in envelope (Commissioner's Eyes Only).

<u>Item 5:</u> Take Item 3 to Commissioner Public Health· City Hall- Wait for his response in envelope (Commissioner's eyes only)

<u>Item 6:</u> Take Item 1 and item 4 back to Chairman's Office Boston Security and Trust—Wait for response in envelope.

<u>Item 7:</u> Take Item 3 to Dr. Richard Folley—St. Anslem's Hospital- Wait for response in envelope.

<u>Item 8:</u> Take Item 6 and Item 7 back to Commissioner Public Health -City Hall Commissioner's eyes only)

<u>Out time EST 1400" Assign comp: EST 1630</u>

Brian was used to the complex type assignment. He also recognized the tight time frame for completion. Two and a half hours to move around heavy City traffic was tough enough but waiting for response was always dependent on the secretaries' breaks and other delays as the subjects quizzed each other about the documents. This was obviously some hot stuff that some big wigs wanted done in quick order. Well, he would do his end. The rest was up to the subject items. As he departed, Eddie requested that he phone in at every stop.

Brian checked out of Patriot dispatch with the envelope containing the ten-thousand dollar check in his courier pouch. He aimed the blue Chevy toward the financial district and Hardly Security and Trust. The trip took about twenty minutes in midafternoon. He parked the car in the loading zone and headed for the twenty eighth floor executive suite. The executive assistant in Mr. Hardly's office presented Brian with a very large promotional type folder that was to be delivered to Commissioner Logan's office. In addition, he was given a smaller envelope containing the private banking account signature cards. He was instructed to wait for Mr. Logan to sign the cards and then bring them back to Mr. Hardly's office. This was generally in accord with Eddie's orders. On his return trip, he would also deliver the envelope listed as Item one. Brian couldn't figure out why he couldn't deliver Item One now but his was not to reason why and orders were orders. He left the Executive Suite and dropped down to the tenth floor per instructions to pick up Item three from the Human Resource Office. The envelope was waiting for him at the reception desk. First phase completed he telephoned Eddie that he was on his way to City Hall.

When Brian arrived at Commissioner Loan's office he was escorted into the Commissioner's office. Mr. Loan asked Brian to sit in a comfortable chair while he examined the documents. It took about twenty minutes for the Commissioner to review the material. Mr. Logan made a phone call to someone who seemed to answer his question about a bank account. Item two was signed and placed back in the envelope. Item three took another twenty minutes of scrutiny before it was signed. Both items were given to Brian after Mr. Logan made copies. Brian called Eddie to report that the stop at the Commissioner's office had consumed an hour of the precious schedule. He departed City Hall and made his way back to Boston Security. He was actually doubling back over his original track. Brian would cover the same route three times. Again, he realized that his job was to follow Eddie's orders. He made a mental note to critique the process with Eddie at his first opportunity. To Brian the process seemed like, "pure bullshit."

Again, Brian managed to avoid the usual downtown traffic snarls. Fortunately, the unloading zone in front of the Bank was vacant. He ran for the elevator destined for the twenty fifth floor just managing to squeeze past the closing door. As he entered the executive suite the assistant waved to him to move ahead of others waiting her attention. At last he sensed some expediency toward restoration of the vital schedule. Then things began to unravel. She explained that the material for Mr. Hardly had to be taken to Mr. O'Shea's office on the twenty second floor. Mr. O'Shea was waiting for the material. He would complete the transaction and authorize the transfer of information back to Mr. Logan. Brian dutifully retreated from the executive suite and caught the elevator for twenty-two. The executive assistant in Mr. O'Shea's office took the envelope containing the check and the envelope containing the signature cards into Mr. O'Shea's office.

The door to O'Shea's office was left open. Brian saw that O'Shea seemed irritated with the material. He made a few telephone calls. Yelled at the ceiling and sent the executive assistant packing the material to an unknown location. Before she departed she made copies of the material and asked Brian for his log sheet that she also copied. She then disappeared and returned in less than fifteen minutes with a few slips of paper in her hand that she gave to O'Shea. O'Shea gave out with a blast of profanity that shocked Brian. Then he came out of his sanctuary with a sealed envelope in his hand. He pushed the envelope into Brian's hand and ordered him to tell Mr. Logan that the money, "where ever it came from," was now in his new account. Brian sensed that the messenger had just been shot. He didn't respond to O'Shea. Verbal messages by courier went out of vogue when Bell invented the telephone. Instead, he quietly retreated to the elevator, got into his car, and headed for his next destination, St. Anslem's Hospital.

Brian's attitude deteriorated completely when he attempted to park at St. Anslem's.

The traffic at the hospital was usually complex but today it was compounded by an unusual number of ambulances delivering nursing home patients for therapies. When he attempted to park in the fire zone next to the main entrance a burley security guard chased him out. He offered little consolation to Brian's plea for temporary parking. Eventually he found an unoccupied handicap slot. Once inside, he found the information clerk busy assisting visitors. She finally found time to direct Brian to Dr. Folley's office located a floor below the main entrance.

Brian was feeling his way toward Dr. Folley's office when he met Cecile. She glared at Brian in her usual manner. Brian had actually never seen Cecile that he could remember, without her hateful stare. He gave her a weak wave and attempted to pass.

Cecile blocked his way. She pushed him against the wall and put a clench fist in his face, "Brian, you worm, where is Jay? I've been trying to contact him for two days. He better return my call. You see to it, dimwit."

The fist was less alarming than her attitude. Brian untypically became somewhat sarcastic, "Cecile, I'm so happy that we had this pleasant chat. As soon as I leave here I'll let Jay out of my trunk so he can give you a call. Now if you'll go back to your cage, I'll get back to work."

The comment accelerated Cecile's anger, "You don't know the meaning of work, you crawling epidemic. Get out of here before you contaminate the place."

Having fired the last volley, Cecile popped back into the Medical Intensive Care Unit. Brian stood in the corridor totally disarmed. His mind was blown. He leaned against the wall pondering the exchange with Cecile. Gradually he remembered the task at hand and proceeded to locate the office of Dr. Richard Folley. The receptionist took the package from Brian and invited him to be seated. Dr. Folley was in conference but had left instructions to be interrupted when the courier arrived. The receptionist reappeared and told Brian that Dr. Folley would be with him in a few minutes. Then she went on break. Thirty minutes later Brian took the initiative and knocked on Dr. Folley's door. Dr. Folley responded with an invitation to come in. When Brian inquired about the package Dr. Folley nodded to the out box on his desk. He stated that it had been ready for the last twenty minutes and waiting for someone to pick it up.

Brian thanked the good Doctor and headed for his handicapped parking place. He headed for City Hall, the final destination. Eddie said he would call the Commissioner's office to let him know that the package was on its way.

It was nearly four thirty and traffic was becoming impossible. Brian arrived at the Commissioner's office at five fifteen. The Commissioner was alone in the office. He was packing files and personal affects in boxes that were stacked in the outer office. Brian handed him the envelope from the bank and the envelope from the hospital. He waited patiently as the commissioner looked them over. Finally, the Commissioner looked up as if to ask Brian if "there was anything else."

Brian caught the signal, "Ah Sir, the gentleman at the Bank asked that I tell you that the money, where ever it came from, was in your new account."

Logan nodded as if relieved, "Thank you. Do you remember who at the Bank gave you that message?"

"Yes sir. It was the gentleman on the twenty second floor, a Mr. O'Shea. He signed for the material I just delivered. Anything else, Sir?"

Michael Logan said nothing in response. He simply gave Brian a wave as a sign of dismissal and continued to pack.

Brian left the Commissioner's office after he had used the secretary's desk phone to notify Eddie that the run was complete. Eddie immediately informed Mr. Meehan who called Patello. Patello was already aware of the matter having, first, been informed by Logan who wanted to know why Mr. O'Shea was so caustic. Patello covered the matter by informing Logan that the signing bonus was provided by anonymous benefactors of the Archdiocese who did not want to reveal their identity. He offered that Mr. O'Shea was irritated that he did not know the source of the donations. He offered to calm Mr. O'Shea by giving him some insight to the signing bonus.

Logan accepted the offer. He also advised Patello that he had signed his letter of resignation and sent it by special courier a half hour ago. He had called the Mayor earlier. The Mayor was going to inform the media tonight and present the resignation as a matter of business at the City Council meeting in the morning.

Patello was furious. Everything had gone fine except that idiot Hardly had to involve O'Shea. O'Shea obviously took careful note of the deposit check. He most certainly realized that the Mayor's endorsement on the check signaled foul play. Nevertheless, he let the deposit go through. Why? Regardless, O'Shea was in the know. This made him a big problem in the conduct of the Waste project and possibly a bigger problem in the future health initiative. The guy had to be reported to the boys in New York. Since it was now a matter concerning the Waste project, Patello thought it best to advise Meehan as well as Mondi. He first called Meehan and told him about the conversation with Logan. Meehan was not aware of the way that Capizzi had arranged the wrapper so could offer little comment. He, nevertheless, did recognize the potential for a massive screw up. His recommendation was that Patello check with Phil Mondi at Patriot to see if the courier experienced anything unusual. Patello took the advice and called Mondi. Mondi promised to interview the courier and get back to him.

As Brian was about to take up where he had left off with Louise earlier in the day, his pager once again let out its annoying tone. This time Brian was being summoned by Mr. Mondi who wanted to meet him in the office immediately. Brian bid a quick farewell to his main squeeze and pointed his trusted Chevy back to the coral. Big Boss Mondi was very kind and grateful to Brian for returning to the office at the late hour. He asked Brian several questions about his afternoon run. Brian gave detailed answers about every stop. He left out the exchange with Cecile but was very explicit about the hassle in Mr. O'Shea's office including the verbal message that he relayed to Mr. Logan. He noticed that Mr. Mondi took careful notes on the part involving O'Shea. Mondi also was interested in the fact that O'Shea's secretary made a copy of Brian's log. He asked Brian for his log and then made a copy for himself. Brian became increasingly nervous during the interview. He wasn't sure if he had screwed up or not. If Eddie suddenly came through the door, Brian would know that he had messed up and Eddie was going to rearrange his anatomy. That never happened. To the opposite, Mr. Mondi shook Brian's hand, gave him five twenty dollars bills, and told him to take his best girl out to dinner. This was definitely a day and night to remember.

Mondi called Patello at his home around nine thirty that evening. He gave him the courier's report. Patello was now very certain that O'Shea was holding some very incriminating evidence. As he pondered the matter the local television stations were reporting the resignation of Commissioner Logan combined with information from a Washington source that Mayor Cowan was to be named as the Under Secretary of Labor. The Mayor acknowledged that Commissioner Logan had resigned to accept a post with the Archdiocese of Boston. However, at this time the Mayor would neither confirm nor deny the Washington report.

In an on-camera interview, Commissioner Logan stated he was very pleased to be joining the Archdiocese as the Director of the Office of Health Affairs. Cardinal McMahon was in Rome and unavailable for comment but a spokesman for the Archdiocese confirmed that Mr. Logan had been employed. No additional information was available at this time from the Archdiocese.

Sister Elizabeth was glued to her television set. The creation of an Office for Health Affairs was a recommendation that she and Sister Celest had made to Cardinal McMahon when he was first installed as the Archbishop of Boston. He rejected the proposal out of hand stating that it represented too much bureaucracy. At the time Sr. Elizabeth had recommended that Sr. Celest could run the office as a part of St. Anslem's Hospital thus avoiding additional expense and bureaucracy. Again, the Cardinal rejected the idea because of more pressing matters. She now recognized that politics of some nature created the moment for the Office. However, the fact that she and the other members of the Board of St. Anslem's were not consulted gave her a stomach ache. Her pain and discomfort was compounded with the realization that the Director of the Office was selected without any input from the Board. Indeed, she would again have recommended Sr. Celest for the job. She suspected that the Terrific Trinity had a hand in this and vowed to raise no small amount of hell at the Board meeting on Tuesday.

CHAPTER TEN

Jay woke early Wednesday. The light of the new day was beginning to filter through the dusty venetian blinds on his shabby hospital window. The previous two days were still a blur. He did recall several conversations with the hospital staff on Tuesday. Nothing of great substance. A few residents checked the progress of his treatment that consisted in the main of medication and bed rest. The lab jockey stuck him a few times and there was the persistent demand that he pea in a bottle. He recalled that Susan was with him for a few hours last night. Boss and buddy, Ken Ryan, also dropped in, said little and left. Susan mentioned that Brian inquired about his health and wished him well. The kids, Benny and James, wanted Dad home for the weekend. Kristie hadn't been told about Dad yet. He and Susan reasoned that Cecile would push Kristie for answers that she didn't have. Besides Jay wasn't sure what his diagnosis was. Nobody had given him the word. Today was supposed to be the day that Jay learned all. The real doctor was supposed to show up early in the morning to explain to him why he had been in captivity for the past two days. Jay had made up his mind that this was his last day in internment. He was going to bust out at noon, doctor or no doctor. He felt fine.

He was just beginning to dig into his breakfast tray when a distinguished gentleman with stethoscope in hand came into his room.

He was the first physician that appeared to be over thirty that Jay had encountered since he was admitted. The doctor introduced himself as Doctor Kenneth, an internist in private practice and part time attending with the St. Anslem's Chemical Addiction Program. He explained to Jay that he had been assigned to his case on the rotation schedule. If Jay preferred another Physician, Dr. Kenneth would make all the necessary arrangements. Otherwise he would continue to direct Jay's care as he had been doing since Jay had been admitted to the Unit. Jay did not have a primary care physician although the HMO required him to name one. He knew that Susan and the kids had docs but Jay couldn't remember their names.

Jay reasoned that accommodating the doctor would be the best tact so he offered a proper reply, "Look, Doctor, I'm sure that you'll do fine. In fact, I think you have done wonders. I feel fine and think I can go home and back to work. I thank you for all that you have done. The staff has been wonderful. About all I need is a discharge order and I'll cease being your problem."

Doctor Kenneth shook his head from side to side as Jay talked. Then he answered, "Jay, you are not well. I'm here to advise you about your illness and work out a treatment plan. You have a long way to go for recovery. We might be able to discharge you from this bed but we cannot in good conscience discharge you from treatment. You have an illness that needs treatment. On the other hand, we cannot force you to follow our direction. This has to be a voluntary decision on your part."

The doctor's comments frustrated Jay. He wanted out of the hospital. He did not want to hear about an illness that he did not believe he had. This time he answered with sarcasm, "What, pray tell, is this terrible disease. Am I going to die? I don't feel like I'm what sick. If you are referring to my boozing, I've heard that song before. Some guy at Waltham Hospital handed me that line on Sunday. Said his name was Hendricks. Know him?"

Kenneth sat on the edge of the bed and looked out the window, "Mr. Marquart, you told the resident about your admission to Waltham's ER on Saturday. You also signed a consent release for us to access your records. We brought your records forward and have consulted with Dr. Hendricks. If you would like him to continue your treatment that can be arranged. Dr. Hendricks and I trained here at St. Anslems. We share a private office practice. In summary, you have a chemical dependency based on a deficiency in your blood. This deficiency causes you to use drugs to offset the imbalance in your system. The problem is that the chemicals that you are using while giving you emotional satisfaction are causing an increasing deficit in the quality of your metabolism. We intend to treat your deficiency with the right chemicals and restore your chemical balance. You also need to know that we suspect that you are developing ulcers. That is very consistent with addicted people. Without treatment, you will continue to experience physical as well as mental breakdowns."

Jay got out of the bed and began to pace around the room. His irritation was now very obvious, "Let me get this straight. You want me to start taking drugs in order to stop taking drugs. That's interesting. You guys have a neat thing going for you. Hendricks scoops 'em up in Waltham's ER and you take a chunk out of 'em at St. A's. Between the two of you every junkie in town gets fixed. Not."

Dr. Kenneth stood up and followed Jay. Eventually he got in front of him and looked Jay in the eye, "Mr. Marquart, I don't intend to argue with you about this. I also don't intend to take any of your crap. Your disease is the most difficult to cure. The main reason is because you and many like you do not believe that they are as sick as they are. A person who experiences cardiac arrest doesn't have to be convinced. They get religion real fast. An addict, in spite of the pain, wants to keep right on punishing himself because he thinks it feels so good. The cost isn't money. The real cost is the loss of dignity, family, and the love and respect of those close to you. You think you can handle it. Well, friend, look around you at your wife and kids and ask if they can handle it. They have to carry the burden."

"Doctor I'm sorry if I offended you." Jay realized that he had angered the physician and probably lost his chance to be discharged, "You've got a tough and thankless job. Yeah, I know that I have a problem. I like to party. Who doesn't? But I pull up short of saying I'm a junkie. I also realize that over doing it can screw me up big time. So, I'll slow down. No reason to quit. Just a little self-control and I can go on living. You take care of the poor bastard that's zonked out in the gutter. I'll take care of good or Jay and stay out of here. Tell me again how you got my record out of Waltham."

Dr. Kenneth backed away and seemed to regain his composure, "Mr. Marquart, I want to treat you now so you avoid being zonked out in the gutter. Your denial of the problem is very typical. I won't bother you anymore today but I will ask our counselor, Bob Markley, to have a chat with you. Will you see him?"

Jay sensed that things were about to go his way, "Sure, if it will make you feel better. Send him around. How about that discharge order? I don't want to walk out of here today against medical advice or AMA as you guys put it. That could screw up the insurance. We can both appreciate that."

Dr. Kenneth closed Jay's chart folder, put his pen in his pocket, and with a sigh followed by a slight wave to Jay walked out of the room. Jay watched the Doctor walk out. In a way he felt sorry for the guy. He had tried his very best to sell Jay a continuing treatment program. The effort and passion that the doctor displayed suggested to Jay that there had to be big money involved. Why else would the doctor try so hard to convince him that he needed the cure. Jay also recognized that the doctor's compassion was genuine. Several of Jay's verbal blasts almost brought the man to tears. "Why couldn't the guy just back off?" he wondered. "No need to make such a big deal out of the problem." Suddenly, he remembered that he had to make some telephone calls. The first one to Susan would be to arrange for her to pick him up this afternoon. He also had to call Ryan and, "oh yeah, the bitch." Must not forget the "bitch."

Jay dressed and packed what few items he had in a hospital container that he found in the closet. Satisfied that he was ready to go, he ambled to the front desk to get permission to use the patient telephone. The desk was unattended except for a gentleman in whites that, because of his somewhat unkempt appearance and relaxed poster, gave Jay the impression that he was a male nursing assistant. The man also looked a little shop worn and long of tooth. His ID badge was clipped on backwards so the name was not visible. His hair was overdue for a trim, the mustache drooping slightly to starboard, and his belly pulled the shirt buttons to maximum tension. The uniform was clean and the white shoes were spotless yet old. When Jay asked for permission to use a phone, the man flashed Jay an infectious grin and passed him the desk phone. Jay punched nine for an outside line and received a weird screech.

The man gently reached over and depressed the button causing disconnect. "Sorry, buddy, No need to punch nine. We now have the most marvelous advanced state of the art telephone system in the world. Administration bought this miracle of modem technology with the money usually paid to us slaves. Now we can call anywhere in the world without punching nine. Try again. Just dial your number. All the comforts of home right here in St. A's. Would you ever have guessed? Just look at the excellent device before you. We still have to train it to say only what we want to hear. I guess that will be part of next year's expensive upgrade. We can hardly wait."

Jay returned the man's smile. He loved the guy's sarcasm. This was the kind of person Jay was attracted to, a real cynic. This time he dialed correctly. Susan answered on the second ring. Jay explained to her that he was, "busting out of this funny farm by four thirty at the latest." The man heard the comment, smiled, and leaned back in his chair as if he was a party to the conversation. Jay noticed his interest and gave him a wink in acknowledgment that also served as an invitation to monitor Jay's particular style and humor. Jay appreciated an audience. He performed well using the best street terms in describing to Susan the quality of care at St. Anslems. He talked about how he humbled Dr. Kenneth and now was waiting for his next victim, "some dweeb named Markley" After he polished off this guy, he was leaving.

Susan was very pleased that Jay was being discharged. Trying to handle Benny and James, make visits to the hospital to see Jay, and run the household was no small challenge. She was looking forward to Jay's homecoming and the coming weekend party. She desperately needed a few belts and a couple of good laughs with Brian and Louise.

Her excitement was evident. "Jay, I'll be there to pick you up at four thirty. I'll bring the kids. They have been concerned about you. Cecile called several times but I told her you were on the road for Action. I think she smells something. Brian met her at the hospital today when he was delivering something. Anyway, she chewed him out about you not returning her call. He called about a half hour ago. He doesn't know where you are either. He thinks you are out of town. Maybe you ought to call him tonight after you get home."

Jay acknowledged the need to call Cecile. He also said he would call Brian that evening. His intent was to call Ryan after he finished his conversation with Susan but the fact that Cecile was making such a fuss motivated him to retaliate. He cut short his conversation with Susan. As he hung up the receiver he asked his new-found buddy if he could place an in-house call. The man nodded in the affirmative and instructed Jay how to locate the number in the house directory. It was a simple matter of dialing the four-digit number.

The unit secretary in the Medical Intensive Care Unit Answered the phone immediately and in response to Jay's inquiry, informed him that Mrs. O'Sullivan was on duty. He was asked if he wanted to hold for a minute until she was available or she could return the call. Jay opted to hold. He reasoned that a return call to the SACAP unit could complicate the conversation.

In less than a minute Cecile answered the phone with her usual professional greeting. "This is Nurse O'Sullivan. How may I help you?"

"Nurse O'Sullivan, this is Mr. Jay Marquart. The question is how can I help you, as if I really cared?"

Cecile was not in the mood for Jay's smart mouth. She fired back with a blast of her own, "Well, Mr. Marquart, your antics of the past week are of sufficient note that my lawyer is preparing the necessary papers to return you to court. You have placed Kristie in harm's way with your habitual and excessive alcohol and drug use. I am advised that I have an obligation to bring your conduct and Mrs. Marquart's conduct as well to the attention of the court that way protecting Kirstie from harm and undue negative influence. You will lose your custody. My call was to advise you that papers would be served to you in the next few days. I will add the information that for the past few days you have obviously been in treatment at St. A's drug unit. We will subpoena your medical record. You know, Jay, I don't care if you and Susan dope yourselves to hell. But there is no way that my daughter is going to be subjected to the influence of her drunken, spaced out father and his junkie wife. You can try to ignore me but that won't matter once we get to court. This time you have really screwed up."

Jay was speechless. He feared that Cecile was on his trail after Kristie spilled the beans about his trip to Waltham Hospital on Saturday. How did the Bitch know that he was at St. Anslem's? Everything was supposed to be so confidential. He thought he was in a protected unit. Suddenly he realized that he had accidentally violated his own confidentiality. As he stared at the marvelous marvel of modem technologic telephone he noticed the small screen LED on the top of the instrument flashing the number of the station he had called and the name of the unit secretary that had answered. Apparently, Cecile was now looking at the LED on her telephone that was flashing the number and name of the Unit from which the call had been placed. He was nailed. He was at the moment too shocked to get angry. Tears filled his eyes and he sobbed. His tough cocky attitude dissipated. Gone was the humor that he had exchanged earlier with the man at the desk.

The man at the desk took note of the change. He got out of his chair, walked around the desk and stood at Jay's side. Gently he placed his hand on Jay's shoulder. The touch of compassion was welcomed by Jay. God, how he was in need of a friend.

Jay struggled to regain his composure and best Cecile, "Cecile you and your lawyer can cram it. You have no right to my medical records and you have no knowledge that would give cause of improper influence on Kristie. I'll have you out of her life for good if you try to disrupt my relationship with Kristie. Kiss off"

Jay slammed the telephone on the desk. Now he was enraged. Inadvertently he swung his fist at the man whom he had befriended a few minutes before.

The man with the skill of a prizefighter gracefully dodged the blow. Jay threw a chair across the room that crashed against the wall then bounced into a lamp that it destroyed. His anger accelerated. Three more pieces of furniture were pitched across the room. The office, reception desk, and adjacent area were systematically reduced into piles of debris. Jay raged, shouted, cursed and beat his fist into the wall.

A Code 777 SACAP was called by the unit head nurse to the hospital communication center and relayed through the entire institution via the audible paging system. Three massive security guards responded, well trained in handling violent patients. As they appeared Jay's new friend waved then out of sight. He allowed Jay to wear out his anger. Eventually, Jay tired. He sat down in the middle of the room, exhausted, and began to cry. His friend sat down next to him among the broken furniture, glass, torn paper, and various personal items from staff lockers. Gently, he placed his arm around Jay. Jay reached up and took the man's hand as a gesture of relief. He was asleep within a few minutes.

Jay's new friend sat in the chair next to the bed and waited. It was well past time for his lunch break but he had missed that many times before. He waited, as he had also done many times before.

After a few hours, Jay opened his eyes. He was still very tired and emotionally drained. He was also bathed in sweat. His clothes were damp and he felt a chill. The very dry condition of his throat was stark contrast. He was in desperate need of water. The shame of his outrage clouded his mind. Above the discomfort and shame was the overriding issue of the pending court fight with Cecile. Martha was his only counsel. He desperately needed to talk to her. Carefully he raised himself up and sat on the edge of the bed. It was then that he noticed the man in the chair next to the bed. It was the same guy that was with him when he lost it at the nurses' station.

The good dude with the quick smile and wicked sense of humor that Jay had tried to cold crock with his famous right hook sat peacefully watching Jay struggle to the edge of the bed. "How you doing, partner? Thirsty I bet. I'm usually thirsty when I come off a tear like that. Man, you messed up the place. Administration's going to flip. Well, they have to have something to do to earn the big bucks. What set you off, anyway? Here, I got you a glass of water."

Jay accepted the glass of water with noticeable gratitude. He raised the glass in salute before he gulped it down. He handed the glass back to the man who poured him another from the pitcher at his side. Again, Jay drained the glass without taking a breath.

On the third glass Jay sipped the contents slowly. He was beginning to regain composure. "You know, buddy, you seem to have been my constant companion for the past several hours and we haven't even been introduced. I'm Jay Marquart, patient extraordinare and self-appointed interior decorator of St. A's drunk tank. Who might you be?"

The man's quaint smile returned, "My name's Bob Markley. I used to have your job and, I might add, did a much better job on a regular basis. Now I'm confined to the payroll as a counselor. I think before the action started that you referred to me as a dweeb. Doctor Kenneth wanted me to chat with you this afternoon. I have to admit, it was an interesting interview."

The comment surprised Jay. He leaned forward and supported himself by spreading his arms to his side and placing his hands on the side of the bed as he sat. "Yeah. You ain't what I expected either. I don't know what to do now. This fucking hospital has messed me up big time. I came in here thinking that I was protected by the usual code of confidentiality. Now that goofy telephone has told the world including my ex-wife that I'm a junkie. Man, I'm gonna sue their ass. She's taking me to court knowing that I'm in here. The goddamn records are open for public scrutiny, she thinks. Where does she come off as a nurse in this hospital exposing the records of a patient? My sister's a lawyer. Man, she is going to sue your ass."

Markley was shaken by Jay's comment about litigation but he remained calm. "Jay, I can't comment on the status of the hospital in your dispute with your ex-wife. I can say that under Federal law if a patient seeks or receives treatment at a general hospital that operates a certified substance abuse program recognized by the Federal Government then the patient's treatment and the patient's records in the program remain confidential. No one, including the courts, can access that information. Any member of the hospital staff in any capacity that uses that information outside of the treatment program is subject to criminal action. St. A's program is fully accredited and certified by the Federal government. You are protected as a recipient of our care. The only way that your records would transfer out of here is if you were never admitted to the program. While you have been in the Unit for the past two days you have been classified as a general hospital patient. What Dr. Kenneth tried so ineffectively to explain to you this morning is that we want to admit you to the program. You rejected the idea but you might want to reconsider in view of recent events."

Jay wasn't sure he had heard what Markley said. "OK, let's see if I got this straight. I join your little dance party and my records get locked up. Nobody gets to them. But if I don't join, then my records are treated like general hospital records. Hell, what's the difference? General medical records are supposed to be confidential."

Markley got out of his chair and placed his hand on Jay's shoulder to emphasize the point, "General medical records are easily subpoenaed by the courts. Lawyers force disclosure through discovery all the time. It's not as easy in substance abuse programs. You can have your lawyer check it out. Anyway, it gives you better protection than you have now. My suggestion is that you voluntarily admit yourself to the program as of your date of admission on Tuesday. You can do that since you have not been discharged. We simply transfer you and your records out of general hospital into the program. Everything is locked up including your trip to Waltham hospital because Dr. Hendricks made a referral in your record to St. A's program. It's a nice neat package."

"What's the catch?" Jay was suspicious.

Markley sensed that he had Jay's attention, "Well you have to be serious about your treatment. If you admit to the program and then withdraw or refuse to accept treatment, which is the same as withdrawal, then you lose the Federal protection. Your records flow back to general hospital for whatever consequence."

The thought of protection was appealing but the thought of continuing treatment was discouraging. "Man, what am I getting into? I thought Dr. Kenneth wrote the discharge order. How we going to get around that?"

Markley waved his hand in the air as if to brush away a fly, "No sweat. I asked him not to make any entry on your chart until we had our little chat. I really didn't have any idea things would shape up this way. I thought maybe I would just beat the hell out of you and leave it at that. So, what do you say? Try it. You'll like it."

Jay was caught by Markley's comfortable manner. "OK sign me up. Did you ever sell used cars or do recruiting for the Marines?"

Bob Markley invited Jay back to the nursing station. Housekeeping had cleaned the place up. Some of the broken furniture had been replaced and there was an odor of fresh paint. Jay attempted a weak apology that Markley discounted. Apparently, the nurses' station and lobby were frequently rearranged by irate clients

The two men entered a very small office in back of the nurse station. Markley produced an admitting form to the Program that Jay signed after giving the small print a quick glance. He also signed another series of consent and release forms. Markley back dated the forms to last Tuesday. He handed Jay several pamphlets about the program that he instructed Jay to keep and use if he ran into questions from family and friends about his disease and treatment. Otherwise there was no need to advertise his condition.

One pamphlet was strictly for the employer. Markley noticed that Jay seemed to be staring at this one, "Jay, you worried about your job?"

"Yeah. My boss and the company nurse brought me in here. They know about me. How they gonna keep this out of my employee file?" Jay's eyes were closed as if experiencing some pain as he mouthed the question.

Markley made a quick check of Jay's medical record, "It says on the record that Action Waste Management referred you to us through their Employee Assistance Program. The only thing that should ever appear in your work record is the time that you are off the job for illness, vacation, and things like that. If you had a medical problem at work that the company nurse assisted with then that would be a part of her daily log. There should be no indication in your work file regarding your dependency problem. If it concerns you, I'll have our staff check your file or you can do it yourself when you get back to work."

The response brought Jay out of his temporary depression, "When can I go back to work? I got things stacked up. I was counting on being there tomorrow."

"Monday at the earliest. That wild spree that you went on a few hours ago is apt to hit you again. We need to get better acquainted over the next few days. You can go home this afternoon but I want you to spend your days here for a while. When you get over the hit that detox gives you then we can let you take a little more mental pressure. It's hard to tell at the beginning what might light your fuse. Apparently, your ex-wife lights you up real easy." Markley knew he had made an understatement.

Anger flared in Jay's eyes. He stood and pounded his fist on the counter, "Yeah, well she's gonna drag my ass into court over custody of my daughter. This goddam place gave her the information she needed to fry my ass. You gotta know that I'm going after her big time. This hospital is in deep shit, I'll own this goddam place before it's over. That fucking telephone system is gonna cost you big bucks. I thought hospital employees were supposed to keep patient information confidential. Seems to me that I could have her nursing license revoked."

Markley tried to appease his patient, "Jay, you are getting agitated and in a few minutes your anger will erupt into violence. I'll see that it doesn't happen. You and I can talk about something else, or if you want, we can talk more about your concern. The key here is that we talk out your anxiety and anger. That's why I want you to spend a lot of time with me over the next few days. You'll meet some other people who understand your problem and the disease that causes it. In time, you will realize how beneficial it is to have someone to turn to when the pressure moves you to a breaking point. You will get to know a lot of people in the many support groups that are available."

The thought of a full-blown counseling program was not what Jay had in mind. "Look, Bob, you know that I'm not really big into this stuff. I'm hiding my record so my Ex can't take my daughter away from me. You gave me the idea. All the rest of this stuff is a little far out. Sounds like you figure me for a head case."

"In a way, you are." Markley came back at him. "What makes you different from a psycho is that the cause of your anger is very evident. You are going through a form of withdrawal. The change taking place in your body chemistry causes a psychic reaction that manifests in violent behavior. Dr. Kenneth will monitor your chemistry and give you supplements that moderate your emotions while your body adjusts to what we expect to be a permanent change in your life style. However, the type of disease that you have cannot be cured medically. It can only be controlled by a combination of medicine and a strong dose of individual will power. Dr. Kenneth will evaluate your physical needs and prescribe the appropriate therapy. I'll be your buddy during this process and together we can work on the will power bit. Take it from me, it's not going to be easy."

It was apparent to Jay that the price of protection from Cecile was cooperation with Markley. With some degree of courtesy, he tried to explain his position, "So you think that between now and Monday I'll get religion. Man, that's far out. I can't wait to get out of here. The only thing that will bring me back is Kristie, that's my daughter. No way am I going to swallow Kenneth's medicine. I told him this morning that taking drugs to stop taking drugs was bullshit. I'll listen to you but I'm not going to start taking those weird pills. You know I used to work in the cath. lab here. I saw those docs pump up the charges on those patients with a lot of stuff that didn't mean shit. What did the patient know? Nothing, man. They just wanted to live. Well, I just want to keep my daughter."

"OK, Jay, we'll take it one step at a time." Markley was satisfied that he had a taker.

One of the first procedures in the first step involved a telephone call to Ken Ryan at Action Waste Management. Jay's call was warmly received by Ken who emoted about the prospect of the Boston project. It was expected to start as early as tomorrow. Ken was in hope that Jay would be back on board. Jay reported that he had to continue treatment through the weekend and would possibly be back to work on Monday. His new buddy, Bob Markley, got on the phone at Jay's request and explained in careful terms that Jay's condition required careful monitoring for the next few days. The call concluded with Ken reporting to Jay that a Mr. Donovan desperately needed to talk to him. He gave Donovan's phone number to Jay.

Jay called Donovan and explained that he had been sick and in the hospital for the past couple of days. He had to stay home for another few days and would be back to work on Monday. Donovan asked Jay to call him tomorrow since it was noised about that the Boston project at Action was going to kick off. The Union contract had to be worked out so that the workers got a piece of the rewards. A good health plan was definitely a part of the discussion. Jay agreed to give Donovan another call in the morning.

At four thirty Susan came into the Unit. Benny and James were left in the main lobby with coloring books being carefully watched by the volunteers on duty. Susan was anxious to get back to her charges and became noticeably irritated when Jay asked her to take a few minutes to meet Bob Markley. She became increasingly agitated as Bob explained that

Jay was not being discharged but allowed to go home in the evenings. His days were to be spent in the Unit through the weekend. Susan realized that somehow Markley had got his clutches on Jay. She feared the goody two shoes life style that often accompanied the reformed. This could mean a damper on the weekend party that she desperately needed.

On the way home, she noticeably pouted about the days ahead. Jay didn't appreciate her attitude. He was concentrating on the legalities ahead of him while trying to form the details in mind so he could give Martha the material to hang Cecile and St. Anslem's in the bargain.

The happy Marquart family arrived home and proceeded to enjoy a welcome home dinner that Susan prepared for their hero. Jay was in very good spirits. In similar circumstances, he would have had two or three gin and grapefruits. Now he was sober and intent on staying that way. Susan missed the usual jag that accompanied the family's good times. Somehow things just didn't seem the same. After dinner Jay moved in front of the TV to take in the sports report on the evening news. His timing was perfect to see and hear the headline story about the pending resignation of the Mayor and the resignation of the Commissioner of Health who was to become a part of the Archdiocesan staff. Jay caught the comment that the former Commissioner was to be the Director of Health so he made a mental note to sue the Church as well as St. Anslem's although he wasn't too sure what he would do with a Church if he won. The kids hung around Jay until they were certain that he was home for the night. Then they disappeared to other haunts.

As the sports reports began, the Marquart telephone broke Jay's attention on the latest Red Sox win. When he answered the phone his concentration remained focused on the interview with the relief pitcher who managed to get the final out on three straight strikes. His attention shifted immediately, however, to Martha's greeting following his bland hello.

Martha was insistent on penetrating the events of the past few days. "Well, my dear brother, what have you been up to the past five days? My guess is that you have teased your former wife to a state of frenzy."

"Martha, thanks for calling." Jay was excited and began to ramble. "We got to talk. Man, that bitch really messed up this time. I want you to sue her ass and St. Anslem's Hospital. We goin' to nail them big time."

The strength of Jay's reply caused Martha to try a counter measure. "She apparently thinks you are the one who messed up. I don't know what to think. Your lawyer that handled the divorce was advised by her lawyer that you are going to be served with papers tomorrow claiming that you are an unfit parent, an alcoholic, drug abuser, and a few other things all of which is intended to return you to court for a custody hearing. He called me and asked me to tip you off. I wanted you to know that you will be served and advise you not to beat the shit out of the process server. Remember that he is a court official. Please be a good boy and accept the papers without contest or comment. Bring them to your divorce lawyer and we can take it from there. What have you been up to anyway?"

Jay detailed the events of the weekend beginning with his trip to Waltham Hospital. He proudly added his new status as Shop Steward with Local 936 and the Action union as prelude to the event Tuesday morning that caused his trip to St. Anslems. He omitted telling Martha anything about his experience at the Troubadour with Cecile's husband but he did explain that his illness of Tuesday was prompted by a drinking and smoking spree with Brian the night before. The big event, from Jay's point of view, was the telephone call with Cecile and the telephone system at St. Anslems. Jay was confident that he had complete immunity from Cecile's charges because of his enrollment in the St. Anslem's Chemical Addiction Program. Martha remarked that she was not familiar with the Federal law regarding substance abuse program immunity. She would check it out in the morning. She also advised Jay to stay cloistered in the SACAP during the day but to expect that the process server would find him at home or at work when he returned.

After some more thought, Martha conceded that Cecile may have compromised herself. Guardedly, she explained, "Jay, off the top of my head, I think that you may have a point about Cecile. She could be in big trouble. The hospital is another story. I'll talk to some plaintiff attorneys about the malpractice issue. If you have a case they'll grab it on contingency. We need to talk about it some more. Let's plan on getting together as soon as you can without messing up your participation in the program at the hospital. You need to maintain your status in that effort. Let me know when you are going to get sprung."

Martha was relieved that Jay was participating in the SACAP program. She and the rest of the Marquart clan knew that Jay needed help for years. Any mention of this to Jay was always ignored or met with angry response. In her own way, Martha prayed that Jay would stick with it this time. She was certain that without the benefit of the program he was without a defense to Cecile's custody challenge. Jay, on the other hand, concluded the call with Martha, encouraged over the prospect of gaining full custody of Kristie, receiving a generous settlement from the Hospital, and forcing Cecile on to welfare as a consequence of losing her nursing license. Things were definitely looking up. He felt good enough to give buddy Brian a call.

Brian answered the phone on the first ring and Jay fired a greeting, "Brian, my main man, I hear tell that the Bitch worked you over yesterday at St. A's. Man, you don't have to take nothing from her. I got her good this time. I been spending some time at St. A's myself, following up on Sunday. How you doing?"

"Hey, Jay. I'm fine, man. How about you? Why they hang on to you so long? You can't pay or something? I got a few bucks and maybe Louise can chip in. Say we get the crowd down at the Waltham to have a charity drink me down for your benefit. What do you say, man?"

The idea of a charity drink fest to help a drunk struck Jay as very funny. He decided to humor his friend in reply, "Well, Brian, the hospital says that I got to cut down on the partying. They got me coming back during the day for a while until I get straighten out. I'll be fine in a week or so. I just been hitting

It's nothing. Hey, we goin fishing Friday night? I got the boat out at Hingham. I hear from the Customer that the Blues are running. It's time we get out there, man. We got skunked last time. Time to get even."

"Not this time, Brian. Benny's got a game again and I got to rest after. The hospital wants me to come in on Saturday. They do a test and I got to be clean. I'm gonna be very dry for a while. Let's get together on Saturday evening as usual. Susan and the kids are looking forward to it."

Brian still didn't quite get the message, "Yeah, man. Louise and I enjoy it to. You want me to come packing? There's some quality joy in town."

"Oh, Brian, my man you are the party mule. I just told you I got to stay clean. You bring what you think you and the girls will want. I'm not having any, thank you."

oOo

Thursday morning was warm, bright and clear. The Mayor enjoyed his stroll to City Hall greeting well-wishers along the way. He was in very good spirits. The night before he had received final notice that he was the Nominee for the position as Under Secretary of Labor for the United States Department of Labor. Washington would release the information from the President's office before noon. The matter had been leaked to the wire services late last night and, therefore, would be the topic of interest by the media at the City Council meeting. His official resignation would take place next week at the Council meeting but would be a matter of routine for him. Siro would gain the spotlight next week. Between now and then it would be Mayor Cowan's time to celebrate and be celebrated by the Boston media. It was a real story about a local boy making it big on the national scene. Just what the Mayor needed to pave the way for his eventual return as the Democratic candidate for Governor. His plan was working well.

As Mayor Cowan entered City Hall a Boston Globe beat reporter came by his side and began asking questions about the transition. The questions were more for the reporter's information than as a matter of report. The Mayor invited the reporter to walk with him to the office where they chatted about several items in the process of resignation. The Mayor appeared successful in cultivating the young reporter. Sharon, the faithful secretary, filled their coffee cups and maintained the process of cleaning the files, packing personal items, and answering the phone that was now constantly ringing. At eight thirty she invited the reporter to step outside while reminding the Mayor that he had to prepare for the Council meeting scheduled for ten o'clock. As the reporter was leaving the office, Council President Alphonse Siro and Commissioner Michael Francis Megan, currently of Parks and Recreation and soon to be of Health and Hospitals, walked in. The reporter decided to wait around in the outer office.

Al Siro had in hand several press releases regarding the appointment of Megan to the Commissioner of health position. Of even greater importance, was the resolution supporting the initiation of a voluntary waste management program for the City of Boston. The resolution made the program effective immediately upon acceptance. The Mayor was quick to approve the resolution and press release. He was also delighted to begin to pass the routine of the Mayor's office to Council President Siro. The two men had conspired to have Siro actually run his office and the Mayor's for the past week and now going forward until after the special election that the City Council had to arrange. The tact was obviously to establish Siro in the minds of the voters so that he would be the choice for Mayor elect.

The three men conferred for about an hour. At nine thirty they left the Mayor's office for the City Council Chambers. The Globe reporter strolled with them as if one of the party much to the chagrin of the reporters from the electronic media crammed in the Council Chambers. The other members of the Council were already present. They surrounded Cowan and Siro as they entered the room. The Mayor accepted the individual acknowledgments with excellent poise. Everyone was very well behaved. Even the media seemed to respect the collegial order that prevailed this important meeting. At exactly ten AM, President Siro called the meeting to order. Several matters of routine business were handled with dispatch. Next on the agenda was the resignation of Commissioner Michael Logan.

Council President Siro asked Mayor Cowan to report the resignation of the Commissioner and to announce his interim successor. Mayor Cowan reported that Commissioner Logan had long sought an opportunity to enter the private sector and become involved in the direct provision of health services.

"It is to his credit and to the credit of the Boston Catholic Archdiocese that their mutual interest can be served by integrating the Church's healing mission with the dedication of a health professional committed to the public's interest" was the opening theme of the Mayor's report. He concluded by praising the work of the Church in carrying for the Boston community saying in conclusion that. "Michael Logan is truly an honorable public servant that deserves credit for his attention to the health needs of the community."

When the Mayor concluded his report, President Siro introduced a resolution of gratitude to Michael Logan. The resolution was passed unanimously.

The Mayor requested the floor again and announced Megan as his choice to replace Logan as Commissioner of Health. Megan needed no introduction to the Council, the media, or to the residents of Boston. His very active manner and enthusiasm for his job had endeared him to the public. He was a budding politician who was cutting his teeth in public service. Someday he intended to be mayor. As for now he was content to share in the bright lights of the Office transition. He was at this time becoming a prominent matter of record. At the Mayor's beckoning, Megan stepped to his side. The Mayor embraced the new appointee as the media cameras recorded the event.

President Siro called the meeting back to order at which time he accepted a resolution to endorse and support Mayor Cowan's appointment of Commissioner Megan as the interim Commissioner of Public Health. Again, the motion was passed unanimously.

The Mayor thanked President Siro and the Council for their supporting resolutions. He then baited the media by stating that the replacement for Commissioner of Parks and Recreation would be announced in the future. Perhaps next week. He however, had no one in mind at his time. The media became drawn to the reality that the Mayor's own resignation would be the topic of the next City Council meeting. The media seemed to surge at the inference. Siro noted the interest and immediately called a twenty-minute recess. The media swarmed to the Mayor and began asking questions about his Federal appointment, his resignation, and plans for transition.

Things were going exactly as planned by Siro and Cowan. They had decided at their morning conference to create a media diversion before the introduction of the voluntary waste management program to the Council. They reasoned that by creating interest in the Mayor before the recess, the media would have filled their notebooks and cameras with sufficient material. As expected, the majority of the electronic media were folding their equipment at the end of the recess time. When President Siro called the meeting back to order only the assigned beat reporters from the local newspapers remained.

Council President Siro introduced the subject of waste management as a matter of concern for the City Council. He explained the history of the project going back at least ten years when the City found it necessary to begin an expensive process of harbor clean up and water reclamation. He pointed out that the project although funded in the main by the Federal government had nevertheless required the City and surrounding Communities to experience the highest water rates in the nation. Now it was time, if not past time, to continue the cleanup of the area through a process of waste control and management of waste disposal. This included a recycling program for the City but more important it had to include a recycling and waste management program for private industry and private residences.

Siro concluded his remarks by pointing out that improper control of waste material and toxic agents was the fifth ranking cause of death in the United States last year. "These agents," according to Mr. Siro, "could be traced to environmental pollutants, food and water contaminants, ingredients in commercial products and many more related health problems." He proposed that the City had a large responsibility dealing with asbestos, childhood exposure to lead, as well as the new large-scale changes that the City needed to contemplate. "Therefore," he concluded after twenty minutes of information that he read from an Action brochure, "the City requires the assistance immediately of a qualified private company to assist in the protection and maintenance of a high standard of health for the citizens of Boston."

Following the presentation by the President of the Council, the Mayor explained that the City was particularly blessed to have the Nation's leading private waste management company located in Boston. This company, at the invitation of the Mayor, had submitted a bid to cover the Boston Hospital's waste management process at a saving of thirty percent under present costs. The City Budget Office had confirmed these savings. With the concurrence of the City Council the Mayor would sign the contract with Action Waste Management to implement a waste management program at City Hospital immediately. President Siro then called for a motion to approve the Action Waste Management/Boston Hospital agreement. Again, the motion passed without opposition.

After the vote on the City Hospital contract, and on cue, a member of the Council called for a vote supporting the voluntary privatization of waste management for the City. "This vote," he explained, "would open the door for private waste management companies such as Action to promote a healthy environment without imposing higher taxes on a community already overtaxed."

This time there was some dissension as several Council members argued that the citizens were not over taxed but perhaps under-served. The debate made for good theater and also served to tire the remaining reporters who were faced with deadlines. Siro allowed the debate to continue until it was obvious that the reporters had enough. He then called for the vote which passed by a sound majority exactly as planned. As the Council meeting came to a close, Siro noted with pleasure that the meeting had extended well beyond the two hour schedule. It was nearly one thirty. The Council had worked through the lunch hour. No one could say that the people were not getting their money's worth from the City Council.

Mark Meehan sat in the back of the City Council Chambers for the entire meeting. He had supplied Council President Siro with pages of material on environmental control. Most of the information had been published by Park in a sales handbook for their respective agencies. With Meehan was the company attorney who noted the time and date of the Council's votes regarding waste management. After the meeting the attorney went immediately to the office of the City Clerk to obtain copies of the resolutions. Meehan went straight to his office filled with the excitement of the Boston Project. It was now official. The project was underway. At his direction, his secretary called another management meeting on the Boston Project. These meetings were turning into daily affairs.

Bob Muldoon was also at the Council meeting. He sat with Meehan and commented from time to time about the actors on the stage. He seemed pleased with their performance. After the final curtain call Muldoon moved to the front of the Council. He sought out his friend, Megan, and congratulated him on his new assignment. Siro noticed Muldoon from across the room and made special effort to come to his side. Siro was very obvious about securing Labor's support in the mayoral special election. Muldoon did not hesitate to offer that support. Their relationship extended over Siro's entire political career. Marty Hart, President of Local 936, the only local in Boston having a contract or near contract with a waste management firm, was also at the meeting. With him was Dave Donovan, Business Manager of 936. They sat apart from Muldoon but moved to his side as he began to talk to Siro. Otherwise the two 936 officials chatted about the situation at Action Waste Management concerning their new shop steward. Donovan was concerned that Marquart was sick at a very critical time. Hart advised him to give it another week. Muldoon introduced his associates to Al Siro who seemed genuinely pleased to have their acquaintance.

Charles Patello was also in the back of the Council Chambers. He and Meehan intended to meet there but Patello steered away when Muldoon moved into the chair next to Meehan. Muldoon was Meehan's problem now. Patello had other matters at hand now that the Waste Management project was under way. There remained the mystery of O'Shea's interest in the check deposited in Logan's account. He left the Council Chambers as the meeting concluded and walked back to his office where he immediately placed a call to Mario Capizzi. Mr. Capizzi was very pleased that all the details for implementing the Action project were now complete save the minor issue of the Mayor's resignation. That was simply a matter of timing since the Mayor had publicly announced that he had accepted the Federal appointment. Capizzi gave Patello a well done and concluded with the question of what was next on Patello's agenda.

Patello saw the question as an opportunity to discuss the O'Shea matter, "Mario, we have one glitch that could be trouble. Boston Security's Executive Vice President, a guy named O'Shea, looked over the bonus check. He apparently noticed the Mayor's endorsement. He sent a verbal message to Logan via the courier that the money where ever it came from is in Logan's account. He essentially told Logan that he thinks the money is dirty. Logan called me to ask what's going on. I told Logan that O'Shea's nose is out of joint because he isn't in the know about the donors. Logan seemed to buy this. Then I told Mondi who checked the courier who tells him that O'Shea made copies of the check, the courier's log and I don't know what all. You know that O'Shea is a member of the

St. Anslem's Board. Hardly, O'Shea and I control the place along with a Dr. Folley, who happens to be O'Shea's son in law. Anyway, O'Shea and Folley pull a fast one on me and convince the Cardinal to make Folley the head of the Office of Health Affairs."

Capizzi was very confused at Patello's rambling explanation, "Charlie, you need to take a little time off. I can't follow you. About all I understand is that some big wig at the Bank is aware that the money in Logan's account came from the Mayor. Now the son of a bitch may have some ulterior motive in pimping Logan about the account. That motive is not clear. He knew that you were involved in cutting the employment deal with Logan but he didn't bother calling you about the check. In fact, he didn't bother calling Logan about the check. He chose, instead, to send a cynical message to Logan that essentially said that he was in the know. You think he might want a piece of Logan? He probably figures that Logan and the Mayor are in a deal. He knows that you arranged for the private bank account but he doesn't know, at least not yet, that you or we paid him a signing bonus. It seems to me that the best thing to do at this stage is nothing. You play it straight like you know nothing about a signing bonus. I doubt that Logan will bring it up to anybody but you. If he does, then we'll come up with a cover story. Right now, the trail is to the Mayor just like we wanted it. This O'Shea guy I bet is on that trail for his own good."

"That's probably true, Mario." Patello began to relax and realized that he had pushed the panic button, "I've been a buddy of O'Shea's since our days at Boston College. I'll tell you this, the guy is just smart enough to make him dangerous. Right now, he has the information about Logan's account that is just like a loaded gun. The fool could pull the trigger without thinking and screw everything up. Remember you put the wrapper on Logan as a trigger to nail the mayor. Now O'Shea has the same gun but doesn't know who or how to fire it."

Capizzi was pleased that Patello had regained control of his emotions, "That's right. If he was straight he would have made an issue about the check and never have processed it into Logan's account. My thought is that he might be smarter than you think and have a target in mind or he might realize that the information has great potential for future return. That's what you would expect from a banker. The bastards are all crooked at heart. Let's wait him out. Keep a close eye on him. Say nothing to anybody about this. Anything else?"

Patello answered, "We have a Board meeting at St. Anslem's on Tuesday. That's when we put Logan into the lineup. We'll see then if O'Shea has anything immediate in mind or is playing for the long run. I'll keep you posted."

In Capizzi's mind he thought it time to end the conversation, "OK. I'll brief Marone and Big Frank. Big Frank doesn't like surprises. You best tell Meehan and Mondi its business as usual. We play out the string as planned. Anything comes of this O'Shea issue we'll deal with it from New York. You keep me posted. You also got to play it cool with O'Shea. He may be looking at you just like you are looking at him. Don't tip your hand."

Patello felt relieved after his telephone conversation with Capizzi. He cleaned up his office, dictated a few letters, and placed a call to Siro for a round of golf later in the afternoon. The courting had begun.

oOo

Joseph Durant sat at his desk studying the Boston newspapers. Both the Globe and Herald devoted the entire front page to the pending resignation of Mayor Cowan. Cowan was glorified by both papers as a visionary Mayor that brought the City to new heights with his programs in environmental control, health and safety, and public recreation. Both papers featured pictures of the Mayor during his campaign talking to the man on the street or riding a fire truck The Globe also carried a side bar story about Commissioner Michael Logan's resignation and his new appointment as Director of the Office for Health Affairs for the Archdiocese. This was the main point of interest for Durant. He was both angry and offended that the Archdiocese hadn't informed him of the new Office. He also wondered if the Office would absorb any of the functions of the Hospital President. The newspaper accounts centered on the accomplishments of the Commissioner with little information about his new assignment.

The Herald carried the same stories about the Mayor but differed in its inside report about Commissioner Logan. It implied that the

Commissioner was over his head in dealing with the complex problems of the City. It pointed out that his extreme dedication to the inner-city health problems was admirable but he left healthcare in general get out of hand. The provision of health services was the City's third largest industry next to State government and Private education. That industry, according to the Herald report, was shameful due to the outrageous profiteering and gouging of the public trust by private hospitals. The report called for the new Commissioner and the Interim Mayor to appoint a special Blue-Ribbon Task Force to investigate the deteriorating status of health services in the Boston Metropolitan area.

The Boston Business Journal was published twice a week. It had been focusing stories about healthcare in Boston for over a year. For the most part, they watched the action of the major downtown teaching hospitals as the barometer of the industry. Hospital profits and executive salaries were a common focus. Their editorials were sharply critical of the major hospital Boards and Presidents. Reporters followed executives on weekends taking special note of their extravagant homes, yachts, and golf club memberships. In recent editions, the Journal had begun a series of reports about the excess utilization of Boston Hospitals. It predicted that Boston's over capacity of hospital beds would be eliminated by the new reimbursement methods currently being implemented by the Health Maintenance Organizations. One writer described it as a gigantic melt down of the healthcare industry that would eliminate over a third of the hospitals in the area and displace over six thousand employees. While not stated, the implication was that the smaller hospitals in the City would succumb to the change. It appeared that the rule of the jungle was being applied to healthcare reform in Boston.

Durant knew that the Journal articles, while colored in rhetoric, were based on fact. The future of St. Anslem's was a matter of great concern to him. He felt a desperate urge to express his anxiety and emphasize the need for survival planning at the Board meeting next Tuesday. Unfortunately, the great Thomas O'Shea had pre-emoted the agenda with his microscopic attention to the details of finance.

Durant nursed his frustration. He told himself over and over again that he could regain control by cooperating with the ridiculous demands of O'Shea. He also resolved in his mind to welcome Logan and the Office of Health Affairs. His intent was to capture the focus of the Office on the survival issue and in that way hopefully redirect the Board to the big picture. He decided not to make an issue about not being informed or included in the formation of the Office. It was best to make sure that his trusted vice president for finance was well prepared with every detail in response to Mr. O'Shea's criticisms of the hospital's fiscal status and operational deficiencies. After about three hours of contemplation he regained his composure and asked his Executive Assistant to arrange a time for him to have a pre-board briefing with Rod Weaver, Senior VP for finance. He also asked the executive assistant to invite Mitch Daly, the hospital's Senior Vice President for strategic planning to attend the briefing.

It was Durant's intent to have Daly well informed on the Board's focus on the fiscal item while Daly prepared the appropriate analysis on strategic issues. Durant intended to redirect the Board's attention to strategy for survival over the next three months as the new fiscal year approached. Strategic planning was an excellent complement to budgeting. The fiscal year for St. Anslem's began on October first. Between now and then Durant intended to combine the talents of Weaver and Daly into the most reliable authority on health services in the area. That team combined with his leadership would be the means by which Durant would lead the Board of Trustees and St. Anslem's into its future as the premier Catholic Hospital in New England.

oOo

While Durant pondered the future of St. Anslem's Hospital, Bob Markley pondered the life and times of Jay Marquart. It was nearly nine o'clock and Mr. Marquart had not appeared in the Unit. Markley was questioning his judgment in letting Jay go home last night. He was still very brittle. If his ex-wife hassled him or if his current wife began to mope, Jay could easily revert. He had not yet taken the first step toward recovery. That precious first step required the addict to admit that he or she was hooked. Markley knew that it would take Jay a while to come to that important conclusion. Durant also recognized in Jay an inner strength to meet the challenge of recovery. He was a fighter and a man with passion. He easily displayed compassion and love for others. On the other hand he required love from others. These were the qualities that Markley recognized as prospects toward recovery. He sat at the desk staring at Jay's chart and said his daily prayer for his friends, the recovering patients.

The telephone in front of Markley reminded him of a more immediate concern. From his point of view, "that damn thing," had indeed violated the rule of confidentiality when it signaled to Jay's ex-wife that he was in the unit. Certainly, the lawyers if they got involved would come up with a thousand mitigating circumstances that obliterated the hospital's liability. In the argument the patient would be lost from recovery. Markley was certain of that. However, Jay's determination to litigate the matter forced Markley to prepare an official hospital incident report that had to be submitted to the Risk Management Director who would notify the hospital's malpractice-practice carrier who would notify a defense attorney who would assign a claim manager who would do whatever it took to blame Jay for the whole thing.

Markley knew he had no choice but to prepare and submit the incident report. But he decided to send the matter through the Director of the SACAP Unit, Dr. Ron Anderson, for review before it was channeled to Risk Management. Dr. Anderson was Bob Markley's hero. He, in Markley's eyes was a miracle worker with addicted persons. A kind and compassionate man who was adept at moving around rules that obstructed patient care, Anderson would recognize the problem and find a solution to the administrative dilemma. Markley inserted the required form in the typewriter and began to peck out the answers to the numbered questions. He was pondering the wording and description of the incident when a shadow moved across the desk. He looked up into the smiling face of Jay Marquart. He extended a hand to him and commented, "Jay, you're late. Good to see you. Have a good night?"

Jay appeared in good spirits, "Yes I did, Bob. Nice of you to ask. I don't recall that you mentioned a starting time. We on a time clock?"

"Not exactly. You do remember that hospitals operate on a certain routine. It's rather convenient to have the patient around when the lab tech shows up to draw blood. Little things like that are seen by some as important. I'll call the lab and tell them that you have arrived. They'll be so pleased. Dr. Kenneth will be in shortly. Glad you arrived before him. Otherwise he would have to make a house call."

Jay was not impressed, "Yeah, right. Look I talked to my Sister last night about this flap with my Ex. Seems that I'm going to be served some papers. Can they do that to me in here?"

Markley was not about to let Jay worry about the presence of a court order, "Jay, no one knows you're here but us chickens. The front desk has you as discharged from general hospital. They don't know where you are. If, by chance, the process server gets by the front desk he won't get into this unit. We have a security force that loves to throw people into the street. You will probably be served at home or at work next week. And, by the way, could you manage to check in here by eight o'clock? We would appreciate it. Here, go pea in this bottle."

Jay complied with the request and returned the specimen to the desk. A Lab tech in a white coat two sizes too small met Jay at the desk and took the urine specimen. He then escorted Jay to a small room where he extracted a small vile of Jay's blood. Jay's attempt to make small talk fell on deaf ears. The tech was not a friendly sort. Jay was prone to suggest that the tech needed a stiff belt but thought differently as he saw Dr. Kenneth enter the Unit. The Doctor began reviewing several charts that Markley had selected for his review. The two men were conferring when Jay walked back to the desk. Markley nodded to Jay and then asked a nursing assistant to take Mr. Marquart to the patient library to view the video presentation. Jay obediently followed the attractive young lady to a former patient room now equipped with a couch and a few recliners facing a television and a VCR All of the furniture had seen better days. On each side of the room were battered bookshelves containing a few books and a lot of pamphlets.

The nursing assistant invited Jay to have a seat and be comfortable. She offered him a cup of juice or water that he declined. She then pulled down the tattered window blinds, turned on the television and started the VCR. As the video began she left the room. Jay realized that they only way he could escape the approaching propaganda was to leave the room or turn off the set. Either option would be seen as discourteous, rude, and obstinate, he thought. There was no need to be that offensive to kind people who seemed eager to be of service. Jay decided to go along with the game. He settled back in his recliner to enjoy the video. The flick began with an assortment of down and out bums aimlessly through littered streets and then panned to a well-dressed, up and coming, Harvard type sitting in a BMW smoking a joint. The scene shifted to a group of business types having lunch with several drinks. As the group departed one member walked to the bar instead of out the door. He ordered a drink and began a casual narrative about his decision to enjoy life by his standards. The key to the good life, according to the drinking narrator was maintaining control of your own destiny. He hastily drank his drink and ordered another. Following the consumption of the second drink and more narrative about his staunch independence he dropped the money on the bar and left, apparently in full control of his destiny. Following scenes depicted his failure to make appointments, loss of customers, arguments with his spouse, divorce, unemployment, fiscal disaster and eventual transition to the street aimlessly walking and looking for his lost destiny. He appeared in poor health. As he collapsed a friend picked him up and escorted him into a shelter where he was given nourishment, clothes, and assistance in his recovery.

The concluding scene showed the recovering alcoholic regaining his dignity and control of his destiny. He explained that controlling his destiny required control of his addiction. That type of control required the understanding of his disease and the benefit of support from others who understood the many difficulties faced by an addicted and dependent person. The final scenes pictured various support groups in the conduct of their meetings and providing individual support. The now recovering narrator praised the work of the groups and offered to be of assistance to the viewer as the telephone numbers of the groups rolled over the screen.

Jay, for lack of anything else to do, watched the video with mild interest He recalled the same type presentations in high school. Then he thought the corny acting was funny. He and his buddies would mock the flicks as they partied after school. Now he began of wonder if the film had some message for him. His life carried some of the tragedy depicted in the story but he had reasonable comfort and happiness. The struggle he had with Cecile over Kristie was rooted, he admitted, in his determination to party above all else. He also realized that his family and his life with Susan was centered on the good times associated with the high that he and Susan so often sought. They were always financially distressed. They were compatible. Were they addicted? He was holding the question in his mind when Dr. Kenneth greeted him from the hall.

Dr. Kenneth's inquiry about Jay's current state of body and mind brought a courteous response from Jay. The good Doctor noticed Jay's change of attitude from their first meeting. This was a definite sign of progress. He invited Jay to walk down the hall to his office. Once there he gave him a standard physical exam. A nurse appeared and stuck a thermometer in Jay's mouth. As Jay's temperature was being recorded, Dr. Kenneth flipped through the chart making various notes.

Kenneth eventually closed the chart, removed the thermometer, looked at it, and put it aside as he addressed his patient, "Jay, your body is responding well to treatment. Your lab and urine tests show that the presence of alcohol and cocaine use are substantially gone. This is normal. But you are in a fragile state. If you consume any substance of that sort over the weekend you could have another incident like the one that brought you in here. Your blood still carries very evident traces of marijuana. That shows little or no decline over the time that you have been with us. This does not necessarily mean that you have used marijuana in the last few days. The chemical trace of that substance in a habitual user will remain for a long time even if the person completely refrains. We should begin to see a decline after a week. It could be a month or maybe two before you test completely clean. That should be your goal. Test clean and then stay that way. In the interim we will provide you with the support that your body needs to adjust to the new you. I would like you to take some medication that will help you overcome your craving for these substances. We also have something that will help you control your anger. Mr. Markley told me about your incident yesterday."

Dr. Kenneth offered Jay three pills and a paper cup filled with water. Jay looked at the pills and reluctantly put them in his mouth, drank the water, swallowed, and attempted to talk. "Doctor, I'll give this medication thing a try. I don't know why but as long as I'm here I might as well play your game. If these things mess me up then you got to know that I won't take another one. I've heard about guys being hooked on methadone. They are as spaced out as dope heads on opium. I'll go cold turkey before I get hooked on that treatment."

Dr. Kenneth explained, "Jay, you are going through withdrawal from three substances, cocaine, alcohol and marijuana. You have used these substances in increasing quantities over the past several. Your dependency obviously was increasing so now we are reversing that biological trend. We are uncertain how you will react to this transition mentally and emotionally. Our attempt with the medication is to fortify you against a convulsive reaction like you experienced Monday and an emotional breakdown like you experienced yesterday. We know from experience that every patient experiencing withdrawal has physical and mental side effects. We can't predict the severity of those side effects. Your situation is better than most because we are treating you before you totally overdosed and experienced a severe major physical and mental breakdown. That's the up side. The down side is that we are faced with greater uncertainty about withdrawal side effects than we would be in treating what you describe as dope heads on opium. We do know that you are experiencing side effects. Markley watched you do it. We are confident that you will have more."

Jay tried to act sincere, "So how long am I gonna be a head case?"

Dr. Kenneth continued, "Well cocaine withdrawal which is the substance having the greatest impact is generally not predictable. We have recognized that cocaine abstinence syndrome has three stages. Phase one could last only a few hours. In some cases, we have seen it last up to nine days. Phase one is the most serious. This is when a patient becomes violent and does physical harm to himself or someone else. In phase two the patient becomes less violent but may experience severe depression. The depression eliminates harm to others but may cause the patient to harm himself. Phase one and two may overlap. There is no clear cut line between them. The second phase may take from one to ten weeks. Phase three is that time when the patient recognizes the problem and struggles to be free of the addiction. A failure in the attempt triggers the effects of one and two. Phase three has an indefinite time phase. It just goes on and on. What is important to the patient's recovery, just as it is to people addicted to alcohol, is the recognition of their addiction and the ability to seek the support from others in helping them avoid the crash. What I'm telling you is that there is no known cure from addiction. The disease can be controlled."

Jay seemed to modify his doubts, "Man this is weird. I been hanging around this place for the past four days and all of a sudden I got an incurable disease."

"Correction. You've been hanging around this place for four days and now know that you have an incurable disease. You were sick when you came in here, remember. You just didn't believe it." Dr. Kenneth tried to regain Jay's attention to the point

Jay remained skeptical, "Yeah, I'm still not completely convinced that I'm sick as you put it. Another way of looking at it could be that I was on a weekend drunk and took a bad trip. You know—like a bad hangover. Otherwise I feel fine."

"I recognize your disbelief" Kenneth attempted to be tactful but direct, "You weren't hit hard enough to be a believer. The guys that get hit the hardest are the first to admit the problem but are usually too far gone to do anything about it. You, at the moment, don't fully admit the problem but have the strength to do something about it. Hopefully you won't wait to get the big hit. This is the time to start your recovery."

"I'm here aren't I? What's the drill?" Jay's anger started to flare, "I give you my blood, pea in a bottle, watch a class B video—that's it? Where's the beef, man?"

"Good questions, Jay. The drill is rather loose except for the medication and observation. We will see that you get plenty of rest over the weekend. Mr. Markley will explain the support methods in place to assist with your recovery and I'll keep tabs on you medically. If you seem to be in control by Monday we will recommend that you go back to work. We'll know for sure by Sunday evening. Depends how you behave over the weekend. That medication that you took will make you drowsy. The nurse will show you a room where you can sleep if you like. Otherwise, feel free to go back to the lounge, have a cup of coffee or whatever. Read or watch television for a while. Bob Markley will catch up with you in an hour or so. He'll start you on the reinforcement. By the way lunch will be served in the lounge. You'll meet some other people there. I'll check in with you tomorrow."

Jay left the doctor's office in a quandary. He still didn't accept the idea that he had a disease. He was beginning to accept the thought that he raised a little too much hell. He began to feel sleepy. A little sack time seemed like a good idea. The nurse at the desk was very responsive to his request to lay down and rest his eyes. She escorted him back to the same room he was in the day before. Jay popped off his shoes, laid down, and fell asleep

The next thing he experienced was someone gently shaking him awake. He opened his eyes to the friendly smile of Bob Markley who extended a friendly greeting. "Wake up, Sunshine. You have been pounding your ear for nearly two hours. Another half hour and you would have missed lunch. Let's go. Got some people I want you to meet."

Jay gave Markley a light jab on the shoulder as he rolled out of bed. It took him awhile to find his shoes since he couldn't remember taking them off. Then he went to the powder room where he discovered that he forgot his comb. After straightening his hair with his fingers, he joined Markley for the walk to the dining room lounge. As they entered the room Jay noticed that the buffet lunch had been well consumed. Markley's estimate that Jay would have missed lunch in a half hour was off by a half hour. Jay picked up some bread, a slice of cheese, and the crumbs of a few potato chips that the swarm had mysteriously overlooked. Some sliced vegetables were all that remained in abundance. Jay filled his paper plate with the residue and took the remaining empty seat. Markley walked around the room greeting each person. Then he walked to the podium placed at the back opposite the food table.

"Good afternoon folks", Markley began, "My name is Bob and I'm a recovering alcoholic. How's everybody today?" Everybody applauded Bob's greeting and seemed to be in good spirits. Bob raised his hands asking for silence. Gradually the group came to order. Markley then continued his greeting, "Ladies and Gentlemen. It's always nice to have you here for our weekly meeting. It's especially nice to see so many of you attending on a regular basis. Now there are a few things, however, that the administration has asked that I point out. First is that you are using too many napkins. If this keeps up the vice president in charge of napkins is going to cut us off and we'll have to go back to using the drapes—that is if they ever get around to replacing the drapes that they took away from us last winter. Also, they have reminded me that we have used up our allotment of used and broken furniture for the remainder of the fiscal year. We will have to wait until next year before we will be given any more broken furniture. Until then we will have to make out with the good stuff. That means we will have to be on our worse behavior. Can you handle it?"

Again, the remarks were answered with laughter, applause, and cheers. The remarks about the furniture caused Jay to blush. He felt as though everyone in the room was looking at him but when he raised his head he saw that he was not being noticed.

As Bob paused in his remarks he looked directly at Jay. "My friends, we have a guest today. I hope my comments made in jest have not given him the wrong impression. You are a wonderful group dedicated to your own recovery and the recovery of those around you. You have done a marvelous if not miraculous service for one another. Some of you will want to talk about that today but before we do I want you to introduce yourself."

Following his comments each person in turn rose and faced Jay. They introduced themselves giving their first name only followed by the comment that he or she was a recovering addict. At the end of the introductions Bob asked Jay to introduce himself

Jay carefully stood before the group uncertain what he was going to say, "Ladies and Gentlemen, ah, I'm Jay. Bob, ah, I mean when Bob said he was going to buy me lunch I didn't know that, ah, he had this in mind. You see I'm, ah, I mean I been getting some treatment here and he said he wanted me to meet some wonderful people. Well, ah, I know what he meant. You are great folks. Thanks for having me."

The people responded with a loud round of applause. A few waved a sign of acceptance to Jay. Another person reached out and shook his hand. Jay was somewhat embarrassed at the friendliness of their reaction. When the group came back to order Bob asked if anyone had anything that they wanted to report or discuss. One by one individuals stood to report on the success or failure of their efforts to stay sober. One man reported in detail about his fall from the wagon and how a friend rescued him. He was back on the road to recovery. Others commented on the days, weeks, or months that they had been clean. They all thanked each other for the support to continue.

After the reports were completed Bob congratulated the group for their continuing success in recovery. He mentioned that the meeting would be held again next week at same time and place. He encouraged them to return and bring a friend in need. As the meeting concluded several of the attendees approached Jay and shook his hand. They stated that they hoped to see him again.

Jay accepted their expressions of friendship with courtesy. He noticed that the group consisted of people several years his senior. They were clean, poorly dressed, but well groomed. Their age was more in line with his parents. He realized that these were not his kind of people. Bob was beginning to pick up the paper plates and cups from the tables so Jay broke off his thoughts and began to help.

Markley, at first, seemed to take Jay's help for granted. Then he casually asked, "So Jay, what did you think of our little gathering?"

Jay was waiting for the question, "Nice people, but I felt really out of place. I mean these people were old enough to be my parents. That really threw me off. I was surprised to hear you admit to being a drunk. You gave me enough hints over the past few days that I should have realized it. Anyway, it was an eye-opener. I couldn't believe how many of these people fell off the wagon. Man, I guess when you been sopping it up as long as they have there ain't no way that you're gonna quit. Right?"

"Wrong!" Markley fired back, "Many of those people have been dry longer than you have been alive. They come here to give help and be an inspiration to the rest of us. We need all the help we can get. The key to recovery is to admit that you are sick and be willing to get help when you need it. Age makes no difference. An addicted person experiences the same difficulties. Help is the answer. That's what I wanted you to see and hear. I want you to have confidence in the ability of others to help you when you are under pressure."

"Man, you guys have been pushing this sick shit at me since I came in." Jay reverted to his defensive style, "I'm not ready to buy it. Sure, I overloaded and had a bust. You guys can dry me out and everything is jake. I go back out on the street and take care of myself No way I want to go through this again. I got that religion, man. Don't need this gang bang routine, no way."

The response caused Markley to put down the paper plates and directly confront Jay, "Jay we know what we know about you. You can't take the street. Eventually you'll find that out. Here's a card with the Unit's call number. Keep this in your wallet.

Right now, I'm your friend as well as your counselor. When the pressure builds call this number. If I'm not in, somebody else just as qualified, if not more qualified than me, win come to your aid. We can even pick you up and bring you in if necessary. Things might get rough for you in your free time this weekend. Remember, Dr. Kenneth explained that you were in Phase One of your recovery. You could experience a serious reaction to your detox. You need to be on guard. You mentioned that you had religion, well say a few prayers that you get by without taking a big hit. I'll say a few for you myself."

"Screw that religion stuff, partner. I'm supposed to be Catholic. Went to a Catholic grade school and had that God stuff crammed down my throat. Never bought it either. This is a Catholic hospital, right? How come they screw me over with their goddamn telephone letting my Ex know that I'm in "Dope-Ville." It's nothing but a freaking racket, man. All they want is money. Bring in my insurance. Too bad you ain't on the cash side of this deal, partner. They got you suckered. Looks like the Pope trained a drunk to dance to his tune and bring in the trade. Shit, I ain't buying."

Jay's anger accelerated. He suddenly grabbed a chair and threw it across the room into the food table. He kicked violently at another chair, missed and slammed his foot into the wall mounted air conditioner. The resulting pain brought his emotions to overload. He screamed and sat down in chair. As he rubbed his aching foot he shouted continuing profanities at the top of his lungs. The head nurse and a nursing assistant heard the commotion and rushed to the aid of Bob Markley. As they entered the room Markley was calmly leaning against the wall waiting for Jay's temper to cool. They opted to stand across the room at the door out or Jay's sight. Eventually Jay began to run out of steam. He placed his face in his hands and his elbows on his knees. He sat that way in silence taking deep breaths.

As his breathing began to slow Markley sat in the chair next to Jay and gently put his hand on Jay's shoulder, "Jay, you've had a long day. It's time for a rest. Let's go back to your room. It's time for another pill. Then you can sleep for a few hours before you go home. I'll be with you and check on you before you go leave. We can pick up on all this conversation in the morning. What do you say?"

"Yeah, OK. I'm sorry about messing the place up. OK?"

"Sure, it's OK, man. It's nothing. Let's go."

Jay got out of the chair unassisted. Markley waved the nurse and her assistant out of the room before Jay noticed their presence. As Bob reached to assist, Jay indicated to him that he could, actually preferred, to walk unassisted. Markley wondered if Jay was signaling that he still denied that he need for help in his recovery. However, Jay did not seem to object to Bob walking beside him to his room. As they neared Jay's room Markley noticed that Jay's energy and good nature had returned.

Jay picked up the pace and gave Bob a smile as they entered the room, "That was a short trip. Hope I didn't break anything expensive."

"Not likely, Jay. The administration gives us the hand me downs that are usually shot to hell by the time we get them. If that stuff wasn't in SACAP in would be in the junk. Feeling Better?"

"Yeah, sure. I don't think I need that pill."

"Take it anyway. That way the Pope won't get upset when the cash is low. I'll check you out about four. If you feel all right then you can go home for the night. OK?"

"Sure." After Jay took the medication Markley busied around the room until he was confident that Jay was relaxed and under control. Then he returned to the nursing station and completed his work on the incident report concerning Patient John Marquart and the St. Anslem's telephone system. He read his description of the incident over several times, uncertain on the emphasis given to the apparent misconduct-conduct of a certain staff nurse. Finally, he put the report in his confidential file for safe keeping. He intended to think it over some more before sending it to Dr. Anderson.

oOo

Joseph Durant, President of St. Anslem's Hospital, habitually arrived at his office every day at seven AM. This Friday was no exception. His diligent executive assistant somehow always managed to arrive at least fifteen minutes before the boss and routinely had the lights on, voice mail recorded, and coffee perking when he came in. Durant's routine was to go through the messages, read correspondence, dictate replies, review the appointments for the day and then begin shouting usually about, "that son of a bitch, Folley," followed by whoever else came to mind. He could never quite handle the fact that while he arrived at seven most of the other executives began filing in after eight. The executive assistant could only shrug when he demanded a stat meeting of his executive staff at seven thirty. The only one available was Dr. Folley who was the last person Durant wanted to see.

Durant's frustration centered on the lack of information for the Board of Trustees meeting agenda next Tuesday. O'Shea, Folley and, "the rest of those bastards that had screwed things up royally with that crap about the expense reports and now the prospect of this Logan character getting into the act," made for more uncertainty. He had tried to call Hardly, Chairman of the Board, on Thursday but he was out playing golf. Hardly eventually returned the call through his secretary who advised Durant to consult with Mr. O'Shea about the board agenda. Durant had that experience last week. No further contact was necessary.

He sat at his desk with his head in his hands wondering who on the Board might have some interest in an agenda and be available for a telephone conversation before eight AM. Suddenly he remembered Sister Mary Elizabeth. Nuns always got up early, went to Mass, and then to work. She would know about Logan and the Office of Health Affairs. After all she was part of the Official Church. He hastily dialed her number. Sr. Mary Elizabeth answered with a cheery good morning. After that it was all downhill.

Sister Mary Elizabeth became emotional when Durant asked her if she could give him any information about the change at the Archdiocese. She pulled up an inch short of using gutter terms in describing the basic intellect of the male dominated Board and the Chancery. She had tried to discuss the matter with Bishop Hanks who said that he would report in full at the St. Anslems Board meeting. Until that time, he in effect told her to cool her jets. He did explain that Dr. Folley had been anointed by the Cardinal as the guru of Health and would be the king of kings as far as the health ministry was concerned. End of report.

As a closing comment Sister mentioned that she had talked recently to Sister Celest who would be calling Mr. Durant in the next week. She concluded by telling Joe that he was constantly in her prayers.

Durant's next move was a call to Bishop Hanks at the Archdiocese. He felt certain that he would get a better reception than Sister Mary Elizabeth. In fact, he got no reception at all. The switchboard operator at the Chancery reported that the Bishop was not available. She took the name and number for an eventual return call. She had no idea when the Bishop would be available.

Charles Patello was a mystery to Durant, He was, on the surface, a very friendly type who always had a useful opinion when asked. At Board meetings, he seemed content to let Hardly get pushed around by O'Shea and Folley. Durant felt that Patello was not a part of the inner circle that ran things for the Archdiocese and the Universe. He observed that Mr. Patello preferred to be removed from the politics of business and government. He was a successful self-made man, content in his own right. It, therefore, seemed inappropriate to call him for an opinion on the agenda and the Office for health Affairs. On the other hand, Mr. Patello was a member of the executive committee. Durant had already called O'Shea, Hardly, Sr. Elizabeth, and Bishop Hanks. To omit calling Patello would appear improper and look like a selective omission if the matter became a topic of discussion. He realized then that he needed to call Mr. Patello and the remaining board members as well. He would first call Mr. Patello. After that he intended to call Mr. Mondi and Mr. Meehan. With luck, he would have made contact or at least attempted to make contact with the entire Board before noon with the exception of that jerk, Folley.

The medical staff was scheduled to have its monthly meeting in the auditorium at noon. Durant usually gave a brief report at the meeting. Folley always showed up for that part. Durant decided to collar him after the medical staff meeting and after he had talked to the other members of the Board.

Durant had seldom called Patello in the past since Patello always seemed as though he preferred to remain distant from the administrative chores of the hospital. However, on this occasion Patello seemed pleased that Durant had called. He answered the phone with a cheery greeting followed by an immediate offer of assistance. Durant first apologized for having to call then explained that the purpose of the call was to determine Mr. Patello's preference in dealing with the formal and informal items that were becoming apparent for the St. Anslem's Board meeting. Charlie Patello replied in a gentlemanly manner with complete courtesy. He stated that he felt the most immediate concern of the hospital and of the Board was the deteriorating fiscal position. He was aware that Mr. OShea was very intent on that point. He also mentioned that he had met Logan and felt that he could be of great help to St. Anslem's especially in getting the hospital into a better competitive position with the leading Teaching Hospitals of the world.

As Patello talked his mind was searching for an opportunity to link Durant's apparent anxiety to Capizzi's suggestion that Durant, "be put in a wrapper." It seemed to Patello that Durant needed a friend in court. There was the opportunity to compromise him. Durant had suddenly walked into his arms. The question was how best to embrace him.

Patello needed time to consult with New York. For the moment he would compromise Durant, "Joe, my friends Mr. Hardly and Mr. O'Shea have been very active with the Archdiocese in bringing about these changes. They have given me some insight to the duties of Mr. Logan but I really don't know enough about it to comment. Dr. Folley has also been involved I believe and as you know he has the ear of the Cardinal. I suspect your best source of information is Dr. Folley. If you haven't talked to him about it I suggest that you do before the Board meeting. Personally, I'm confused how your position and Logan's interact. I consider the CEO of the Hospital as the key person in the health structure. We need to make sure that is the way things are structured."

Durant was relieved to gain a friend on the Board, "Thanks Charlie. Obviously, you realize that I'm concerned about this new structure. Of course, the Cardinal has every right to make whatever changes he wants in the conduct and direction of his health ministry. I'll go along no matter what but in this very competitive environment we cannot afford expensive duplication of executive talent and complicated levels in decision making. The Mass General and Brigham merger has eliminated a big hunk of bureaucracy. They are streamlined. Our decision making must be very accurate and timely."

"Joe, I know far less than you do about health reform and what's going on in Boston," confessed Patello. "The newspapers carry a story everyday about the changes taking place. St. Anslem's is never mentioned in the new networks that the downtown hospitals are forming. It seems to me that we need to move rapidly before we are left out completely. With all the pressures, you have in just trying to make ends meet it must be nearly impossible to keep up the pace. Mr. Logan will be able to help I'm sure. However, we need to develop a plan that fits the future. We need a true strategic plan. I have used national consultants in my business and have been amazed and pleased at the amount of insight that a large national firm can give you. I would like to recommend to the Board that we form a strategic planning committee and hire a national consulting firm to help us. I'll fix it so you direct the effort. What do you say?"

"Yeah, that's great." Durant was elated. "Mitch Daly our Planning VP, as you know has been bugging me to hire a consultant to help us do a strategic plan. The problem is money. We are struggling to meet payroll. O'Shea is constantly raising hell about the deficit. I understand that a major consulting job could go over a hundred grand. In all good conscience, I couldn't spend that kind of money when I'm laying people off. How are we going to justify it?"

Patello saw the opening but decided to play it slow and easy, "At the moment I don't have an answer. Let me explore some options. I have some contacts with national organizations that have provided grants and planning assistance to charitable agencies in various parts of the Country. I'll make a few phone calls and see if I can come up with something. I'll get back to you on Monday. In the meantime, just enjoy the weekend. You're a boater, aren't you? I understand that it's supposed to be a great weekend for sailing."

"Actually, I'm a power boater. We don't always appreciate high winds like the rag flappers but I expect to get out for a few hours on Sunday. How do you intend to bring this planning effort up to the Board?" Joe asked.

"Tactically, I think it best that the agenda remain as loose as possible," commented Patello, "That way I can slip it in when the opportunity presents itself. My guess is that Kevin will let things just happen as he usually does. Tom will want to beat you on the head about money. Bishop Hanks will want to tell us about Folley and Folley will tell us about Logan. The combination of all of this will create enough confusion for me to suggest that we bring about order through a strategic plan. The other Board members will welcome the comic relief."

Durant was relieved, "OK. I'll stop worrying about an organized meeting and agenda and let things just happen. I was going to call Mr. Mondi, and Mr. Meehan for their input. Should I still do that? What does the Bishop have to tell about Dr. Folley?"

The question about the Bishop brought Patello up short. Suddenly he realized that by pressing his interest to compromise Durant he had inadvertently tipped his hand that he was in the know more than he wanted Durant to realize. At this point Folley's appointment as Secretary of Health for the Archdiocese was only known to a few insiders. Patello did not want Druant to see him as a member of the Cardinal's gang. On the other hand, to deny having any knowledge about the appointment and have Durant learn later that he was one of the first informed would destroy the trust with Durant that he was now trying to firmly establish. Patello opted to give an honest reply.

"I'm sorry, Joe. I thought that Dr. Folley might have informed you. The word I got from Bishop Hanks is that the Cardinal has named Dr. Folley to be his Secretary of Health. Logan will be reporting to Folley as I understand it. I expect that the Bishop will report that to the Board on Tuesday."

The news was a real downer for Durant, "Christ! That really sucks, Charlie. How in the hell can I run this hospital to the satisfaction of the Cardinal, the Board, that jerk Folley, and Logan, who I've never met? That really sucks!"

Patello recovered, "Well it only serves to justify the need for an organized plan of action. Let's get the planning committee organized. Maybe Mondi and Meehan could serve on the Committee with you and me. That would create some balance while Logan, Folley, O'Shea and Bishop Hanks handle the fiscal crisis. Hardly can be the mediator. Why don't you let me talk to the others? That way you won't be seen by O'Shea and his associates as an insurgent."

Suddenly Durant remembered, "How about Sister Mary Elizabeth? Where does she fit in? Her nose seemed well out of joint when I talked to her about an hour ago. Think she would fit into the planning committee?"

"Good question, Joe. I'm not really sure. Let's give it some more thought and talk on Monday."

As the conversation ended Patello felt certain that he had gained the trust of Durant. Even more important he felt that Durant had allowed himself to become dependent on Patello for leverage against the apparent power play that Folley had engineered by his appointment as Secretary of Health. A side bar advantage is that the counter move the planning committee could cause O'Shea to expose his motive for holding the evidence about Logan's bank account. This was a long shot worth taking. Now Patello needed the assistance of Park consulting. Tony Marone wasn't in to answer his call but got back to him within the hour. Charlie detailed the conversation with Durant to Marone who immediately opted to consult with Cappizi and get back to Patello. Three hours later a meeting had been arranged for Monday morning in Patello's office. Capizzi and Marone would be there. Tom Callahan, world class health consultant of De bur and Tandy, would also be with them.

Durant was fuming mad. Twice he picked up the telephone to call Folley. Each time he thought better of it and returned the phone to the receiver. He pounded the desk in anger, shouted at the ceiling, and yelled for his executive assistant. She walked into his office and calmly sat in the chair in front of his desk. Her matronly deportment and professional style caused the near mad executive to reign in his own emotions. They sat looking at each other for a few minutes before he spoke.

"Dam it, that jerk Folley has got me by the shorts. I need to have a stat conference with Weaver and Daly. Get 'em here in the next fifteen minutes. Tell 'em whatever they are doing can wait. Have you mailed out anything for the Board meeting?"

The executive assistant was very curious about the Folley remark. Some rumors about the good Doctor becoming Durant's boss had been circulating among the secretaries. Obviously, this was not the time to engage the boss in small talk about a trivial thing like his job. She thought it best just to answer his question. "The only thing that has been sent to the Trustees is the meeting notice, Mr. Durant. I expected to fax an agenda to everyone today. Do you have it ready?"

"Negative. We'll surprise them with some of Hardly's mystic commentary. Folley can do the dance of the Seven Veils and I'll do some slight-of hand tricks with the cash balance. For my big finish, I'll make Weaver disappear. That ought to make 'em go bananas"

This was the opening the Executive Assistant had been waiting for. Now was the time to pop the question, "You are obviously upset about the meeting. What has Dr. Folley done this time?"

Durant's anger brought him out of his chair. He paced back and forth as he began to explain to the faithful executive assistant, "God's gift to the medical profession, one Dr. Folley, has apparently used his clinical relationship with the Cardinal as a means to achieve prominence and glory in the Chancery. He got himself appointed Secretary of Health for the Archdiocese. I think the son of a bitch is running for Pope. The Cardinal had to be drunk when he made that decision, Jesus!"

Having extracted the information of interest, the executive assistant redirected Durant back to the business at hand, "Mr. Weaver called earlier for an appointment. I gave him one o'clock. Usually Mr. Daly prefers to meet with you on Monday morning. Should I cancel his Monday meeting and bring him in at one with Mr. Daly?"

The relationship between Weaver and Daly had always been strained. Weaver by nature and profession was cautious. Every detail needed to be accounted for in an exact fashion. Accounting was an art that Weaver mastered and bookkeeping was an exact science that he commanded. Daly was an artist of a different sort. Since his days as a student activist during the Viet Nam War, Daly had used estimates and trends as a gauge of measurement. Details were always contained but hidden in the packaged conclusion. Durant had discovered that Weaver's exact nature in budgeting and Daly's wide lens approach to planning often led to the same conclusions. When that happened the hospital could set a course with accuracy. When the two perspectives differed, Durant took the time to analyze the differences in depth before proceeding. During the analysis of the difference Durant would attempt to get the two executives to collaborate and come to a uniform compromised conclusion. Collaboration was difficult and often forced. The two men were not only professionally different but were on the opposite extremes politically. Weaver epitomized the arch conservative while Daly was an outspoken liberal who still wore a Castro style beard. Bringing the two together in a small conference or in a general executive staff meeting was always potentially explosive. Apart each man was extremely competent and possibly the best in their respective positions in all of the Boston area hospitals, a fact not fully known therefore not appreciated by the Board.

Durant intended to inform Weaver and Daly about the conversation with Patello at the same time. He wanted to measure their individual reactions and see if they could come to an immediate common perspective on the conduct of a strategic planning process.

It was important that the executive staff have a united effort in order to keep planning under management control. He would emphasize that point by telling the executives about Folley's latest claim to glory. The political strategy within the Board would be obvious. No need to explain all of this to the executive assistant.

Instead Durant gave a simple answer to her question, "No. Let Daly's Monday meeting stand. Tell him to be here at one for a discussion with Rod on strategic planning. We can detail today's meeting on Monday. Schedule Rod to come back on Monday. That Way they'll both be upset."

Actually, one PM was the best time for Durant to meet with Weaver and Daly. The General Medical Staff meeting was less than an hour away by the time he had finished his morning routine, called the board members, ranted and raved, then had a discussion with his executive assistant. For the next thirty minutes Durant would busy himself making notes for the President's report to the Medical Staff. The meeting would begin at noon and usually conclude by one. He could then move immediately to the meeting with his two senior vice presidents.

At eleven forty-five Durant entered the hospital's main auditorium. Several physicians had arrived and were enjoying the buffet lunch. Physicians are customarily attracted to a free lunch. It is an integral part of their residency training that lasts through out their entire career. Hospital Presidents are taught to always cater to the physicians. Gradually the room became crowded as the teaching faculty, hospital based specialists, and community based physicians assembled for their obligatory meeting. Some signed the attendance forms, ate lunch and left. Most stayed obediently through the reports and presentations. The agenda for the general staff meetings is purposely short since the physicians attend a number of departmental quality review sessions on a routine basis. In addition, the medical staff has a major scientific session each month called grand rounds that is always very well attended. Actually, the general staff meeting was more of a social gathering where the elected leadership of the medical staff would report on medical administrative matters and the members of the medical staff could register a complaint about parking, medical record transcription, or anything else that came to mind. The president of the medical staff moved quickly through the agenda to the concluding item, The Hospital President's Report.

Durant's style in dealing with the general medical Staff was to be concise, factual, and always upbeat. His years of experience had taught him that placing a burden on the physicians with a lot of crape hanging always generated a negative reaction. This was especially true in the current environment where the specialists were losing income because of the increasing denial rate by Health Maintenance Organizations. The primary care physicians were becoming busier but they were also being held far more responsible and accountable under the capitation payment method.

Durant cautiously steered around conflict between members of the staff. He began his report by thanking the physicians for their continuing support during these difficult times. He noted that the occupancy of the hospital was nearing a record low but the diagnostic and therapeutic procedures were running ahead of last year. From a fiscal perspective, the hospital's cash flow was excellent. Days in the accounts receivable were slightly under this same period last year. The employee to patient ratio was on the decline. Spending was being modified to become consistent with revenue. He concluded his remarks, as he began, by thanking the physicians for their loyalty and support.

As Durant was giving his report, most of the physicians were finding another cup of coffee, talking to a colleague, or lining up a consultation. No one seemed to realize that the President's report was packed with bad news. The Hospital was losing money. Admissions were at a record low. Intensity was declining. Expenses were being cut. Employees were being laid off. Revenue was declining. As always Durant asked if anyone had any questions or comments. Hearing none he returned the podium to the President of the Medical Staff who adjourned the meeting.

Durant lingered in the auditorium as the physicians filed out. Some of the doctors remained in little groups chatting about matters of practice and referrals. Others socialized and talked about the Red Sox, golf, or vacations. Often individual physicians would take the time to whisper the latest gossip in Durant's ear. He wondered if anyone would bring Folley's latest escapade to his attention. None did. He also noticed that Dr. Folley, Chairman of the Department of Medicine at St. Anslem's Hospital, Member of the Board of Trustees, Professor of Medicine Tuft's University School of Medicine, Distinguished servant of the Commonwealth and City, gentleman, scholar, man of letters, and soon to be announced Secretary of Health for the Boston Catholic Archdiocese was not present. "Good" thought Durant, "this is not the time or place for a confrontation."

While Durant was hanging around the auditorium, Weaver and Daly had arrived at his office. Daly was the first. He properly announced himself to the executive assistant and took a chair in the office reception area. Weaver arrived within minutes of Daly. He walked past Daly without comment, waved to the executive assistant, entered the President's office and sat down. Both executives remained in their own solitude until Durant arrived. As the boss entered his office Daly walked in and took a chair opposite Weaver at the small conference table. Durant joined them and sat at the end of the table so that he was flanked on both sides by his capable assistants. The boss tried to warm the meeting by commenting about the weather, the week end relaxation, and some trivial gossip about who was doing what to who. As the execs took to the discussion with their own commentary Durant carefully measured the compatibility scale.

When he determined the time was right, he brought their attention to the purpose of the meeting, "Boys we have another interesting challenge given to us by the great Dr. Richard Folley. This time he has managed to get himself appointed Secretary for Health on the Cardinal's Cabinet. He has also been appointed boss of the new Office for Health for the Archdiocese. I'm sure that you have heard that former City Commissioner Logan is going to direct that office. What we don't know at this time is how all of this impacts on our work in administering St.

Anslem's. I expect to be enlightened at the Board meeting on Tuesday. There are some Board members who feel that the CEO of St. Anslems should be the principal agent for the Board of St. Anslem's. They are going to recommend that St. A's establish its destiny through a strategic planning effort led by the administration of the hospital. We need to be prepared to take charge of the planning effort. I wanted to have an initial discussion about this with the two of you today so you could begin to prepare your thoughts over the week end. We will meet again on Monday morning to begin to flesh out our approach."

Daly sat up straight and began to be energized by Durant's comments. His black eyes flashed from Durant to Weaver and back. As Durant finished his comments Daly jumped in, "This could be the opportunity that we have been looking for to focus the Board on the changing pattern of health delivery going on in Boston and away from the micro perspective of money. The only reports they ever see are financial. Has anyone thought about a planning committee?"

Weaver slumped in his chair and began rubbing his temples. He seemed irritated by Daly's eagerness. With a quick flick of the wrist he popped open his ever-present Briefcase, laid copies the draft financial operating statement for the recent month on the table, and began his commentary. "What we need to plan is how we are going to get out of the toilet. We went down a million two hundred and change the past month. If this keeps up the only viable plan is bankruptcy. Folley and that goddamn Department of Medicine is way under budget in revenue and way over on expenses. That jerk needs to start cutting losses. Why don't we start with him and bounce his ass full time to the Archdiocese? Another cut could be in administration by chopping back on wild hair planners who only know how to plan to spend. We need more tertiary admits to cover the overhead load. O'Shea will jump all over this planning shit."

Durant took quick notice of Weaver's slam at Daly. Daly hadn't missed it either. He was leaning forward in his chair as if he was about to lunge at Weaver. Durant came forward in his chair in an attempt to separate the two. "Look guys what I need is your collective wisdom not your antagonism. We know that this place has got warts. We also know that O'Shea is screaming about the losses. If our only answer is to gut this place with layoffs and cutbacks then we are in a death glide. I'm not ready to admit that, although it might be the fact. We owe it to the Board to do a very careful review of our situation and look for viable alternatives. Maybe the Office for Health can help generate more referrals to St. A's. We ought to at least get the Catholic market."

With a wave of his hand Weaver dismissed Durant's comment. "Boss you are kidding yourself if you think the Catholics are going to let the Archdiocese tell them where they are going to get health care. Have you been to Church lately? The place is nearly empty on Sunday. People listen to the HMO's. Our docs have to sell their excellence to the HMO's. That's where the action is. The only thing you are going to get from that stupid Health Office at the Archdiocese is a bill to pay for Folley and Logan. That's the only kind of plan they care about."

Daly remained focused on Weaver but directed his remarks to Durant. "I believe the only way out of the fiscal crisis is to reposition the hospital into new markets. Our emphasis on cardiac disease has brought us into the most competitive market. We might have the best product but who knows it. If we are going to stay with that emphasis then we have to put big bucks into the marketing end. We could be a small player with high quality in cardiac and create another high- profile service that draws the referrals. A planning effort would help determine where the new markets are. Again, my learned fiscal wizard, you better be prepared to open the purse strings because a real planning effort costs money."

As Daly concluded his comment, Weaver leaned forward and put his fist in the middle of the table. He glared at Daly. "If I'm a wizard you're a mystic. What in the hell do we need to spend money on? We need to stop spending, not start, for Christ's sake. Your goddamn planners and consultants are not going to tell us anything that we don't know. What we need to do is kick some ass. Let's start with Folley."

Daly sat back in his chair and seemed to relax. He looked at Weaver with a slight smile before commenting, "Rodger, my dear friend, you are a real asshole."

Before Durant could call for order, Weaver jumped from his chair and made a move for Daly. Daly, the smaller of the two but far quicker, was on his feet in time to duck Weaver's blind punch. Weaver's second punch landed harmlessly on Daly's upraised arms. The two combatants then went into a clinch and proceeded to waltz around Durant's office knocking pictures off the wall and rearranging the top of the boss's desk.

Durant was at first speechless and then began to repeatedly shout, "knock it off!" to little avail except to draw the executive assistant into the office. She watched the dance for a few seconds before announcing that, "You two jerks couldn't get noticed at a walrus convention." That comment ended the fray.

Weaver and Daly picked up their material and left together. Durant wondered if they were headed for the parking lot to finish the battle. As the door closed he joined his faithful executive assistant in putting the office back in order. "Another executive conference brought to a productive conclusion," he thought. It was now three thirty on Friday afternoon. Time to start the week end. Durant turned out the lights in the office and went home.

As he drove home, Durant worked over in his mind the exchange between his two capable Vice Presidents. He dismissed the physical combat as something of no consequence. Instead he searched for a common point to base a planning review. Points of agreement were the fiscal crisis and low occupancy. There seemed to be mixed attitudes about the hospital's emphasis on cardio vascular disease. Yet, putting the insults aside, the two executives seemed to acknowledge that as the hospital's strong suit. Neither seemed to suggest that the hospital had any other area of prominence. Daly would not acknowledge that cost reduction methods were required. Weaver, on the other hand, felt that immediate cutbacks were necessary. On the last point, Durant completely agreed with Weaver. Monthly losses of over a million dollars could not be sustained. The hospital was required to drastically scale back its spending. The challenge was to reduce spending without impacting the revenue base. On the other hand, revenue enhancement would be served if the doctors would become salesmen to the HMO's, as Weaver had suggested, and if the hospital would find new profitable markets as Dally had suggested.

In summary Durance focused on three combined efforts. The first would be a detailed fiscal analysis of all hospital functions. Those that were not essential would be eliminated. The second analysis would be a review of all hospital services from a revenue to cost perspective. Those services that were not profitable would be eliminated unless they materially contributed to enhancing revenue for another service such as the cardiac catheterization laboratory in medicine contributing to the volume of cardiac surgery. The third analysis would be the strategic planning effort. The intent of that effort would be determining new markets that offered opportunity for growth and prominence.

This last analysis is where Durant intended to focus the planning committee. He prayed that Patello would find a funding source for the planning program. Such a find would eliminate the objection that Weaver raised about the cost of consultants. In his heart, Durant felt that Weaver was being the Devil's advocate as a conditioner for O'Shea. "Yes, all things considered it was a productive meeting," was his last thought on the subject as he turned into his driveway.

ALL THE CARDINAL'S MEN AND A FEW GOOD NUNS

ALL THE CARDINAL'S MEN AND A FEW GOOD NUNS— PART TWO

CHAPTER NINE

Jay Marquart was in a funk. Friday, his second favorite day, was spent at St. Anslem's chemical dependency unit talking with Dr. Kenneth about his "disease" as the doctor described it, listening to a variety of lectures about physical and mental deterioration caused by substance abuse, and chatting with seasoned veterans in the struggle to recovery. It was hard to deny the logic of the presentations. He was convinced that he was going to die a painful death and bring no end of hardship and ruin to those who loved him if he gave no effort to reform.

"OK, you got me," he thought as he looked at the fourth video in a series of six.

But recognizing the problem and doing something about it seemed impossible. It was Friday and for as long as Jay could remember, Friday afternoon he went on a jag that carried him to Monday morning. His life style was built on the practice of substance abuse. He smoked and drank when he went fishing on Friday night. Or was it more correct to state that he fished when he went smoking and drinking. Jay was puzzled over what came first.

"It's that damn medication" he thought, "it's messing up my head." If he was going to be a recovering addict as, everybody seemed intent on making him, then he would design his own method of recovery. He began a careful reflection of his lifestyle and decided that he could maintain the practices that he enjoyed absent of the excessive consumption of substances. A troublesome point in the analysis was that his spouse was a happy participant in his excess. There was no way that Jay was going to disrupt the loving relationship that he had with Susan. They shared good times centered on booze, pot, and coke. That's what brought them together and nothing, especially abstinence, was going to separate them. Jay concluded that for the sake of his family he would need to continue to consume some form of intoxicating substance. He would explain that requirement to Bob Markley at their next session.

Staying off the stuff on a Friday night wasn't enough of a downer but he had to check out of his fishing trip with Brian in order to meet with Martha about his intent to sue the Hospital and, "nail dear old Cecile to the wall." Martha had researched the Federal law on record confidentiality and wanted to go over it with him. She wanted to make sure that while he was hanging around the hospital over the weekend he did not do anything that would void his protection. Their meeting was scheduled to follow Benny's baseball game.

Cecile's process server had yet to catch up with Jay and give him the summons to return to court for the custody battle over Kristie. That was another downer. There was a big legal fight brewing that Jay did not have the money to sustain. Lawyers, other than Martha, expected to be paid. She and Jay were also going to discuss that monstrous problem at their Friday night session.

If he survived Friday night, he had to look forward to coming back to St. A's and hanging around in the morbid surroundings while his yard was left unattended. Saturday morning was the time that Jay had dedicated to mowing the lawn and trimming the place to perfection. He was proud of his yard. He also enjoyed the three or four beers that it took for him to complete the job. Afterwards it was playtime with the kids until Brian and Louise arrived. Then it was party time all night long. Brian was scheduled to show up with the usual goodies. Sunday morning, instead of sleeping off the jag, he was scheduled to check in again at St. A's.

"Bummer. This is a goddamn bummer. Ain't no way that I'm gonna make it through the weekend. No way!" was the thought in his mind as Jay laid down for his afternoon nap.

Bob Markley had purposely avoided Jay on Friday. He had a legitimate reason. It was time for Jay to reconcile his dependency in his own mind by coming to grips with the activities in his lifestyle that catered to his problem. Jay also needed to build support relationships on a broader base than Markley. However, if Jay entered into a crisis, the staff had been informed to call Bob to the scene. Markley and Dr. Kenneth felt that Jay was not out of the woods emotionally but could still experience a violent reaction to the detoxification.

Another reason for the distance that Markley sought from Jay was to establish some objectivity in thinking about the incident report sitting in his desk drawer. Markley feared that the report once submitted to the risk manager would bring Jay's former wife under investigation by a nursing review board. This would give her reason to create a defense, he thought, that would subject Jay to intense pressure. He feared that Jay would crack under the pressure and revert to substance abuse. On the other hand, if Markley did not submit the report and Jay sued the hospital the same pressure would be caused as the hospital applied its defense. Markley's interest in Jay as a patient was overshadowing his obligation as an agent representing the institution's best interest. The pressure of being in the middle was very familiar to Markley. He had cracked under that same type of pressure in the past and well understood the familiar sensation to find an escape.

About the time that Joseph Durant was pulling into his driveway in Hingham after an exciting day at St. Anslem's, Jay Marquart was entering his driveway in Waltham after a non-eventful day at the same place. As Jay left the Jeep, he was mobbed by Benny and James. Kristie was not scheduled to visit until Sunday night. Susan had prepared a snack for him that he gobbled before he changed into shorts and a Tee shirt. Once properly dressed, the whole family piled into the Jeep and headed for the Waltham Little League Ball Park. This was the final game of the schedule. Rumors around the dugout indicated that if Benny had a good game he would be selected as the first alternate on the League All-Star Team. The prospect of such an honor registered little with Benny as he toyed with his brother in the back seat. Jay, however, was visibly excited about the prospect. He kept explaining the fine points of the game to Benny as they negotiated around the usual five o'clock traffic. Susan listened to Jay and observed that Benny was not at all on the same wavelength. When they arrived at the ballpark, Benny jumped from the Jeep and ran to his team mates already taking in-field practice. Jay gave him a parting pat on the back and shouted encouragement to the back of the running boy.

As Jay was walking toward the bleachers he noticed a familiar person sitting prominently in the third row where Jay usually perched. It was none other than his new-found friend of last Friday, the owner of the Oldsmoble that James had marked on the door and forever in Jay's mind. "What's that son of a bitch doing in my place, Susan?" was his first verbal reaction. "I'll kick his ass," was the second.

Susan tried to direct Jay around to the other end of the bleachers while trying to calm him down, "Jay, the man can sit wherever he wants. We don't own the ballpark. Let him be." Her appeal had the right effect as Jay followed her lead but continued to mumble. They found a vantage point behind home plate but with an obstructed view of second base where Benny was positioned.

As the game began with Benny in the starting lineup, Jay began pacing in front of the bleachers shouting encouragement to Benny while standing for brief periods in front of his former advisory. Eventually the Oldsmobile owner moved to the top of the bleachers above Jay's intended obstruction.

As the inning came to a close and Benny returned to the dugout, Jay returned to his seat beside Susan. "Fixed his ass good, Susan. Did ya see him move? Man, he knows I ain't gonna take nothing from him," Jay proudly announced loud enough to cause people near them to turn around. With his emotions in high, Jay stood on the bleachers and directed more remarks toward the top row, "Hey man, you want to talk about this? We can do some battle or we can wimp out? Shit, man, I know what you want to do"

The man to whom Jay had directed the remarks looked toward the field in apparent disregard of Jay. Susan's embarrassment was at its peak. Gently she pulled at Jay's trousers in an attempt to get him to direct his attention elsewhere. Fortunately, before the matter reached a climax little Benny was at bat. Susan brought this to Jay's immediate attention. Jay became focused on the ball game once again and seemed to forget the Oldsmobile owner. It took seven pitches for Benny to earn a walk. Jay yelled base stealing instructions, told him when to tag, suggested he keep his eye on the pitcher, and generally announced strategy to all within ear shot. Benny made it to third on a throwing error to second by the catcher and two pitches later ran home on a pass ball. Jay was elated. At the end of the first inning Benny's team held a comfortable six run lead. Jay was now relaxed and focused on the rest of the game without incident.

Benny's team coasted to victory in four innings thanks to the merciful eleven run rule. As the team assembled at the Dairy Queen, Benny's manager informed Susan and Jay that Benny had been selected as an alternate to the All-Star squad and would be assigned as a regular since another player was forced to drop out due to a conflict with the family vacation. Benny was an all-star. Susan and Jay were proud parents. Normally this would be cause for a few drinks and a family celebration into the wee hours of Saturday morning followed by the ritual of Saturday night. Jay couldn't wait to tell Brian but it would keep until tomorrow when he and Louise came over.

As he sat in the Dairy Queen pondering the glorified status of Susan's son, Jay lost all thought of St. Anslem's, Cecile's lawyers, and a disease that he didn't think he had. None of that for now. It was a time to rejoice.

The Marquart family Jeep pulled into their Waltham estate about seven thirty. Susan was primed for a grapefruit and gin in Benny's honor. Jay was still in a good mood but stuffed with a quart of frozen yogurt and hot fudge. Normally he would have forgone the ice cream for a few stiff drinks but suddenly he remembered the blood and urine test in the morning. He realized that one drink would lead to another and then to countless others ending in a super jag. This was the picture vividly explained to him over the past three days in his rehabilitation. Some of it was beginning to sink in. As an alternative, he ordered the largest serving of frozen yogurt that was available and loaded it with hot fudge. He tried to get Susan to join him in the quasi-celebration but to no avail. She appeared to Jay to be somewhat depressed.

The prospect of a continuing celebration at home diminished more as Susan noticed Martha's car parked on the street in front of their home. Jay made the same observation but with positive interest since Martha had promised him information about the Federal law on patient records and the prospect of a malpractice-practice action against the hospital.

As the family piled from the Jeep, Martha walked into the driveway from the backyard where she had been sitting on a swing enjoying the summer sunset. James was the first to greet Aunt Martha with great news that Benny was going to be in the sky with the moon because he was going to be a star. Martha accepted the information with parallel happiness to James' but was confused as to what was actually being said. Susan greeted her Sister-in-Law and detailed the good news. She also offered to fix Martha a refreshing drink as an adjunct to her relaxing moments. Martha was quick to accept. Jay interjected a request for an ice tea that Susan promised to supply as well. Jay and Martha returned to the backyard swing to watch the final hour of a beautiful sunset. Within moments Susan joined then with a tall ice tea for Jay and a couple of equally large gin and grapefruits for Martha and herself.

Jay felt the surge of anger toward Susan and Martha. It seemed to him to be totally inconsiderate of the struggle he faced. "Don't they realize that I am in a world of hurt," he thought. "How can they drink in front of me when I need their help and support?" was the question that raced through his mind as his anger surged toward an uncontrollable rage. "This is a test," he reasoned, "yeah a goddamn test. Markley said I would be tested over the weekend. If I break now and get pissed then I fail the test and will probably have to start that rehab crap all over again. I'll have something to tell Markley in the morning. No way am I gonna let these two broads mess me up"

He felt an inner strength and frustration at the same time that caused him to stand. He at first turned away from the women then turned to face them, "Martha, I need to be briefed on the deal about the Federal law. You thought you would know something about the suit I want to bring against the Hospital. Maybe we ought to go inside where it's cooler and better light."

With a nod Martha and Susan carried their drinks inside to the kitchen table where they sat with Jay. Susan placed a bowl of pretzels on the table as Martha began her report.

"Jay, the hospital gave you the straight dope on the Federal law. Essentially, the Law enacted in 1975 established that any patient in a

Federal qualified substance abuse program was guaranteed confidentiality. However, the Department of Health and Human Resources was charged with enforcement of the Law and with establishing the appropriate regulations for implementing and enforcing the law. A revised set of regulations was published by the Department in 1987. These new guidelines apply to any hospital or treatment program operated under Federal License or certification. The guidelines do allow a general hospital to determine that only the distinct substance abuse program falls under the regulations."

Jay was eagerly following Martha's commentary. He held up his hand as if to ask a question but began with an explanation, "OK, so Markley was right in telling me that I had to sign in the program. Otherwise they could have released my general medical record. Sounds like we got 'em by the short and curly. They blew my cover with their damn telephone."

Martha gave a slight shrug and continued her report, "Jay, as we know the law is seldom black or white. According to the regulations, the focus of enforcement depends on how the hospital organizes its substance abuse program. If a patient receives treatment in a general hospital that does not operate a program or have specialized personnel whose primary function is treatment, diagnosis or referral of substance abuse patients then the record is not protected under the law. On the other hand, if the hospital does have an organized program with the requisite personnel and certification, then the law does apply, St. Anslem's has all the necessary qualifications to bring it under the Law. Now we have to be aware that the regulations allow for exceptions."

Jay's face reddened as Martha mentioned exceptions. He stood and began to pace around the kitchen. "Martha what exceptions? They flat out broke the law, right?"

"Jay, there are always necessary reasons to except rules and regulations," Martha straightened her glasses and looked at Jay as if she were talking to a client, "The law recognizes this. In this case the Federal regulations allow for patient information to be given if the patient authorizes it. Most patient authorizations are to qualified service organizations such as research firms, data processing organizations, insurance payers, and laboratories, legal or medical professional services, even collecting agencies. However, once the information is given to the agency, they must agree to retain its confidentiality. You can see that as the information gets spread around to so many different places the ability to enforce the law becomes mute."

"Hell Martha, I ain't gonna authorize any release of information to anybody." Jay pounded the table to give emphasis, "They can't make me, can they?" Jay's expressed concern brought him back to his chair.

Martha looked at Susan and pointed to her glass for a refill. Susan was quick to oblige. Jay's ice tea was half full but Susan topped it off. This time Jay didn't notice. He was concentrating on Martha's every word. She continued to explain, "There are other exceptions for minors, incompetent patients, and such that don't apply to you. And there are a lot of wrinkles in the patient authorized disclosure that we need to be careful about. You may have authorized certain agencies to receive information when you signed the admitting form to the program. For example, your insurance company may be an authorized agency. We'll have to check it. The point is that your release of information on the admitting form may give the hospital its defense."

Jay hit the table again with his fist and scared both Susan and Martha. "That's bullshit, pure bullshit. That's no defense against their damn telephone, I didn't authorize that telephone on my admitting form. No way!"

Martha raised her hands as if to calm him, "Jay, I'm only trying to demonstrate the complex side of the issue. We will have to explore the hospital policies of patient confidentiality on and off the substance abuse unit. There's a lot we don't know and will need to know to determine if we have a case that will stand up in court. I'll need to talk to a few more med-mal lawyers. This is a legal specialty in which I have limited experience and then only on the side of the defense. Now before you go off on another tear let me advise you that there is another category of exception known as disclosures without patient consent that allows for access to your record in case of a medical emergency. That's an obvious one except you need to know that if you are severely injured from whatever cause the treating person or institutional is entitled to your medical history. The last category is one that merits our careful concern. Your records could be disclosed on a court order if you refuse to voluntarily disclose your medical history to the court. This allows an attorney, even in a civil suit, to apply to the court for a court order to release the information. What I fear is that Cecile's attorney could make that application in your custody hearing. You see how complex this can be? You also need to know that if you are involved in any sort of criminal action the judge can order the immediate release of your medical records. Do not, I repeat, do not get involved in any violation of the law—even a speeding ticket or worse yet using or trafficking drugs—until we have a chance to sort all this out.

Jay was visibly shaken by Martha's last remarks. He felt a familiar pain in his stomach as he remembered the episode on Monday night at the Troubadour Lounge. Was he at that time involved in a criminal act? Should he tell Martha about the incident? Did Officer O'Sullivan have enough information to link him to Brian and the delivery? Did that Cop tell Cecile about her Ex running dope to a queer bar?"

Jay decided on the spot not to tell Martha about his escapade but to ponder the questions for future response as Martha advanced his cause. "Deni, I'm off the stuff I hope for life. I don't want any more to do with it. I'm sober and intend to stay that way. I admit that I'm habitual and will need a lot of help and support to stay clean but I'm gonna do it. It's like a disease that can't be cured but only controlled. I'm gonna control it. It's not going to control me anymore."

The three sat in silence. Martha's eyes filled with tears as she reached across the table and put her hands over Jay's clenched fists. Jay sat slumped with his head down and eyes closed. Susan sat wide eyed with her mouth open as if she had just had the shock of her life. In fact, she had just received the shock of her life. She was firmly convinced that Jay's daily trek to St. A's was simply a front to dodge the obnoxious pressure from the docs who wanted him on the wagon. She thought that as soon as he could ditch their action it would be back to party time. Now he had bought into their routine and was swearing off. This was serious if true. On the other hand, he might be playing out the magnificent hoax. Jay was a great actor. Could be that he was acting serious to build up Martha's confidence in representing him. Susan remained confident that Jay would repent his new-found ways as soon as the coast was clear. He would let her know when.

Martha saw the expression on Susan's face and decided that the evening conference was over. After a few minutes of silence, she stood up. "Susan, thanks for the hospitality. It's really nice to visit a family and relax. Benny and James are the cutest. Tell Benny that I'll try to make the all-star game."

Jay and Susan both stood as Martha was speaking and walked with her out to her car. Martha kept the conversation alive with small talk about the yard, neighbors, and the heat and humidity.

As she opened her car door Jay shook her hand, "Martha, thanks for everything. I'll call you when and if I ever get those papers from Cecile's lawyer."

Susan nodded her agreement with Jay. Martha closed her car door, opened the door and started the car while making a parting comment. "Well I'm certain that the two of you will be served by Monday night at the latest. They usually don't deliver legal documents on Saturday or Sunday. Don't be shocked at what they say. Remember the other side has to make the case. We defend. I'm not worried. Don't you be worried."

After Martha left Jay and Susan walked into the back yard and sat together on the swing. Jay put his arms around Susan and held her close. She returned the embrace with a kiss. Their evening ended in love. The weekend had begun.

Jay got up early on Saturday and drove to St. Anslem's. It was raining and cool so he really didn't mind the imposition on his time in the yard. If it wasn't for this hospital thing he would be sitting around the house bored stiff waiting for the rain to stop. He parked his car in one of the free out-patient parking spots next to the doctor's office building and casually walked in the hospital's main entrance. The hospital was routinely quiet on Saturday. Ambulatory service was about half the volume of a weekday and in- patient occupancy was about forty percent of capacity. General staff on weekends was reduced to the minimum. Everything was slow and easy.

Jay remembered the hospital week end drill well from his days in the cath. lab: Check in early. Tidy up the lab and the lab office. Make sure everything is set for the occasional emergency. Do the odd jobs scribbled on the note pad by the supervisor. Check the battery in the beeper. Let switchboard know that the lab was on stand-by. Head for the cafeteria for donuts, coffee, and to place a bet.

Placing a bet in the cafeteria was one of St. Anslem's unusual qualities that set it apart from just about any other hospital in Boston. It was not, however, a featured service of the institution since only the rank and file employees were aware of its availability. Administration seemed to be in the dark about the little man who sat in the cafeteria every morning except Sunday from seven to nine reading the sports page from the Herald. He nibbled on a donut, slowly drank: his coffee, and had an occasional conversation with the hospital employee who would make a brief stop at the table and chat about the prospective outcome of the Bruins, Patriots, Celtics or Red Sox. He wore a Boston College cap that served as his advertisement. Indeed, the BC Eagles were the focus of his enterprise. He, as a special service to his established customers, would scalp tickets to the big games such as Notre Dame or Michigan.

Jay, while employed at St. Anslem's, had used Tommy the Tout on several occasions and at one time found himself seriously in Tommy's debt. When he became delinquent on payment a rather large muscular patient transporter took a few minutes of his time to explain to Jay that Tommy expected prompt payment and that Jay should perhaps borrow the necessary funds to cover the debt otherwise he might have a sudden accident. Jay got the message and mooched the money from his Dad. Tommy was impressed with Jay's immediate response and from that day forward held Jay in high esteem.

The thought about his old friend Tommy caused Jay to amble into the Cafeteria for a cup of coffee and donut before checking into SACAP. He was still early and Saturday was casual time. Not surprisingly, Tommy was on his perch with the Herald spread on the table before him. Jay paid the cashier for the donut and coffee and took the table directly across the aisle from Tommy.

Without looking up Tommy greeted his old friend, "Jay, how you doing? Looks like the Sox are on a run. They win 'em both this week end and they are in third place. Looks to me like they got a good shot at it. What do you say?"

Jay was practically knocked off his chair by Tommy's comments. He hadn't seen Tommy for nearly eight years since he had graduated from UMass. The fact that he remembered Jay's name was remarkable. Before responding Jay picked up his donut and coffee and moved to Tommy's table for a chat. Just like he had done many years ago.

"Tommy how in the hell did you remember my name? Man, that's remarkable."

Tommy liked the praise but decided to be humble, "Not so remarkable, Jay. You remembered my name. Why? Because we had dealings that left a lasting impression. Some people you never forget."

Tommy never looked up from his newspaper as he spoke. Jay stared at the unseen face and pondered the remark about Cecile's cop before he answered, "Tommy, Cecile and I couldn't make it work. Happens to a lot of couples. That cop is better for her. Seems to be more her type."

"Yeah, well maybe so," commented Tommy, "You know I do some business with the boys over at the Precinct and the talk I hear is that he's a switch hitter. Maybe he should play for the Sox. You want any action?"

Jay noticed that Tommy looked up when he mentioned action. "Not today, Tommy. I'm just passing through. Got an appointment in a few minutes. I'll be back and we can chat some more. Maybe you'll give good odds on BC making it to the Sugar Bowl"

"Don't laugh. They been there before. See ya around, Jay. Stop back when you got time"

Jay walked toward the SACAP Unit thinking about his conversation with Tommy. He realized that the Hospital cafeteria was the universal communication center for all things personal and private. Talking to Tommy was a mistake he thought, "If he mentions the conversation to an employee who mentions it to another eventually the whole world will figure out that ol' Jay is in SACAP working off a drunk. Nothing is confidential among hospital types just like nothing is confidential among cops. Put the two together and nothing is sacred. Pretty soon Cecile will hear from her hubby that I was at the Troubadour and she'll tell him that I'm on junk then the two of them will throw me in the slam and take away my kid,"

Jay's depression was beginning to mount when he checked into the Unit. It climbed another notch when he was told by the nurse that Bob Markley had the week end off. Another counselor would work with him today. She gave him his morning medication that he took reluctantly. A lab tech obtained the usual specimens and disappeared down the hall toward a room with a screaming patient going through initial detox. Jay wondered if he had made such horrible sounds. The nurse informed him that Dr. Kenneth would be making rounds in about a half hour. She suggested that Jay rest in a room assigned for his use today. Instead he opted to walk up and down the corridor while he continued to ponder his awkward predicament involving Officer O'Sullivan.

There was something wrong with the picture that he couldn't figure out. Gradually he began to realize that Tommy, with reason or not, was sending Jay a message of some kind. Jay's mind was spinning as he tried to reason the situation, "What was it he said about Cecile's cop? He's a switch hitter! The guy is half gay maybe even full time. Yeah. OK. What about it? Was he in the Troubadour for business or pleasure or both? What if the guy is a gay user cop? Man, that's heavy. So could be that he's as scared of me as I am of him. That so, then he ain't gonna say nothing to Cecile. I'm safe."

The thought of being off the hook with Officer O'Sullivan gave Jay a boost out of his depression so he thought. Actually, the medication he had taken a few minutes before was more of an assist. He began to put a little bounce in his step as he paced in front of the nursing station. The nurse made a clinical note about his obvious change in attitude. Jay started another lap around the Unit as Dr. Kenneth came through the door. He greeted Jay but made no attempt to interrupt the wandering soul. Jay was actually humming a song as he returned Dr. Kenneth's greeting with a wave. Kenneth was pleased with Jay's demeanor. It Action with the positive progress notes in his medical record. It seemed possible to Dr. Kenneth that Jay would escape from Phase one of his detoxification in another day and return to work on Monday in reasonably good shape. He reviewed the Nurse's notes on the record and followed her comments with his own entry about Jay's progress. Just as he completed the daily entry Jay rounded the comer in front of the station. Dr. Kenneth flagged him down and invited him to go to his office for a chat.

Dr. Kenneth sat at his desk. Jay was hyped and chose to stand. He continually rocked back and forth as the good Doctor talked to him, "Mr. Marquart, you have made steady progress over the past few days. We note that your depression and anger have become more controlled. The medication that we have been using is having the right effect. You're a little manic right now so we will have to make some adjustments in the dosage. If we can keep your chemistry in balance you will have a much better chance of building your will power to stay clean. Congratulations. You seem to be on the way to recovery. We'll watch you for a few more hours today then you can go home early and enjoy the rest of the day with your family. You haven't seen much of them this week. Tomorrow will be a short day as well. We want to give you some more medication. If the dosage seems right then you can go home. Monday it's back to work. Bob Markley will set you up with the right amount of support for your continuing recovery. You'll check in with us once a week for a while then you can fly on your own and just call when you need help."

Jay listened to Dr. Kenneth and was recalling his conversation with Martha the night before at the same time. The prospect of being out of the daily clutches of the Unit was excellent. Being on his own was trouble. Martha had warned him that screwing up in public would void his Federal protection. He knew that he was still very attracted to the "stuff'. Markley understood the problem. Jay wanted Markley at his side. He wanted his freedom but he wanted help. He suddenly realized that he was beginning to act like a recovering addict. He was not the same belligerent that broke up the place a few days ago. He had developed respect for the very people who he had ridiculed. Had he inadvertently taken that first step that Markley had talked about? If so he didn't remember taking an oath or pledge that put him officially on the wagon. Dr. Kenneth was great but he was no junkie. That was for sure.

Jay wanted to talk about this with Markley before he stepped back into the cold cruel world and Action Waste Management. He tried to explain this to the Doctor, "Dr. Kenneth, I appreciate all that you and the nurses have done. I feel pretty good right now. Staying off the stuff ain't going to be easy. I know that. I told you when we first met that I didn't want to take drugs to help with my recovery. I still feel that way. That medication messes me up. I need to be able to work things out in my own mind. I'll come in tomorrow for my last dose. Let's see what happens without any drugs after that."

Kenneth sensed that Jay was trying to escape, "Jay, going bare is a mistake. Your chemistry is still subject to wide fluctuations that could cause you severe depression and violent behavior. We want you to avoid that."

"But you said that I made good progress. Hell, I haven't busted up a thing or anybody for a couple of days now. You think I'm bye Phase one. So let's go with the flow"

"There could be a relapse," commented Kenneth "you know, an overlap between the Phase one and Phase two cycles. These things aren't exact. If you insist on going bare then we will probably have to double or even triple the usual support base. You up to that?"

Jay gave an emphatic nod, "Whatever it takes. But no drugs. Where's Markley? He's never around when we need him. He ought to be in here holding my hand. Seriously, I want to talk to him about this before I go back to work on Monday. Is he available?"

Dr. Kenneth thought for a while before he answered. As he pondered Jay's question he slowly shook his head from side to side in a negative fashion. "Bob Markley, for, ah, personal reasons has been given every week end off. He takes call but doesn't come in except for extreme emergencies. I know how to reach him so I'll call him tonight and try to arrange for him to meet you tomorrow. When you check in tomorrow we'll let you know the arrangements. You coming in after Mass?"

The question caught Jay off guard. He hadn't been to Mass since he graduated from the eighth grade. He gave Dr. Kenneth a look that caused the learned man of science to blush. "Yeah, right, after Mass. I'll see you about ten. OK?"

Jay escaped the confines of St. Anslems at noon. He arrived home in time to join Susan and the kids for lunch. On impulse, he called Cecile's in an attempt to talk to Kristie and to arrange for her visit on Sunday evening. Cecile was not in but Michael O'Sullivan obligingly gave Kristie the phone to talk to her Daddy. The conversation centered on her many activities of the week that included swimming, dance lessons, and a visit to a pre-school that Kristie had attended. Daddy reminded her that she was coming to Daddy's house for dinner Sunday evening. Kristie seemed excited about the event. At Jay's request, Michael got back on the line to talk about the arrangements. Michael explained to Jay that Kristie would be at Cecile's parents on Sunday for a visit and Jay could pick her up there at five PM. The arrangement was fine with Jay as long as he didn't have to spend time chatting with Cecile's parents. That was always a painful experience. Jay completed his conversation with the man of the house and hung up. He had been tempted to make some small comment about the Troubadour but could not find the right approach. Afterwards he was relieved that he had not opened the subject. More research on the mysterious Michael O'Sullivan was definitely in order.

Susan seemed to be in a rare sullen mood. She appeared cool toward Jay but attentive. Her facial expressions signaled Jay that something was amiss. He took special care to show extra affection to her as he sought out the cause of her suspected malady. Susan recognized Jay's very obvious attempt to communicate with affection. This was a pleasant change in his usual disregard. She decided to nurse him along and get the most mileage out of his affectionate maneuvers. After a while of being exceptionally nice Jay seemed to tire of the effort. The sun was breaking through the clouds and the temperature had risen to near normal. The grass was still too wet to mow but the driveway was dry enough for some hoops. Jay dismissed his attention to Susan and joined Benny and the basketball, Susan nevertheless enjoyed the past hour stringing him along. She also knew that she had him hooked for the rest of the day. He was set to be her obedient servant.

By late afternoon the skies had completely cleared. It was going to be a beautiful evening but a little on the cool side, a definite reminder that September was less than a month away. The usual backyard cook out with Brian and Louise was right on schedule. The party couple had arrived exactly at five. Brian and Jay had enlisted Benny and James for a two on two basketball game while the charcoal in the old Webber began its progress to white hot. Brian would break out of the game now and then for a quick sip of beer. He hadn't given any notice that Jay was sipping an ice tea carefully placed near the grill.

Inside Louise and Susan sat at the kitchen table chatting about Jay's recent illness. The standard tall gin and grapefruit was placed in reach as they conversed while preparing salad and side dishes. Louise opened her hand bag to show Susan the small bag of cocaine that Brian had supplied for a late-night sniff. Susan was pleased to see that the usual party was in the offing. Her concern was that Jay in his new temperate mentality would deny the recreation to the rest of them.

She felt a need for reinforcement that caused her to talk to Louise about Jay. "Louise, I'm worried about Jay. You know that he went back into the hospital for two days and has been going in for treatment every day this week?"

Louise was taken back by Susan's concerned expression. After a deep breath she responded to Susan, "Brian mentioned that Jay had to go back in on Monday. Jay told him about it the other night. Is he really sick? How serious is this, Susan?"

Susan laughed at the question and tried to imagine the seriousness of sobriety. "Oh, Louise, he isn't going to die or anything like that. He's decided to go sober. I mean he thinks that he can quit booze, pot, coke, and whatever just like that. I can't believe it! I mean how am I going to live with him in that condition? I don't know how to handle this"

Louise closed her handbag before she responded, "Well knowing Jay you won't have to live with it for long. He'll have his nose into the candy tonight I bet. We both know that Jay and Brian have been using since they were thirteen maybe before. They won't quit. Jay especially. He's got to have a mighty big reason to keep him sober. I mean a mighty big reason."

Suddenly Susan's sense of humor disappeared. She appeared to have tears in her eyes. "Kristie is the big reason, Louise. He's doing it for Kristie. Cecile is taking him back to court on custody. Jay thinks that she is going to convince the judge that he's a drunk and an unfit parent. Jay is determined to stay sober to keep Kristie. I don't understand it all but Martha tells Jay that he's got to stay out of trouble or the kid is lost. I want to help him, Louise, but I'm not a drunk. Why should I have to give it up?"

Louise took Susan's hand in sympathy, "Did Martha say you had to give it up? How about Jay? Did he ask you to go sober? I don't think you have to enter into this do you?"

"Oh, Louise I just don't know." Susan's depression increased, "I don't want something like this to come between us. It shouldn't matter if I have a few drinks. Jay can stay off it. I'll even help him if I can. I love him. But you got to remember that I've been using since I was thirteen too. We were in the same class."

The conversation was interrupted by the sudden ring of the telephone. Susan answered it immediately. Bob Markley was calling for Jay. Markley was a familiar name to Susan. Jay had mentioned his new friend to her several times during the past week. Hearing his voice made her feel like he had been listening in on the conversation she had been having with Louise. She almost made a comment about him not taking her seriously but managed to simply extend her greetings with the comment that she had heard Jay mention his name. Bob responded with the hope that would have the opportunity to meet in the near future. Susan gave a polite response and asked Bob to please hold until she could call Jay to the phone

Jay came quickly to the phone as Susan announced that Mr. Markley was holding.

The two ladies noticed Jay's relieved expression as he greeted the caller. Jay, noticing their intense interest in his conversation, moved out of the kitchen to the living room stretching the phone cord to its maximum length. After thanking Bob for calling he unlaced a barrage of criticism about his goofing off on week-ends.

Then in a conciliatory manner Jay got to the point, "Bob I appreciate you getting back to me. You see Kenneth says that I can go back to work on Monday. That's great except he wants me to stay on the meds. I think that stuff messes me up and I don't want to be screwed up at work. So he says that I can stay off the meds if we can triple the support. Hell, I don't know how we can do that. I figure I got to talk to you about it. You got time tomorrow?"

Markley seemed to hesitate before he answered, "Sure Jay, we can get together and talk about it. The support that you will require is not all that time consuming. It just requires that you get help at the first sign of pressure rather than trying to tough it out. You partying now?"

"Yeah we got some people in. No big deal. Why?"

"Well I imagine that some of you are having a few drinks and such. As the night goes on you will feel like having a belt or two yourself just to join the fun. That leads to trouble. I don't know how long your friends have been with you but if they have started drinking you are already experiencing pressure. If not right now then in a little while. So what Kenneth was saying is rather than wait for the urge to down a few, you use your will power when you expect pressure and call for support. I thought that maybe you were calling for help now."

Jay was impressed with Markley's ability to understand what was going on, "Yeah in a way I am. This action will go on for a while. Ice tea won't make it past dinner, then I'll look to kick back. But you got me peeing in a bottle in the morning so I'll stay off the stuff. It's not much pressure—just a little."

Markley moved to conclude, "Well if you think you are in trouble later on give the Unit a call. There's someone on duty that can help you. If you need me they can reach me. Otherwise I'll see you at St. A's about ten. OK?"

"Yeah that's OK. Ten is fine." Jay tried to lighten up the conversation, "Gives me time to go to Mass like the Doctor ordered. You going to Mass?" quipped Jay.

Markley was quick in reply, "Sure thing my man. See ya at ten sharp. Don't be late."

Jay pushed the disconnect button and walked back into the kitchen to replace the phone in the wall mounted cradle. It was obvious by the look on Louise's face that she had heard his part of the conversation. Susan was standing by the kitchen counter preparing some vegetables. Jay stared at Louise for a brief moment to register his dislike for her eavesdropping, then gave Susan a sharp slap on her behind as he moved out the door to rejoin the basketball game. He felt rejuvenated. The party would be the same and he would have a good time without the need of a buzz. "Let the good times begin" he thought.

The party followed its usual format. The steaks were done to everyone's preference by a sober chef. Brian swilled his usual eight beers waiting for the food. After each one he offered to bring one to Jay as he opened the cooler for another. Jay's constant refusal did not make an impact until he began asking Brian to run into the kitchen for a refill of his ice tea. After a second trip Brian asked if Jay was on the wagon. When Jay answered yes, Brian took it as a matter of the moment and hardly let it register.

However, both Susan and Louise were carefully monitoring Jay's actions. Neither one mentioned it during the dinner. They were preoccupied with getting the kids fed and after a while directed to a shower and bed. By the time the ladies returned to the picnic table Brian was well past sobriety and Jay was still nibbling on a piece of Susan's chocolate cake. The two women had been on a constant intake of gin and grapefruit for the past three hours and were sharing a nice glow. As was customary at this hour on a Saturday night Louise opened her purse and put the little bag of white powder on the table. She opened it carefully and stretched the lines to accommodate the consumers. Brian immediately inhaled the first line. Susan followed and then Louise. Jay sat at the table and watched the action. He leaned toward the remaining line then stood and walked to the opposite end of the table. Susan followed him and gave him a loving hug and kiss. She felt him tremble and saw that he was sweating. In spite of her now heavy jag she recognized his need for compassion and understanding.

Louise recognized the situation and placed the cocaine into her purse. Brian saw that Jay was abstaining so he began to inhale the remaining line. Louise gave him a quick jab in the ribs that caused Brian to suddenly realize that the party had experienced a mood change. "What's going on?" was his flustered reaction to Louise. Then he saw Susan holding Jay as she helped him sit down. "Jay getting sick again?" was Brian's second question that went unanswered. Susan sat next to Jay. Louise steered Brian onto the bench across from them.

Jay regained his composure and spoke to Brian, "Brian I'm feeling better now. I was hurting a few minutes ago because I'm on the wagon and I desperately wanted to take a sniff with you all. But I ain't going to 'cause I got to test clean in the morning. I'm hooked on dope. Hell, I guess we all are. But I got to get clean and stay that way or I stand a chance of losing Kristie. Can you dig that?"

Brian blinked and put his hands on his head. "Wow, yeah I can dig that. How is Cecile gong to bust you, man? You got rights. Shit, she can't just walk in and take the kid. She's got to go to court, man. How they going to know that you been flying? Shit. She messed with you and I'll have Eddie bust her ass. Shit!"

Brian's expression of support was refreshing to Jay. All evening he felt that he was being criticized for attempting to stay sober. He extended a high five to Brian who responded with a double grip. Jay was pleased that he had his friend's moral support if not his understanding.

Jay gave Brian a nod and commented, "Brian, my main man, I'll need you to carry me through this. I don't know if all this is really necessary. Last Saturday you and Louise carried me to the hospital when I was in a world of hurt. Tuesday the same thing. Now I feel fine but the doctor tells me that if I keep hittin it I'm gonna bust. I think I got to stay clean for a while till my insides get better than I can go back on if I stay low. You know, kinda nice and easy. Cecile is serving papers that say, I guess, that my boozing and partying is a danger to Kristie. That way she can take her away from me. I ain't gonna let that happen. I got to stay completely clean till the legal stuff is resolved. You dig? Hey, man, you been back to the Troubadour and see those dudes you met last Monday?"

Jay's sudden interest in the Troubadour crowd escaped Brian. He was more intent on his friend's struggle to retain the partial custody of Kristie. "Jay, man, you got whatever help I can give. That Bitch, Cecile, worked me over good at St. A's. Hell, I was only there trying to do my job. She yelled at me like I was some scuzz or something. Man, that broad has a big problem. Somebody got to take her out. Maybe Eddie's got an idea. You want I should ask him?"

Susan listened to the conversation in silence until Eddie was mentioned. She stood, walked in front of Brian and proceeded to get in his face. "Let's keep things in proper perspective, Brian my good fellow. Eddie has two sons that have a pretty good life right now without him around. We don't need his help and we certainly don't need to be in his debt. You have to work for the bastard and you have my sympathy. I'm free of him and I want to keep it that way. I have custody of my kids. There's no way I want him to even think of getting next to them again. Keep him out of our family affairs!'

Jay put his arm around Susan's waist and pulled her back from Brian while giving her an affectionate hug. He felt her relax. She was on a heavy jag that caused wide emotional swings. Jay realized that it was time for the party to come to hopefully a peaceful end. "Yeah Brian. Susan's right! We don't need Eddie to get involved. I think I got Cecile anyway. She screwed up big time last week. I can't talk about it now 'cause the lawyers got to work it through. We're in good shape. Hey I really appreciate the way you all are backing me on this. Things will be back to normal in a few weeks. What do you say we call it a night? I got to meet a guy in the morning."

Louise was pleased with Jay's suggestion that the party end. She had been uncomfortable with the affair since she first learned of John's intent to remain sober. In her own mind, she harbored a fear that he would in some way influence Brian to change his ways. In a protective way, she put her arms around Brian and expressed her concern that Brian needed his rest after a long day making special trips for Patriot. She properly avoided mentioning that Brian was making the trips at Eddie's direction.

In custom with their usual routine the two couples busied themselves cleaning up the back yard, putting things back in order, and taking the remaining food back into the kitchen. Usually the cocaine had been consumed on previous Saturdays. This time Louise opened her purse and placed the half-used bag on the kitchen counter. She then asked Susan if she wanted the remainder since Jay had always split the cost with Brian. The leftover was rightfully Jay's since he was the only one who didn't take a sniff Susan was grateful to Louise for making the offer. She took the small bag and placed it high and deep in a kitchen cabinet.

When the cleanup details were completed Brian and Louise bid their farewells and left. Jay and Susan sat in their living room completely exhausted. It was eleven thirty and time for bed, nearly four hours ahead of the usual Saturday night schedule.

oOo

Sunday morning at Mass Joe Durant followed his wife back to their pew after receiving Holy Communion. His mind repeated the standard prayers of thanksgiving and praise. He knelt in the pew with his head bowed in the same fashion that he had been taught by the good Sisters when he first received this Sacrament over fifty years ago. The peaceful meditation quickly bounced his mind back to the St. Anslem's fiscal crisis and political reorganization that he had been concentrating on all morning. As the Priest descended the altar to give the final blessing, Joseph Durant was damning the stupidity of the terrific trinity of Hardly, O'Shea and Patello and the inflated ego of one Dr. Richard Folley. He thought of the open warfare between his two vice presidents on Friday afternoon with the resolve to kick them in the butt if it happened again. His anger was at a flash point as the Priest, servers, cantor and lecturer processed from the altar to the back of the Church in the concluding act of the service. Indeed, Joseph Durant had fulfilled the obligation of the faithful to attend Mass on Sunday but his attention was at best divided between matters spiritual and temporal or perhaps moral and immoral if subject to penitential reflection. He felt the subtle nudge from his wife signaling time to leave the pew and depart the Church.

The warm sun felt good after the overly cooled air-conditioned Church. It was a typical failing of New Englanders to run the air conditioning at full blast when the temperature outside hovered at the seventy-five degree mark. "They don't know heat," Durant thought, "Cold they know heat they don't. They put in air conditioning and think it's going to make it snow in August. They should spend a summer in Cincinnati."

As he walked by the elderly Priest greeting the parishioners on the way out of the Church, Durant was tempted to complain that the Church was too cold. However, the good nature of the Priest gave him pause to reconsider. He decided against the complaint and moved to his car parked across the street. His wife had preceded him to the car and was waiting for him to unlock the doors. He saw her waiting and pushed the unlock button on his security case. The double beep of the alarm system caused his wife to jump and then to give him an angry look as she opened the door. That look was his first humorous event of the day and caused him to focus on the freedom and relaxation of a beautiful Sunday. After he slipped behind the wheel he lowered the windows on his BMW to enjoy the refreshingly warm breeze. His wife promptly raised the window on her side.

Ten O'clock Mass was too late for Joe. By the time Mass was over and they returned home it was almost Noon. Mrs. Durant would fix some brunch and proceed to read the Sunday Globe. Joe's preference was to go to the earliest Mass possible, run home, change clothes, and buzz down to the Marina. Joe loved to spend time on his twenty-eight-foot Carver cruiser. An early start gave him time to set up the electronics, tinker with whatever needed tinkering and shoot the breeze with adjacent boat owners. Unfortunately, his routine on this Sunday was restricted due to his wife's insistence that they attend ten o'clock Mass. By the time they got through brunch, read the paper, and drove the three miles to the Marina it was nearly two PM. Another hour of tinkering put him out of the Marina on a cruise of Boston Harbor as other boats were returning. To be running against the trend was frustrating to Durant and caused his emotions to begin to peak. Besides the late hour of the afternoon signaled his physic to begin to prepare for the usual intellectual combat that a hospital administrator experiences as the week begins.

As they returned from their afternoon cruise Joe's mind was dealing with the problems of St. Anslem's. He was making an approach to the Marina's gas dock to refuel and miscalculated his speed. The Marina's dock hand made every attempt to signal Joe to back down and then to slow the boat with his own weight on the line that Joe's wife had passed. Joe came too just as his cruiser began to climb the stern of an ancient blue Sea Sprite tied up at the forward pumps. He immediately reversed both engines but not in time to avoid giving the old boat a bump sending its owner over the windshield onto the bow. Dockhands successfully secured both boats without further incident.

The owner of the Sea Sprite crawled off the bow of his boat and onto the gas dock. He began shouting at the dockhands who seemed willing to take his wrath. Suddenly he turned to Joe and began calling him everything but human. Joe at first attempted to apologize but saw that the man was not about to be placated. Joe also noticed, as did everyone else, that the man was totally stoned. His threats and vulgarity caused the gas attendant to call the harbor master who arrived immediately. The Harbor Master somehow managed to calm the man and then suggested, since there was no apparent injury or damage to either vessel, that the two boat owners exchange names, addresses, telephone numbers, and insurance carriers as required by law.

Joe's wife had anticipated the information and had it prepared on one of Joe's business cards. The owner of the Sea Sprite grabbed a piece of scrap paper from the glove box on his dash and scribbled out the information that he handed to the Harbor Master who handed it to Joe. He looked at the information and found it barely legible but adequate. Then to his surprise he noticed that the man had written the information on the back of a delivery receipt for a package from Patriot Transport and

Courier Service that had a special thank you note on the bottom from Philip Mondi, President of Patriot and parenthetically a trustee of St. Anslem's Hospital. The package had been delivered on Friday by a special courier named Brian who had also signed the receipt. Joe thought he might get an insight on the man from Mr. Mondi at the Tuesday board meeting. Carefully he placed the information in his wallet.

oOo

Jay slept in Sunday morning. It was almost nine thirty when he jumped out of bed remembering with a start that he had an appointment with Bob Markley at St. A's at ten. After a quick shower, he dressed and jumped in his Jeep. Susan and the kids were at the breakfast table as Jay made his Dagwood exit. They waved to their disappearing Dad and accepted Susan's assurance that he wouldn't be gone long. Jay pointed the Jeep toward Brighton and hit the gas pedal.

He pulled into the out-patient free parking at ten fifteen, bailed out of the vehicle and ran to the Unit. The nurse at the station was unaware that Jay had an appointment with Markley. It wasn't on the schedule. She was also not aware that Markley was coming in. She was aware that he had not yet appeared in the Unit. Nevertheless, she invited Jay to be comfortable in the "lounge." She also offered to notify another counselor if Markley didn't show.

With his confidence in Markley beginning to slip Jay nursed his anxiety as he waited in the lounge. He had managed to beg a cup of coffee from the nurse at the station and was beginning to relax when he heard Markley greeting the nurse down the hall. A few minutes later he stuck his head into the "lounge" and invited Jay to meet with him in Dr. Kenneth's office. When they were both seated Markley offered an apology for being late but did not attempt any explanation.

Jay did not require an explanation but felt slightly offended that none was offered. He, nevertheless accepted the apology and began the conversation, "Bob, like I explained last night, Kenneth has released me to go back to work tomorrow and that's great. But he wants me to stay on the meds. I don't want any more of that shit, I got to go bare and he says that I'll need triple support.

"Right Jay." Markley was reassuring, "I talked to Dr. Kenneth last night. He feels that you are not completely through your detox. Something could trigger a violent response that you might not be able to control. You have a temper that gets out of control very easily. That's because you are an emotional guy. You love and hate to extremes. When you go on a hate you could hurt someone or someone could hurt you. The worst result is that you would seriously hurt someone that you love. Some guys have never come back from that kind of a trip."

Jay was not convinced, "Well I haven't lost it in a while. You know that I've taken all kinds of crap without bustin' anybody. You know I'm under control."

Markley was reassuring, "You're under control because you have been taking medication for the past six days. You have a buildup in your system that will carry you for an indeterminable amount of time. As that stuff wears off you will either go back on drugs and/or go crazy and hurt someone. Believe me. I've been there. We can't make you take the medication. You can do as you please. What Kenneth wants me to do is keep a real close check on you, like every couple of hours, to see if we can anticipate when you are going to crash. Then we send over a truck and haul you back in here for a dope job."

Jay was not amused, "So how is this supposed to work? You call me every couple of hours at work to see if I'm still among the sane and living. Suppose I ain't at my desk? Then What? You send over the dope mobile? People will think the place has turned into a trauma center. You got to come up with a better system."

Markley gave Jay a direct answer, "The best system is for you to take the medication. That way we can trust your emotions. Otherwise we have to keep you in a net. We don't have the high- tech stuff like cardiology. There are no Holitor monitors in our arsenal. Just plain old infantry is all we have. Here's what we can try. Your medication has been given once a day at around ten AM. You're just overdue. Suppose you take a dose now and another tomorrow morning before you go to work. Then I check on you tomorrow afternoon around three or so. If things are cool, then we try to get by Tuesday but I check on you throughout the day just to be safe. You take another dose on Wednesday and we try to stretch it out to Saturday. Gradually you come off the stuff in about two weeks."

"Ween me off is what you mean." Jay was adamant, "No way. I'll take a dose now like you want. Then we talk about it some more on Wednesday. If I'm still in good shape then we go another couple of days. You can call all you want in the meantime"

Markley was now on the defensive and looking for an out, "Jay I just thought of something. Suppose we do it like you just said except that you come to our support groups on Tuesday and Thursday nights. You take a little extra time to pea in the bottle like you do now. That way we can keep tabs on each other and maintain the emotional support therapy as well. Is it a deal? Think about it. You have the weekends free."

Jay heard the sound about the weekend. He was growing weary of the haggling over the medication. The meeting with Markley had not been as sympathetic as he had hoped. He was being pressured to continue a process that he wasn't convinced he needed. Yet he knew that the legal fight over Kristie would require him to have some demonstration of sobriety. Grudgingly he accepted, "OK, Robert, you got a deal"

Markley was pleased that Jay was willing to attend two support groups during the week. That was actually his goal in the first place but he had to get Jay to buy the idea. There was one other point that needed to be accomplished, "Good Jay. It's not the ideal method but it will do I suppose. You drive a hard bargain. Remember this is in your best interest. I don't get a damn thing out of helping you. You're just like any other drunk to me. You see it any different?"

Jay's anger peaked, "Don't get anything out of helping me! Markley, you hypocritical son of a bitch. You get off helping drunks and dopers. You need me and everyone like me. Man, you are so full of shit."

"Yeah, right," Markley fired back—"I really need you. You and this load of junkies. You think that you qualify as an addict? Man, you got to feel that hook before you know you're on."

Jay countered, "I'm on baby. I know that. I'll admit it. But I'll control it. Yeah, you watch."

"That's it" thought Markley, "The kid just said the magic words, 'I'll admit it'. Now if I can just get him to admit that he needs help to control it then he is on his way in the never-ending struggle toward recovery, Yeah"

The conversation between Jay and Markley lasted about a half hour. As they were completing their discussion Dr. Kenneth came in to make his Sunday morning rounds. Bob and Jay both reported the outcome of their conversation after which Dr. Kenneth gave Jay his last dose of medication. Then he wrote the appropriate note in the record authorizing Jay's return to work. The nurse on duty filled out the form for Jay to turn in to the EAP supervisor at Action Waste Management. The form stated that Jay had received treatment at St. Anslem's for a medical disorder and was now able to resume duties.

Markley gave Jay a schedule of the support groups that meet on Tuesday and Thursday evenings at seven PM in the hospital cafeteria. He explained to him that he could report into the Unit at six thirty and give his urine specimen before the meeting began. With sincere appreciation Jay shook Bob Markley's and Dr. Kenneth's hands and left the Unit to drive home. He turned into his driveway at about the same time that Durant arrived home from Mass.

Kristie was waiting on the front porch of her maternal grandparents at precisely five PM as scheduled. Jay drove the Jeep into the driveway and waved for Kristie to get in the Jeep. She ran immediately to the car but Jay had second thoughts. As she entered on the right-side Jay exited on the left. He went to the front door and knocked. Cecile's father answered after a brief wait. Jay explained that Kristie was in his care. He thanked the old man for having her ready. Cecile's father appreciated Jay taking the time to come to the door. He offered a cold beer to Jay and seemed to want to talk. Jay again thanked the man for his kindness but used the excuse that dinner was waiting for back home. He concluded the conversation with a promise to take Cecile's father fishing in the near future. With that finished he re-entered the Jeep and headed for Waltham.

When they arrived home, Susan had a well prepared dinner waiting. The Marquart family enjoyed the meal. Afterwards they played in the yard until dark. Susan supervised the baths and Jay read stories. When the right hour came, Susan put Benny and James to bed while Jay drove Kristie to Roslindale. She was in her Mother's arms by ten PM.

CHAPTER TEN

Summer haze destroyed the view of Boston Harbor as Charles Patello drove North on Interstate 93. The sun was barely visible as it appeared to rise out of the distant ocean in the east. In a couple of hours, the heat from the rising sun would dissipate the fog and give way to a clear warm day. For the time being motorists would occasionally use their windshield wipers to clear the damp fog. Headlights were on and speeds were moderate except for a few reckless souls seemingly in a hurry to begin the day's labor. It was only six fifteen in the morning but traffic was bumper to bumper caused by late week-enders returning to Boston for an early Monday morning start. Patello was on schedule, however, as he pulled off the Interstate at exit 19 and into the financial district. His office was only three blocks from the main traffic artery giving him easy in and out to the City.

The first order of the day was preparation for an important meeting with Frank Cappizi, Tony Marone, and Tom Callahan. The New York trio was due in on the shuttle from LaGuardia at nine o'clock. The time from Logan Airport to Patello's office was less than an hour in traffic which meant the meeting could begin before ten. Between now and then Patello intended to pull his extensive file of St. Anslems for review by Callahan, He would also make copies of special items like the work done by Hardly Security and Trust's planning wizards that justified the Office of Health Affairs for the Archdiocese.

Another item on Patello's agenda for the week was to further conversations he had over the week end with several prominent, wealthy individuals who held stock in Cambridge Banks. Patello spent most of Sunday in the locker room and bar of the exclusive Oceanview Country Club courting the ear of the investors. Everyone he talked to in friendly and informal conversation was attracted to the idea of merging the two banks held by the Hardly boys. Patello had offered to expand the idea with some initial fiscal analysis that he promised to provide in a very confidential way. Uncle Frank's idea had taken root.

Joseph Durant left his home in Hingham at six thirty and arrived at St. Anslem's at seven fifteen. He did his usual routine and then checked with his faithful executive assistant to be sure that Abbott and Costello, otherwise known as Daly and Weaver, would be in his office at exactly eight AM. She confirmed that both executives had been notified on Friday that the meeting was so scheduled. Durant became tense. He ordered his assistant to begin immediately to find the executives and make sure that they were on time. He was determined to make them disciplined.

Ken Ryan was in the shower at six thirty. He intended to be at his desk at Action Waste Management an hour ahead of his usual start time in order to prepare the day's work schedule. The Boston Project was in process. Boston Hospital had signed on Friday thanks to the enlightened Commissioner of Health, Michael Megan. Now the wandering intellect of Action's crack sales manager, His "Worthlessness", Mr. Veto Celi, was to be displayed at the President's office at St. Anslem's Hospital to explain the advantages of a waste management contract with Action. Considering that Mr. Celi was an expert in propositions that one could not refuse, it was a forgone conclusion by Mr. Ryan that he would have his staff actively engaged in the St. Anslem's contract by noon. Ryan intended to use Jay Marquart as the lead technician on the St. A's agreement.

By seven thirty Dr. Ron Anderson, Medical Director of SACAP, had reviewed the Medical Record of Jay Marquart. He had also studied the incident report clipped to the back of the chart. If anything, he felt that Bob Markley had understated the importance of the incident. Dr. Anderson asked his secretary to call Mr. Markley to come to his office for an urgent conference on the Marquart affair. He also asked her to invite Dr. Kenneth to the meeting. For the present time, however, he felt the matter should be restricted to the three of them.

Bob Markley came into the Unit just as Dr. Anderson's Office called for the meeting. The unit secretary handed him the phone. After he hung up, he informed the nurse that he was headed for the Big Office. On the way, he popped into the cafeteria for a cup of coffee and a donut. "Anderson wouldn't mind a twenty-minute delay en route" he thought, "he takes that long to come up with his next word." As Bob sat munching his donut he noticed the hospital chaplain having a conversation with Tommy the Tout. "Gezz, there goes the Mass card money." was his first reaction. Then he saw Tommy give the Priest some money. "My God, Father won!" was his second take. On his third glance, he noticed that Tommy held a Mass card in his hand. Obviously, Tommy the Tout had invested in the spiritual welfare of the dearly departed, most certainly one of his customers who hadn't welched. In Tommy's mind, he was covering the spread.

With renewed faith in God and man, Bob Markley finished his donut and coffee, took his cup and saucer to the dish conveyer, and walked to Dr. Anderson's office. When he arrived, the secretary ushered him into the office of his leader. Ron Anderson was a diamond in the rough. He hated administration but was a very capable administrator in his own right. That is to say he did things by his own rules instead of the rules of the institution. The Jay Marquart incident frustrated him because he couldn't figure out a resolution to the problem without using the standard administrative procedure for potential mal-practice claims. His reason for inviting Markley and Dr. Kenneth to a meeting was to see if the three of them could conjure up a better way of disposing of the incident.

As Markley entered his office, Anderson gave him a typical Anderson greeting, "Well pickled brain you got this one really messed up. What's your answer to this mess? What took you so long to get here anyway?"

Markley was accustomed to the gruff talk of Anderson. Indeed, it was his frank nature and direct approach that had contributed so well to Markley's road to recovery. After which Markley found that his own personality was a good match for Anderson. As a team, they had formed the SACAP program that was just beginning to be recognized by the medical staff as successful. Anderson had carefully selected community based primary care practitioners to be the medical staff in the Unit while Markley had carefully worked with nursing to develop the support staff. Dr. Kenneth was one of the first physicians to join the team. He had completed a medical residency at St. Anslem's several years before. During those years he was seen as one of the most promising physicians in his class and was elevated to the position as Chief Resident. In that capacity, he and Dr. Anderson quickly established a strong sense of mutual admiration that carried forward into his private practice.

As Markley was attempting to respond to Anderson's opening inquiry, Dr. Kenneth arrived. Kenneth greeted both men and immediately inquired about the nature of the meeting. Without saying a word Anderson handed Kenneth the Incident Report and Markley's notes. The three men sat in silence as Kenneth reviewed the information.

Kenneth completed reading the report and placed the information on Anderson's desk. As he did so Anderson began to offer his analysis, "This is the first I was aware that Jay was thinking of suing the hospital. He is somewhat difficult but manageable I thought. He never said anything to me about the conversation with his ex-wife. The fact that she works here is in the notes. Bob charted the incident when Jay broke up the lounge the first time. The record does note that he reacted following a telephone conversation. I didn't know that crazy telephone system was really the cause. It seems to me that the nature of this incident could cause the hospital a lot of trouble. There does not seem to be any basis for professional malpractice which would make this a general liability case. I guess the lawyers will decide that."

Markley nodded his agreement before commenting, "Jay signed into the program in an attempt to maintain confidentiality of his medical record. The hospital through its telephone system violated the patient's right to confidentiality. We screwed up plain and simple. I think the man has a good case that could cost the hospital big bucks but worse than that we could lose our Accreditation and Federal Certification. We lose that and there goes the revenue. Durant would close us down in a New York minute. Count on it."

"A couple of things come to mind," commented Anderson, "First I think there is a professional malpractice act by the patient's ex-wife. If she uses this information for her personal intent then she has violated her professional ethics and the ethics of the hospital as well. Secondly, I agree with Bob's observation that Administration would close us down. Even with our accreditation in good order, I'm being badgered to cut the program back to nothing in order to break even. A big law suit would take us off the board for good. Anybody have an idea how we can get around this?"

Anderson's two colleagues looked at one another in silence. This was the first time that either of them had ever heard their leader ask them for a way around an administrative problem. He was the one who always had a way of dealing with the issue at hand. He had never lost in an administrative contest of rules. Now it appeared that he was helpless in circumventing the incident.

After a brief period of silence, Kenneth made a suggestion, "This may seem reckless, Ron, but why don't we play it by the book. You know, send in the report through channels and let administration find a way out. Hell, we didn't buy the phone system. Durant and his band of merry men put the thing in. Nobody asked us if it violated patient confidentiality. My guess is that the hospital lawyers will do everything they can to avoid looking stupid as rocks. This thing will never get to court. How can Durant justify the stupidity of administration? If he tries to close us down as a cover up he really sticks his foot in it. I bet the lawyers will tell him to keep us going no matter what. This thing could really be our salvation."

Markley realized that it was his turn to speak. "Dr. Kenneth, if we do as you suggest then we are hanging a nurse out to dry. This thing will fall on her like a ton of bricks. It seems to me that a lawyer would reason that the telephone system, as faulty as it is, is inhuman and therefore incapable of violating confidence. Only a person can do that and the person who did it is a nurse in the employ of St. Anslem's. She has a reason for using patient information for her own intent. The hospital will have to defend her but only to the point that she violated the hospital rules. After that she is on her own. She could lose her license over this."

Kenneth felt uncomfortable defending his point considering Markley's comment. He gave a slight wave of his hands as a signal that the nurse was not his concern. Anderson caught the signal and decided to speak to the idea, "Bob, the nurse is responsible for her own actions and therefore her own defense. She is not a nurse on our Unit so we have no control of her actions. She is the one who committed the malpractice, allegedly. If we try to cover this matter then we become an accomplice to the act. I think Kenneth is right. Maybe we should do it by the book. That, at least, would throw administration. They hardly expect me to follow procedure. I might go one better than expected and bring this matter personally to the attention of Folley and Durant. I'll ask them both to meet with me on an urgent matter. That way I'll have them off guard. Just as soon as I get the meeting, I'll see that risk management gets the incident report at the same time so they can't blame me for hiding anything. On the other hand, once Risk Management has the report they have to process it so Durant can't cover it up by sticking it in my ear. I'll try to move this thing this morning. It'll make Folley's day."

Markley saw the lights go on. The Old Man was back in charge. He would blow administration away with the realization that their decision to install a stupid telephone system was the cause of a major problem that not only threatened the hospital's reputation but brought into question the professionalism and ethics of its nursing staff "Kenneth could be right," he thought, "this might be a blessing in disguise."

oOo

Mitch Daly walked into the President's office at seven fifty-five. He was always early. Rod Weaver by contrast was always late. Daly intended to make Weaver's delinquency evident by his early arrival. In his usual aggressive manner, he announced himself to the executive assistant and walked immediately into Durant's office acting as though he expected the meeting to be in session. Durant was still fusing to himself about Folley and at first tried to ignore Daly's presence.

Daly, detecting the cold shoulder, asserted himself into the Boss's presence by making conversation, "As usual Rod is late, Joe. If you like we can begin to discuss the planning process. I don't think Rod will be able to contribute much to the conversation anyway. That was pretty disgusting conduct on Friday. You handled it well. I made some calls on Friday and have some good advice on strategic planning. I have copies of my notes that we can go over anytime that you want."

Durant realized that he could not easily escape this conversation without throwing Daly out of his office. This would not only frustrate him but would cause more delay in developing a planning format for presentation at the Board meeting tomorrow morning. Since he did not want to start the meeting without Weaver, he decided to humor Daly until Rod made the scene.

Durant stood up and walked over to his office door. "You want some coffee, Mitch? I'm going to have some. That was a very unsatisfactory scene Friday. I hope you two have gotten it out of your system so we can have a productive session this morning."

Daly was relieved that the subject had been brought up. He was not the type who apologized but who always sought out the opportunity to rationalize his every action. He walked with Joe to the coffee pot in the reception area but did not accept the offer of the senior executive to pour him a cup of coffee. Instead he commented, "Joe, you noticed I'm sure that the confrontation was initiated by Rod's refusal to accept the need for a strategic plan developed by market analysis. He will not accept any data that he hasn't had the opportunity to massage into his own format I believe he refers to it as 'cooking' the facts. He does it every month with the financial statements. You know that. Well if we are going to have an objective planning effort I'll have to be put in charge of the data gathering and Rod will have to keep his hands off."

Durant was intent on keeping the team approach intact. He was not interested in excluding Weaver from the data. "Mitch, we can discuss the details of information at our gathering when Rod arrives. I'm sure each of you have sources that are unique to your position. I know, for instance that Rod has some very reliable data concerning the cost of operations in the various Boston teaching hospitals. I imagine that information will be very helpful. You have shown me market data and utilization reports for the entire State that we can incorporate in our analysis. I believe that both of you are vital to this project."

"But somebody has to be in charge" insisted Daly, "That corn fed accountant will procrastinate forever. I said Friday that we had to regain control. We have to move fast to compile a set of facts that are objective so we can formulate an objective plan. Creative accounting won't work in these changing times. You know that I'm right."

The two executives walked back into Durant's office and sat at the small conference table. Durant was thinking about how to respond to Daly's comments when the executive assistant came into the office and announced that Rod Weaver had called in to report that he was caught in traffic the Mass Pike. He estimated his time of arrival at ten AM. She also informed Mr. Durant that a Mr. Veto Celi of Action Waste Management was waiting to see him. She placed Mr. Celi's card on the table and left.

Durant had completely lost his concentration on Daly's suggestion. He was barely able to control his anger toward Weaver who should have left home earlier to avoid the usual traffic snarls on the Pike. This only tended to authenticate Daly's point about Weaver. It also meant that without Weaver the present meeting was a Daly benefit. It seemed to Durant that to continue the discussion with Daly was useless unless he was willing to put Daly in charge.

"On second thought" he concluded, "maybe if I give the lead to Daly, Weaver will be more responsive to protecting his turf and therefore more of a contributor to the process." With that in mind he responded to Daly. "Mitch, we are obviously not going to get much accomplished in the time we have this morning but I want to be prepared to give the Board a review of our planning process tomorrow. You put one together for me to review later this afternoon. If it looks OK then you can present it to the Board. I'll explain this to Weaver when he shows up."

Daly was elated with the charge. He immediately pulled an outline out of his briefcase and put it on the conference table. Durant waved his hand across his chest to cancel the move. "Mitch, I'm pressed for time right now. We can go over this later today. There's a gentleman waiting to see me and I guess a few others that are pressing the schedule. We'll talk about this later. Please excuse me."

The expression on Daly's face was reminiscent of a scolded child. He slowly retrieved the outline and placed it back in the briefcase. As he walked out of the office he reminded Durant that he had put him in charge of the process. He also reminded Durant that it was vital to the conduct of the strategic plan for Weaver to be subordinated. Durant had his orders.

As Daly left the office Durant collapsed in his desk chair. His emotions were about spent in one meeting trying to corral the slippery intellects of Daly and Weaver. Unfortunately, he had no choice but to continue the effort since the pressure caused by O'Shea, Folley and now Logan had to be offset by a dramatic counter move. He scribbled a note to call Patello before noon. As he moved the note pad next to his telephone his eye caught sight of a short burly gentleman with no neck and a flat bent nose standing at this desk.

When Joe looked up the man sat down and introduced himself. "Joe Durant, I'm Veto Celi with Action Waste Management. You probably forgot that I was here so I came on in. We got to talk about your waste. You got a problem."

Joe Durant felt the intimidation as it was offered. He also realized that this was no ordinary salesman. "Mr. Celi, I apologize about the delay. I had an appointment with a gentleman who just left and I was making a few notes. What is this problem about waste? St. Anslem's has a very satisfactory arrangement with the City for waste handling that we intend to keep in effect."

Veto leaned forward and placed a small plastic bag on Durant's desk. "Yeah, well you had an arrangement with the City. You got canceled this morning. No more waste handling. Here's why."

Celi popped opened the plastic bag and dumped the contents on Durant's desk. Several syringes, IV tubing, bloody bandages, and various pieces of paper with the St. Anslem's logo were spread before the hospital chief executive. "You see all this was found in your last load that was supposed to be clean waste. You ain't separating your trash right so the City ain't gonna haul it no more. We're gonna do it for you and we are gonna see that you do a good separation job. We'll take care of everything. No hassle. You sign now and we can have our guys on the job tomorrow. You got no worries. The press ain't aware of any of this cause the new Commissioner is looking out for the hospitals."

"More intimidation," thought Durant, "This thug has got a pair. He also has me by the trash if he is right about the City canceling the waste contract."

In response Durant attempted a counter bluff. "Mr. Celi, we have no information about this from the City. If they do intend to cancel our arrangement then they have to give us proper notice. I believe the contract calls for a sixty-day notice of cancellation. If we are to use a private service we would select the company on a bid basis. Your offer of immediate support is appreciated but I don't think it's necessary."

Veto Celi leaned back in the chair and rested his large folded hands on his portly expanse. "Durant, you got no contract with the City. They been doing the trash because of the Ordinance that got changed last week. Private companies are in the business now. The City can cancel who it wants anytime it wants. Now, you want to do business with someone else. OK. Find another Company that's ready to go. There ain't any. So, you haul your own trash, or let it pile up and face a big fine, or do business with us. You probably got called from the City on Friday. You take the day off?"

Durant was uncertain about Celi's comments. It was true that he had not seen a contract with the City for trash hauling. The subject had never come up before. The arrangement was taken for granted. If the City had called to cancel on Friday, a message would have been noted by the executive assistant or if the call came after hours it would have been registered on the voice mail system.

Durant tried to reason again, "Sir, I can assure you that I have not received any call from the City canceling our waste hauling agreement. As far as I know we still have the service."

Celi remained unmoved, "OK. Look maybe they talked to someone else. Who you got in charge of trash? They got a call I bet. You better check with them."

Without hesitation Durant hit the speed dial button for the hospital's chief operating officer. The COO was making administrative rounds when Durant called. However, the secretary in the office acknowledge that the hospital's Director of Environmental Services had been notified by the City just an hour ago that they had discontinued the waste hauling service. She also reported that the COO and the DES were going to meet in an hour to determine how to solve this crisis. Durant explained to her that he had the solution near at hand and asked that the two managers meet with him in his office at the scheduled time.

As Durant hung up the phone, Celi again propped himself on the desk, "You got the word like I said, right? Now we can do business. Here is the standard contract that you sign. We send in some people to do a special review then we write up the extras. You always got to have extras. Like I said, we can start today or tomorrow on a hand shake. You can trust me and I know that I can trust you. We gonna get along fine."

Durant took the contract from Celi's extended hand. He gave it a fast review and noted the unilateral advantage to the seller. The price was pre-printed in the contract as a base on which the extras would be added. The initial fee was thirty thousand dollars plus a monthly service fee of twenty-five thousand dollars. Before any extras were figured in the annual expense in the first year of the agreement was a minimum of three hundred and thirty thousand dollars. This was pure expense add on. No replacement of existing costs or revenue offset. The total amount fell right to the bottom line as another increase to the rapidly growing deficit. "Weaver would love this deal," he thought, "Just one more item to make the fiscal wizard an unhappy camper."

The irritation had to be evident on Durant's face. Nevertheless, Celi gave no solace. He, instead, pushed the point, "You want to talk it over with your people? OK. Call me this afternoon so I can arrange for a pick up in the morning. Like I said we can do business now on a handshake. That number on my card will go directly to Mr. Meehan's office. He's the big shot at Action. He tells me he knows you and the hospital. Anyway, he'll let me know when you decide. It's a pleasure doing business with you. I got to run along."

As Celi stood to leave he extended his hand to Durant. Joe was sensitive to Celi's prompting him to do business on a handshake. He doubted that this clod recognized the fine points of contract, but a handshake at this point was establishing a contract. Joe did not take Celi's hand but put his own hand on Celi's back and politely escorted him out of the office with the understanding that Mr. Durant would call Mr. Meehan's office with a response in the next few hours.

Rod Weaver had finally arrived and was chatting with the executive assistant when Celi walked out of the office escorted by Durant. As they passed, Weaver hastily moved into Durant's office and settled down. He had the up to date financial report spread out on the conference table when Durant returned.

"Boss, we went down another million five last month but I covered some of it with prior period adjustments," Weaver explained without looking up from the report, "We still lost over a million at the operating line and about three hundred thou bottom line. That's what I was working on this morning early. I figured you would want me to finish this instead of bull shitting with Daly."

Durant couldn't make up his mind on where to begin. His first instinct was to chew Weaver out for disregarding the directive to attend the meeting with Daly. He also had to find the appropriate way to tell Weaver that he had put Daly in charge of the planning effort. More pressing was the matter with waste hauling that was going to add over three hundred thousand dollars to the operating loss now projected at fifteen million dollars.

Durant chose to initiate the discussion about the waste. "Rod, we have been blessed with another challenge. It seems that the big change in City Hall last week not only gave us Mr. Logan but it also gave us three hundred thousand dollar increased expenses in the environmental services budget. We have, or are about to have, an exclusive agreement with Action Waste Management to haul our waste and manage our waste control. You have the assignment to find the money to pay for it."

Weaver remained calm, "The only way is to start cutting out programs that aren't self-sufficient. That means we have to take on the docs especially Folley. He pisses it away faster than anybody. Hey, isn't Action owned by one of our trustees. We can't do business with them. It's a breach of the conflict of interest regulation. You going to bring that up tomorrow?"

Durant looked at Weaver with shock, "Come on, Rod. The whole damn board is one big conflict of interest. We do our banking with Boston Security run by Hardly and O'Shea. Sr. Elizabeth and Bishop Hanks have spiritual equity and Dr. Folley earns his daily bread here, more or less. Now that Meehan is dipping in, that only leaves Patello and

Mondi without a piece. I bet if we look hard enough we would find that they have something going for them too. Best we don't look and I sure as hell am not going to raise the conflict of interest issue. I'll report the waste contract matter and see what happens."

Carefully, Weaver folded the financial report and placed it back in his briefcase, "Boss, three hundred thousand is going to look like a good deal compared to what I figure the Cardinal's Office for Health Affairs will cost. I estimate it at over a million dollars for salaries, wages, supplies and rent. We don't have that in the budget either. Two months of that will add another couple hundred thousand to this year to date deficit with only two months left in the fiscal year. Next fiscal year, starting in October, we predict another twenty percent drop in revenue. Something has got to give. We better let the board in on this disaster."

Durant was quick to reply, "Rod, I suspect that Mr. O'Shea will expand on that topic quite adequately. How Folley and Logan will react is beyond me. I do know that Patello is going to work with us in an attempt to regain control through the planning effort. That's what I needed you for this morning. Since you were engaged in other happier things like the deficit I told Mitch to take charge and develop the process. I'll see his outline this afternoon and he'll present it to the board with Patello tomorrow."

Weaver began to react but was cut short by Durant who moved to answer the phone. The executive assistant reported that Dr. Anderson was holding on a matter of urgency. He insisted that she interrupt the meeting with Weaver adding parenthetically that Weaver never had anything of substance to talk about anyway.

Durant excused Weaver, subject to recall later in the day, and took the call from Anderson, "Dr. Anderson, and good morning. What pray tell is of such great urgency that you would interrupt my discussion about the deficit to which you contribute so generously?"

Anderson accepted Durant's jab in good humor since he was often prone to taking a few good- natured shots at the President. "Joe, we have a situation in SACAP that could mean big trouble. I've filed an incident report but think that you, Folley and I should review this matter and decide how we keep it under control. It's either a big malpractice mess or gigantic general liability problem. Apparently Folley is available now if you are."

Durant's many years as a hospital administrator had sensitized him to malpractice and the delicate process of discovery so rigidly applied by plaintiffs' attorneys. He had often painfully collected all records pertaining to an incident in response to interrogatories and had sat for hours giving depositions or serving as witness at trial. If the incident that Anderson was reporting was as serious as it seemed then the meeting that he was asking for would eventually be discovered and subject to examination by the plaintiff. The only way to avoid having the meeting subject to discovery was to meet under the hospital's professional review and quality assurance process that was privileged from discovery under Massachusetts' law. Until that could be arranged Durant knew that it was best for him not to be informed or involved.

The Risk Manager at St. Anslem's reported to the Director of Professional Review and Quality Assurance who reported to the Professional Review Committee of the Board of Trustees. The President of the hospital served as a member of the committee but like all other members could not influence the agenda of the meeting. That method of organization assured that all incident reports regardless of nature or severity were reported and reviewed by the Committee. The only way an incident could avoid review was if it were not reported to risk management or if risk management omitted the incident from the committee report. In either case the individual responsible for the omission became personally liable. As a consequence, the risk management process at St. Anslem's was excellent. Conversely the quality of care at St. Anslem's was also excellent. The entire staff took great pride in the very low frequency of incidents and the very rare mal-practice law suits.

Durant was very curious about Anderson's incident report but did not want to violate the privilege process by having an impromptu meeting. Instead he offered an alternative approach, "Let's have your meeting, Ron, but do it under the auspices of the Professional Review Director. That way the meeting will be a part of his investigation that he will report to the Board Committee. If this thing is as hot as you say then we don't want to get caught outside of privileged communication. We have to keep it under wraps. OK? Now as far as a big rush is concerned, the Professional Review report for the Board is complete for tomorrow. The next full meeting of the Board is two months from tomorrow so if any Board action regarding the incident is necessary it will have to wait that long. In the interim, we'll have the insurance company involved and the lawyers and whoever else is necessary to keep it in control."

Anderson remained insistent but amiable toward the process. He, nevertheless, had to suppress his anger as he responded to Durant. "Joe, I realize the need to keep this thing privileged so if you want to have the Quality Director at the meeting that's OK with me. My only concern or I should say my greatest concern is that the people involved will be in a civil action that will bring us to the front in less than the two months it will take to get this to the Board. I don't think it matters if you report it to the Board tomorrow or not. What really matters to the hospital is our reputation that could be smeared all over page one. We have employees violating patient confidence. We have a goofy telephone system that does the same thing. We have a possible violation of Federal Law and our Joint Commission Accreditation at stake. Now, do you want to talk about this or not?"

Durant was not persuaded, "Ron for the second time this morning I have been given a proposition that I cannot refuse. I'll try to arrange something today or first thing tomorrow after the Board meeting. As usual, it's been a pleasure talking to you."

Durant hung up the phone and glanced at his watch. It was almost eleven thirty. In the past few hours he had been conned by one vice-president, snubbed by another vice-president, shaken down by a hit man turned salesman, told that the place was going bankrupt, and informed by a physician that the hospital had screwed up royally. All things considered it was a fairly typical Monday morning.

A brief walk in the summer air before lunch seemed like a smart idea. Durant waved to his executive assistant as he passed her door. Once outside his office he sensed the freedom to think. The walk around the hospital campus at noon always gave him time to reflect on the morning's events. The most important thing in his mind was the need to formulate a planning proposal for the Board. Daly had to be the front man, He knew that Weaver would be supportive in the meeting. Weaver in spite of his unusual character was loyal and a team player especially when the chips were down. He made up his mind not to attempt to change the spots on his two vice presidents at this critical time. The hospital's fiscal problem was certainly obvious to everyone on the Board. O'Shea could scream and holler all he wanted but it would not make a difference. It was curious how O'Shea could support the idea of an Office for Health Affairs if Weaver's projections were right that a million dollars were to be added to the hospital's expenses. Durant from Action Waste Management bothered Durant. One of the Hospital's trustees had apparently sent this goon over to break St. Anslem'ls leg. Since there was obviously no alternative for the hospital, it seemed that the approach could have been more subtle. He made a mental note to ask Meehan about it in the morning.

All things considered the Anderson matter seemed to be the least significant. He intended to ask the Director of Professional Review and Quality Assurance to pull the incident report and call a special meeting as part of his routine investigation. "No sense making it a Federal case just yet." he thought. "These malpractice matters take a long time to resolve anyway."

As he returned to his office, the executive assistant handed him a note to call Dr. Folley immediately on a very urgent matter. Durant's first inclination was to throw the note in the waste basket which he did. Talking to Folley was the last thing he wanted to do in view of the morning's events. As he began to read the day's correspondence the private line to his office lit up as the phone rang.

The private line by passed the executive assistant and was seldom used except in extremely important and highly confidential matters. Its main function was for out-going calls. Since in-coming calls was not the purpose of the extension, the number was not listed in the hospital's directory. To Durant's knowledge the number was known only by his executive assistant and his wife. Most of the time in-coming calls were wrong numbers. He casually lifted the hand set and said hello.

There was a pause before the caller reacted to the bland greeting "Hello! Is that how you answer your phone? You're supposed to be the chief executive officer of Boston's most prestigious Catholic hospital and you answer with a stupid hello. It's no wonder people have no respect for us. Did you get my message that I wanted to talk to you?"

Durant took a deep breath as a way of warding off the temptation to slam the receiver down. "Yes Dr. Folley I did get your message and I intended to call you at the first opportunity. How's Mrs. Folley and the kids? Well I hope. And does all go the same with you?"

"Durant don't hand me any of your smooze. Save it for the Nuns. They buy it. Where do you come off telling my Director of SACAP that you're not going to meet with me about the screw up in the Unit. Now let me tell you how it is. I'm not going to meet with you. No Sir! You are going to meet with me. For the record, the SACAP incident is a matter of concern to the Cardinal and his Director of Health Affairs. As Secretary to the Cardinal, I will conduct a personal investigation of this incident. You see to it that all the appropriate records are on my desk this afternoon. This is now Archdiocesan business. Your job is to serve the cause. Do you understand?"

Durant was totally disarmed by Folley's outburst. Carefully he tried to recover from the apparent emotion of the caller to a point of reason. "Look, Richard, I don't know what happened in SACAP except that Ron thinks it's serious enough to prompt mal- practice litigation. My response to Ron was in the interest of putting the discussions into a privileged forum. You might want to consult with the Archdiocesan attorney before you get too involved. Right now, the Cardinal is not likely to get sued but you could change that very easily. I'll have all the records dumped on your desk by this afternoon."

"No, I don't need the records as long as I have your report." responded Folley.

"You look into this thing and give me a report. I am a trustee of this hospital entitled to this kind of information when and if I want it. Just do it and report to me." Folley demanded.

"As you wish Herr Doctor. But if you want fast information why don't you act like a Department Chairman and talk to your Director of SACAP? Seems to me that you would be getting first-hand information rather than something I might edit. I'm sure Dr. Anderson would want to fill you in. You really don't need me in the conversation. I'll get involved when you need a solution to whatever the problem is."

Suddenly Folley was silent. The reality that he could be involved as the Chairman of the Department of Medicine had never occurred to him.

It was beginning to be evident that his many hats as Secretary of Health, Hospital Trustee and Department Chairman was confusing his already complex and gigantic ego. He was now caught up in the confusion and desperately needed to retreat.

The circumstance caused Folley to have a sudden mood change, "You make a good point, Joe. I'll talk this over with Ron. We'll keep our conversations off the record. You don't need to be involved at this stage. I'll call you if I need you. Thanks for returning my call."

With all the confusion surrounding the SACAP incident Durant forgot about the meeting he had requested with the Chief operating officer and the Director of Environmental Services. After he had finished his conversation with Dr. Folley the executive assistant advised him that she had delayed the COO meeting until he had a break. They were now available and waiting in the reception area. Durant asked them into the office and again the small conference table became the locus for decision making. In response to Durant's questions the DES advised that the City had canceled the waste hauling agreement effective at eight AM this morning. There were no other private waste management companies in Boston other than Action that was capable of handling hospital waste. And finally, the price was high but under the amount estimated for the hospital to handle its own waste disposal.

The Chief Operating Officer offered the concluding comment, "We have no choice, Joe. Let's take the deal and look for a way out down the line. As soon as Action gets some competition the price will become more reasonable. In the meantime, we pay through the nose."

Durant nodded in agreement. After the two executives left the office Durant called Action and confirmed the acceptance of the contract.

Mark Meehan wasn't in his office when Durant called to accept the Action offer. Joe was disappointed in not being able to attempt to negotiate some improvement to the arrangement. The need to get the agreement in place immediately caused him to give Meehan's secretary the message that St. Anslem's Hospital was now a customer of Action and that Mr. Durant would like to speak to Mr. Meehan about the contract terms. The Secretary took the message and, as previously instructed by Mr. Meehan, relayed the message to Mr. Celio. Celi just grunted and notified the back office that St. Anslem's was now an Action Waste Management Customer.

The back office at Action had been notified last week that the Boston project would start with hospital contracts at Boston Hospital and St. Anslem's. The Boston Hospital agreement came in on Friday and a project team had been immediately assigned. On Monday morning they had moved on site to begin to scope the project. St. Anslem's was expected to be in place on Monday so the back office was standing by waiting for the signal to begin.

Celi's call to Action's production manager triggered the first phase of the St. Anslem's project design. Kevin Ryan, as director of quality control for Action, had the assignment of doing an assessment of each project in the pre-design phase. The assessment was conducted by a team of waste management technicians who would go to the project site and completely review the existing waste handling methods and waste requirements. After the review, the technicians would present a list of recommendations for the project that Ryan would in turn present to the production manager who would send the project design to cost accounting who would determine the cost of the add-ons to the base price that also included the standard thirty percent markup. This final document would go to Mr. Meehan for signature.

Celi would not see the final contract. That was a confidential matter between Meehan and Muldoon. Meehan would add Muldoon's cut to the contract as part of the mark-up before letting Muldoon see the final price. When the customer signed the contract, Action gave Muldoon his ten percent and Muldoon would think about giving Celi a piece.

oOo

Jay Marquart returned to work Monday morning on time. He felt good but was uneasy about his reception in the office. His exit last Tuesday was a bit spectacular as he experienced the trauma of detox. To his surprise and comfort, he soon realized that only Ken Ryan and the EAP director knew the true nature of his illness. The others could only speculate and few seemed to be interested in the nature of the illness but many inquired about his health while welcoming him back. It was refreshing. Jay dug in to the unfinished work on his desk and was well on the way of catching up by lunch time.

When he returned form lunch Mr. Donovan, business agent for Local 936, was waiting at his desk. For the first time Jay felt the pressure that Markley had warned him about. Donovan had a cheery smile on his face when he greeted Jay, "Hey how are you feeling? Good to see you back on the job. You know I'm sorry to have to come here on your first day back but we are a little behind on getting this contract thing worked out. You know?"

"Yeah I'm OK. Good to see you too, Donovan." Jay was immediately suspicious, "What's the agenda. I'm still new at this you know. Only been in the Union a week and sick most of the time. Any connection?"

Donovan dismissed the humor, "No connection, Jay. The purpose of the Union is to make the workers well and whole at the same time. Best we get to it." Donovan opened his briefcase and placed a copy of the standard Union agreement form on Jay's desk. He explained each article to Jay and how each point was intended to benefit the workers. The distinction between the non-economic and economic issues were explained in a manner that began to detail the preliminary bargaining strategy.

Jay became fascinated with the information and the relevant process. Several times he interrupted Donovan to ask questions. Donovan tolerated the interruptions as a coach would accept strategy questions from a quarterback. The relationship between the two men was growing stronger. Jay though his fascination was rapidly becoming an advocate for the collective bargaining agreement. Donovan was a true labor pro who took note of Jay's attitude with growing pride.

Jay and Donovan had been in session for about an hour when Ken Ryan came by the desk and asked Jay to meet with him. Donovan courteously greeted Ken and acknowledged that he and Jay had about finished their conversation. Jay told Ken that he would be with him in a few minutes. As Ken left the desk Donovan continued the conversation by pointing out that a meeting of the Action union members would be held in a few days. At that meeting Donovan would explain the contract form to the workers. Jay's assignment would be to take special note of the questions asked and by whom. Then in the next few days after the meeting he was to circulate among the employees and get their opinions and answer their questions. Then, in a week or so there would be another meeting where Donovan would present a list of union demands that would be presented to management at the first negotiation session. Jay would be present at the negotiations and communicate progress to the employees. Donovan concluded the meeting by saying that he would keep in close touch with him over the next few days. Jay walked Donovan to the door and then returned to Ken's desk.

Ken seemed frustrated with the work load of the Boston project. Boston Hospital's administration was apparently not cooperating with the Action project team. Staff in the Environmental Services department had refused to take the project team on tour they were forced to undertake an unguided exploration of the mammoth institution to find the various trash collection points. Nursing personnel were equally uncooperative in giving time to the surveyors for review of the waste management processes in patient care areas. All things considered the first day of the Boston project was turning into a disaster. Action's production manager had called an emergency supervisors meeting to regroup the effort when it became apparent that the Boston Hospital staff was intent on sabotaging the program. As the meeting was in process the manager received word that St. Anslem's had accepted the Action proposal and trash pick-up and disposal was to begin tomorrow.

Ken Ryan was instructed to have a survey team ready to go to St. Anslems for initial analysis in the morning. Ken explained all of this to Jay before informing him that he was to be the lead technician on the St. Anslem's part of the Boston Project. Jay couldn't believe what Ken was saying. The lead technician would be required to spend two or three weeks at St. Anslem's in the design phase and another month on a part time basis helping with the implementation. He would practically be a member of the St. Anslem's staff again but with complete freedom to roam the house looking into every nook and cranny. Ken's main concern was that St. Anslem's waste management program be designed and implemented without conflict. He had selected Jay because he was knowledgeable about hospital routine and was acquainted with the staff at St. Anslem's. Jay seemed like the perfect choice to head the project. Ken was unaware that Jay intended to sue the hospital. Jay, on the other hand, felt that piece of information was not germane to the discussion so he didn't mention it to Ken as they discussed the St. A's program.

Neither Jay nor Ken was aware that Veto Celi had conned Durant into accepting Action's contract. No one except Durant and Weaver was aware that St. Anslam's could not afford to pay for all the good service that Action intended to provide. Ken and Jay decided to outline the study phase of the program for St. A's this afternoon and go over to the hospital in the morning to meet with the appropriate members of the hospital staff to discuss the project. Ken had asked Mr. Celi to arrange the meeting. So it was that Action's finest trash men, Ken Ryan and Jay Marquart, leaped into the fray confident of success.

After Jay had accepted the assignment Ken moved to another subject. He carefully inquired about Mr. Donovan's visit. Jay felt that the matter would soon be general knowledge when Donovan distributed the contract form to the employees so he filled Ken in on the process of negotiation that Donovan had described. He also mentioned that he was a member of the negotiation team. Ken commented that with Jay's assignment at St. A's and his Union position he was a man of dual status.

"Not bad for a drunk." Jay thought.

As Jay returned to his desk he received a call from the receptionist informing him that a gentleman was in the lobby who wanted to discuss a legal matter. Jay's first thought was that the person was a cop waiting to arrest him for drug trafficking at the Troubadour. When he asked the receptionist to tell the man that he wasn't in she said that he *was* aware that Mr. Marquart was at his desk and had asked permission to meet him there. Jay knew the day was going too well. Something like this was bound to happen. Suddenly he felt the rush of pain and concurrent anger that caused him to destroy the SACAP lobby last week. Jay told the receptionists to, "send the son of a bitch in" and slammed the phone. He stood at the side of his desk and clenched a paper weight in his right hand. "No way I'm gonna take a dive from that queer bastard O'Sullivan," he pledged in his mind. "I'll knock that weirdo silly. Then they can send in the swat team to get me out of here."

A small man with glasses dressed in an open collar shirt, no jacket, with faded blue jeans walked up to Jay from the opposite direction that he was facing. "Good afternoon, Mr. Marquart. Thank you for seeing me."

Jay turned abruptly and dropped the paper weight when he saw the small man. He broke into a wry smile as he greeted the alien. "Well how do you do little fella? What pray tell brings you to my den? Need your ashes hauled perhaps?"

The grunt looked at the paper weight on the floor and then into Jay's eyes, "Mr. Marquart I am an official of the Court here to present you process and notice ordering you to appear before a Judge on the date and time specified in the documents as noted. My I see your driver's license as identification?" The man sat at Jay's desk and pulled several sets of legal looking documents from his heavy bag.

Jay was stunned at the sudden direct manner. He pulled out his wallet and without any comment produced his driver's license for the man's inspection. The runt looked at the license with a nod returned it to its owner. Then he handed the papers to Jay who took them without comment. The little man then asked Jay to sign a paper certifying that process had been served. A copy of the signed paper was given to Jay and the little man disappeared.

The papers, as Jay had realized when they were presented, were the anticipated summons from Cecile's attorney. He recalled Martha's warning that they would get to him on Monday. He also remembered her warning him not to kill the messenger. She said that they would be cut throat documents that would be very irritating. Carefully he began reading the first document and wondering if his emotions could take it. He was not up to it. Halfway through the first document he let out a scream that brought Ken running to his desk. Jay was shaking with anger as Ken put his arms around him and walked him out of the building.

After two laps around the employee parking lot Jay seemed to regain composure. Ken stayed by his side but said nothing. Gradually Jay began to open up, "Christ, Ken, I'm sorry about that outburst. That dirty bitch, Cecile, has served me with papers to take Kristie away. Goddam it, the things in those papers are bullshit, Ken. Pure bull shit! Man, she has started a war that she is gonna lose. I'll fry her ass. Goddamn it, Ken, she can't do that. She's gonna pay."

Ken was sympathetic. His divorce had been pure hell. The hatred between him and his first wife was intense for the first two years but gradually disappeared. Now they were friendly and occasionally met on social occasions. The fact that no children were involved in Ken's divorce made it easier to adjust the anger. That was very different from Jay's situation. Ken's second marriage produced a child that brought him to focus on the happiness of marriage and family. The pain of the first difficult experience was over. Jay's anguish brought back the memories of that experience.

Ken knew how Jay felt and he was intent to ease his pain. "Jay. I got a pretty good idea what you are going through. I'll give you whatever help I can. How you fixed for a lawyer? You need a mean legal jock that will ride her ass. My man might be the guy you want. He hits hard and takes no prisoners."

Jay was grateful for Ken's assistance. It was very necessary support that caused him to remember that he was due to attend a support session at St. A's that evening. "There's no escaping the place," came out as a sudden burst from Jay that caused Ken to give him a bewildered look. Jay continued, "Ken, I've got a ton of problems with this damn divorce thing. I need to call my Sister and arrange to have her go over these damn papers. She'll help with the legal stuff and probably hook me up with the guy I used the first time. If not, then I'll mention your attorney. She knows who's who. If you can spare me for the rest of the day I'll come in early tomorrow and prep for the St. A's meeting. I won't let you down on the Project, I promise. Right now, I got to start with the legal stuff. By the way I'll be over to St. A's tonight. Sort of a therapy session."

Ken looked at his watch. The day was about shot. He patted Jay on the back and told him to get lost. After Jay drove out of the parking lot Ken returned to his desk and began planning the approach to St. Anslem's management. A quick check with Celi revealed that the earliest Action's crack sales manager was able to arrange a meeting with the hospital administration was Wednesday morning at nine o'clock. "Good," thought Ken, "that gives me an extra day to prepare and extra time to get Jay back on track."

oOo

Tom Callahan, Mario Capizzi, and Tony Marone walked into Charlie Patello's office a few minutes after ten. They looked refreshed and ready to work. After an exchange of greetings, the four men went into the conference room and spread out around the large round table. Patello had purposely removed chairs from the room in order to give each participant lots of elbow room. Fresh coffee, juice and Danish were on a side table. In front of each chair at the table was a set of documents pertaining to St. Anslem's Hospital. Audit reports, minutes from board meetings, the famous Boston Security Trust planning review, organizational charts, and a file on the top executives including Joe Durant, Rod Weaver, and Mitch Daly were at the ready. Patello had also prepared a summary report of each of the board members. Dr. Richard Folley's report was extensive and was his father in law's report by Thomas O'Shea. The rest were one page documents extracted from the Boston Register.

Patello suggested that the first hour of the meeting be spent in silence while each person did their own review of the documents. After the review, he would answer questions about the information or as requested get additional data to supplement the information at hand. He then suggested that following the data review: The meeting be divided into three segments. The first segment would be a tactical discussion about Park's entry into the Boston health care market. The second segment would be an analysis of St. Anslem's potential as an assist to Park's objectives. The third and concluding segment would be a detailed plan for the invasion of the Boston Health care market using St. Anslems as a resource when and if appropriate.

Torn Callahan was impressed with Patello's organization of the meeting. He complemented Charlie and suggested that some additional information that he had brought along regarding the Health Maintenance Organizations be distributed and included in the first hour information review session. Charlie was quick to agree. He also asked Tom to lead the discussions in the following three segments. Tom, true to his consultant status, was pleased to accept the assignment.

Mario took off his coat, filled his coffee cup, and directed a comment to Tony, "Christ, I guess we are back in school. You and I will sit here with our hands folded and do our homework. Sounds like we are in for a serious session."

The real Boston Project was about to begin. The document review session took less than an hour. It was apparent to Callahan that the three men were ready for discussion after about forty-five minutes. Patello had left the room to make a phone call, Capizzi was staring out the window at Boston Harbor, and Marone was in the men's room. As soon as they returned, Callahan brought the document discussion to order. Callahan offered the first observation that St. Anslem's seemed to have a complete lack of corporate direction. He also observed that the Health Maintenance Organizations were moving into exclusive arrangements with providers that could offer organized delivery or health service networks. St. Anslem's had no affiliation with the existing area networks. He reasoned that St. Anslem's absent of a network affiliation would experience rapid market decline to the point of dissolution. Since this was so obvious, he asked Patello if the hospital had developed a plan for becoming part of a network or developing a network of its own. Patello reported that he and the Hospital's CEO had discussed the need for a planning effort. The conduct of that effort would be the center of the discussion in the third session.

Mario Capizzi was openly disgusted at the lack of fiscal stability exhibited by St. Anslem's. In his opinion, the Archdiocese would be better off closing the place and going into some other "racket". He expressed the concern that if Park used St. Anslem's as the entry to the Boston health market it would be a venture destined to fail.

Tony Marone was silent. He seemed depressed after reading the information. Patello noticed his body language and asked him to comment. Tony kept his eyes down as if in deep thought as he responded, "I was told by my Mother that if I couldn't say anything nice I should keep my mouth shut. May Mother forgive me, this is a big freaking mess. Charlie, you been hanging out with this Catholic gang for a long time. What's with it? These board meeting minutes are all about politics. Who's watching the store? O'Shea sounds like a real hitter but that's the guy we got some trouble with. Right? What about Hardly? Who owns him?"

Patello was about to respond to Capizzi and Marone when Callahan interrupted. "Gentlemen, your questions are well directed. They express the obvious point that St. Anslem's is not moving progressively with the changing Boston market. Without re-direction, the hospital will dissolve. I believe we all agree on this. Now our purpose is to find opportunity in the market, not to invest in St. Anslam's as our own. Let's hold our opinions and concerns for now and deal with them after we consider Park's interest in Boston healthcare. Allow me to reflect on the decision of the NAI Board. This is in tune with Charlie's agenda for our second topic. NAI recognized that the disruption in the health care market place was caused in the main by payers modifying the insurance coverage in order to tap into the profits of the providers, especially hospitals. Because of the success of that effort hospitals are now losing money and the HMO's are making it. Things have gone nearly one hundred eighty degrees in just a few years. Now the hospitals are countering with networks in order to force the HMO's into sharing the wealth. Meanwhile the purchaser, area employers, are demanding a piece of the action by a reduction in the premium. Things are very confused. NAI is looking for the opportunity to profit by the confusion. NAI's intent is to tap into the revenue stream of the HMO's and the networks, extract maximum return, and divest at the first sign of order or regulation that is bound to happen."

This was the first time that Patello had heard the details about the NAI decision. He immediately recognized the wisdom of a fast hit into the market and running with the money when the slow down became obvious. The history of health care suggested that government regulation would follow as soon as the big investors had accumulated the maximum return. Some politician would see the advantage in demanding that the poor be given equal access to health care financed by a method of indirect or direct taxation.

That would socialize the industry and cause private enterprise to divest. Then the healthcare business would return to the not for profit status that it originally had with rigid government regulations. Insurance would be replaced by a government controlled single payer mechanism that would shut off cash flow to the private HMO's and insurance companies. At the present time health care was enjoying a period of deregulation that offered the window of opportunity. He and Callahan entered into a lengthy dialog about the timing of a Federal sponsored health reform and then evolved into discussion about the prospect of a

State reform effort that would close the window of opportunity in the near future.

Patello reported that Governor Dukar was solidly controlled by private enterprise, especially the insurance industry. His re-election assured that private investment in health care would be protected through his next term. On an even brighter note he pointed out that it was the intention of the party to move Dukar into the National picture as a Presidential candidate by the year 2000. Key to his re-election as Governor, however, was moving Mayor Cowan out of the picture as an opponent. NAI's assistance in placing Cowan in a Federal post was very much appreciated by the local establishment who would be, therefore, supportive of NAI's adventure in the Boston health market as long as it did not conflict with the progress of the other major players.

Callahan jumped on Patello's comments, "There's the opportunity to get in and out of our window, Charlie. We get involved in the segment of service that the other networks can't crack or don't want to crack. We do it with the understanding that eventually the market that we control will be dissolved to the benefit of the major participants. They let us alone until we finish milking the cow then it's all theirs. I'm talking the Catholic market. No one wants to compete with God. So, we become God's agents and eventually integrate with the unholy. There are three pieces to this puzzle. The first is the payer. That's where the cash flow originates. The second is the physician who inadvertently directs the distribution of dollars by directing care. The third piece is the institution that still demands the lion's share of the money. We want to tap in at all three points."

Capizzi was beginning to track on Callahan's evolving strategy, "If I'm following you right, Tom, you are beginning to make the point that the weaker elements in the three categories offer us the opportunity to get involved. Seems to me that speed is important. We probably have to buy in at all three levels. That's going to mean heavy cash. The ROI will be stressed."

Callahan was quick to respond, "Not necessarily, Mario. We can use leverage on the buy in and, in St. Anslem's case, we might not have to spend a dime. I think we can acquire that hospital in time by relieving the Archdiocese of the debt Then we sell the assets at a profit to another provider, like the doctors. You see, the doctors, especially the primary care guys, are the main support of the hospital and the specialists. We get control of the hospital by buying the practices of the primary care docs then organize a network of physicians that includes the key specialists at St. A's. Once we get control of the docs, we have control of St. A's. After that we set up a system where the cash flows through the network that we own before it flows to the hospital. We got the hospital by the shorts and it doesn't cost us any more than we had to invest in the docs."

The conversation was moving too fast for Tony Marone. He waved his pencil back and forth as the three other men injected their comments. Finally, he held up both hands as an appeal to be heard, "Look I'm only the trash man in this outfit so you gotta excuse me if I get lost in this medical stuff. I'm interested in how we get control of the cash flow in the first place. Seems that we got to start an insurance company and sell policies to employers. You got to understand that I haven't done any policy work since I was helping my old man run numbers. How we going to get into this end of the business, Tom?"

"We take over an existing HMO that's on the edge" was Callahan's quick reply. Callahan was prepared for the question. He asked the participants to open the HMO information that he had distributed at the beginning of the meeting. Inside the folder were summary financial statements of the major competing HMO's in the Boston market. All of the reporting payers displayed significant improvement in operating results except Bay Area Health Maintenance. Their five percent operating deficit the prior year had slipped to seven percent in the current year in spite of increased enrollment.

Callahan brought this distinction to the attention of the assembled, "Gentlemen, Bay Area has grown in number of lives enrolled every year. Yet it continues to lose money. Their figures show the highest case cost per hospitalization, the longest length stay, the most hospital days per thousand enrollees, and the highest charge per physician visit. In view of their lack of provider discipline they are obviously pricing their product below cost and below market. Why? Because the shareholders realize that a high market penetration will attract a takeover if they get a buyer before they face bankruptcy. At the moment, they lack the market penetration to make them a favorable hit. They are also facing a significant cash squeeze. If their financial institution forces them to lose their line of credit then we ride to the rescue. "Patello smelled the smoke, "What Bank is on the hook, Tom, as if I didn't have a pretty good idea?"

"My up-front opinion is that the Bank's Board of Directors to which I belong will be anxious to support the takeover," responded Patello, "If Hardly can be easily convinced. O'Shea will have little to say about the deal but he might smell what is happening if he realizes that I'm directly involved. We have to be very careful of Mr. O'Shea right now."

Callahan was not aware of the intrigue involving O'Shea and Mr. Logan's special account. He nevertheless knew by the look of agreement on the faces of Cappizi and Marone that whatever the issue it best not be discussed. Instead he continued to explain the plan.

Callahan continued, "The doctors must believe that they are in charge of the process. To give it the right look we set up a holding company that owns a subsidiary HMO. We manage the subsidiary and charge a management fee. That fee comes off the top. We also share in the profits that will eventually result when we get the utilization under control."

"That's the same process that we use in the waste management business," quipped Marone, "Park rakes it in on the consulting fee and comes back in for a piece of the profit. Same game, right?"

"Right," answered Callahan, "The Catholic hospitals sponsored by Religious Orders have essentially used the process ever since Medicare began. That's how they were able to support the Sisters' retirement and maintenance. They are now dissolving their operations because the new organizations or networks won't carry the extra cash load that the system office used to put on the hospitals. The hospitals aren't the revenue centers anymore. They are simply another element of cost. The Catholic hospitals and others like them are going through a lot of change. The Sisters are getting out of the business. There's more opportunity for us."

"Things are a little different in Boston" Patello asserted, "St. Anslem's is the major Catholic hospital. It doesn't belong to a system. All of its profits and cash have been held for its own use. Now the Archdiocese, at our urging, has set up a central office that Logan is going to run. That could be expensive for the hospital. How do we cut ourselves in?"

"That Archdiocesan office has all the importance of an udder on a bull," quipped Callahan, "Logan will have to find something to do. We need to make him our friend very fast so he appreciates the advantage to the Catholic market in associating with the Park Medical Service Network that we form and has control of the primary care physicians at St. Anslam's and the other area Catholic hospitals. By the way Park Medical Service Network is a subsidiary of none other than Park Medical that also holds Bay Area."

Patello held up his hand as if asking permission to speak. Callahan noticed the gesture and give him the opportunity. "Actually, Tom, Logan is a tool of ours as it is. He is also under the control of an egomaniac. I'm speaking of my very good friend, Dr. Richard Folley. Folley won't let Logan take a pea without permission. If we concentrate on Logan we will be wasting valuable time. I suggest that we go all out to compromise Folley. Logan will fall right in line."

Cappizi, taking his cue from Patello, jumped into the conversation, "This stuff Charlie gave us about Dr. Folley tells me he is a sucker for a pat on the back. No brains but a hell of a lot of pride. What's his thing Charlie, broads, booze or bucks?"

Patello laughed at the thought of the great Dr. Folley being compromised by a cheap whore in a waterfront tavern. "I don't think the standard methods are applicable, Mario. The man is a pseudo intellectual that feeds his ego from a position of prominence. He needs to be in charge but never accountable. That way he gets all the glory of success and is the first to condemn others for failure. He hates Durant, the hospital CEO, because Durant has a higher position from a social perspective. So he managed to gain a higher perch by convincing the Cardinal that he should be the Secretary of health overseeing the so called health ministry. The Secretary, you see, has no accountability for the conduct of the hospital. That's Durant's job. If the hospital fails, Folley tells the Cardinal that Durant is incompetent. The Cardinal admires Folley's perceptive wisdom and cans Durant. Now Folley has another kind of problem. If he is put in charge of the hospital directly he becomes accountable and subject to criticism. Criticism is something he cannot stand. He desperately needs to appoint another shill as the hospital CEO to insulate him from the heat. All we need to do to push Folley over is in some way make him accountable. On the other hand, if we want to keep him in place as our shill then all we have to do is be his protection from accountability."

Callahan was actively making notes as Patello described Dr. Folley. He suddenly looked up and interrupted the conversation, "I think this all fits together rather well. We give the good Dr. Folley a prominent position at the corporate board level of Bay Area and another corporate board position with Park Medical Services Network. We convince him that a man of his prominence is important for our success. He then becomes our advocate for the development of the network and our ally in the implementation of utilization control. If he steps out of line we expose his gigantic conflict of interest. He could go to jail because of his ego but he probably will just melt from humiliation."

Patello felt a need to review the plan as it had developed so far, "OK, Tom, let's review where we are. The first priority is to acquire the Bay Area HMO by underwriting its loans with Boston Security. We have to discuss how we are going to sell this to the Bank. The second priority is to establish a holding company known as Park Medical Services. This will become the holding company for Bay Area and eventually for Park Health Services Network. Third, but concurrent with the second priority, is to establish the Park Health Services Network. Fourth is activating PHSN to acquire the primary physician practices affiliated with St. Anslem's and other Catholic Hospitals? Is that it?"

"Generally, that's it," replied Callahan, "The details of each priority need to be worked out. Let's make some assignments. The Bank deal with Bay Area should best directed by Charlie, I think. Corporate formation belongs to Mario and Tony. Anybody have a suggestion how we proceed with the primary docs?"

"Let me provide some input," offered Patello. "I think I should be the invisible man getting things pointed in the right direction. The Bank deal and Bay Area is tricky. My suggestion is that we get a brother Knight to call on Hardly. Hardly controls the Board of Security. If his brother in arms wants the deal for the good of the Church. Hardly will go to hell and back to deliver. Mario, we can discuss who in New York should contact Hardly. I can arrange for the details of incorporation of the holding company and the subs but Mario and Tony will square the set with Park and NAI. Now as far as getting to the docs, I think we could do that with the cooperation of the Hospital's Board of Trustees. You see, St. Anslam's CEO wants me to help form a long-range plan. I suggested that we required a consultant to steer the process. I also said that I could possibly arrange for a planning grant. My thought is that the affiliated companies of NAI employ Debur and Tandy to do a strategic plan for St. Anslem's. Callahan comes in and does a complete review of the hospital. The outcome of the review points the hospital the way we need it to go. However, in the process of the review Callahan gets to know where the docs are. He feeds the information to us and we go after the docs. Folley could even be our front man. How's it sound?"

"Sounds like a go to me," offered Marone. "How long before we get it squared away?"

Callahan eagerly responded to the question, "We can get the business set up in less than a month. Cash should start coming our way in six months. That means late winter early spring. I'll have to clear with corporate to do the St. Anslem assignment. They might want to use our Boston office. Maybe NAI should consider it part of the National contract. Charlie, can you get this approved by the St. Anslem's Board very soon?"

Patello gave a quick reply, "Hope to get the strategic planning proposal approved at tomorrow's board meeting, Tom. Ok if I use your name?"

"Sure, Charlie. Let me know when they want me to start. Give me as much lead time as possible." answered Callahan.

Mario Capizzi noticed that the discussion had evolved to a point of conclusion. At his suggestion Callahan was delegated to formalize the morning's discussion into a corporate plan for the directors of Park. That plan would be the document authorizing the development of the corporate structures. He suggested that the meeting was concluded. Then the New York contingent called a cab and rushed to Logan Airport in an attempt to catch the one o'clock plane to LaGuardia.

oOo

Jay drove directly to Martha's office after he left work. He bolted into the waiting room like a man on a mission. The apprehension on his face more than his demand for immediate service caused the receptionist to inform Martha that she had a client with an emergency. Jay appreciated the extra attention. His anxiety level had been on a steady increase since leaving work. The legal language in the documents served to him seemed oppressive. In spite of the cooperation given to him up front, he still was asked to wait until Martha finished her conversation with a client who was in the middle of an appointment. The wait lasted twenty minutes during which time Jay paced back and forth in the small reception area. Only the receptionist was more relieved than Jay when Martha finally appeared.

Martha allowed Jay time to emote about Cecile, her crooked lawyer, and his vengeance to the, "Bitch." When he began to settle down due to physical exhaustion she asked to see the documents that he was clutching in his hands. Jay timidly gave her the papers then renewed his wrath.

"Martha, that bitch has really done it this time. You got to nail her. That crap in there is not true. I mean its bullshit. What's gonna happen now?"

The documents were about as Martha had expected. She noted that Cecile's attorney was regarded as one of Boston's leading divorce lawyers. Not the same one that had represented her in the divorce. That was significant. It signaled that Cecile was going for it all by retaining a respected and very expensive attorney. The pleadings were designed to force Jay into economic ruin in defense. This was a very expensive case that Jay could ill afford. The stage was definitely set for a compromise rather than a bare-knuckle brawl in court. Without some unknown leverage Jay would lose more than he would gain if a deal had to be struck. Martha realized that this was not the time to inform her brother that he was in deep trouble. The original divorce decree had contained a Judgment of Dissolution governing the relationship of the parties to the divorce in matters of child support, custody, and visitation. Cecile through her attorney was asking for modification of the original judgment to revoke joint custody and increase support payments based on the allegation that Jay's income had increased substantially over the amount he was making at the time of the divorce. Cecile was asking at minimum the twenty percent allowed by law of Jay's current income. The second modification request was revocation of custody based on the allegation that Jay and Susan were not fit to care for Kristie because of their substantiated use of chemical substances. Martha noted with particular concern that the petition to the court made special mention that Susan was a habitual user of intoxicating substances.

The surprise package that concerned Martha the most at this time was an Emergency Petition to the Court to immediately revoke custody because of immediate endangerment to Kristie based on the substantiated information that Jay's use of chemical substances has resulted in an overdose. This would require that Jay's medical record be presented as evidence to the court. To that end, a Discovery Document was included that required Jay to present all of his medical records from all doctors and medical institutions from whom and in which he had received care in the past five years. The discovery specifically mentioned Waltham Hospital.

Another clever part of the pleadings was a Petition to the Court for ruling to show cause that Jay had missed several support payments. This was a diversion to create the perception that Jay was, in addition to being a junkie, a dead-beat Dad. The discovery document requested that he present all of his financial records for the past five years to include paychecks, bank statements, loans and mortgage documents, and all other personal financial documents.

Finally, the package included two notices of Hearing. The first hearing was of an immediate nature to deal with the Child Endangerment Emergency. The second Hearing was attentive to all other matters of petition pertaining to the modification of the Judgment of Dissolution. Martha realized that the emergency hearing could be scheduled within two weeks from time of service. The Petition for Modification would be heard by the Court sometime in November was her first guess. She was consumed with anger over the issue affecting Kristie but also realized that Cecile was being represented by a professional who knew that emotion served his cause. Job number one at this time was to keep Jay under control and get him properly represented on the custody matters,

Carefully, she began her explanation of the issues, "Well, my brother, we have our work cut out for us. I'll get with a good divorce lawyer in the morning. Mark Addison, the man that represented you at the time of your divorce is with another firm so I'll have to see if he is interested in continuing, I recommend that you stay with him. He has an excellent reputation in these matters. He'll have to charge full fees so we will have to talk about that after he gives me some idea about what to expect. I'm going to suggest to him that we team up on the defense in the Emergency Petition. I'm probably better prepared on the medical record confidentiality issue. We'll see."

Jay's anger seemed to abate but he remained emotional, "Martha, I don't have any money. I'm supporting three kids and a wife on my income. Cecile makes nearly twice what I make. How can she expect me to pay more support? Between her and her weird cop husband they must be knocking down a hundred grand. I'm barely meeting expenses. How am I going to pay Addison? I think he ripped me off last time."

Martha was extremely sensitive to Jay's remarks about Mark. He had given Jay every possible consideration in fees to the extent that the Firm had been critical of him continuing the case. Only Martha's association with the firm had prevented him from withdrawing. Carefully, she commented, "Jay, you have to realize that lawyers need to get paid for their work. I'll try to work something out for you but it's still going to cost. You need to be prepared for that."

"Well he needs to be prepared to deal with a guy that runs a little short. Maybe he'll take my credit card if it isn't over the limit." was Jay's reply

For the first time since last Thursday Jay felt the surge of uncontrollable anger that caused him to react violently. Suddenly he experienced the familiar pain in his chest and a sudden shortness of breath that caused him to double over.

"Jay, are you all right? Should I get you some help? What's going on?" were three rapid questions asked by Martha that Jay could not answer because of the increasing pain now moving from his chest to his stomach. He could only look at her with a very painful expression.

Gradually Jay relaxed and the pain decreased. "Deni, I think I'll be all right. I'm might go over to St. A's. I have to do a urine test and then hang around for a support group session. If I get in trouble someone there will help. Otherwise I'll just drive home. Could you do me a favor and call Susan? Tell her what's going on just in case I decide to go in. I don't think I will but I can't tell. Man, my gut hurts."

"Sure, I'll call her. You want me to drive you to the hospital?" Martha offered.

Jay had managed to stand and was feeling less pain. He felt certain that the physical crisis had passed. His emotions were also stable at the moment. "Thanks, Den. I just had some sort of a jolt. I'll be all right, I think. I can drive. Tell Susan that I should be home soon. Are you going to call me tomorrow after you talk to Addison?"

Martha moved to his side, "I'll call you early afternoon. You had better be prepared to give this matter a lot of time. We'll talk tomorrow. "She took Jay by the hand and gave it an affectionate sisterly squeeze. Then she escorted him through the now vacant reception area. Jay gave her a hug and went out the door. By the time he arrived home the pain was gone.

oOo

Joe Durant was pleased to see Monday end. It seemed that nothing good had happened. Tomorrow's board meeting appeared to him as the mother of all disasters. Monday's little problems were nothing compared to the battle that awaited the mom. He was holding his head in his hands while sitting at his desk in apparent deep contemplation when Rod Weaver and Mitch Daly walked in. They seemed to be in a collegial mood as they jointly greeted their depressed mentor. Joe had forgotten that he had demanded that the two appear before him to discuss tactics for the AM on-onslaught. With a pained expression, he returned their greeting and moved with them to the well-used small conference table.

Eagerly, Mitch Daly distributed his plan for planning that he had tried to force on Durant earlier in the day. With a nod from Durant he began his explanation, "Boss since you put me in charge of this project I thought we ought to have a common understanding of the approach I will take at the Board meeting. I want to be sure that you and fiscal are in sync in case any questions are directed at you during or after the meeting. OK? Now I will distribute this outline that has three major phases. The first phase is organization. As I understand it, Joe, Mr. Patello has agreed to chair a planning committee. We'll let him pick the board members who will serve but I think we should name the administrators. Obviously, the three of us would be the ones to serve. Medical staff should be represented on the committee. The president of the medical staff should be invited or his representative. I imagine Folley will want to play God and name the physician. Any way the Committee should be in place within a week after the meeting. Second phase is plan function. I will select a consultant with the approval of the committee. Several firms have been contacted that are sending me information and ballpark prices. We definitely need a consultant to move this along. The last phase is timing. You notice that I intend to complete the planning project in eight months. That includes the conferences and special interest reviews that will need to take place. How's it sound?"

"Expensive" was Weaver's quick answer, "How in the hell do you intend to pay for an army of consultants hanging around her for eight months? God created the universe in seven days. That ought to be good enough for you."

"Actually, it was six days, Rod. Remember he took Sunday off," commented Durant, "Your plan for planning outline has some merit. Mitch, but I anticipate that Mr. Patello has a consultant in tow that we will use. If I'm right, he also has a means to pay for the process. That being the case then we'll take our directions from the consultant, I imagine. Patello called me about an hour ago and said that he had what we wanted. His only concern was convincing the rest of the Board. I guess he is taking care of the politics. We can only wait and see."

"Well the price recommends it," said a smiling Weaver, "If Patello wants to pay the fiddler it's only right that we let him call the tune."

Daly was showing signs of depression, "So if I'm supposed to be in charge of the process and Patello and his consultant are actually running it what do I do?"

"Whatever they ask," responded Durant.

With that comment, the meeting came to a close. Weaver left first. Daly followed in a few minutes after starring in silence at his boss. Durant was unmoved by Daly's silent emotion. His day had been a sequence of disasters. A disgruntled vice president was the least of his concerns.

CHAPTER ELEVEN

Kevin Hardly was up by five AM. He did his usual exercises, showered and had breakfast before six. He drank his coffee, had some juice, and read the paper as he sat on the patio of his mansion on his well landscaped estate. This was to be Kevin Hardly's day. He was to conduct the meeting of the St. Anslem's Board of Trustees, an assignment bestowed on him by the Deity. Otherwise his position as Chairman of one of Boston's most prestigious Banks was somewhat mundane compared to the responsibility of doing God's work at the leading Catholic Hospital in the area, if not the world. The Cardinal had impressed him with the awesome responsibility when he asked Hardly to serve the Church in that capacity. He had accepted the assignment just as eagerly as he had accepted the leadership of the Knights of the Holy Cross. This was God's work that had to be done and he was the man to do it. The Cardinal, himself, had said so.

At exactly six fifteen he backed his Mercedes out of the garage and aimed it toward St. Anslem's Hospital. The half hour drive would put him there fifteen minutes before the seven o'clock starting time. "Plenty of time to get organized," he thought.

Joe Durant had a different perspective on the board meeting. He had arrived at the Hospital at six AM and began to assist the housekeeping and food service personnel arrange the hospital's spacious board room for the meeting. Durant felt that the board room was obscene but his opinion was of no consequence. It's think panel walls, expensive drapes, false sky lights, religious art, plush chairs, and a custom-built table that would hold thirty-five people was way beyond good taste. The adjacent kitchen and serving area with wet bar that opened into the main room also seemed pretentious.

The entire board suite was commissioned and paid for by Kevin Hardly as a gift to the Hospital following his appointment as Chairman of the Board. Three adjacent storerooms had been absorbed by the designer and decorator for the project. Walls had been removed. New ceiling, carpet, thick panel walls and a full kitchen with food serving area added. Hidden microphones recorded every word spoken and amplified every sound. Picture screens descended from the ceiling at a touch on a control panel at the Chairman's place. Television, VCR's, and projectors all were at the ready in a rear projection booth also commanded by the Chair.

Hardly had assigned the interior decorator of Boston Security to the task of designing, building and equipping the suite without regard to cost. Consequently, the room was named the Hardly Board Room. A portrait of the great and generous man hung in an ornate frame on the wall at the end of the mammoth table. On the wall, opposite and above the chairman's position, hung a picture of His Eminence, Francis Cardinal McMahon.

The food service personnel were assigned the task of preparing the extensive breakfast buffet that was the trademark of the Board meetings. Grommet dishes were always plentiful. Delicious Danish, bagels, and sweet rolls from the City's best bakeries adorned the table as did a variety of juices. A chef was available to prepare custom omelets for those with expanded appetites. Waitresses were assigned the task of replenishing beverages and removing the dishes.

Customarily the people attending ate and discussed the business of the hospital at the same time in a rather informal manner. The conduct and ambiance of the meeting was Kevin's idea because he thought that God would have conducted the meeting in a friendly relaxed way. Occasionally the discussions were replaced by a formal presentation but that was rare. A staff of six people from the Environmental Services department had arrived at five thirty to thoroughly clean the entire suite.

Durant could not remember anytime that the Board meeting ever included material of such consequence that environmental and food service personnel could not be present. Hardly ran an open and informal meeting. Rarely did the minutes reflect the actual conduct of the meeting since Durant wrote the minutes to accommodate the regulatory requirements. Confidential matters were always slipped into the minutes after the fact and authenticated by approval of the minutes at the following meeting. Everyone seemed content with the loose conduct. This time Durant expected a rather large explosion of emotions as the hospital finances were discussed, the waste management contract was reported, the planning committee was proposed, and the Bishop announced the impact of Dr. Folley's and Mr. Logan's positions with the Archdiocese, as well as the ongoing discussion regarding the serious fiscal plight of the hospital.

This was a very important meeting that Durant felt required the Chairman to conduct in formal fashion. So convinced was Durant that he had placed a copy of Robert's Rules of Order at the Chairman's place. He had also directed the food service and environmental staff to leave as soon as the Chairman began the meeting.

Hardly was the first member of the Board to arrive. He strolled into the Board room and extended a cordial greeting to the employees. Then he walked over to Durant, shook his hand and presented him with a thick envelope that held the crest and return address of the Knights of the Holy Cross.

Joe looked at the envelope with question as Hardly began to explain, "Joseph, it's time that you became a Knight. That envelope contains the application form and information about the Order. It's true Catholic action that you will want to be a part of. We'll give it fast process. I'm sure the Cardinal will approve it. We can have you ready for the October installation. Your wife will become a Lady in the Order and join with you. It's all explained in the material. Don't forget to give us your sizes so the good Sisters can have your capes ready for the installation. The capes are made to order by a cloistered order of Nuns in Canada. They need a month lead time at least. It will be good to have you join us. I expect that Mr. and Mrs. Logan will be installed in the same class with you."

Durant was taken off guard by Hardly's invitation. He could only express his gratitude to Hardly for considering him for the honor. Hardly seemed pleased with Durant's attitude and followed with a lengthily explanation about the New England Platoon of which he was the Leading Knight. The discussion became extended and offered no time for Durant to prepare Hardly for the coming onslaught.

Just as Durant sensed an opening in the conversation, Dr. Folley arrived with a gentleman unknown to Durant but who was recognized from his picture in the media as Mr. Michael Logan. Folley ignored Durant as he introduced Logan to Hardly. Hardly graciously greeted Mr. Logan and invited him to be a regular guest at all St. Analem's board meetings and functions. He then produced another Holy Cross envelope that he presented to Logan with the same lengthily explanation.

Bishop Hanks was next to arrive. He noticed Folley and Logan talking to Hardly and immediately joined them. Hardly informed the Bishop of Logan's intent to become a Knight which sparked another round of conversation about the Order. By now Durant realized that any preparation time was lost. The remaining Board members were now present and seated at the table where breakfast was being served. Patello was among them but distant from Durant denying them the opportunity to communicate.

Sister Mary Elizabeth was the last to arrive. When she greeted the Bishop, it diverted Hardly from his recruiting speech. Hardly noticed that the Board had assembled in their usual informal fashion so he took his place at the head of the table and ordered his favorite omelet from the waiting chef.

Although the meeting lacked formality there was a customary seating arrangement that was always adhered to: Kevin Hardly sat at the head of the table with the portrait of the Cardinal looking over him. Thomas O'Shea sat on Hardly's right and Charles Patello sat on his left. Durant sat next to Patello and Folley sat next to O'Shea. The remaining board members sat anywhere they pleased but never in the designated chairs. Durant was moving to his customary place when he noticed that Dr. Folley had placed Logan in the chair that Joe usually occupied. Hardly seemed pleased with the arrangement that left Durant to find a place most distant from the Chairman. This caused him to take a place at the end but next to the friendly Sister Mary Elizabeth. Sister Elizabeth greeted Joe warmly. She had noticed the social slam by Folley and expressed her resentment of the action as she gave Joe an affectionate pat on his hand.

Joe had desperately wanted to inform Chairman Hardly about the special features of the meeting not the least of which was that he had invited Rod Weaver and Mitch Daly to attend as guests. Weaver and Daly walked into the Board room unnoticed by Hardly. Durant motioned them to join him at the table. He then hastily explained to the two executives that they were there at his invitation only since he had not had the opportunity to clear their attendance with Hardly. Weaver was his usual casual self and ordered a lavish breakfast. Daly became very nervous. His hand seemed to shake as he attempted to drink the glass of juice put before him.

Another custom of the Board was the prayer used to start all of their gatherings. Kevin had the prayer composed by a Trapist Monk for which he had made a sizable contribution to the monastery. He tapped his water glass to get everyone's attention and then asked Bishop Hanks to lead the Board in the recitation of the special prayer. The good Bishop always accommodated Kevin's request to recite the Monk's prayer and routinely added a few prayers and petitions of his own that served to allow everyone's eggs to get cold. Following the prayer Kevin invited the members to continue enjoying their breakfast. He then invited Dr. Folley to introduce a very special guest.

Dr. Folley remained seated and continued to hold his fork that he pointed at Logan as he began the introduction, "Kevin and members of the Board, it is with pleasure that I introduce you to Mr. Michael Logan who I'm sure you already know because of his outstanding work with the City. Michael has accepted the challenge of working with me as we start the much-needed Office for Health Affairs for the Archdiocese. Bishop Hanks will explain the Cardinal's intent for this important office. Allow me to say that Mr. Logan will be instrumental in organizing and directing the various health institutions and services provided by the Archdiocese. Putting it all together makes us the largest provider of health care in the

State bar none. Mr. Logan's background and experience will be of great help as we expand our Catholic network."

The Board gave a muffled applause as Dr. Folley concluded his remarks. He turned to Logan and asked if he had anything to say. Michael felt inclined to stand and make his comments but he succumbed to the informality and remained seated, "Thank you for the warm greeting. I am excited about this association with the Church and its health ministry. Dr. Folley has told me about your dedication and I am most anxious to join you in carrying out the mission of St. Anslem's and the Church. I look forward to getting to know each of you personally."

As Logan concluded his comments, Dr. Folley again took the lead in the discussion "Kevin, I think that this is the right time for us to hear from Bishop Hanks about the Cardinal's decision to establish an Office for Health Affairs." Kevin simply nodded at the request. Bishop Hanks wiped his mouth with his napkin and prepared to speak.

Dr. Folley then signaled that he had a few more words to say causing the Bishop to yield. "Before you get to that, Bishop, I suppose that I ought to express my gratitude to you and the Cardinal for listening to my recommendations about the function of the Secretary for Health. Cardinal McMahon asked me to meet with him on several occasions last month to work out the details of the assignment. I can say to you that he is very excited about this post and I am very excited about being the first person, religious or lay, to be selected for the task. Bishop Hanks was most kind in recommending me for the job and I thank him for that. Bishop, please continue."

Bishop Hanks seemed skeptical that he was actually being allowed to speak. He recalled that he had actually recommended that the Cardinal appoint a priest to the secretariat post instead of Dr. Folley. He hadn't said as much to the Cardinal but he thought Folley was a, "pompous ass." The Cardinal had already promised the job to Folley when he asked the Bishop's opinion.

Carefully he thought out his comments so that the Cardinal would be protected from any bad consequence of the decision. "My friends, His Eminence has a very high regard for the laity. We have more lay people in key posts within the Archdiocese than any other diocese in the United

States. We also have the largest percentage of Catholic population of any major metropolitan area in the Country. The services provided by the Church to the people of Boston are numerous. That is why the Cardinal felt that a professional such as Dr. Folley should be the one to guide those health services in the true interest of the Church and the community the Church serves. We are fortunate that Dr. Folley can find the time from his very pressing duties here to attend to the challenge offered by the whole Archdiocese."

Sister Mary Elizabeth was unconvinced. With no hesitation, she fired a shot across the Bishop's bow. "Bishop, it seems to me that the Cardinal sought little counsel on the need for the Office. Many of us would have advised him against it. Health care is going through a massive restructuring that may move the ministry in an entirely different direction. I believe the matter should have been discussed openly in the Priests' senate if nowhere else. Where is the Office to be located and how are we going to pay for it? It seems to me that these are questions that should have answers before men are appointed to new positions."

Bishop Hanks had feared Sister's reaction. He took special note of her use of the word "men" in the spicy retort. The flush in his cheeks betrayed his embarrassment as he fumbled for an answer.

It was at this point that Thomas O'Shea saw the opportunity to relieve the Bishop and redirect the focus of blame. "Kevin, before we get into much more detail I want to know why certain uninvited people are in this room. Aren't the Board meetings supposed to be confidential? We have two vice presidents sitting at the table who usually don't come into these meetings until they are called and then excused. Why are they here?"

Kevin hadn't noticed that the hospital wait staff, per instructions of Durant, had disappeared when the discussion started. He also hadn't noticed that Weaver and Daly were seated at the end of the table. He had no idea how to respond to his friend and associate, O'Shea.

Durant relieved him of the pressure by firing back at O'Shea. "These gentlemen are here at my direction to serve as resource to this Board on two very important subjects, finance and strategic planning. Perhaps we should get into these items and then they could be excused."

Hardly responded, "Yes, all right, we can do that. Joe would you like to lead us through the latest financial report. Is that all right with you, Tom?"

Thomas O'Shea was determined to control the discussion of the finances. He had studied Weaver's report to the last item. "Kevin, as Treasurer of the Hospital's corporation I think it would be more in tune with my responsibility if I gave the report and then we can ask management to reply. There are significant problems apparent in the operating statement that Mr. Durant will need to address. If you will so allow me, I'll pass out a copy of the latest statement and a copy of my own notes. I want you to know that I had to make a demand for this information to Mr. Weaver who finally sent me the statements late yesterday afternoon. One of our major problems, as you can see, is the lack of current information."

Hardly nodded his consent as O'Shea began distributing the documents. Weaver leaned over to his boss and in a stage whisper stated another problem was that, "the Treasurer didn't know his ass from third base about a hospital financial operating statement." The people seated near Durant chuckled when the comment was made. Sister Mary Elizabeth simply nodded. Durant actually blushed.

O'Shea paused when the humor became apparent but he had not heard the comment. He could only stare at Durant with contempt. Weaver was gratified that the Treasurer had been disarmed by the interruption He sat back in his chair and flashed a big smile at Mr. O'Shea that brought him back to the task of distributing the material. Thomas O'Shea, regardless of Weaver's opinion, was an expert in financial analysis. His many years directing the fiscal affairs of Boston Security had made him expert in all forms of fiscal reporting. The hospital method of accounting had been foreign to him when he first became involved with St. Anslem's but he soon mastered the information. He knew that St. Anslem's was in a "death glide" as he described it to the Board. The escalating monthly deficits were pointing to a year end disaster that would reduce the Hospital's equity by nearly twenty million dollars. This equity reduction would break the bond covenants and require extensive debt reduction that the hospital was ill-prepared to do.

The immediate requirement proposed by Treasurer O'Shea was, "an all-out reduction in spending by a minimum of thirty percent within the next thirty to sixty days. While that reduction could not offset the expected loss for the current year, it would be sufficient to convince the Rating Agencies that the hospital could regain stability with a projected break even or better result in the next year. What we need from management is their plan for expense reductions and a positive margin." When his remarks were completed the mood around the table was somber.

Hardly was unsure what to do or say next. No one seemed ready to ask questions or even move.

Durant realized that, ready or not, he had to seize the moment before the Board turned their attention to O'Shea's demands and took management to task. He pulled his emotions under control and formally addressed the Chair, "Mr. Hardly, I thank Mr. O'Shea for his excellent analysis of the many challenges facing St. Anslem's. Our fiscal position has deteriorated rapidly this year. We have been adjusting our spending to match the declining revenue but, unfortunately, the change in the case mix intensity has reduced the average case revenue faster than we can adjust costs. To accommodate the thirty percent reduction that Mr. O'Shea proposes requires elimination of programs that are not carrying their own weight and/or are not feeding patients to the more profitable services. What I'm proposing is that St. Anslem's only provide those services that are profitable. However, those services that we provide must be suitable to our mission of teaching and research. The determination of our service base must be carefully reviewed."

Patello had been silent up to this point. Suddenly he caught the cue from Durant about the determination of service being an overture to the planning program. Without pause or permission he injected himself into Durant's comments, "We have the prospect of a major disaster if we cut expenses without reason other than to offset the deficit. If making money was our mission then we would sell this place and put the money into a saving account at O'Shea's bank. Mr. Durant is right about the need to analyze our services in respect to our mission. I also think that we need an expert to assist us with the process. This is a major consulting job."

Kevin Hardly suddenly came to life at the suggestion of a consulting job. "We have a great amount of expertise at the Bank that could be used by the hospital at no charge. Our planning and marketing staff has two very well qualified people who did the work for the Archdiocese on the Office for Health Affairs. They could be made available to assist the hospital and this Board."

The look on Patello's face at the mention of "Laurel and Hardy," crack planners from Boston Security made O'Shea laugh out loud. Normally O'Shea was a man completely divorced from humor but when Hardly trumped Patello's ace, he couldn't control the expression.

Patello was rendered speechless by Hardly's remarks so O'Shea took up the void. "Kevin, the Bank's staff is involved in a major project at this time that would prevent them from giving the hospital the attention it deserves. My thought is that Mr. Logan could direct the planning effort. He could use our marketing and planning staff for special reviews."

Durant sensed the loss of control as Logan was mentioned. He interrupted as O'Shea was about to speak, "Excuse me, Mr. O'Shea, but we have a qualified planner on our executive staff who is prepared to direct the planning effort. Mr. Daly is not only a qualified and experienced planner of health facilities and functions he is also knowledgeable about St. Anslem's, I would like to propose that Mr. Daly be empowered to formalize the planning effort and that a consultant as offered by Mr. Patello be used as back up to the program."

"The point I'm trying to make is that we have no confidence in management to lead us in anything," O'Shea stood and pounded the table to give emphasis to his verbal reaction. "Joe Durant has led this hospital to the point of fiscal failure and now he wants us to trust him to lead us out of it. We need new leadership to give us a better focus on the impact of health reform. Joe is old school. Let Logan, a fresh face, take over and preserve the ministry. That's what he is supposed to do under Richard's guidance. Right, Richard?"

Sr. Elizabeth suddenly jumped into the debate. The little nun had a hot disposition that tended to explode when she became frustrated. The discourteous assault on Joe Durant by O'Shea brought back to her mind the same mean tactics that the Cardinal's "men" had employed to discredit Sr. Celest.

"No more of this" she thought and rose from her chair. "Mr. Hardly, I am ashamed to be party to this juvenile bickering. Why are we being so critical when we have never expressed any dissatisfaction with our managers in the past? Yes, we have good reason to be concerned but Mr. Durant has stated that concern and has requested an opportunity to undertake corrective steps. We, or at least Mr. O'Shea, seems determined to replace Mr. Durant with Mr. Logan. I'm certain that Mr. Logan is a fine gentleman but so is Mr. Durant. Mr. Durant is also known to us as a capable administrator is spite of Mr. O'Shea's opinion. I, for one, will not go along with Mr. O'Shea's suggestion. I implore you, Mr. Hardly, to bring this discussion under control. It's your job as Chairman to properly direct this meeting and I suggest that you do it."

Hardly had the look of a second grader being scolded by the Sister. He sat with his hands folded in good parochial school fashion. He lowered his head when Sr. Elizabeth leveled her criticism at him. His embarrassment was obvious as the room became deathly quiet. Hardly was emotionally wounded and rendered speechless. The great lay member of the Church's nobility was now a silent Knight divorced of sword or speech. He had no quick response to this professed Lady of the Church who had humbled him and now stood before his table in his court demanding that he be responsible to his charge.

The silence continued. No one seemed to move. Sr. Elizabeth remained standing and took time to look into the eyes of each member of the board. Some made eye contact. Others like Hardly and O'Shea kept their eyes lowered. Sr. Elizabeth was for the moment in charge of the meeting. Hardly, unable to respond, had effectively abdicated to Sister.

It was an opportunity to correct a wrong. Sister took full advantage of her position and began her commentary, "As a Board of Directors we have been lax in our responsibility. This hospital has been governed by a process of absentee decision making that we have accepted without question. Why was the Office for Health Affairs established without our input? Why was Dr. Folley appointed to the Secretariat without consideration being given to other interested people, religious or laity? Why was Mr. Logan employed without the benefit of executive search? Why, then, should we be held accountable for the status of this hospital if we are not to be involved in the major decisions affecting our responsibility? How can we plan the future of this hospital as a service to the ministry when we are excluded from ministerial direction? I believe we need to have direct communication with the Cardinal in order for us to fulfill our responsibility."

Sister Elizabeth looked directly at Bishop Hanks as she paused. The Bishop was now staring back at Sister and opened his mouth to speak. Sister was not ready to yield. Still standing she continued her filibuster, "I want to know what the Office for Health Affairs is going to cost and who is going to pay for it. Do we have a say in that? We are expected to maintain fiscal stability. In view of our current instability I presume that the Cardinal has found other resources to support the Office that has so much importance. Where is this Office to be located? Several months ago, we agreed to hire more surgeons and cardiologists. They have occupied every available space in the hospital. Are we now expected to reduce our patient capacity to accommodate the Secretary and Director as well as a supporting cast of thousands? Do we have any say in this? Indeed, we need to plan. But we cannot plan in a vacuum. The Cardinal must be part of the planning process and be transparently honest in dealing with us. We cannot be expected to guess at his interests. The preservation and conduct of the healing ministry requires total cooperation and honesty. I am determined to see that this Board has every opportunity to fulfill its responsibility. Therefore, I request, no I demand, to be given the Chair of a Planning Committee for this Hospital that will deal with the full scope of the healing ministry as it may apply to St. Anslem's."

Hardly had regained some composure but was still emotionally off balance. Sister's demand to be named Chairperson of the yet to be formed Planning Committee was ringing in his ears. He desperately needed help.

Bishop Hanks seemed to be riding to the rescue when he began to counter Sister's comments. "Sister, I apologize for not communicating with you and the rest of the Board when the Office was formed. The Cardinal asked that I attend to all the details. Obviously, I was lax in several matters. The Cardinal has no funds to support the Office. The expenses are to be paid by St. Anslems at first and as the other Catholic hospitals in the Archdiocese join the system they will help defer the costs. Mr. Logan is very qualified to create the system of Catholic Health Services. That's why he was employed. It was not intended that he would be directly involved in the management of St. Anslem's. Your point is well taken. I, for one, welcome your leadership in the development of the health ministry. You are the right person to orient Mr. Logan on the scope of the ministry and the content of the health system. As we form our recommendations, I'm confident that His Eminence would join us for discussion. I'll tell him that you and your committee will be working with Mr. Logan and Dr. Folley on the plan for the System. I know that he will be pleased."

Sister felt the all too familiar kick upstairs. By moving her to the System formation the Good Bishop had effectively moved her away from the details of the hospital plan. However, she was unsure if that was his intent or if he was just being the usual tactful clergyman. She decided to test his sincerity. "Thank you for the vote of confidence, Bishop. I assume that you will join us on the committee. Have you any suggestions for other members?"

The Bishop had played the game of Church politics many times. He was a seasoned veteran of the clerical wars and recognized the clever move of this cagey nun. If he yielded to her intent to block involvement by the terrific trinity he would gain counsel in dealing with the problems of the women religious' defiance toward the official Church. On the other hand, if he suggested one of the terrific trinity it was a message to her that the committee was a chosen battle ground for the conflict of the religious sexes in the Boston Archdiocese. That was a war for a different time and place.

In reply he opted for the middle ground. "Sister, I have no specific recommendations. Please choose whoever you think will best serve the purpose. Of course. I'll be on the committee as you ask."

Sister received the Bishop's communique and acknowledged it with a smile. The Bishop signed off the net with a nod of respect leaving her to play the next card. That card was selection of another member to the committee that would be an acceptable party to the Bishop and still supportive to her cause. That meant someone with influence but apparently neutral to the terrific trinity.

Sister replied, "Thank you for the support, Bishop. I suggest that Mr. Mondi would be an excellent addition to our committee. You, Mr. Mondi and I will team with Dr. Folley and Mr. Logan to plan the purpose and function of the Office for Health Affairs. We can coordinate with the planning function at St. Anslem's that Mr. Durant will conduct."

Not only had the good Sister taken over control of the Arch Diocese Office for Health Affairs, she was now moving in as chairman of St. Anslem's. Hardly realized what was happening but was a victim of his informal style. He was at a loss to recover the mantle from this black clad whirlwind. O'Shea also recognized that the Bishop and Nun had worked a combination that effectively moved the terrific trinity to the sidelines. This could be bad for business if left alone. Mondi was unknown to O'Shea except that he was a loyal knight that Hardly had recommended to the Cardinal. For the moment O'Shea counted him on the side of the trinity. O'Shea concluded that the new Committee was controllable. He opted not to create any obstruction to its function. Of greater importance was to maintain control of St. Anslem's governance.

To that end O'Shea decided to form an alliance with Patello. "Sister, your idea of relating the plan for the Health Office with the plan for the hospital is excellent. But it seems to me that the Office and the Hospital are somewhat at opposite extremes. The Hospital is in desperate need of a business plan to offset the growing deficit. Related to this, as we heard from Mr. Durant, is the need to determine the appropriate products for the hospital to deliver. Therefore, I suggest that the hospital plan be held separate from the Office until it is concluded and then be coordinated. Otherwise we could be out of money before we have these things properly thought out. Earlier Mr. Patello suggested that we use a consultant to assist the hospital. I now believe that we should accept that suggestion in order to expedite the planning process."

O'Shea's comments keyed Hardly's return to authority. Before Sister Elizabeth could respond the Great Knight regained the Chair, "Thank you, Tom. You have brought us back to the original concern of the hospital's finances. Let's give that matter some thought before we decide to use a consultant. Tom, I believe you said that we needed to reduce our expenses by sixty percent in the next thirty days. Correct"

"Actually, it was thirty percent in sixty days, Kevin" was O'Shea's glib response.

"Well whatever, we need to be at it," continued Hardly. "Now Mr. Weaver is here. Perhaps he can give us some insight as to how we might accomplish this."

Rod Weaver had been enjoying the heated exchange and political maneuvering of the board members. It was better than Monday Night Football of which he was an avid observer. The sudden call to participate came unexpectedly. He was caught off guard.

A quick look to Durant signaled his panic and caused Joe to respond in his behalf. "Mr. Hardly, I can speak for Rod on this matter. He has studied our fiscal situation in depth but is not prepared at the moment to make any definite recommendations. I asked him here today to explain what Mr. O'Shea has eloquently stated and to ask the Board to allow us to prepare a cost reduction program as Mr. O'Shea has proposed. With your permission, we can be prepared to present that plan to the Board by next week. We have already advised management in all areas of the hospital to prepare for significant reductions in the work force. Unfortunately, as we prepare for the reductions our situation becomes worse by changes in the local environment. The recent modification in the City ordinance regarding waste management will add another three hundred thousand dollars to our expenses in the next year. Sister has also raised the question about the expense of the Office for Health Affairs. Mr. Weaver has estimated that will cost us another one million dollars. These additions compound the thirty percent reduction already required."

Hardly's response did not garner the sympathy that Durant was seeking. "Joe, every business in town is affected by City Hall. We have to accept it as the cost of doing business. So should you. If these additions require more belt tightening then we just have to do it. If the members agree, we can have a special meeting of the Board next week to review the cost reduction plan. Tom, I expect that you and the Finance Committee will review the plan ahead of our meeting."

Tom O'Shea was quick with a reply, "You can count on it, Kevin. Remember that the Finance Committee consists of Dr. Folley and me. I suggest that Mark Meehan join us. That gives the committee good balance. OK with you, Mark?"

Mark Meehan had been quiet and comfortable during the meeting. He was confident that ultimately the great Charlie Patello would surface and destroy all this political intrigue. Durant's comment about the waste management costs caused him some anxiety. Now O'Shea, either purposely or accidentally, had put his feet to the fire by asking him to serve on the Finance Committee. Perhaps O'Shea had done this to give Meehan some protection since the Committee would control the cost analysis. The impact of the waste management contract could be covered by other reductions. He reminded himself of Hardly's comments that sought to admonish administration's criticism of the change in Civic policy. Without speaking, Mark Meehan nodded his agreement to serve as a new member of the finance committee. If necessary he could always resign.

Kevin Hardly felt that he had regained control. His intent was to adjourn the meeting before he lost it again. The time served that purpose well. Kevin had always promised that the seven AM start time for the Board meetings allowed those attending to be at their offices by eight thirty providing the meeting ended by eight. He had never failed to close the meeting by that time. Today was not to be an exception. A glance at his watch registered the time to quit. He then began his closing commentary. "Bishop Hanks, Sister Elizabeth, I want to thank you for your leadership today. You have advanced the ministry with your commitment to assist the new Office for Health Affairs. I also want to thank the Board members who have agreed to accept new committee appointments. Indeed, all of you are to be commended for your commitment to our ministry. This has been a very important meeting. It's now eight o'clock and time to adjourn. Mr. Durant's office will inform you soon about the date, time and place of our special meeting next week. Thank you for coming."

The Board members reacted without hesitation at Hardly's call to adjourn. They stood almost in unison and began to exit. However, each one took the time to shake Michael Logan's hand as they departed. Michael was un-steady in his response to the welcome comments. His mind had been blown by the conduct of the Board meeting. Certainly, as a public servant and a member of the Mayor's cabinet he had been subjected to vicious political in-fighting. He had expected it and was prepared for it. However, he was not prepared and certainly did not expect to experience the scope of bickering that seemed to pervade this Catholic hospital. He kept reflecting in his mind that on his second day on the job, at his first meeting of the St. Anslem's Board, he became the target of a Sister's wrath. Her anger caused the creation of a committee that had the prospect of replacing him or at least reducing him to an errand boy. He felt that he had been had. He wanted out.

Joe Durant was also frustrated as the meeting came to a close. He had hoped to initiate a planning process that would give administration the opportunity to continue managing the hospital. Instead he had to be content with Sister Elizabeth's system planning i.e. watch dog committee and a cold-blooded cost reduction finance committee that expected miracles in a week. Remarkably, Rod Weaver seem pleased with the challenge. He positioned himself at the door of the Boardroom and exchanged pleasantries with the members as they left. Mitch Daly was in a quandary. He simply hung back waiting for the chance to reconcile with his boss.

Charlie Patello was the big loser. His intent to establish a planning committee under his control with the consultants was deterred by a crafty Nun who had another agenda. Now the inside track to the health care business sought by Park was on hold until another avenue could be found. Charlie noticed that Joe was hanging back waiting for the room to clear. Hardly and O'Shea had already left. Logan was still chatting with Sr. Elizabeth and Dr. Folley.

As Charlie approached the door he caught Durant's eye and motioned for him to step into the hall. Durant made an immediate move for the door with Daly following. Outside and out of sight from Folley, Charlie offered the services of the Consultants to Durant at no cost. Patello proposed that the consulting expertise could be a valuable assist to the hospital's administration in developing the cost reduction plan. Durant was elated with the offer and accepted on the spot.

Daly listened intently to the conversation between his boss and the Board member. Afterward, he reminded Durant that he had been placed in charge of the planning process which meant that the consultants were to be in his charge. Durant again explained to Daly that the immediate problem was cost reduction in concert with planning. That meant that he and Weaver would be working in tandem with the consultants. Durant decided that he would personally direct the process.

Rod Weaver was finished working the crowd. He was noticed by Durant as he escorted Sr. Elizabeth toward the door. Since Daly was already standing by lobbying for control, Durant thought it a good time to get his two senior executives primed for the task ahead. He asked Daly to follow Rod to the door and then escort him back to the President's office for a brief post mortem. Daly obediently went after Weaver as Durant returned to his office.

A few minutes later Daly and Weaver came into the President's office already engaged in heated debate over the process of cost reduction versus strategic planning. Weaver was adamant that the process as requested by the Board should be led by the Fiscal officer. Daly insisted that the cost reduction program was a feature of a bigger effort in strategic planning and therefore should be lead and coordinated by the professional planner. Durant patiently listened to the debate until he suspected that his two valued assistants were about to resume physical combat.

At this vital point he explained the process by handing out specific assignments accordingly: "Gentlemen, the Board in its usual fashion was not clear what it expected to see in the next week. It did mandate a plan for a thirty percent cost reduction over the next year. That means immediate cutbacks. Rod, pull together the other members of the executive staff for an emergency session. Operations will have to carry the ball with the initial layoffs. After the first hit of a general cut we'll go after the programs that are free standing and in deficit. SACAP is one that comes to mind. The next level of cost reduction is modification of those programs that are high cost and primary to our mission statement. Things like teaching, research, and tertiary care are examples of the third level. At the third level we will want to consider spreading the cost of programs by arranging affiliations with other teaching and research institutions in the City. This means a loss of autonomy. It might also lead into a merger. Mitch, this is where you come in. I want you to become very valuable to Sr. Elizabeth and her committee. Give them all the staff support they can handle. Become valuable to Logan. He has no staff for planning so you become his staff. Just remember, you still work for me. When the consultants get involved they will function out of my office but will work with each of you as we progress through the three phases. Now, gentlemen you have the outline for the cost reduction plan that will be explained to the Board next week. I'll have the consultants put this forward as their recommendation so we can by-pass Folley's usual objection to whatever we suggest. Any questions?"

Daly was energized by the assignment. Durant's organized approach to the effort was exciting. It seemed to create a clear path that everyone would follow. This was Daly's style. He loved having everyone marching to a common drummer even though he preferred to march to his own beat. He seemed confident in his assignment but sought some clarification. "Joe, if I'm reading you right you want me to contact Sr. Elizabeth and offer her help with her committee. That will bring us into some discussion about phase three details in the cost reduction program including affiliations and possibly merger. You think the Bishop will even allow us to talk about that?"

Durant took some time to think before he answered, "I don't know, Mitch. You recall that Sister mentioned that we couldn't plan in a vacuum. She wanted the Cardinal's input and direction. Talk of a merger will force him to speak although it may be in Tongues. I read in the last issue of Health Progress from the Catholic Health Association that some Religious Orders of Women are restructuring their health ministry and repositioning away from the institutional acute care business to non-institutional services for the poor such as half way houses, nutritional support, and day care centers. If his Eminence wants to make that switch in Boston, the next year seems to be the open window."

Weaver sat wide eyed listening to the conversation. When Durant mentioned repositioning to non-institutional service Rod broke in, "Not in a million years! He can't afford to get out of acute care. We've got too much debt. He'll never file Chapter Eleven. That's the only way he could dump the bond holders. St. A's balance sheet after this year's deficit won't be able to satisfy our capital debt out of equity. We would have to dissolve. The Cardinal wouldn't have a nickel to support those charity programs. That could take down the whole Archdiocese. He's broke as it is. It seems to me that we are in one hell of a bind."

"We'll never know unless we force the conversation to the surface, Rod" Durant remained pensive as he responded. "The ethical issues are also beginning to mount. Assisted suicide is going to be as big as abortion. If State or Federal action supports that as a right I question if the Church will be able to remain in the acute care business regardless of the fiscal issues. That's something else that Sister's committee will need to discuss, I guess."

Suddenly Daly appeared uncomfortable. "Joe, I don't think I can lead any discussion on the ethical things. I don't know anything about the Church except what I hear around here." Daly's agnosticism was well known throughout the hospital. He was firm in his social stance that belief in a Supreme Being was a very personal matter not requiring an open ecclesiastical forum. Therefore, Church in any form was not a part of his thinking.

Durant was tolerant of Daly's point of view and sheltered him from the ritual of the Catholic hospital in order to avoid any mutual embarrassment. "Don't worry about leading that discussion, Mitch. It will happen without your urging. If nothing else the Cardinal and Bishop Hanks will work it out in a closed session and then bring the answers if there are any to the committee. All you have to do is make sure that the ethical issues are recorded when they come up."

"Let's get back to the cuts," urged Weaver. "You want me to get operations to chop across the board on the first run then we go back and knock off the losers. Why don't we do 'em both at the same time?"

"That's fine. Do them both at the same time if you can" Durant was agitated at Weaver's apparent criticism. "Do you know or are you sure who the winners and losers are? It seems to me that some review is in order before we just chop off a department or program."

"Not all of' 'em" quipped Weaver, "but we have some that are no brainers. You mentioned SACAP. That's a big loser. We could save a ton if we closed it today. Not only do the dopers not pay but they routinely bust up the place. I think we should convince Folley to fold it up. On the first cut I think we should ask for a twenty percent cut back in staffing then settle for fifteen. How's that sound?"

Durant was skeptical, "Rod, it sounds like a wild guess. You probably have reason for suggesting that number but I beg you to support it with fact. We'll have a hell of a time convincing the management staff to do the cuts not to mention the skepticism of O'Shea. Work it up and be prepared to present it at a general management meeting in a few days. Meanwhile I'll see that Human Resources gets with you to work out the proper notices and placement services. You have any trouble with that?" As Durant finished his reply he signaled the end of the meeting. Daly and Weaver left abruptly without further comment. The cost reduction program had begun.

oOo

Dr. Folley quit the Board meeting in good spirits. He always maintained an appearance of self-esteem and control no matter what pressures he might be facing. This was in stark contrast to Michael Logan who Folley had in tow. Logan was visibly distressed after the meeting. His depression was apparent in his manner and his conversation with the trustees who took the time to speak to him. Folley noticed his state of mind and decided to change the young man's attitude with a little counseling in the great man's office.

The office of the Chairman of the Department of Medicine at St. Anslem's Hospital well represented the status of the Chairman and well as the incumbent's ego. Originally the single office was adequate to hold a desk, credenza, small conference table, and several comfortable chairs. Soon, after being named to the post Dr. Folley removed the adjacent walls of the office tripling its size. He added paneled walls, thick carpet, expensive book shelves, a miniature library, communication and entertainment center, two comfortable sofas, and innumerable pictures of the great Physician with heads of State, Cardinals, Popes, Corporate Presidents, Athletes, Royalty, and Television Personalities not to mention one picture of his wife and daughter.

Logan was welcomed into the plush accommodation and given an in depth commentary about each person with whom the great man was pictured. Then they sat on the comfortable couch and had a father to son type conversation.

Folley intended to convince Logan that they were in control of the hospital and its administration. Sister Elizabeth had distorted that concept in the Board meeting and somehow had manage to wrestle the control of the Office of Health Affairs hack into the arms of the clergy. He began the conversation with a direct approach. "Michael, regardless of what this morning's meeting might lead you to think, I am in charge of the health affairs of the Archdiocese. That position takes precedence over any board or committee. As far as you are concerned, you only report to me, not to Sr. Elizabeth or anyone else. I'm the boss. St. Anslem's is run by Tom O'Shea and me. Hardly is our support. No one else counts. What we say goes."

This type of reaffirmation was very much needed by Logan. His confidence was lost by the conduct of the meeting. Folley seemed to reinstate some of the foundation but he retained an uneasy feeling about the ability of Folley to exercise the authority he claimed to have. His inclination was to directly question the great man on the stability of the Secretary appointment and his own position as Director of the Office. Instead he opted to be polite and talk around his concerns.

Logan began to comment, "The meeting was an eye opener, Richard. The quality of the people on the Board is very impressive. Everyone seemed eager to participate. You must enjoy the collegial activity."

The attempt to catch Folley in a soft contradiction by referring to collegiality was missed by the great Doctor. He responded with a flurry of compliments about the members of the Board and concluded with praise for his counter parts. "You know, Michael, we have some of the best minds in healthcare gathered at St. Anslem's. The people on the Board respect that and add to our excellence. They are the true leaders of the Boston community. It's an honor to be part of this organization. They have attended to the needs of the institution and have guided us to greater heights. We are truly blessed to have a Board with such dedication and influence. You will come to appreciate them in a very short time."

Logan could see that his meeting was more "bullshit" than "applesauce" as they used to say at City Hall. He began to plot his escape from the den of greatness. "We need to get our office set up, Doctor. I have an appointment with a rental agent who wants to show us some new space in Wellesley, I understand that would be close to your home. Would you like to see it with us?"

The good Doctor hated these details. He preferred to be accommodated in accord with his status. Shopping was not part of that accommodation. "Michael, I know that you will do an excellent job in choosing the right spot. Wellesley would be very nice. If it looks good to you sign the deal. I'll arrange for the bills to be paid by the hospital."

Michael Logan said his good bye to Dr. Folley and walked to the hospital's lobby.

Mitch Daly spotted him near the door and ran to catch up. He reintroduced himself to Logan in a friendly way. Logan was impressed with Daly's professional demeanor and his friendship. The prospect of friendship was more the attraction since Logan felt a strong need for a friend in what he believed to be a hostile environment. Daly sensing the acceptance walked with Logan to the parking garage. The two men chatted generally about the Board meeting. As they were about to go their different ways, Daly nonchalantly offered to help Logan with the work of the planning committee, Logan accepted without hesitation.

Within minutes after Logan departed for his appointment with the real estate agent, Daly informed Durant that he had infiltrated the Office of Health Affairs. Durant was pleased.

Durant, while pleased with Daly's initiative, could not give him much time to relay all the details of his successful encounter with Logan. Waiting outside the President's office were two representatives from Action Waste Management who had arrived for their appointment to discuss the design and implementation of the waste control program for the hospital. Durant had summoned his Operations Officer and Director of Environmental Services to join them. Neither had arrived as yet and Durant was reluctant to meet with the Action "hoods" alone. "They can wait," he thought as he began to scribble the first paragraphs of what would eventually be the minutes of the recently concluded Board meeting.

Outside of Durant's office Ken Ryan and Jay Marquart waited patiently for the meeting to begin. Ken was nervous about the presentation that he had outlined the day before and explained to Jay that morning. He and Jay had rehearsed for about two hours before driving to the hospital. Jay was excited about the prospect of meeting the hospital "big shot." He had mentioned to Ken that after they made their pitch he intended to tell the "cheese" some things about his hospital that needed "some work." Ken at first pleaded and then emphatically instructed Jay to set his own problems aside and attend only to the task of the company. Jay, with a hurt expression promised to behave himself and stick to the script as Ken had it written. He still nursed the fantasy of convincing the boss that a certain nurse in the Medical Intensive Care Unit was, "a big ass problem that had to go."

The Hospital's Chief Operating Officer and the Director of Environmental Services arrives about five minutes after the time of the appointment. As they entered the President's waiting area, the Executive Assistant introduced them to Ken and Jay. They were involved in conversation when Joe Durant opened his office door and invited them to come in. The five men sat around the well-used small conference table. Ken introduced Jay to the Hospital President as his assistant and technical advisor for the St. Anslem's contract. Jay, in very proper business like fashion shook Durant's hand and commented about the excellent reputation of the hospital. He concluded his statement with an expression of pleasure in being associated with this premier institution.

Durant was pleasantly surprised at the quality of Action's representatives. He had expected another "knee capper" like Veto Celi. Ken Ryan was, first of all, a gentleman and secondly a true expert in the process of waste management. "The technical guy is a bit of a bull shitter but seems like he could adapt to the hospital scene." was the mental note that Durant made as Jay was introduced. He also realized that he was captive to the contract so to make the most of it he decided to listen rather than argue with the presentation. If any contest was in order he knew that he could rely on his COO and DES to carry the ball.

Durant countered Ryan's remarks with an explanation of the hospital's organization and conduct. He emphasized the priority of patient care while pointing out that the hospital functioned around the clock. Therefore, all patient support services, especially sanitation was a perpetual need. Waste services had to be continuous.

Ryan was attentive to the admonitions of the chief executive. He addressed the need to be always supportive of the patient and the caregiver. To accomplish the intent of the contract which was in another sense a patient care activity, Action intended to do a complete review of the hospital's waste handling systems to insure the sanitary quality of the institution was maintained and enhanced.

Ken Ryan explained that, "The Company's leading technician. Mr. Jay Marquart, will supervise a team of four people who will spend two weeks around the clock reviewing all procedures of waste disposal. After the review has been completed we will make specific recommendations on improved methods that we will discuss with the hospital. We will also train your personnel on the new methods of dealing with hazardous and infectious waste products. After the training is complete we will do continuous spot reviews and upgrades on methods and equipment. We have a twenty-four hour on call service that will respond in case there is a special problem like a radiation spill or contamination. With your permission, Mr. Durant, I would like Jay Marquart to explain more about the survey process."

During the rehearsal Jay had been short and bland as he explained to Ken how he thought the survey should be conducted. His descriptions were not very impressive compared to Ken's style but adequate to convince the hospital management that Action had some idea what it was about. Durant's nod to Ken's suggestion for Jay to proceed created a transformation of Jay's rehearsed stoic personality to the great orator. With persuasive animation he walked and talked about the details of the hospital's systems. He knew the trash collection regimens of the environmental services personnel, the location of the trash chutes, and the special handling of waste from the infectious cases, surgery, and post anesthesia recovery. He talked about double bagging, red bagging, incineration, liquid waste, and equipment sanitation. He even talked with knowledge about the Joint Commission on Accreditation of Healthcare Organizations' safety and sanitation standards and the State regulations pertaining to AIDS. He was in his element and he knew it. After about fifteen minutes he had blown their minds.

The hospital's Director of Environmental Services was amazed at Jay's detailed knowledge of the housekeeping policies and procedures. His instinct was to offer Jay a job on the spot. The Chief Operating Officer was equally impressed and, in his mind was thinking that Jay would be an excellent replacement for the DES. Durant was wondering if Jay's knowledge would lead to significant cuts in the Environmental Services staff that would offset the cost of the waste management contract. For the first time Durant was optimistic about the invasion of the hospital by Action Waste Management. "These guys are pros" he said to himself, "Where in the hell did they get that thug, Celi? That part still doesn't fit."

The presentation plan that Ken had prepared called for him to follow Jay with more rhetoric about the depth of Action's quality control. As Jay concluded his comments, Ken realized that Jay was a tough act to follow. He recognized that the hospital's executives were literally, "in the bag" as far as Acton was concerned. To belabor the pitch would be overkill that could possibly dull the edge that Jay had so skillfully honed. Instead he opted to conclude the promotion and move into details.

Ken concluded, "Mr. Durant, we can have our team here tomorrow to meet whatever staff you would like to have involved with us in the survey. Mr. Marquart has been cleared from his other assignments to give St. Anslem's first priority. We are ready."

Durant was sold as was the COO and DES. He actually thanked the Action representatives and then asked the COO to take charge of the project. The COO immediately bucked it to the DES who responded to Ryan. "Gentlemen, I suggest that you have your team available to meet with supervisory staff from environmental services, nursing, engineering, and ancillary support services tomorrow afternoon at one thirty. I'll arrange the meeting. Here's my card. If your secretary could contact my office after ten tomorrow we can tell you where the meeting will be. I expect we will have present about fifteen or twenty persons. That will be the first team. Others will come on board as you move through the house. You'll find St. A's people a delight to work with."

Ryan recognized a good ending. He rose from his chair and shook the hand of each of the hospital executives. "We will be here tomorrow at one thirty. This has been a very enjoyable and productive session. Action is honored to be a part of the St. Anslem's tradition. Thank you very much."

As Ken spoke he passed out his business card. Suddenly he realized that the star of the show, one Jay Marquart, had not been blessed with business cards since he was not a part of management or sales. Awkwardly he asked Jay to write his name on the back of his card so that the hospital executives would be able to contact him. Jay obediently retrieved the cards and printed his name and desk extension on the back of Ken's card.

Durant was amused at Ken's embarrassment. "You'll have to get the kid a promotion so he can have his own cards," he quipped.

As Durant was concluding his meeting with the Action reps, Dr. Ron Anderson was entering the sanctuary of Dr. Folley. He carried the medical record of Jay Marquart and a copy of the incident report filed by Bob Markley. The Board meeting and the postmortem session with Logan had caused Folley to forget the little problem in SACAP. When Anderson entered his office Folley was curious why he was there. Anderson impatiently explained that the meeting was Folley's idea. Apparently the great one felt a need for an off the record report about the Marquart incident. Gradually Dr. Folley's mind adjusted to the particulars of the incident. He asked Ron to sit down and give him a full verbal report.

Anderson was irritated that the matter had not been officially reviewed by the administration. He let Folley know in no certain terms that the hospital was running a major risk if it did not take proper steps to offset what could be a major lawsuit. "If it is necessary to protect the investigation from discovery by classifying it as professional review then let's get it done!" shouted Anderson. "Risk management should have been on top of this the minute they got my report."

Folley listened patiently to his super star for a few minutes and then held up his hands to call for a pause, "Ron, so far you've told me how upset you are, how administration is dragging its feet, and what a hell of a mess we're in. Somehow you have managed to avoid telling me what happened to cause this sad state of affairs. Could you possibly get to the details?"

Anderson reacted, "Yeah, sure. In a nutshell this fellow, Marquart, a patient in the program, uses the unit phone to call his ex-wife, a nurse in MICU. She sees on the caller screen that he's in SACAP and runs to her lawyer who files to revoke his joint custody of their kid. Now I think he's got us on violation of the confidentiality provisions, both State and Federal, and I imagine he's got her on several violations of the Nurse Practice Act. She could lose her license. We could lose ours. He could get a big settlement. That's it in a nutshell."

Folley sat up in his chair. His eyes opened wide at first and seemed to begin to squint as he thought about Anderson's comments, "If what you say is true then we need to reach a settlement with this patient. On the other hand, if the telephone made the mistake, then the hospital is not at fault but the nurse is in deep trouble. My thinking is that he used the phone for his own benefit, not for ours. In a way, it was an unauthorized use of hospital equipment. I could argue that he doesn't have a case."

Anderson stood and began to pace as he responded to Folley's observations, "I thought of that too. Then Markley busted by bubble when he told me that he gave Marquart permission to use the phone. I think that brings us back into the problem."

The complexity of the issue caused Folley to have a headache. He wanted to delegate this mess but his immediate subordinate to whom he would refer the matter stood before him seeking guidance. The pressure of accountability caused him to abdicate. "OK. Let's give this to risk management and professional review like Durant wants. I'll tell him that it's being forwarded by Department so he has to keep me involved as the Chairman and referring party. You and Markley are parties to the fact. We point at the nurse. I imagine that the hospital will eventually have a disciplinary hearing and will be forced to report the misconduct of the nurse to the State. That could screw her out of her career."

Without further comment, he dialed the number of the Risk Management office and directed the manager to refer the incident report to the Director of Quality Assurance for immediate review. Dr. Folley also advised that he would sign the report as Dr. Anderson's supervisor.

oOo

Susan Marquart hated the summer. During the winter Benny was in school and was the teacher's problem. Now he was hers. James wasn't old enough to realize that Mom needed a few drinks in the afternoon to move her from one hour to the next. Benny was old enough to understand and even ask questions. He was out of the house at the moment, playing ball with the neighborhood kids in a vacant lot. James was taking a nap. Carefully she recovered the bag of white powder that Louise had so generously left after the party Saturday night. She inhaled the cocaine and felt the pleasure with relief from the problems of the day. She, for the moment, couldn't even remember the problems.

Carefully she stretched another line. Life was comfortable again. The ringing seemed distant so she attempted to ignore it. Then it started again and seemed to be closer and closer. Awkwardly she grabbed the phone and gave a mumbled greeting. The person calling her tried repeatedly to communicate with her. She also tried to cooperate but her mind was not functioning on what was being said. "What? Who is this? This is Susan. Who are you calling? What? Who Is This?"

"Susan, this is Eddie. You know. Eddie, the father of your boys. Hey, you on something? Hey, com'on now. You sober up. I wanna talk. Man, you ain't changed at all. You gotta be missin' old Eddie now that your hero is goin' clean."

The fog covering Susan's mind was beginning to clear. Eddie's name registered strong with her. He caused her to tremble and chill. "Eddie, why are you calling? I don't need you."

Eddie laughed, "You'll always need me, honey, or someone like me 'cause I got what you need to face your miserable life. But that's not the only reason I'm calling. I hear from our mutual friend, Brian, that my kid is on the All-Star team. So, when does he play? I gotta see the game."

Susan's emotions bounced from anger to calm. Eddie had not exhibited any interest in the boys from the time of their birth. He had beaten her when he learned that she was pregnant claiming that she purposely conceived to trap and enslave him to a responsibility that he didn't want. Now he seemed to want to be part of the boys' life. Benny had asked her about his real father on several occasions. He was interested in his father even though his father did not seem interested in him. Jay had attempted to be a true surrogate with reasonable success. Benny liked Jay and well appreciated the special attention that Jay gave him, especially in baseball. If Eddie attended the game Jay may become offended and retreat from the close affection that had developed between the two. She also realized that she could not stop Eddie from attending the game. He could easily find out from the Waltham Recreation Department when the game was going to be played. He had called her for another reason. Benny, the All Star, was his excuse."

The first round is Wednesday at six." she reported, "If they win they play again on Saturday. Are you really going to be there? Why don't you bring your support payments with you? That way I won't have to bother the judge."

The comment caused Eddie to chuckle, "Well, darling, you know that I don't need a hassle with a judge. Maybe you and I could work out some sort of trade. You know, maybe I could supply you with a needed commodity. Brian tells me that your old man isn't buying anymore. That means you are on the wagon unless you have resources that we don't know about. I can start hanging out with Benny and James now and then like a good daddy. They could deliver the mail between us. It sort of gives the kids a sense of responsibility. Can't get 'em started too early. What do you say?"

Susan was furious, "Eddie, you no good son of a bitch! You want my kids to be a mule for their goddamn worthless father. You son of a bitch! Maybe I will explain this to the judge when I drag you into court." Her audible sobs caused her to choke as she tried to scream her response.

Eddie seemed unmoved by her emotional outburst. "Whoa. Hold on there, Sweetheart. I'm trying to make things simple and easy for us. Now if you bring the judge into the deal he's gonna expect that you have mended your sorrowful ways. I might go to the slam but you, my dear, go on the wagon with your hubbie. From what I hear that's the last thing you want to do. Right? So, what I suggest is that you and me come to terms. Like, I give you a reasonable discount on your personal needs and you layoff on the support thing. You don't want the kids as the go between, that's OK. Then we got to work something else out. I think it's best we do it my way. I still am going to Benny's game. You want to talk some more there? I'm willing to listen. See you Wednesday?"

"Yeah. OK. We can talk Wednesday!" As Susan hung up the phone she broke into a sweat. Her hands trembled. She knew that she had to accept Benny's offer. The problem was explaining to Jay that Benny's real father was taking an interest in his son and then explaining why the support payments stopped. The inconsistency of the two actions would cause Jay to eventually discover that Eddie was her supplier. She would also have to pay the balance to Eddie from the meager house allowance that Jay was able to afford her. This was a very dangerous and delicate operation that required a cool approach. She also reasoned that Benny as the go between might inadvertently say something to Jay that would cause the upset. An alternate was necessary. "Perhaps Louise could help" she thought, "She seemed to understand the problem."

Susan was uncertain about Louise as a friend. She was very supportive of Susan in dealing with the pressure that Jay's reformation was causing her. But could she be trusted to be a mule for her in bringing the goods from Eddie? Brian, as a professional mule worked for the syndicate under Eddie's supervision. Would Eddie tell Brian about the link? Then Brian would tell Jay because of their long standing friendship. The set up was full of faults but there seemed to be no alternative. She decided to call Louise and discuss the proposition when the telephone rang.

When she answered Jay greeted her with bubbling excitement. "Suse, I really scored big! Ken Ryan asked me to be the lead tech at St. A's so we made the proposal this afternoon and I wowed 'em. They want me bad. Anyway, I met the head guy who thinks I'm great. I'm gonna be spending a lot of time surveying the joint. Hell, maybe I can convince the boss to can Cecile. Then I'll sue his ass with less prejudice. Anyway, I called to let you know that I'm doing some overtime then I'll go direct to St. A's for my support therapy. Oh yeah, Martha called. Seems my emergency hearing is set for Friday morning. I'll meet with my lawyer tomorrow. Then Martha and I are gonna have a special session on Thursday before I go to my support thing. That means I won't be able to make the start of Benny's game but I'll get there before it's over. How's things with you?"

Susan sensed an opportunity to set the stage for her own arrangement. Jay's good mood allowed her to inject the presence of Eddie at the game without causing Jay depression or anger. Eddie would serve as Jay's substitute. It was worth the gamble. "Jay. I've had a bit of a shock that I'm still trying to recover from. That bastard, Eddie, called and told me that he was going to Benny's game. He said that he wanted to watch his son play in the All-Star game. I told him that I thought he had a lot of nerve."

Jay reacted in a strong but calm manner, "Boy that takes a pair. He doesn't even give the kid a birthday present but he wants to take pride in the fact that his son is on the All Stars. He's really messed up. You better tell Benny that his father is gonna be at the game. It's probably a good thing that I'm gonna be late. I don't want to have to talk to the guy. You can do that."

Susan was surprised and more than a little hurt at Jay's reaction. While it was what she had hoped for it nevertheless left her with the definite and distinct impression that she was secondary in Jay's life. He cared not that Eddie was re-entering her life and the lives of Benny and James. He definitely was totally focused on Kristie and his legal bout with Cecile. She felt the pangs of jealously. After a few minutes of contemplation, she called Louise.

Jay and Ken Ryan sat at a table in the cafeteria at Action Waste Management. Food service had been discontinued for the day except for the coffee pot that was always available for employees on break. Jay talked incessantly about the St. A's project. He explained the survey approach, waste collection points, employee training programs, and recycling. Ken took extensive notes as Jay rambled and occasionally inserted his own observations. The two men were as excited as college students planning a road trip. They were having fun being a success. Ken needed this session with Jay in order to compile the program plan for the St. Anslem's project. That plan, formally prepared and submitted under Ken's signature, would go to Mr. Meehan for final approval and pricing. Then the final document would become a part of the contract including all the extras that Celi would deliver to Mr. Durant by the end of the week. Ken expected to have the draft of the plan completed this afternoon and had asked Jay to hang around to review the draft. Jay, contrary to his usual reaction, was eager to participate. His only concern was that he not be late for his evening therapy support session at St. Anslem's.

Ken Ryan was a quick study when it came to creating a written proposal. He picked up Jay's ideas and polished them to perfection. Within an hour after he had returned to his desk the first draft was being reviewed by Jay who made several suggestions. Jay was equally excited about the creative function. He sat with Ken as the proposal went in and through the word processor. Another draft was produced that required little revisions. By six PM the team of Ryan and Marquart delivered the final proposal for the St. Anslem's project to the in-basket on the secretary's desk in Mr. Meehan's office. There was no doubt that the two men had prepared a masterpiece for the company. Under usual circumstances they would have washed down their euphoria with several beers before arriving home late and too tired to explain to the waiting spouse what caused this celebrate binge.

That was the way a working man, or woman perhaps, was expected to give emphasis to the import of their labors. It is a long-respected custom. But no longer is it the custom for Mr. Jay Marquart. Mr. Marquart's excitement for the day is followed by a rush trip to St. Anslem's Hospital where he will pea in a bottle and cavort with his fellow junkies and drunks. Jay Marquart is establishing a new ritual in an attempt to rid himself of the habitual effect of an old custom.

The adrenaline was flowing as Jay made his way back to St. Anslem's. He arrived a few minutes late for his lab test but sufficiently ahead of the time for the start of the support group session. Bob Markley met him in the Unit and offered Jay the specimen bottle. That was all Jay required in the way of instruction. He proceeded to the rest room, filled the much too little bottle with urine, applied the safety cap, and returned the specimen to the waiting Bob Markley.

Bob noticed the spirited attitude of Marquart and had to comment. "Jay, you look like a high school kid that just landed his first date. You really that turned on about going to a support group?"

"Oh no, man. I scored big at work today," bubbled Jay, "As a matter of fact I set this place up with a hell of a deal. You are going into a waste management program that will make this place the talk of the town. Man, you are going to have the best recycling system in the whole Country. Count on it, baby. And old junkie Jay set it up. You may applaud."

Markley shook his head in disbelief at the pride his patient exhibited. Then he glanced down at the memorandum on his desk from Mr. Weaver's office that summoned him to a crisis meeting to discuss and implement a minimum twenty percent cut in expenses. Now he learned from a popular drunk that the hospital was adopting a waste management program on top of a twenty percent cut back. "Durant has really lost it this time," he mumbled as Jay marched around the room acting like a proud Caesar.

Markley took a deep breath that caused his emotions to gain control. With some remorse, he looked at Jay now perched on his elbows across the desk. "OK, Napoleon, let's go join the party of our peers."

Somehow Markley had persuaded the hospital administration to let the SACAP Support Group use the hospital cafeteria for its Tuesday and Thursday night sessions. This meant that the Cafeteria had to be closed to the public by seven o'clock on those particular evenings. It also meant a loss of revenue from the regular use of the cafeteria coupled with the fact that the support group did not pay for the use of the room or the coffee they consumed. This was another coup for Markley over administration. Weaver had wanted to charge the revenue loss to the SACAP budget but Dr. Anderson raised so much hell that Durant caved in. Markley was concerned that the mess that the group caused plus the occasional fight that broke up the furniture would give emphasis to Weaver's point and cause Durant to change his mind regardless of Anderson's wild temper. Fortunately, Durant was far too occupied with the escapades of Dr. Folley to worry about a few broken tables and chairs. At the moment, the party seemed secure.

Bob Markley and Jay entered the cafeteria a few minutes after seven. The meeting was well attended. At least thirty qualified members were present who politely applauded when Bob arrived. Instead of moving to the podium as Jay expected, Bob took a seat in the third row next to several elderly participants. Jay hastened to sit next to him. The room came to near order as an elderly gentleman, facilitator for the evening, came to the front. He asked everyone to rise and join him in the opening prayer. Jay was not ready for a religious experience. The idea of a prayer seemed to turn him off from a party that he was not overly excited about to begin with. With reluctance he stood and prepared himself for the usual Our Father, Hail Mary, fair for which Catholics were famous. Instead the assembled stood and began to recite The Twelve Steps of Alcoholics Anonymous from small pamphlets that were on each chair. Markley was most vocal in his recitation, from Jay's observation.

The elderly gentleman asked for order following the opening prayer since several members decided to have another cup of coffee and continue to socialize. Gradually the members returned to their chairs. Once order was returned, the facilitator asked each person to introduce themselves. As usual each person began with the admission that they were a drunk or an addict, gave their first name, and then reported how long they had been sober. The times ranged from over twenty years to less than a day. To Jay's surprise, Markeley reported only a ten-month period of sobriety. Some members omitted the statistic that caused Jay to recognize that the information was not obligatory.

When it was his turn, Jay made the admission and reported one week of success on the road to recovery. As he was speaking he noticed for the first time that several of the attendees were close to his age. That gave him some encouragement and comfort in realizing that he was not confined to an old man's club. Following the introductions, the facilitator asked the audience to take time to meet and become acquainted with the person near them or if already acquainted then find a new friend. The purpose, as everyone seemed to know, was to create a network of acquaintances who could help in a crisis.

Again, the meeting became animated and seemingly unruly. Jay wanted to converse with Bob who had turned to the person on the other side leaving Jay to find another friend. He sat in silence for a brief time until he felt a tap on his shoulder.

The man introduced himself as Herb. He was dressed in an open collared sport shirt and a pair of Dockers. His Rockport dock siders covered sockless feet. Jay estimated his age at around forty. He was well spoken and conveyed a professional attitude. Jay shook the out-stretched hand and accepted the suggestion that they move to a less crowded part of the room. Herb told Jay that he had worked the investment desk at a large investment firm and was well on his way to making big money when he was caught by his boss coming in an hour late after a liquid lunch. Fortunately the boss recognized the symptoms of a problem drinker and sent him to the company employee assistance program. Herb objected to the inference that he had a problem and resigned. After several weeks of unemployment and constant drinking he found his way back to the program. He was re-employed on a probationary basis and now was on the way to recovery.

Herb had also found Jesus as he traveled the way on his journey. Jesus was his inspiration and his guide to a new life and the life hereafter for there was no life without Jesus. He wanted Jay to understand that Jesus could be his friend as well and help him through the pain and suffering that was part of the recovery process but more important Jesus would be his strength as he faced the temptation to again use the destructive substances.

Jay became increasingly uncomfortable as Herb continued to ramble about his born-again status. He looked for an opportunity to break off the conversation. Several times Jay glanced over toward Bob Markley who was engaged in conversation with several people. No chance for rescue.

Jay sensed that the only way to divert the conversation was to become confrontational, a method that well fit his personality. "Herb, I guess that Jesus is the right way for you but I believe in myself as the only source of power to overcome my problem. You see I'm responsible for what I do. No other person or God directs my will. What I do I do myself. If I need help then I get that help from my friends."

To Jay's surprise, Herb seemed pleased with the comment. His eyes brightened and he again took Jay by the hand. "You see, my friend, how you admit that an inner strength is necessary for recovery. I felt the same way but eventually I realized that the inner strength was the true Spirit of Jesus Christ born within us. That's the answer to the problem we face. By increasing our faith we build inner strength of mind and soul that carries us through our trials. You will come to realize that the dependency that you have on yourself is really a dependency on Christ Our Savior. Study His life and you will see yourself. Then you will have strength because you will have knowledge and inspiration."

Jay realized that Herb was very serious about his religious perspective. He was not evangelizing. He stated his opinions about Jesus in a calm but definite manner. Herb was a true believer. The man deserved respect. He was sincere in presenting Jay with a perspective that he believed would help his recovery. It was difficult to simply confront the man.

On the other hand to accept his point of view could result in an acquaintance that Jay did not really want. "What the hell" Jay thought, "I guess I'll just have to give it to him straight. Herb, as I understand this session we are supposed to be getting acquainted so we can help each other when we are about to fall off the wagon. Now it seems to me that you and I have different attitudes about who gives us our strength when we need it. I say it's strictly up to me and you say it's Jesus. Now with that difference I don't see that we could be of help to each other. Hell, man, if you start preaching to me about Jesus you can be damned sure that I'm gonna take a stiff drink and keep on rollin. If fact I feel like one right now."

Herb was not about to be deterred, "The truth is, Jay, we always feel like taking a drink and keep on rolling. Falling off the wagon is what we do best, I guess. It takes strength to hold on. You know that Jesus fell three times on His way to His death and resurrection. His crucifixion is a reflection of our own. We can be renewed through Him. Think about it. Maybe we shouldn't be together at the time of our crisis but we are together now and you have been an inspiration to me to keep my faith. Perhaps I have been of some help to you. I pray that this conversation creates an awareness that Christ is your strength and that someday you will realize that. Anyway we have met as fellow travelers. We'll see each other again. Remember, live and let live."

Herb stood, gave Jay a pat on the shoulder, and walked across the room where he easily entered another conversation. Jay was left alone and somewhat bewildered. Now that the conversation had ended he was a bit remorseful. It didn't seem that he had offended Herb. Jay actually hoped that he would have the opportunity to meet him again. The fact that he had been influenced by a "Jesus freak" was fascinating.

Anxiously he sought the opportunity to review the experience with Bob Markley who was roaming about talking to everyone he could. Jay walked toward him and was about to corner him when the facilitator again called for order. When all were seated he introduced a lady by her first name who came forward to lead a review in "The 24-Hour Plan" The "plan" was a simple process of concentrating on keeping sober for the current twenty-four period. Essentially the plan was to merely put off taking a drink until tomorrow. Jay found the concept amusing but controlled his expressions. Others in the room nodded their agreement with the concept but humorously chided the presenter who also took humor in her presentation.

"For a bunch of drunks" Jay thought, "these guys are a ton of laughs"

The meeting concluded exactly at eight. Markley and a few others policed the cafeteria and rearranged the tables and chairs. Jay assisted Markley with the cleanup detail. He wanted to talk to him about the meeting anyway. It only took about a half hour to complete the detail. Jay noticed that the Environmental night staff was poised outside the cafeteria waiting to finish the process so the cafeteria would be ready to reopen for the night shift. Markley did a final check and then signaled the cleaning staff to come in. He put his arm around Jay's shoulder and thanked him for his help. Jay acknowledged and asked if Bob had a few minutes to chat. Markley looked at his watch as if to signal limited time and suggested that they go over to the Unit.

They sat at the desk since the staff was busy making patient rounds. Markley asked Jay what was on his mind. Jay wasn't sure how to address the subject but made a straight forward attempt; "Bob, this session tonight was a little weird from my point of view. I mean I can't see how this buddy, buddy shit does any good. I've been sober for only a week so why make a big thing out of it. Those guys seem like they want to celebrate every minute off the stuff. I'm not sure that I belong. Then I meet this guy Herb who gets off telling me about how he found Jesus. Man, I know that I don't belong. You got to help me in a different way, man. This is definitely not my style."

Markley gave Jay an understanding glance, "Jay, you do belong but we don't want to force you to realize your dependency on others. We want you to discover it by becoming acquainted with people who you can depend on to help you in a crisis. Sooner or later you will want someone to help you through a situation. You will reach out for them. I expect that, at this time in your recovery, you would call me since you know me the best. Eventually you might find reason to call Herb or somebody else that you will meet in future sessions. As you become better acquainted you will have a circle of associates and will only come to the meetings occasionally. A lot of people come now only to offer to be of help to others. They have their problem under good control but none of us are ever cured. You have to remember that. That's why we emphasize mutual support. You may not believe this but you are still in a withdrawal stage. Hopefully you have moved to phase three where the impact of the change in you physically is minor. However you could be at the phase two level where your emotional reaction to the physical withdrawal could be severe. In other words you could be a living time bomb emotionally. Something could set you off and you could become violent. You have demonstrated your temper to us on a few occasions. What I am attempting to do by having you attend these sessions is to build a network of people who you can call when you feel a violent reaction coming on. Most if not all of the people at the meeting tonight have experienced this kind of reaction. They know what to do."

Jay waved his disbelief at his friend, "Yeah, right. I've got some poor sum bitch by the neck ready to pound on him and buddy Herb shows up and gives me a Jesus lesson. That's really gonna help, man. Why can't I just rely on my on mental strength to get through? How come I got to have all this help? "Jay's climbing irritation served as a good case in point as he banged the desk for emphasis.

Bob recognized that Jay was losing his control. He thought of bringing that to his attention as an example of the emotional imbalance that could erupt into violence but opted to pursue the content of Jay's remarks. "Eventually you will build more inner strength, Jay, but until you have that strength you will need help from others. At this stage of your recovery you are emotionally weak. You need to condition yourself emotionally. It's like training for the Olympics. Right now you have the desire to win but you haven't a prayer of pulling it off. You need to train for the event. Many people use religion as a platform to build their inner strength. It's a very good base. Herb discovered that. Another good base to stabilize the emotions is prescribed medication. A combination of the two is a very good choice. Remember you have already decided against that medical advice. Now you seem to want to reject social support. Well, I assure you my friend, you will need all the help you can get. Don't cut yourself off completely."

Jay decided to take one more jab, "So if I'm gonna train for the Olympics in Doping Off I need a good coach. Don't tell me Herb is my main man. I need you. You gonna be my coach?"

Markley was reassuring, "Sure. Jay. I'm your coach at least for a while. You still need a network in case I'm not available. Come to the sessions for a while. Eventually you'll get with the program."

Jay noticed that Bob glanced at his watch as he made his last comment. This was definitely a signal that their session was coming to a close. With a polite" thank you" Jay stood and began to leave. Bob remained seated but smiled at Jay as a sign of friendship and encouragement. It was enough to restore Jay's confidence in the program at least for the moment.

.Jay said good bye to Bob and walked toward the main lobby. As he passed the President's office Joe Durant and Rod Weaver were standing in the corridor. Jay greeted the President who seemed pleasantly surprised to see him. He introduced Jay to the Senior Vice President for Finance as the chief consultant for Action Waste Management. He also assumed that Jay was in the hospital as part of his consulting assignment. The three men chatted for a while until Durant commented that it had been an exceptionally long day. Weaver and Marquart were both quick to agree as they separated to find their cars in the nearly vacant parking garage.

When Jay arrived home Susan had his dinner waiting. She asked about his day and he was anxious to tell her every detail. He emoted over and over about his presentation to the Hospital's executive staff and his participation in the contract proposal for Mr. Meehan. It seemed to be a near perfect day from Jay's point of view. He even made favorable comments about his support group session commenting briefly about his Jesus freak friend.

Susan sat listening to Jay ramble. She sipped slowly on a tall gin and grapefruit. Jay, in his excitement, had not even noticed. As he stopped to take a bite of food Susan reminded Jay that Benny's father had called to inquire about the all-star game. Jay seemed as though he was going to choke but then swallowed hard before he reacted. This time he was less controlled than when Susan had mentioned Eddie to him on the phone. Jay became agitated. His eyes narrowed and he pounded the table. Without a word he left the table and walked into the living room where he starred out the window. The anger consumed him to a point of violence. Had Susan followed him into the living room he most certainly would have struck her. He was out of control but had not yet acted. Eddie was a hot button and Susan had punched it. His mind suddenly focused on the gin and grapefruit that Susan was drinking. He hated her for having that drink. He wanted to punch her senseless. His mind made a quick shift again and the nerd Herb came flashing before his eyes. He hated Herb and he hated Jesus. The thought of Jesus made him sick and he felt a need to get to the bathroom. Then, as he closed the door behind him the anger began to dissipate. He broke into a cold sweat, laid down on the hard tile floor, and fell asleep. It had been an exceptionally long day.

THE END OF BOOK ONE—ALL THE CARDINALS MEN AND A FEW GOOD NUNS.

<u>AUTHORS NOTE:</u> The Book ends but the story continues. Continuing challenges remain for St. Anslem's Hospital, Jay Marquart, Joe Durant, and Bob Markley and the Board, Physicians and staff. Please read BOOK TWO—ALL THE CARDINALS MEN AND A FEW GOOD NUNS—DIAGNOSIS, THERAPY AND OUTCOME to learn the final conclusion.

ABOUT THE AUTHOR

Ted Druhot, author of ALL THE CARDINAL'S MEN AND A GEW GOOD NUNS, is a retired Hospital Administrator. He spent thirty-five years in this profession as a personnel director, executive vice president and president of large Catholic sponsored metropolitan teaching hospitals. He graduated from Xavier University with an MBA degree and a concentration in hospital administration. His undergraduate degree was from John Carroll University with a major in sociology. In addition to hospital administration, Ted taught part time business administration subjects at a local university.

He was inspired to write this book after retiring and reflecting on the many interesting and challenging experiences during his tenure in hospital administration. All of the various activities within the novel actually happened, although separated by time and location. On reflection, Ted thought it would be interesting to combine all of these events into one place and time. Thus. the novel was born.

One of the book's primary characters, Joe Durant, who is the administrator of St Anslem's Hospital in the novel is a reflection of the author's personal experiences. The other characters that are prominent within the story are also based on actual associates of the author in his time as a hospital executive. The events within the story also happened but at different times and places.

ALL OF THE CARDINAL'S MEN AND A FEW GOOD NUNS is Ted Druhot's first novel. However, throughout his career he published many articles in professional publications. One article titled LIFE IN THE SWAMP OR MUCKING AROUND WITH ALLIGATORS, a commentary of the challenge of being a healthcare administrator, was made into a booklet and circulated nationally to hospital association members.

A subtle purpose of the novel is to cause the reader, especially those with hospital patient experience, to realize that every care giver has a personal life that they set aside to provide the necessary care to the patient. In addition, both professional and personal status of the health care workers tend to collide as they unite as a team to provide coordinated patient care. The coordination of care is constant from the bedside to and thru the patient room, hospital floor unit, patent service departments and all aspects of administration. Patient care is orchestrated with the physician as the conductor but, as with a team on the field, each person has a special job to do and for the success of the effort, each team member must do it right. Administration is the coordinator of patient care.

Self-publishing is very challenging, especially to first time authors. Scam artist are constantly in contact with authors who lack professional publishing support. These scammers will make telephone proposals to promote a novel with suggested returns. The author is required to pay $5000 or more to obtain these unknown returns. Dealing with these constant appeals has been the most frustrating part of self-publishing this novel.